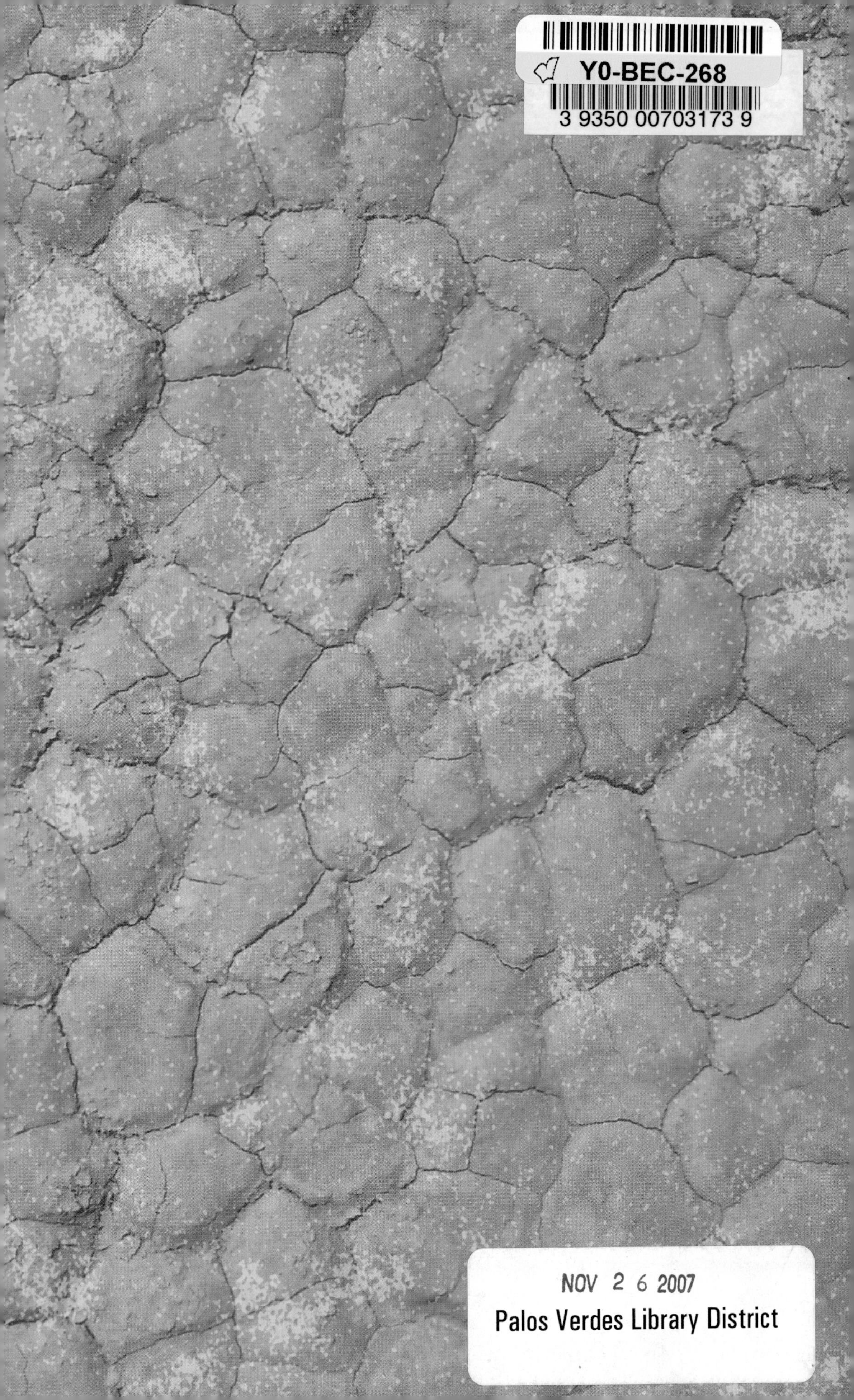

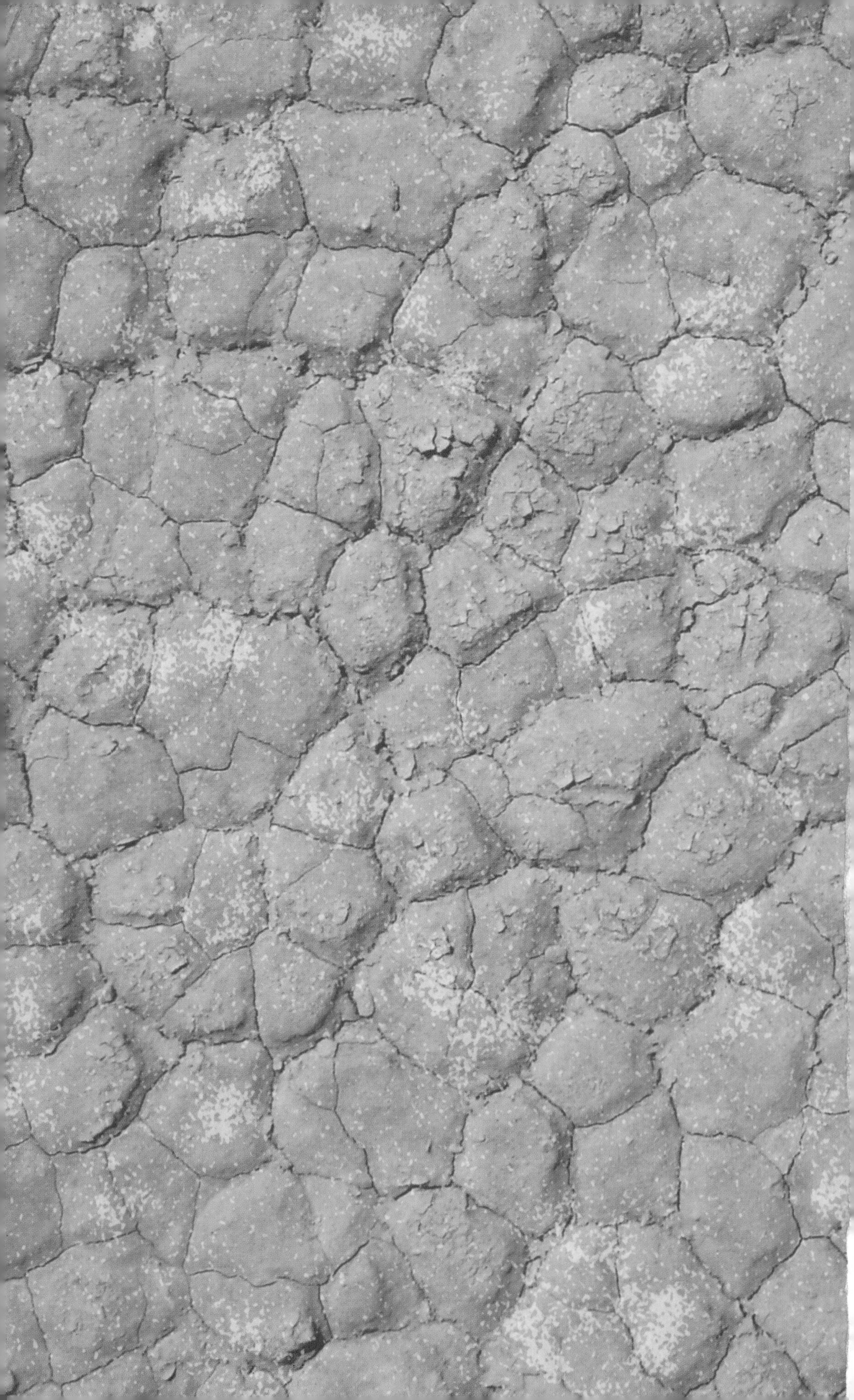

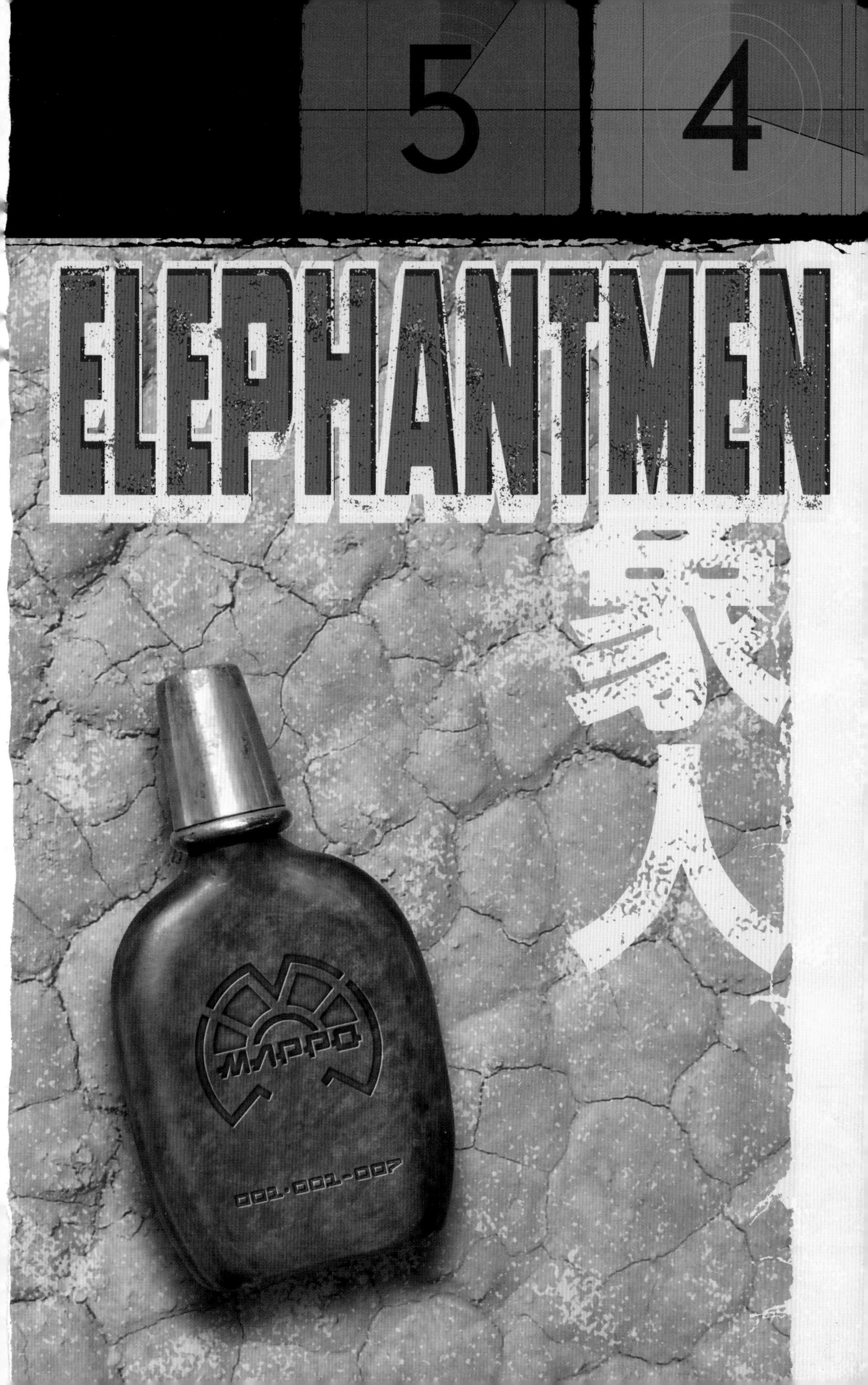
5
4
ELEPHANTMEN
象人
MAPPO
001-001-007

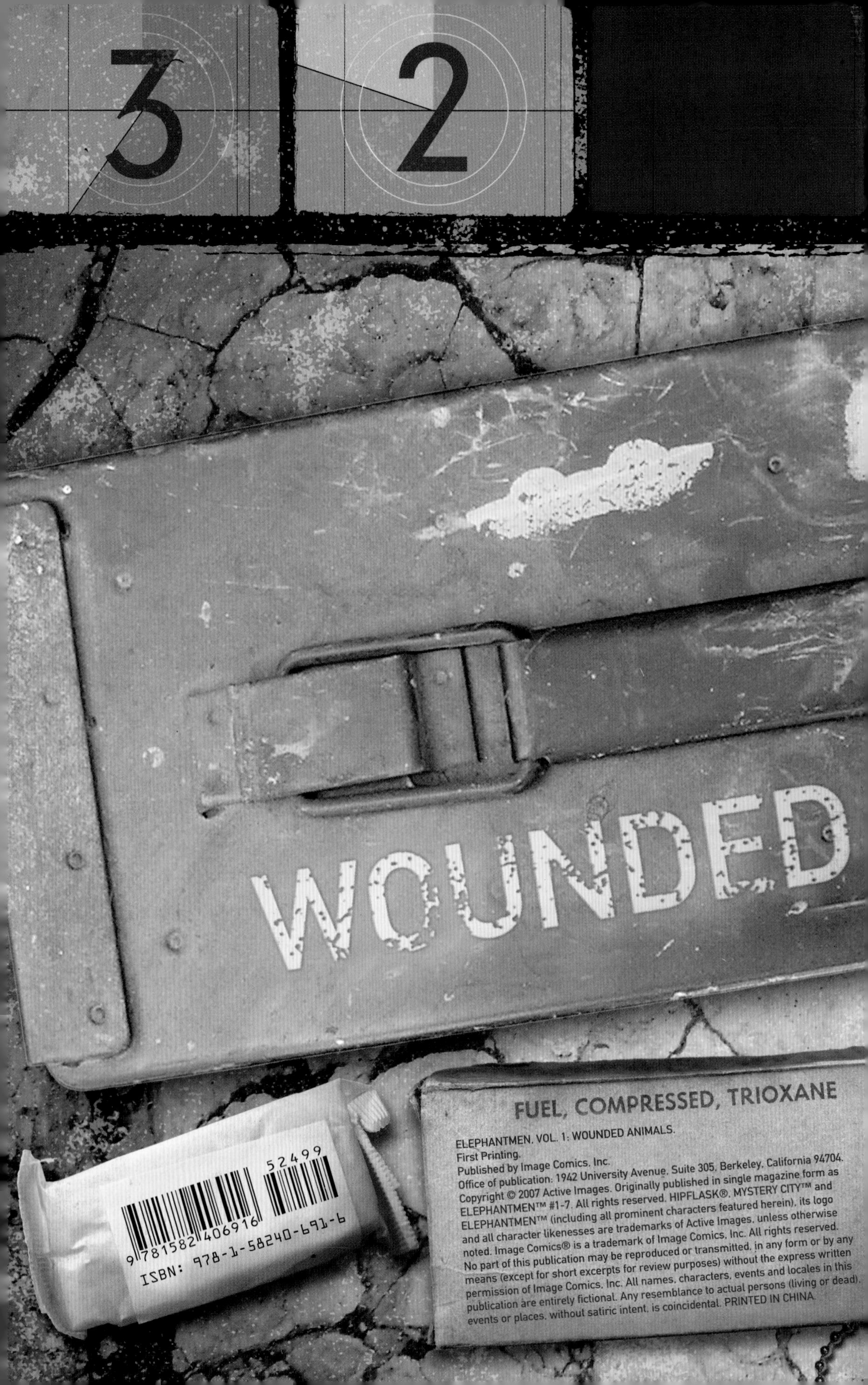
3
2
WOUNDED
FUEL, COMPRESSED, TRIOXANE
ELEPHANTMEN, VOL. 1: WOUNDED ANIMALS.
First Printing.
Published by Image Comics, Inc.
Office of publication: 1942 University Avenue, Suite 305, Berkeley, California 94704.
Copyright © 2007 Active Images. Originally published in single magazine form as ELEPHANTMEN™ #1-7. All rights reserved. HIPFLASK®, MYSTERY CITY™ and ELEPHANTMEN™ (including all prominent characters featured herein), its logo and all character likenesses are trademarks of Active Images, unless otherwise noted. Image Comics® is a trademark of Image Comics, Inc. All rights reserved. No part of this publication may be reproduced or transmitted, in any form or by any means (except for short excerpts for review purposes) without the express written permission of Image Comics, Inc. All names, characters, events and locales in this publication are entirely fictional. Any resemblance to actual persons (living or dead), events or places, without satiric intent, is coincidental. PRINTED IN CHINA.
52499
9 781582 406916
ISBN: 978-1-58240-691-6

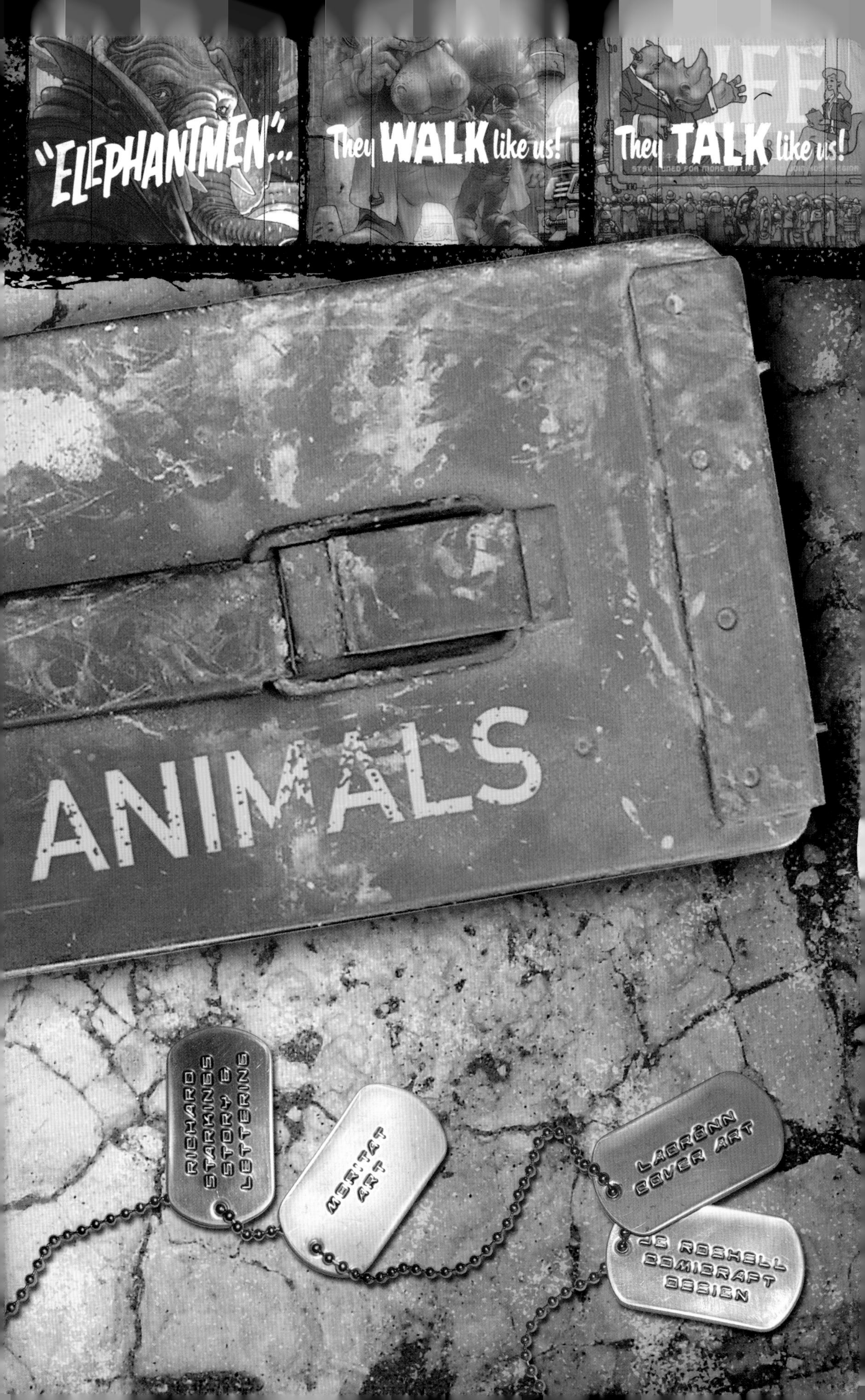
"ELEPHANTMEN"...
They WALK like us!
They TALK like us!
STAY TUNED FOR MORE ON LIFE
ANIMALS
RICHARD STARKINGS STORY & LETTERING
MORITAT ART
LADRÖNN COVER ART
JG ROSHELL COMICRAFT DESIGN

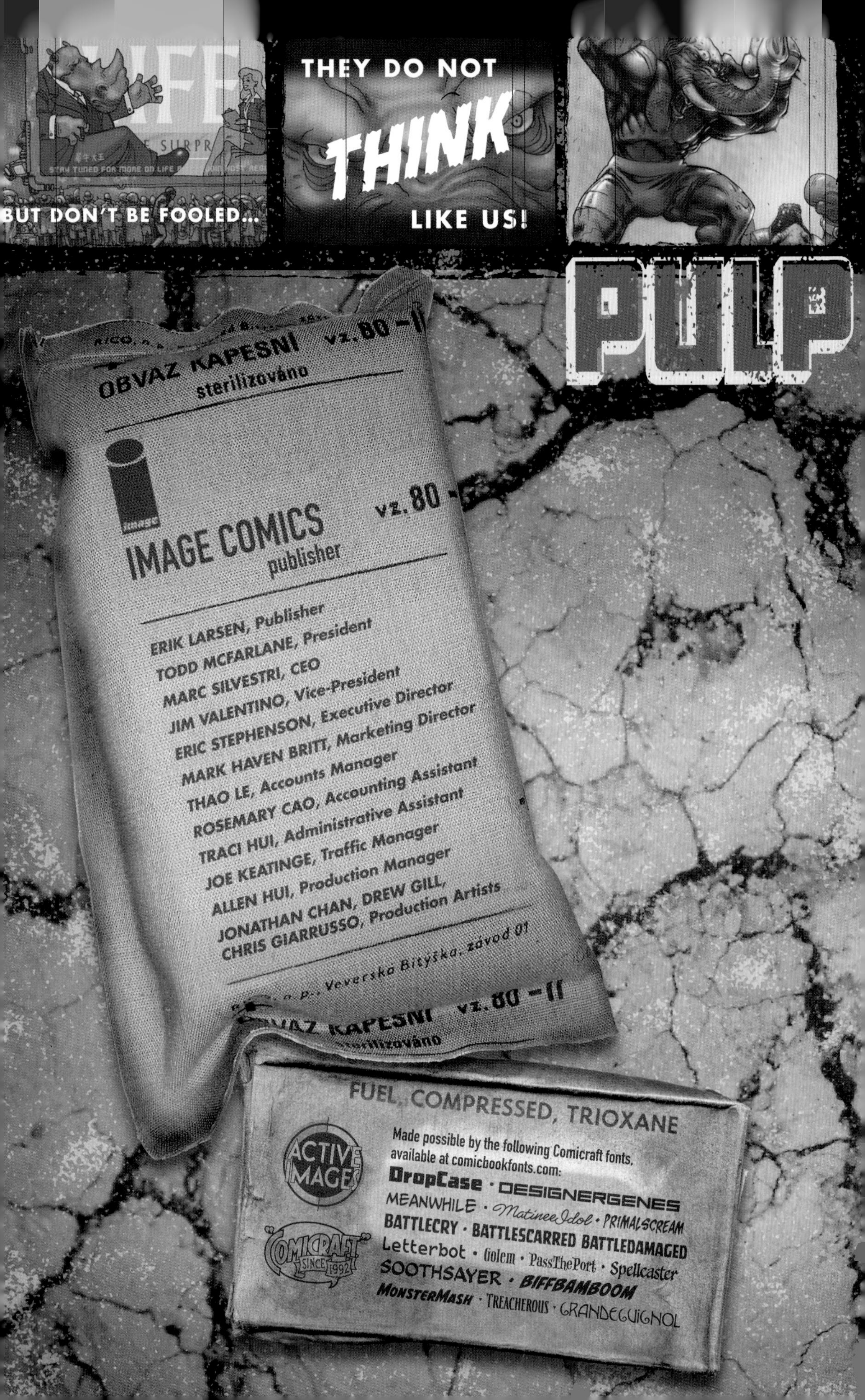
BUT DON'T BE FOOLED...
THEY DO NOT
THINK
LIKE US!
PULP
OBVAZ KAPESNI vz. 80 -11
sterilizováno
IMAGE COMICS
publisher
vz. 80 -
ERIK LARSEN, Publisher
TODD MCFARLANE, President
MARC SILVESTRI, CEO
JIM VALENTINO, Vice-President
ERIC STEPHENSON, Executive Director
MARK HAVEN BRITT, Marketing Director
THAO LE, Accounts Manager
ROSEMARY CAO, Accounting Assistant
TRACI HUI, Administrative Assistant
JOE KEATINGE, Traffic Manager
ALLEN HUI, Production Manager
JONATHAN CHAN, DREW GILL,
CHRIS GIARRUSSO, Production Artists
Veverska Bityška, závod 01
FUEL, COMPRESSED, TRIOXANE
ACTIVE IMAGES
COMICRAFT SINCE 1992
Made possible by the following Comicraft fonts, available at comicbookfonts.com:
DropCase · DESIGNERGENES
MEANWHILE · MatineeIdol · PRIMALSCREAM
BATTLECRY · BATTLESCARRED BATTLEDAMAGED
Letterbot · Golem · PassThePort · Spellcaster
SOOTHSAYER · BIFFBAMBOOM
MONSTERMASH · TREACHEROUS · GRANDEGUIGNOL

THEY ARE
ANIMALS!
EMOTIONLESS
WAR
MACHINES!

SCIENCE FICTION

READY TO BELIEVE?

Countdown
NO.
1
FREE
GIANT SPACEFACT WALLCHART with STAMPS
DOCTOR WHO
THUNDERBIRDS
CAPTAIN SCARLET
UFO

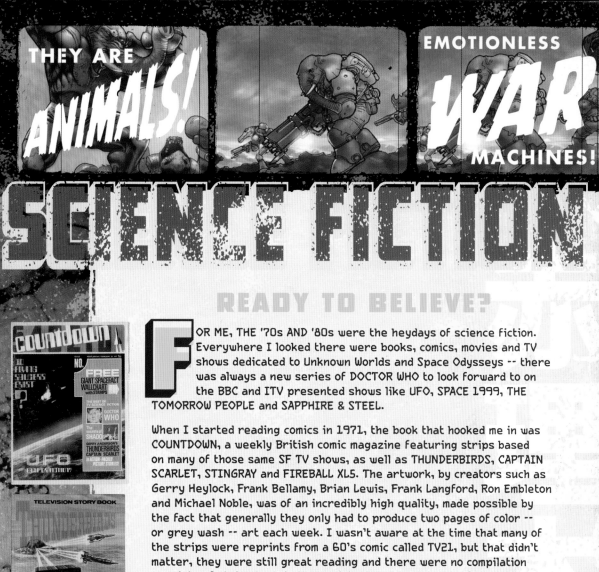

FOR ME, THE '70s AND '80s were the heydays of science fiction. Everywhere I looked there were books, comics, movies and TV shows dedicated to Unknown Worlds and Space Odysseys -- there was always a new series of DOCTOR WHO to look forward to on the BBC and ITV presented shows like UFO, SPACE 1999, THE TOMORROW PEOPLE and SAPPHIRE & STEEL.

When I started reading comics in 1971, the book that hooked me in was COUNTDOWN, a weekly British comic magazine featuring strips based on many of those same SF TV shows, as well as THUNDERBIRDS, CAPTAIN SCARLET, STINGRAY and FIREBALL XL5. The artwork, by creators such as Gerry Heylock, Frank Bellamy, Brian Lewis, Frank Langford, Ron Embleton and Michael Noble, was of an incredibly high quality, made possible by the fact that generally they only had to produce two pages of color -- or grey wash -- art each week. I wasn't aware at the time that many of the strips were reprints from a 60's comic called TV21, but that didn't matter, they were still great reading and there were no compilation reprints of strips back in those distant days -- the era of the trade paperback was still far, far away. Unfortunately COUNTDOWN only lasted two years but was replaced for me by LOOK-IN, another weekly based on TV shows with top artists drawing strips such as KUNG FU, TIMESLIP or MAN FROM ATLANTIS by Michael Noble, THE SIX MILLION DOLLAR MAN by Martin Asbury, THE BIONIC WOMAN featuring the beautiful early work of John Bolton and THE TOMORROW PEOPLE by John M. Burns. The stories in both COUNTDOWN and LOOK-IN were written mostly by Alan Fennell or Angus Allan respectively, and were often more imaginative and engaging than the TV shows that inspired them. I also loved THE TRIGAN EMPIRE by Don Lawrence, a beautiful original painted SF story that was the only comic strip in the educational children's magazine LOOK AND LEARN.

TELEVISION STORY BOOK
THUNDERBIRDS
TV21
BOOK

ON THE BALL JIMMY GREENHOFF
Look-in
THE TOMORROW PEOPLE RETURN WITH A FREE GIFT!
MEET THE NEW TOMORROW PERSON!
ALL ACTION COLOUR PICTURE STRIP!

In those dim and distant magical days, every kid at school was fascinated by the NASA moon landings and every boy had made the AIRFIX Saturn V kit, or was collecting PG TIPS' RACE INTO SPACE cards. Paintings of unfeasibly large spaceships by Chris Foss graced the covers of every other science fiction paperback and albums like ELO's OUT OF THE BLUE and JEFF WAYNE'S WAR OF THE WORLDS eagerly carried science fiction into the mainstream consciousness.

SCI-FI
MONTHLY
STAR TREK: THE KIRK STORY
BACK STAGE WITH DR. WHO!
ENTERPRISE BRIDGE BLUE-PRINT
PLUS: THE

As a teenager I was strongly affected by SF shows with more serious, down-to-Earth themes such as DOOMWATCH and SURVIVORS, and at the pictures I sought out movies such as PLANET OF THE APES, LOGAN'S RUN, SOYLENT GREEN, THE OMEGA MAN, SILENT RUNNING, ALIEN and

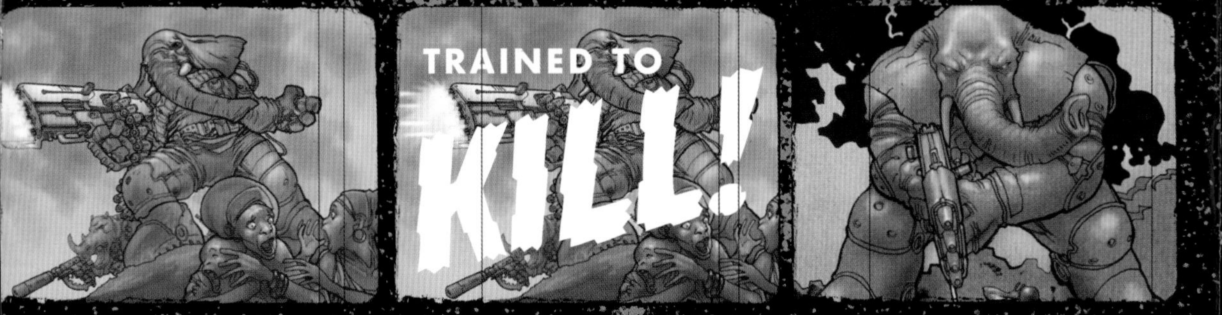
TRAINED TO
KILL!

BLADE RUNNER. In 1978 the fortnightly comic book STARLORD led me to 2000AD and the incredible work of writers John Wagner and Pat Mills and top British artists like Brian Bolland, Dave Gibbons, Kevin O'Neill, Mick McMahon and Ian Gibson. 2000AD presented a host of fantastic characters, outrageous stories and mind boggling concepts every week, including JUDGE DREDD, RO-BUSTERS, STRONTIUM DOG, ROBO HUNTER, HARLEM HEROES and NEMESIS. SF concepts and ideas flew so thick and fast it was easy to take the quality and volume of the work for granted, and even easier to forget that there had not been a comic like this before. In the same way that Stan Lee, Jack Kirby, Steve Ditko and Marvel Comics brightened up American comics in the sixties, the 2000AD creators revitalized British comics in the seventies.

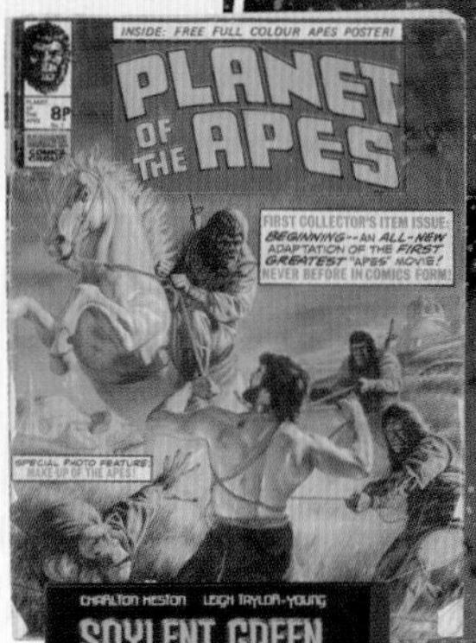
INSIDE: FREE FULL COLOUR APES POSTER!
PLANET OF THE APES
8P
FIRST COLLECTOR'S ITEM ISSUE: BEGINNING--AN ALL-NEW ADAPTATION OF THE FIRST GREATEST 'APES' MOVIE! NEVER BEFORE IN COMICS FORM!

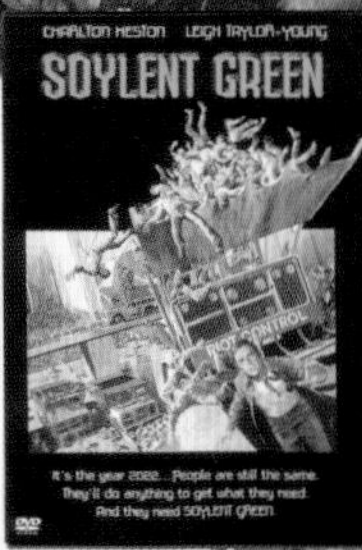
CHARLTON HESTON LEIGH TAYLOR-YOUNG
SOYLENT GREEN

DO YOU REMEMBER when SPIDER-MAN, THE UNCANNY X-MEN, THE FANTASTIC FOUR, SUPERMAN and BATMAN were not movie franchises but simply exciting comics full of interesting new characters, ideas and stories? Did it matter to you that characters like the Toad Men or the Terrible Tinkerer weren't entirely plausible? Were you excited by the idea of cities in bottles and Superman as a ghost or did you dismiss them as silly? How about Superboy engaged in fierce midair battle with a Sharkman? Concepts that might seem goofy or childish to you when you get older are always full of wonder and excitement to kids. For them, every turn of the page is another step into the Twilight Zone of imagination and possibility -- children don't need rhyme or reason, they're ready to believe. My favorite American comic book character was always The Thing -- "THIS MAN, THIS MONSTER!" -- a big guy turned into a pile of rocks by cosmic radiation? Give me a break!

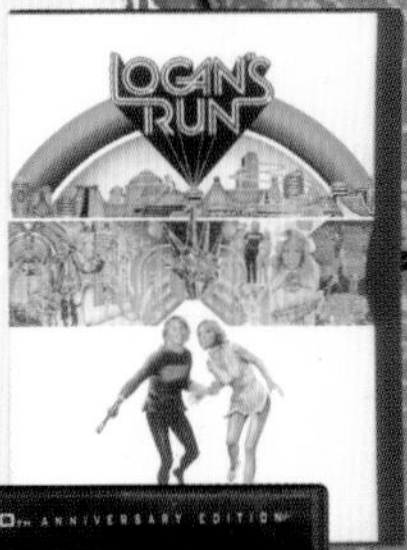
LOGAN'S RUN

I created HIP FLASK and the ELEPHANTMEN with the intention of filling a series of comic books full of implausible ideas and impossible characters. Evil scientific genius? Check. Mutant hippos, rhinos, crocodiles and elephants? Check. Robotic frog? Check? A cybernetic assassin? Check. Hot girls hanging around misunderstood male leads with deep dark secrets? Check. A time travel experiment with disastrous consequences? Check. Action, Adventure and Really Wild Things? Check, check, CHECK! I was also eager to create a strong, heroic character who, like The Thing, The Hulk, Superman and Spidey, didn't rely on guns or knives to make his point. Comics have been taken over by the First-Person-Shooter-Ask-Questions-Later mentality so prevalent in videogames and movies like The Matrix, but I've always felt that true heroes carry their strength and motivation inside, they don't wave it around in the faces of their ideological opposites threatening to pull the trigger. The heroes of my youth were adventurers and explorers who realized that with great power comes great responsibility -- they were all about saving people, not killing them!

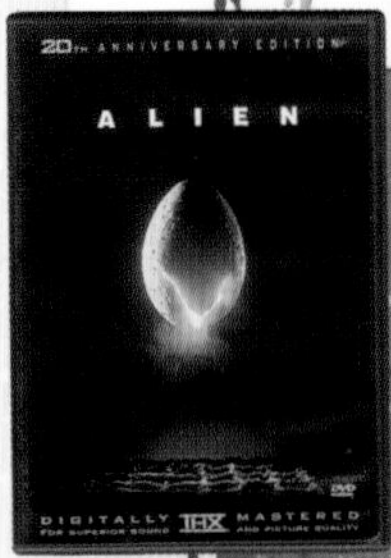
20th ANNIVERSARY EDITION
ALIEN
DIGITALLY THX MASTERED

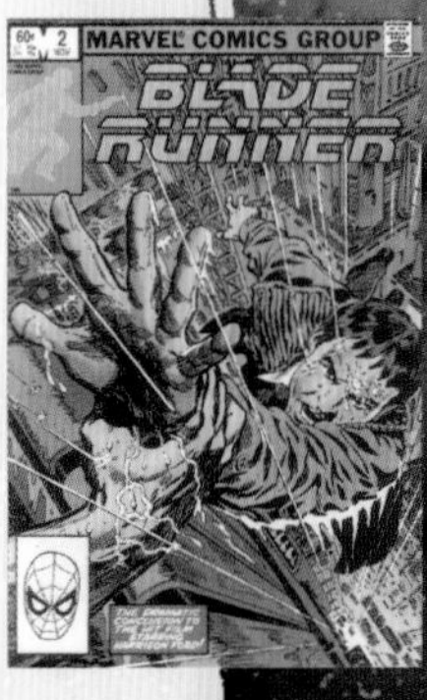
MARVEL COMICS GROUP
BLADE RUNNER

I call it Pulp Science Fiction, a term which not only covers those great 60's Marvel comics and 70's issues of 2000AD that introduced new ideas and characters every issue, but also DOCTOR WHO, THE AVENGERS TV show, THE TWILIGHT ZONE, STAR TREK and all those great Gerry Anderson TV series and comic strips.

DESIGNED TO
CHILL
YOUR VERY SOUL!

BE WARNED!

KEEP YOUR CHILDREN AWAY FROM THESE
MONSTERS!

THE WORLD'S GREATEST COMIC MAGAZINE!
Fantastic Four
51
12¢
"THIS MAN... THIS MONSTER!"

THE MIGHTY WORLD OF
MARVEL
INCREDIBLE HULK!
BANISHED TO OUTER SPACE!
SPIDER-MAN

THE MIGHTY THOR!
SPIDER-MAN
COMICS WEEKLY
ONE OF THE WILDEST OF ALL SPIDEY'S BATTLES!
"SPIDEY SMASHES OUT!" AGAINST THE LETHAL LIZARD!

45p
SCI-FI SPECIAL
STARRING JUDGE DREDD
64 PAGES

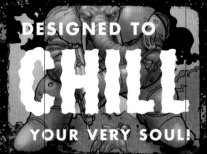

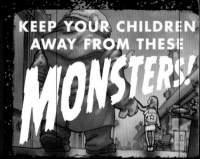

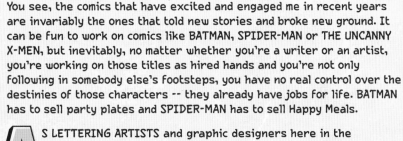

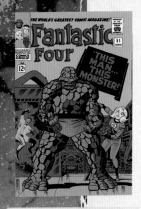

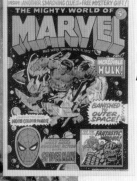

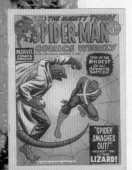

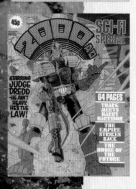

Hopefully, when you picked up this book you didn't know what to expect, and that's the key to science fiction isn't it -- the excitement of Not Knowing? I felt that way when I sat down to write the first issue with nothing more than the image of Elephantman Ebony Hide standing on the street in Santa Monica. What kind of character had I created? How would he tell his story? What the heck was he doing outside HOOTERS?! I couldn't wait to find out.

You see, the comics that have excited and engaged me in recent years are invariably the ones that told new stories and broke new ground. It can be fun to work on comics like BATMAN, SPIDER-MAN or THE UNCANNY X-MEN, but inevitably, no matter whether you're a writer or an artist, you're working on those titles as hired hands and you're not only following in somebody else's footsteps, you have no real control over the destinies of those characters -- they already have jobs for life. BATMAN has to sell party plates and SPIDER-MAN has to sell Happy Meals.

AS LETTERING ARTISTS and graphic designers here in the Comicraft studio we've had the privilege to contribute to exciting and new creations such as ASTRO CITY, BATTLE CHASERS, DANGER GIRL, STEAMPUNK and THE RED STAR -- and those projects have proved to be the most inspiring, challenging and stimulating books we've worked on simply because no one has made rules for us to follow; we had to invent them for ourselves! That's the atmosphere and excitement we've sought to bring to you in the pages of ELEPHANTMEN, and I'm indebted to the creators of those other books -- Kurt Busiek, Joe Madureira, J Scott Campbell, Joe Kelly, Chris Bachalo and Christian Gossett -- for leading the way, and of course to Image Comics for creating the playing field for all of these titles and creators to play in way back in 1992!

Those of you checking in on the HIP FLASK mythos for the first time should also know that you can read more about our affable Information Agent in the pages of two hardcover volumes, written by yours truly -- with the assistance of GØDLAND's Mighty Joe Casey -- and illustrated by our amazing cover artist, Ladrönn, currently available in all good comic book stores or via Amazon.com.

HIP FLASK: UNNATURAL SELECTION tells the story of the origin of the Elephantmen by Doctor Kazushi Nikken and the evil MAPPO corporation. HIP FLASK: CONCRETE JUNGLE catches up with Hip Flask two years after the events that are unfolding in the regular ELEPHANTMEN series, wherein Hip and his associate, Vanity Case, become involved in a time travel murder mystery of epic proportions. That story, entitled THE BIG HERE AND THE LONG NOW will be continued in two one-shots from Image Comics -- watch the pages of ELEPHANTMEN for further news on exactly when you'll be seeing them in comic book stores. For Ladrönn, every page has been a labor of love, and he has produced them with the same attention to detail and care that the artists who worked on COUNTDOWN and strips like THE TRIGAN EMPIRE applied to their work in the '70s.

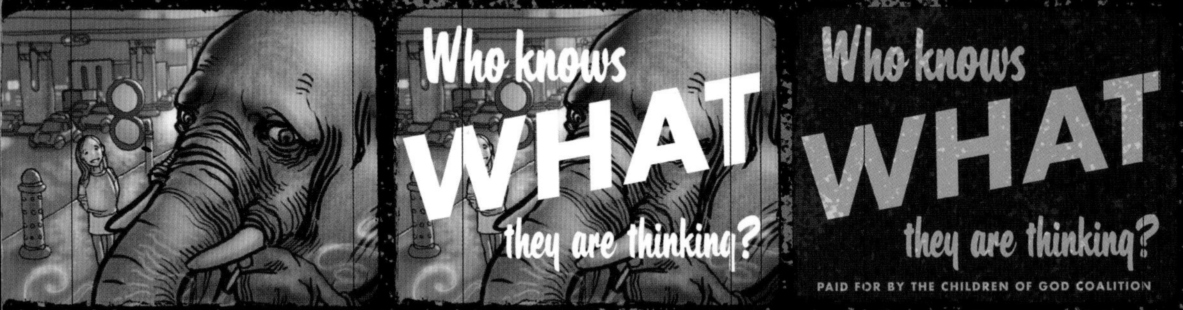
Who knows
WHAT
they are thinking?
Who knows
WHAT
they are thinking?
PAID FOR BY THE CHILDREN OF GOD COALITION

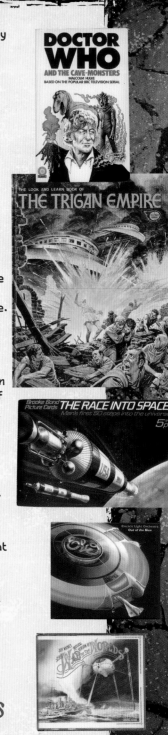

Those of you who just can't wait for collections and need a monthly ELEPHANTMEN fix should check out our monthly series. Thanks to the agile and amazing artistry of Moritat -- who sometimes operates under the unlikely alias "Justin Norman" -- we've been bringing you at least 22 pages of Pulp Science Fiction for just $2.99 every month, and plan on continuing to do so for the foreseeable future. Note that Moritat's not just penciling the book, he's inking and coloring it! If all you've seen of his work is the graphic novel, SOLSTICE -- which he illustrated for Steven Seagle over ten years ago and which, funnily enough, my own publishing company Active Images published in 2005 -- then you'll see in these pages how much he's grown as an artist. Moritat is the perfect collaborator -- he imbues each and every character with the exact amount of horror, humour or humanity they require -- I am, as Ladrönn has often said to me, a Very Lucky Man.

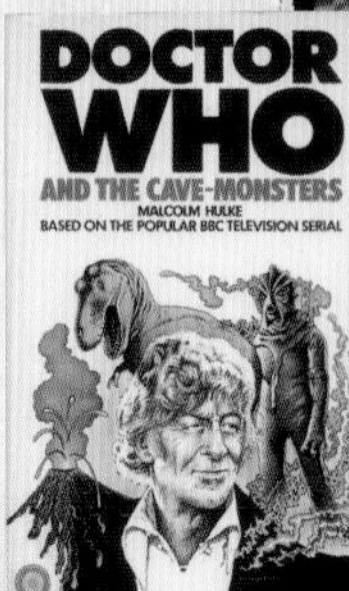
DOCTOR WHO
AND THE CAVE-MONSTERS
MALCOLM HULKE
BASED ON THE POPULAR BBC TELEVISION SERIAL

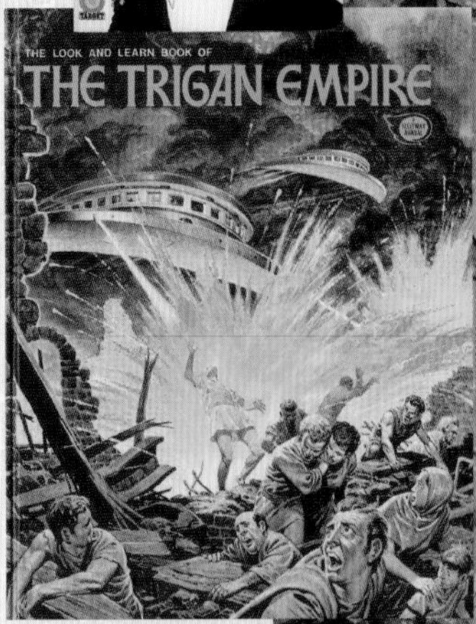
THE LOOK AND LEARN BOOK OF
THE TRIGAN EMPIRE

Naturally, I know that people who've become familiar with Ladrönn's definitive take on HIP FLASK will be concerned that the book won't be the same without him, but I'm happy to say that Ladrönn is onboard, as cover artist, character designer and cheerleader for every issue. His role on the new title is very much like Alex Ross's involvement in Kurt Busiek's ASTRO CITY title. Each issue of ELEPHANTMEN sports a painted cover by Ladrönn, as well as a peek at his sketches and concept art for the series. Ladrönn and I spent many long evenings discussing what happened in the world of the Elephantmen inbetween the first two volumes of the HIP FLASK series, and you'll see many of those stories unfold in our book every month.

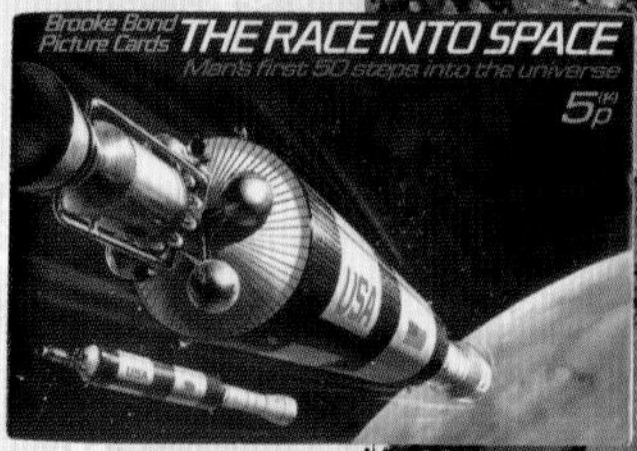
Brooke Bond
Picture Cards
THE RACE INTO SPACE
Man's first 50 steps into the universe
5p

The collection you hold before you features no less than twelve great stories, including four by our tremendous guest artists: Henry DREDD/ALIENS Flint, Tom GØDLAND Scioli, David SPAWN Hine, and not forgetting the wonderful CAPTAIN STONEHEART story by Joe SUPERGIRL Kelly, Chris X-MEN Bachalo and Aron DEAD SAMURAI Lusen.

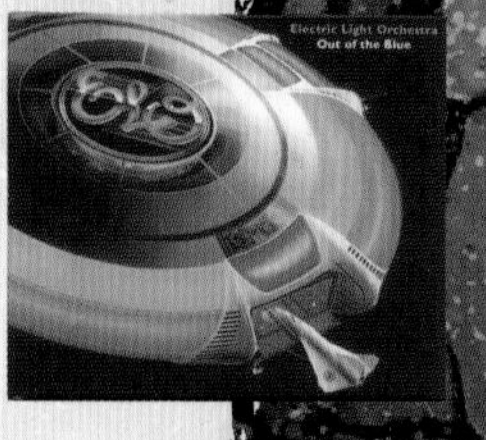
Electric Light Orchestra
Out of the Blue

Last but definitely not least; ELEPHANTMEN just wouldn't exist without the support and enthusiasm of Comicraft's Secret Weapon, John 'JG' Roshell. When JG isn't trying to convince his son, Stone, that A NEW HOPE is way better than ATTACK OF THE CLONES, he's building the HIP FLASK website (hipflask.com), making ELEPHANTMEN flash movies and sanding down the covers of our monthly issues to give them just the right amount of weathering for the war torn design of this first ELEPHANTMEN hardcover volume.

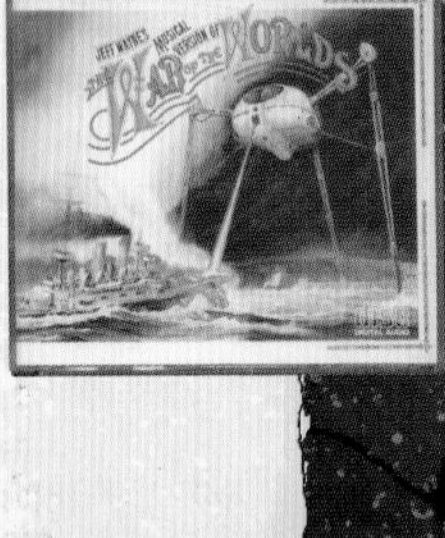

Truly, this is a Team Supreme! All in all ELEPHANTMEN is turning out to be one big long rollercoaster ride. Strap in tight -- 'derm isn't all we're packing!

Richard Starkings

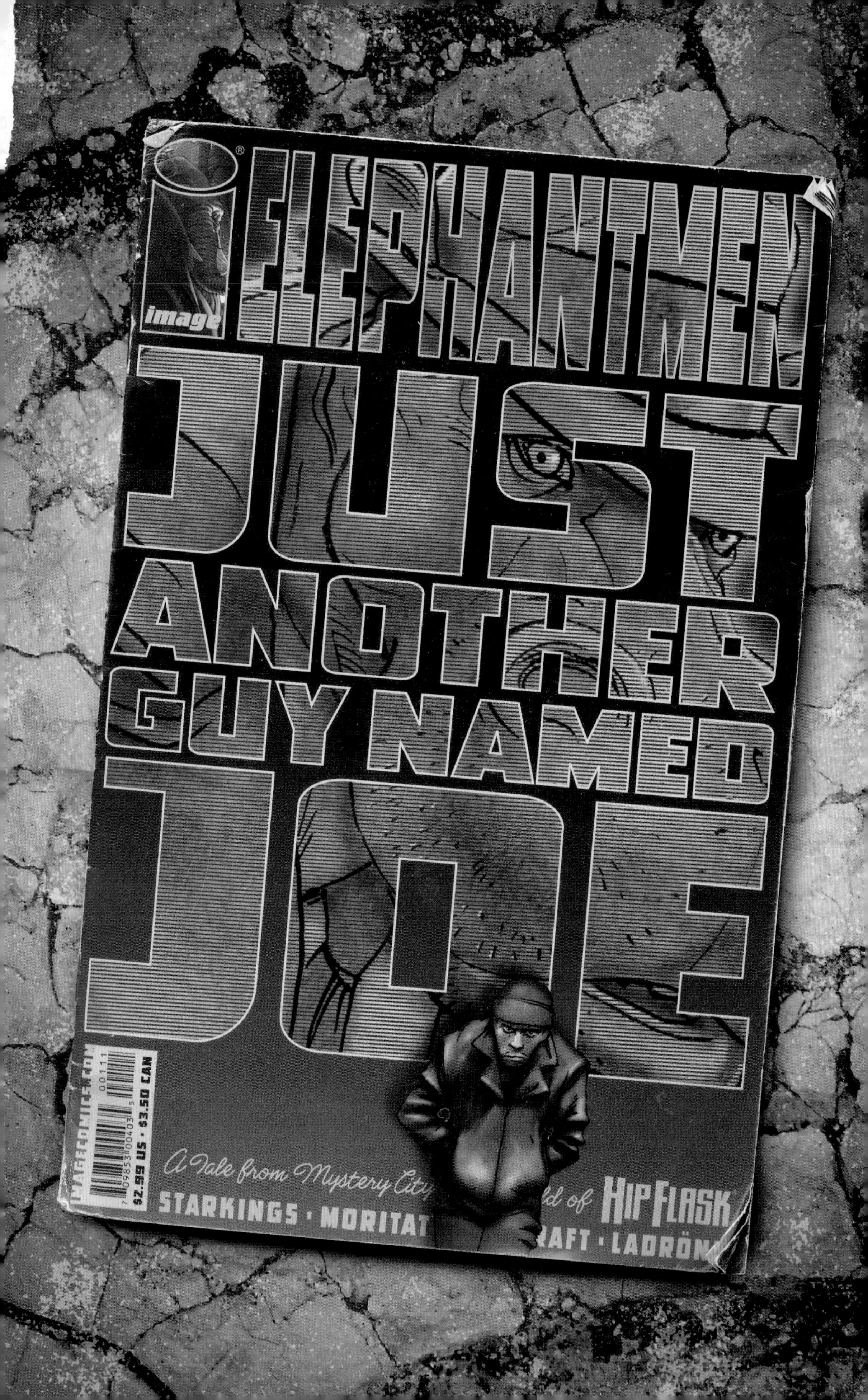
image
ELEPHANTMEN
JUST ANOTHER GUY NAMED JOE
IMAGECOMICS.COM
$2.99 US · $3.50 CAN
A Tale from Mystery City
ld of HIP FLASK
STARKINGS · MORITAT
RAFT · LADRÖN

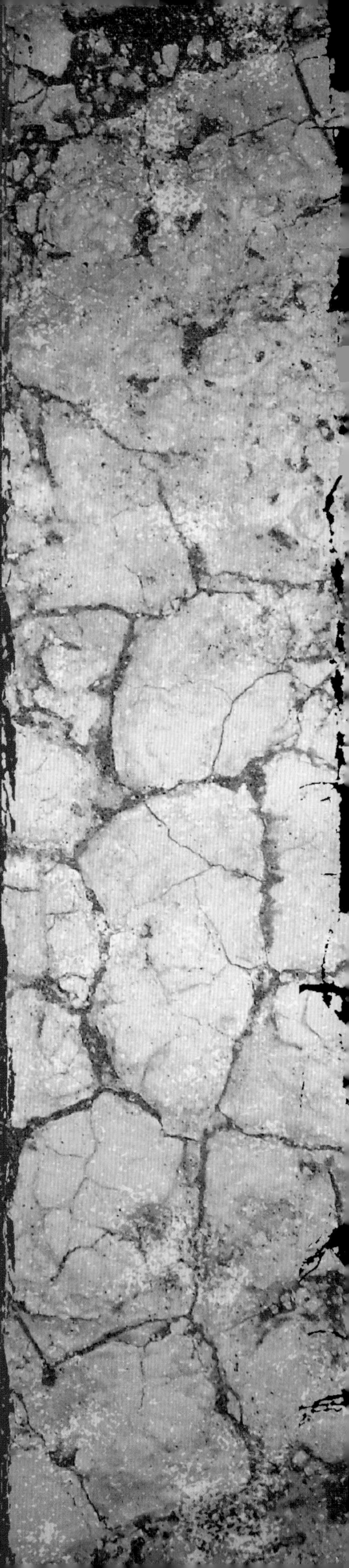

"NEVER TELL GOD YOU DON'T LIKE ONE OF HIS CREATIONS."

ANONYMOUS

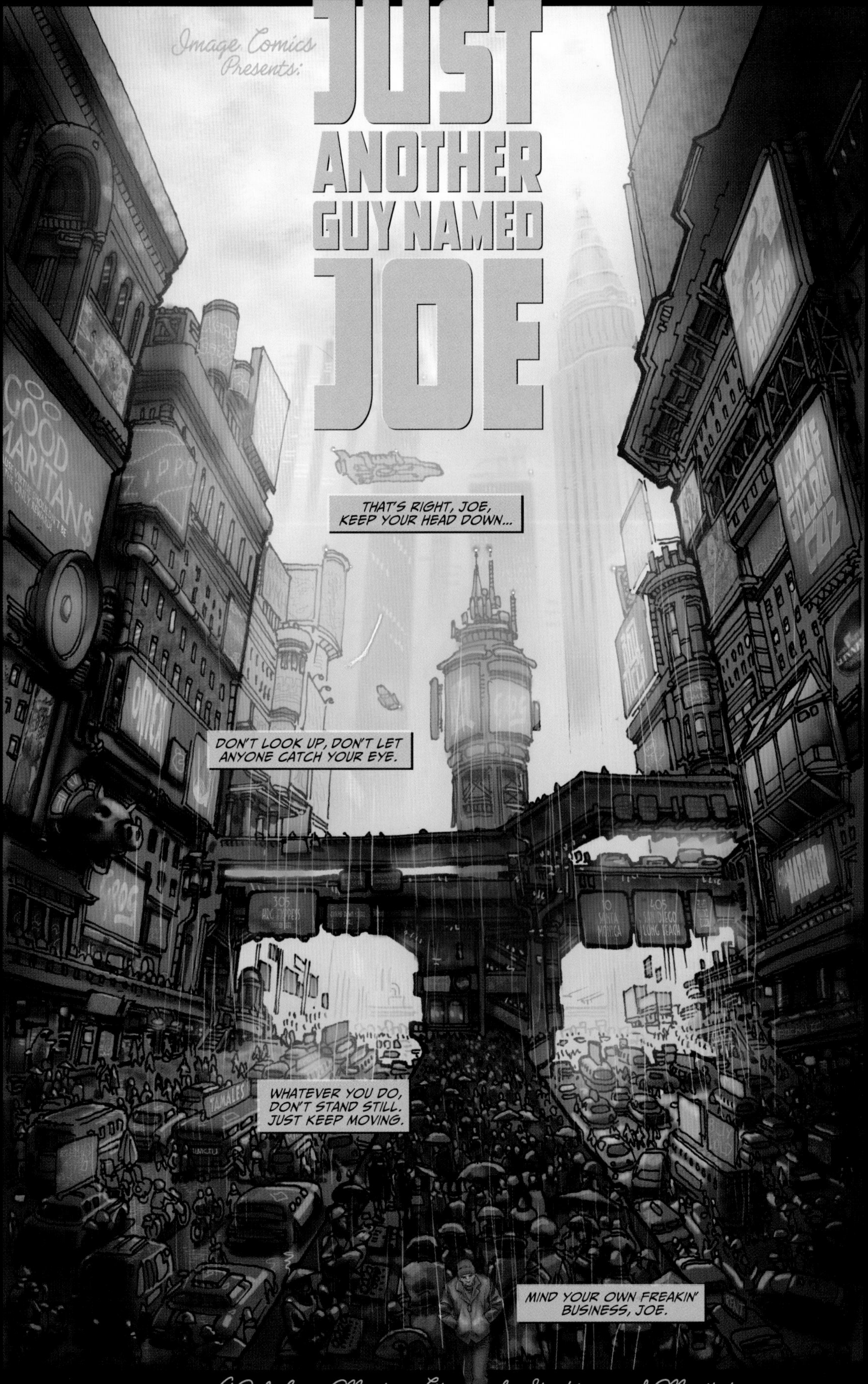

A Tale from Mystery City by Starkings and Moritat

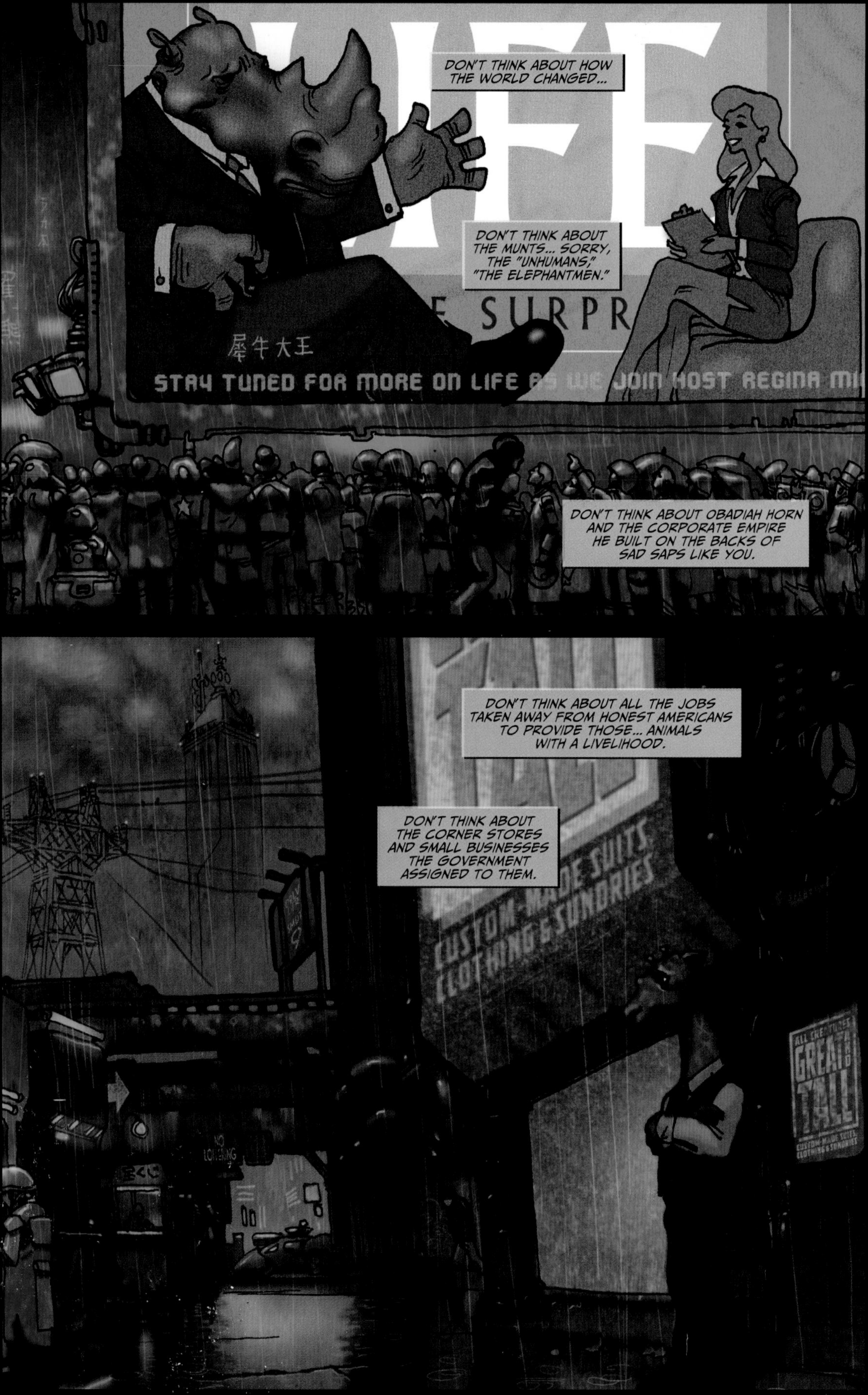
DON'T THINK ABOUT HOW THE WORLD CHANGED...
DON'T THINK ABOUT THE MUNTS... SORRY, THE "UNHUMANS," "THE ELEPHANTMEN."
犀牛大王
STAY TUNED FOR MORE ON LIFE AS WE JOIN HOST REGINA MI
DON'T THINK ABOUT OBADIAH HORN AND THE CORPORATE EMPIRE HE BUILT ON THE BACKS OF SAD SAPS LIKE YOU.
DON'T THINK ABOUT ALL THE JOBS TAKEN AWAY FROM HONEST AMERICANS TO PROVIDE THOSE... ANIMALS WITH A LIVELIHOOD.
DON'T THINK ABOUT THE CORNER STORES AND SMALL BUSINESSES THE GOVERNMENT ASSIGNED TO THEM.
CUSTOM-MADE SUITS CLOTHING & SUNDRIES
NO LOITERING
GREAT TALL

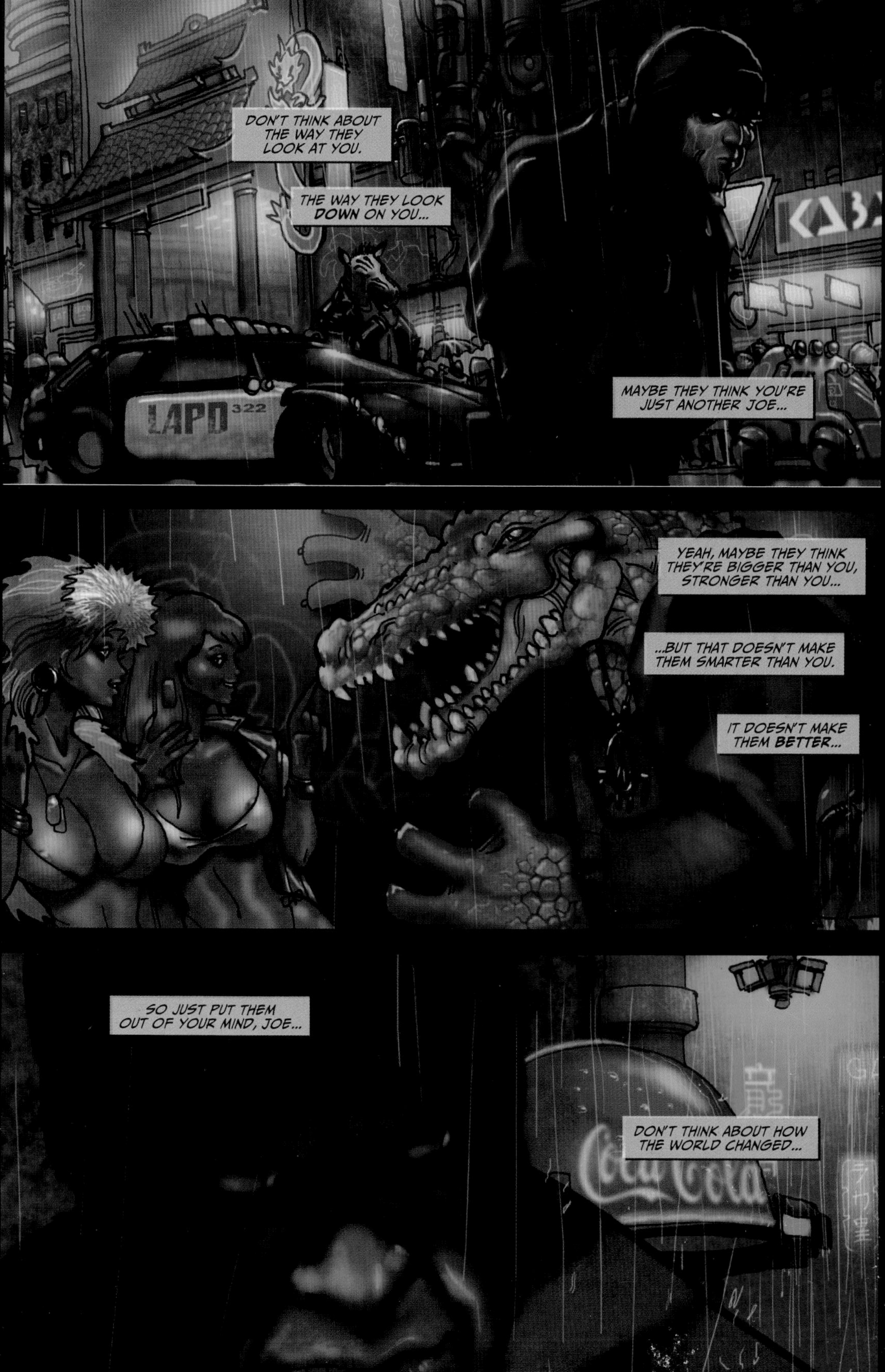
DON'T THINK ABOUT THE WAY THEY LOOK AT YOU.
THE WAY THEY LOOK DOWN ON YOU...
LAPD 322
MAYBE THEY THINK YOU'RE JUST ANOTHER JOE...
YEAH, MAYBE THEY THINK THEY'RE BIGGER THAN YOU, STRONGER THAN YOU...
...BUT THAT DOESN'T MAKE THEM SMARTER THAN YOU.
IT DOESN'T MAKE THEM BETTER...
SO JUST PUT THEM OUT OF YOUR MIND, JOE...
DON'T THINK ABOUT HOW THE WORLD CHANGED...
Coca-Cola

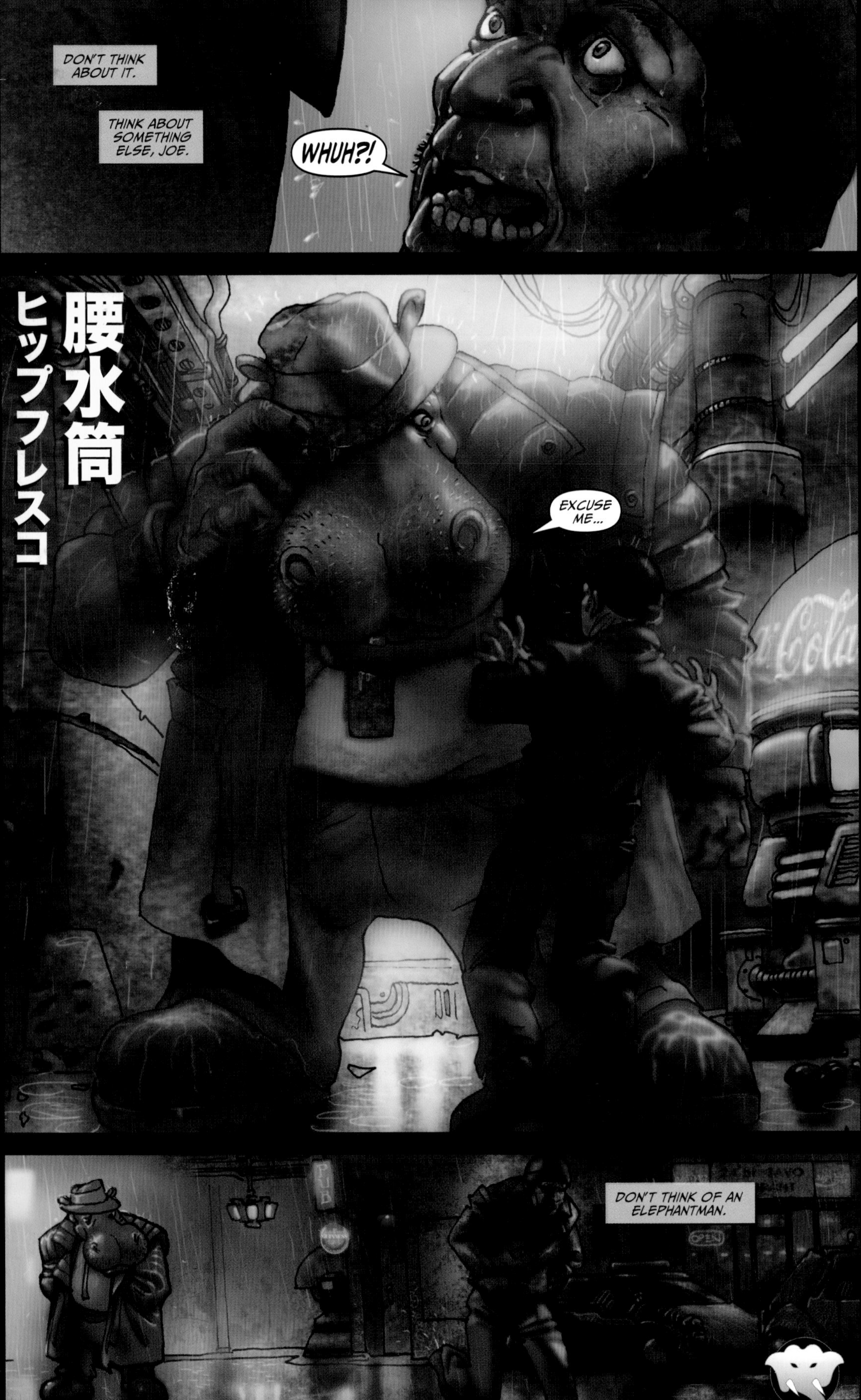
DON'T THINK ABOUT IT.
THINK ABOUT SOMETHING ELSE, JOE.
WHUH?!
腰水筒
ヒップフレスコ
EXCUSE ME...
DON'T THINK OF AN ELEPHANTMAN.

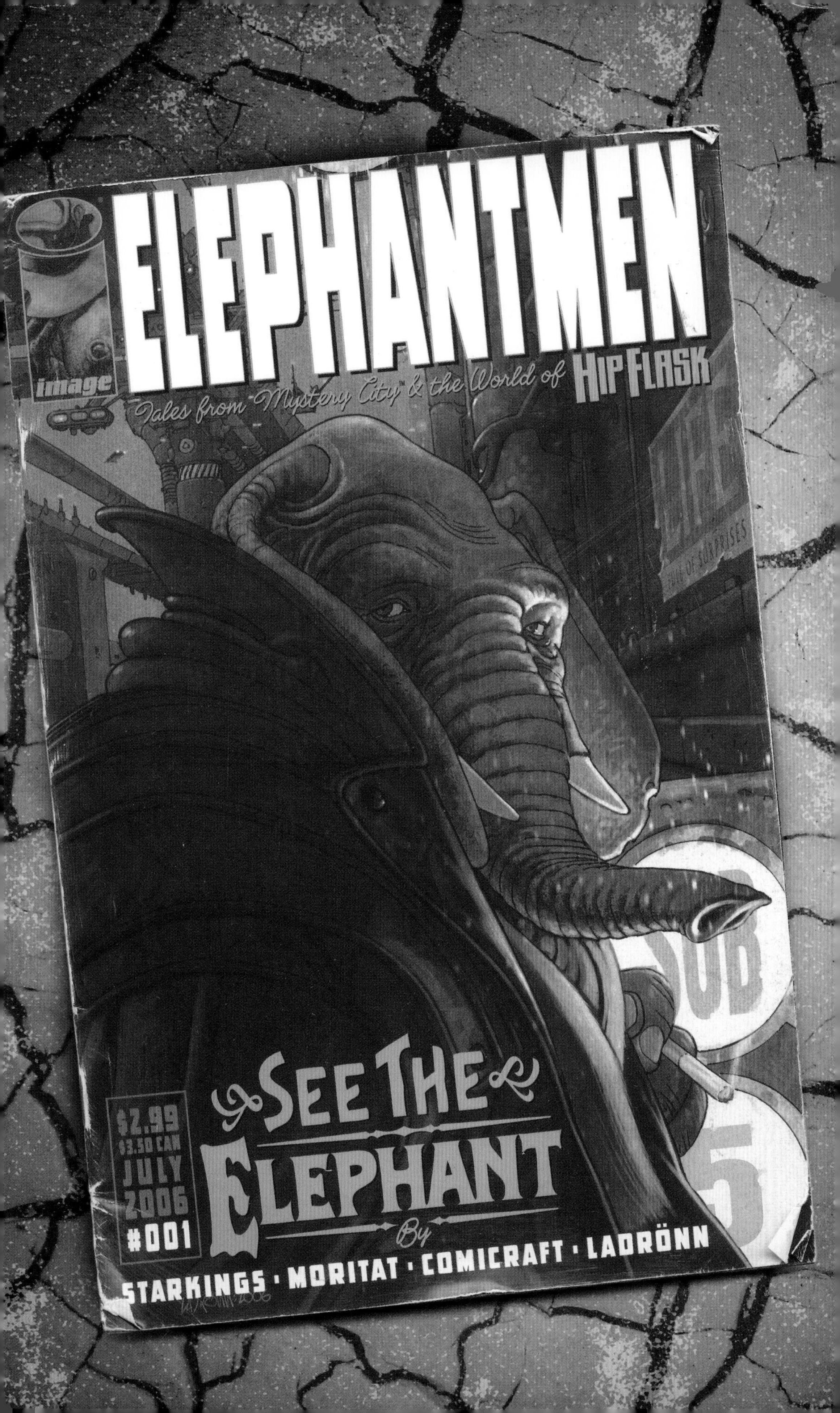

ELEPHANTMEN
image
Tales from Mystery City & the World of HIP FLASK
SEE THE ELEPHANT
By
STARKINGS · MORITAT · COMICRAFT · LADRÖNN
$2.99
$3.50 CAN
JULY
2006
#001

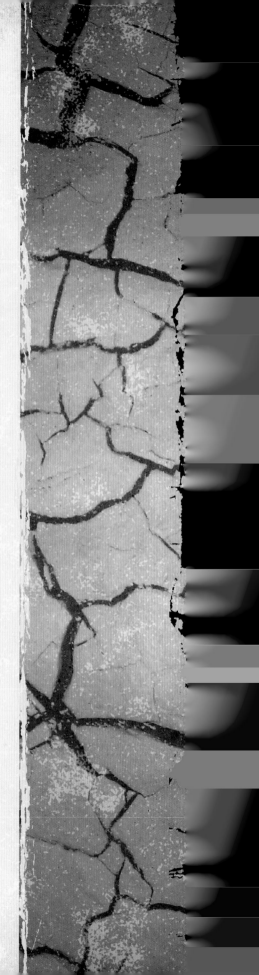

"A HOPEFUL SOCIETY HAS INSTITUTIONS OF SCIENCE AND MEDICINE THAT DO NOT CUT ETHICAL CORNERS AND THAT RECOGNIZE THE MATCHLESS VALUE OF EVERY LIFE.

"TONIGHT I ASK YOU TO PASS LEGISLATION TO PROHIBIT THE MOST EGREGIOUS ABUSES OF MEDICAL RESEARCH: HUMAN CLONING IN ALL ITS FORMS; CREATING OR IMPLANTING EMBRYOS FOR EXPERIMENTS; CREATING HUMAN-ANIMAL HYBRIDS; AND BUYING, SELLING OR PATENTING HUMAN EMBRYOS.

"HUMAN LIFE IS A GIFT FROM OUR CREATOR, AND THAT GIFT SHOULD NEVER BE DISCARDED, DEVALUED OR PUT UP FOR SALE."

GEORGE W. BUSH
STATE OF THE UNION
ADDRESS 2006

"NATURE FALLS UNDER MY COMMAND NOW."

DOCTOR KAZUSHI NIKKEN
2218

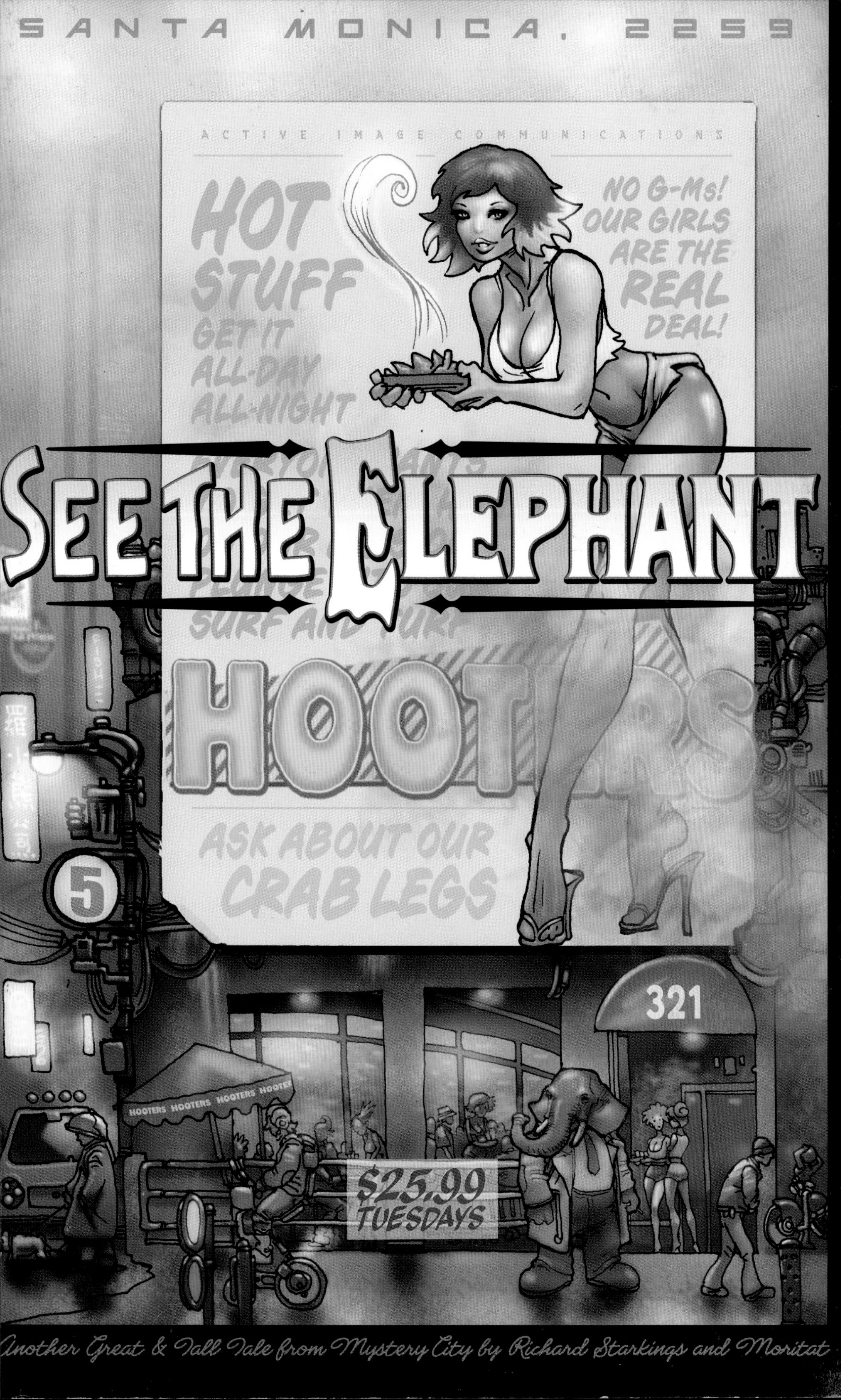

SANTA MONICA, 2259
ACTIVE IMAGE COMMUNICATIONS
HOT STUFF
GET IT ALL-DAY ALL-NIGHT
NO G-Ms! OUR GIRLS ARE THE REAL DEAL!
SEE THE ELEPHANT
SURF AND TURF
ASK ABOUT OUR CRAB LEGS
5
321
HOOTERS HOOTERS HOOTERS
$25.99 TUESDAYS
Another Great & Tall Tale from Mystery City by Richard Starkings and Moritat

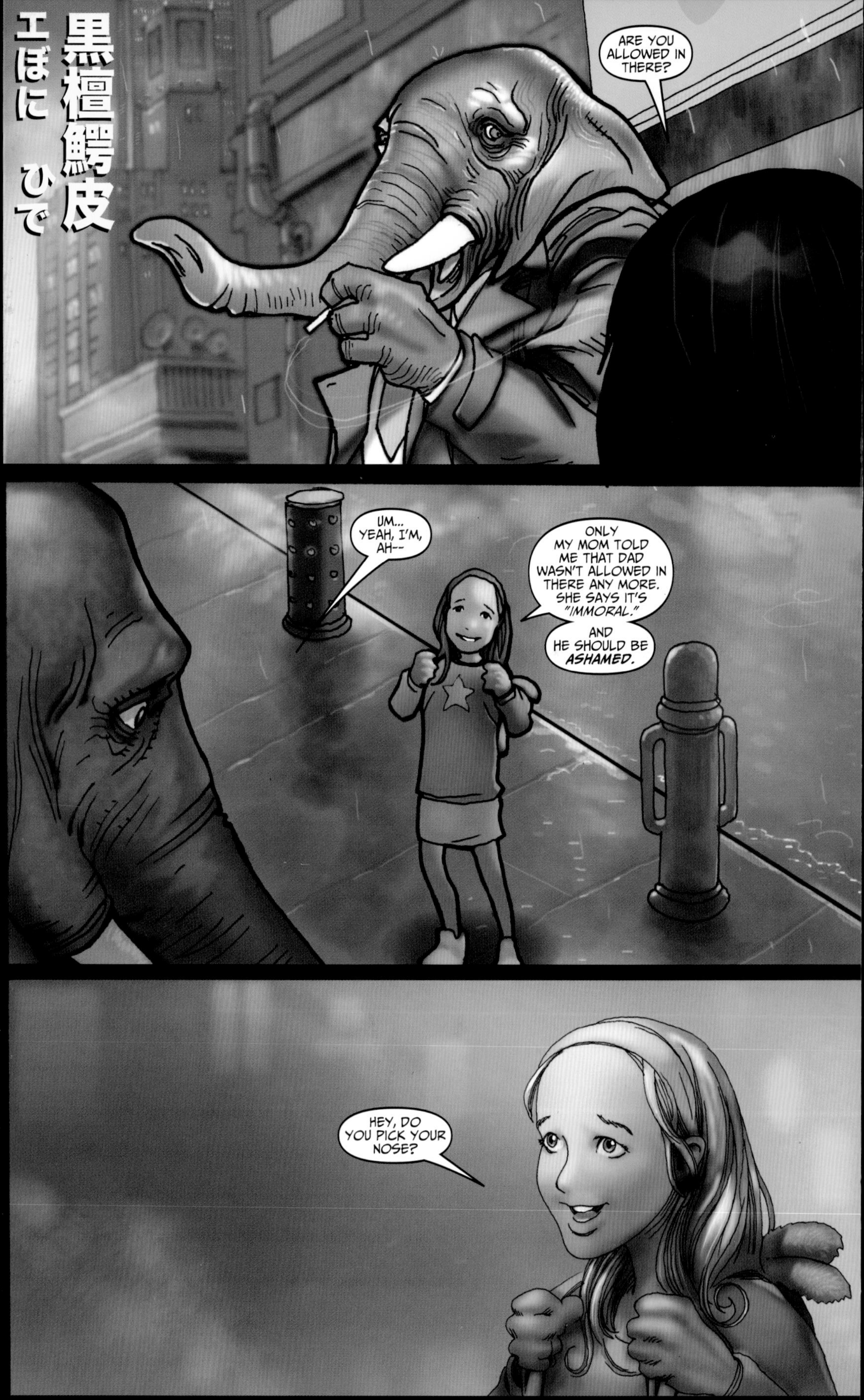
黒檀鰐皮
エぼに ひで
ARE YOU ALLOWED IN THERE?
UM... YEAH, I'M, AH--
ONLY MY MOM TOLD ME THAT DAD WASN'T ALLOWED IN THERE ANY MORE. SHE SAYS IT'S "IMMORAL."
AND HE SHOULD BE **ASHAMED.**
HEY, DO YOU PICK YOUR NOSE?

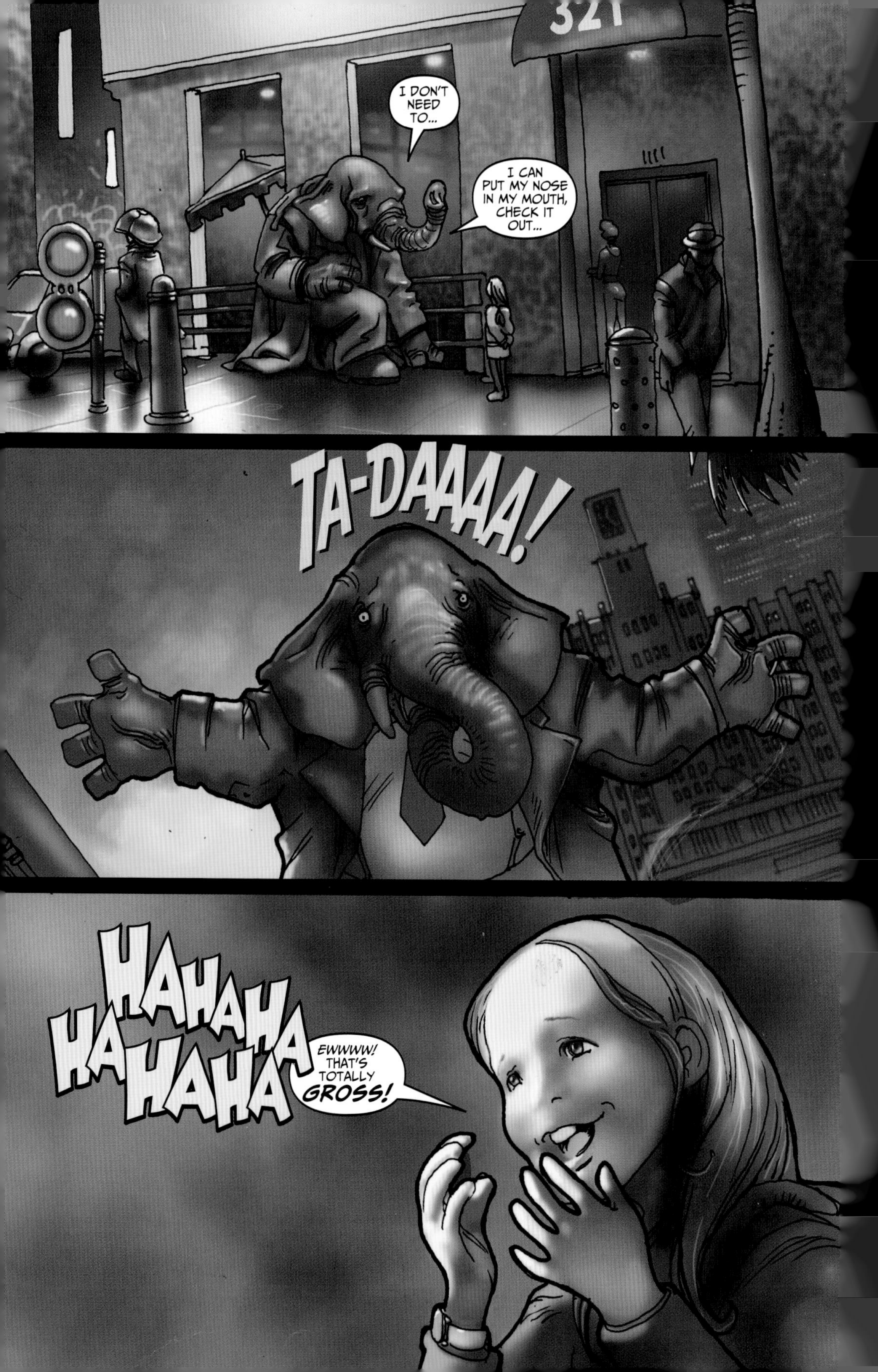
321
I DON'T NEED TO...
I CAN PUT MY NOSE IN MY MOUTH, CHECK IT OUT...
TA-DAAAAA!
HAHAHA HAHAHAHA
EWWWW! THAT'S TOTALLY GROSS!

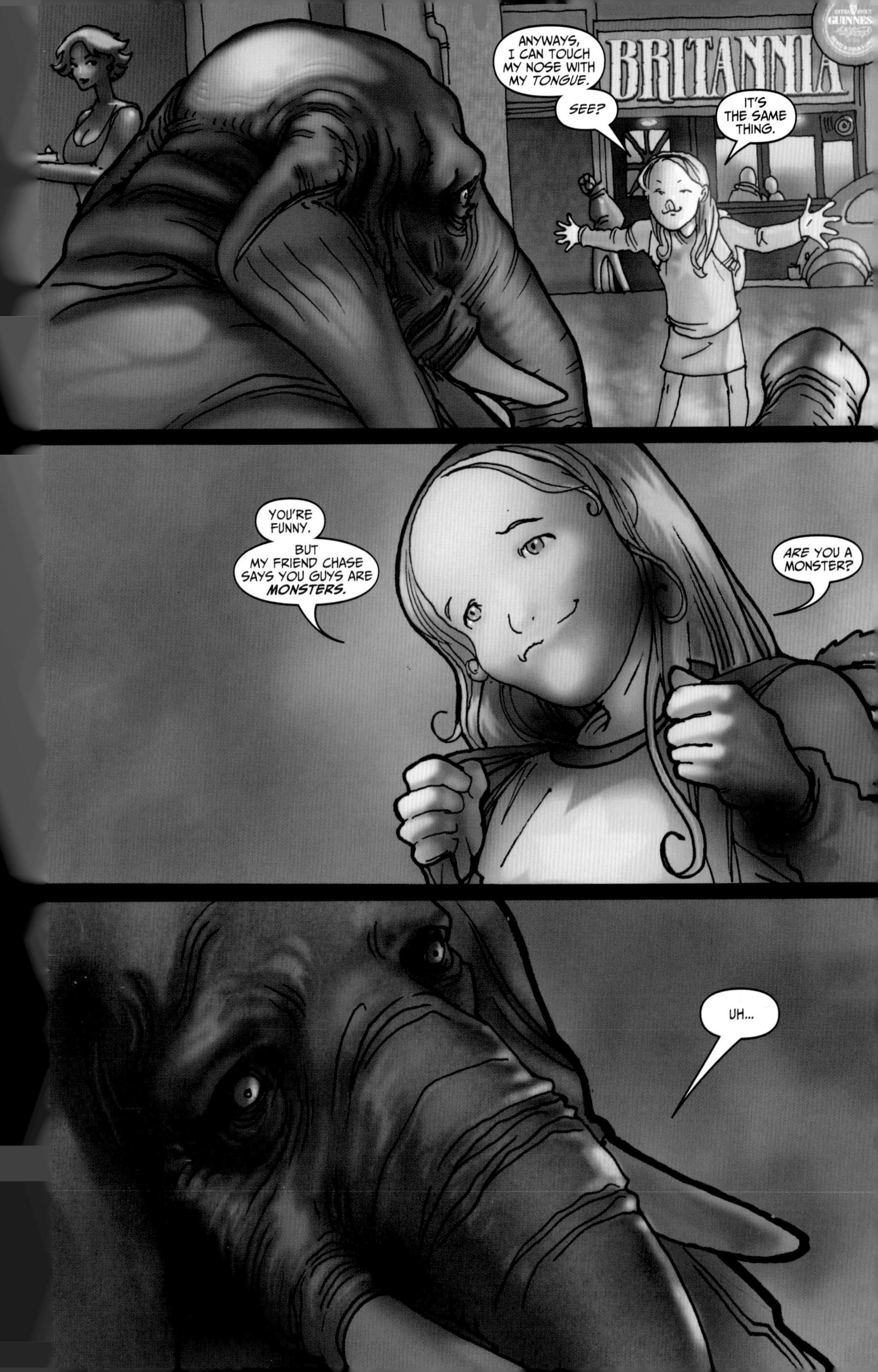
BRITANNIA
ANYWAYS, I CAN TOUCH MY NOSE WITH MY TONGUE.
SEE?
IT'S THE SAME THING.
YOU'RE FUNNY.
BUT MY FRIEND CHASE SAYS YOU GUYS ARE MONSTERS.
ARE YOU A MONSTER?
UH...

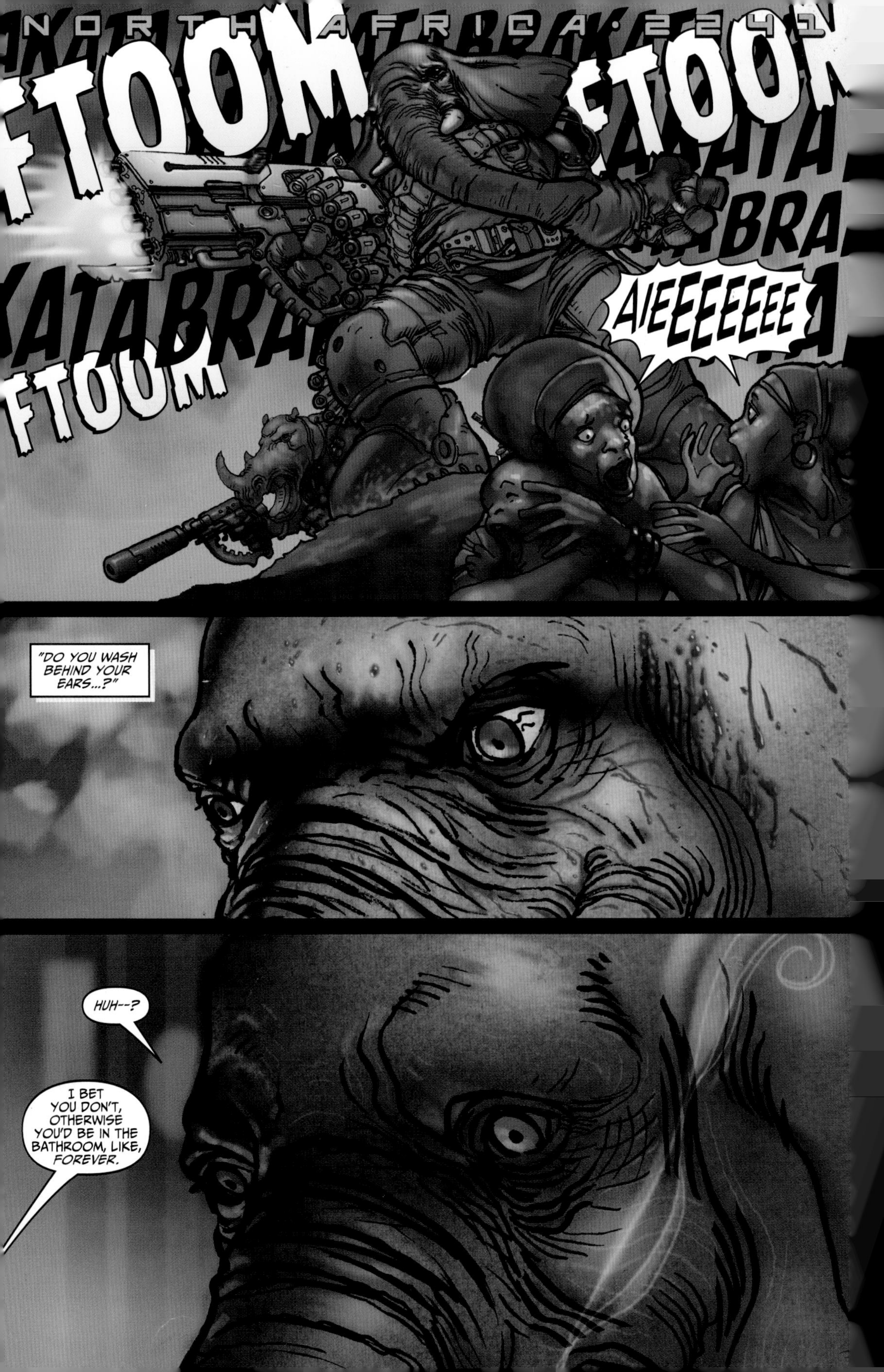
NORTH AFRICA · 2241
FTOOM
FTOOM
KATABRA
KATABRA
FTOOM
AIEEEEEEE
"DO YOU WASH BEHIND YOUR EARS...?"
HUH--?
I BET YOU DON'T, OTHERWISE YOU'D BE IN THE BATHROOM, LIKE, *FOREVER.*

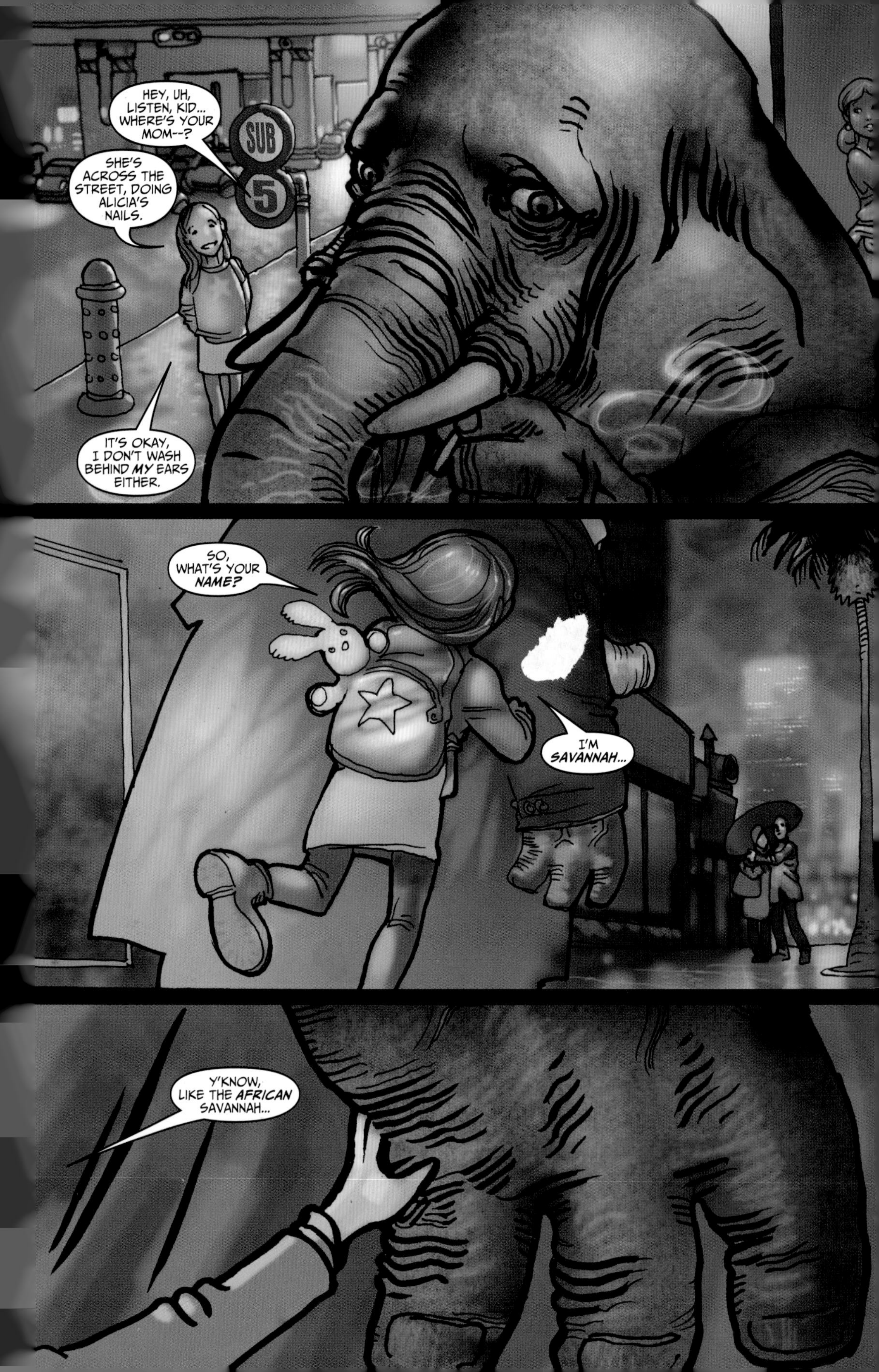
HEY, UH, LISTEN, KID... WHERE'S YOUR MOM--?
SHE'S ACROSS THE STREET, DOING ALICIA'S NAILS.
IT'S OKAY, I DON'T WASH BEHIND MY EARS EITHER.
SUB
5
SO, WHAT'S YOUR NAME?
I'M SAVANNAH...
Y'KNOW, LIKE THE AFRICAN SAVANNAH...

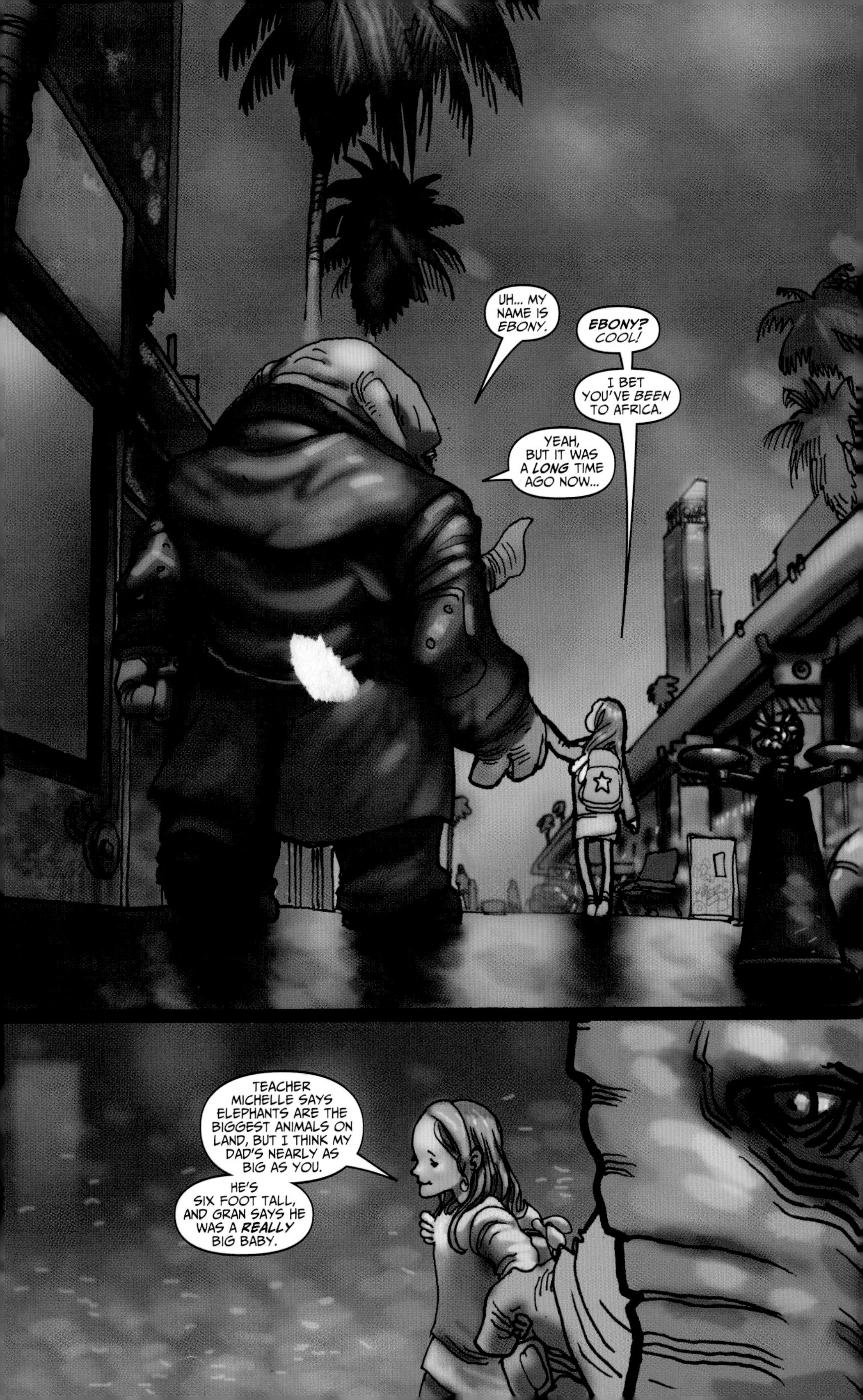
UH... MY NAME IS EBONY.
EBONY? COOL!
I BET YOU'VE BEEN TO AFRICA.
YEAH, BUT IT WAS A LONG TIME AGO NOW...
TEACHER MICHELLE SAYS ELEPHANTS ARE THE BIGGEST ANIMALS ON LAND, BUT I THINK MY DAD'S NEARLY AS BIG AS YOU.
HE'S SIX FOOT TALL, AND GRAN SAYS HE WAS A REALLY BIG BABY.

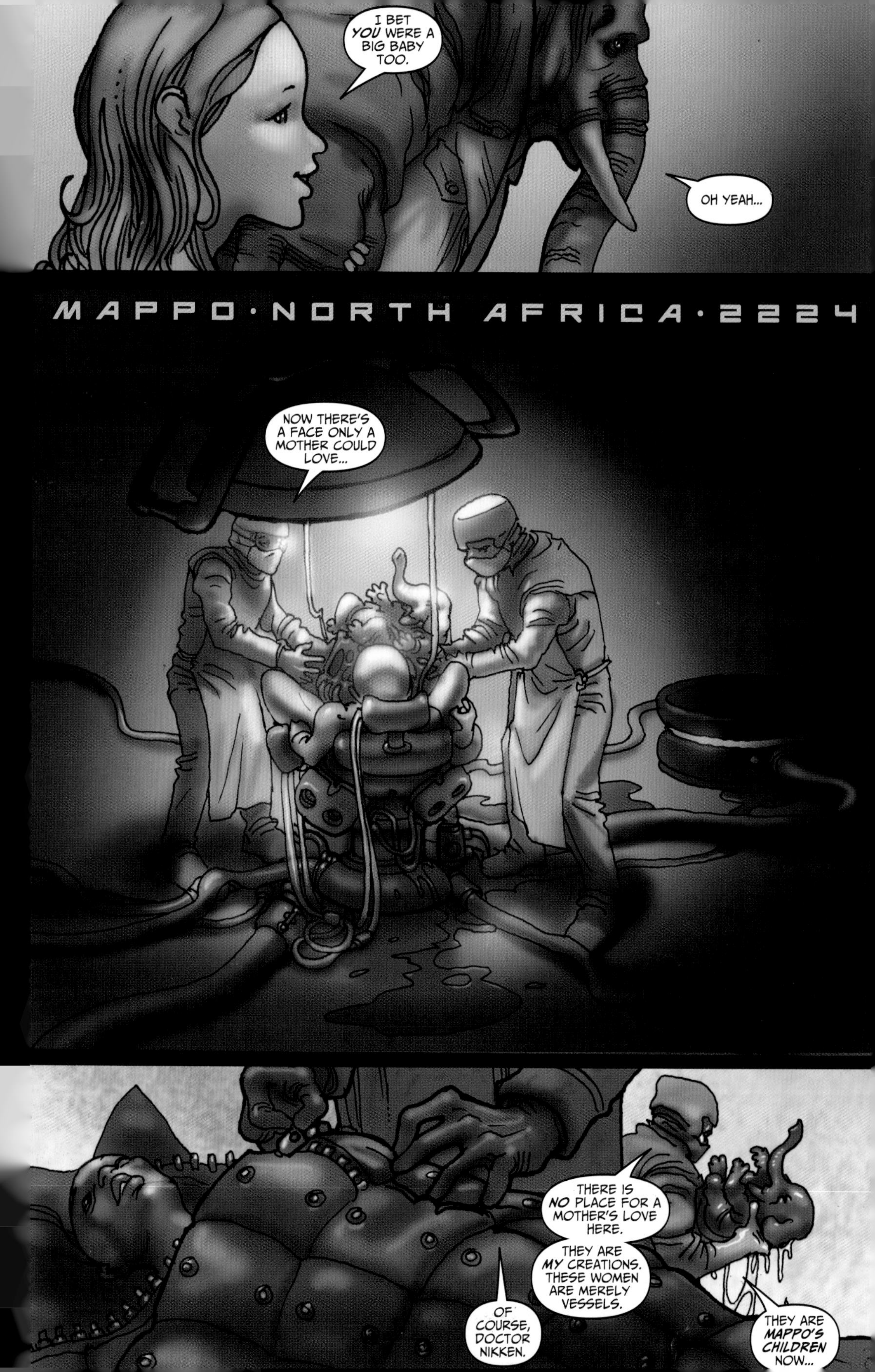
I BET YOU WERE A BIG BABY TOO.
OH YEAH...
MAPPO · NORTH AFRICA · 2224
NOW THERE'S A FACE ONLY A MOTHER COULD LOVE...
THERE IS NO PLACE FOR A MOTHER'S LOVE HERE.
THEY ARE MY CREATIONS. THESE WOMEN ARE MERELY VESSELS.
OF COURSE, DOCTOR NIKKEN.
THEY ARE MAPPO'S CHILDREN NOW...

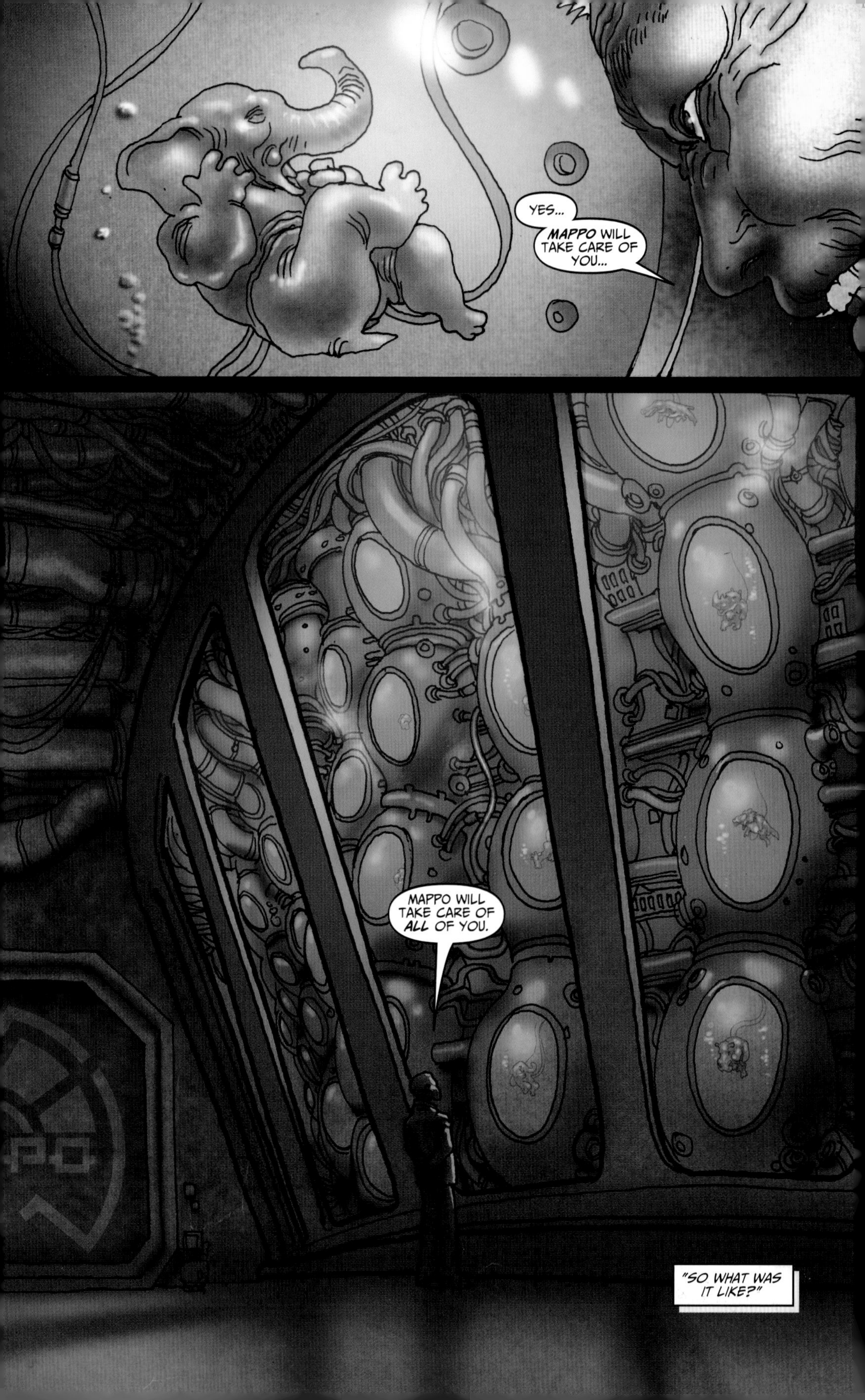
YES... MAPPO WILL TAKE CARE OF YOU...
MAPPO WILL TAKE CARE OF ALL OF YOU.
"SO WHAT WAS IT LIKE?"

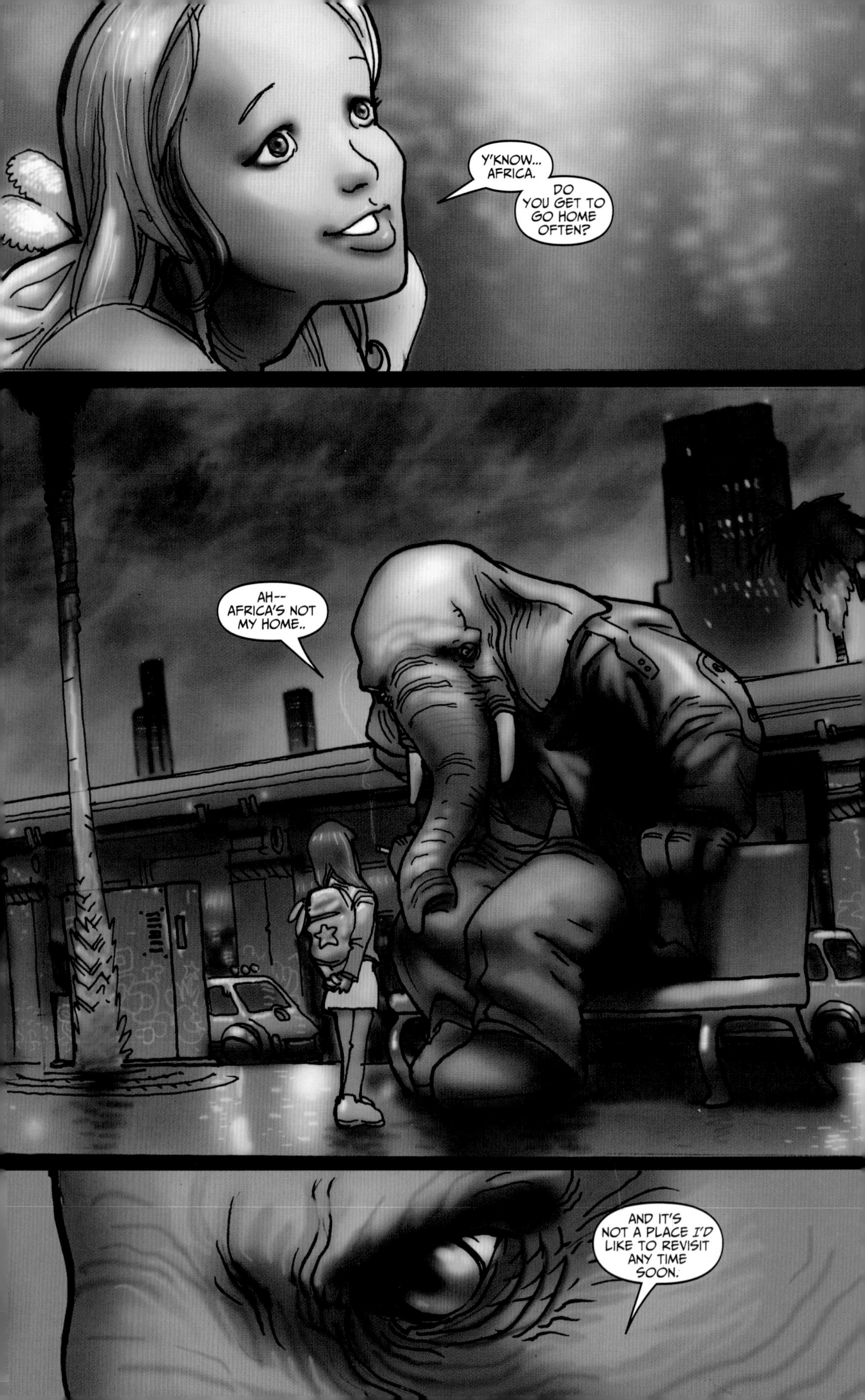
Y'KNOW... AFRICA.
DO YOU GET TO GO HOME OFTEN?
AH-- AFRICA'S NOT MY HOME..
AND IT'S NOT A PLACE *I'D* LIKE TO REVISIT ANY TIME SOON.

NORTH AFRICA · 2240

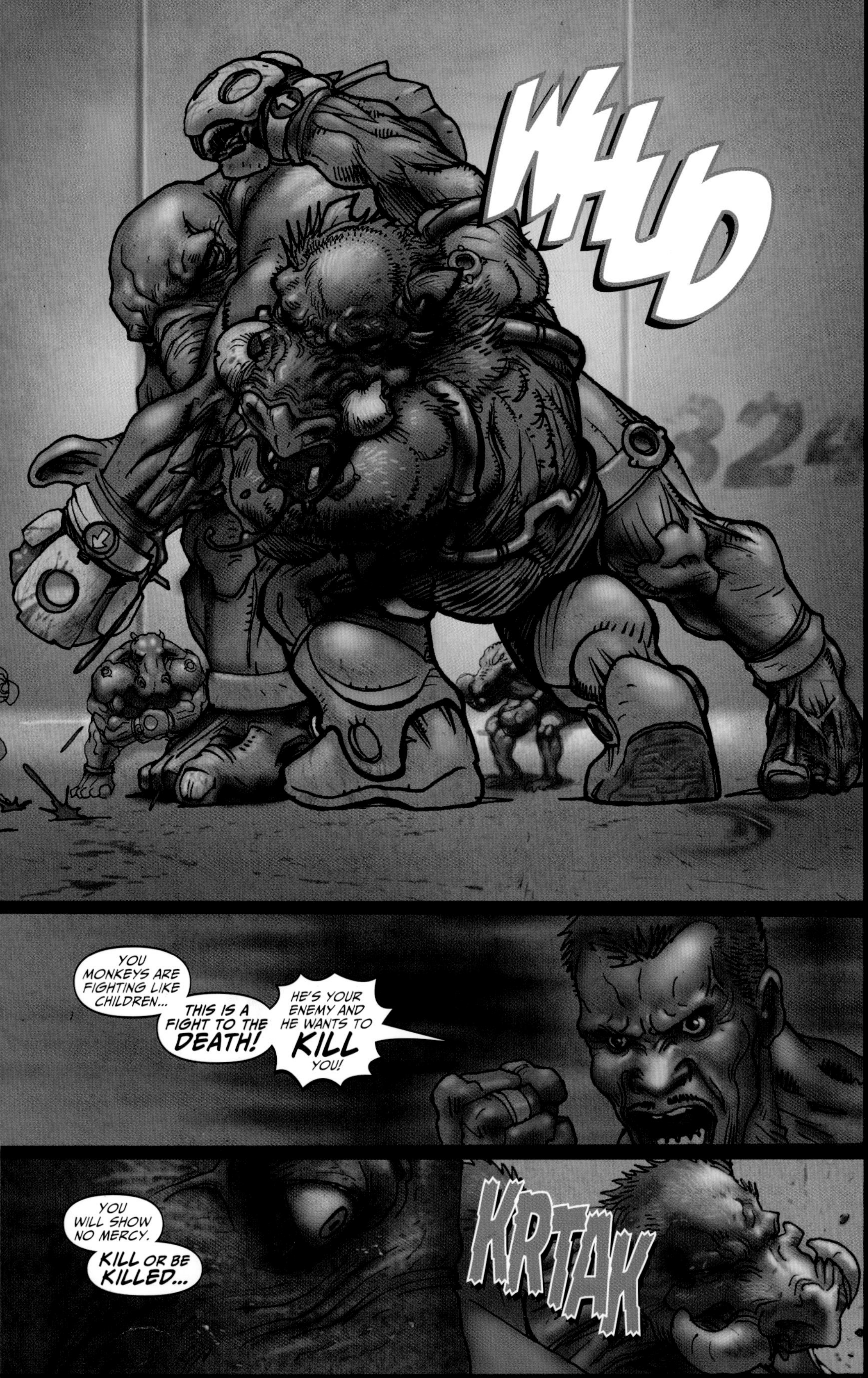
WHUD
YOU MONKEYS ARE FIGHTING LIKE CHILDREN...
THIS IS A FIGHT TO THE DEATH!
HE'S YOUR ENEMY AND HE WANTS TO KILL YOU!
YOU WILL SHOW NO MERCY.
KILL OR BE KILLED...
KRTAK

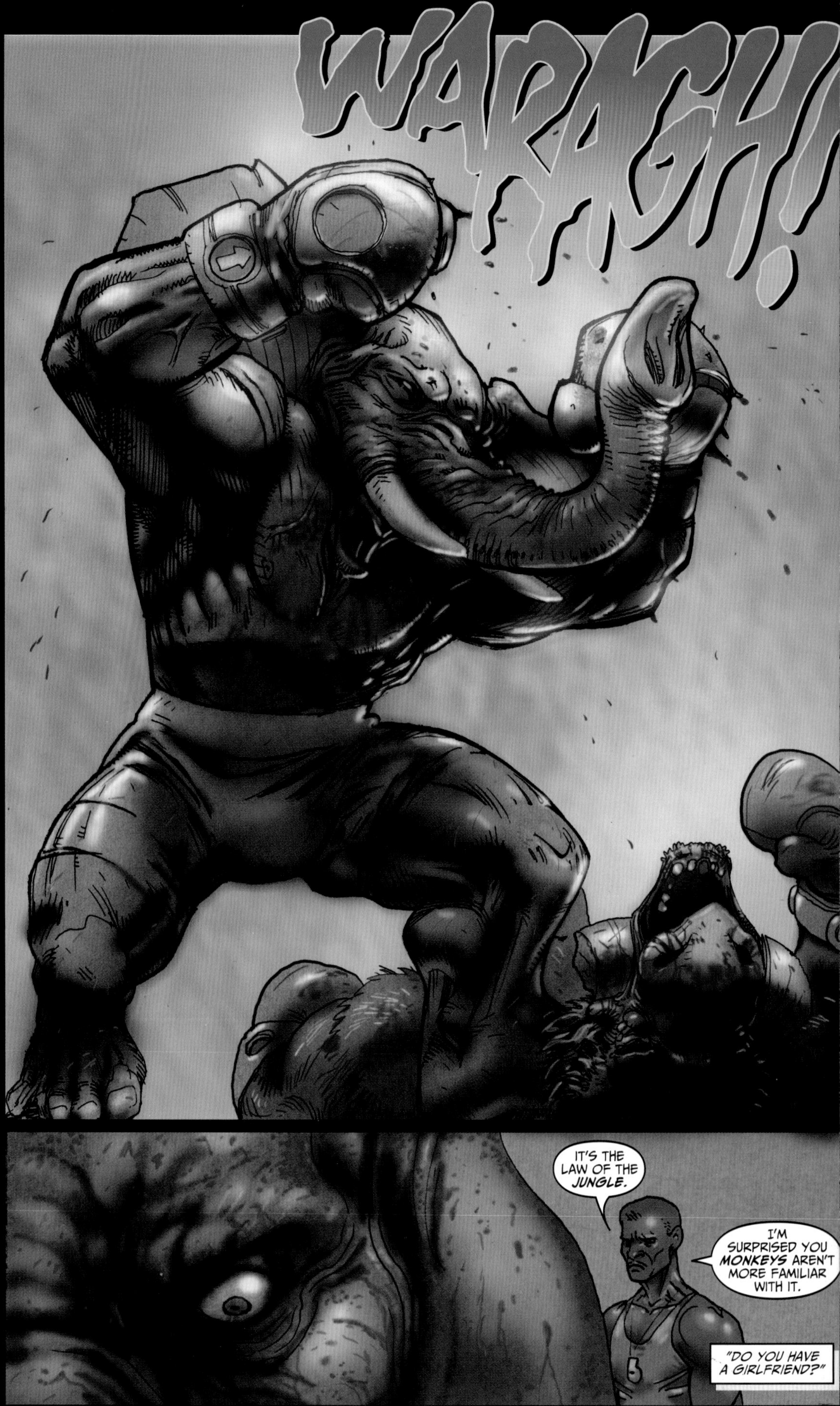
WARAGH!
IT'S THE LAW OF THE JUNGLE.
I'M SURPRISED YOU MONKEYS AREN'T MORE FAMILIAR WITH IT.
"DO YOU HAVE A GIRLFRIEND?"

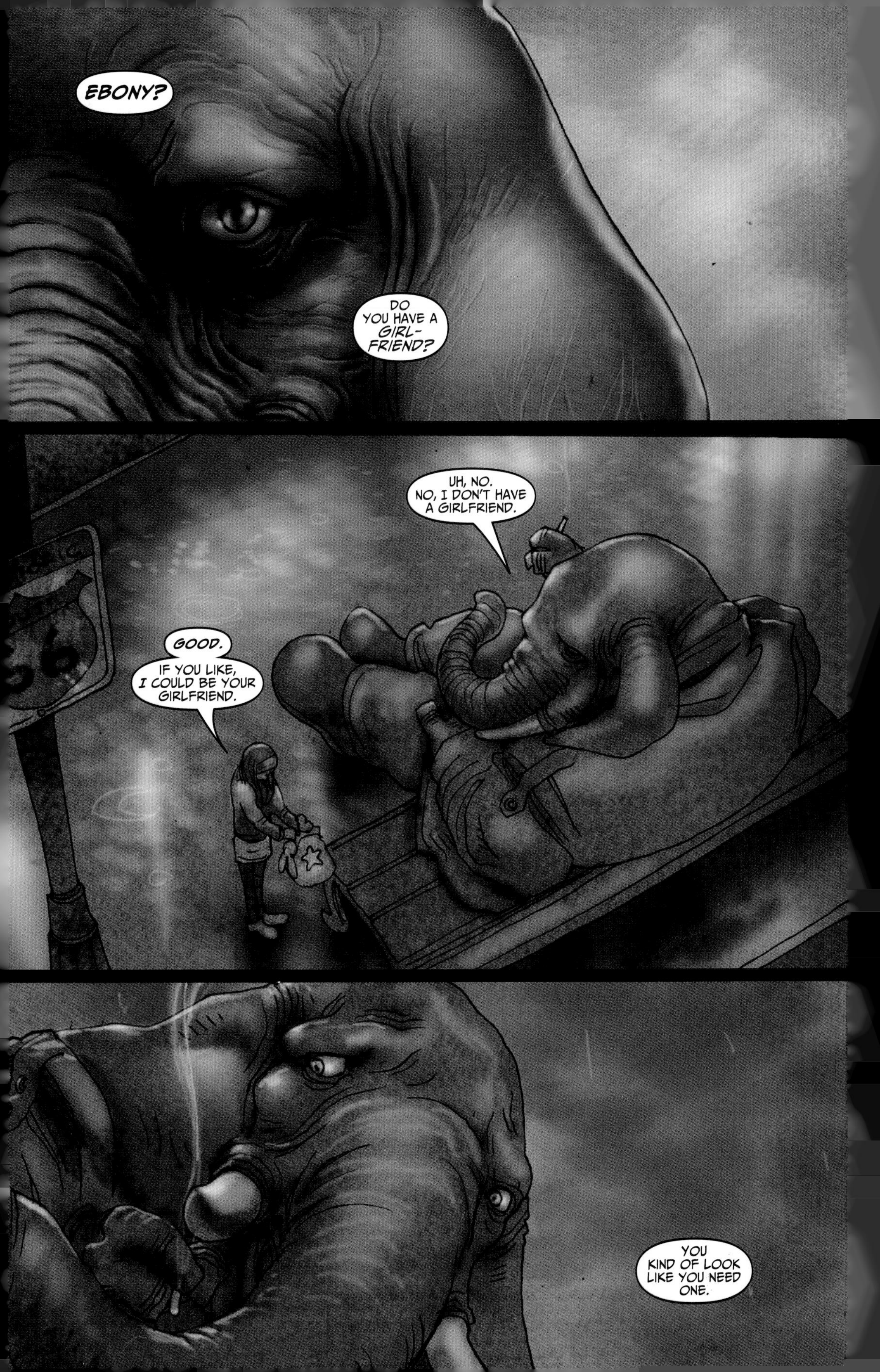
EBONY?
DO YOU HAVE A GIRL-FRIEND?
UH, NO. NO, I DON'T HAVE A GIRLFRIEND.
GOOD.
IF YOU LIKE, I COULD BE YOUR GIRLFRIEND.
YOU KIND OF LOOK LIKE YOU NEED ONE.

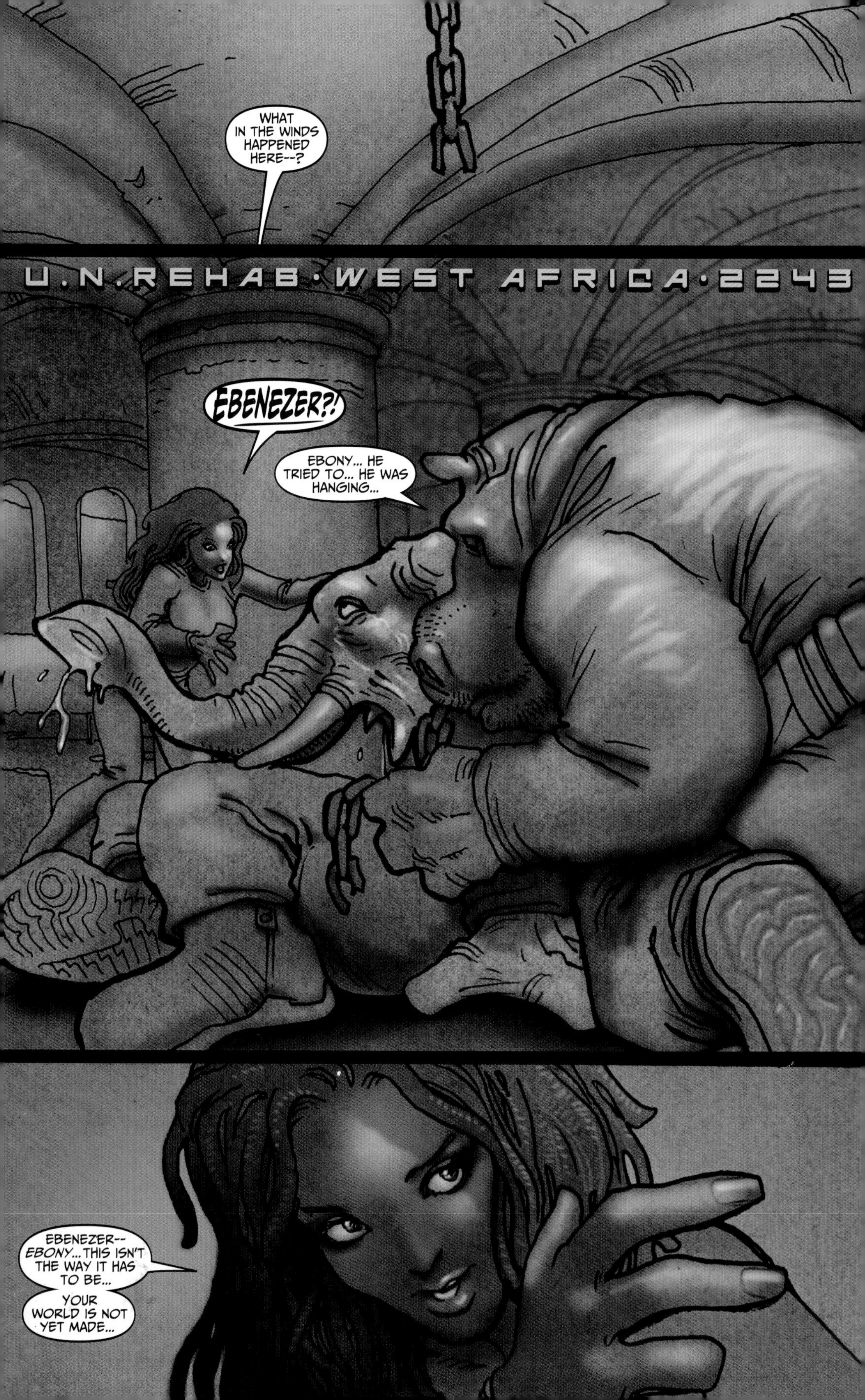
WHAT IN THE WINDS HAPPENED HERE--?
U.N. REHAB · WEST AFRICA · 2243
EBENEZER?!
EBONY... HE TRIED TO... HE WAS HANGING...
EBENEZER-- EBONY... THIS ISN'T THE WAY IT HAS TO BE...
YOUR WORLD IS NOT YET MADE...

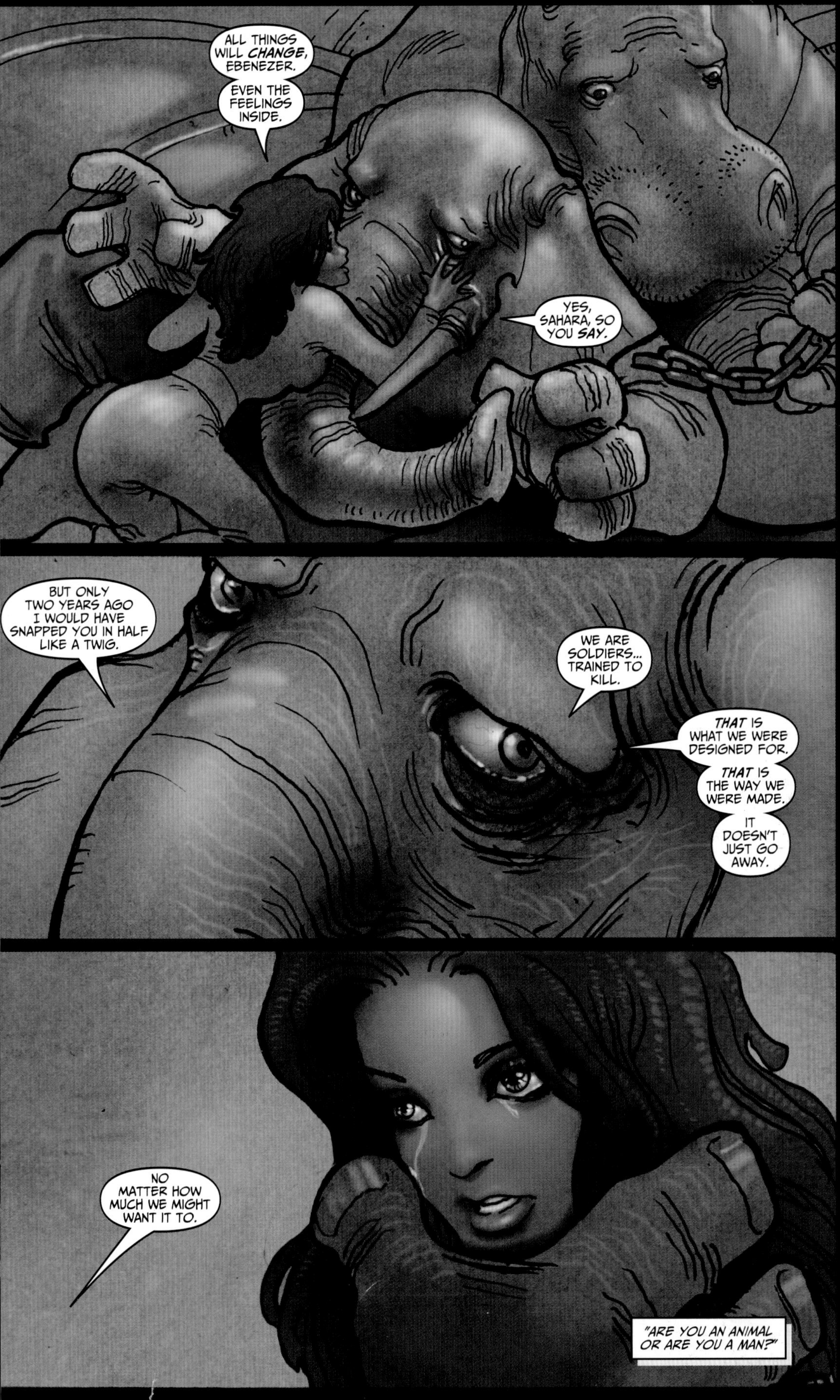
ALL THINGS WILL *CHANGE,* EBENEZER.
EVEN THE FEELINGS INSIDE.
YES, SAHARA, SO YOU *SAY.*
BUT ONLY TWO YEARS AGO I WOULD HAVE SNAPPED YOU IN HALF LIKE A TWIG.
WE ARE SOLDIERS... TRAINED TO KILL.
THAT IS WHAT WE WERE DESIGNED FOR.
THAT IS THE WAY WE WERE MADE.
IT DOESN'T JUST GO AWAY.
NO MATTER HOW MUCH WE MIGHT WANT IT TO.
"ARE YOU AN ANIMAL OR ARE YOU A MAN?"

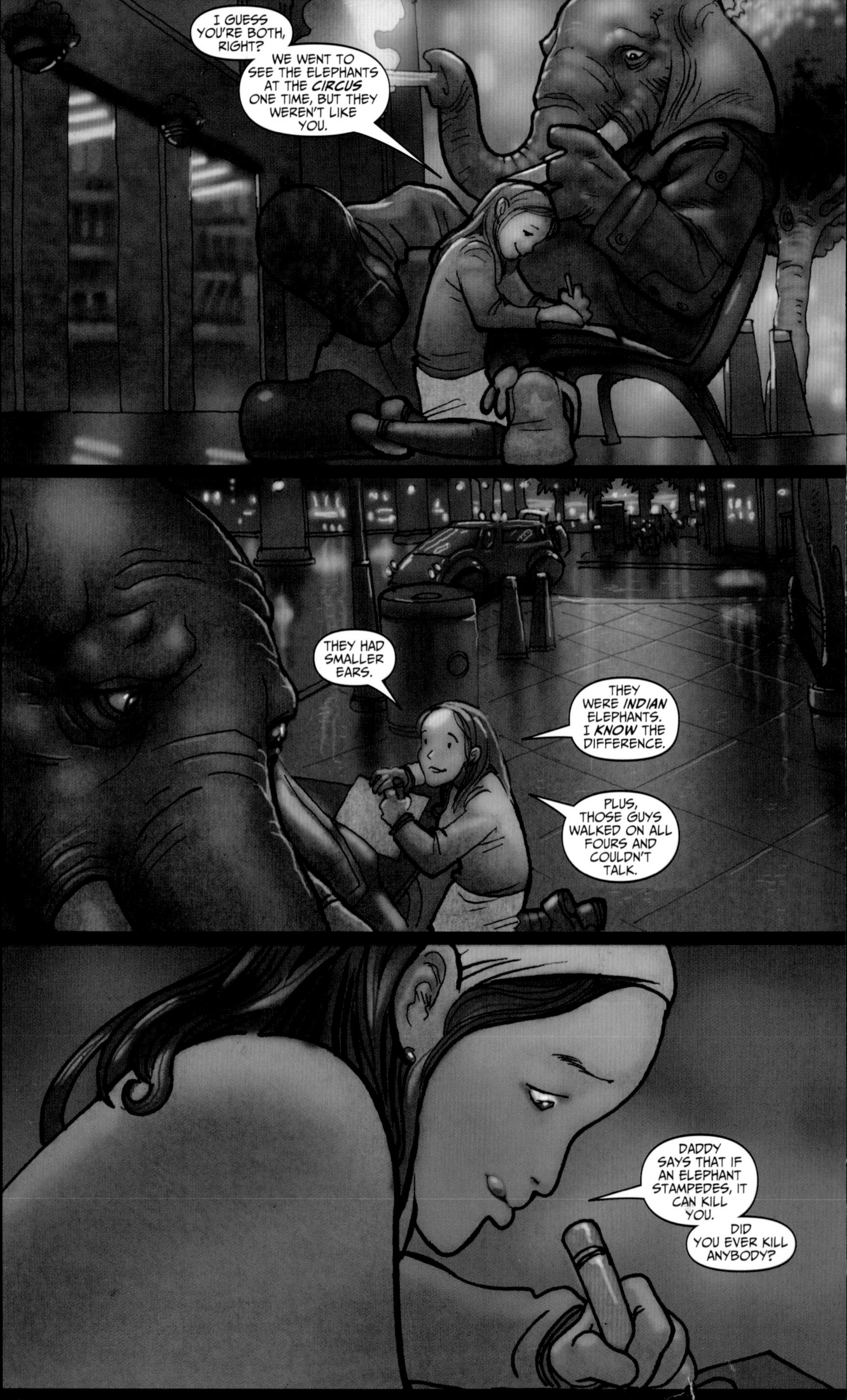
I GUESS YOU'RE BOTH, RIGHT?
WE WENT TO SEE THE ELEPHANTS AT THE *CIRCUS* ONE TIME, BUT THEY WEREN'T LIKE YOU.
THEY HAD SMALLER EARS.
THEY WERE *INDIAN* ELEPHANTS. I *KNOW* THE DIFFERENCE.
PLUS, THOSE GUYS WALKED ON ALL FOURS AND COULDN'T TALK.
DADDY SAYS THAT IF AN ELEPHANT STAMPEDES, IT CAN KILL YOU.
DID YOU EVER KILL ANYBODY?

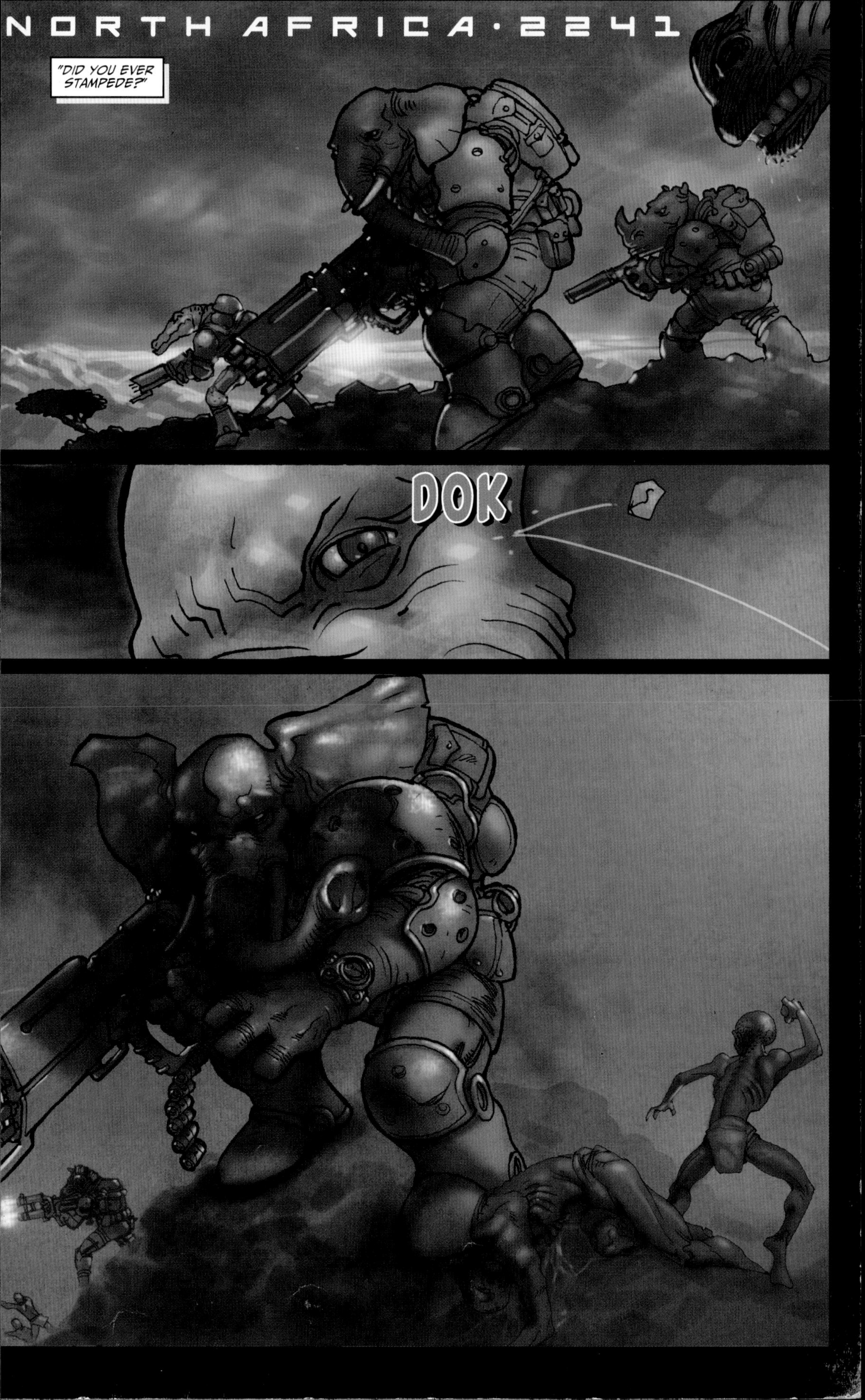
NORTH AFRICA · 2241
"DID YOU EVER STAMPEDE?"
DOK

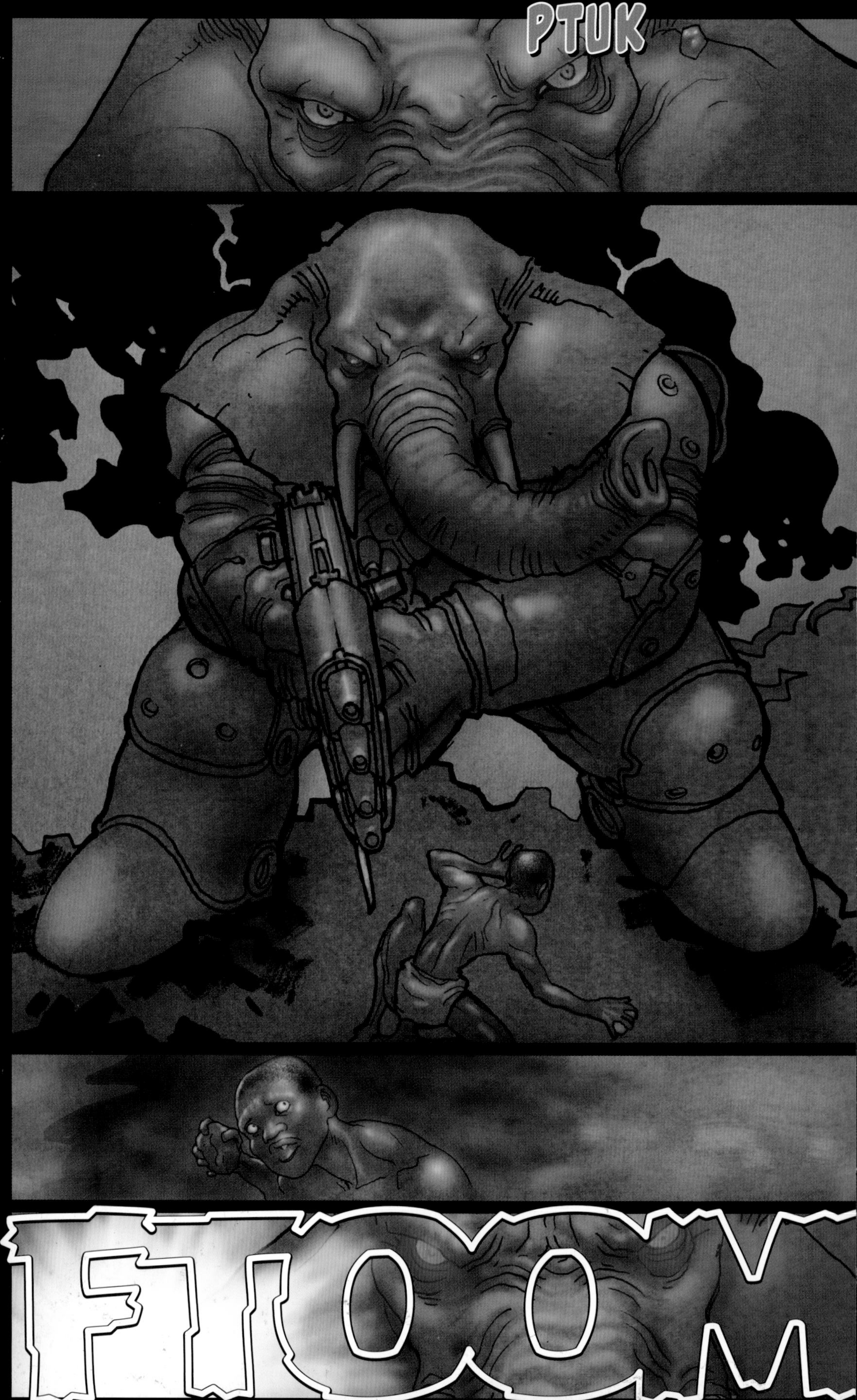
PTUK
FTOOM

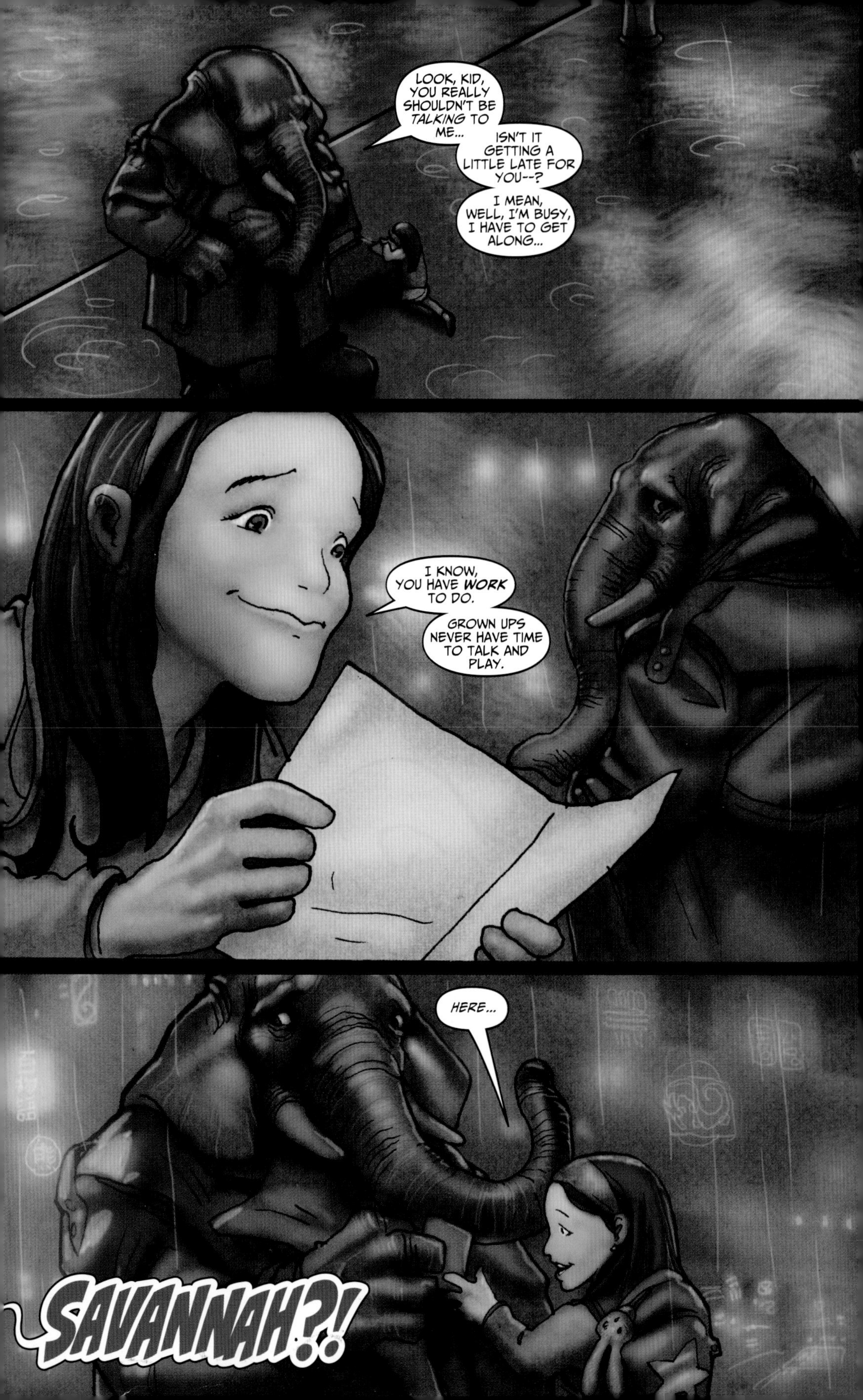
LOOK, KID, YOU REALLY SHOULDN'T BE *TALKING* TO ME...
ISN'T IT GETTING A LITTLE LATE FOR YOU--?
I MEAN, WELL, I'M BUSY, I HAVE TO GET ALONG...
I KNOW, YOU HAVE **WORK** TO DO.
GROWN UPS NEVER HAVE TIME TO TALK AND PLAY.
HERE...
SAVANNAH?!

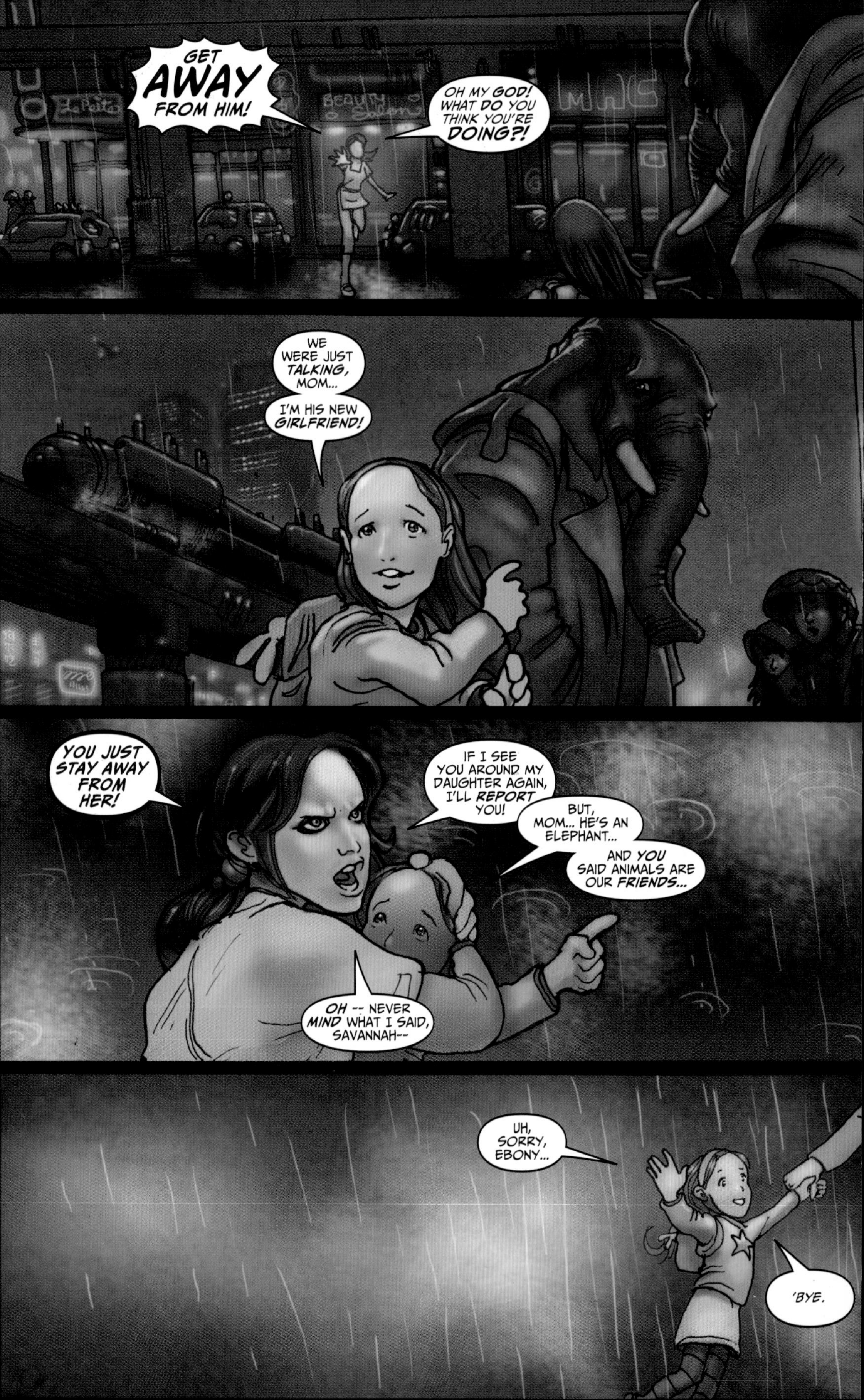
GET AWAY FROM HIM!
OH MY GOD! WHAT DO YOU THINK YOU'RE DOING?!
WE WERE JUST TALKING, MOM...
I'M HIS NEW GIRLFRIEND!
YOU JUST STAY AWAY FROM HER!
IF I SEE YOU AROUND MY DAUGHTER AGAIN, I'LL REPORT YOU!
BUT, MOM... HE'S AN ELEPHANT...
AND YOU SAID ANIMALS ARE OUR FRIENDS...
OH -- NEVER MIND WHAT I SAID, SAVANNAH--
UH, SORRY, EBONY...
'BYE.

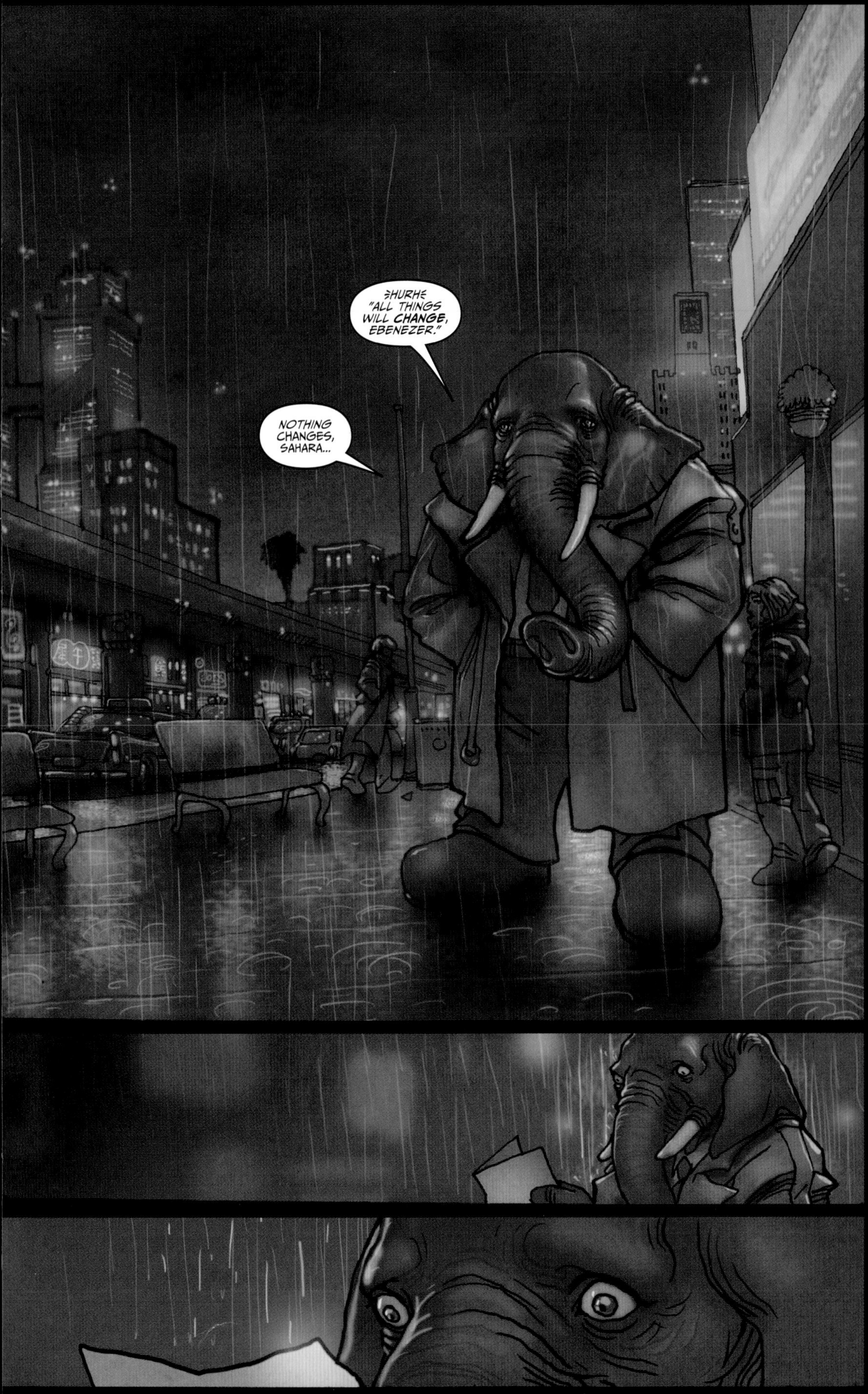
HURH "ALL THINGS WILL CHANGE, EBENEZER."
NOTHING CHANGES, SAHARA...

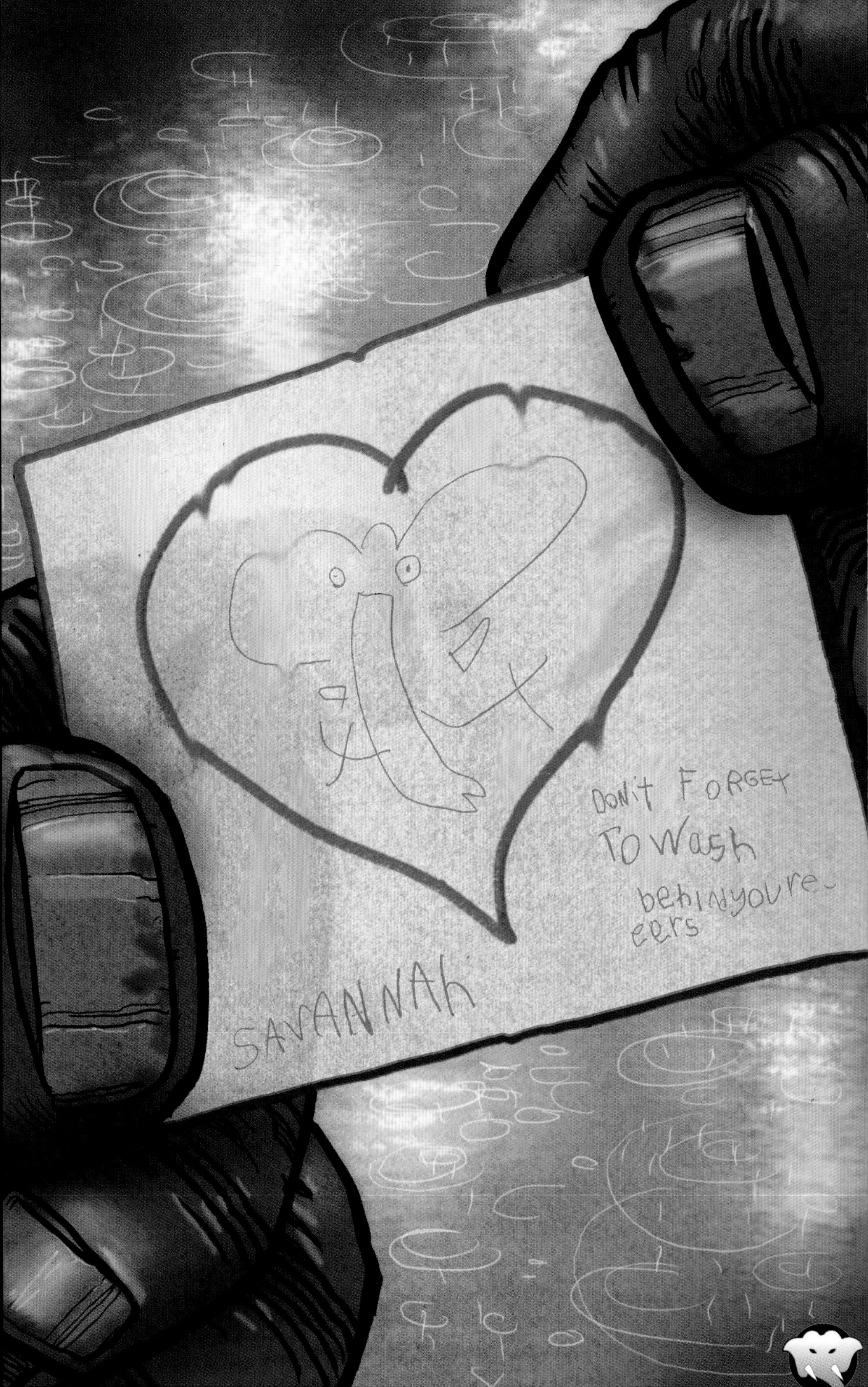
DON'T FORGET
TO Wash
behindyoure-
eers
SAVANNAh

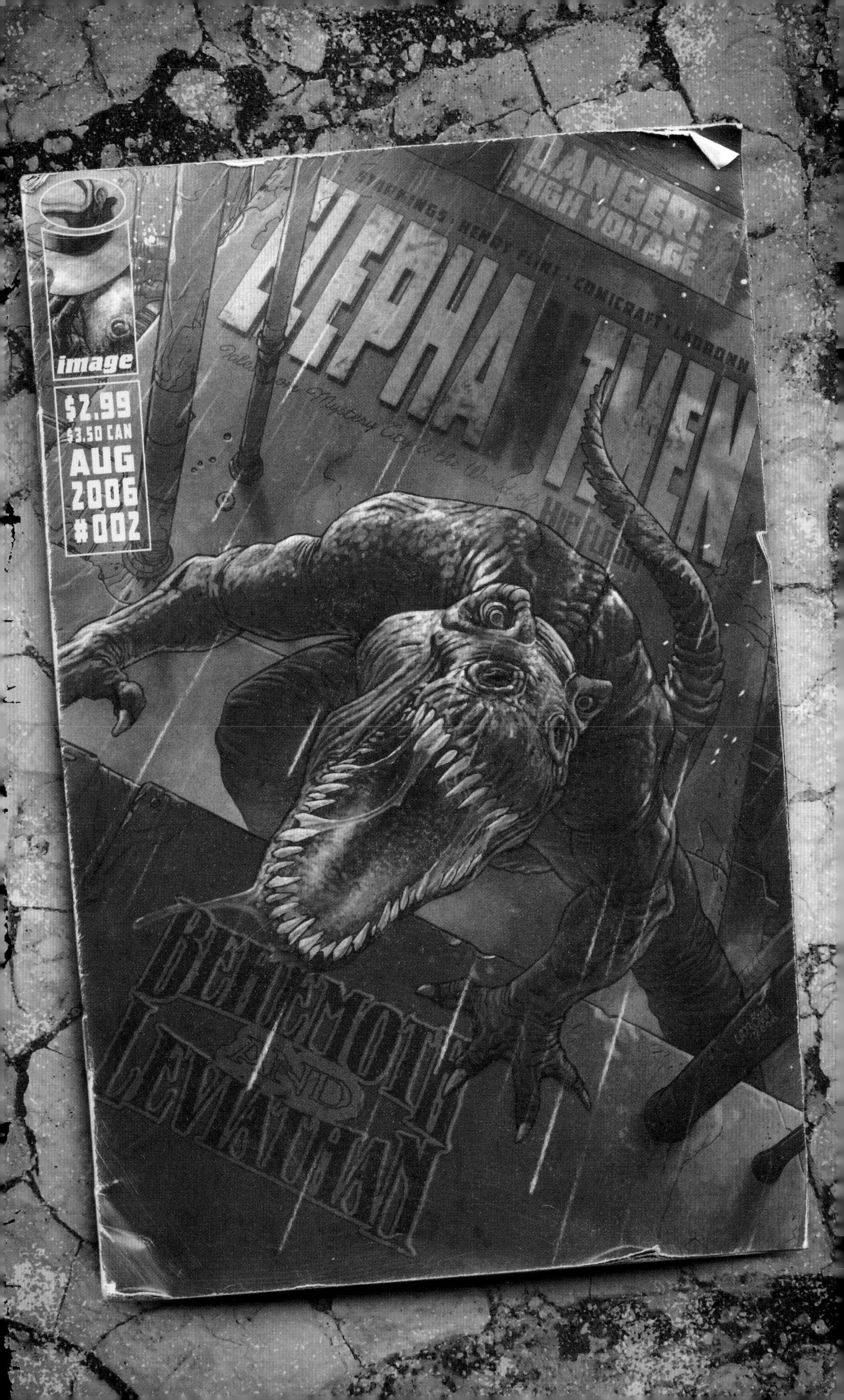
DANGER! HIGH VOLTAGE
image
$2.99
$3.50 CAN
AUG
2006
#002
BEHEMOTH AND LEVIATHAN

"AND GOD SAID, LET THE EARTH BRING FORTH THE LIVING CREATURE AFTER HIS KIND, CATTLE, AND CREEPING THING, AND BEAST OF THE EARTH AFTER HIS KIND: AND IT WAS SO.

"AND GOD MADE THE BEAST OF THE EARTH AFTER HIS KIND, AND CATTLE AFTER THEIR KIND, AND EVERY THING THAT CREEPETH UPON THE EARTH AFTER HIS KIND: AND GOD SAW THAT IT WAS GOOD.

"AND GOD SAID, LET US MAKE MAN IN OUR IMAGE, AFTER OUR LIKENESS: AND LET THEM HAVE DOMINION OVER THE FISH OF THE SEA, AND OVER THE FOWL OF THE AIR, AND OVER THE CATTLE, AND OVER ALL THE EARTH, AND OVER EVERY CREEPING THING THAT CREEPETH UPON THE EARTH.

"SO GOD CREATED MAN IN HIS OWN IMAGE, IN THE IMAGE OF GOD CREATED HE HIM; MALE AND FEMALE CREATED HE THEM. AND GOD BLESSED THEM, AND GOD SAID UNTO THEM, BE FRUITFUL, AND MULTIPLY, AND REPLENISH THE EARTH, AND SUBDUE IT: AND HAVE DOMINION OVER THE FISH OF THE SEA, AND OVER THE FOWL OF THE AIR, AND OVER EVERY LIVING THING THAT MOVETH UPON THE EARTH."

GENESIS 1:24-28

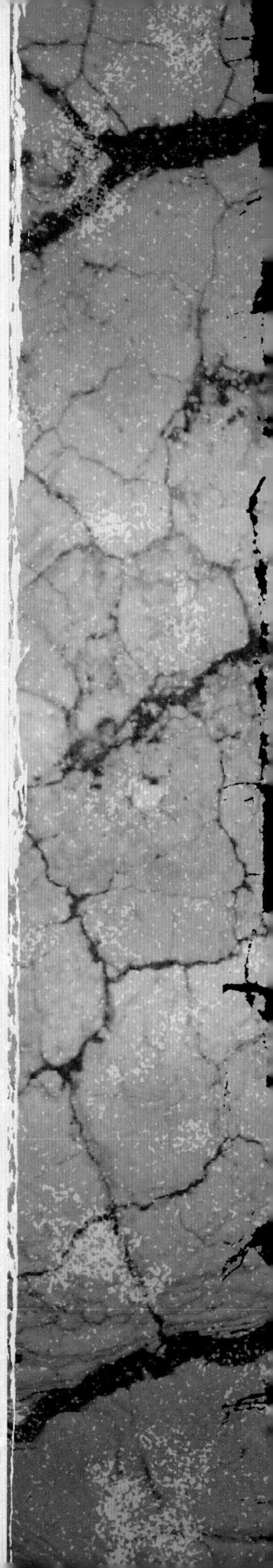

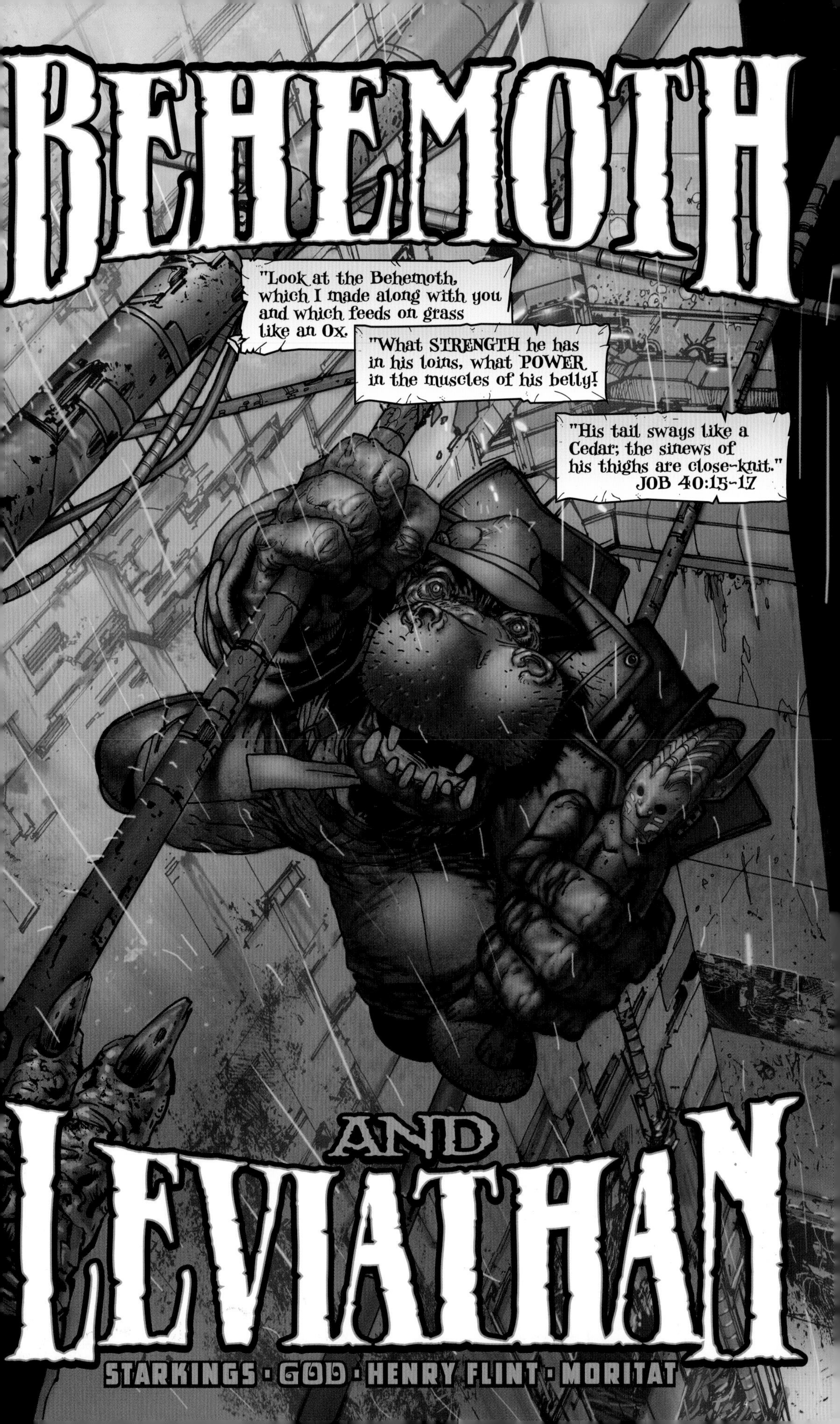
BEHEMOTH
"Look at the Behemoth, which I made along with you and which feeds on grass like an Ox.
"What STRENGTH he has in his loins, what POWER in the muscles of his belly!
"His tail sways like a Cedar; the sinews of his thighs are close-knit." JOB 40:15-17
AND
LEVIATHAN
STARKINGS · GOD · HENRY FLINT · MORITAT

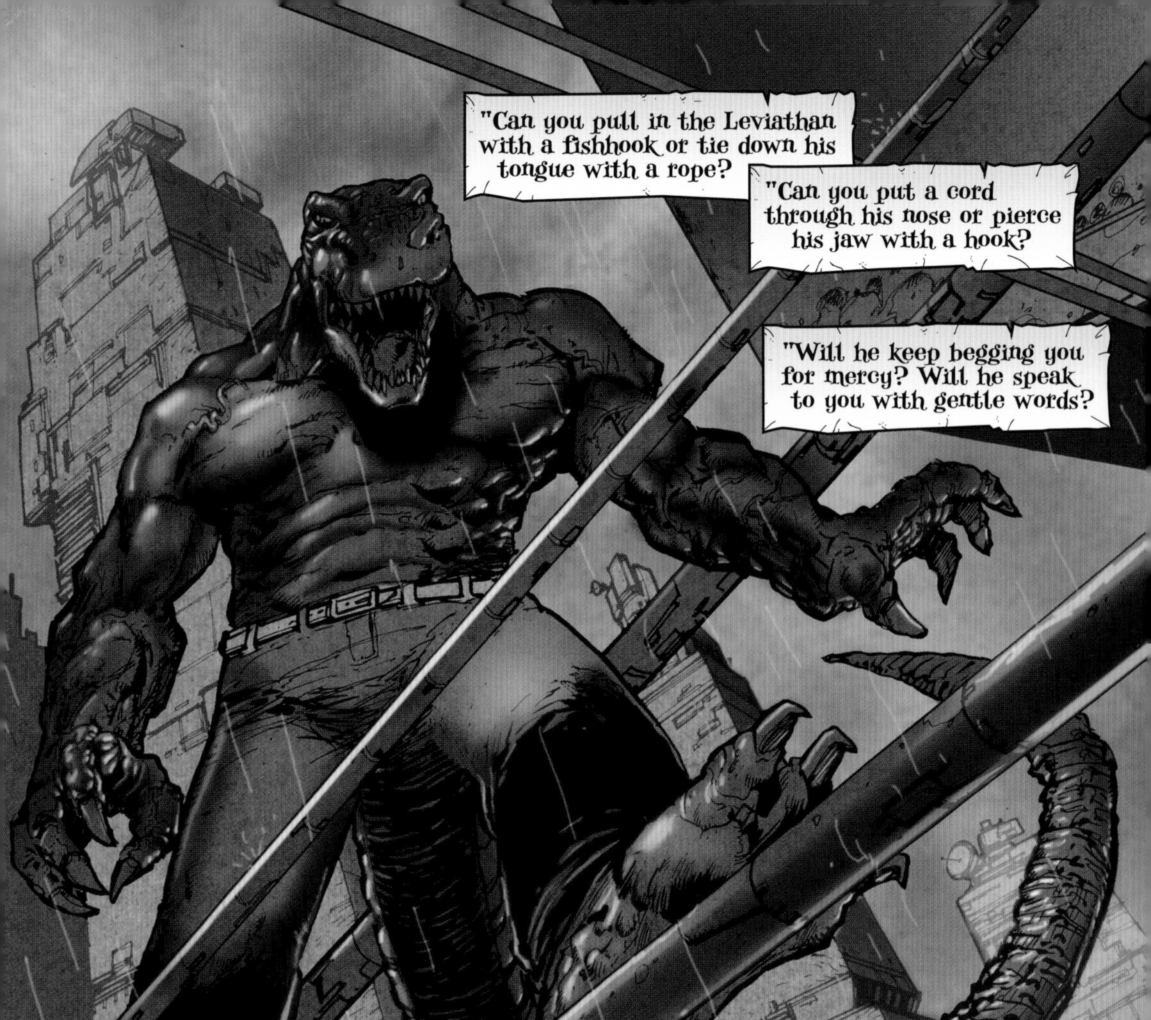
"Can you pull in the Leviathan with a fishhook or tie down his tongue with a rope?
"Can you put a cord through his nose or pierce his jaw with a hook?
"Will he keep begging you for mercy? Will he speak to you with gentle words?
"Will he make an agreement with you for you to take him as your slave for life?" JOB 41:1-4
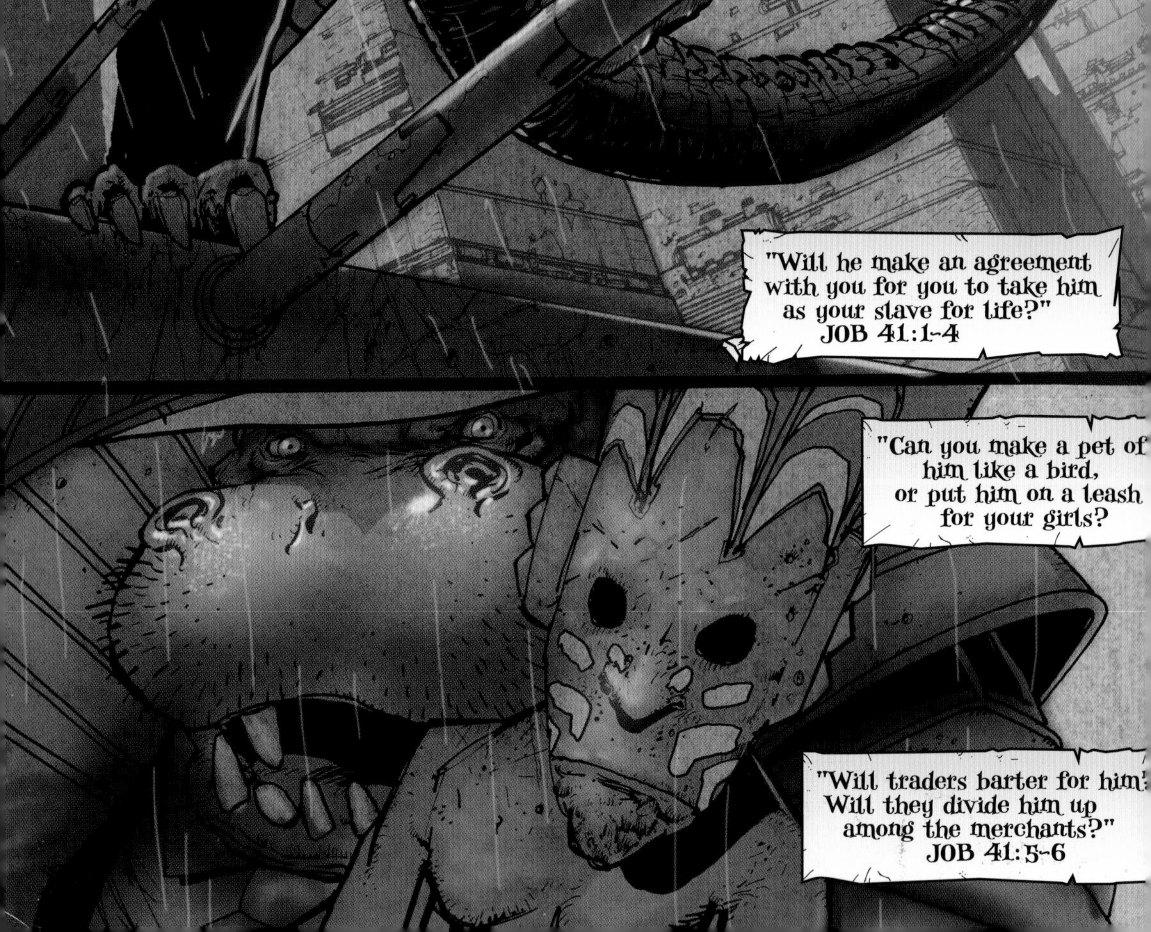
"Can you make a pet of him like a bird, or put him on a leash for your girls?
"Will traders barter for him? Will they divide him up among the merchants?" JOB 41:5-6

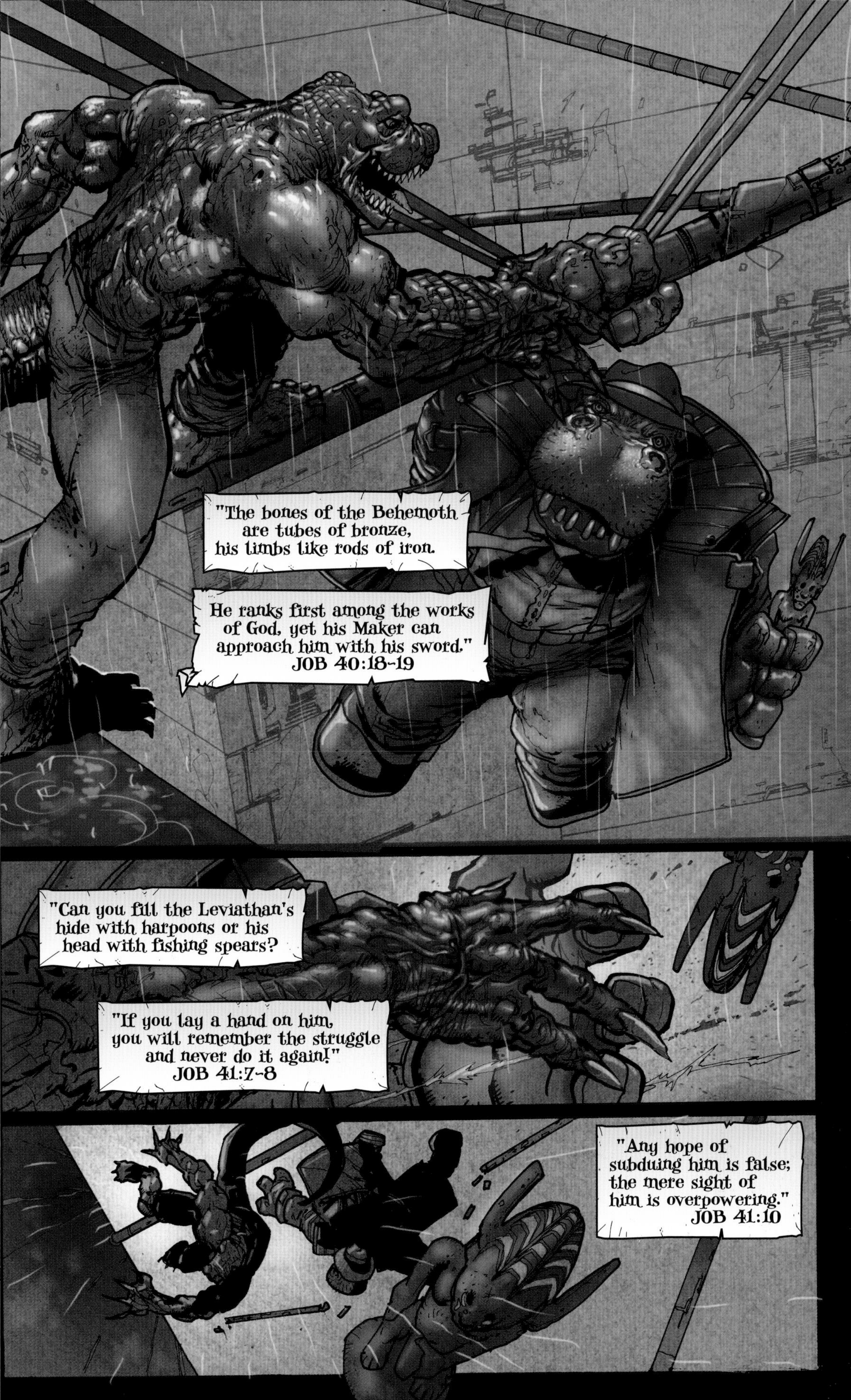
"The bones of the Behemoth are tubes of bronze, his limbs like rods of iron.
He ranks first among the works of God, yet his Maker can approach him with his sword." JOB 40:18-19
"Can you fill the Leviathan's hide with harpoons or his head with fishing spears?
"If you lay a hand on him, you will remember the struggle and never do it again!" JOB 41:7-8
"Any hope of subduing him is false; the mere sight of him is overpowering." JOB 41:10

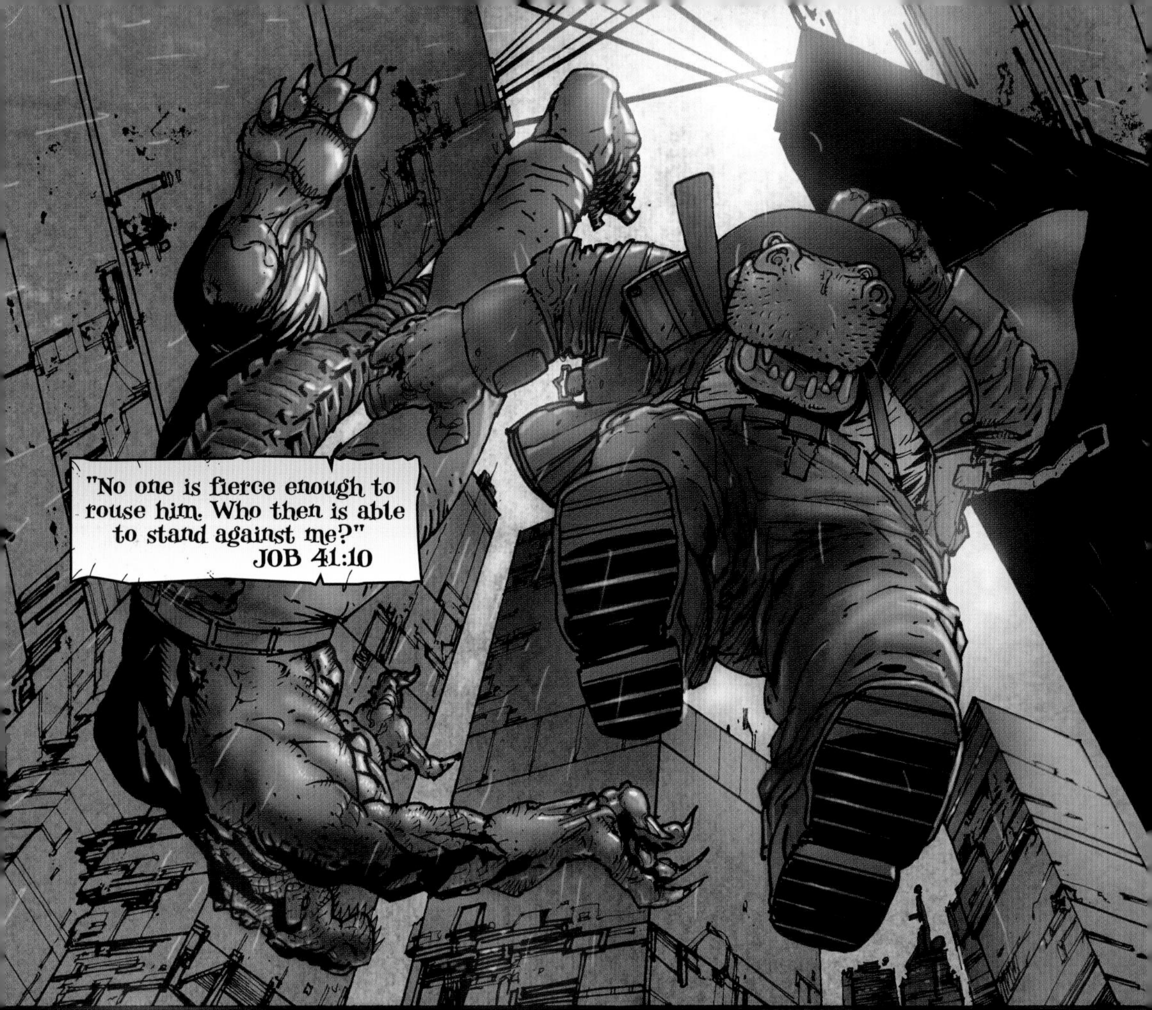
"No one is fierce enough to rouse him. Who then is able to stand against me?" JOB 41:10

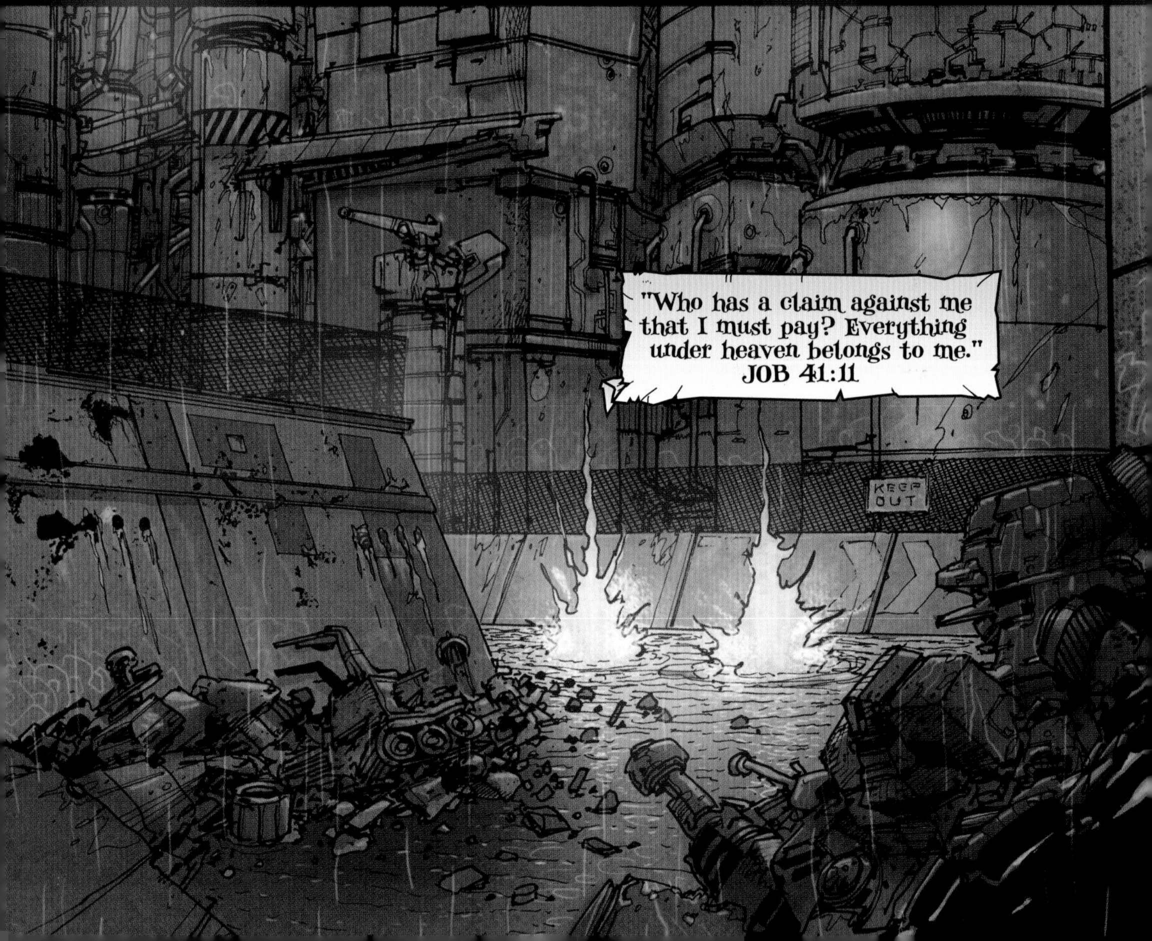
"Who has a claim against me that I must pay? Everything under heaven belongs to me." JOB 41:11
KEEP OUT

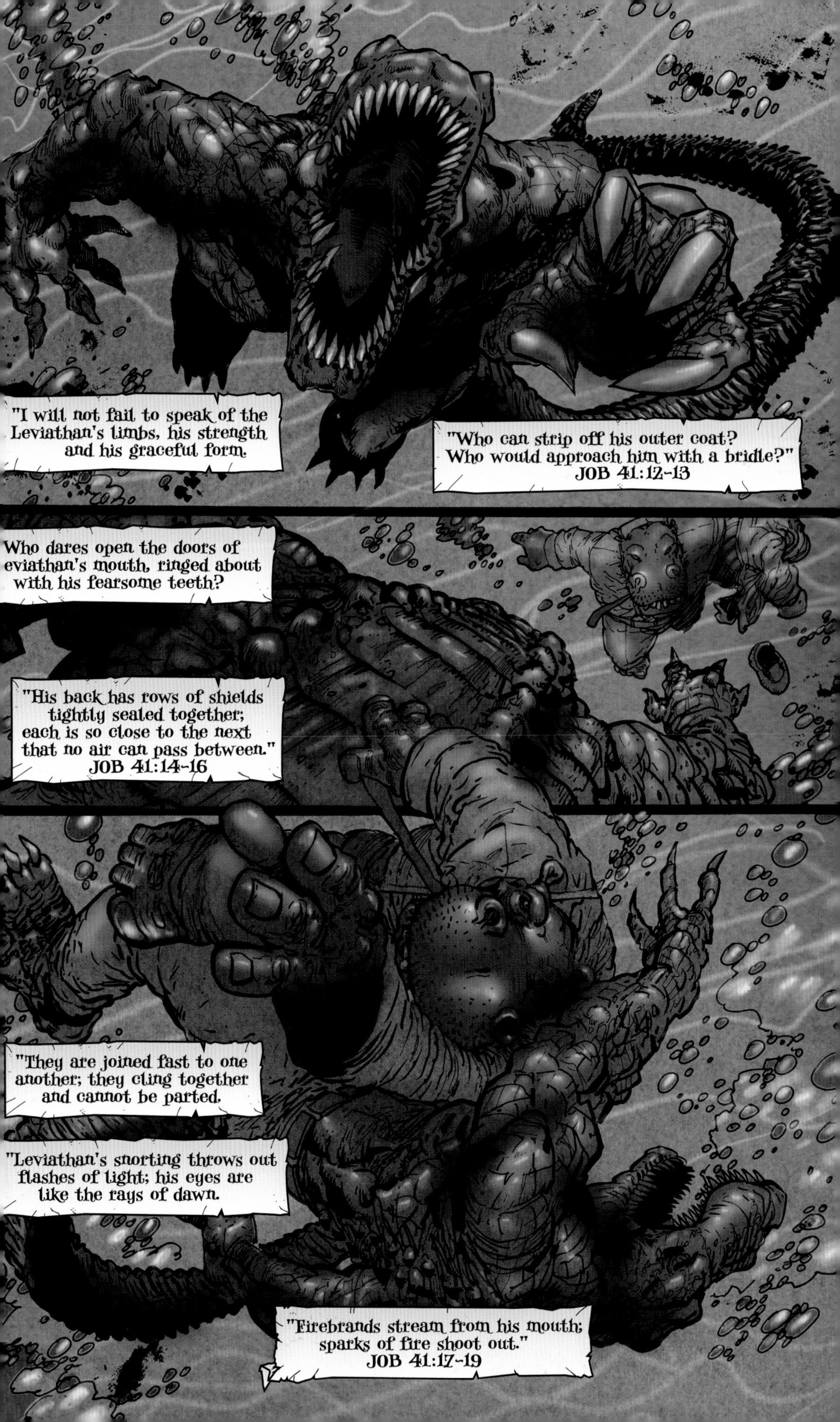
"I will not fail to speak of the Leviathan's limbs, his strength and his graceful form.
"Who can strip off his outer coat? Who would approach him with a bridle?" JOB 41:12-13
Who dares open the doors of eviathan's mouth, ringed about with his fearsome teeth?
"His back has rows of shields tightly sealed together; each is so close to the next that no air can pass between." JOB 41:14-16
"They are joined fast to one another; they cling together and cannot be parted.
"Leviathan's snorting throws out flashes of light; his eyes are like the rays of dawn.
"Firebrands stream from his mouth; sparks of fire shoot out." JOB 41:17-19

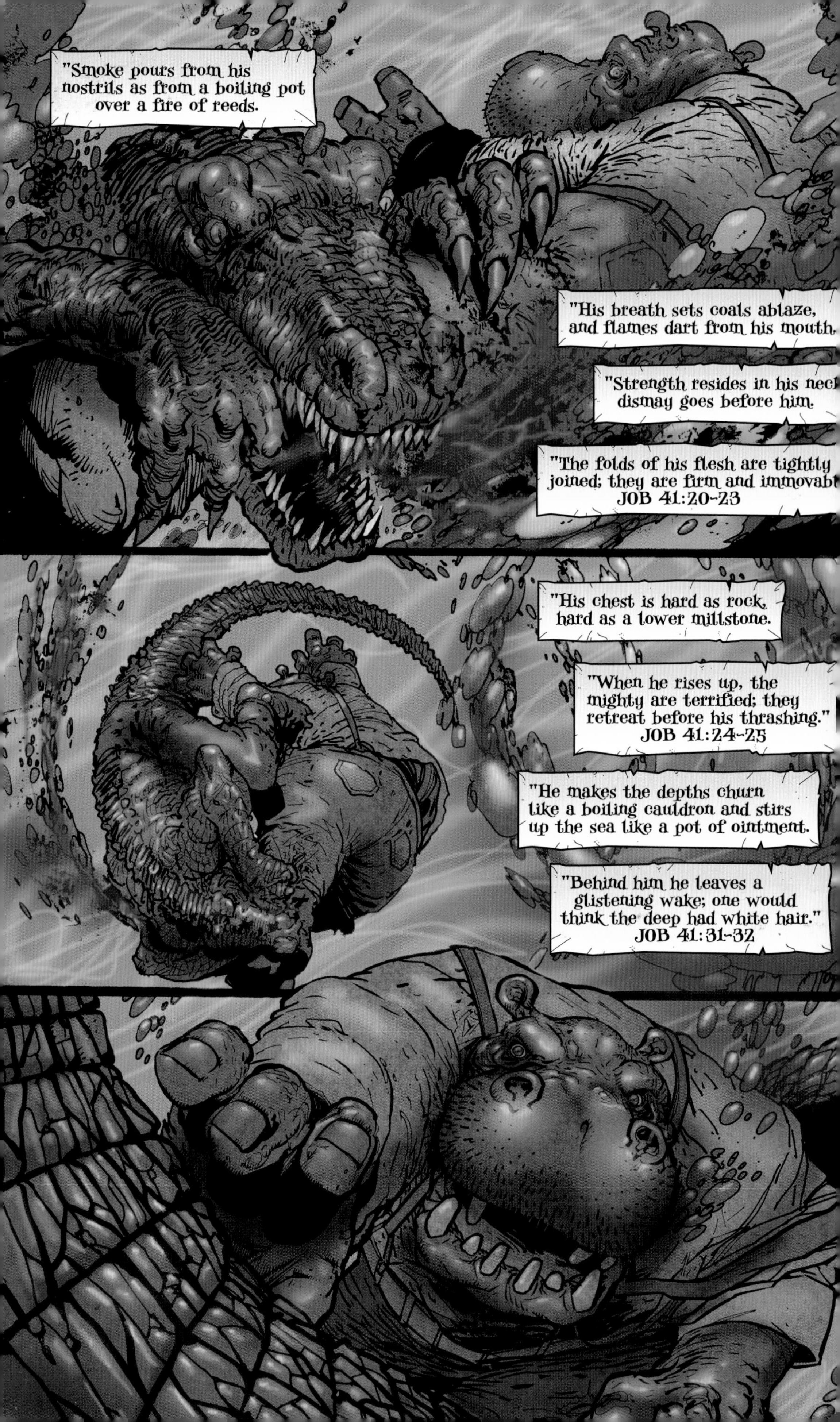
"Smoke pours from his nostrils as from a boiling pot over a fire of reeds.
"His breath sets coals ablaze, and flames dart from his mouth.
"Strength resides in his neck dismay goes before him.
"The folds of his flesh are tightly joined; they are firm and immovab
JOB 41:20-23
"His chest is hard as rock, hard as a lower millstone.
"When he rises up, the mighty are terrified; they retreat before his thrashing."
JOB 41:24-25
"He makes the depths churn like a boiling cauldron and stirs up the sea like a pot of ointment.
"Behind him he leaves a glistening wake; one would think the deep had white hair."
JOB 41:31-32

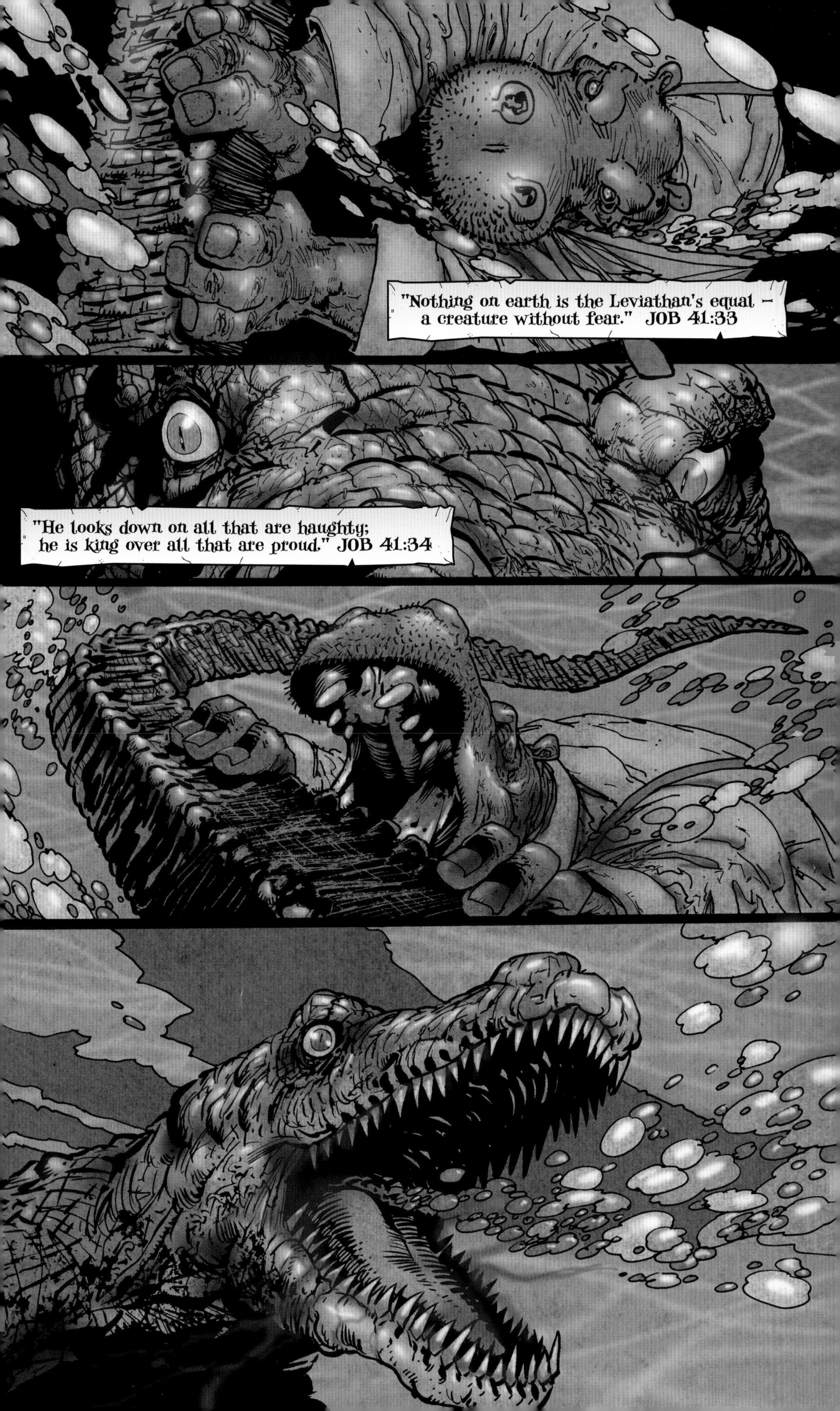
"Nothing on earth is the Leviathan's equal – a creature without fear." JOB 41:33
"He looks down on all that are haughty; he is king over all that are proud." JOB 41:34

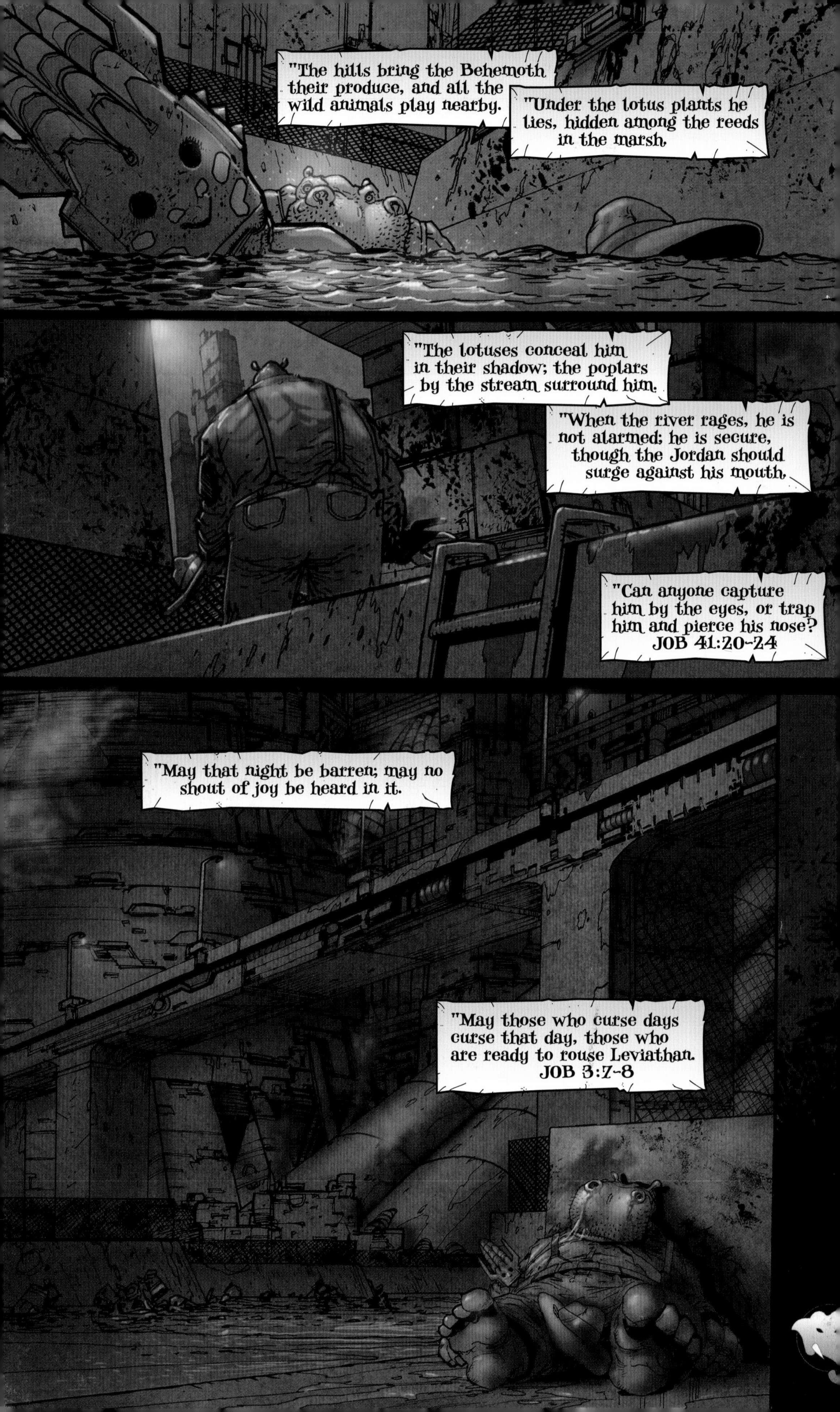
"The hills bring the Behemoth their produce, and all the wild animals play nearby.
"Under the lotus plants he lies, hidden among the reeds in the marsh.
"The lotuses conceal him in their shadow; the poplars by the stream surround him.
"When the river rages, he is not alarmed; he is secure, though the Jordan should surge against his mouth.
"Can anyone capture him by the eyes, or trap him and pierce his nose? JOB 41:20-24
"May that night be barren; may no shout of joy be heard in it.
"May those who curse days curse that day, those who are ready to rouse Leviathan. JOB 3:7-8

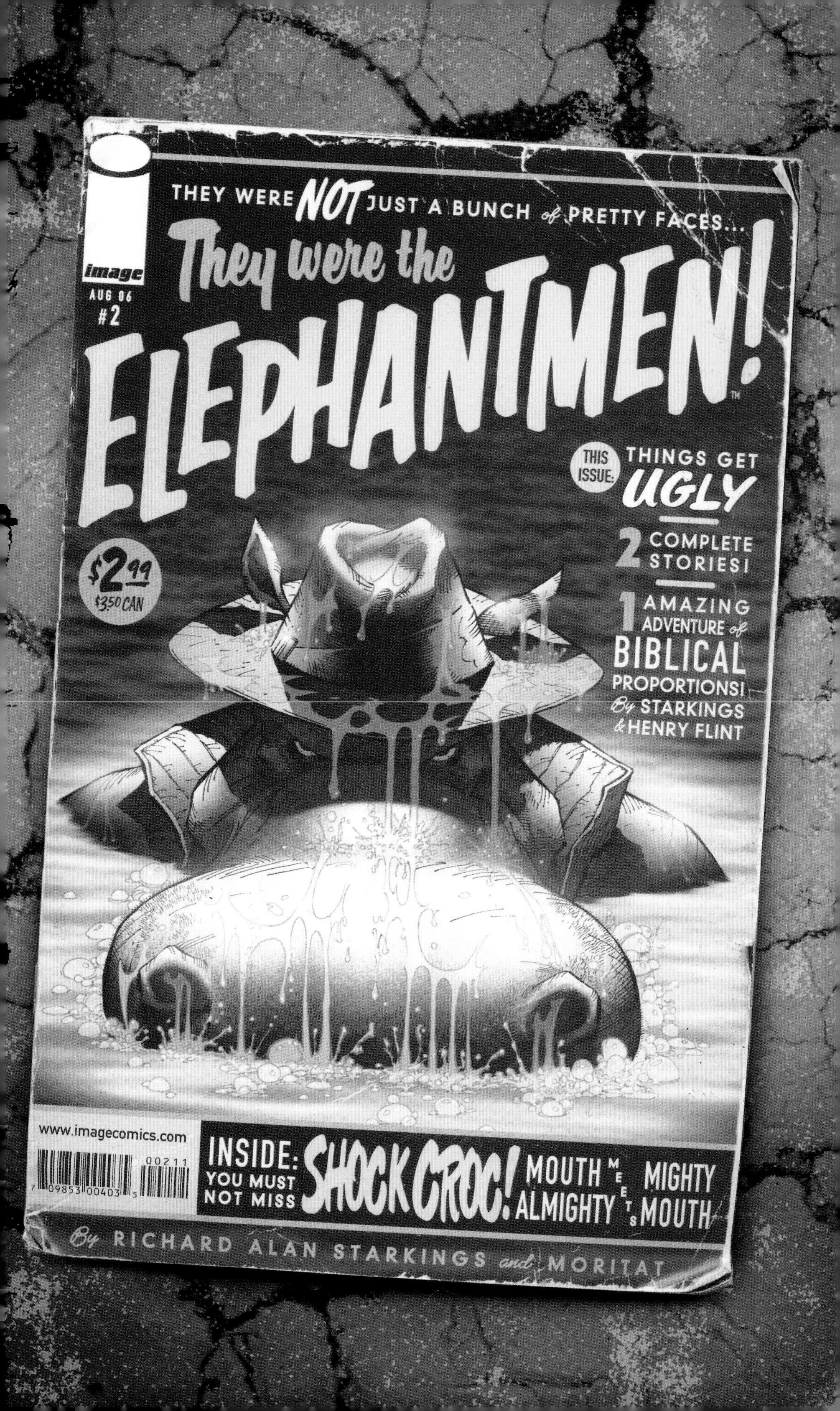
AUG 06
#2
THEY WERE NOT JUST A BUNCH of PRETTY FACES...
They were the
ELEPHANTMEN!
THIS ISSUE: THINGS GET UGLY
2 COMPLETE STORIES!
1 AMAZING ADVENTURE of BIBLICAL PROPORTIONS!
By STARKINGS & HENRY FLINT
$2.99
$3.50 CAN
www.imagecomics.com
INSIDE: YOU MUST NOT MISS
SHOCK CROC!
MOUTH MEETS MIGHTY
ALMIGHTY MOUTH
By RICHARD ALAN STARKINGS and MORITAT

"THE PRESS IS NOT
ONLY FREE, IT IS
POWERFUL. THAT
POWER IS OURS.
IT IS THE PROUDEST
THAT MAN CAN
ENJOY."

BENJAMIN DISRAELI
1804-1881

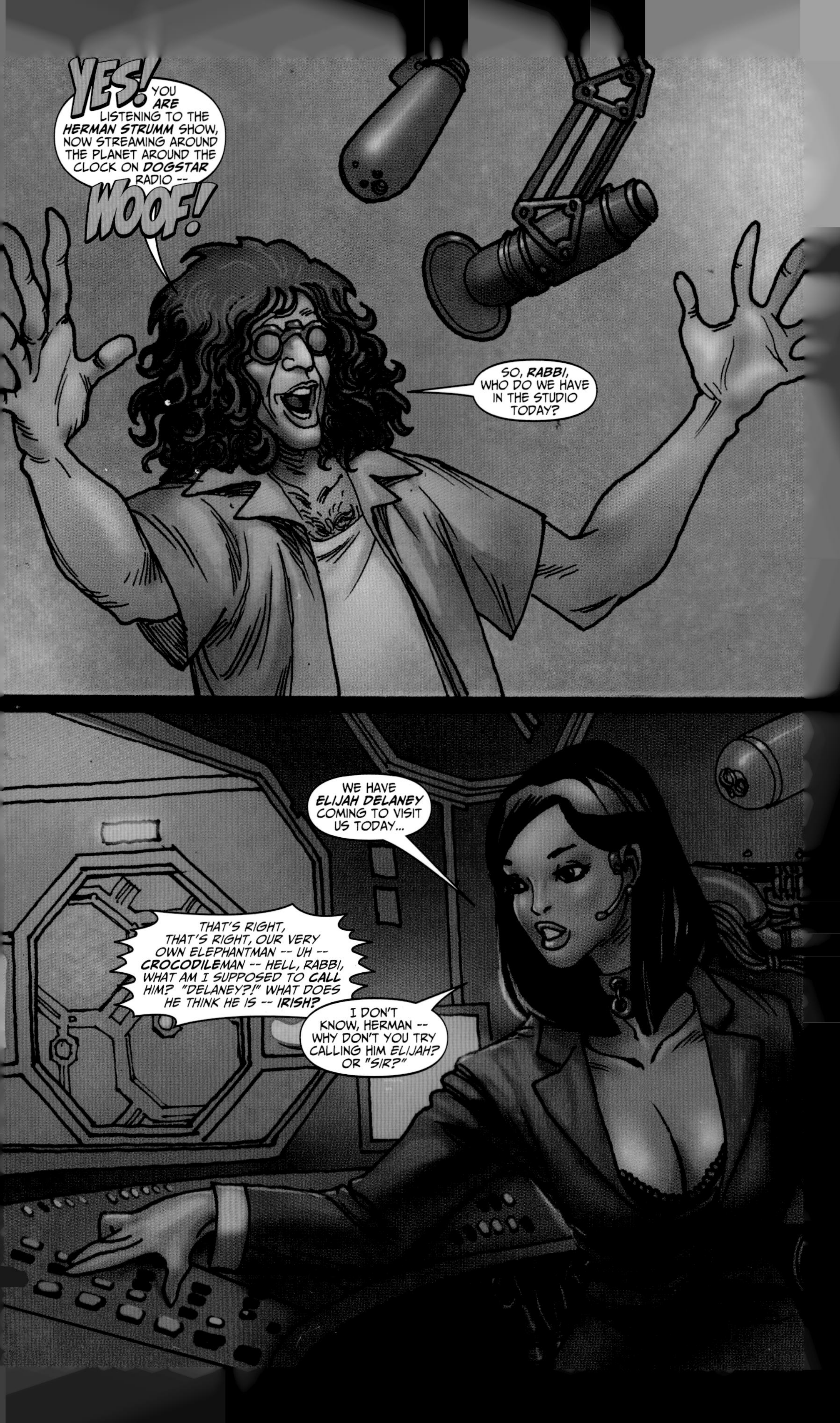
YES! YOU ARE LISTENING TO THE HERMAN STRUMM SHOW, NOW STREAMING AROUND THE PLANET AROUND THE CLOCK ON DOGSTAR RADIO -- WOOF!
SO, RABBI, WHO DO WE HAVE IN THE STUDIO TODAY?
WE HAVE ELIJAH DELANEY COMING TO VISIT US TODAY...
THAT'S RIGHT, THAT'S RIGHT, OUR VERY OWN ELEPHANTMAN -- UH -- CROCODILEMAN -- HELL, RABBI, WHAT AM I SUPPOSED TO CALL HIM? "DELANEY?!" WHAT DOES HE THINK HE IS -- IRISH?
I DON'T KNOW, HERMAN -- WHY DON'T YOU TRY CALLING HIM ELIJAH? OR "SIR?"

Y'KNOW, YOU'RE RIGHT, HE'S, WHAT, 550 POUNDS, ALL MUSCLE, HE'S GOT A MOUTHFUL OF RAZOR SHARP TEETH... "SIR" SOUNDS ABOUT RIGHT...

AND I DO NOT WANT TO OFFEND THE ELEPHANTMEN, AT THE LAST COUNT THERE WERE, WHAT, FIFTEEN THOUSAND OF THESE GUYS?

HELL, I KNOW MY PLACE.

I SERIOUSLY DOUBT THAT, HERMAN...

THIS IS DOGSTAR FIVE TO DOGSTAR CONTROL... WE HAVE A V-I-P ONBOARD, PLEASE CONFIRM CLEARANCE FOR DOCKING, OVER...

ROGER, DOGSTAR FIVE... CLEARANCE CONFIRMED, YOU'RE GOOD TO GO.

ACTIVE ___S & IMAGE COMICS present:

SHOCK

By STARKINGS & MORITAT with COMICRA

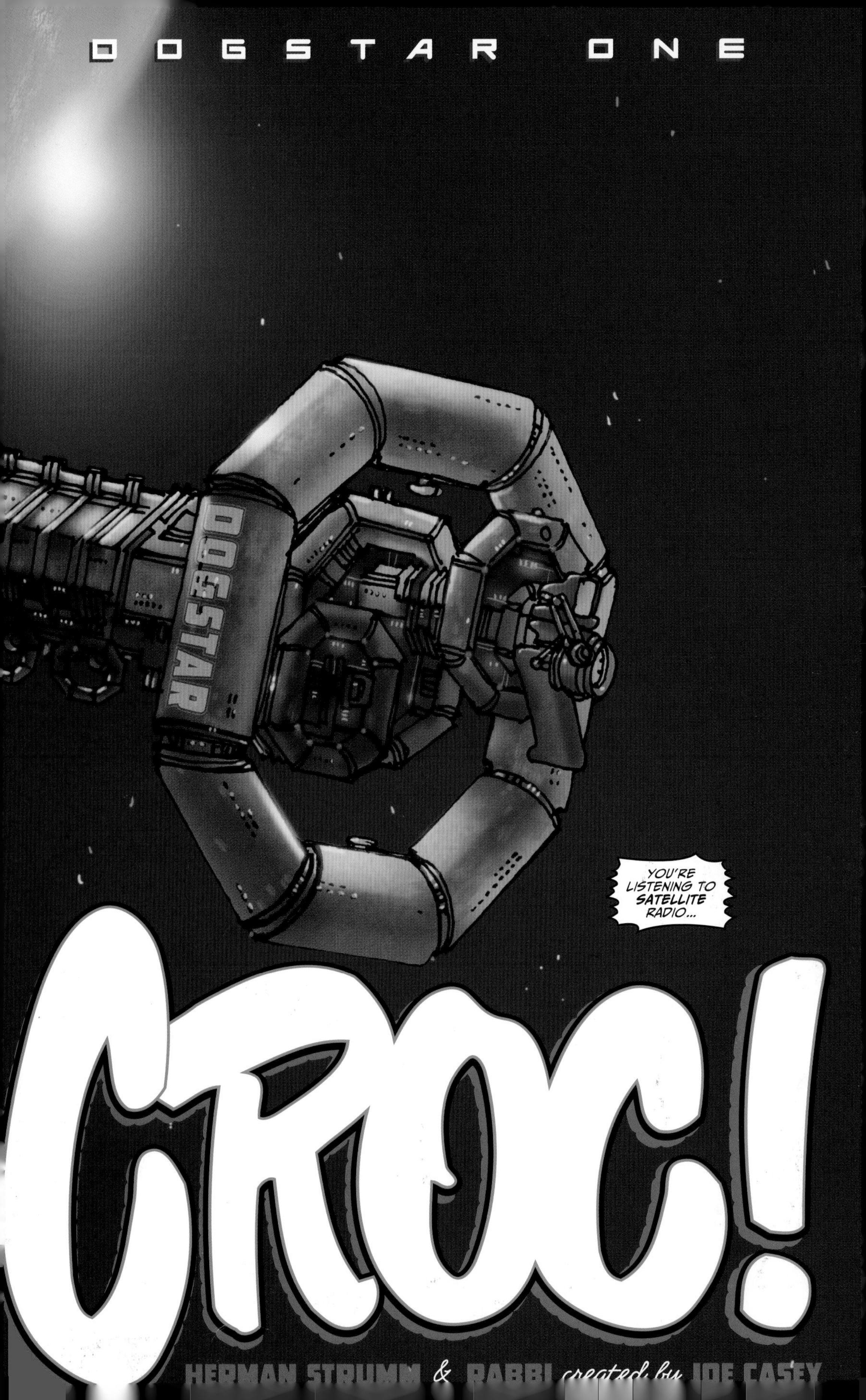
DOGSTAR ONE
DOGSTAR
YOU'RE LISTENING TO SATELLITE RADIO...
CROC!
HERMAN STRUMM & RABBI created by JOE CASEY

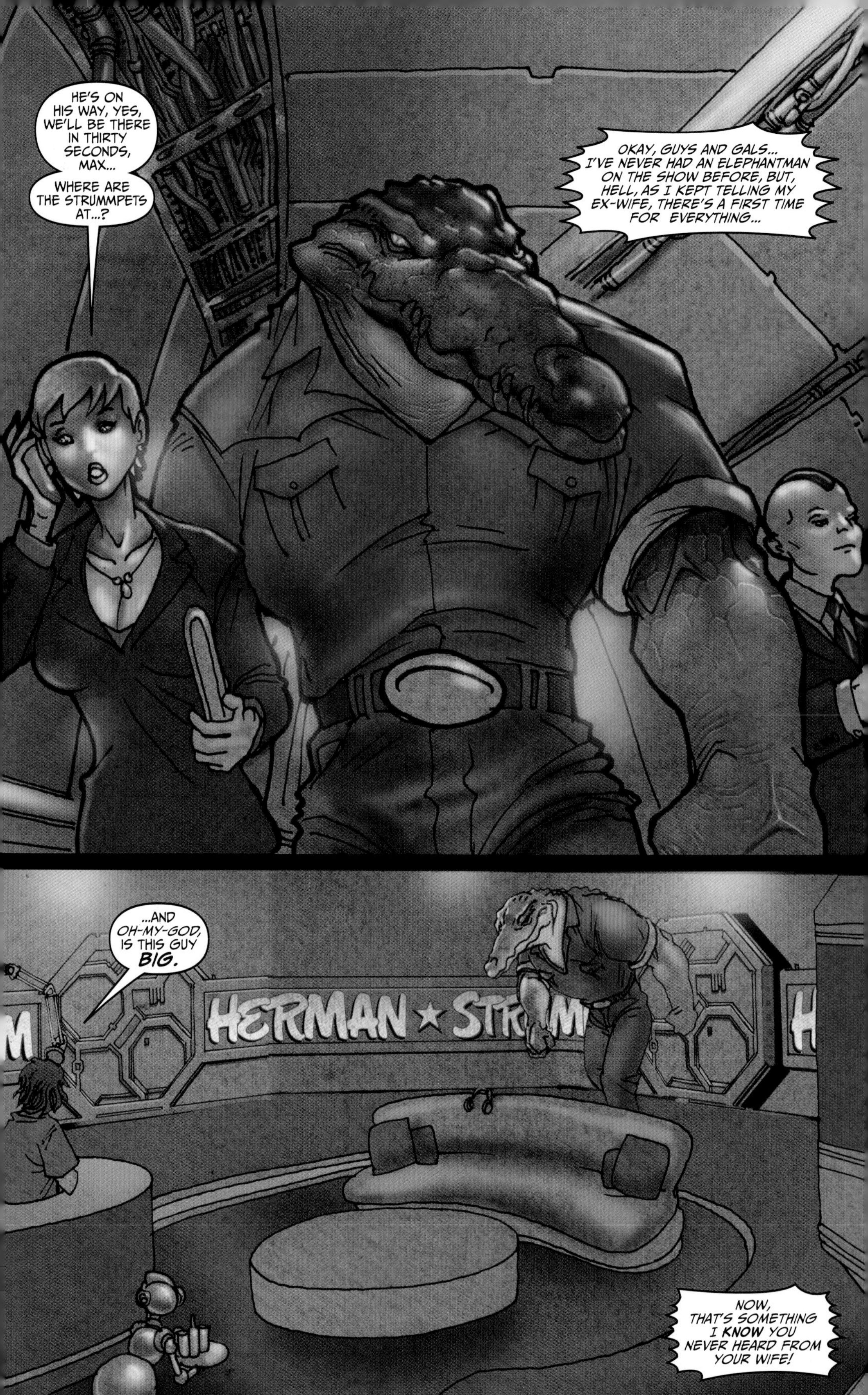
HE'S ON HIS WAY, YES, WE'LL BE THERE IN THIRTY SECONDS, MAX...
WHERE ARE THE STRUMMPETS AT...?
OKAY, GUYS AND GALS... I'VE NEVER HAD AN ELEPHANTMAN ON THE SHOW BEFORE, BUT, HELL, AS I KEPT TELLING MY EX-WIFE, THERE'S A FIRST TIME FOR EVERYTHING...
...AND OH-MY-GOD, IS THIS GUY BIG.
HERMAN ★ STR
NOW, THAT'S SOMETHING I KNOW YOU NEVER HEARD FROM YOUR WIFE!

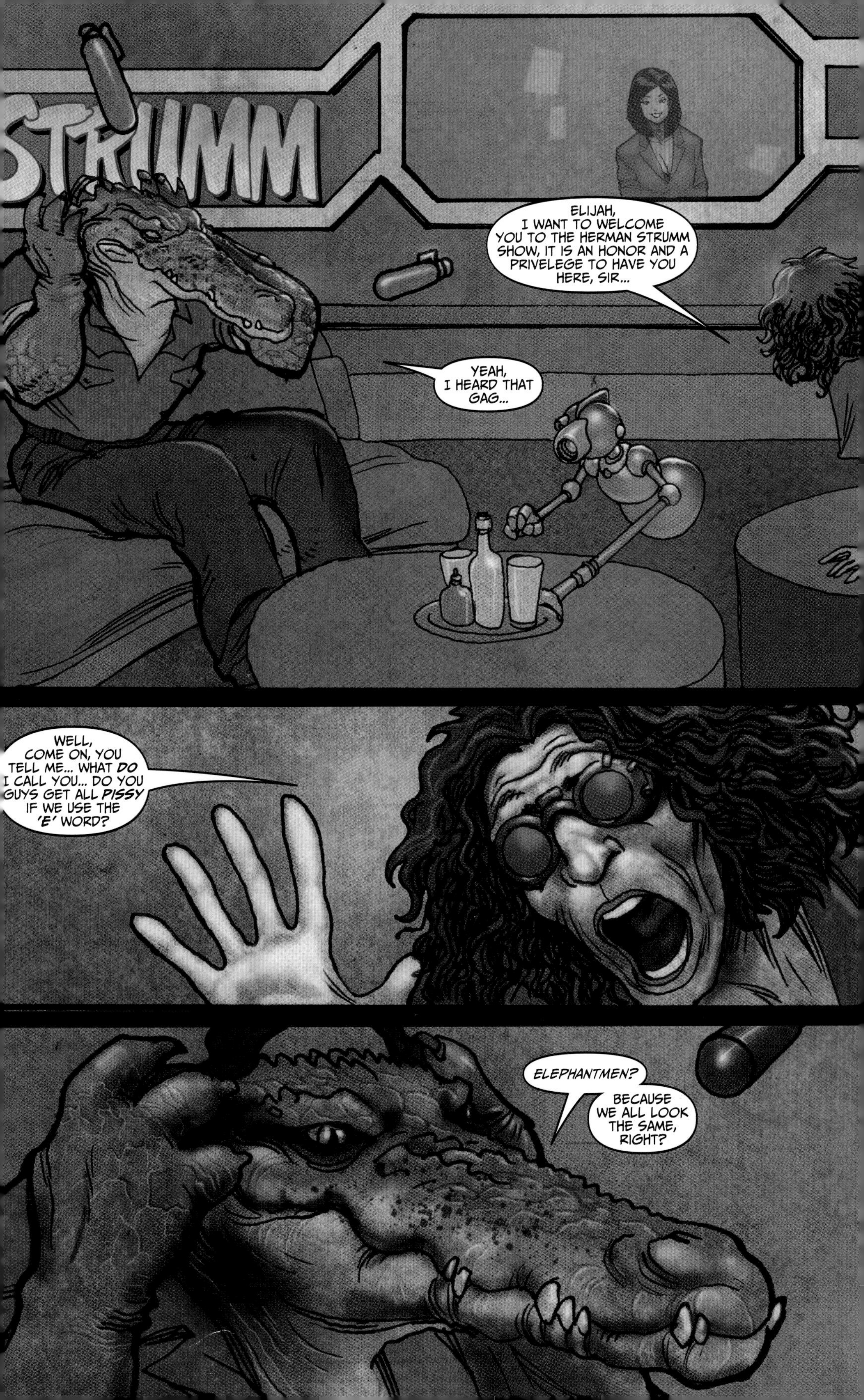
STRUMM
ELIJAH, I WANT TO WELCOME YOU TO THE HERMAN STRUMM SHOW, IT IS AN HONOR AND A PRIVELEGE TO HAVE YOU HERE, SIR...
YEAH, I HEARD THAT GAG...
WELL, COME ON, YOU TELL ME... WHAT *DO* I CALL YOU... DO YOU GUYS GET ALL *PISSY* IF WE USE THE *'E'* WORD?
ELEPHANTMEN?
BECAUSE WE ALL LOOK THE SAME, RIGHT?

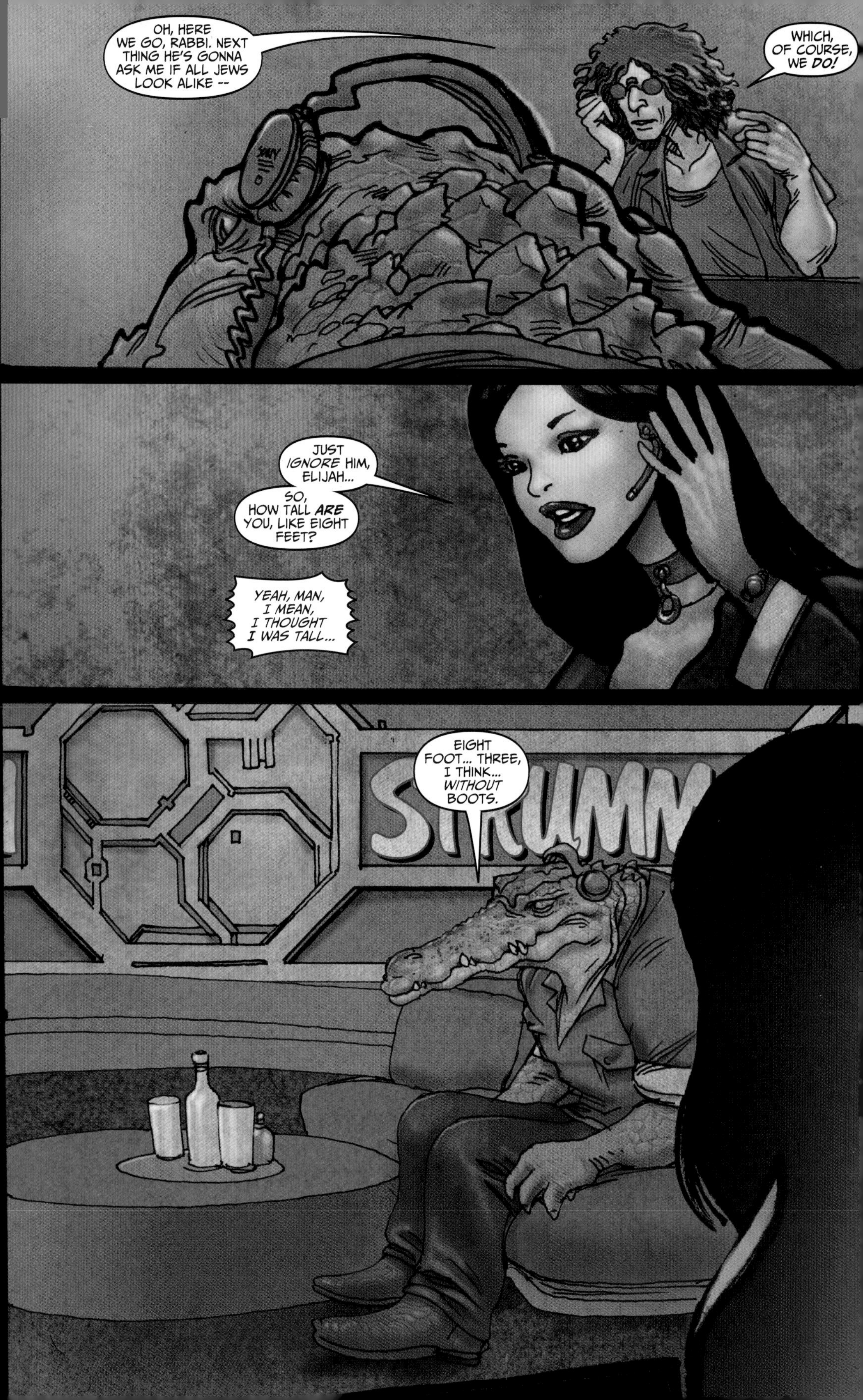
OH, HERE WE GO, RABBI. NEXT THING HE'S GONNA ASK ME IF ALL JEWS LOOK ALIKE --
WHICH, OF COURSE, WE *DO!*
JUST *IGNORE* HIM, ELIJAH...
SO, HOW TALL **ARE** YOU, LIKE EIGHT FEET?
YEAH, MAN, I MEAN, I THOUGHT I WAS TALL...
EIGHT FOOT... THREE, I THINK... *WITHOUT* BOOTS.

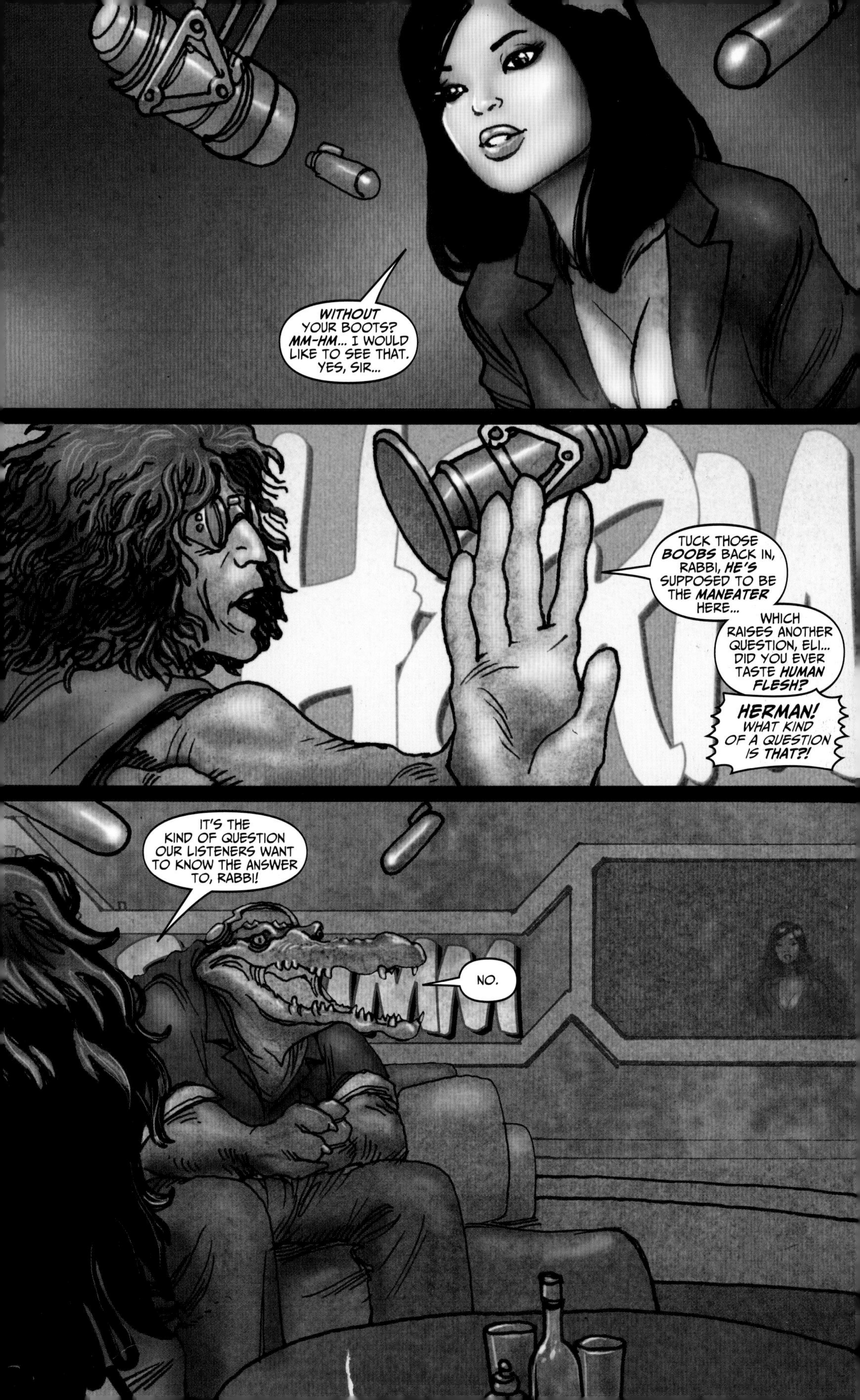
WITHOUT YOUR BOOTS? MM-HM... I WOULD LIKE TO SEE THAT. YES, SIR...
TUCK THOSE BOOBS BACK IN, RABBI, HE'S SUPPOSED TO BE THE MANEATER HERE...
WHICH RAISES ANOTHER QUESTION, ELI... DID YOU EVER TASTE HUMAN FLESH?
HERMAN! WHAT KIND OF A QUESTION IS THAT?!
IT'S THE KIND OF QUESTION OUR LISTENERS WANT TO KNOW THE ANSWER TO, RABBI!
NO.

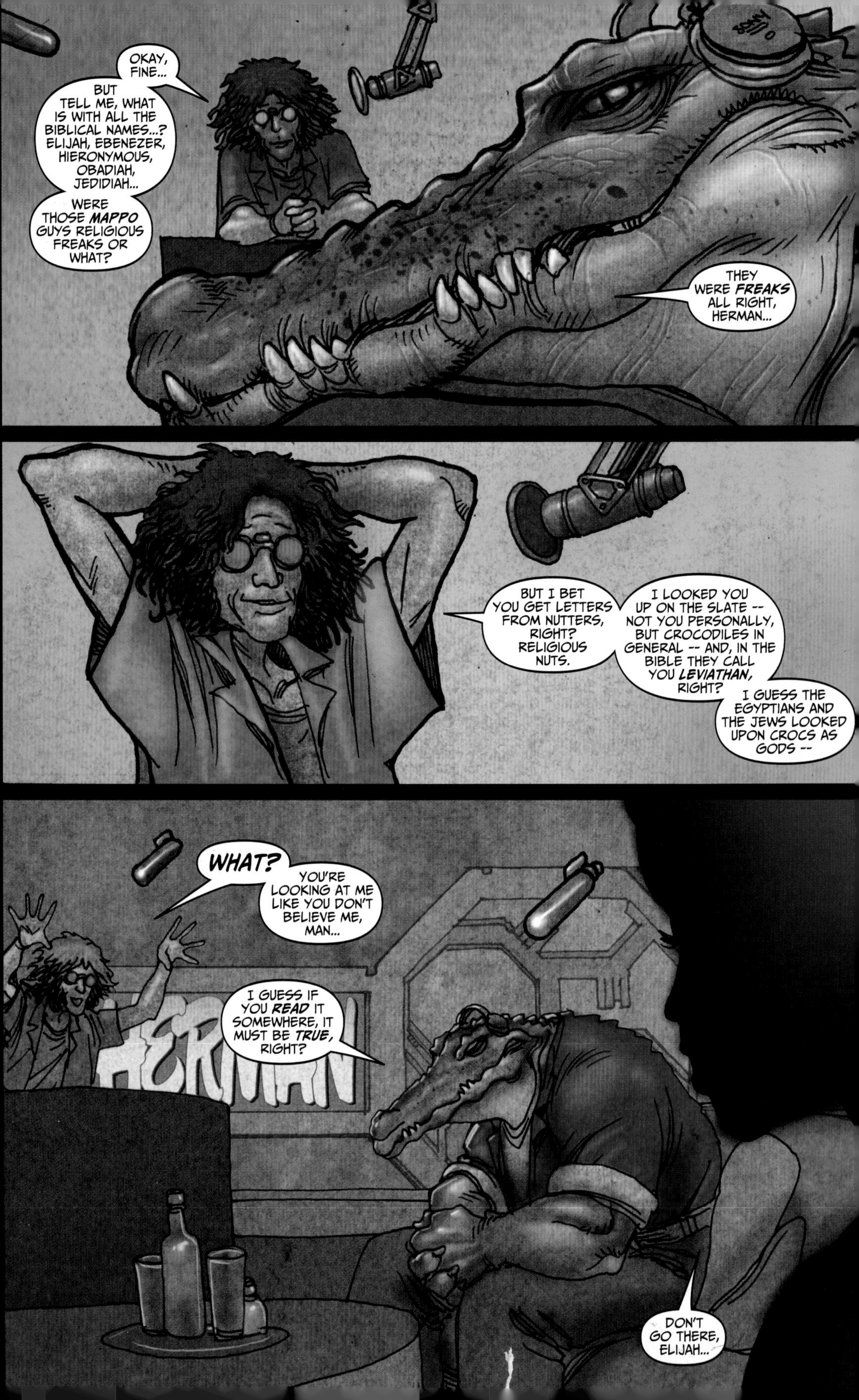
OKAY, FINE...
BUT TELL ME, WHAT IS WITH ALL THE BIBLICAL NAMES...? ELIJAH, EBENEZER, HIERONYMOUS, OBADIAH, JEDIDIAH...
WERE THOSE MAPPO GUYS RELIGIOUS FREAKS OR WHAT?
THEY WERE FREAKS ALL RIGHT, HERMAN...
BUT I BET YOU GET LETTERS FROM NUTTERS, RIGHT? RELIGIOUS NUTS.
I LOOKED YOU UP ON THE SLATE -- NOT YOU PERSONALLY, BUT CROCODILES IN GENERAL -- AND, IN THE BIBLE THEY CALL YOU LEVIATHAN, RIGHT?
I GUESS THE EGYPTIANS AND THE JEWS LOOKED UPON CROCS AS GODS --
WHAT?
YOU'RE LOOKING AT ME LIKE YOU DON'T BELIEVE ME, MAN...
I GUESS IF YOU READ IT SOMEWHERE, IT MUST BE TRUE, RIGHT?
HERMAN
DON'T GO THERE, ELIJAH...

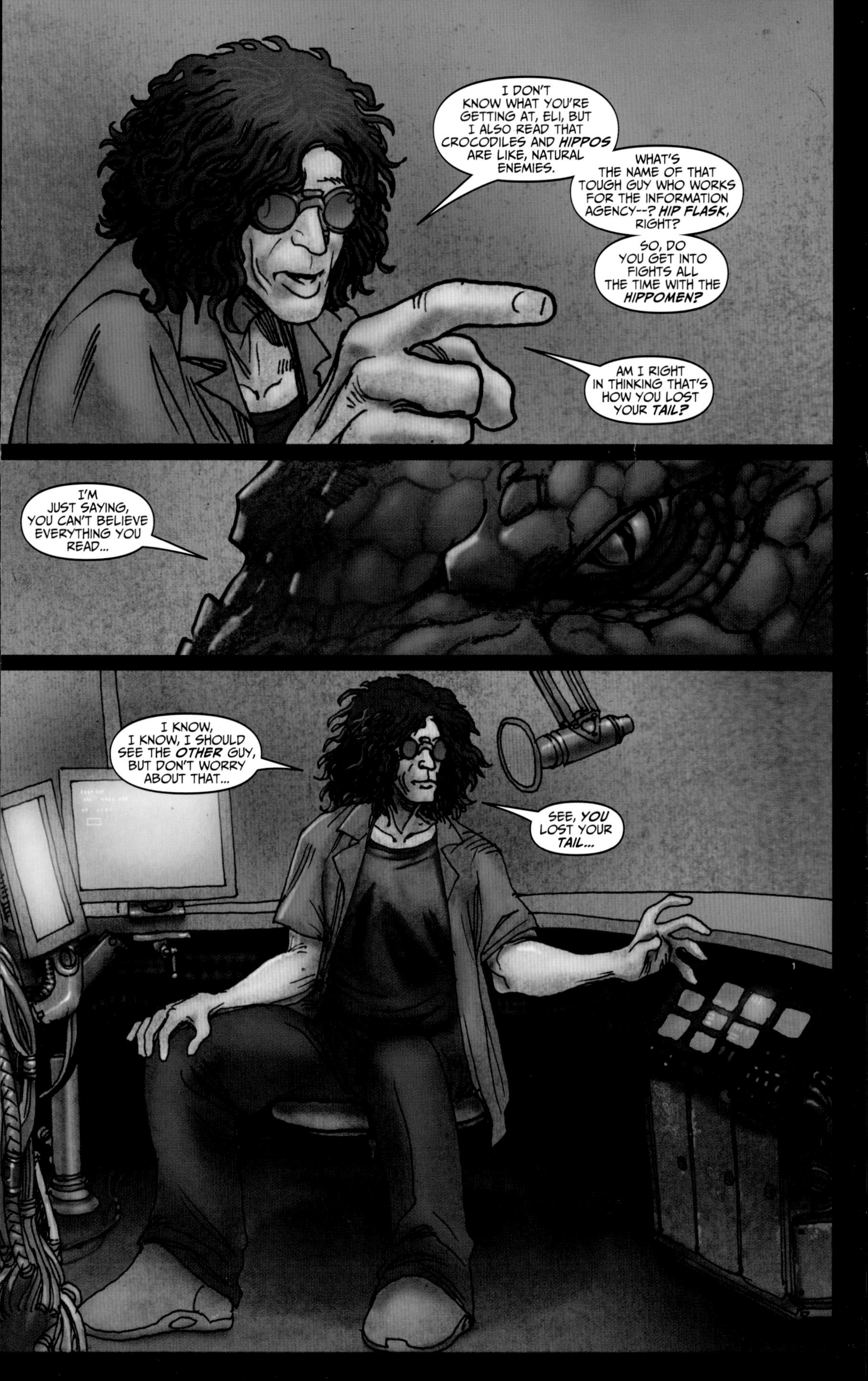

I DON'T KNOW WHAT YOU'RE GETTING AT, ELI, BUT I ALSO READ THAT CROCODILES AND *HIPPOS* ARE LIKE, NATURAL ENEMIES.
WHAT'S THE NAME OF THAT TOUGH GUY WHO WORKS FOR THE INFORMATION AGENCY--? *HIP FLASK*, RIGHT?
SO, DO YOU GET INTO FIGHTS ALL THE TIME WITH THE *HIPPOMEN?*
AM I RIGHT IN THINKING THAT'S HOW YOU LOST YOUR *TAIL?*
I'M JUST SAYING, YOU CAN'T BELIEVE EVERYTHING YOU READ...
I KNOW, I KNOW, I SHOULD SEE THE *OTHER* GUY, BUT DON'T WORRY ABOUT THAT...
SEE, *YOU* LOST YOUR *TAIL...*

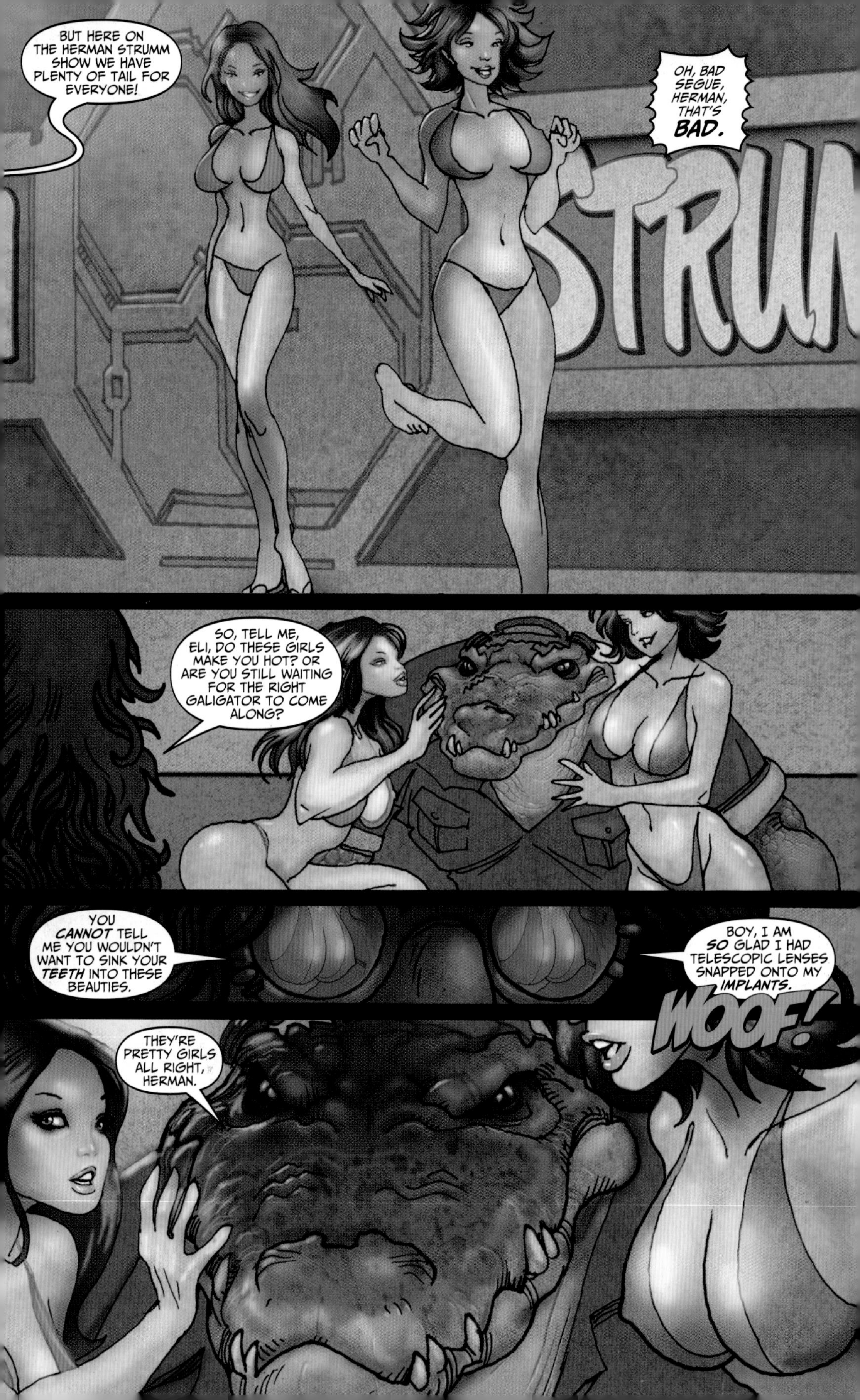
BUT HERE ON THE HERMAN STRUMM SHOW WE HAVE PLENTY OF TAIL FOR EVERYONE!
OH, BAD SEGUE, HERMAN, THAT'S BAD.
STRUM
SO, TELL ME, ELI, DO THESE GIRLS MAKE YOU HOT? OR ARE YOU STILL WAITING FOR THE RIGHT GALIGATOR TO COME ALONG?
YOU CANNOT TELL ME YOU WOULDN'T WANT TO SINK YOUR TEETH INTO THESE BEAUTIES.
BOY, I AM SO GLAD I HAD TELESCOPIC LENSES SNAPPED ONTO MY IMPLANTS.
WOOF!
THEY'RE PRETTY GIRLS ALL RIGHT, HERMAN.

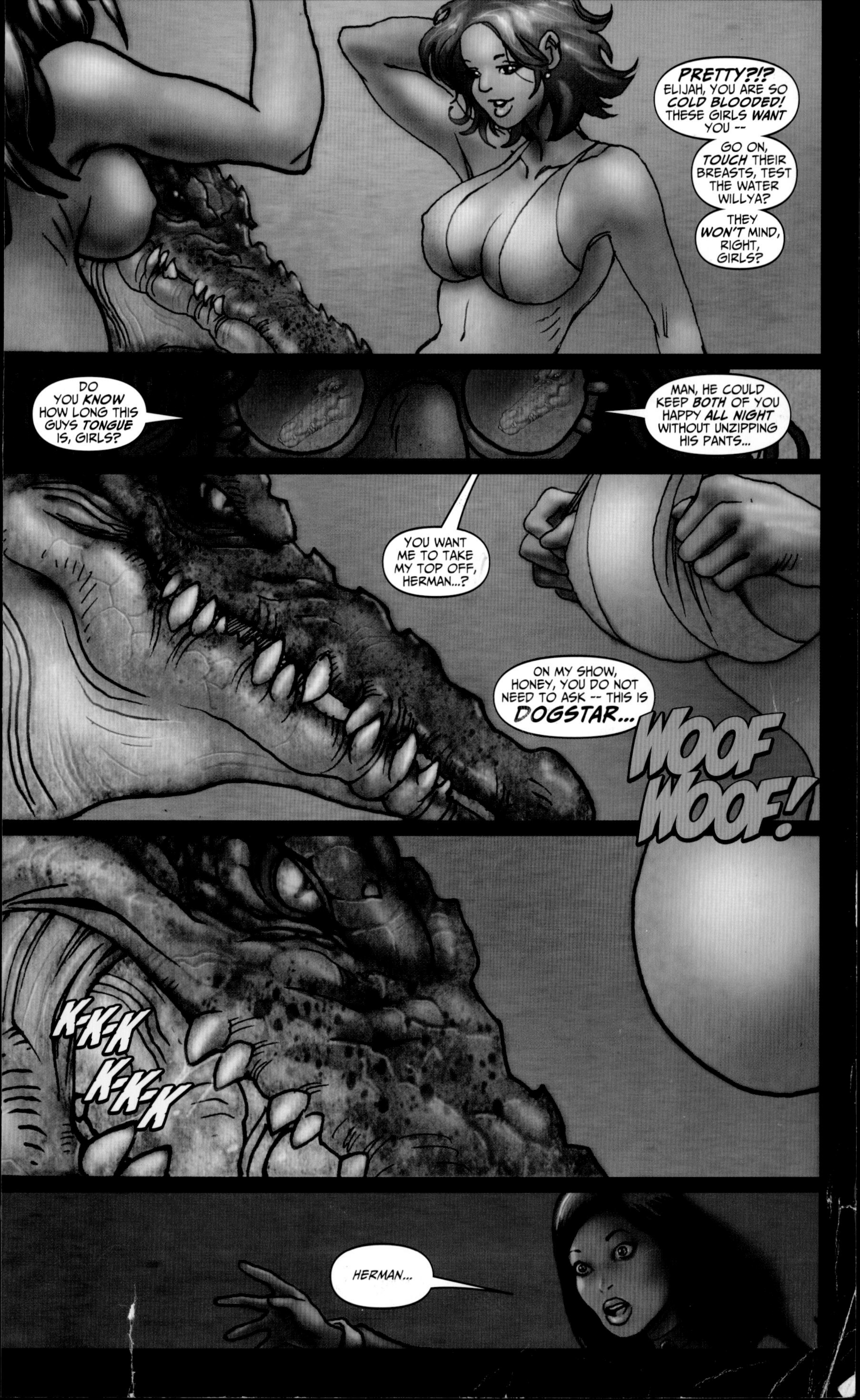
PRETTY?!? ELIJAH, YOU ARE SO COLD BLOODED! THESE GIRLS WANT YOU --
GO ON, TOUCH THEIR BREASTS, TEST THE WATER WILLYA?
THEY WON'T MIND, RIGHT, GIRLS?
DO YOU KNOW HOW LONG THIS GUYS TONGUE IS, GIRLS?
MAN, HE COULD KEEP BOTH OF YOU HAPPY ALL NIGHT WITHOUT UNZIPPING HIS PANTS...
YOU WANT ME TO TAKE MY TOP OFF, HERMAN...?
ON MY SHOW, HONEY, YOU DO NOT NEED TO ASK -- THIS IS DOGSTAR...
WOOF WOOF!
K-K-K K-K-K
HERMAN...

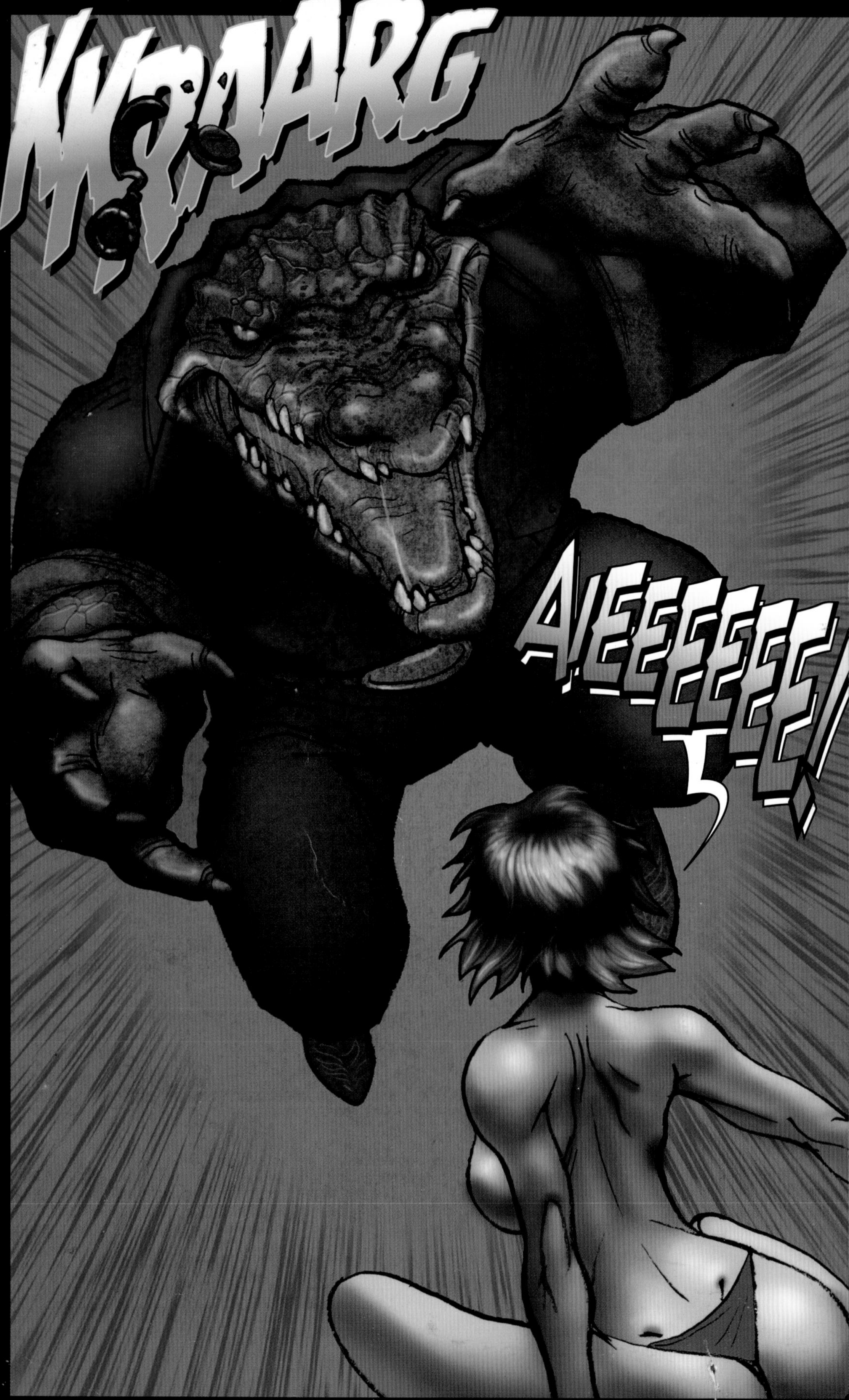
AIEEEEEEE!

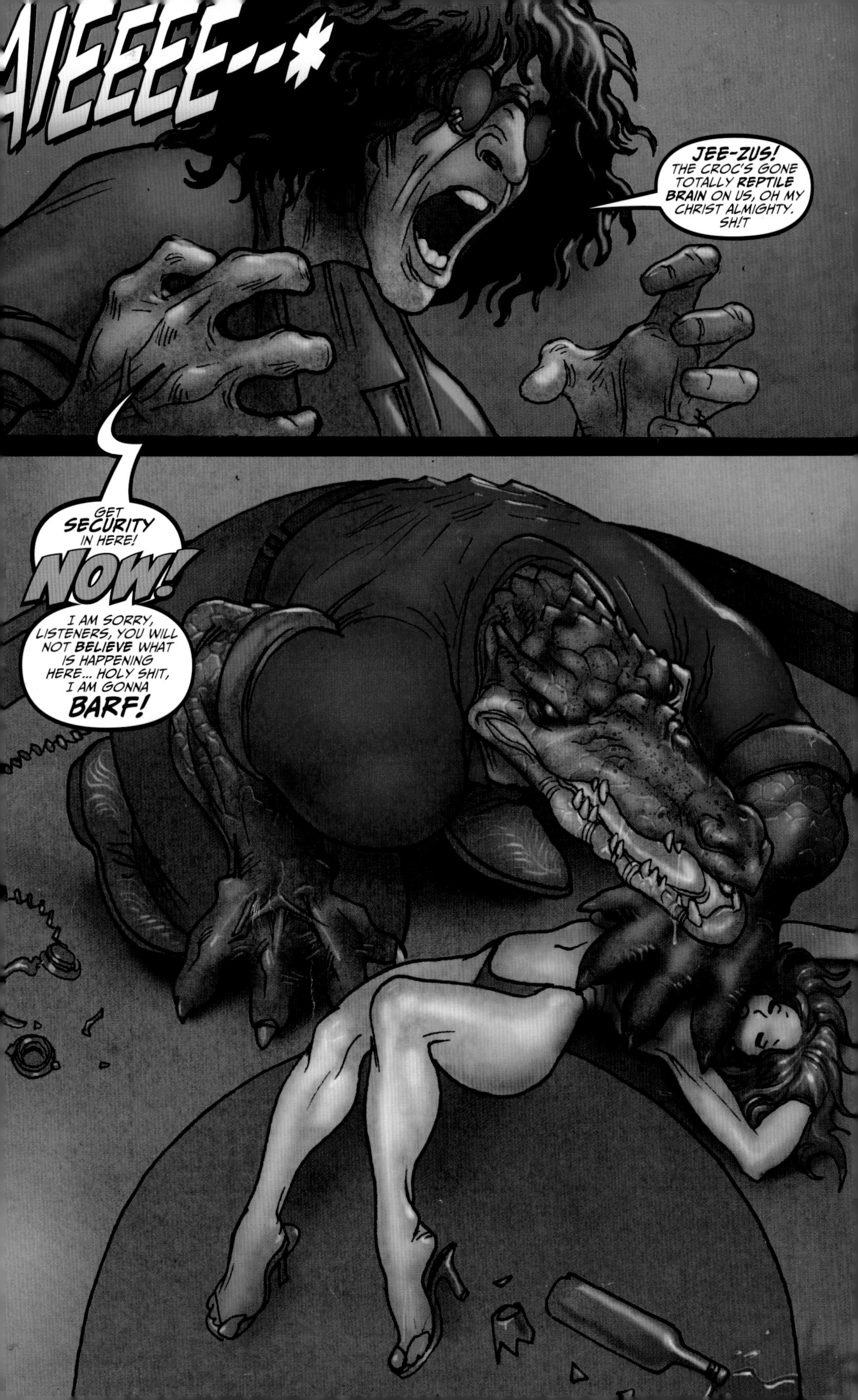
AIEEEE--*
JEE-ZUS! THE CROC'S GONE TOTALLY REPTILE BRAIN ON US, OH MY CHRIST ALMIGHTY. SH!T
GET SECURITY IN HERE! NOW!
I AM SORRY, LISTENERS, YOU WILL NOT BELIEVE WHAT IS HAPPENING HERE... HOLY SHIT, I AM GONNA BARF!

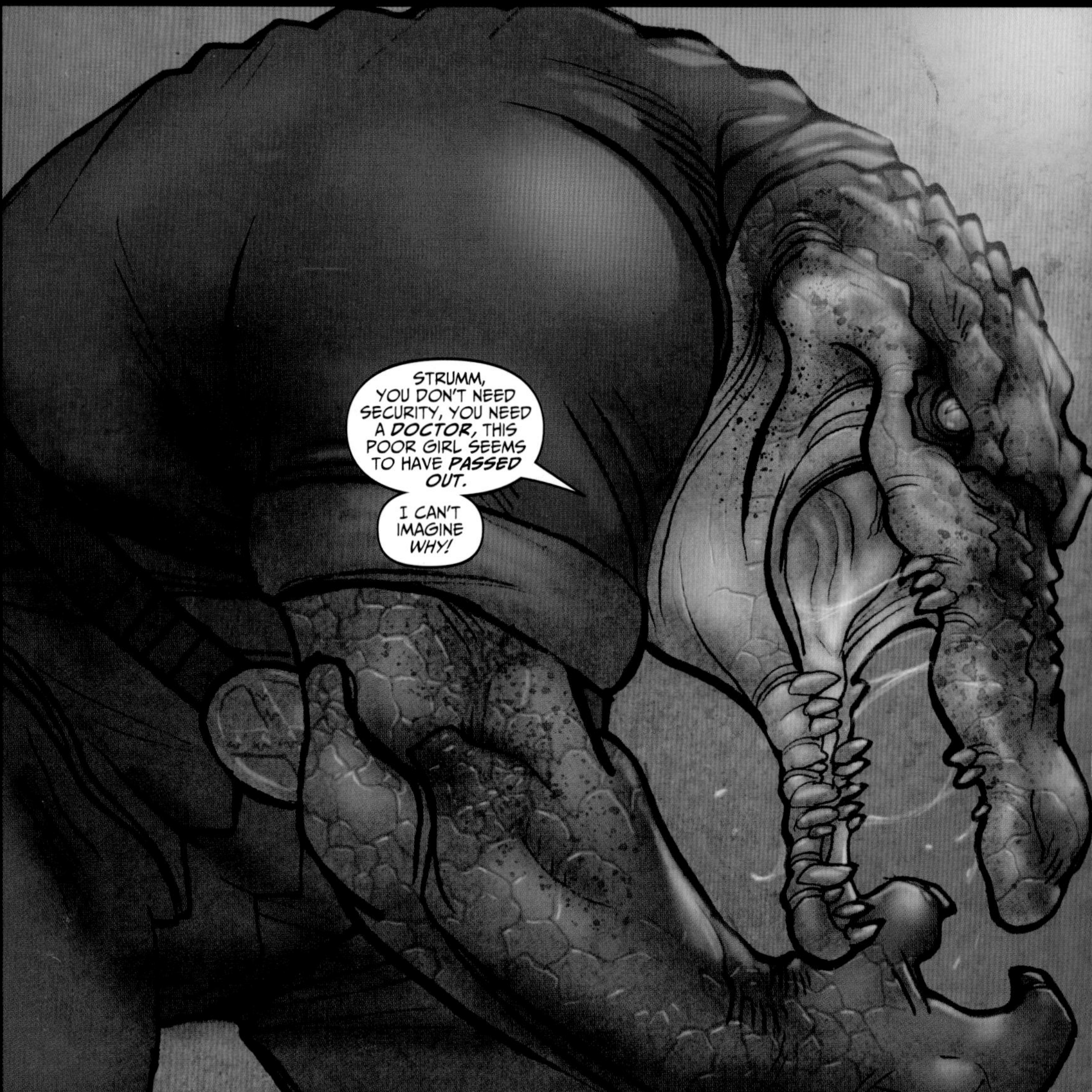
STRUMM, YOU DON'T NEED SECURITY, YOU NEED A *DOCTOR*, THIS POOR GIRL SEEMS TO HAVE *PASSED OUT.*
I CAN'T IMAGINE *WHY!*

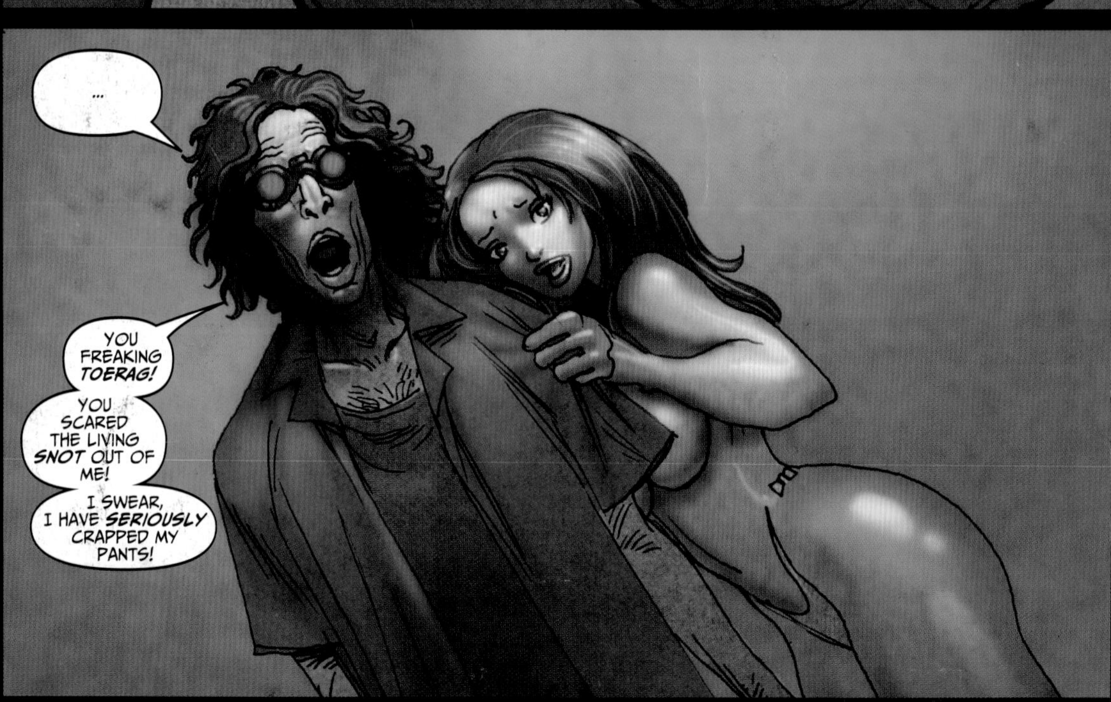
...
YOU FREAKING *TOERAG!*
YOU SCARED THE LIVING *SNOT* OUT OF ME!
I SWEAR, I HAVE *SERIOUSLY* CRAPPED MY PANTS!

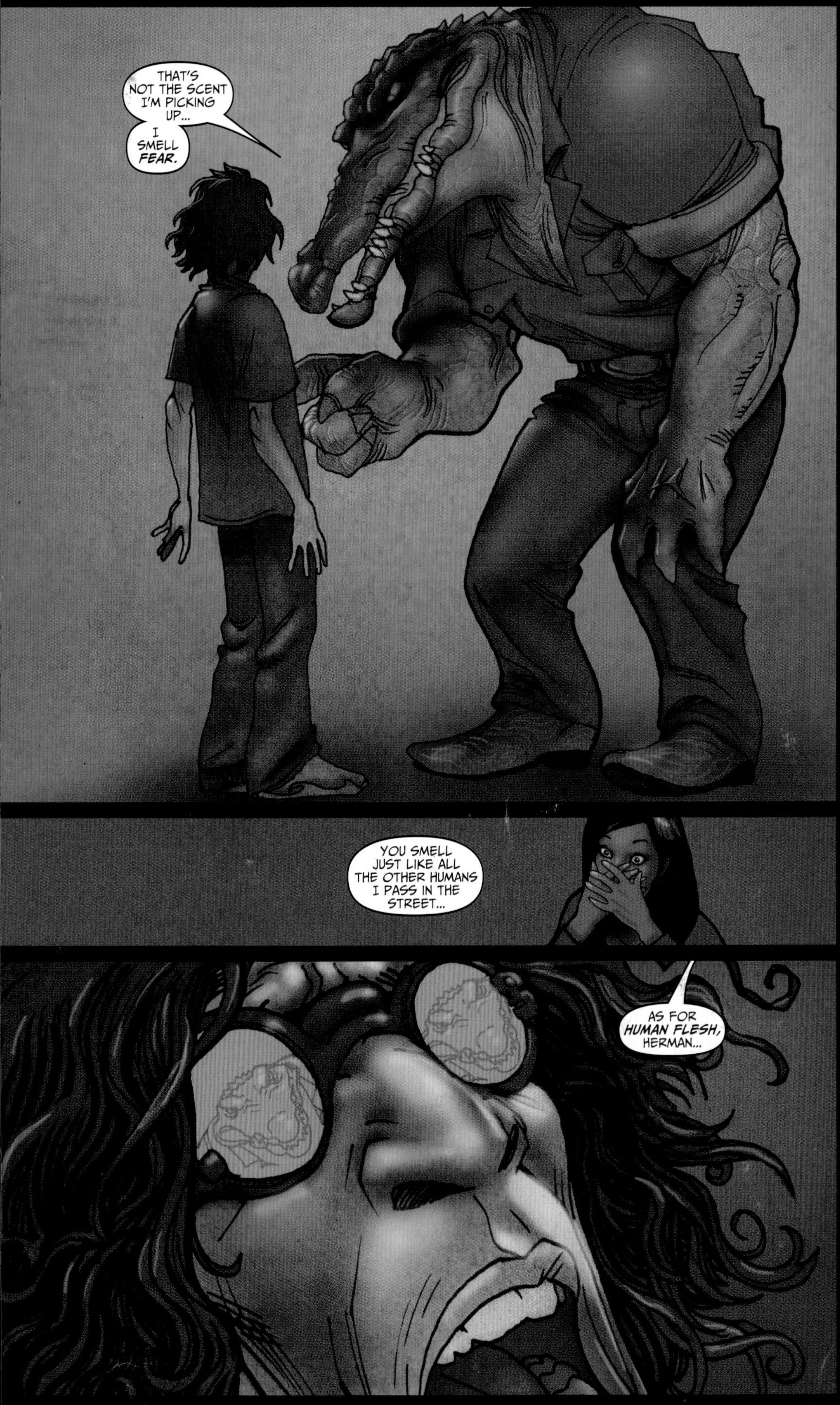
THAT'S NOT THE SCENT I'M PICKING UP...
I SMELL *FEAR.*
YOU SMELL JUST LIKE ALL THE OTHER HUMANS I PASS IN THE STREET...
AS FOR *HUMAN FLESH,* HERMAN...

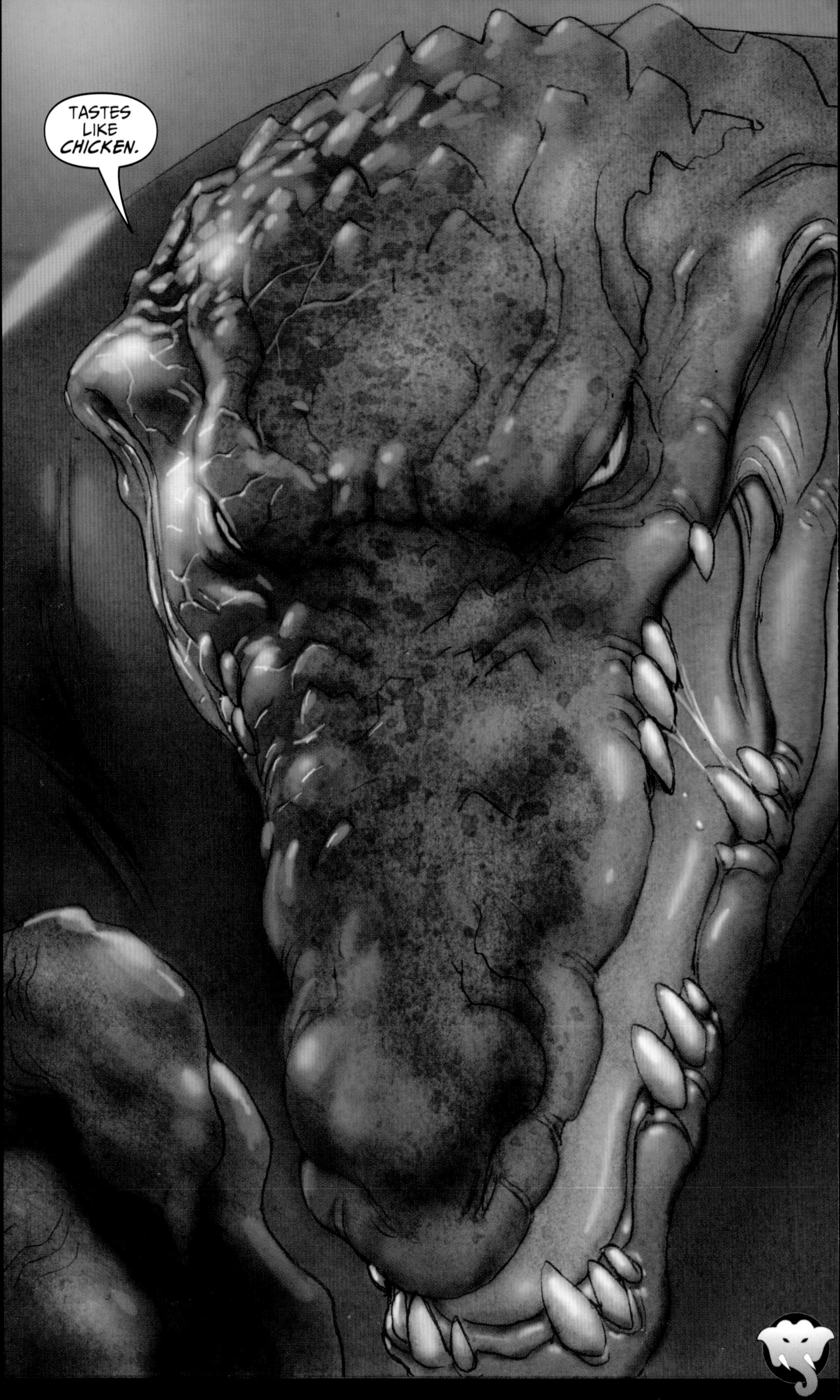
TASTES LIKE CHICKEN.

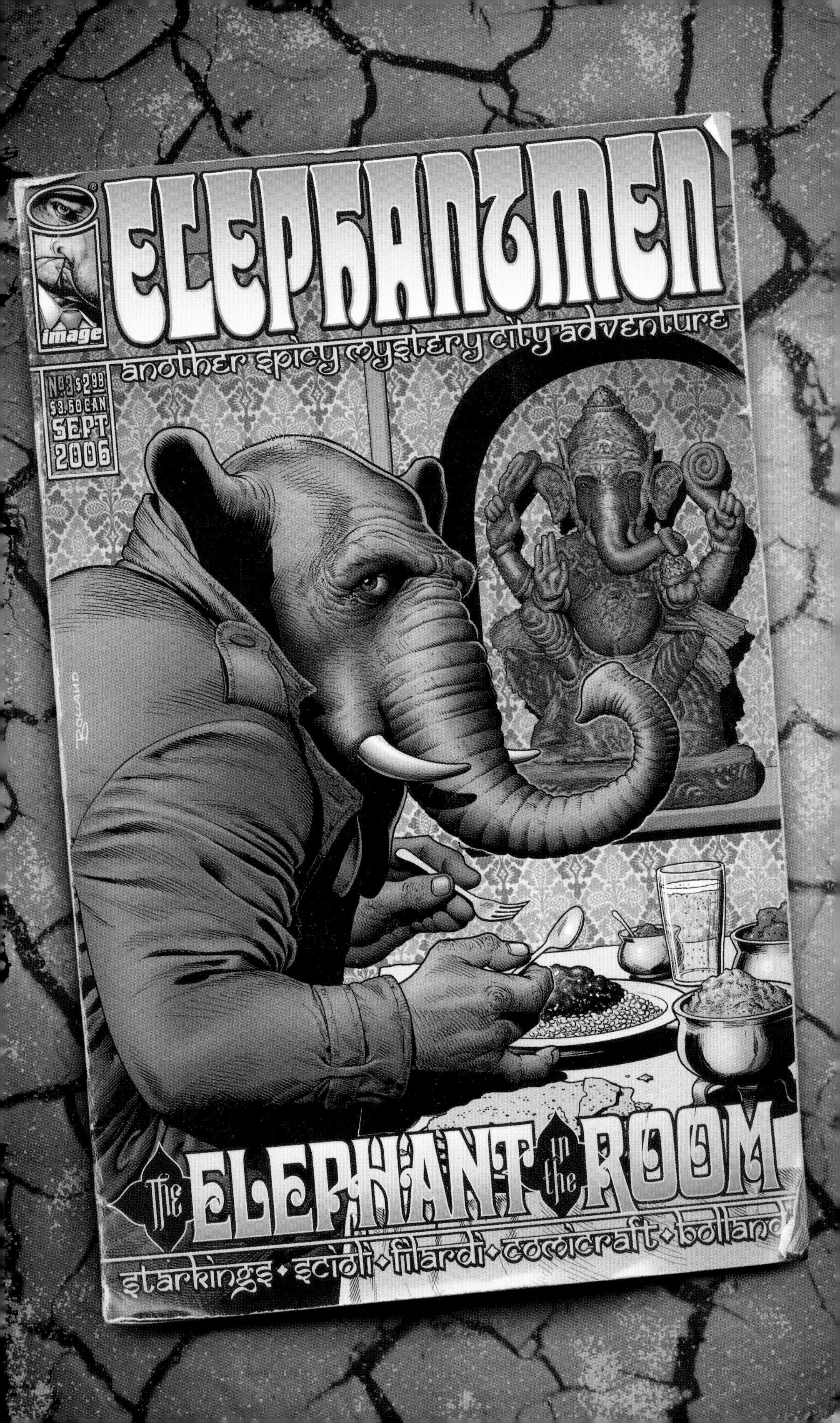

image
ELEPHANTMEN
another spicy mystery city adventure
No 3 $2.99
$3.50 CAN
SEPT
2006
BOLLAND
The ELEPHANT in the ROOM
starkings • scioli • filardi • comicraft • bolland

"IT IS CERTAIN THAT ASSOCIATED
ANIMALS HAVE A FEELING OF
LOVE FOR EACH OTHER, WHICH IS
NOT FELT BY NON-SOCIAL ADULT
ANIMALS. HOW FAR IN MOST CASES
THEY ACTUALLY SYMPATHISE IN THE
PAINS AND PLEASURES OF OTHERS,
IS MORE DOUBTFUL. IT IS OFTEN
DIFFICULT TO JUDGE WHETHER
ANIMALS HAVE ANY FEELING FOR
THE SUFFERINGS OF OTHERS OF
THEIR KIND. WHO CAN SAY WHAT
COWS FEEL, WHEN THEY SURROUND
AND STARE INTENTLY ON A DYING
OR DEAD COMPANION?

"DOGS POSSESS SOME POWER
OF SELF-COMMAND, AND THIS
DOES NOT APPEAR TO BE WHOLLY
THE RESULT OF FEAR. THEY WILL
REFRAIN FROM STEALING FOOD IN
THE ABSENCE OF THEIR MASTER
AND HAVE LONG BEEN ACCEPTED
AS THE MODEL OF FIDELITY AND
OBEDIENCE. BUT THE ELEPHANT IS
LIKEWISE VERY FAITHFUL TO HIS
DRIVER OR KEEPER, AND PROBABLY
CONSIDERS HIM AS THE LEADER OF
THE HERD. DR. HOOKER INFORMS
ME THAT AN ELEPHANT, WHICH HE
WAS RIDING IN INDIA, BECAME SO
DEEPLY BOGGED THAT HE REMAINED
STUCK FAST UNTIL THE NEXT DAY,
WHEN HE WAS EXTRICATED BY
MEN WITH ROPES. UNDER SUCH
CIRCUMSTANCES ELEPHANTS
WILL SEIZE WITH THEIR TRUNKS
ANY OBJECT, DEAD OR ALIVE, TO
PLACE UNDER THEIR KNEES, TO
PREVENT THEIR SINKING DEEPER
IN THE MUD; AND THE DRIVER WAS
DREADFULLY AFRAID LEST THE
ANIMAL SHOULD HAVE SEIZED DR.
HOOKER AND CRUSHED HIM TO
DEATH. BUT THE DRIVER HIMSELF,
AS DR. HOOKER WAS ASSURED, RAN
NO RISK. THIS FORBEARANCE UNDER
AN EMERGENCY SO DREADFUL FOR
A HEAVY ANIMAL, IS A WONDERFUL
PROOF OF NOBLE FIDELITY."

CHARLES DARWIN
THE DESCENT OF MAN

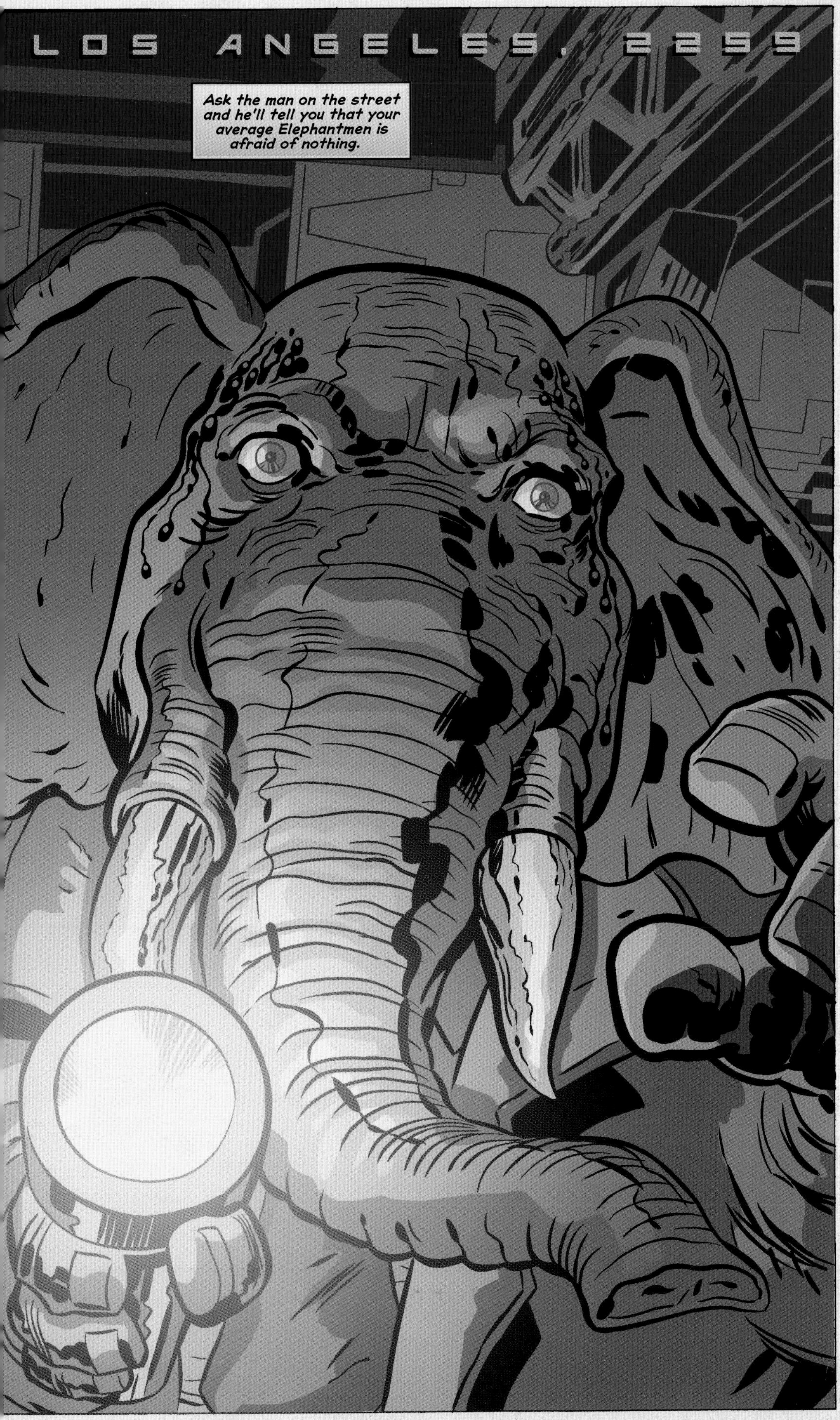
LOS ANGELES, 2259
Ask the man on the street and he'll tell you that your average Elephantmen is afraid of nothing.

ORIGINALLY PRESENTED IN ELEPHANTMEN #3

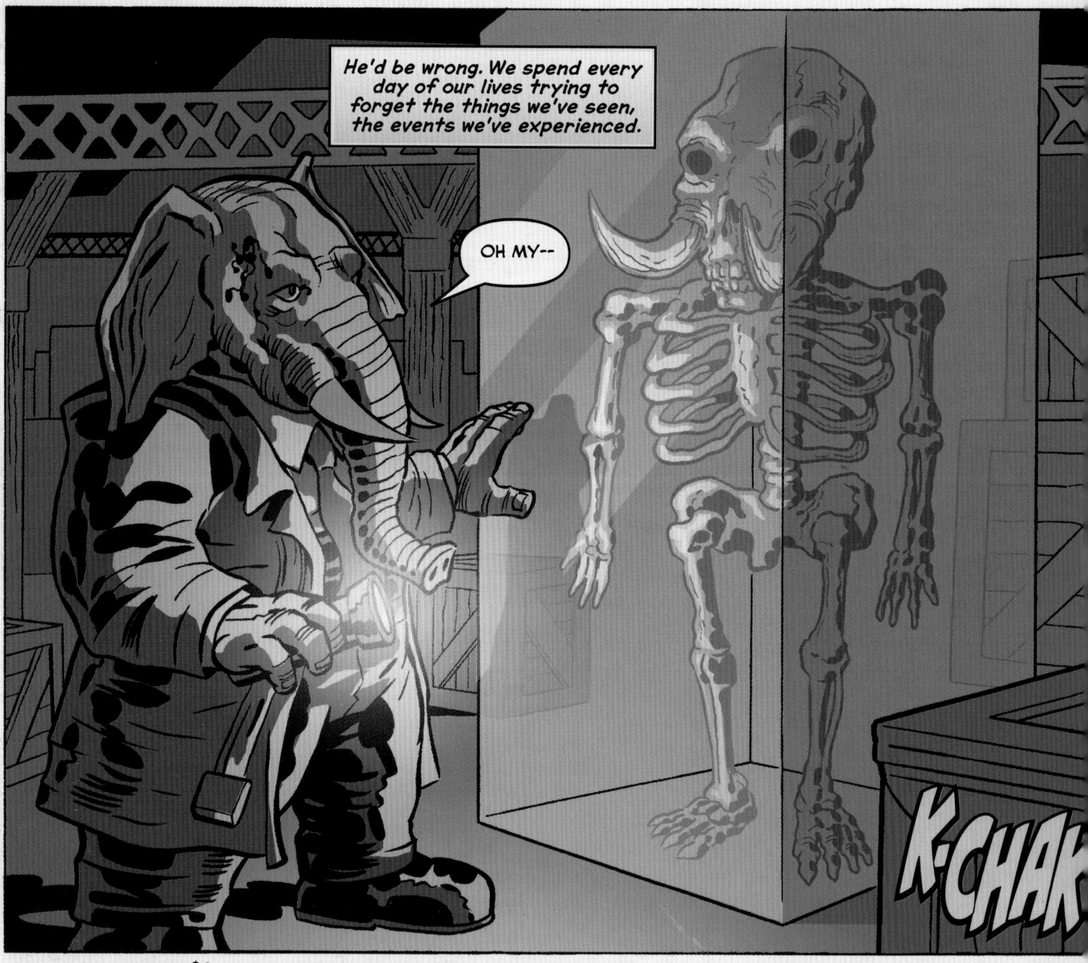
He'd be wrong. We spend every day of our lives trying to forget the things we've seen, the events we've experienced.
OH MY--
K-CHAK

The ELEPHANT in the ROOM!

By RICHARD STARKINGS & TOM SCIOLI with NICK FILARDI cover by BRIAN BOLLAND

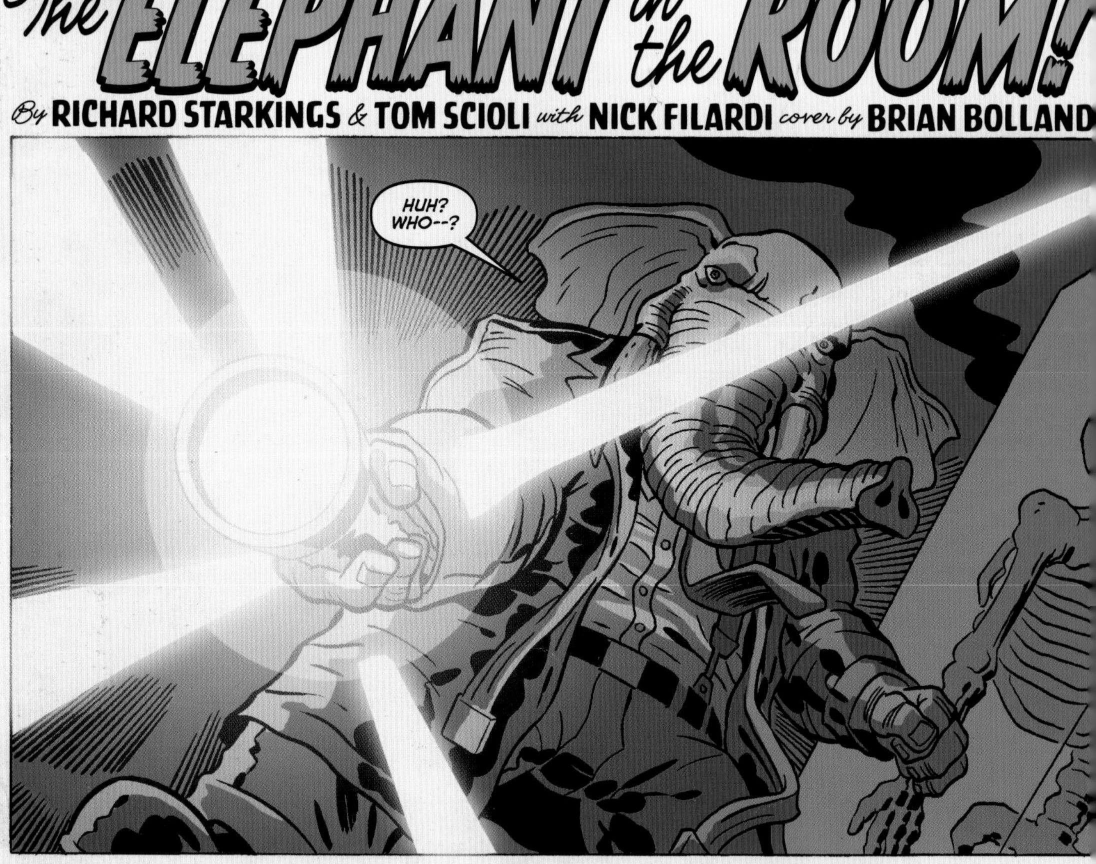
HUH? WHO--?

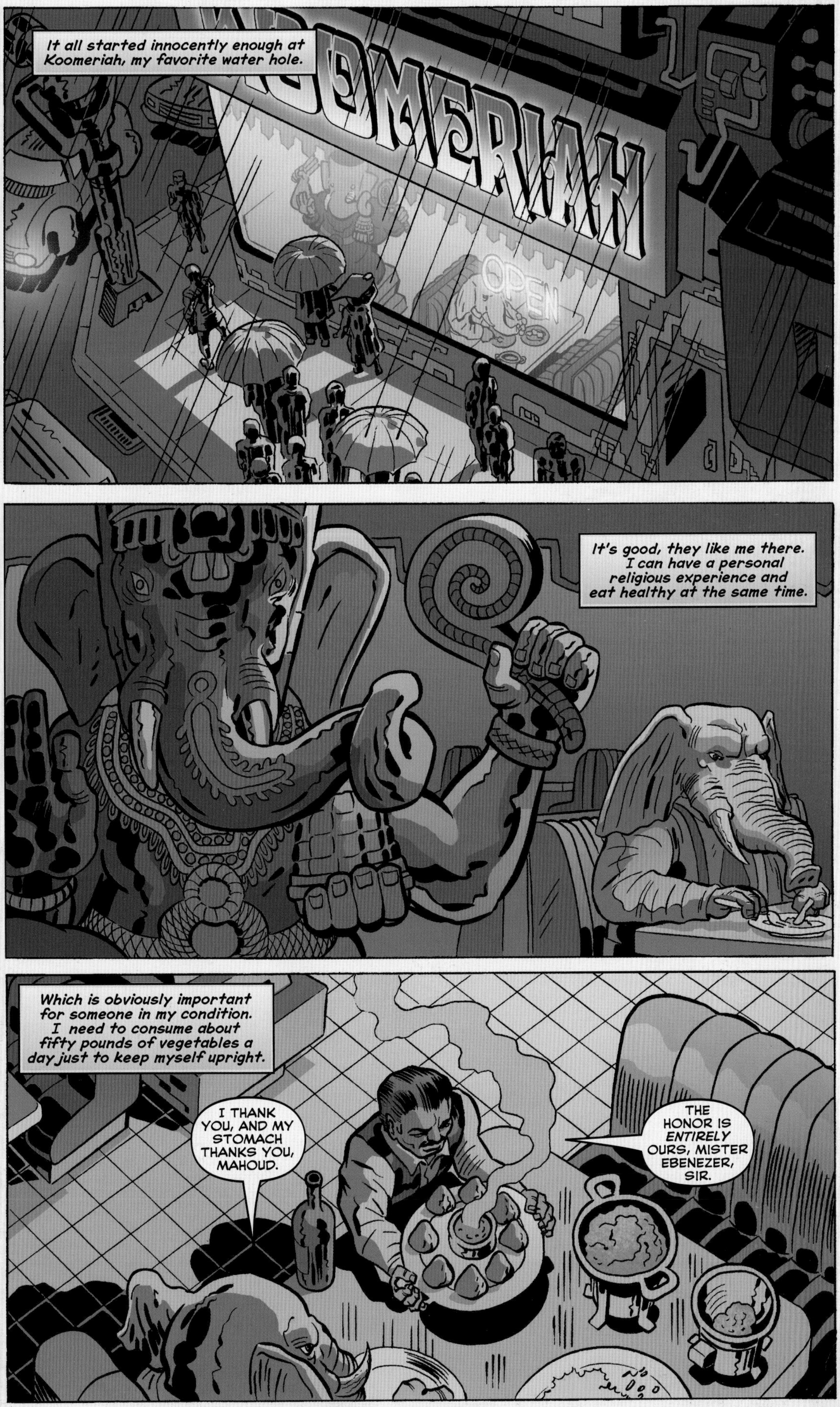

It all started innocently enough at Koomeriah, my favorite water hole.
KOOMERIAH
OPEN
It's good, they like me there. I can have a personal religious experience and eat healthy at the same time.
Which is obviously important for someone in my condition. I need to consume about fifty pounds of vegetables a day just to keep myself upright.
I THANK YOU, AND MY STOMACH THANKS YOU, MAHOUD.
THE HONOR IS *ENTIRELY* OURS, MISTER EBENEZER, SIR.

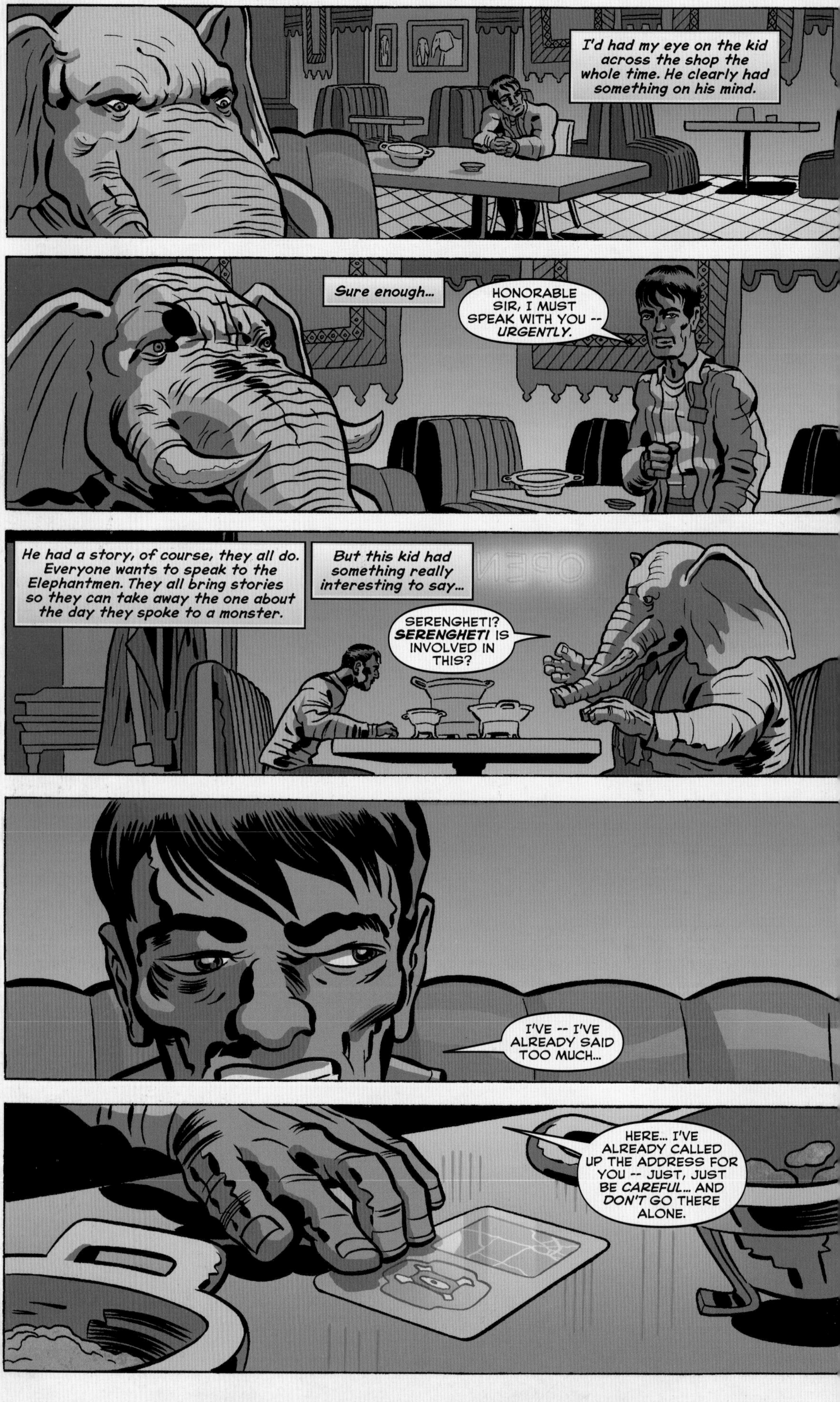
I'd had my eye on the kid across the shop the whole time. He clearly had something on his mind.
Sure enough...
HONORABLE SIR, I MUST SPEAK WITH YOU -- URGENTLY.
He had a story, of course, they all do. Everyone wants to speak to the Elephantmen. They all bring stories so they can take away the one about the day they spoke to a monster.
But this kid had something really interesting to say...
OPEN
SERENGHETI!? SERENGHETI IS INVOLVED IN THIS?
I'VE -- I'VE ALREADY SAID TOO MUCH...
HERE... I'VE ALREADY CALLED UP THE ADDRESS FOR YOU -- JUST, JUST BE CAREFUL... AND DON'T GO THERE ALONE.

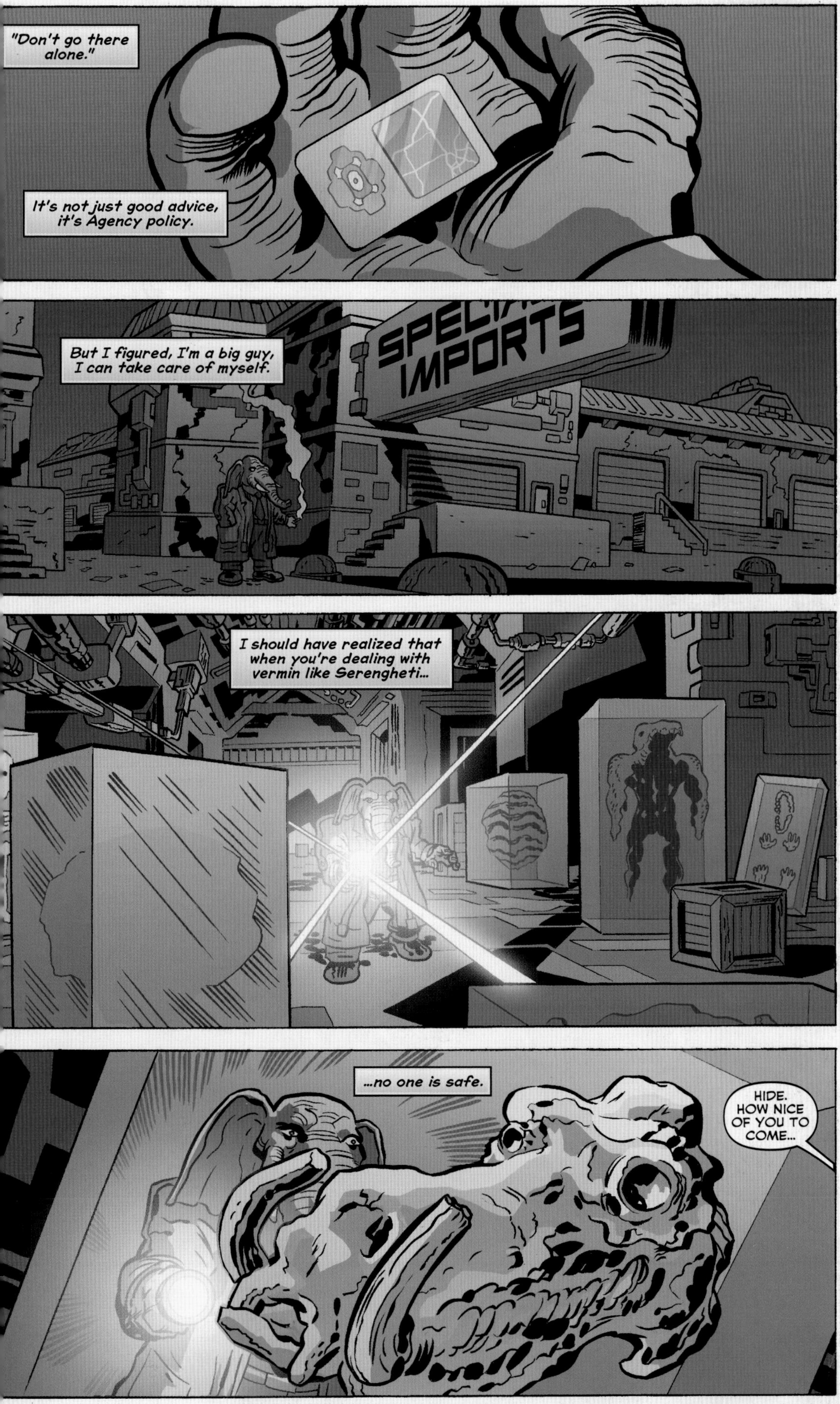
"Don't go there alone."
It's not just good advice, it's Agency policy.
But I figured, I'm a big guy, I can take care of myself.
IMPORTS
I should have realized that when you're dealing with vermin like Serengheti...
...no one is safe.
HIDE. HOW NICE OF YOU TO COME...

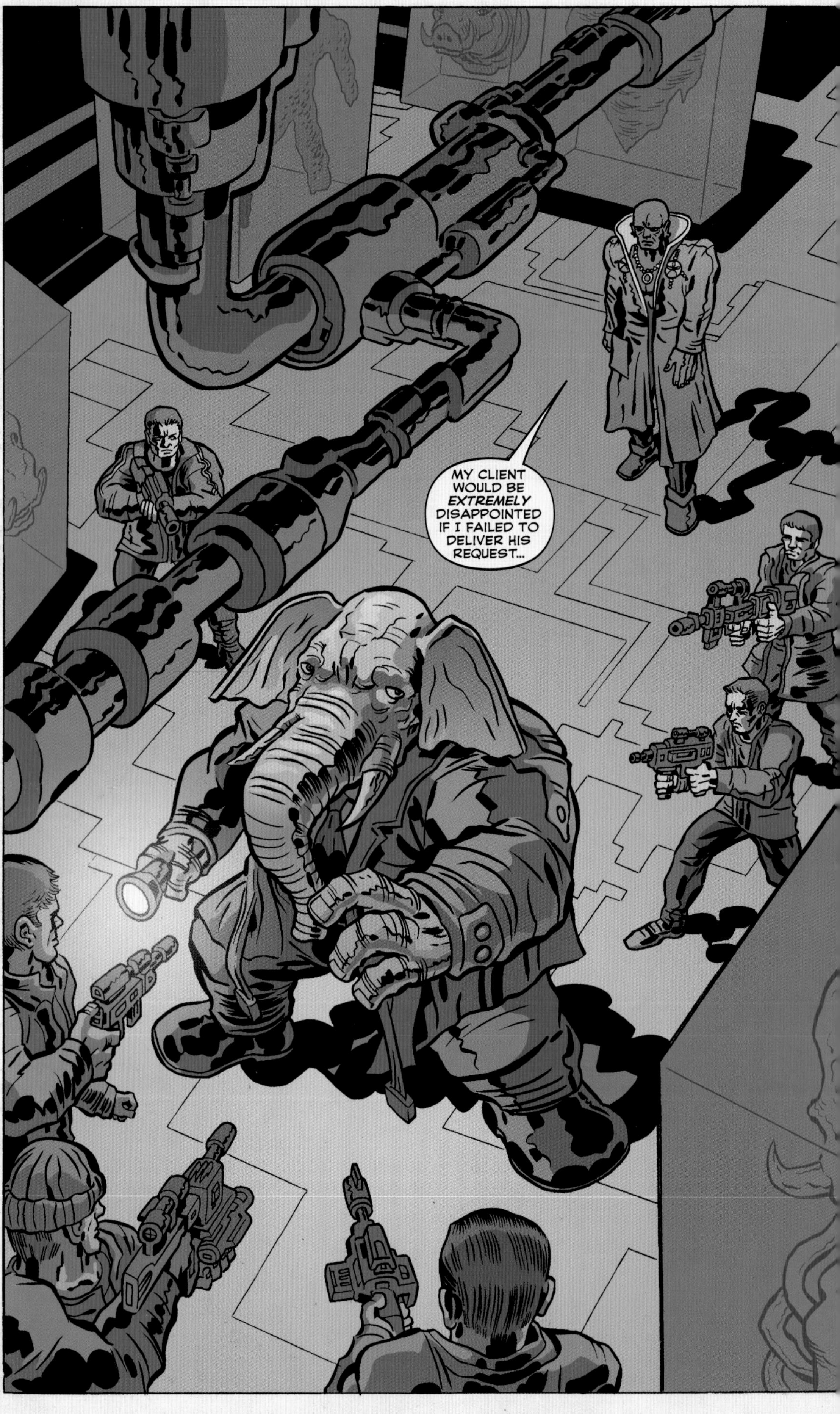
MY CLIENT WOULD BE *EXTREMELY* DISAPPOINTED IF I FAILED TO DELIVER HIS REQUEST...

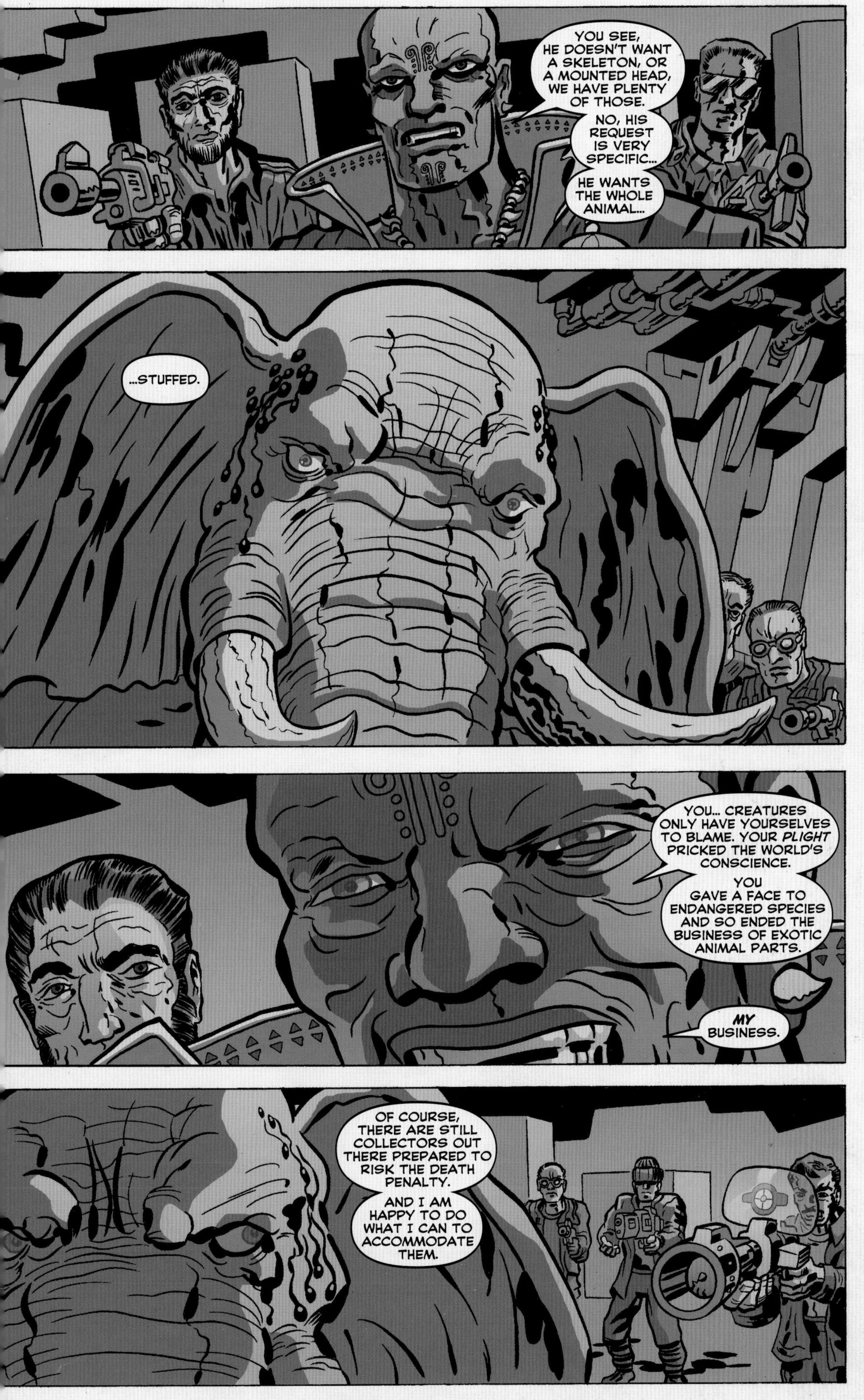
YOU SEE, HE DOESN'T WANT A SKELETON, OR A MOUNTED HEAD, WE HAVE PLENTY OF THOSE.
NO, HIS REQUEST IS VERY SPECIFIC...
HE WANTS THE WHOLE ANIMAL...
...STUFFED.
YOU... CREATURES ONLY HAVE YOURSELVES TO BLAME. YOUR *PLIGHT* PRICKED THE WORLD'S CONSCIENCE.
YOU GAVE A FACE TO ENDANGERED SPECIES AND SO ENDED THE BUSINESS OF EXOTIC ANIMAL PARTS.
MY BUSINESS.
OF COURSE, THERE ARE STILL COLLECTORS OUT THERE PREPARED TO RISK THE DEATH PENALTY.
AND I AM HAPPY TO DO WHAT I CAN TO ACCOMMODATE THEM.

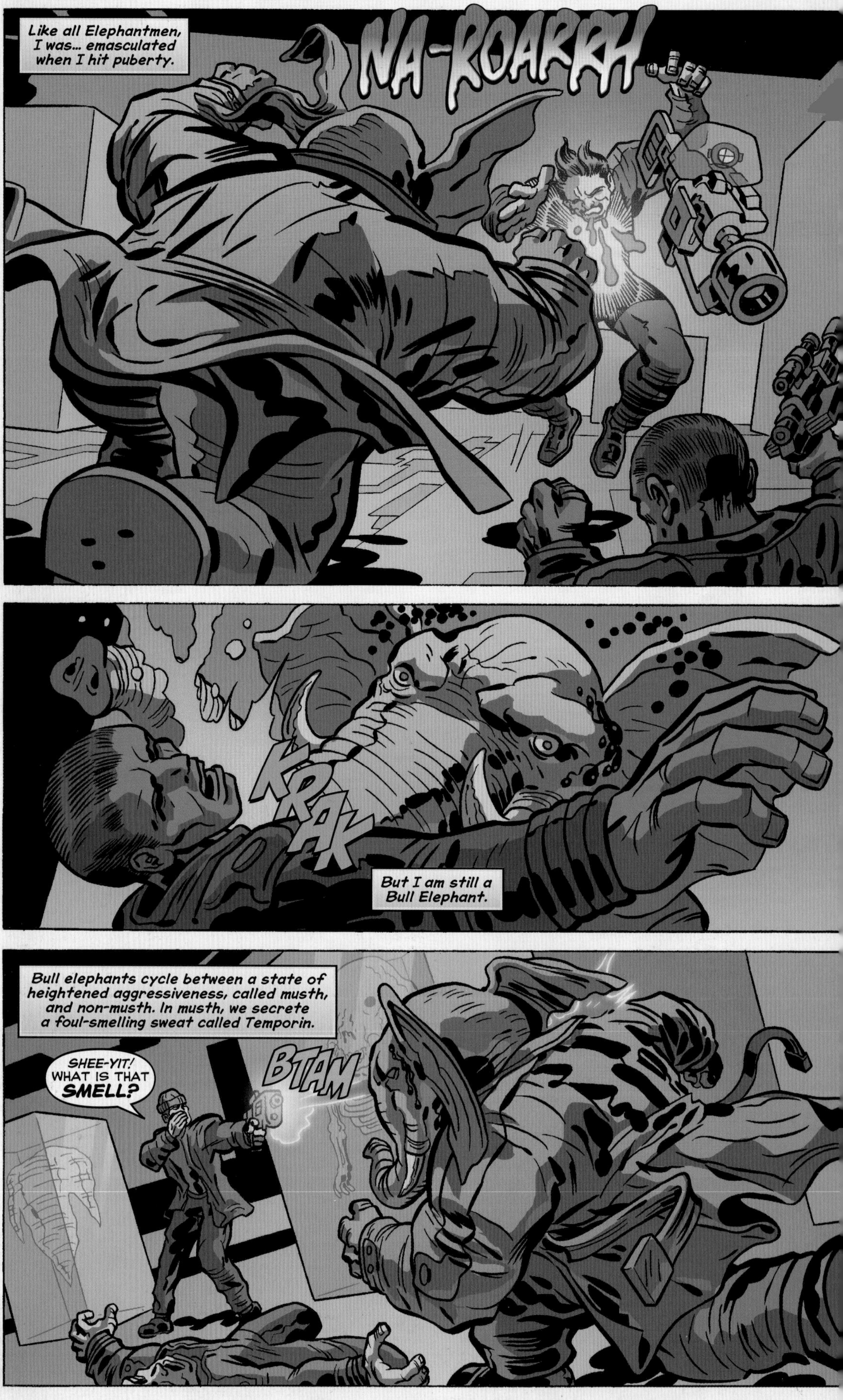
Like all Elephantmen, I was... emasculated when I hit puberty.
NA-ROARRH
KRAK
But I am still a Bull Elephant.
Bull elephants cycle between a state of heightened aggressiveness, called musth, and non-musth. In musth, we secrete a foul-smelling sweat called Temporin.
BTAM
SHEE-YIT! WHAT IS THAT SMELL?

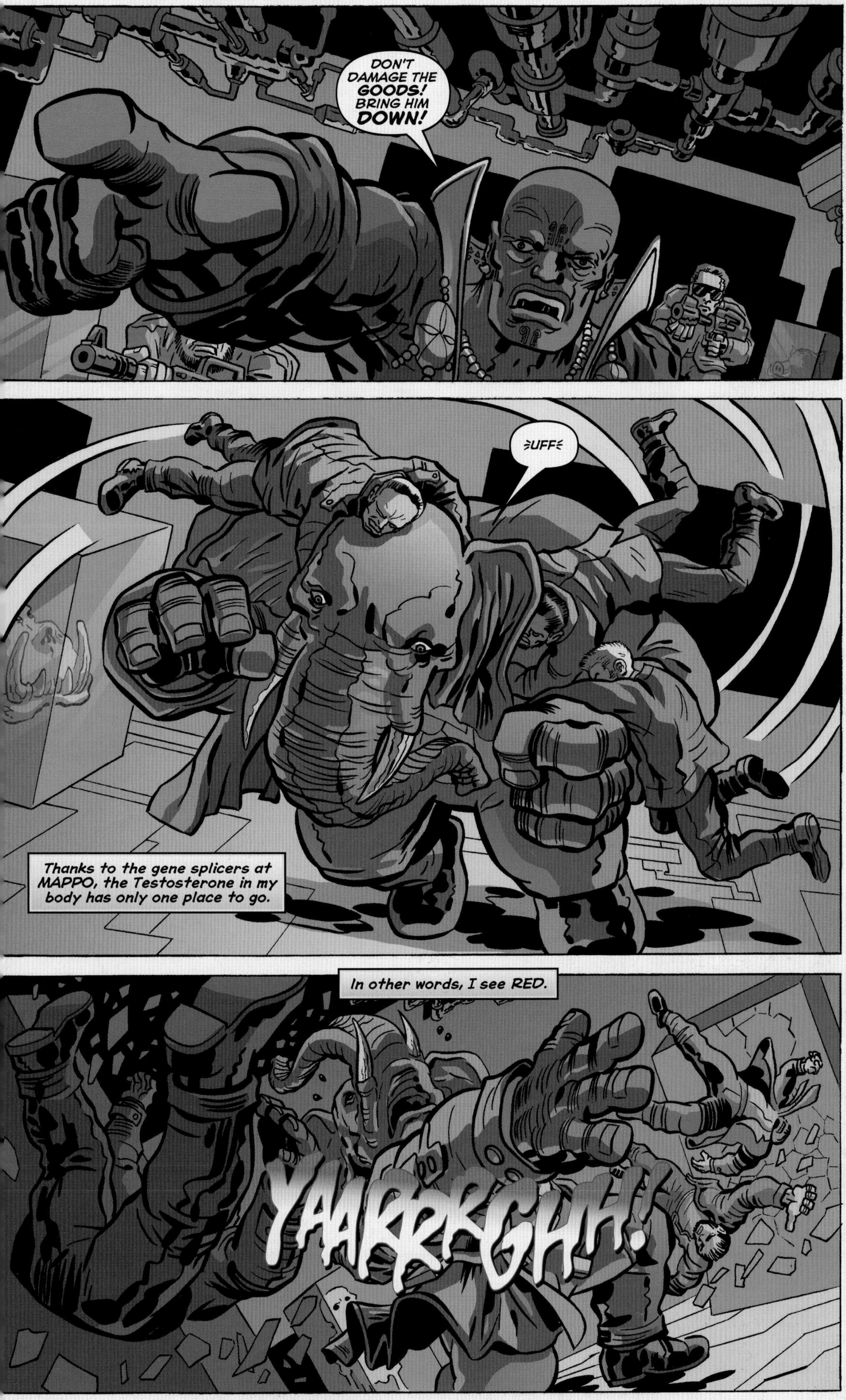
DON'T DAMAGE THE GOODS! BRING HIM DOWN!
UFF
Thanks to the gene splicers at MAPPO, the Testosterone in my body has only one place to go.
In other words, I see RED.
YAARRGHH!

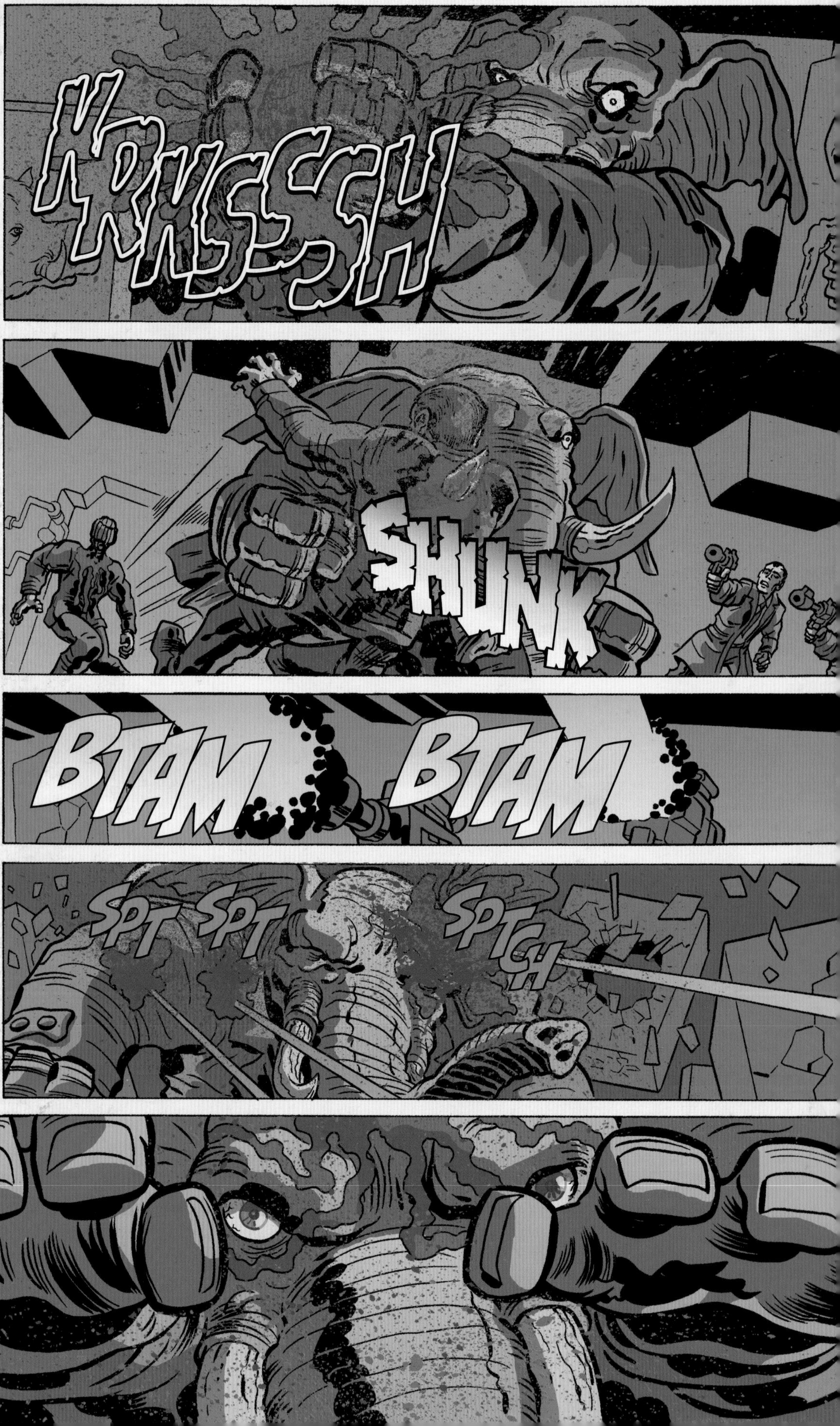
KRNSSCH
SHUNK
BTAM BTAM
SPT SPT
SPTCH

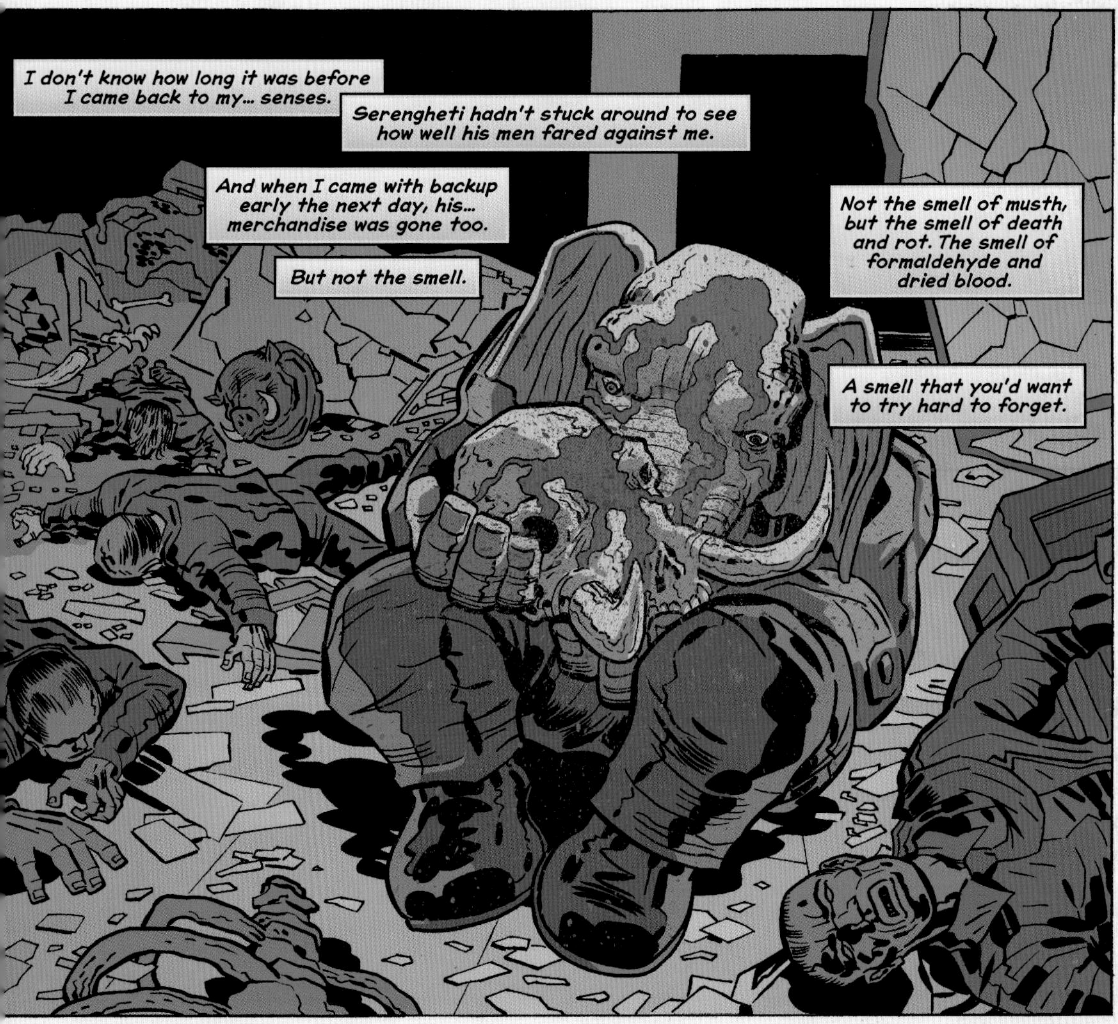
I don't know how long it was before I came back to my... senses.
Serengheti hadn't stuck around to see how well his men fared against me.
And when I came with backup early the next day, his... merchandise was gone too.
But not the smell.
Not the smell of musth, but the smell of death and rot. The smell of formaldehyde and dried blood.
A smell that you'd want to try hard to forget.

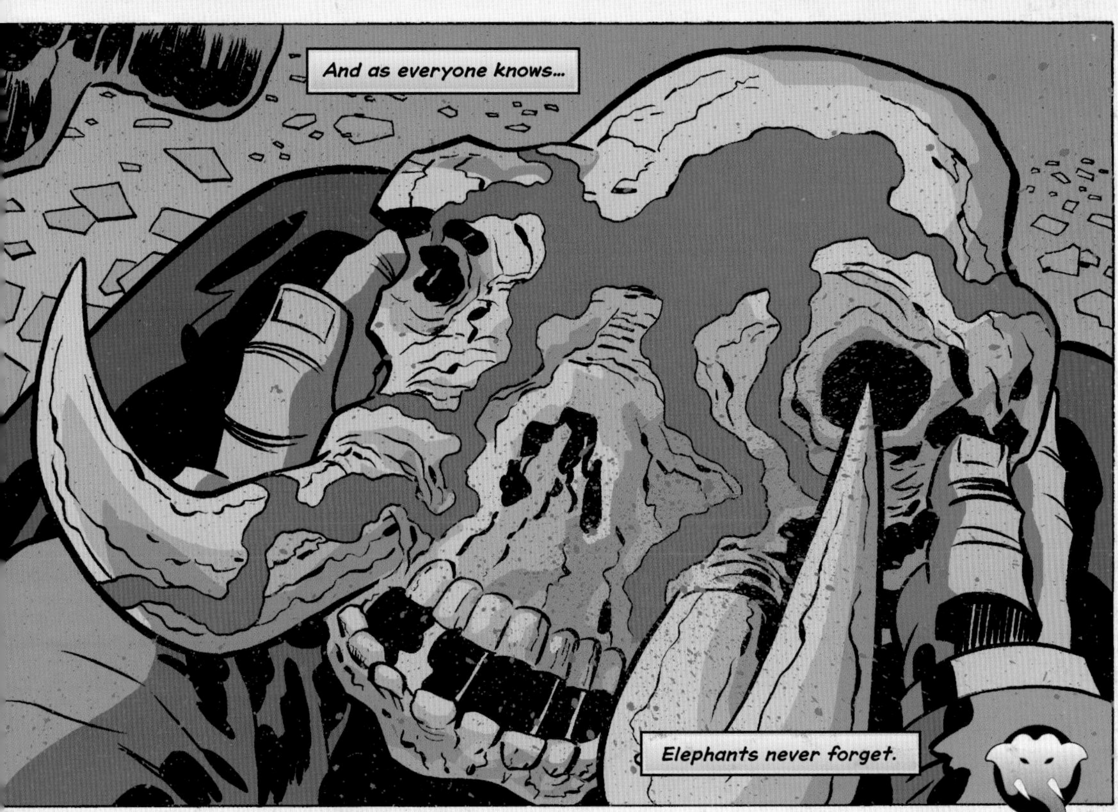
And as everyone knows...
Elephants never forget.

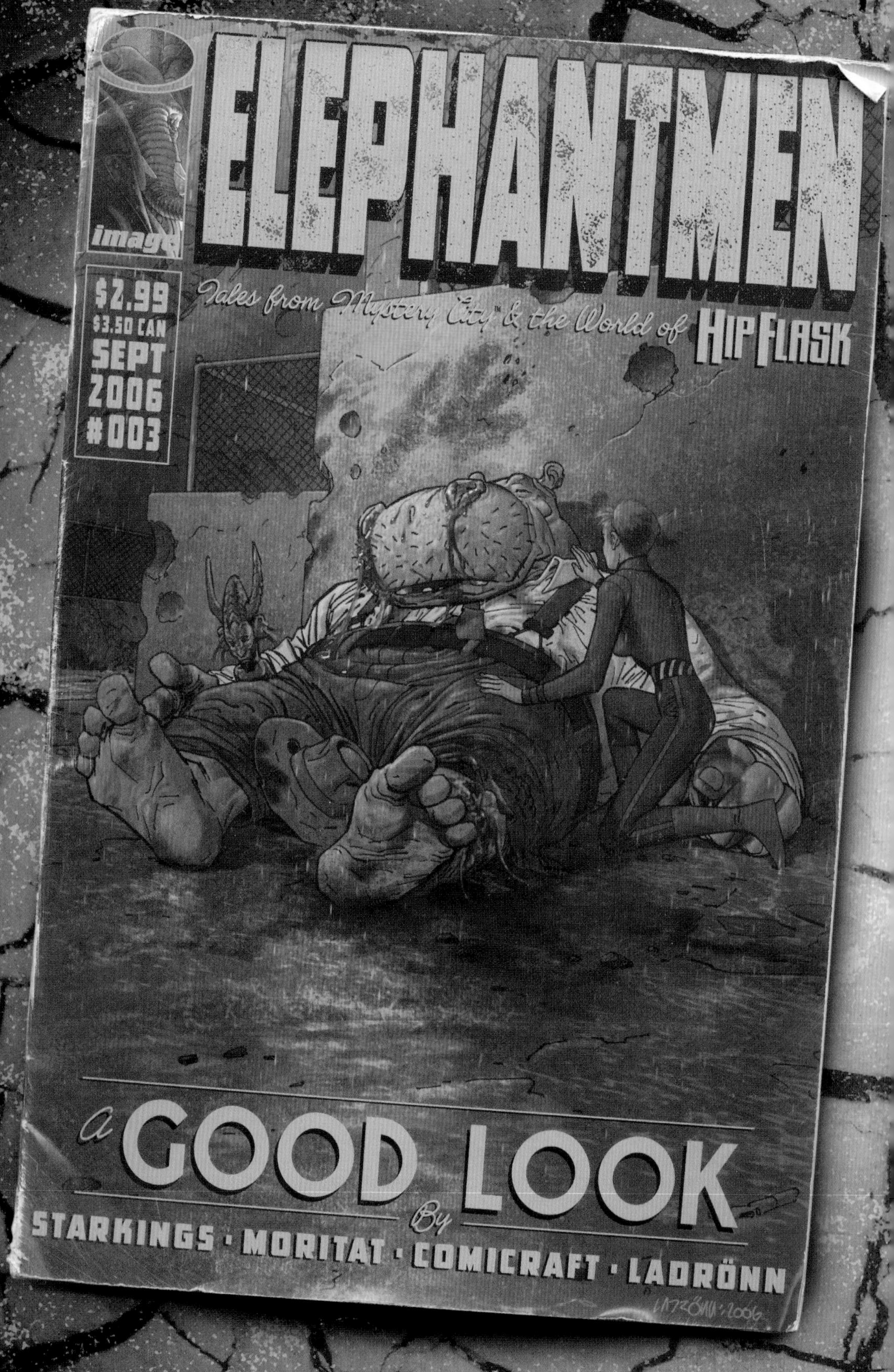

image
ELEPHANTMEN
$2.99
$3.50 CAN
SEPT
2006
#003
Tales from Mystery City™ & the World of HIP FLASK
a GOOD LOOK
By
STARKINGS · MORITAT · COMICRAFT · LADRÖNN

"FROM THE OYSTER
TO THE EAGLE, FROM
THE SWINE TO THE
TIGER, ALL ANIMALS
ARE TO BE FOUND IN
MEN AND EACH OF THEM
EXISTS IN SOME MAN,
SOMETIMES SEVERAL
AT THE SAME TIME.
ANIMALS ARE NOTHING
BUT THE PORTRAYAL OF
OUR VIRTUES AND VICES
MADE MANIFEST TO
OUR EYES, THE VISIBLE
REFLECTIONS OF OUR
SOULS. GOD DISPLAYS
THEM TO US TO GIVE US
FOOD FOR THOUGHT."

VICTOR HUGO
LES MISERABLES, 1862

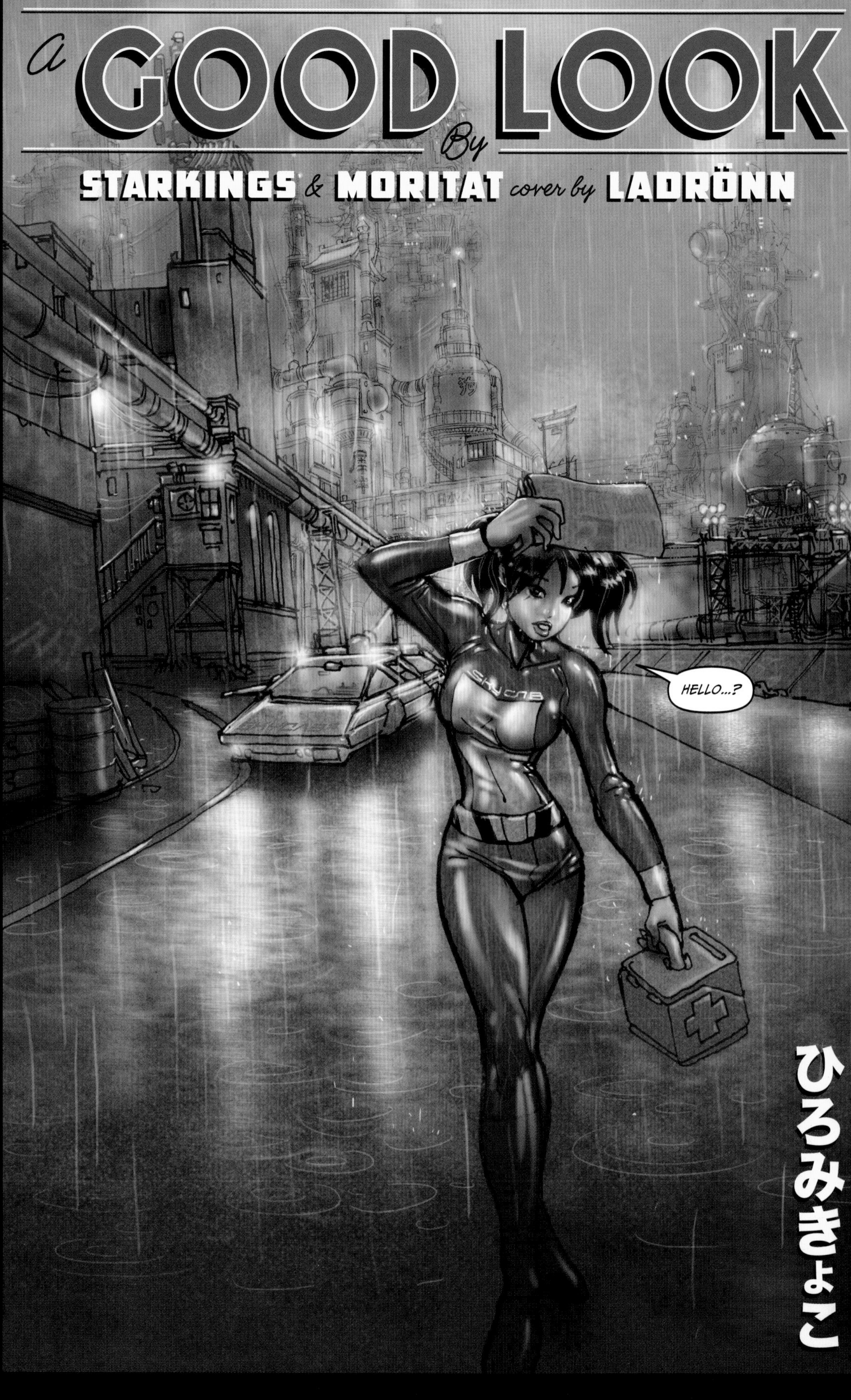
A GOOD LOOK
By
STARKINGS & MORITAT cover by LADRÖNN
HELLO...?
ひろみきょこ

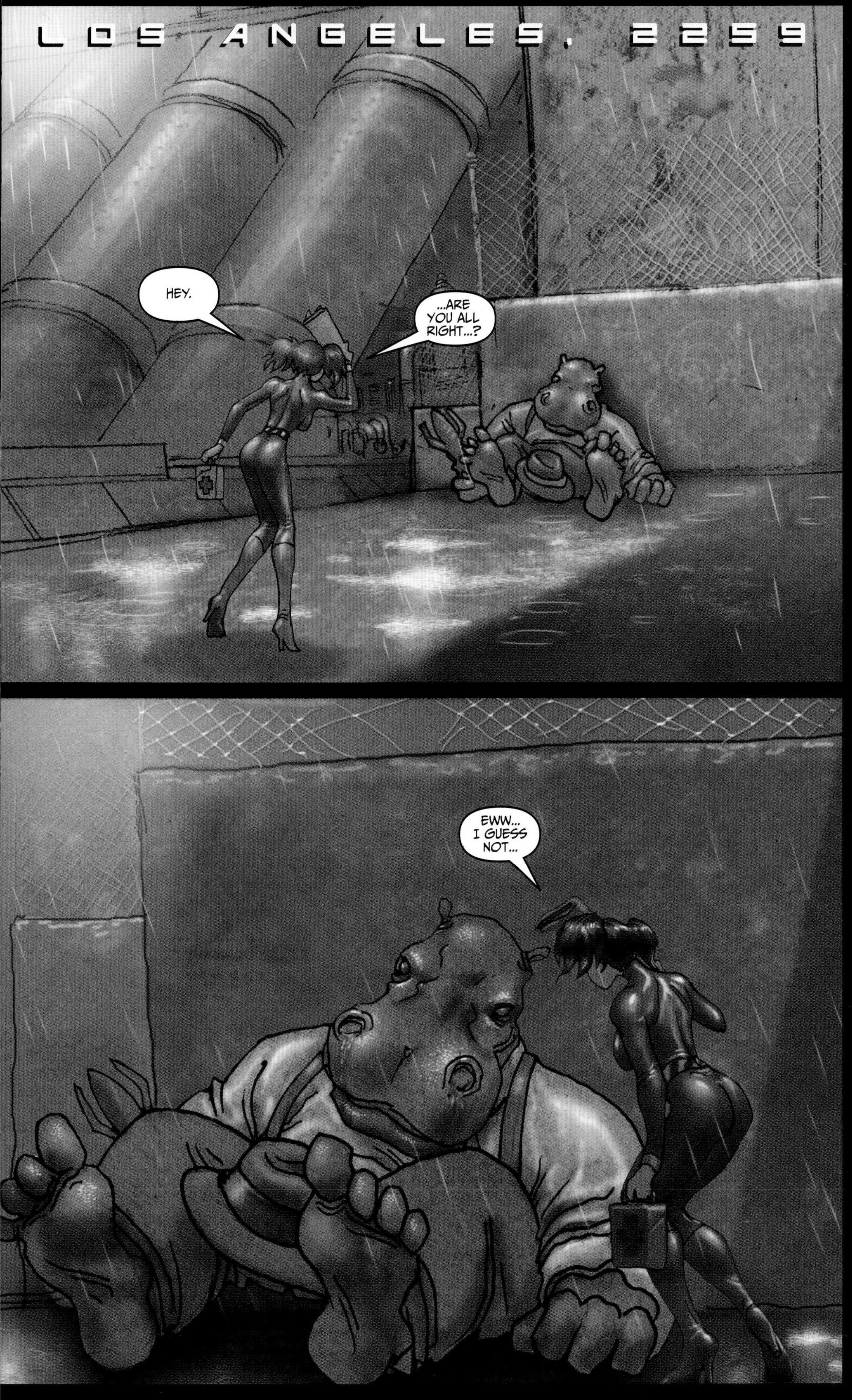
LOS ANGELES, 2259
HEY.
...ARE YOU ALL RIGHT...?
EWW... I GUESS NOT...

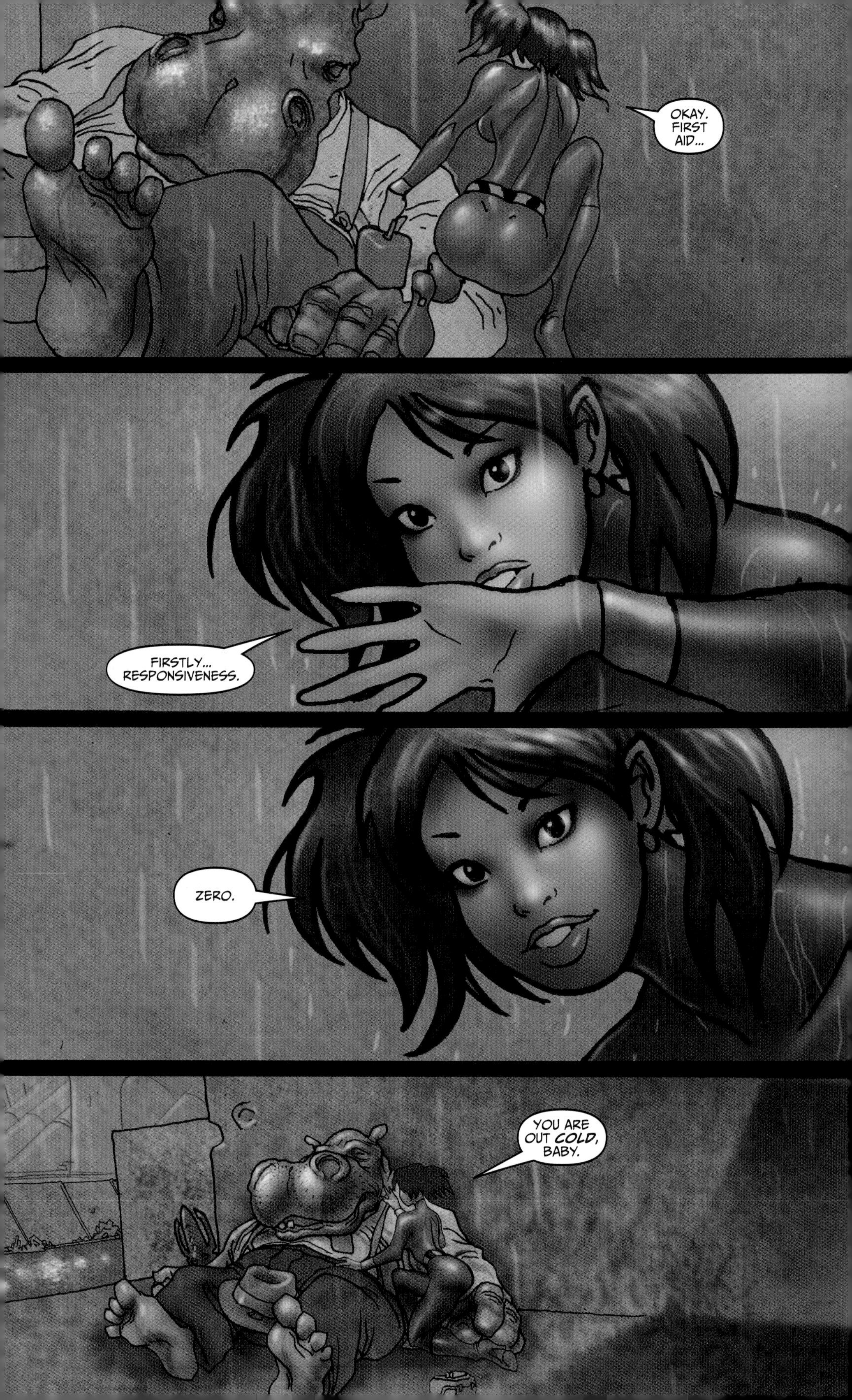
OKAY. FIRST AID...
FIRSTLY... RESPONSIVENESS.
ZERO.
YOU ARE OUT COLD, BABY.

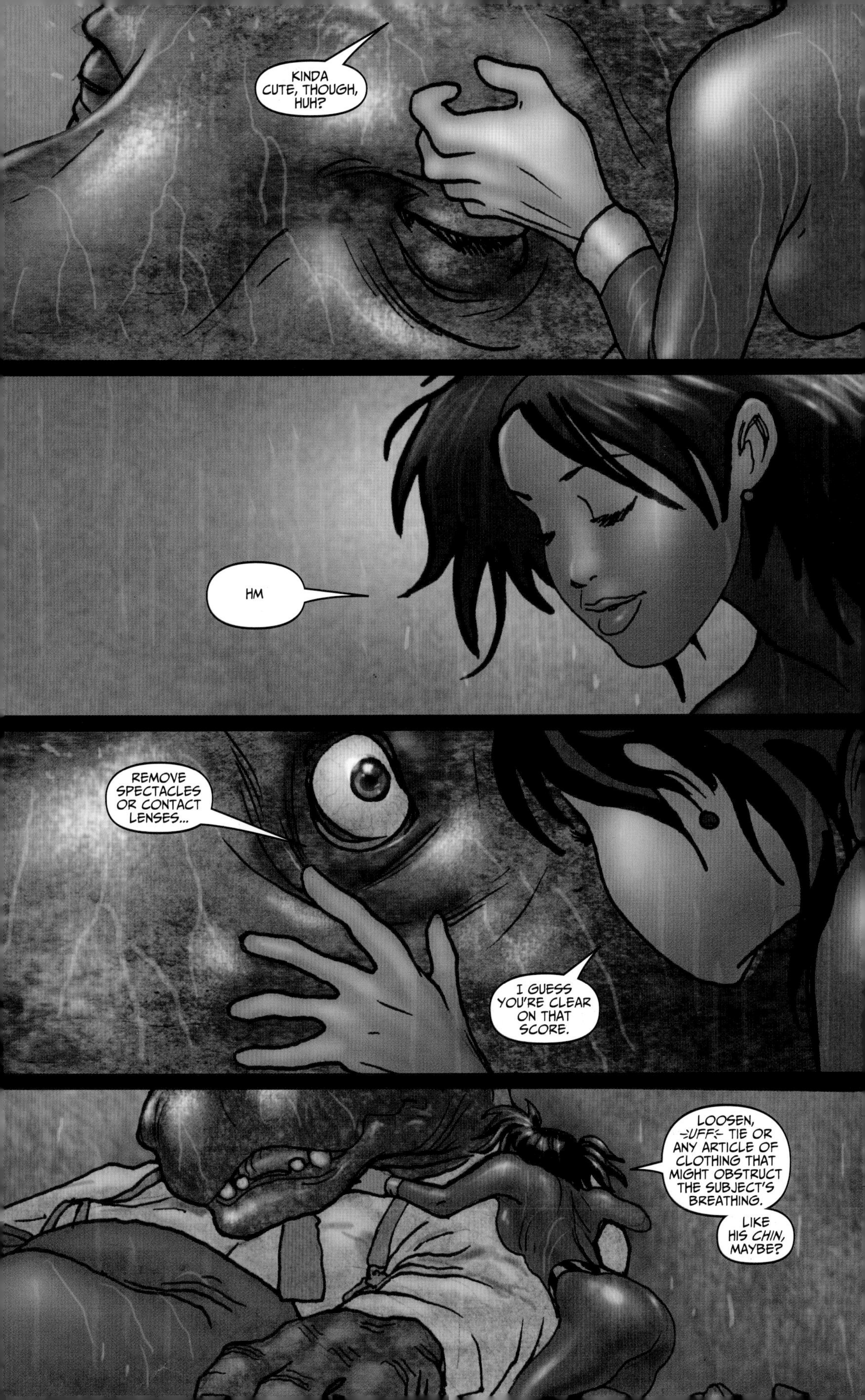
KINDA CUTE, THOUGH, HUH?
HM
REMOVE SPECTACLES OR CONTACT LENSES...
I GUESS YOU'RE CLEAR ON THAT SCORE.
LOOSEN, =UFF= TIE OR ANY ARTICLE OF CLOTHING THAT MIGHT OBSTRUCT THE SUBJECT'S BREATHING.
LIKE HIS *CHIN*, MAYBE?

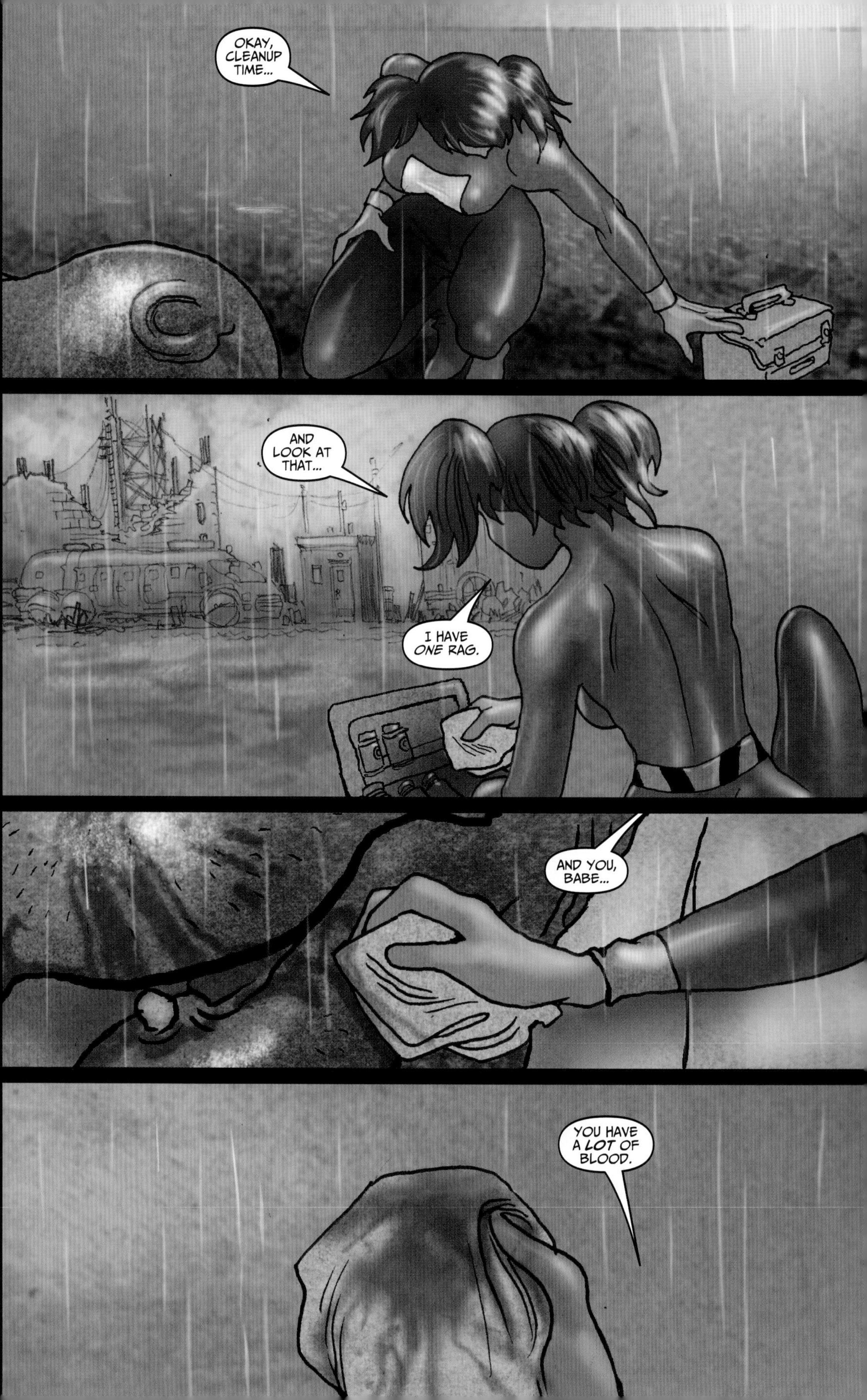
OKAY, CLEANUP TIME...
AND LOOK AT THAT...
I HAVE ONE RAG.
AND YOU, BABE...
YOU HAVE A LOT OF BLOOD.

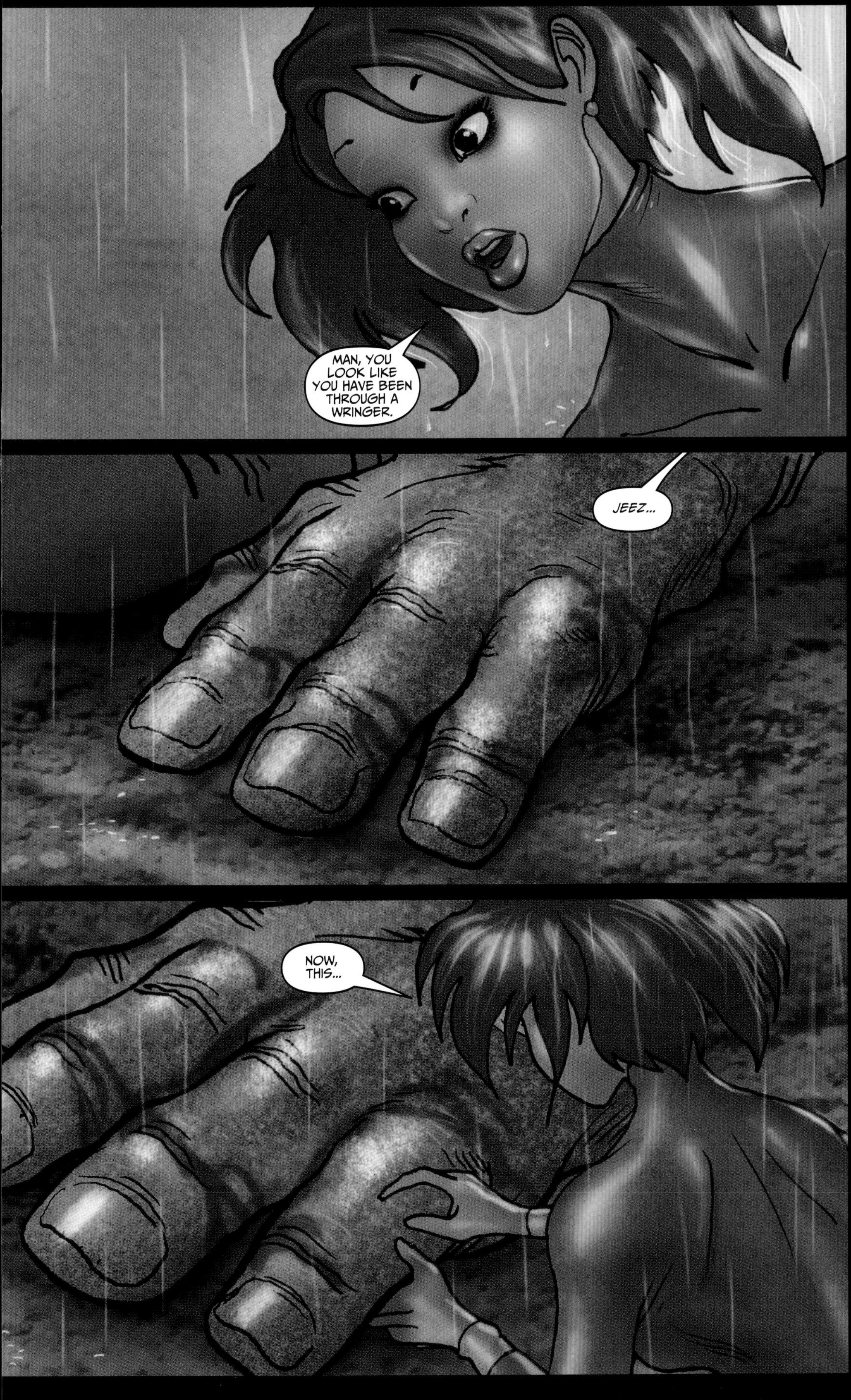
MAN, YOU LOOK LIKE YOU HAVE BEEN THROUGH A WRINGER.
JEEZ...
NOW, THIS...

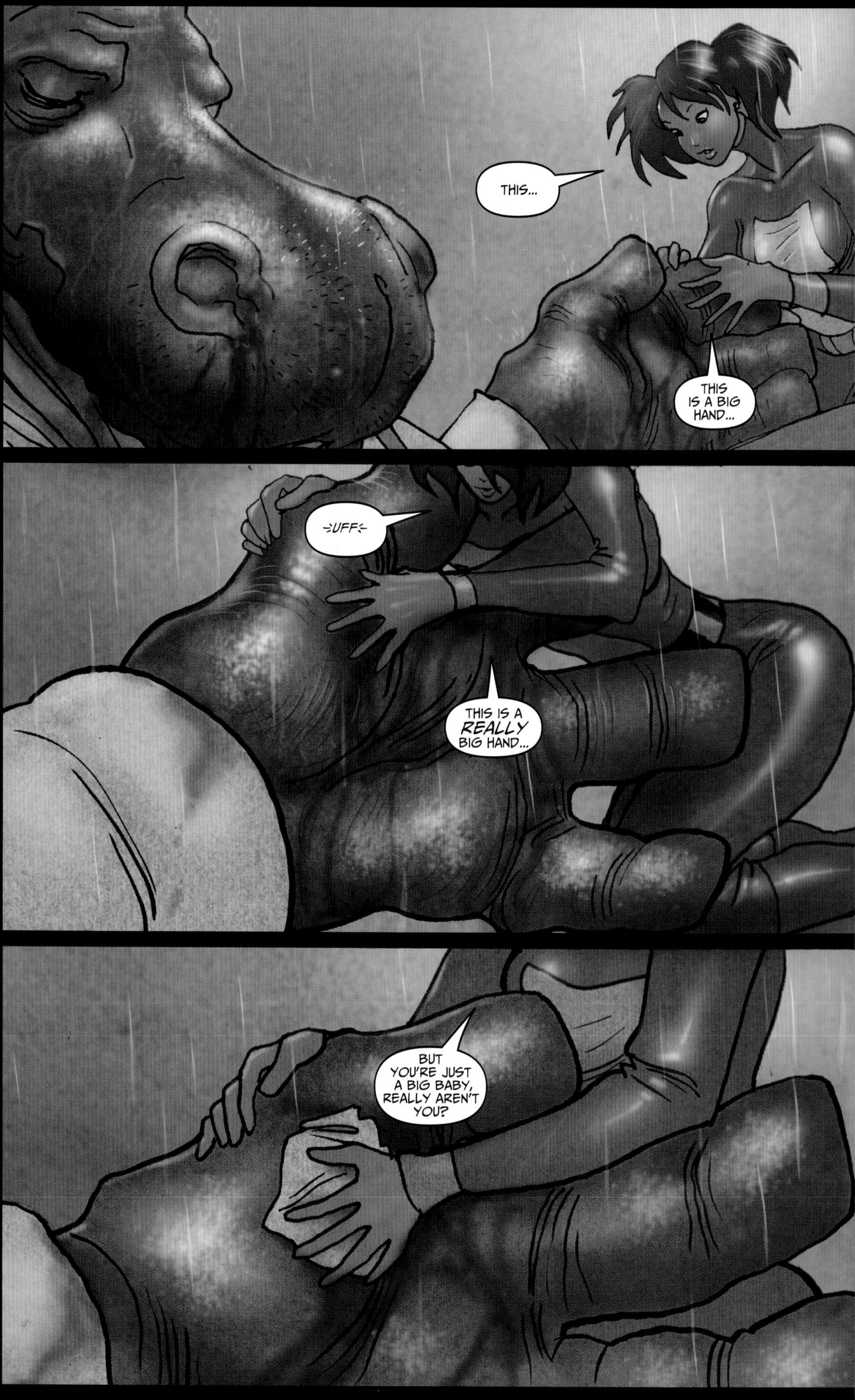

THIS...
THIS IS A BIG HAND...
-UFF-
THIS IS A REALLY BIG HAND...
BUT YOU'RE JUST A BIG BABY, REALLY AREN'T YOU?

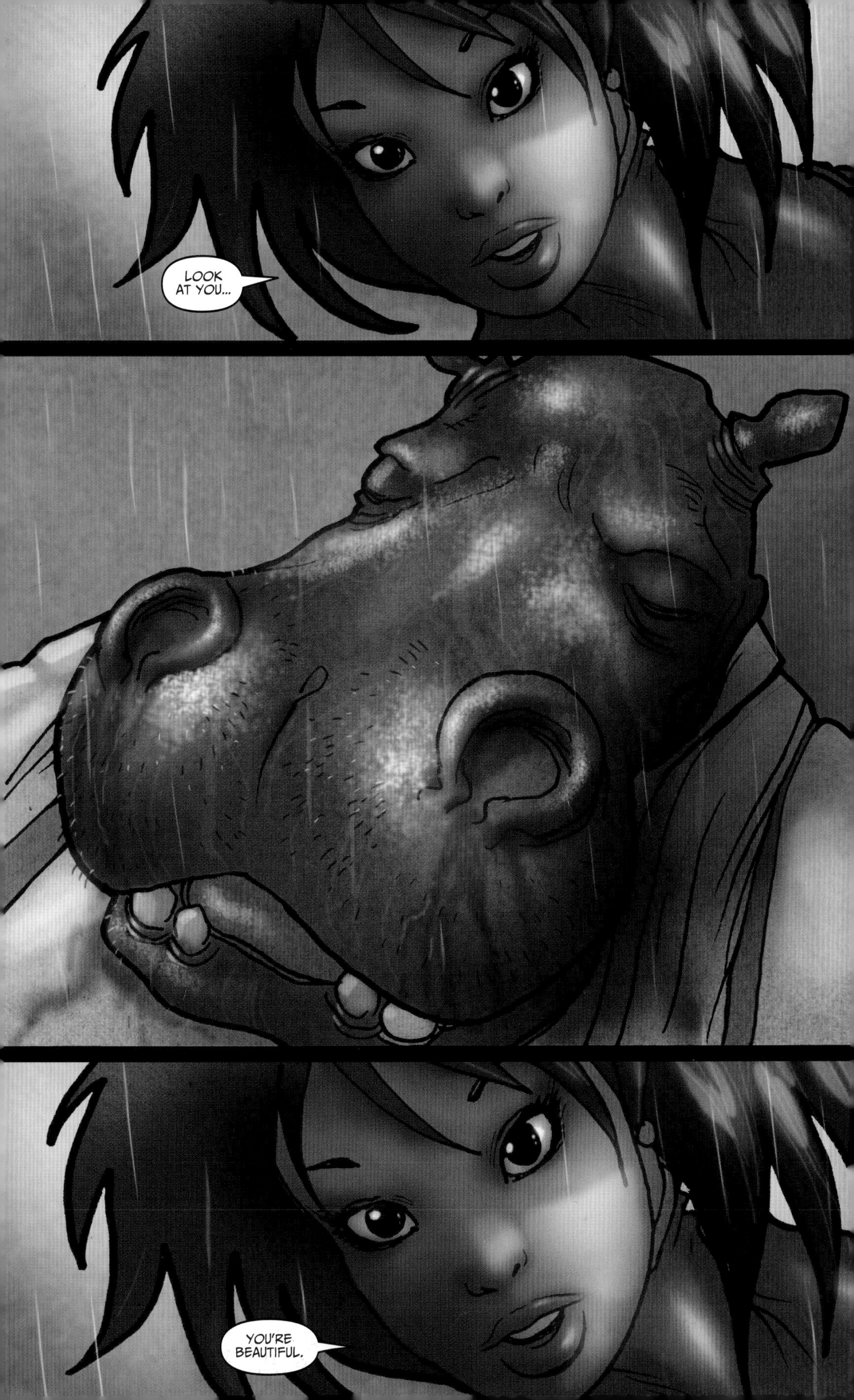
LOOK AT YOU...
YOU'RE BEAUTIFUL.

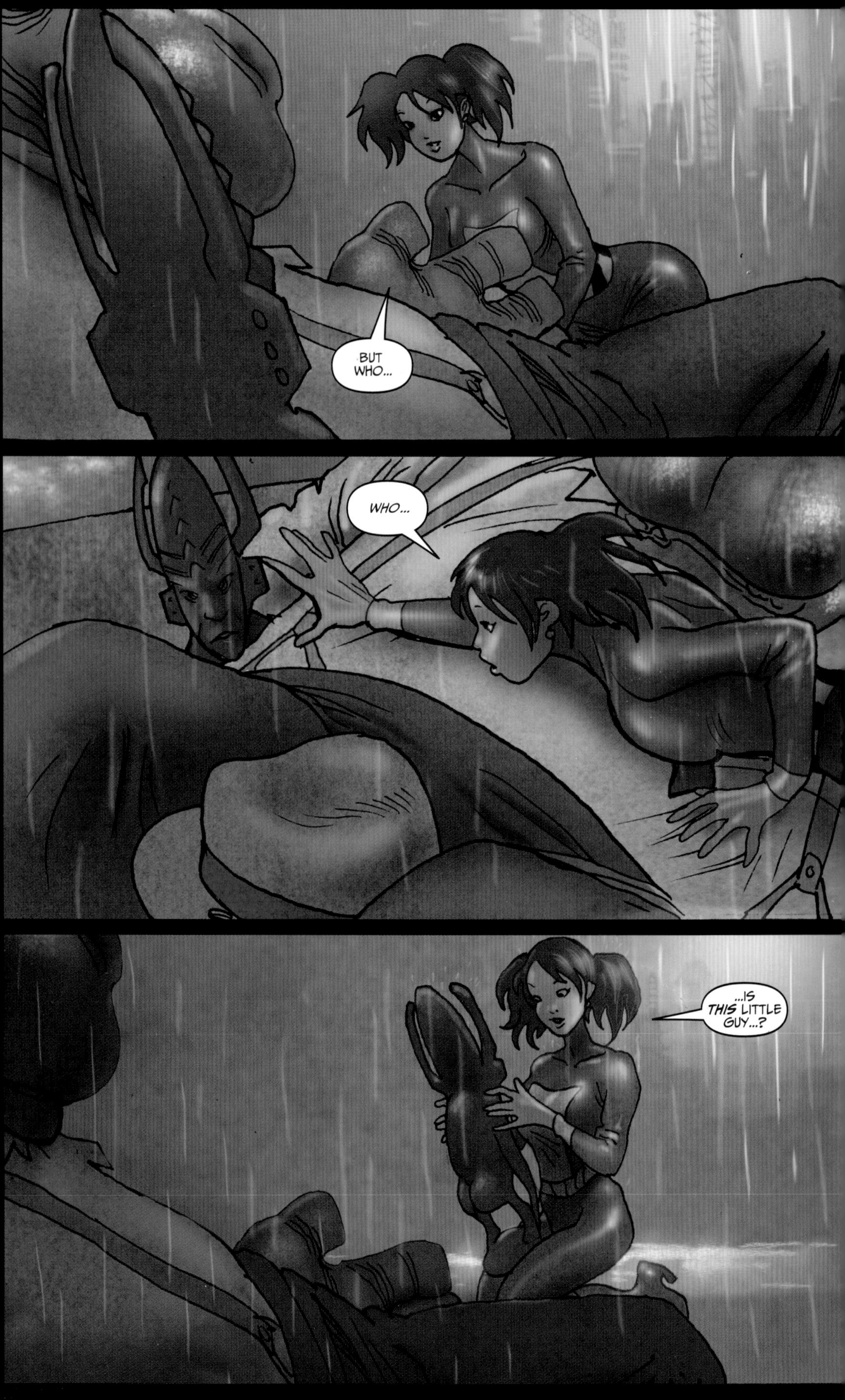
BUT WHO...
WHO...
...IS *THIS* LITTLE GUY...?

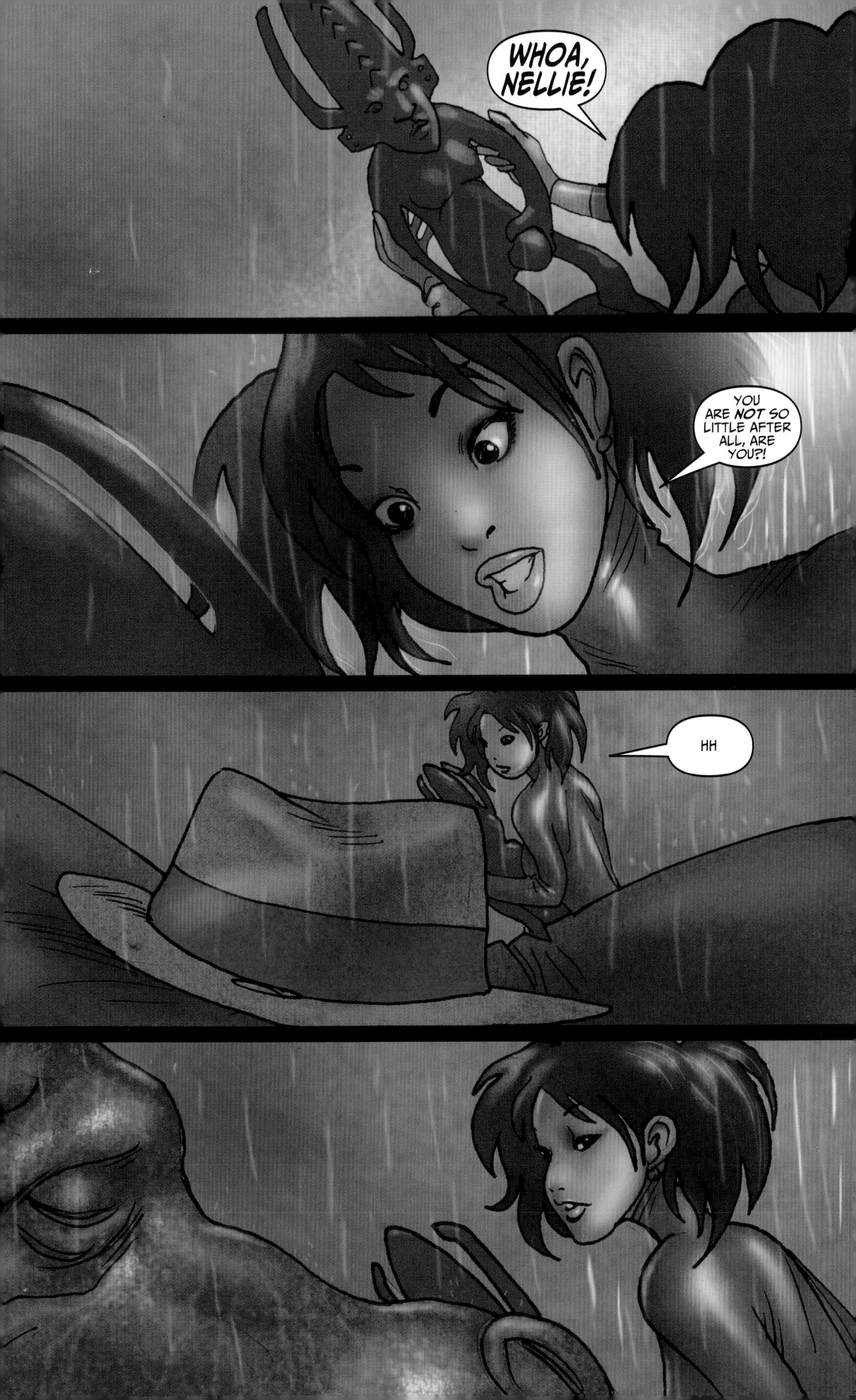
WHOA, NELLIE!
YOU ARE NOT SO LITTLE AFTER ALL, ARE YOU?!
HH

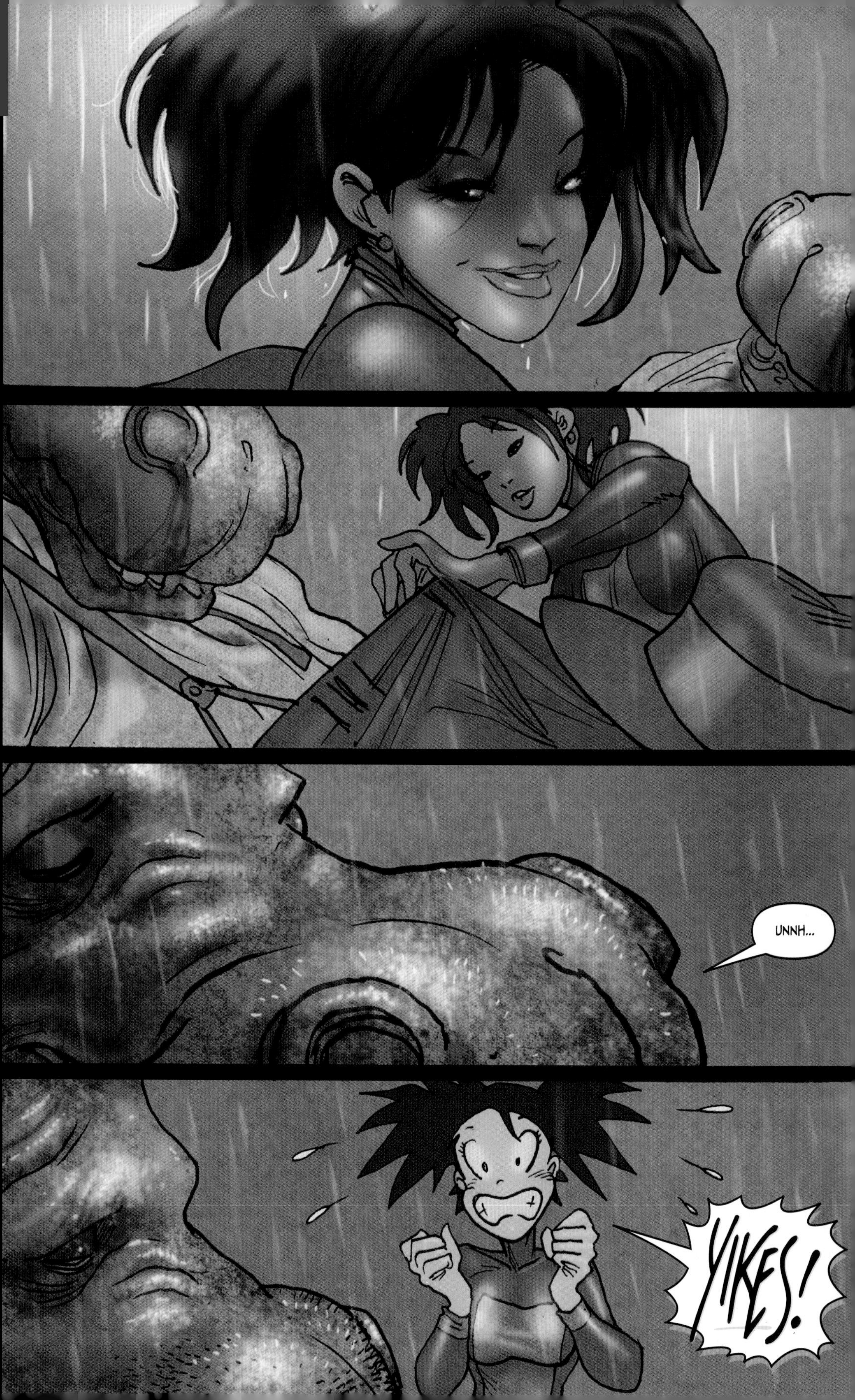
UNNH...
YIKES!

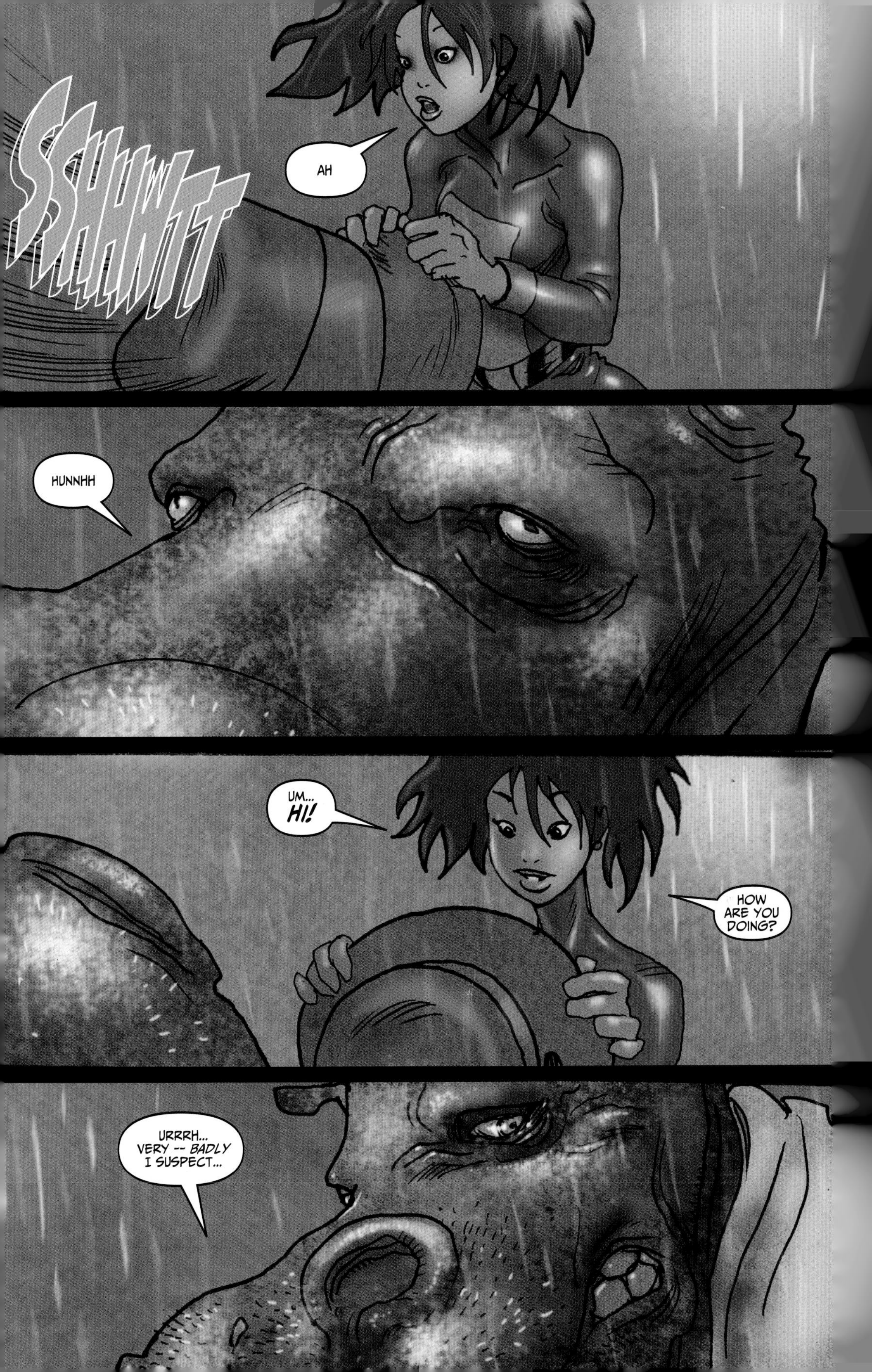
SSHWTT
AH
HUNNHH
UM... HI!
HOW ARE YOU DOING?
URRRH... VERY -- BADLY I SUSPECT...

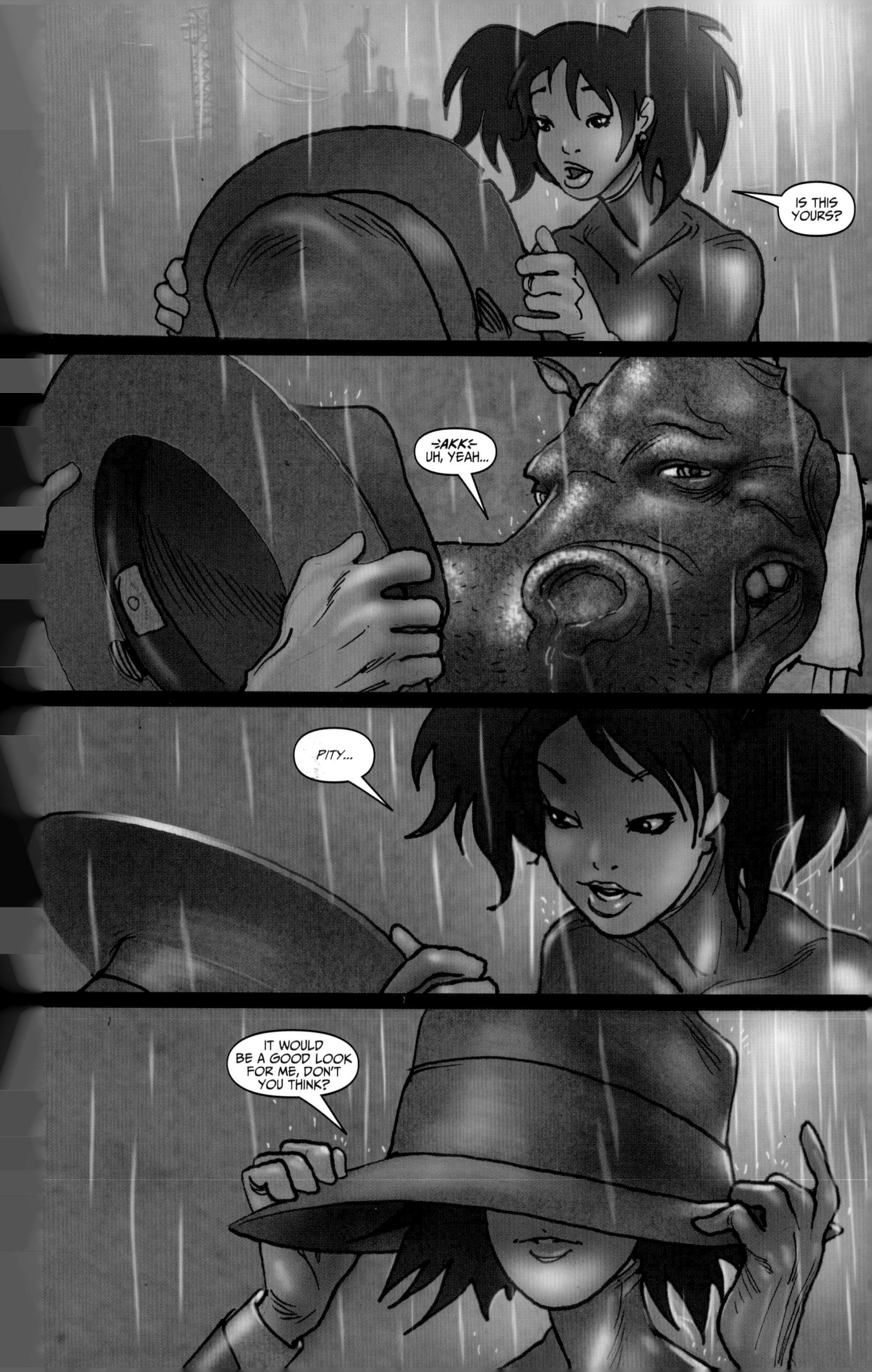
IS THIS YOURS?
-AKK- UH, YEAH...
PITY...
IT WOULD BE A GOOD LOOK FOR ME, DON'T YOU THINK?

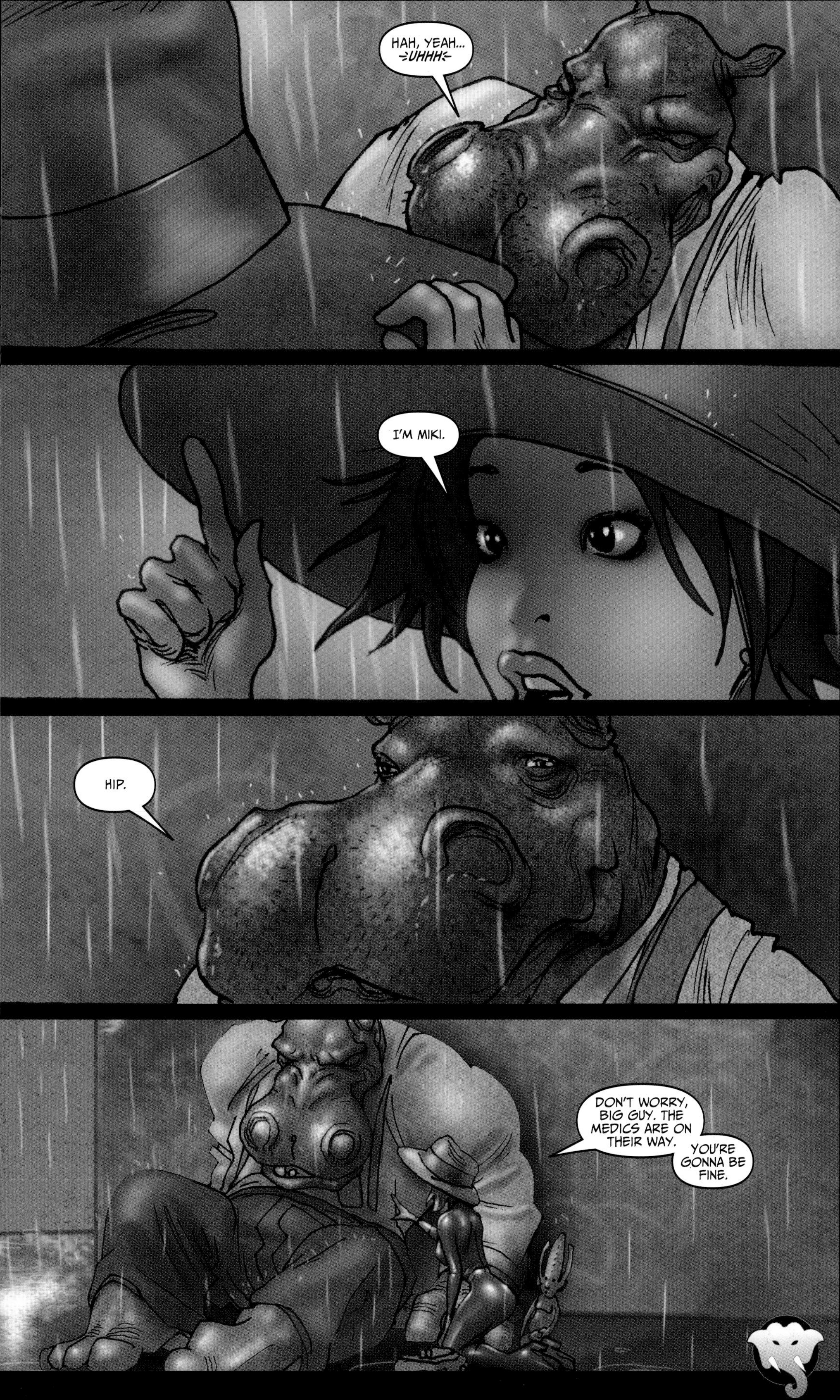
HAH, YEAH... UHHH
I'M MIKI.
HIP.
DON'T WORRY, BIG GUY. THE MEDICS ARE ON THEIR WAY.
YOU'RE GONNA BE FINE.

ANIMALS AND HAZARDOUS MATERIALS

Any research or instructional use of hazardous materials in live animals requires the submission of an Animal Use Protocol to the appropriate Animal Care and Use Committee. The Protocol must be fully approved before any researcher may acquire, house, or use animals.

IMPORTANT: With the increasing prevalence of animal testing, there comes a greater need to protect researchers. Consider both the direct hazards associated with research animals and the hazardous metabolic byproducts produced by research animals.

ANIMALS AND RECOMBINANT GENETIC MATERIALS

Animal research with recombinant DNA (rDNA) must be conducted in accordance with NIH guidelines and TAMUS-HSC requirements. Containment and disposition is a critical concern, all experiments involving rDNA or genetically altered animals (including recombinants, transgenics, and mosaics) must receive prior approval from the appropriate TAMUS Institutional Biosafety Committee.

ANIMALS AND RADIOACTIVE MATERIALS

The component Radiation Safety Officer must approve the use of radioactive materials in animals. Authorization and permits to use radioisotopes must be acquired through the appropriate office or contact the Director of Administration. Always refer to your components Radiological Safety Manual for information.

SOURCE: TEXAS A&M HEALTH
SCIENCE CENTER WEBSITE 2006

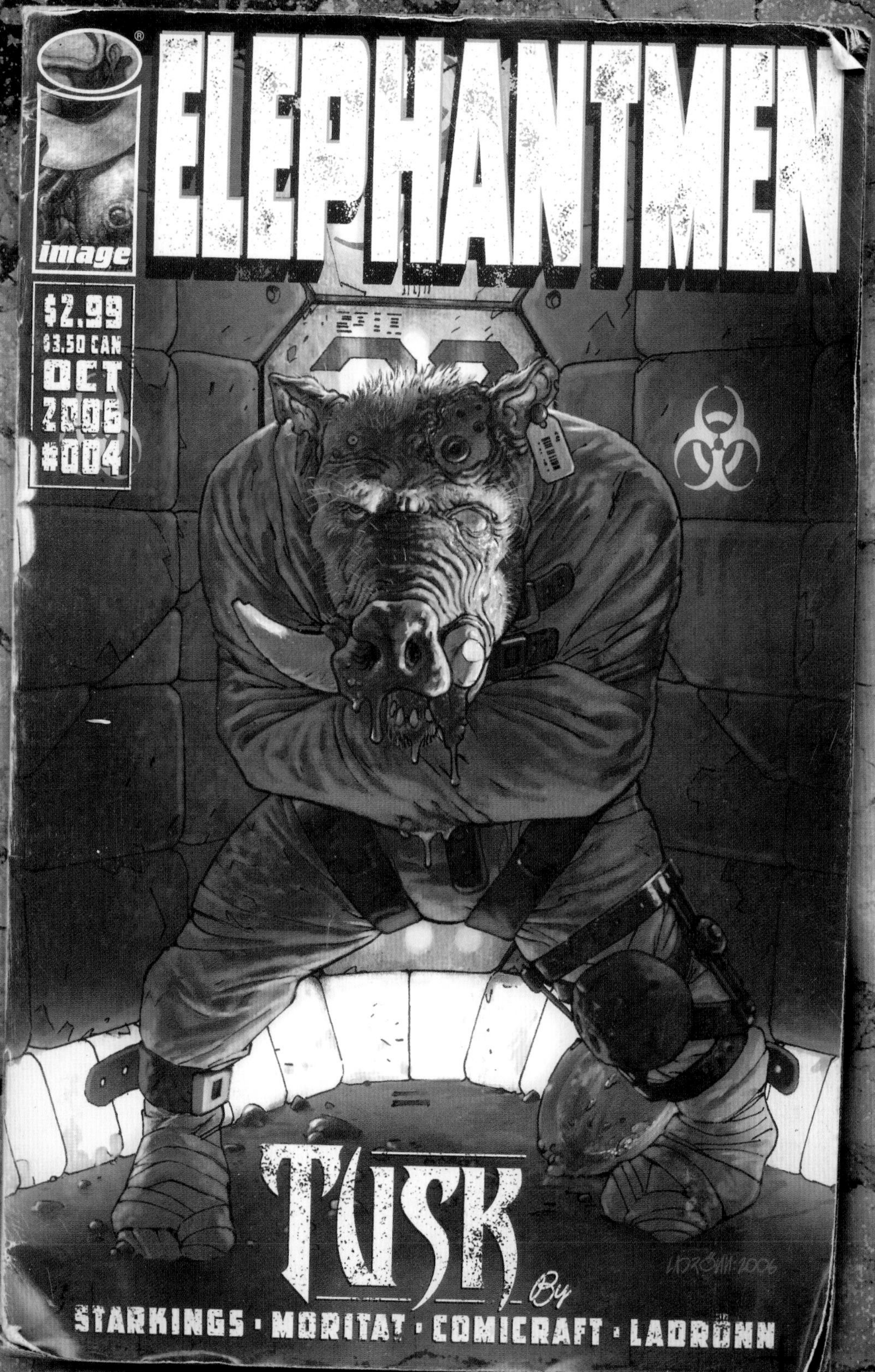
ELEPHANTMEN
image
$2.99
$3.50 CAN
OCT
2006
#004
TUSK
By
STARKINGS · MORITAT · COMICRAFT · LADRÖNN

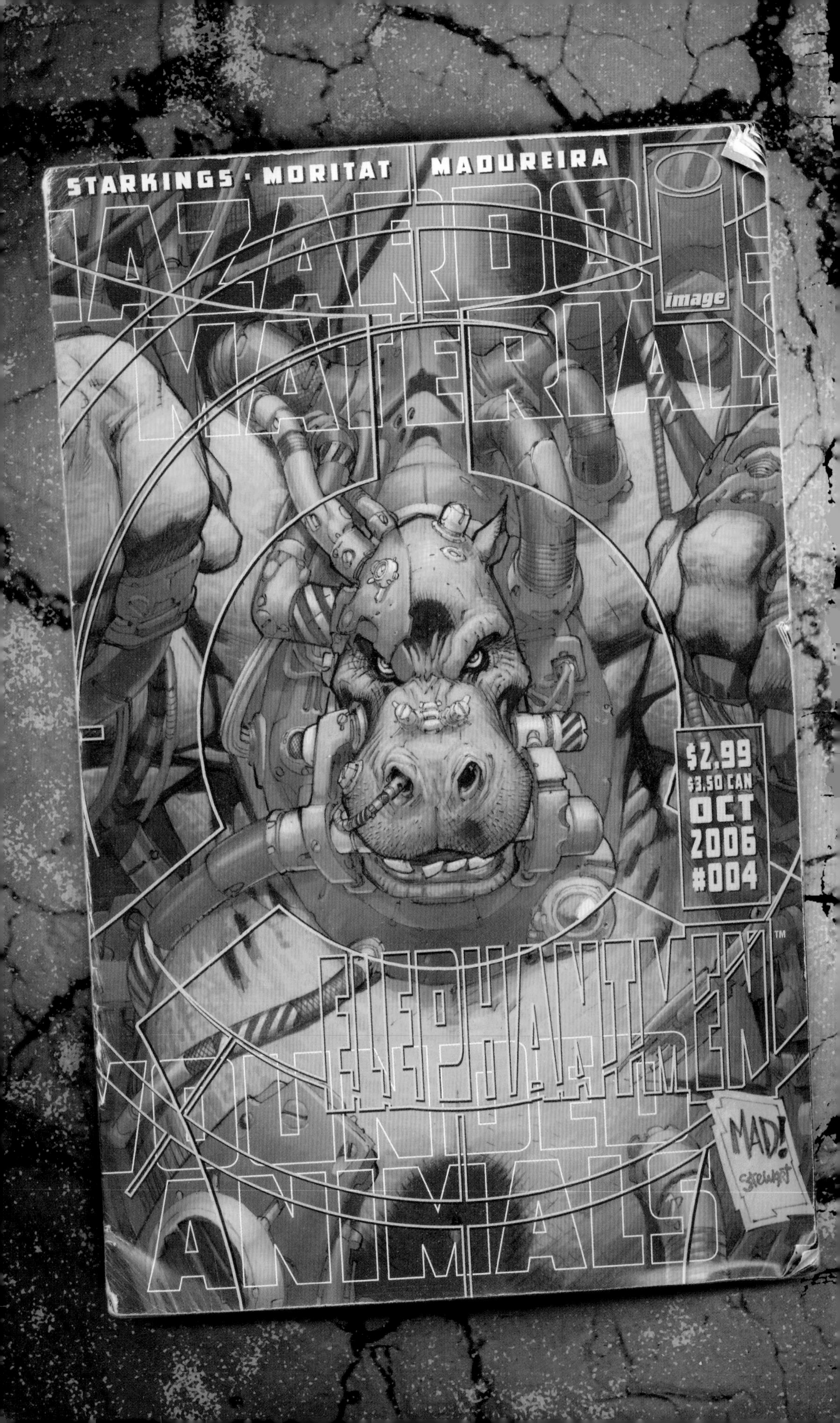
STARKINGS · MORITAT
MADUREIRA
image
MATERIALS
$2.99
$3.50 CAN
OCT
2006
#004
ELEPHANTMEN™
ANIMALS
MAD!
STEWART

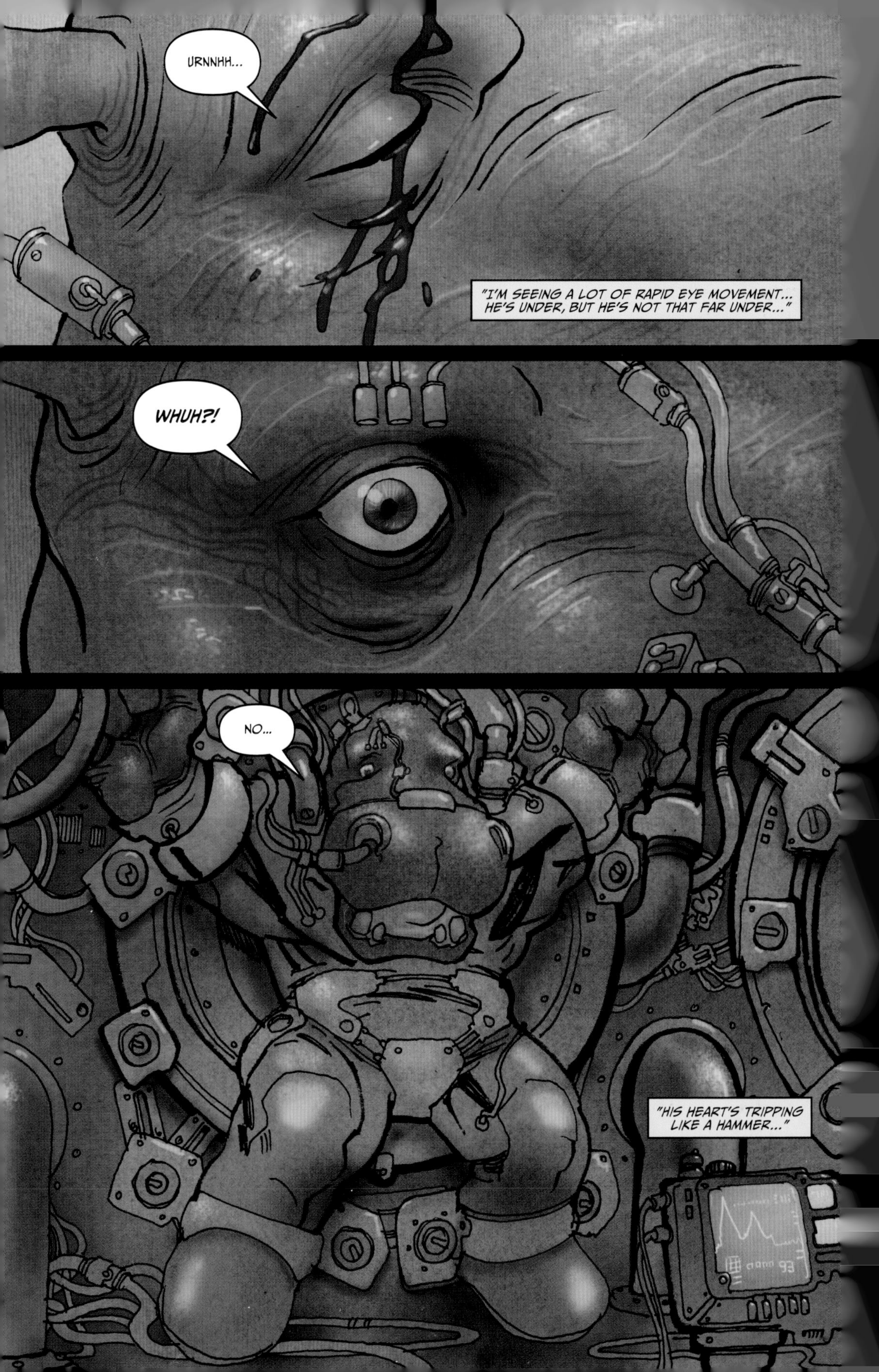
URNNHH...
"I'M SEEING A LOT OF RAPID EYE MOVEMENT... HE'S UNDER, BUT HE'S NOT THAT FAR UNDER..."
WHUH?!
NO...
"HIS HEART'S TRIPPING LIKE A HAMMER..."

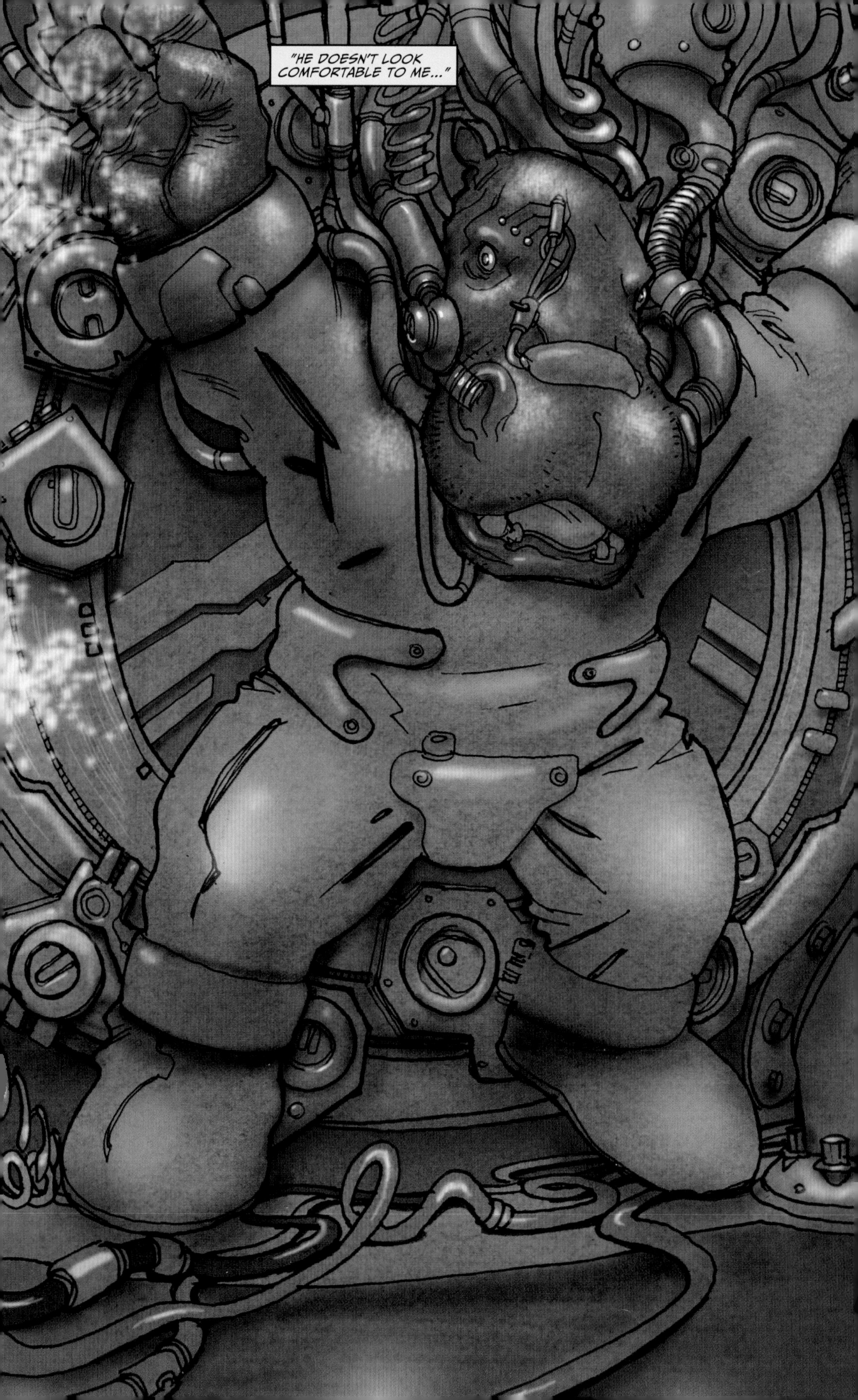
"HE DOESN'T LOOK COMFORTABLE TO ME..."

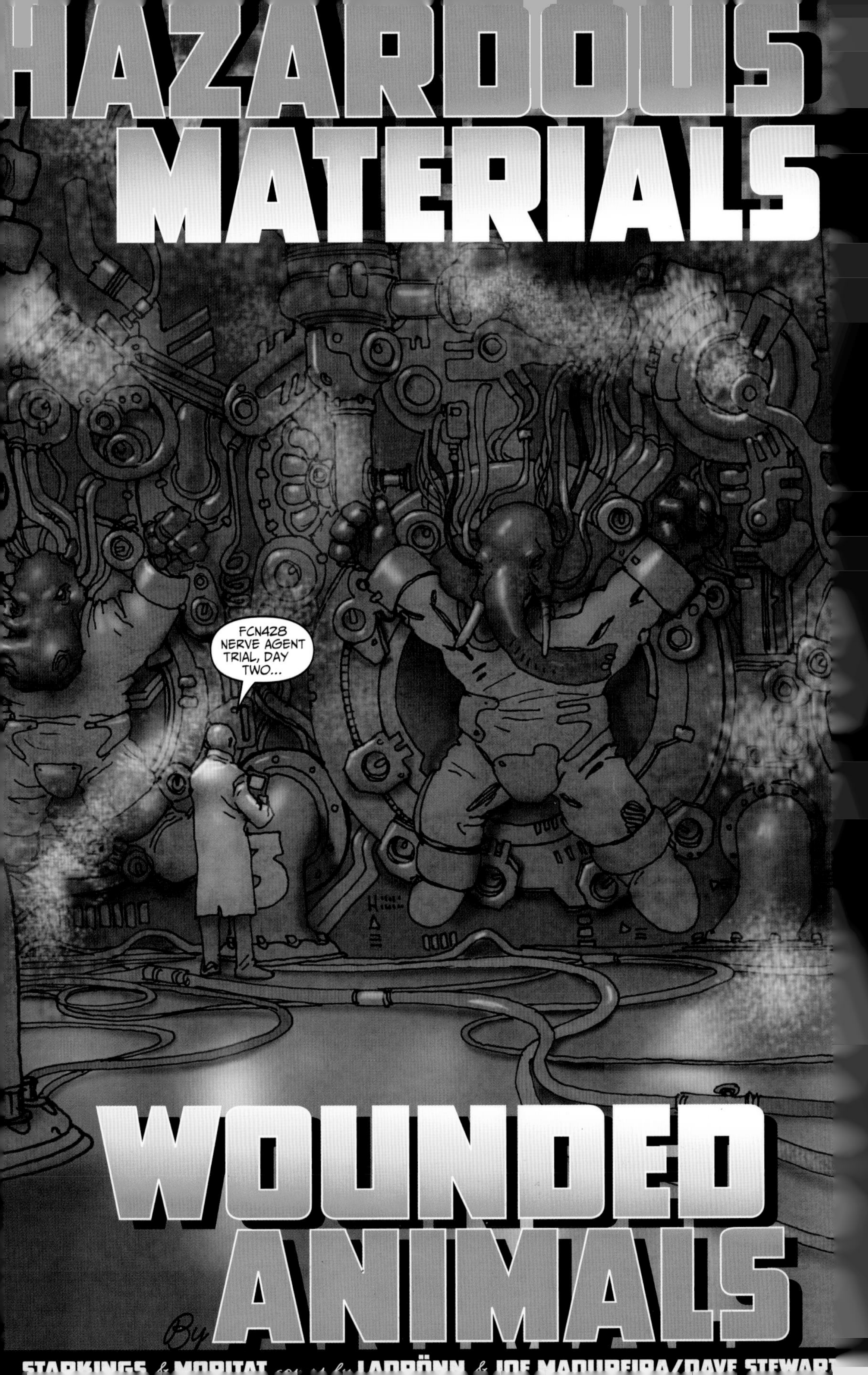
HAZARDOUS MATERIALS
FCN428 NERVE AGENT TRIAL, DAY TWO...
WOUNDED ANIMALS
By

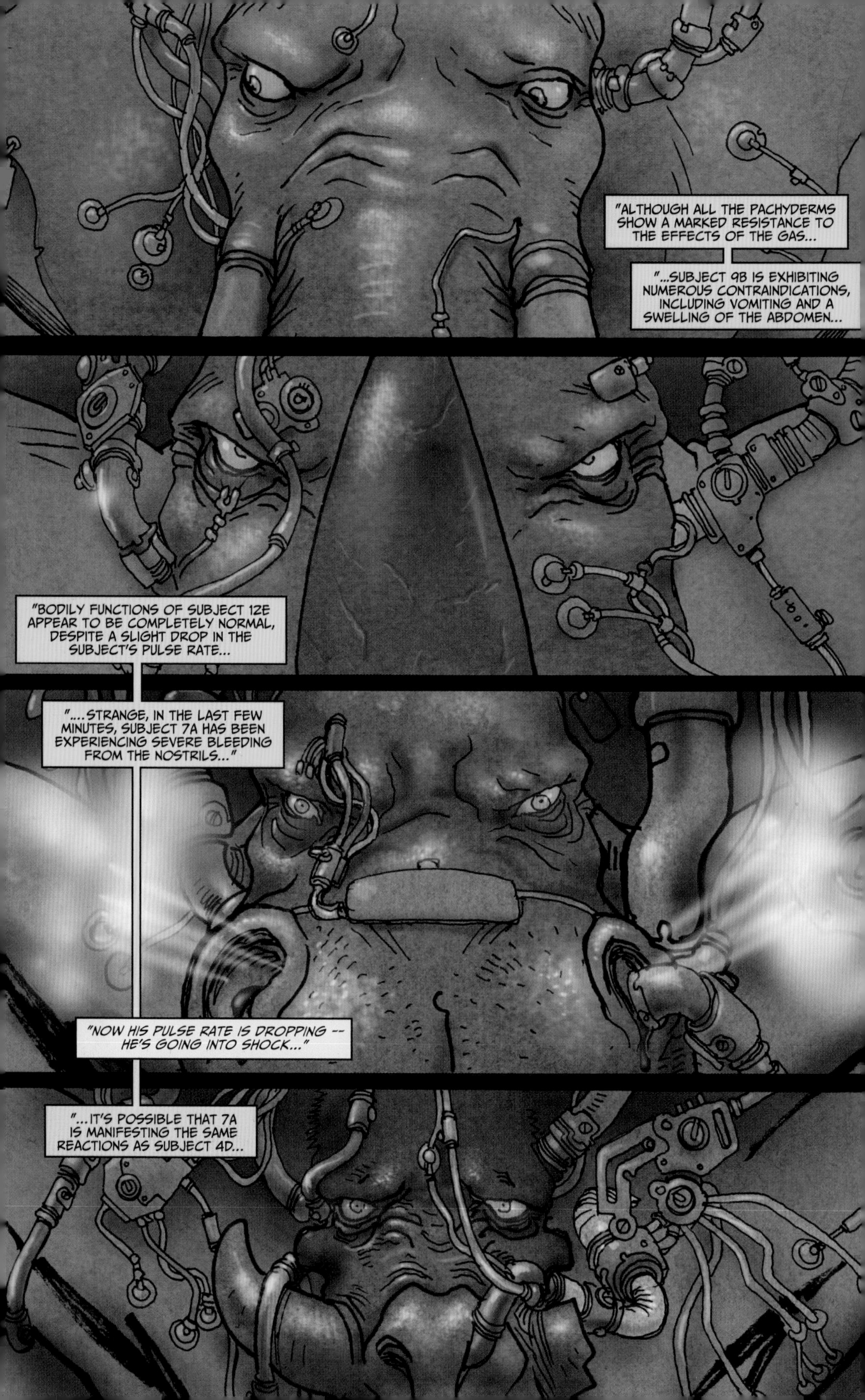
"ALTHOUGH ALL THE PACHYDERMS SHOW A MARKED RESISTANCE TO THE EFFECTS OF THE GAS...
"...SUBJECT 9B IS EXHIBITING NUMEROUS CONTRAINDICATIONS, INCLUDING VOMITING AND A SWELLING OF THE ABDOMEN...
"BODILY FUNCTIONS OF SUBJECT 12E APPEAR TO BE COMPLETELY NORMAL, DESPITE A SLIGHT DROP IN THE SUBJECT'S PULSE RATE...
"....STRANGE, IN THE LAST FEW MINUTES, SUBJECT 7A HAS BEEN EXPERIENCING SEVERE BLEEDING FROM THE NOSTRILS..."
"NOW HIS PULSE RATE IS DROPPING -- HE'S GOING INTO SHOCK..."
"...IT'S POSSIBLE THAT 7A IS MANIFESTING THE SAME REACTIONS AS SUBJECT 4D...

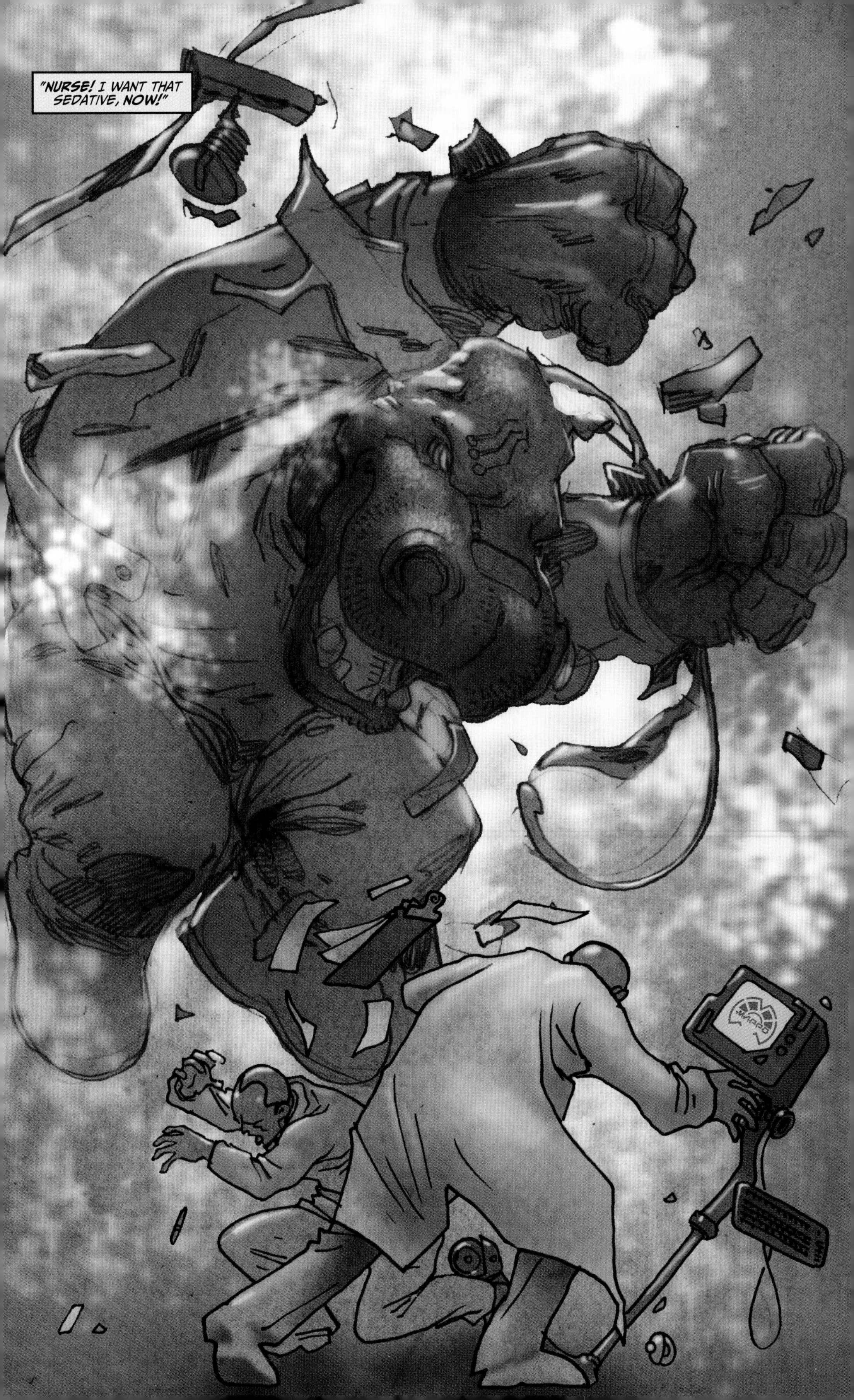
"NURSE! I WANT THAT SEDATIVE, NOW!"

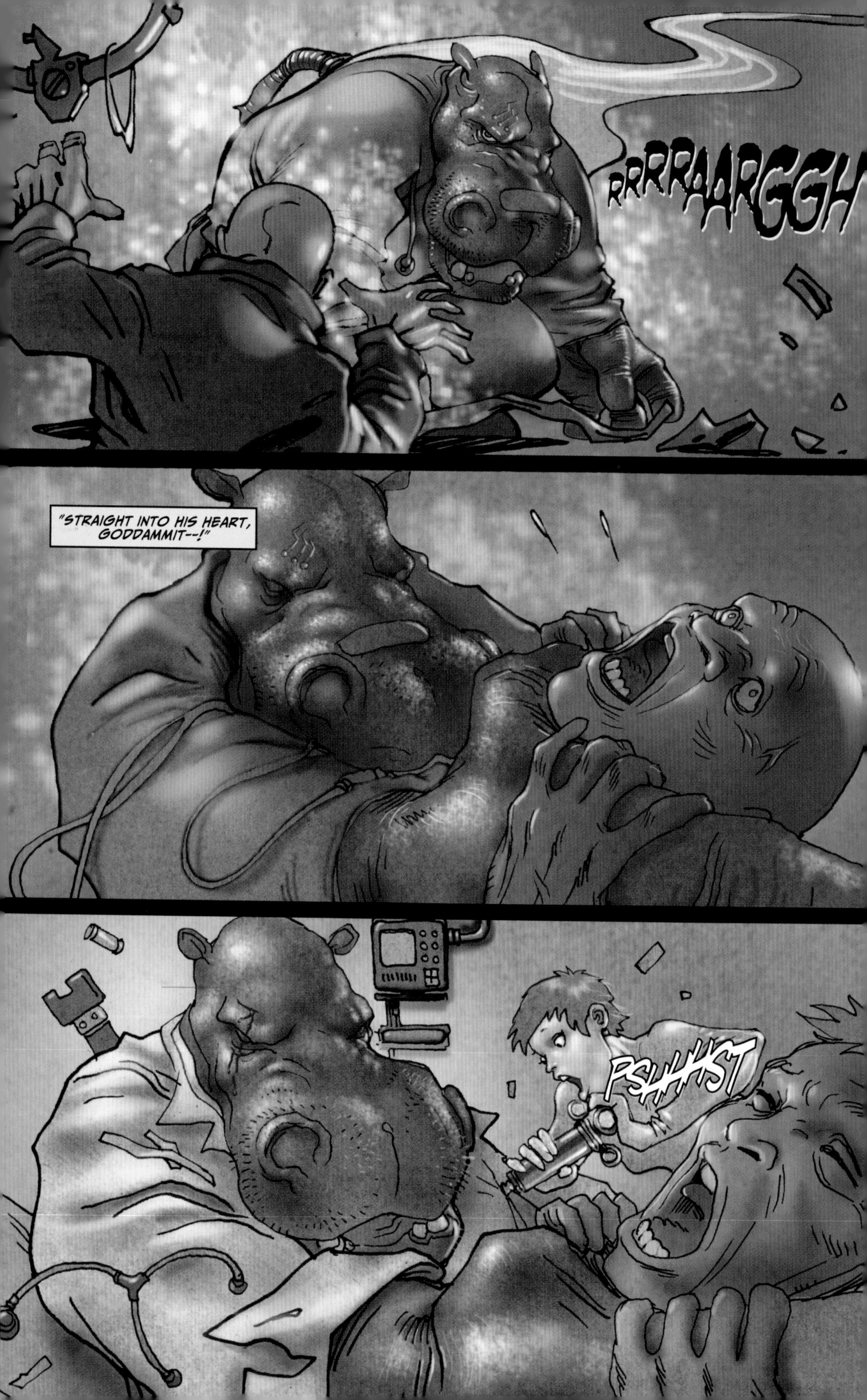
RRRRAARGGH
"STRAIGHT INTO HIS HEART, GODDAMMIT--!"
PSHHHST

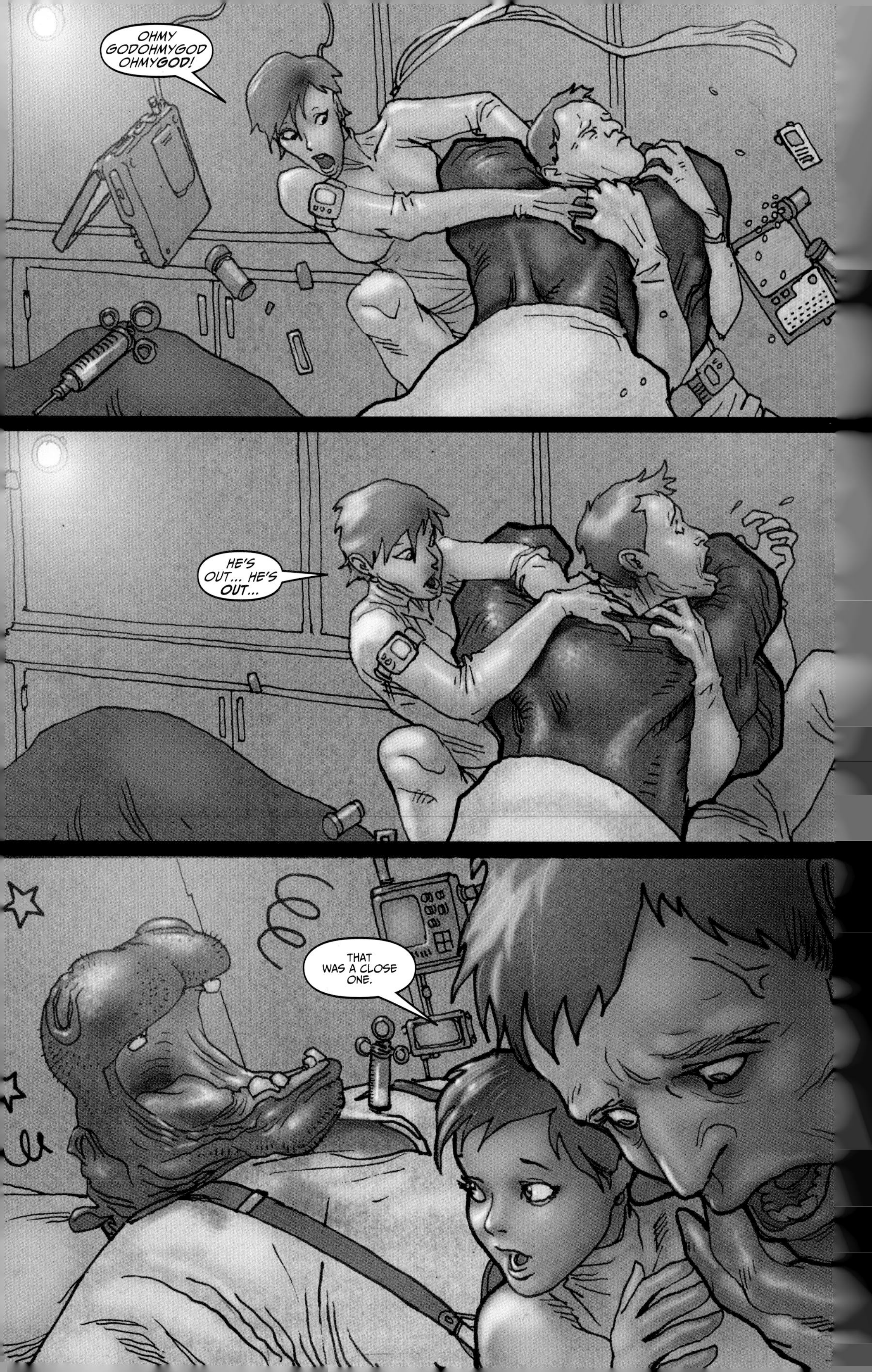
OHMY GODOHMYGOD OHMYGOD!
HE'S OUT... HE'S OUT...
THAT WAS A CLOSE ONE.

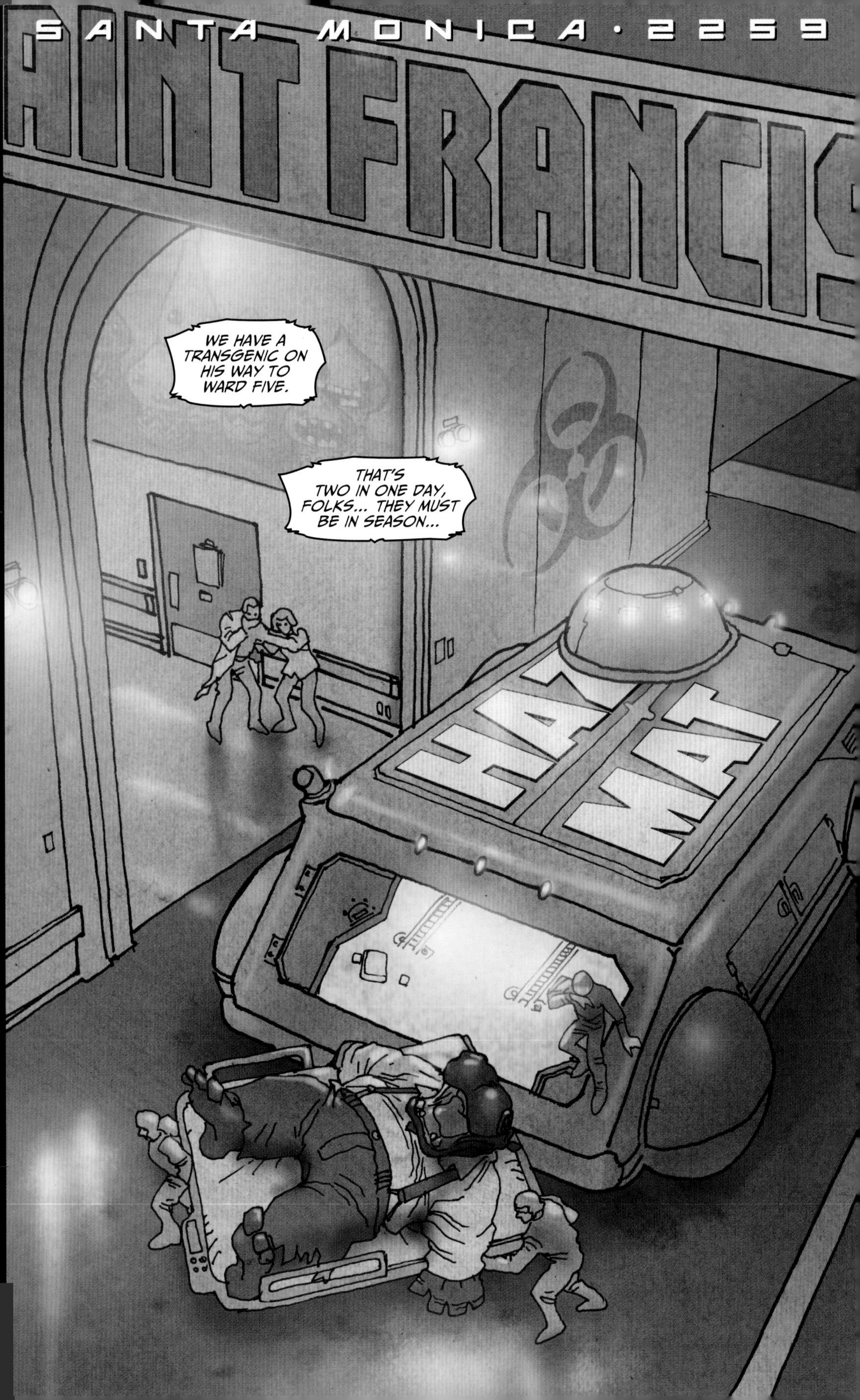
SANTA MONICA · 2259
AINT FRANCIS
WE HAVE A TRANSGENIC ON HIS WAY TO WARD FIVE.
THAT'S TWO IN ONE DAY, FOLKS... THEY MUST BE IN SEASON...
HAZ MAT

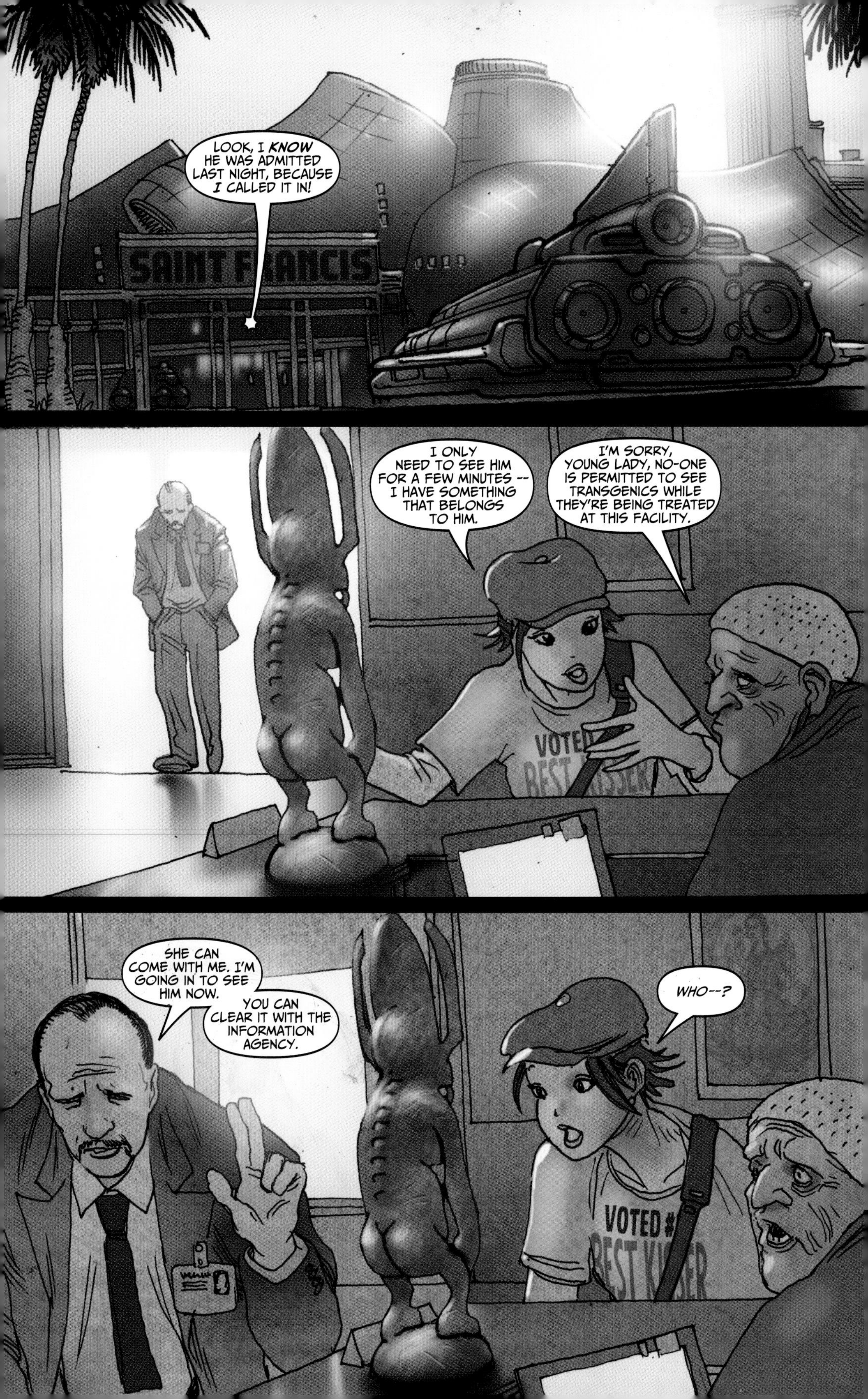
SAINT FRANCIS
LOOK, I KNOW HE WAS ADMITTED LAST NIGHT, BECAUSE I CALLED IT IN!
I ONLY NEED TO SEE HIM FOR A FEW MINUTES -- I HAVE SOMETHING THAT BELONGS TO HIM.
I'M SORRY, YOUNG LADY, NO-ONE IS PERMITTED TO SEE TRANSGENICS WHILE THEY'RE BEING TREATED AT THIS FACILITY.
SHE CAN COME WITH ME. I'M GOING IN TO SEE HIM NOW.
YOU CAN CLEAR IT WITH THE INFORMATION AGENCY.
WHO--?

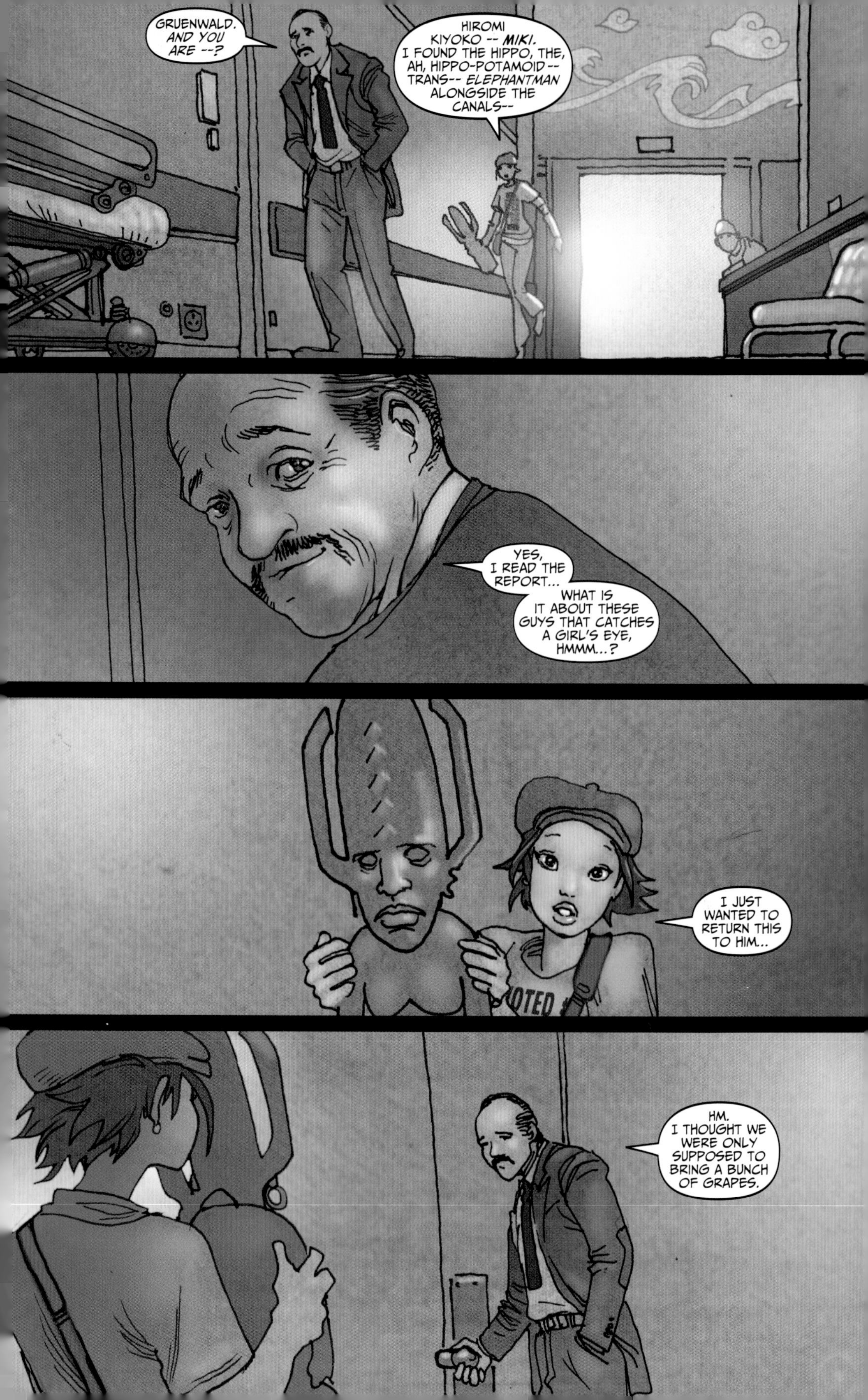
GRUENWALD. AND YOU ARE --?
HIROMI KIYOKO -- MIKI. I FOUND THE HIPPO, THE, AH, HIPPO-POTAMOID -- TRANS-- ELEPHANTMAN ALONGSIDE THE CANALS--
YES, I READ THE REPORT...
WHAT IS IT ABOUT THESE GUYS THAT CATCHES A GIRL'S EYE, HMMM...?
I JUST WANTED TO RETURN THIS TO HIM...
HM. I THOUGHT WE WERE ONLY SUPPOSED TO BRING A BUNCH OF GRAPES.

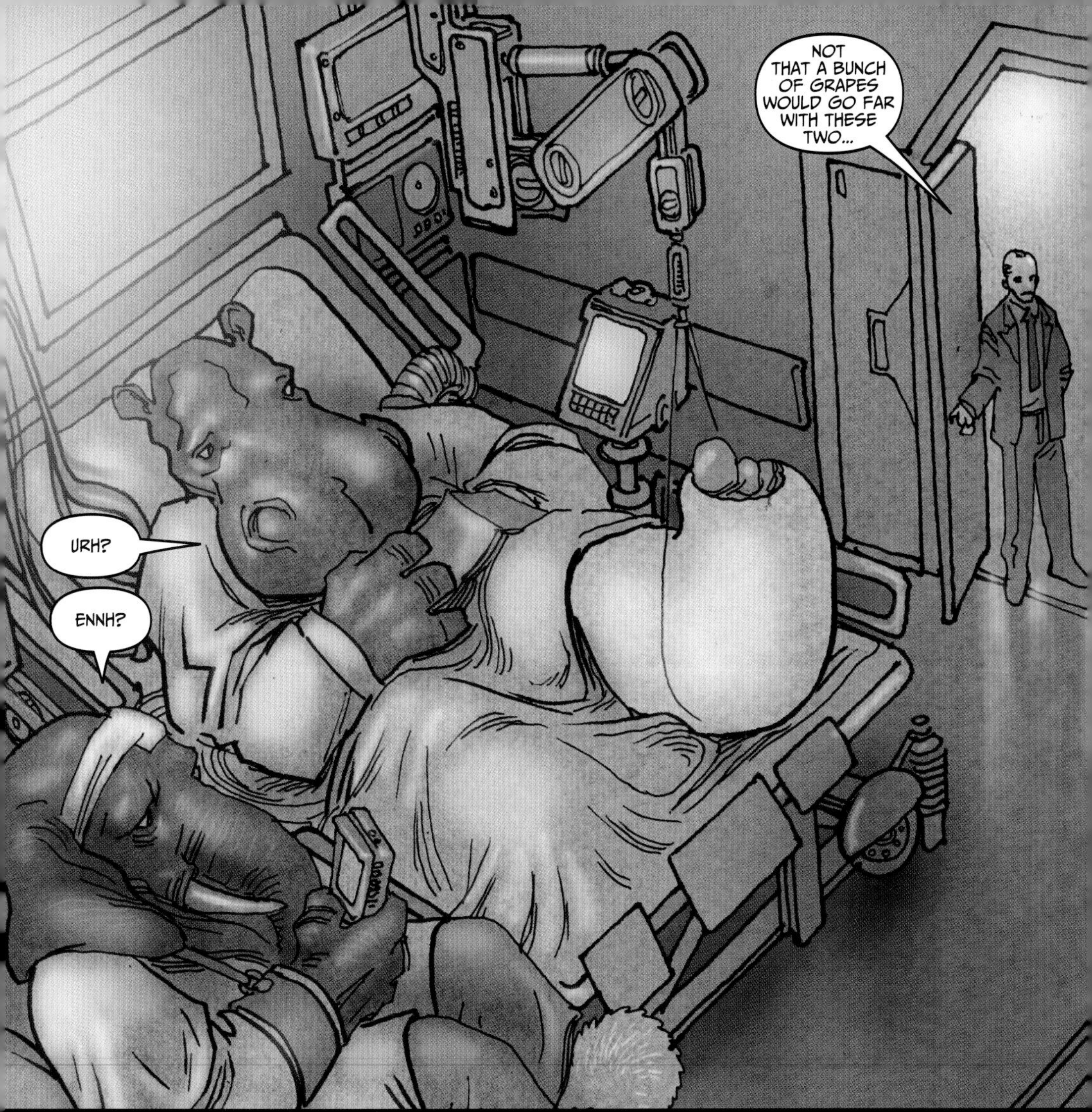
NOT THAT A BUNCH OF GRAPES WOULD GO FAR WITH THESE TWO...
URH?
ENNH?

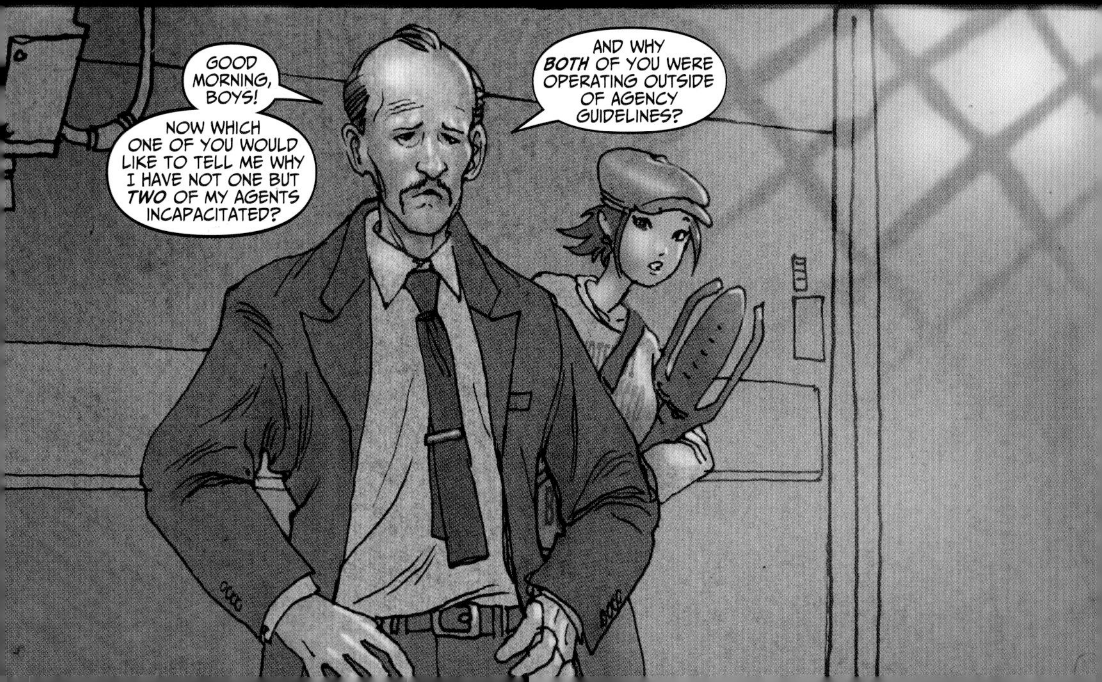
GOOD MORNING, BOYS!
NOW WHICH ONE OF YOU WOULD LIKE TO TELL ME WHY I HAVE NOT ONE BUT *TWO* OF MY AGENTS INCAPACITATED?
AND WHY *BOTH* OF YOU WERE OPERATING OUTSIDE OF AGENCY GUIDELINES?

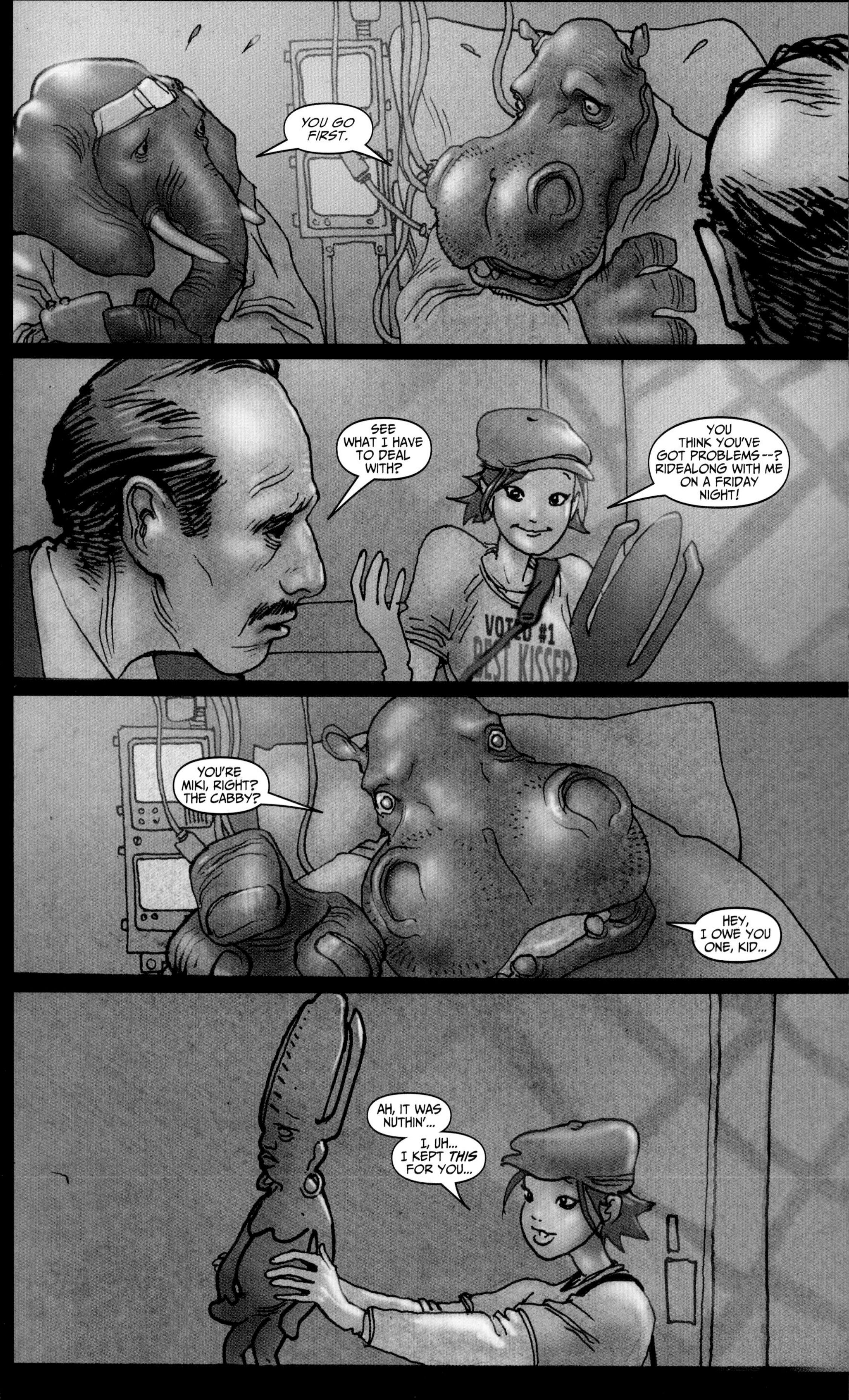
YOU GO FIRST.
SEE WHAT I HAVE TO DEAL WITH?
YOU THINK YOU'VE GOT PROBLEMS--? RIDEALONG WITH ME ON A FRIDAY NIGHT!
VOTED #1 BEST KISSER
YOU'RE MIKI, RIGHT? THE CABBY?
HEY, I OWE YOU ONE, KID...
AH, IT WAS NUTHIN'...
I, UH... I KEPT *THIS* FOR YOU...

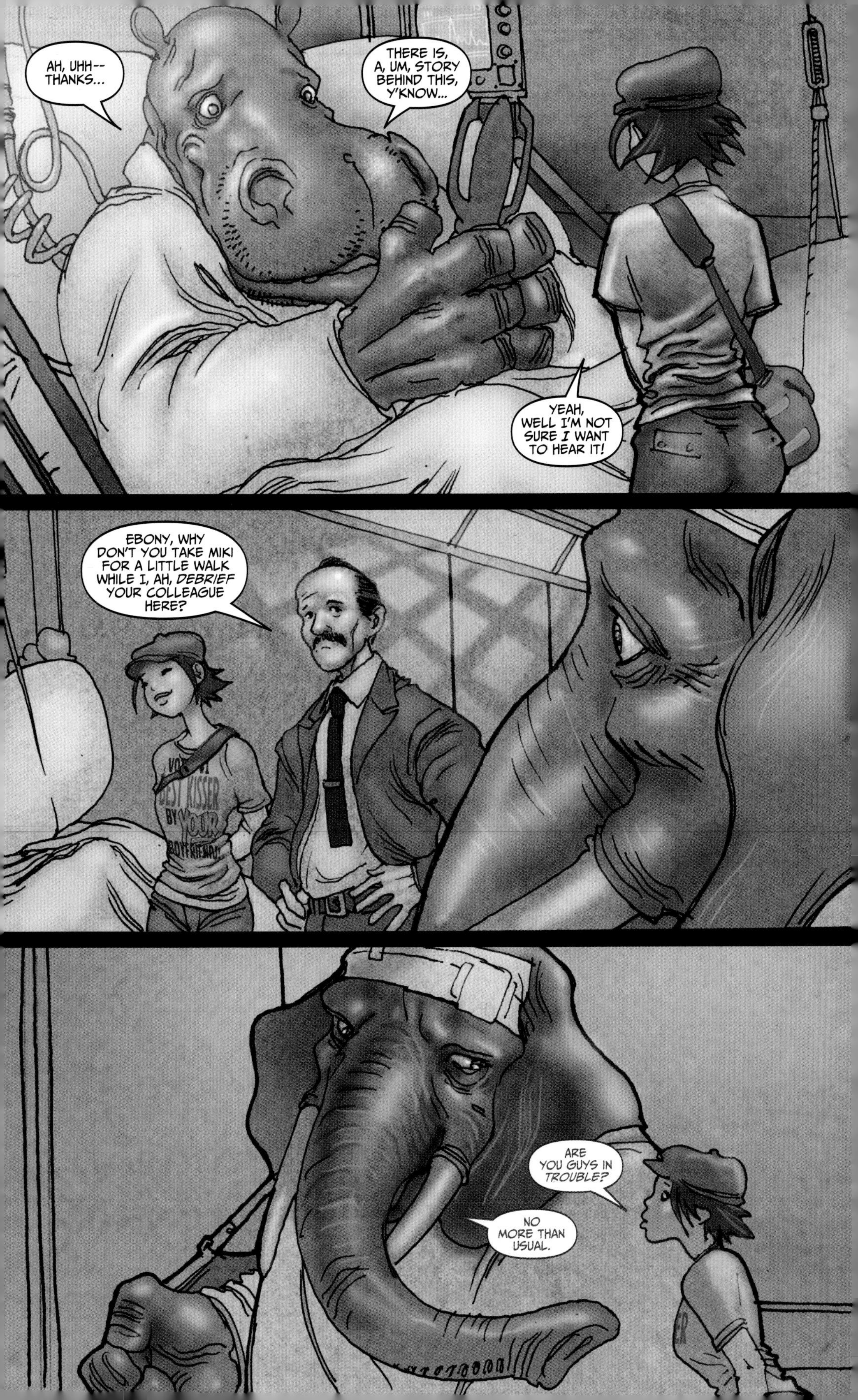
AH, UHH--
THANKS...
THERE IS, A, UM, STORY BEHIND THIS, Y'KNOW...
YEAH, WELL I'M NOT SURE *I* WANT TO HEAR IT!
EBONY, WHY DON'T YOU TAKE MIKI FOR A LITTLE WALK WHILE I, AH, *DEBRIEF* YOUR COLLEAGUE HERE?
#1 BEST KISSER BY YOUR BOYFRIEND!
ARE YOU GUYS IN *TROUBLE?*
NO MORE THAN USUAL.

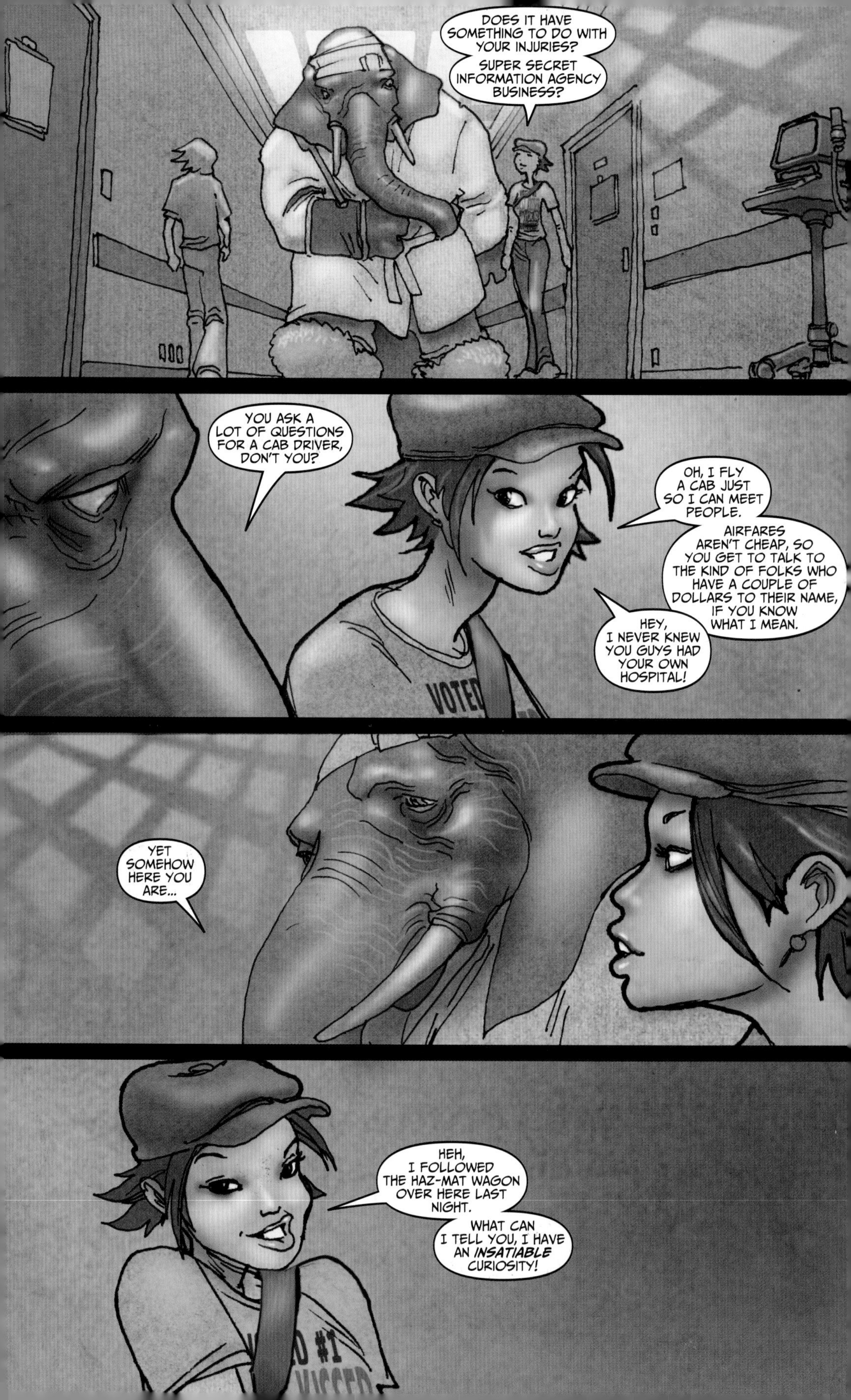
DOES IT HAVE SOMETHING TO DO WITH YOUR INJURIES?
SUPER SECRET INFORMATION AGENCY BUSINESS?
YOU ASK A LOT OF QUESTIONS FOR A CAB DRIVER, DON'T YOU?
OH, I FLY A CAB JUST SO I CAN MEET PEOPLE.
AIRFARES AREN'T CHEAP, SO YOU GET TO TALK TO THE KIND OF FOLKS WHO HAVE A COUPLE OF DOLLARS TO THEIR NAME, IF YOU KNOW WHAT I MEAN.
HEY, I NEVER KNEW YOU GUYS HAD YOUR OWN HOSPITAL!
YET SOMEHOW HERE YOU ARE...
HEH, I FOLLOWED THE HAZ-MAT WAGON OVER HERE LAST NIGHT.
WHAT CAN I TELL YOU, I HAVE AN *INSATIABLE* CURIOSITY!

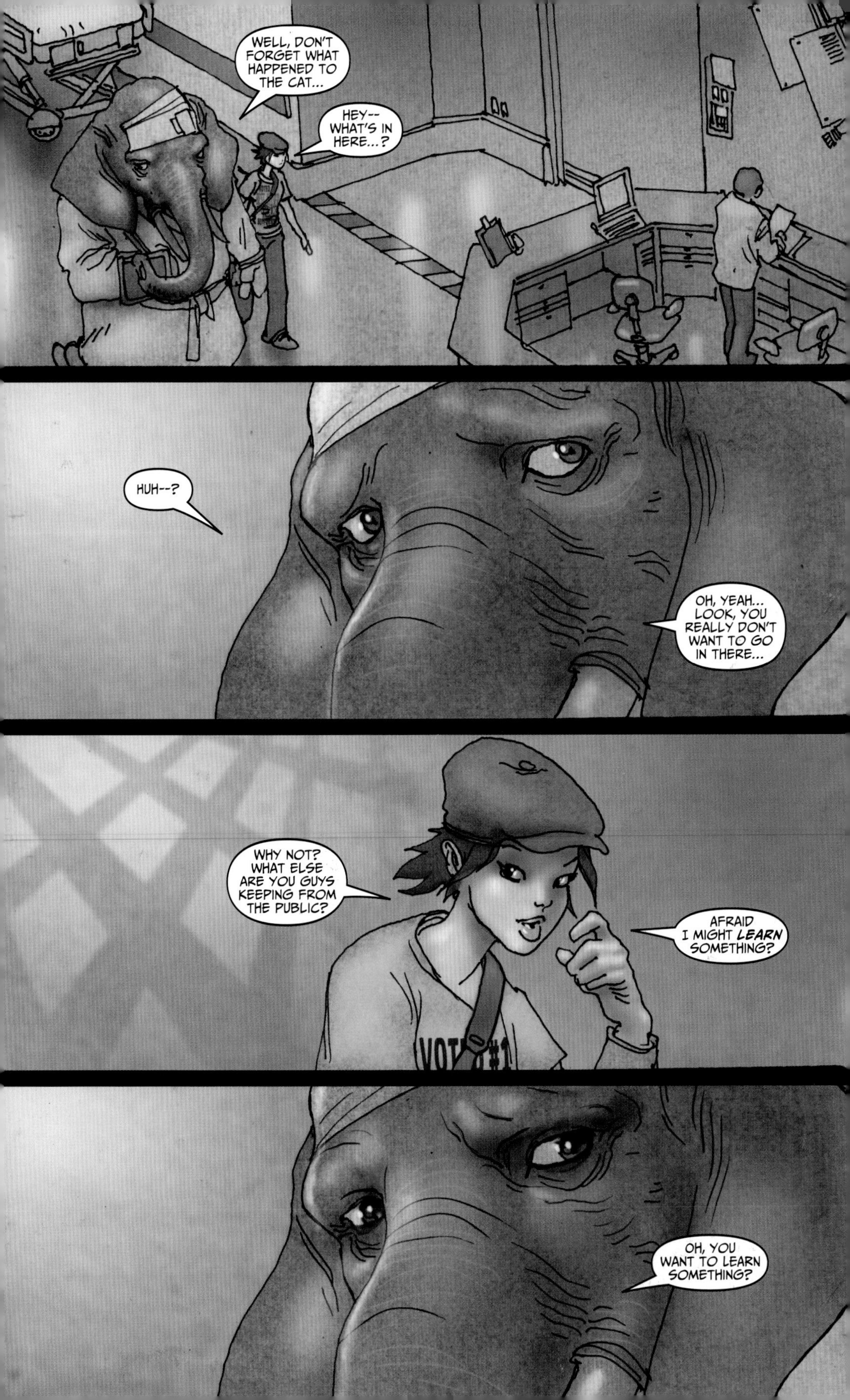
WELL, DON'T FORGET WHAT HAPPENED TO THE CAT...
HEY-- WHAT'S IN HERE...?
HUH--?
OH, YEAH... LOOK, YOU REALLY DON'T WANT TO GO IN THERE...
WHY NOT? WHAT ELSE ARE YOU GUYS KEEPING FROM THE PUBLIC?
AFRAID I MIGHT LEARN SOMETHING?
OH, YOU WANT TO LEARN SOMETHING?

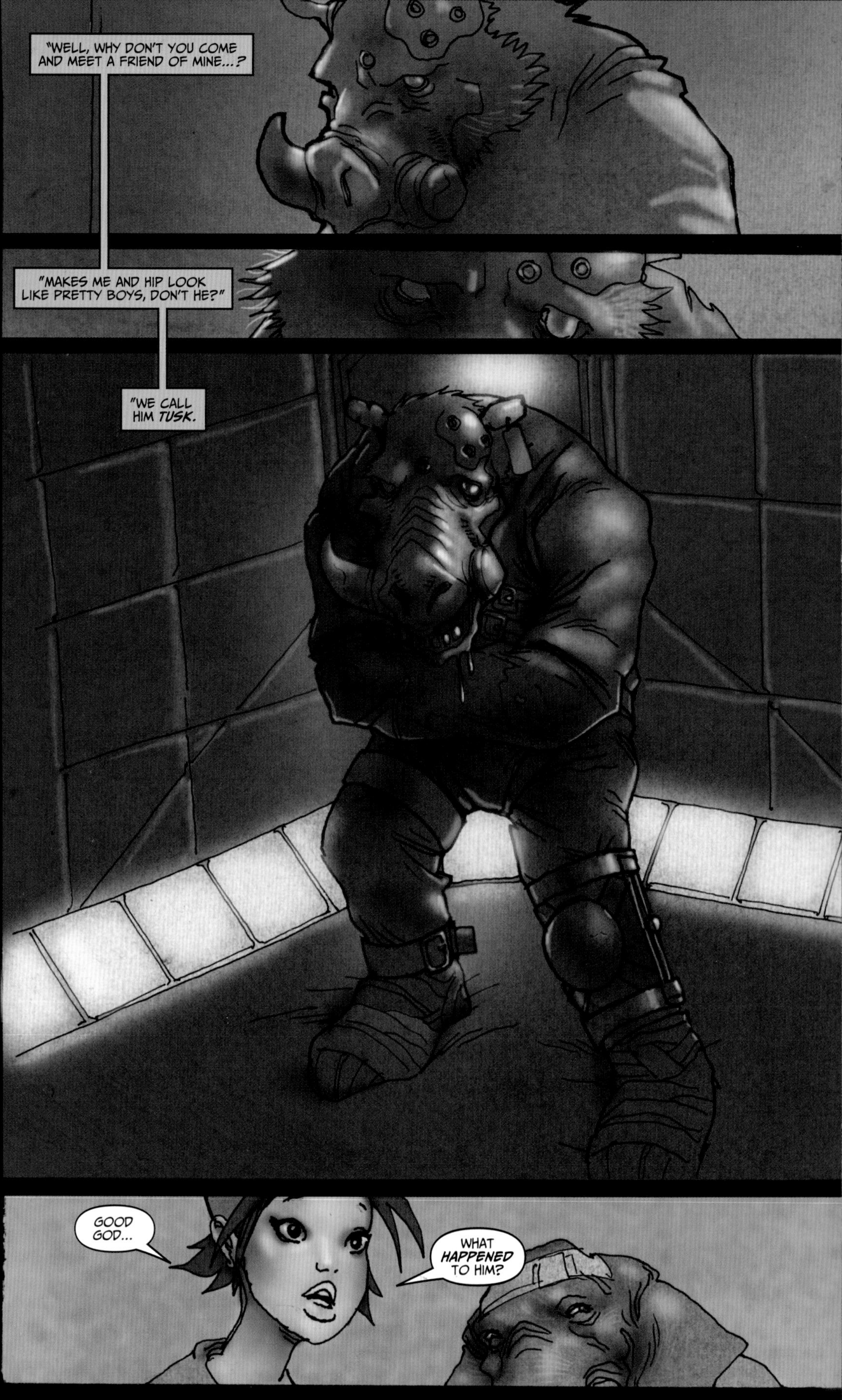
"WELL, WHY DON'T YOU COME AND MEET A FRIEND OF MINE...?
"MAKES ME AND HIP LOOK LIKE PRETTY BOYS, DON'T HE?"
"WE CALL HIM *TUSK*.
GOOD GOD...
WHAT *HAPPENED* TO HIM?

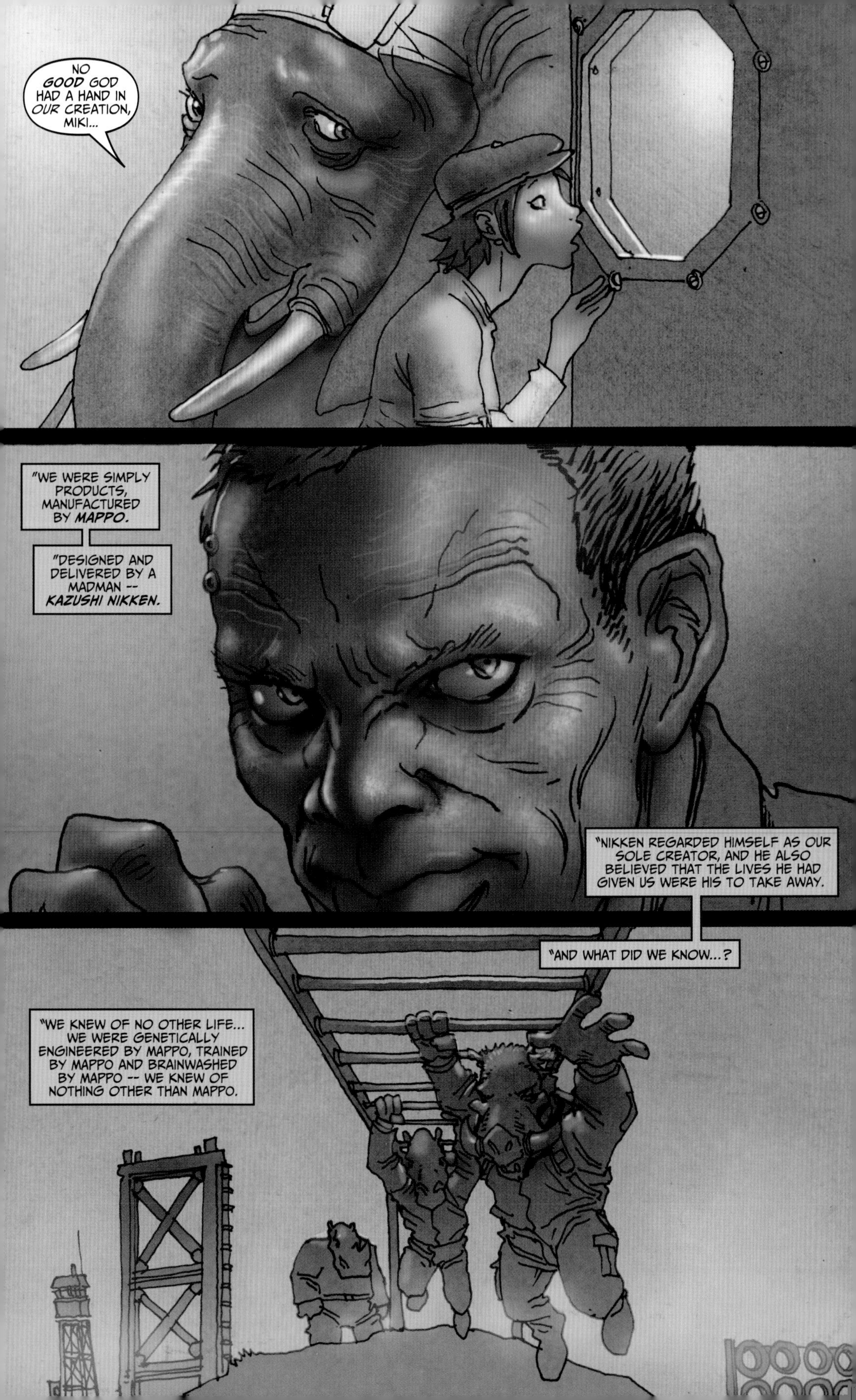
NO GOOD GOD HAD A HAND IN OUR CREATION, MIKI...
"WE WERE SIMPLY PRODUCTS, MANUFACTURED BY MAPPO.
"DESIGNED AND DELIVERED BY A MADMAN -- KAZUSHI NIKKEN.
"NIKKEN REGARDED HIMSELF AS OUR SOLE CREATOR, AND HE ALSO BELIEVED THAT THE LIVES HE HAD GIVEN US WERE HIS TO TAKE AWAY.
"AND WHAT DID WE KNOW...?
"WE KNEW OF NO OTHER LIFE... WE WERE GENETICALLY ENGINEERED BY MAPPO, TRAINED BY MAPPO AND BRAINWASHED BY MAPPO -- WE KNEW OF NOTHING OTHER THAN MAPPO.

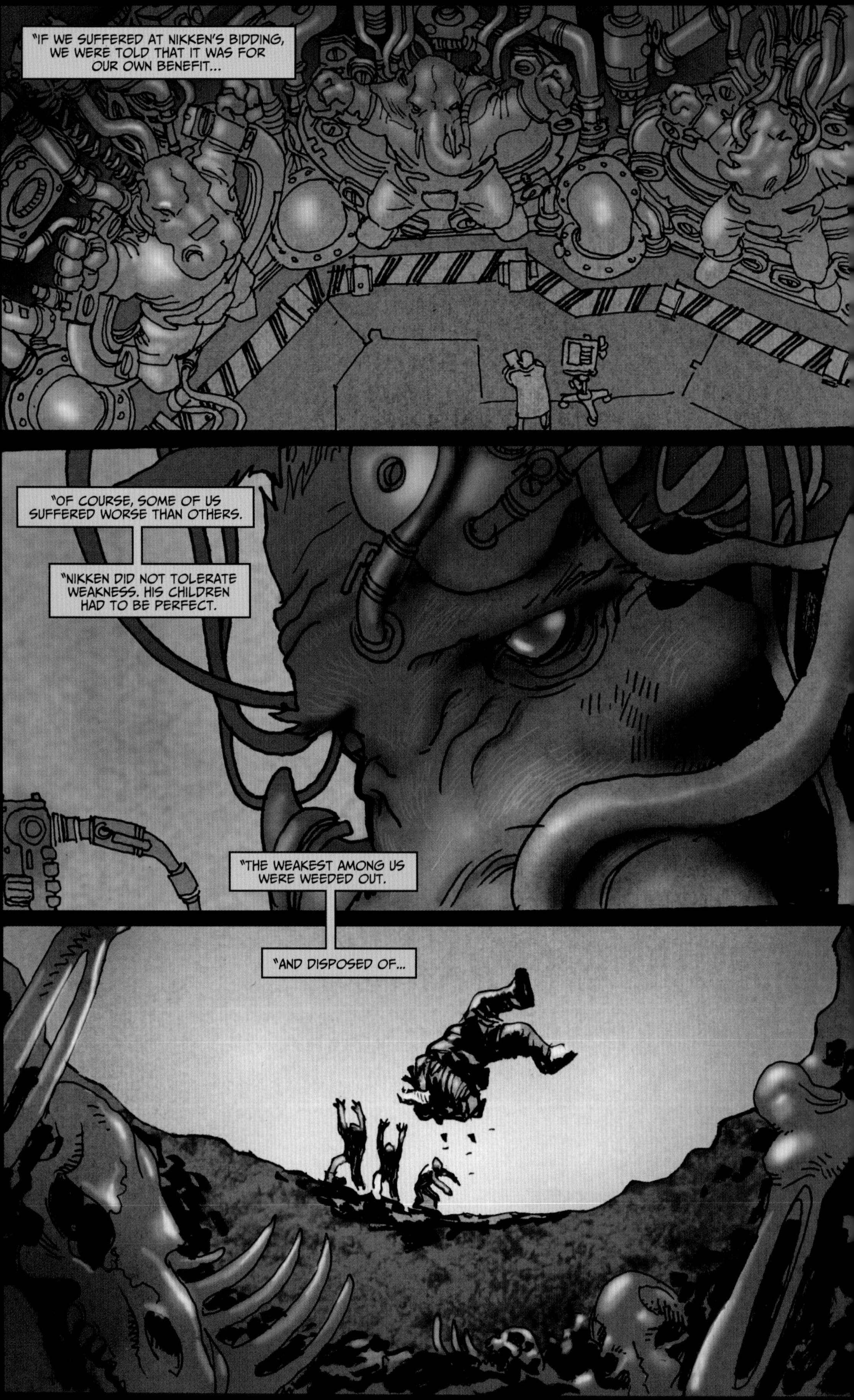
"IF WE SUFFERED AT NIKKEN'S BIDDING, WE WERE TOLD THAT IT WAS FOR OUR OWN BENEFIT...
"OF COURSE, SOME OF US SUFFERED WORSE THAN OTHERS.
"NIKKEN DID NOT TOLERATE WEAKNESS. HIS CHILDREN HAD TO BE PERFECT.
"THE WEAKEST AMONG US WERE WEEDED OUT.
"AND DISPOSED OF...

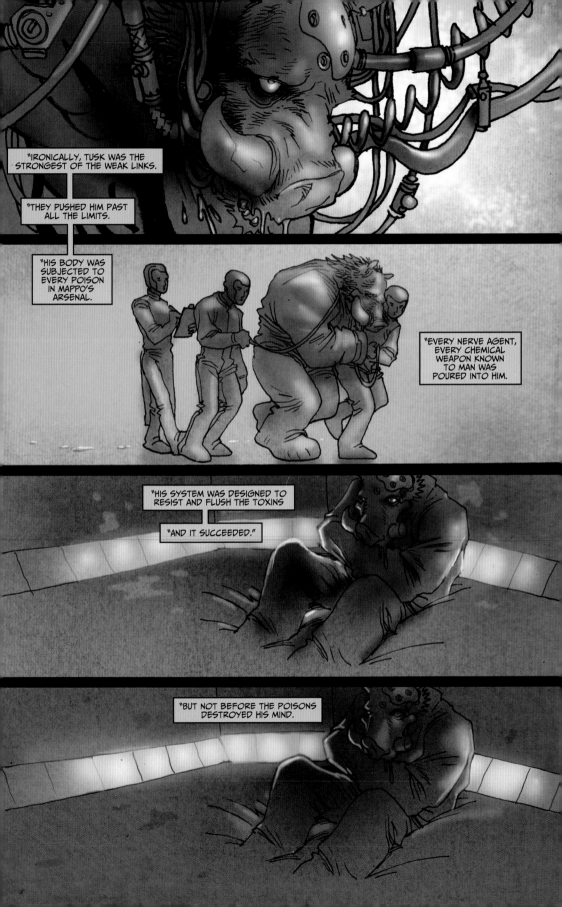

"IRONICALLY, TUSK WAS THE STRONGEST OF THE WEAK LINKS.

"THEY PUSHED HIM PAST ALL THE LIMITS.

"HIS BODY WAS SUBJECTED TO EVERY POISON IN MAPPO'S ARSENAL.

"EVERY NERVE AGENT, EVERY CHEMICAL WEAPON KNOWN TO MAN WAS POURED INTO HIM.

"HIS SYSTEM WAS DESIGNED TO RESIST AND FLUSH THE TOXINS

"AND IT SUCCEEDED."

"BUT NOT BEFORE THE POISONS DESTROYED HIS MIND.

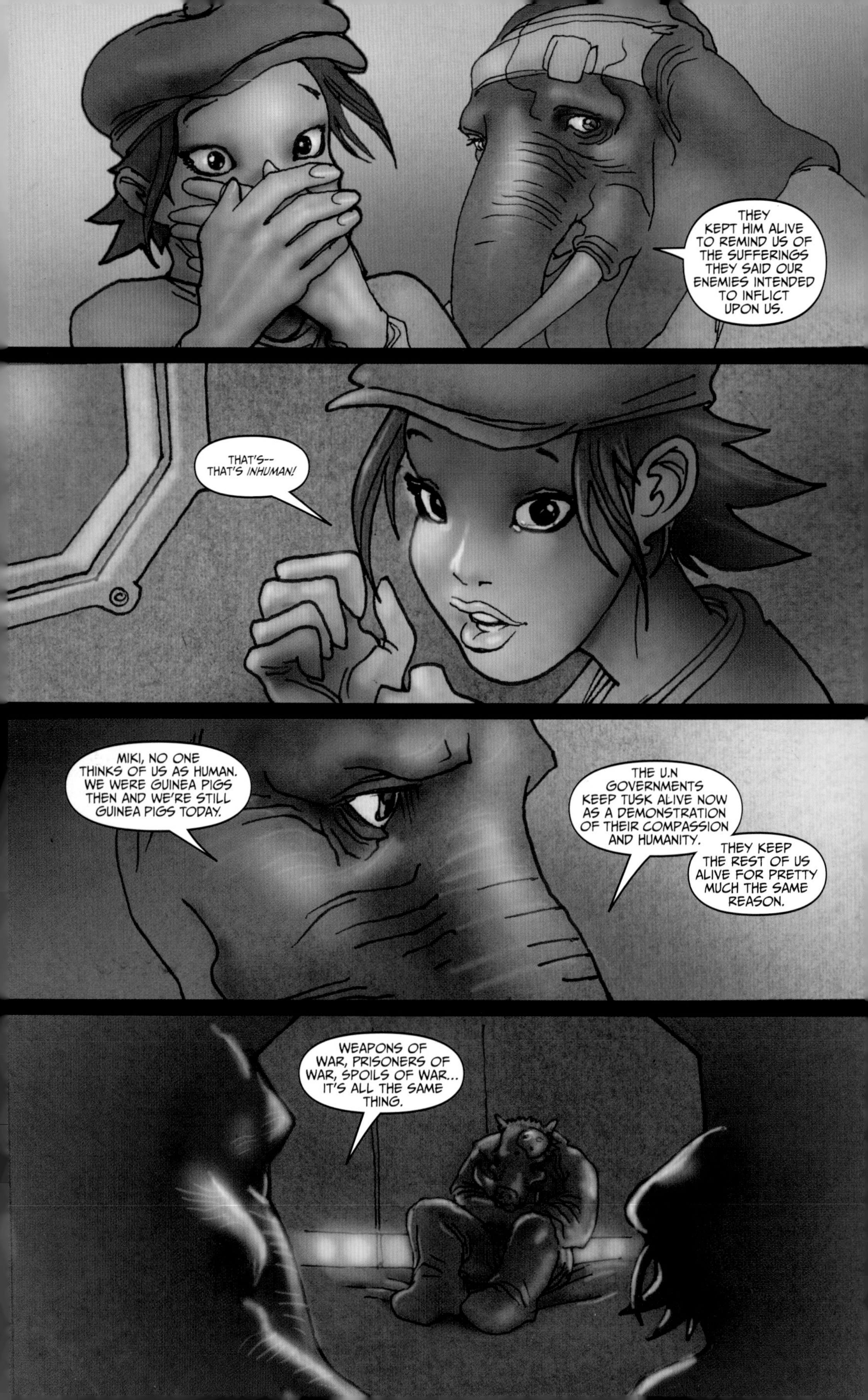
THEY KEPT HIM ALIVE TO REMIND US OF THE SUFFERINGS THEY SAID OUR ENEMIES INTENDED TO INFLICT UPON US.
THAT'S-- THAT'S *INHUMAN!*
MIKI, NO ONE THINKS OF US AS HUMAN. WE WERE GUINEA PIGS THEN AND WE'RE STILL GUINEA PIGS TODAY.
THE U.N GOVERNMENTS KEEP TUSK ALIVE NOW AS A DEMONSTRATION OF THEIR COMPASSION AND HUMANITY.
THEY KEEP THE REST OF US ALIVE FOR PRETTY MUCH THE SAME REASON.
WEAPONS OF WAR, PRISONERS OF WAR, SPOILS OF WAR... IT'S ALL THE SAME THING.

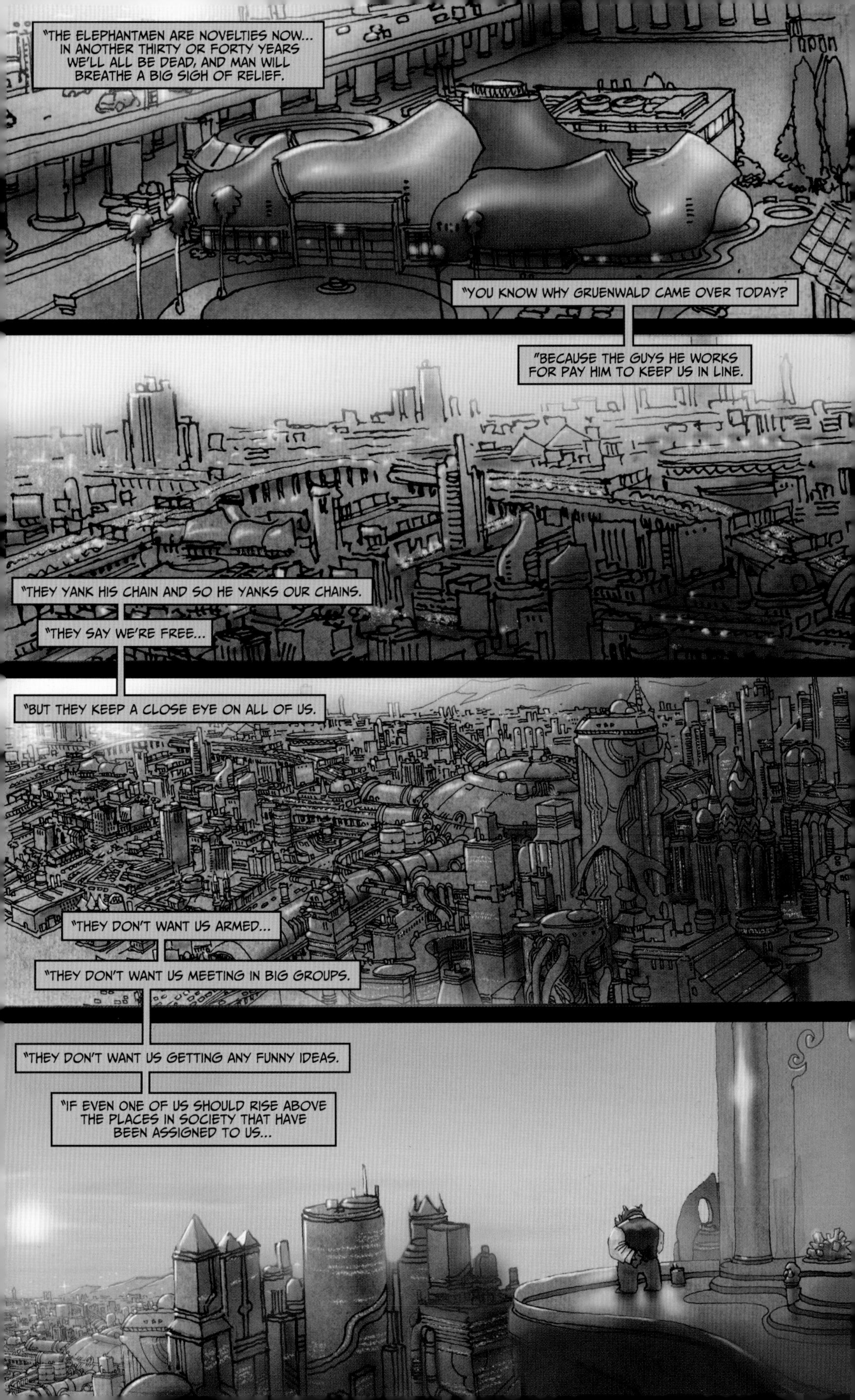
"THE ELEPHANTMEN ARE NOVELTIES NOW... IN ANOTHER THIRTY OR FORTY YEARS WE'LL ALL BE DEAD, AND MAN WILL BREATHE A BIG SIGH OF RELIEF.
"YOU KNOW WHY GRUENWALD CAME OVER TODAY?
"BECAUSE THE GUYS HE WORKS FOR PAY HIM TO KEEP US IN LINE.
"THEY YANK HIS CHAIN AND SO HE YANKS OUR CHAINS.
"THEY SAY WE'RE FREE...
"BUT THEY KEEP A CLOSE EYE ON ALL OF US.
"THEY DON'T WANT US ARMED...
"THEY DON'T WANT US MEETING IN BIG GROUPS.
"THEY DON'T WANT US GETTING ANY FUNNY IDEAS.
"IF EVEN ONE OF US SHOULD RISE ABOVE THE PLACES IN SOCIETY THAT HAVE BEEN ASSIGNED TO US...

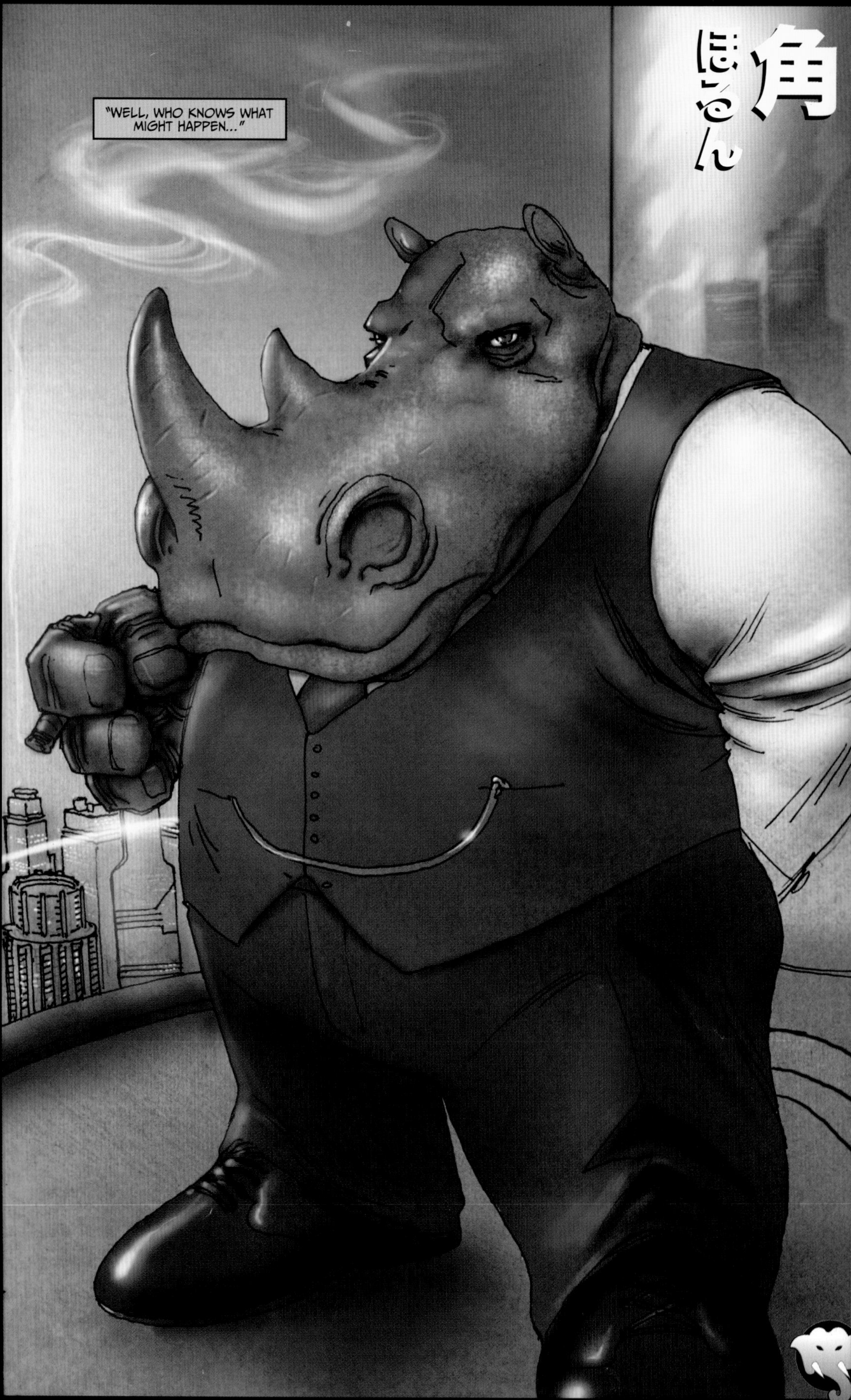
角
ほるん
"WELL, WHO KNOWS WHAT MIGHT HAPPEN..."

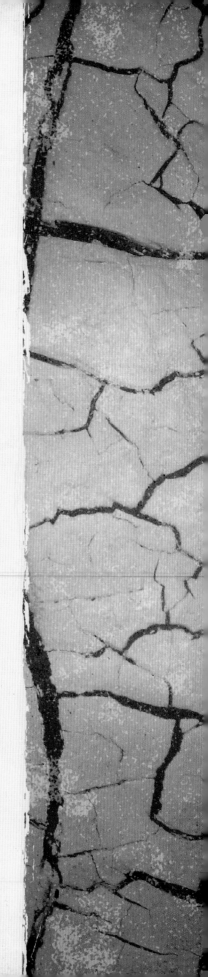

PLAN TO CREATE HUMAN-COW EMBRYOS

Fergus Walsh
BBC News Medical correspondent

UK scientists have applied for permission
to create embryos by fusing human DNA with
cow eggs. The hybrid human-bovine embryos
would be used for stem cell research and
would not be allowed to develop for more
than a few days.

Liberal Democrat MP Dr. Evan Harris
of the Commons Science and Technology
Select Committee said: "If human benefit
can be derived by perfecting therapeutic
cloning techniques or from research into
subsequently-derived stem cells, then it
would actually be immoral to prevent it just
because of a 'yuck' factor."

The problem is that human eggs for
research are in short supply and to obtain
them women have to undergo surgery. That
is why scientists want to use cows' eggs
as a substitute. They would insert human
DNA into a cow's egg which has had its
genetic material removed, and then create
an embryo by the same technique that
produced Dolly the Sheep. The resulting
embryo would be 99.9% human; the only
bovine element would be DNA outside
the nucleus of the cell. It would, though,
technically be a chimera -- a mixing of two
distinct species into one. The aim would be
to extract stem cells from the embryo when
it is six days old, before destroying it.

But some argue that the research
undermines the distinction between
animals and humans. Calum MacKellar, of
the Scottish Council on Human Bioethics,
said: "In the history of humankind, animals
and human species have been separated.
In this kind of procedure, you are mixing
at a very intimate level animal eggs and
human chromosomes, and you may begin to
undermine the whole distinction between
humans and animals.

"If that happens, it might also undermine
human dignity and human rights."

news.bbc.co.uk/1/hi/health/6121280.stm

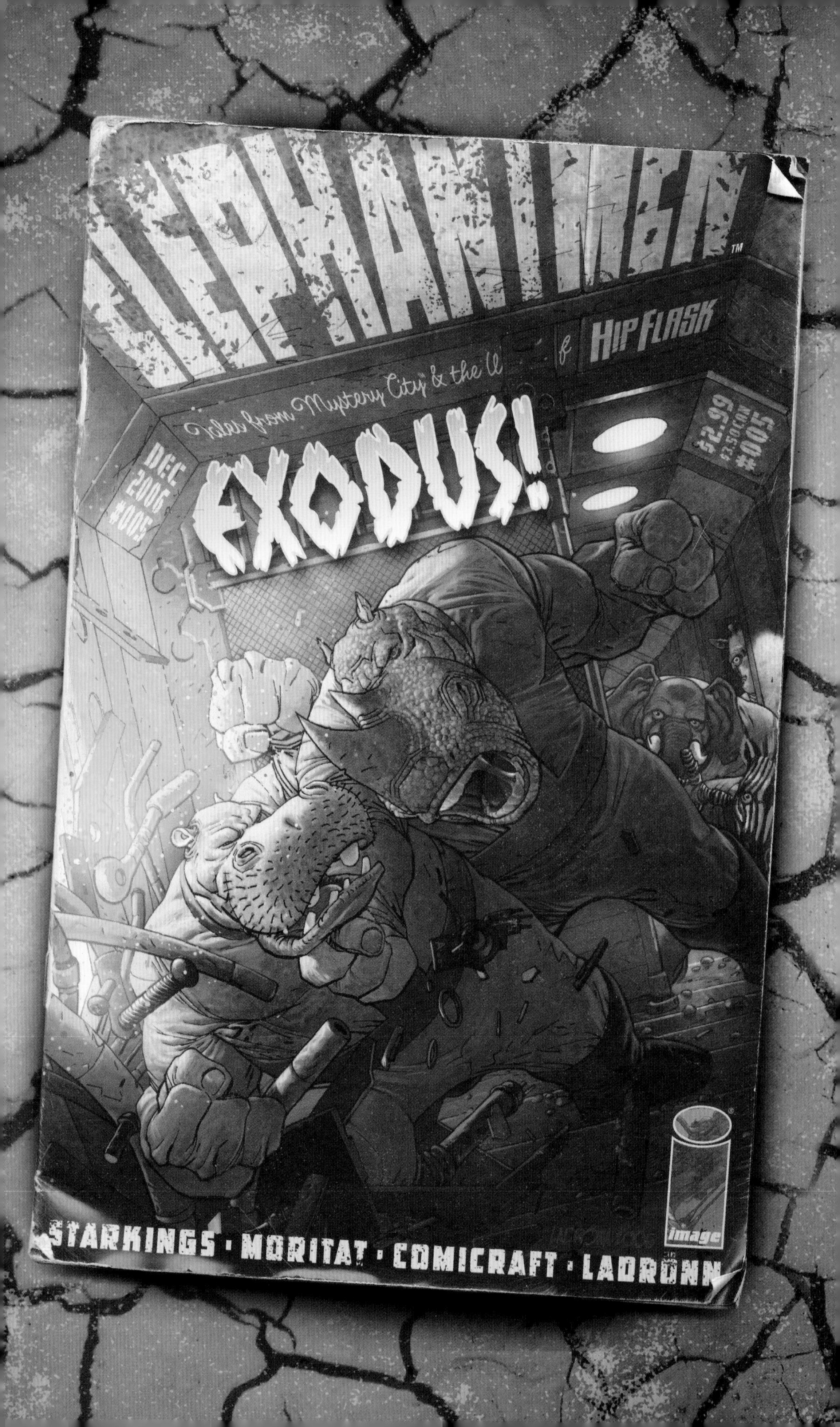

& HIP FLASK
Tales from Mystery City & the U
DEC 2006 #005
$2.99 $3.50 CAN #005
EXODUS!
image
STARKINGS · MORITAT · COMICRAFT · LADRONN

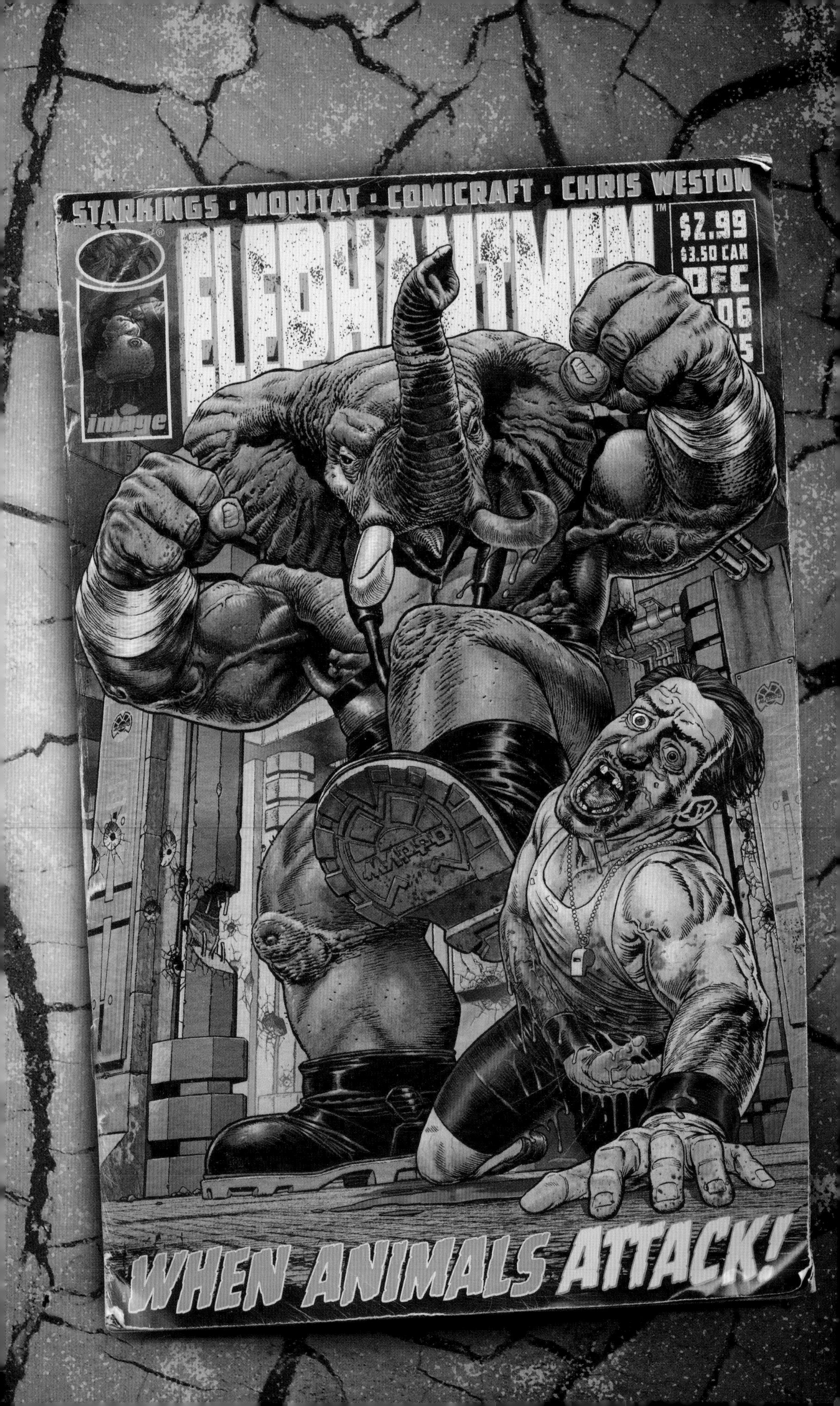
STARKINGS · MORITAT · COMICRAFT · CHRIS WESTON
ELEPHANTMEN™
$2.99
$3.50 CAN
DEC
image
WHEN ANIMALS ATTACK!

HORN INDUSTRIES TOWER

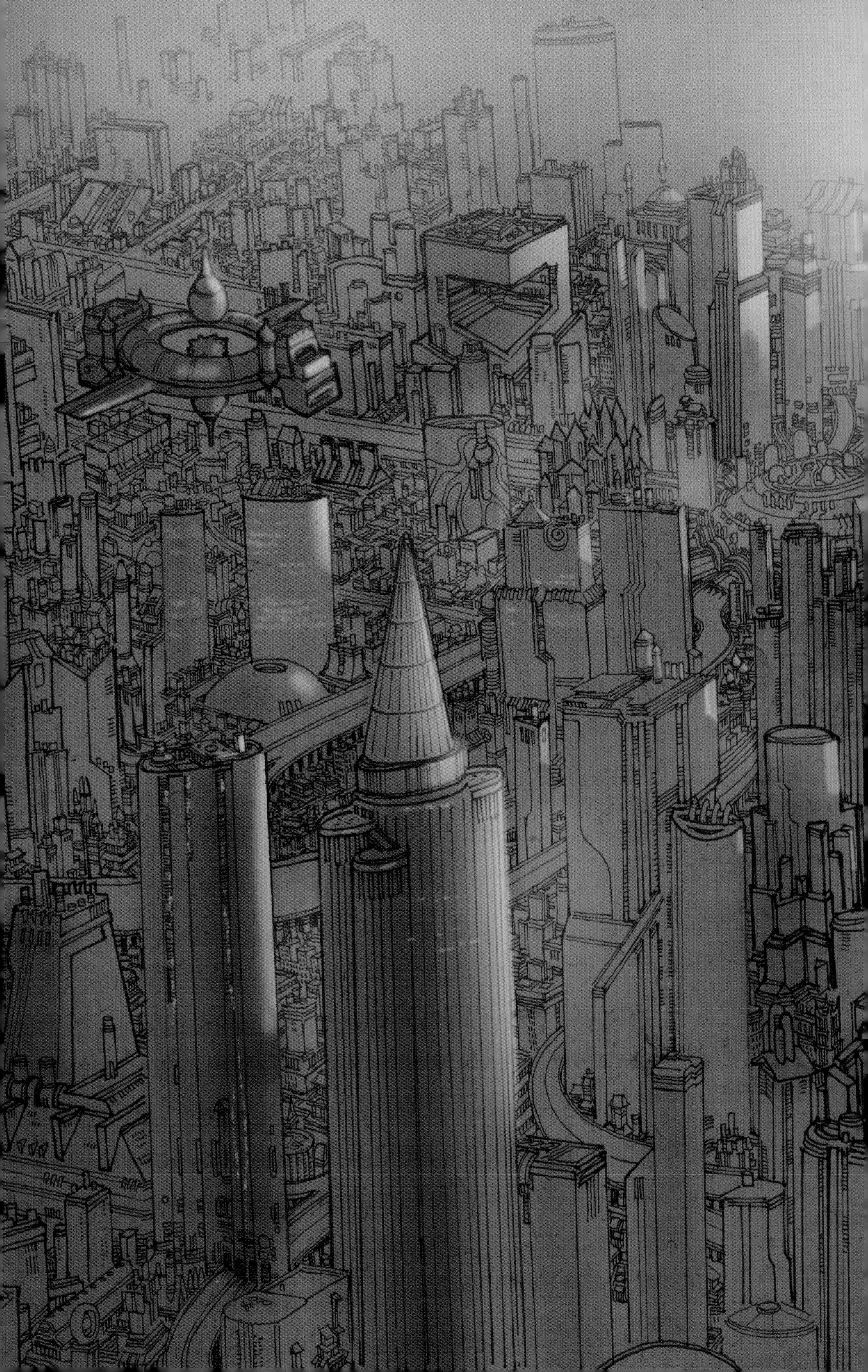

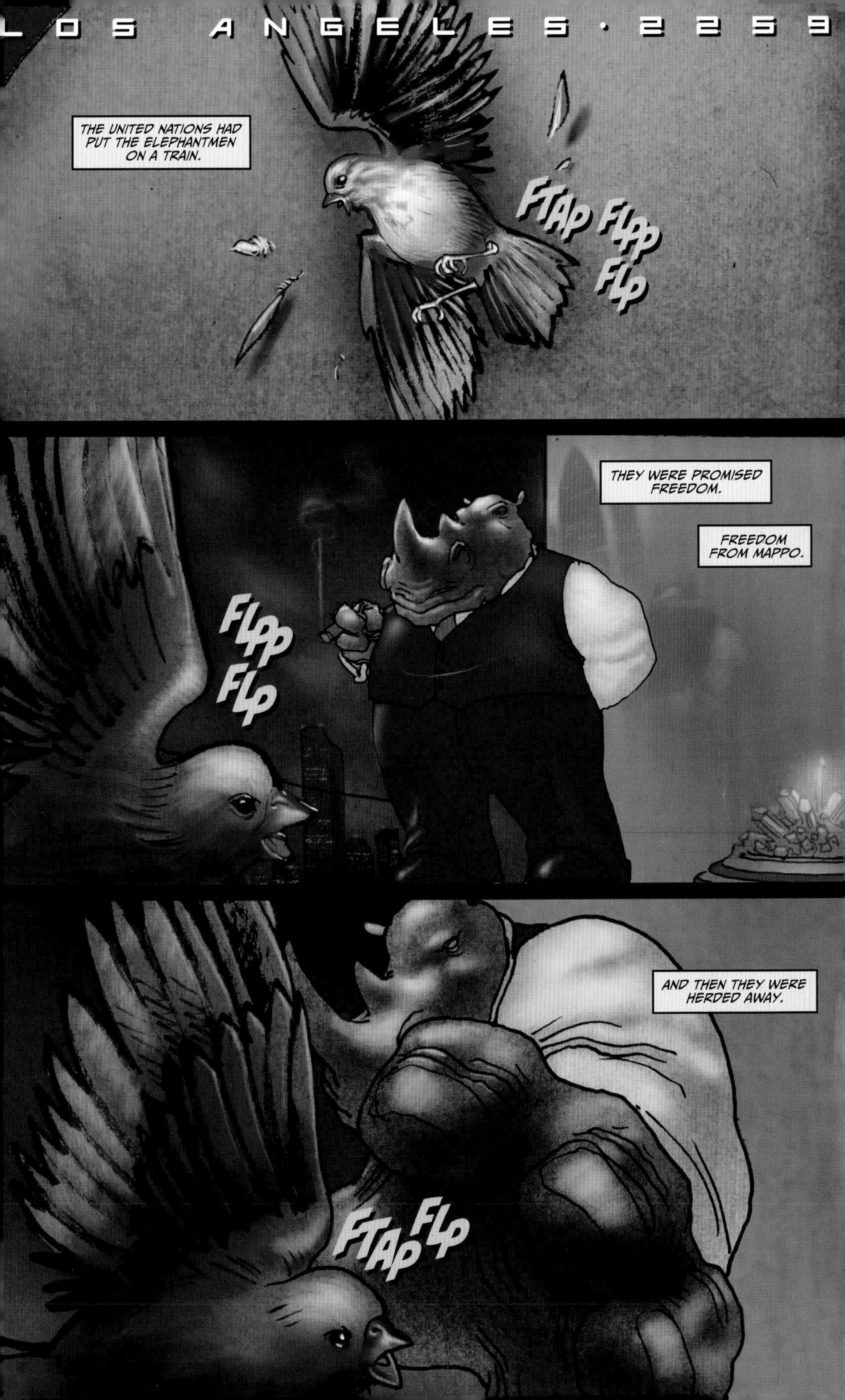
LOS ANGELES · 2259
THE UNITED NATIONS HAD PUT THE ELEPHANTMEN ON A TRAIN.
FTAP FLPP FLP
THEY WERE PROMISED FREEDOM.
FREEDOM FROM MAPPO.
FLPP FLP
AND THEN THEY WERE HERDED AWAY.
FTAP FLP

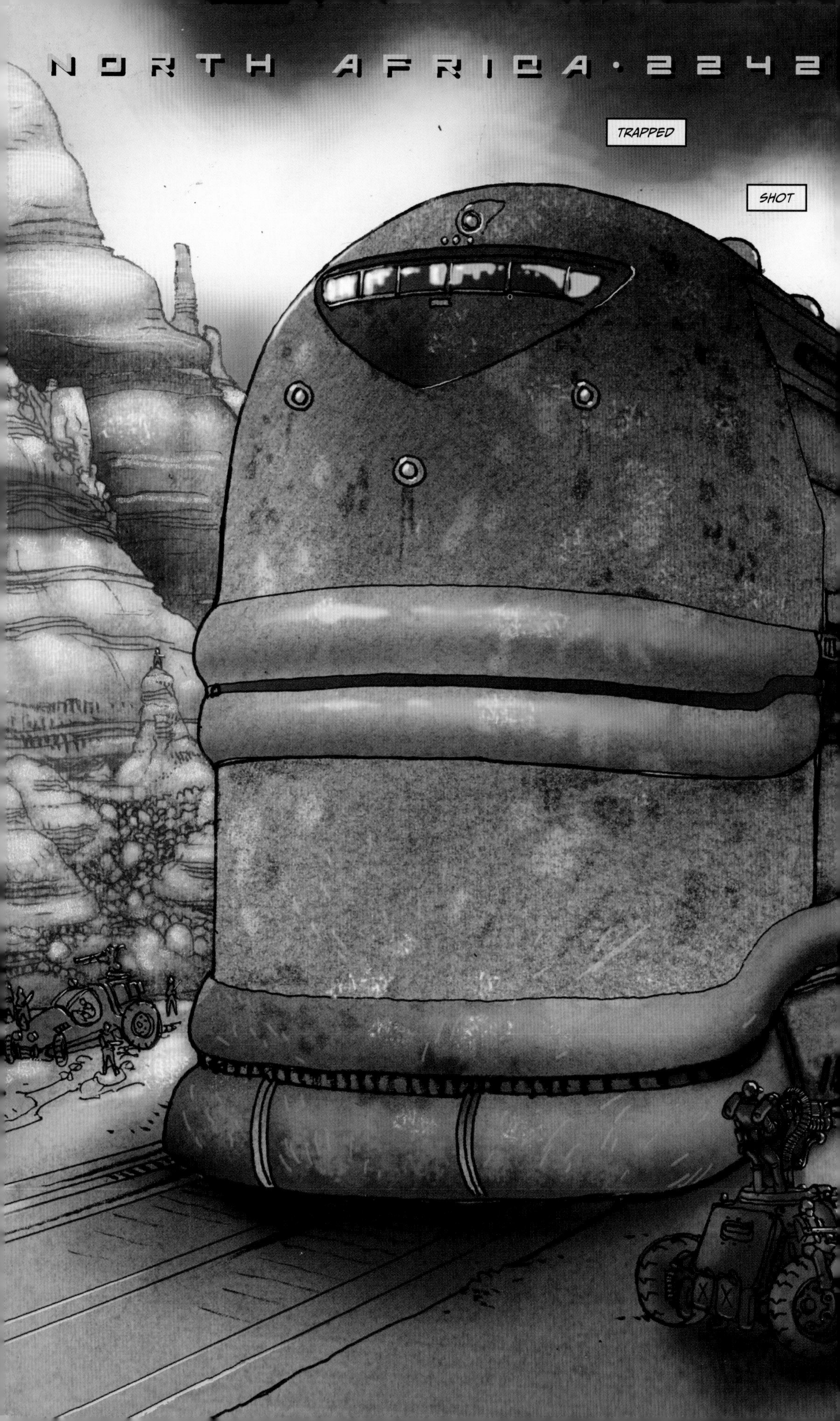
NORTH AFRICA · 2242
TRAPPED
SHOT

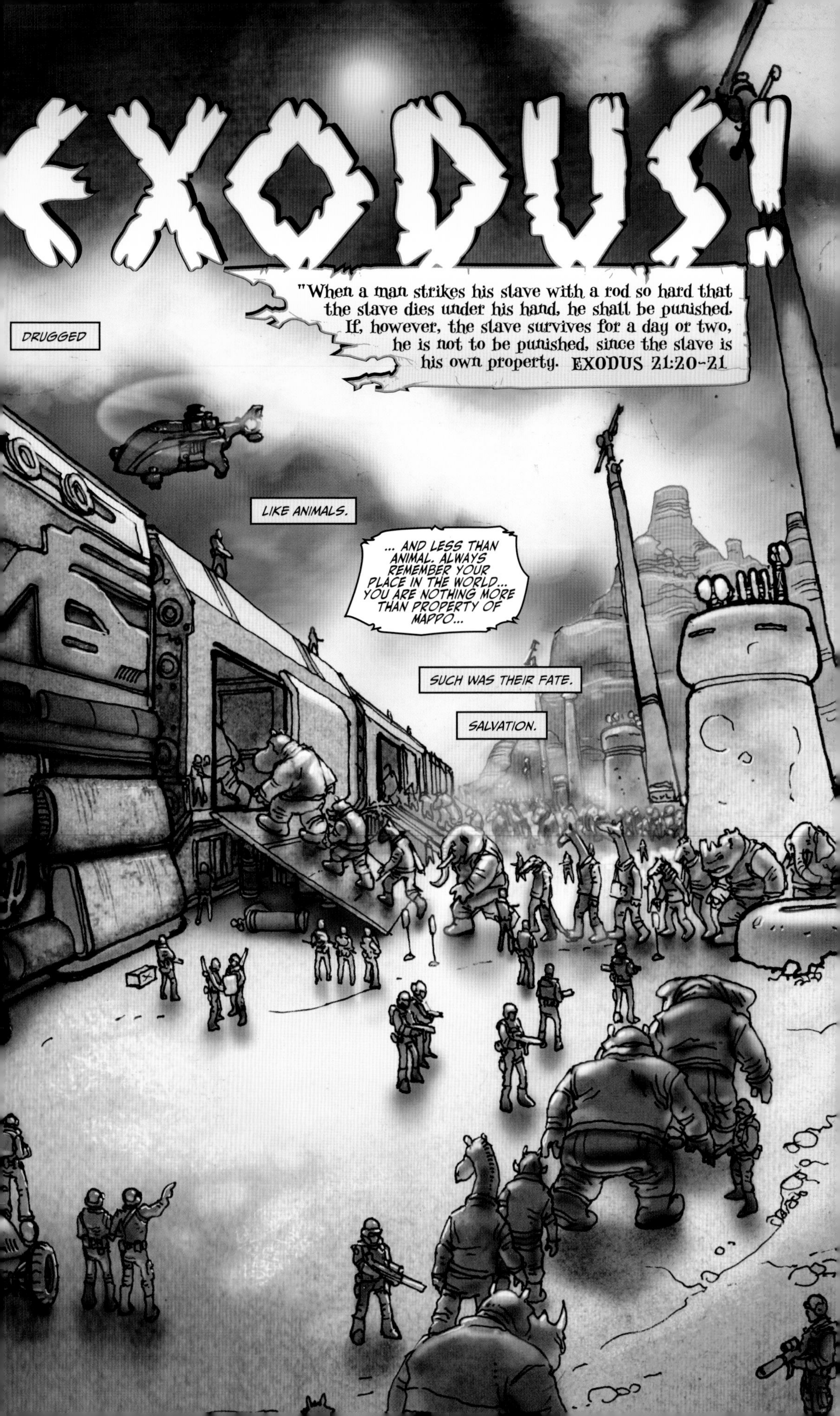
EXODUS!
"When a man strikes his slave with a rod so hard that the slave dies under his hand, he shall be punished. If, however, the slave survives for a day or two, he is not to be punished, since the slave is his own property. EXODUS 21:20-21
DRUGGED
LIKE ANIMALS.
... AND LESS THAN ANIMAL. ALWAYS REMEMBER YOUR PLACE IN THE WORLD... YOU ARE NOTHING MORE THAN PROPERTY OF MAPPO...
SUCH WAS THEIR FATE.
SALVATION.

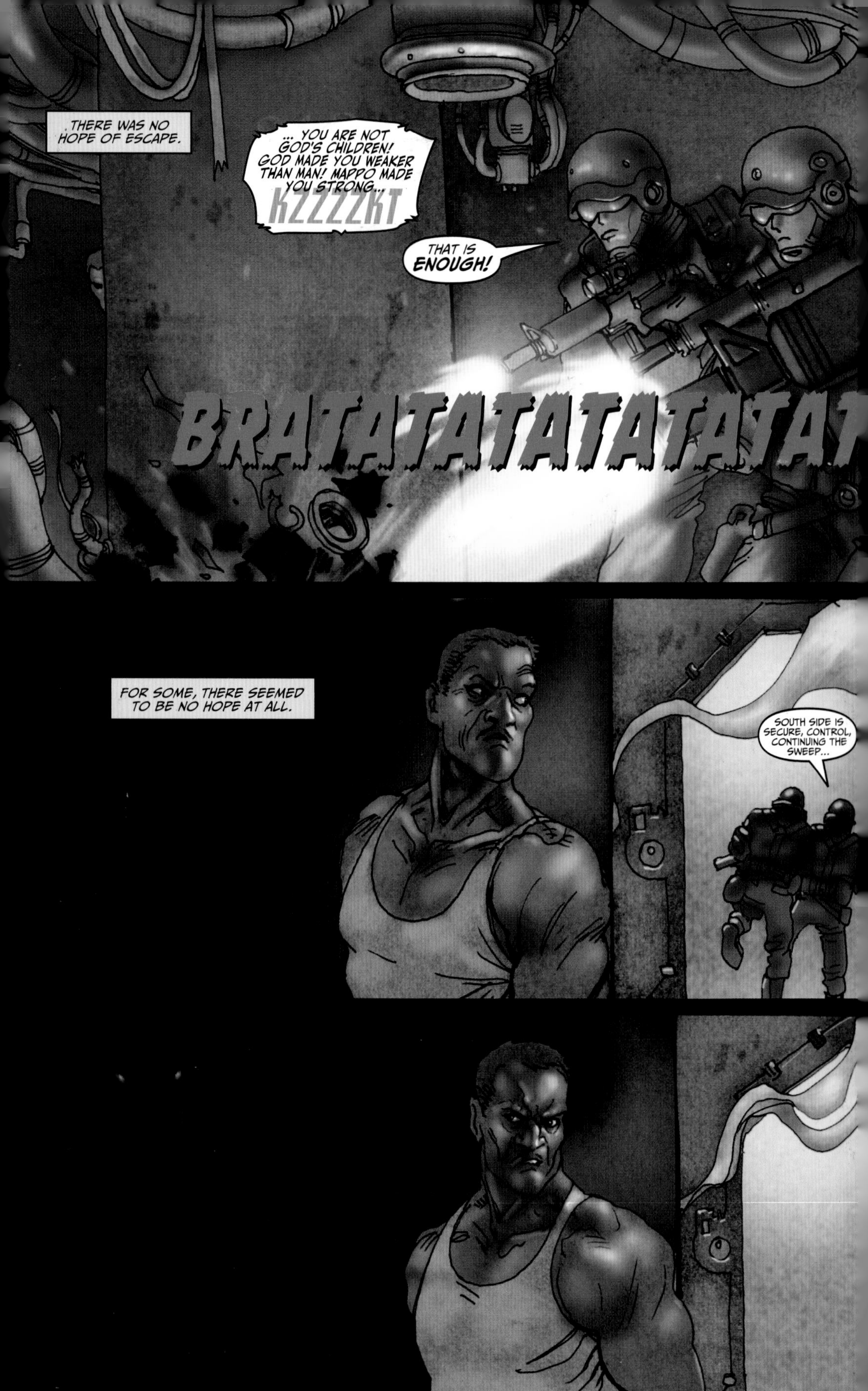
...THERE WAS NO HOPE OF ESCAPE.
... YOU ARE NOT GOD'S CHILDREN! GOD MADE YOU WEAKER THAN MAN! MAPPO MADE YOU STRONG...
KZZZZKT
THAT IS ENOUGH!
BRATATATATATATATAT
FOR SOME, THERE SEEMED TO BE NO HOPE AT ALL.
SOUTH SIDE IS SECURE, CONTROL, CONTINUING THE SWEEP...

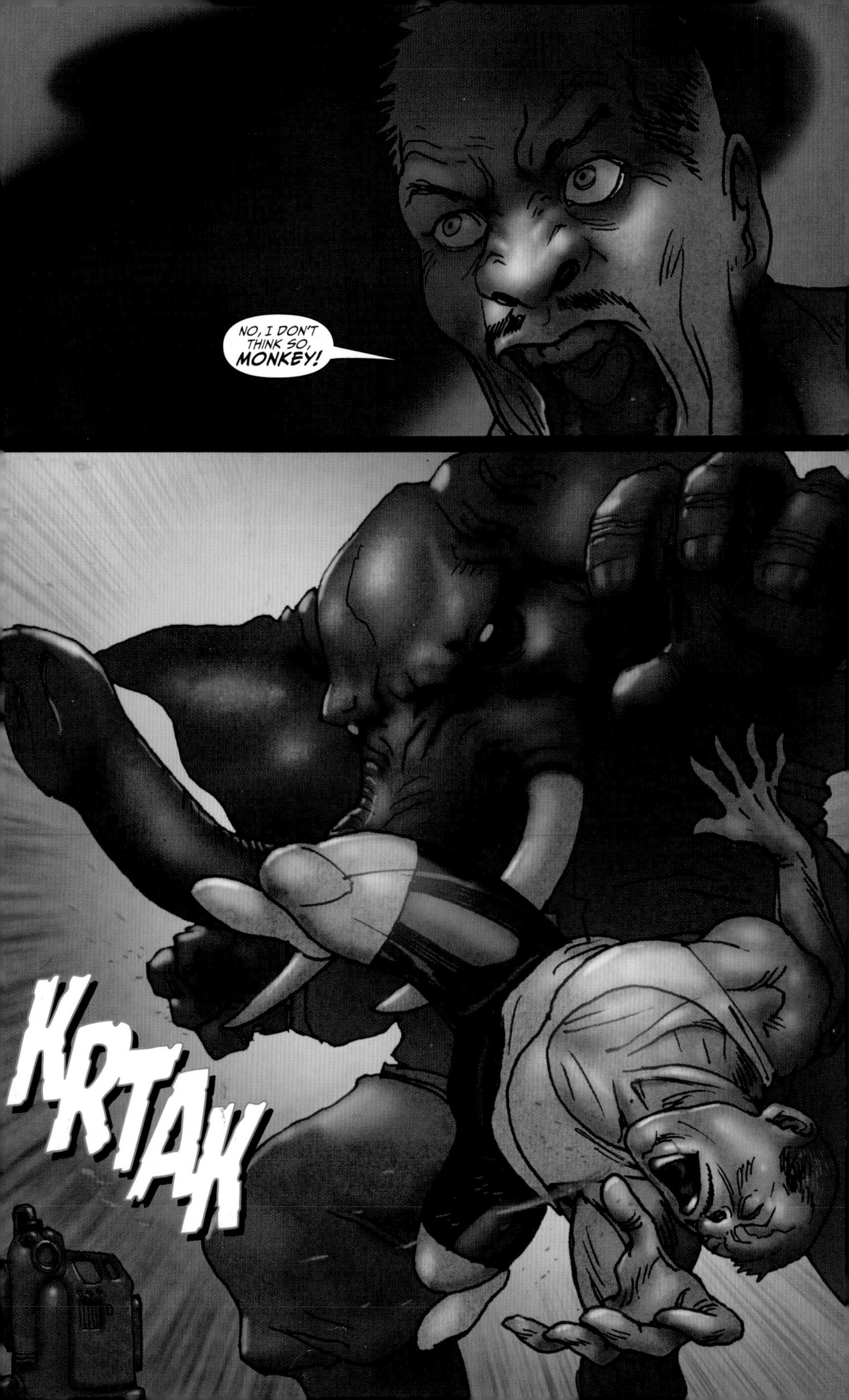
NO, I DON'T THINK SO, MONKEY!
KRTAK

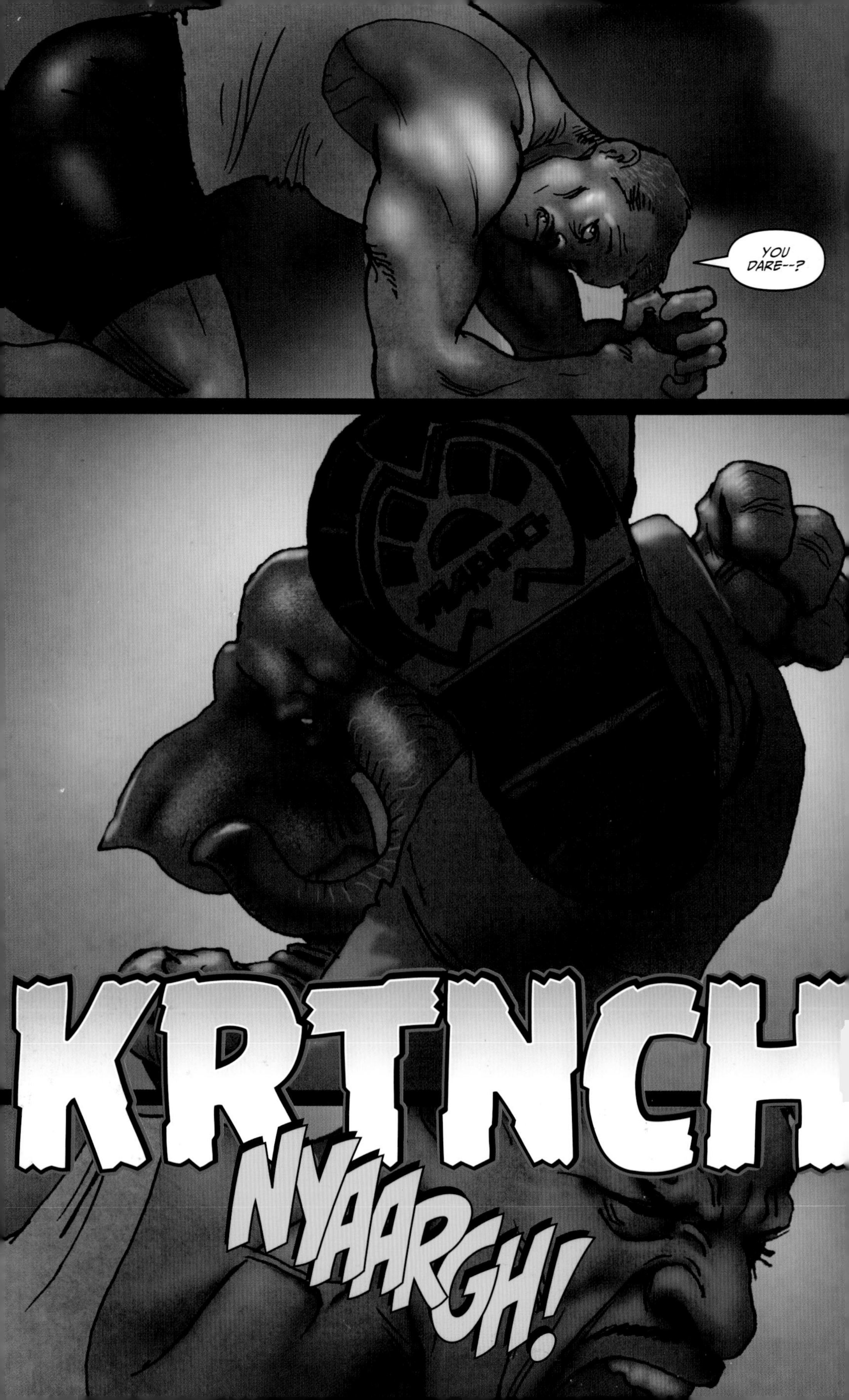
YOU DARE--?
KRTNCH
NYAARGH!

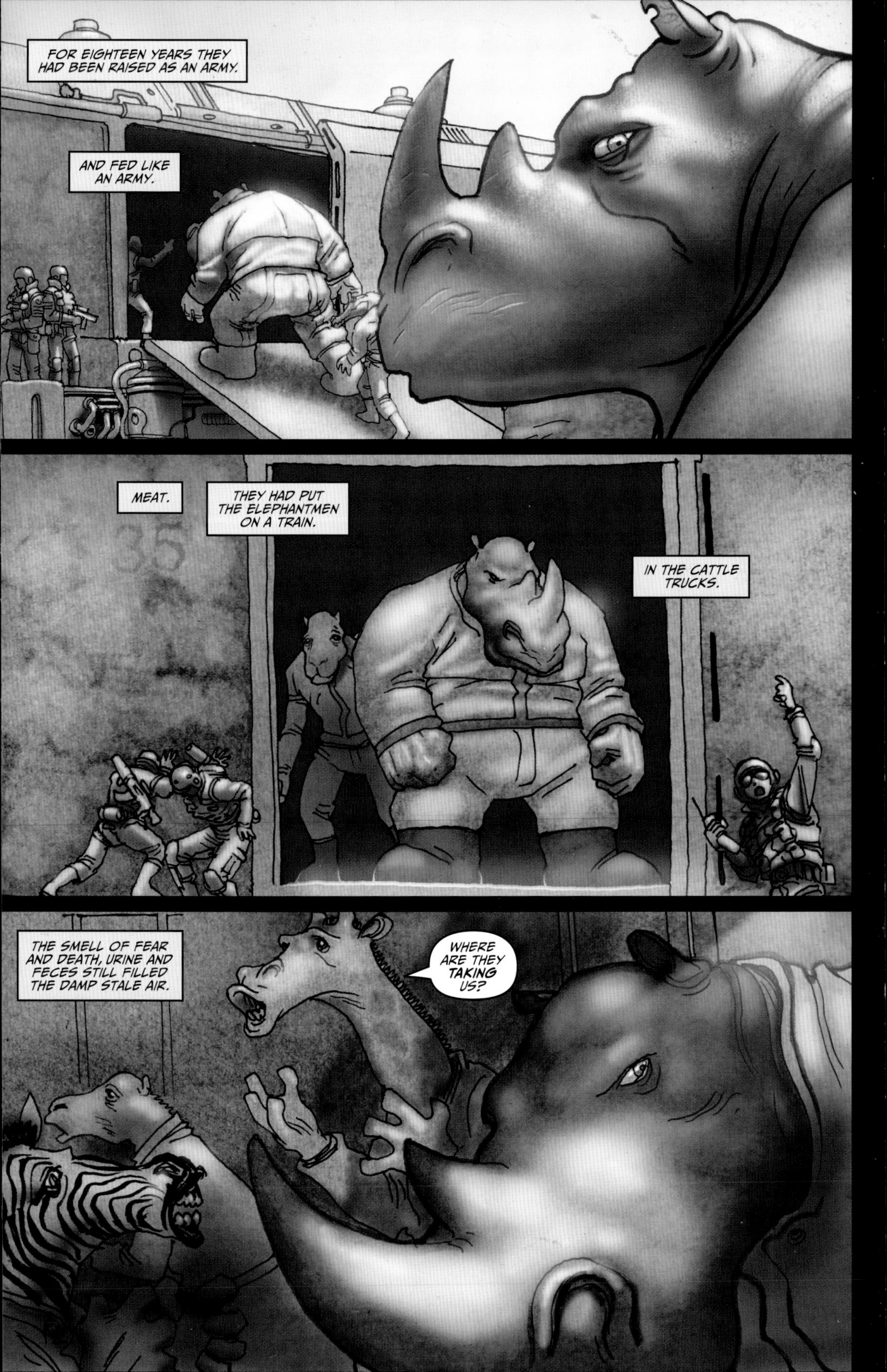
FOR EIGHTEEN YEARS THEY HAD BEEN RAISED AS AN ARMY.
AND FED LIKE AN ARMY.
MEAT.
THEY HAD PUT THE ELEPHANTMEN ON A TRAIN.
IN THE CATTLE TRUCKS.
THE SMELL OF FEAR AND DEATH, URINE AND FECES STILL FILLED THE DAMP STALE AIR.
WHERE ARE THEY TAKING US?

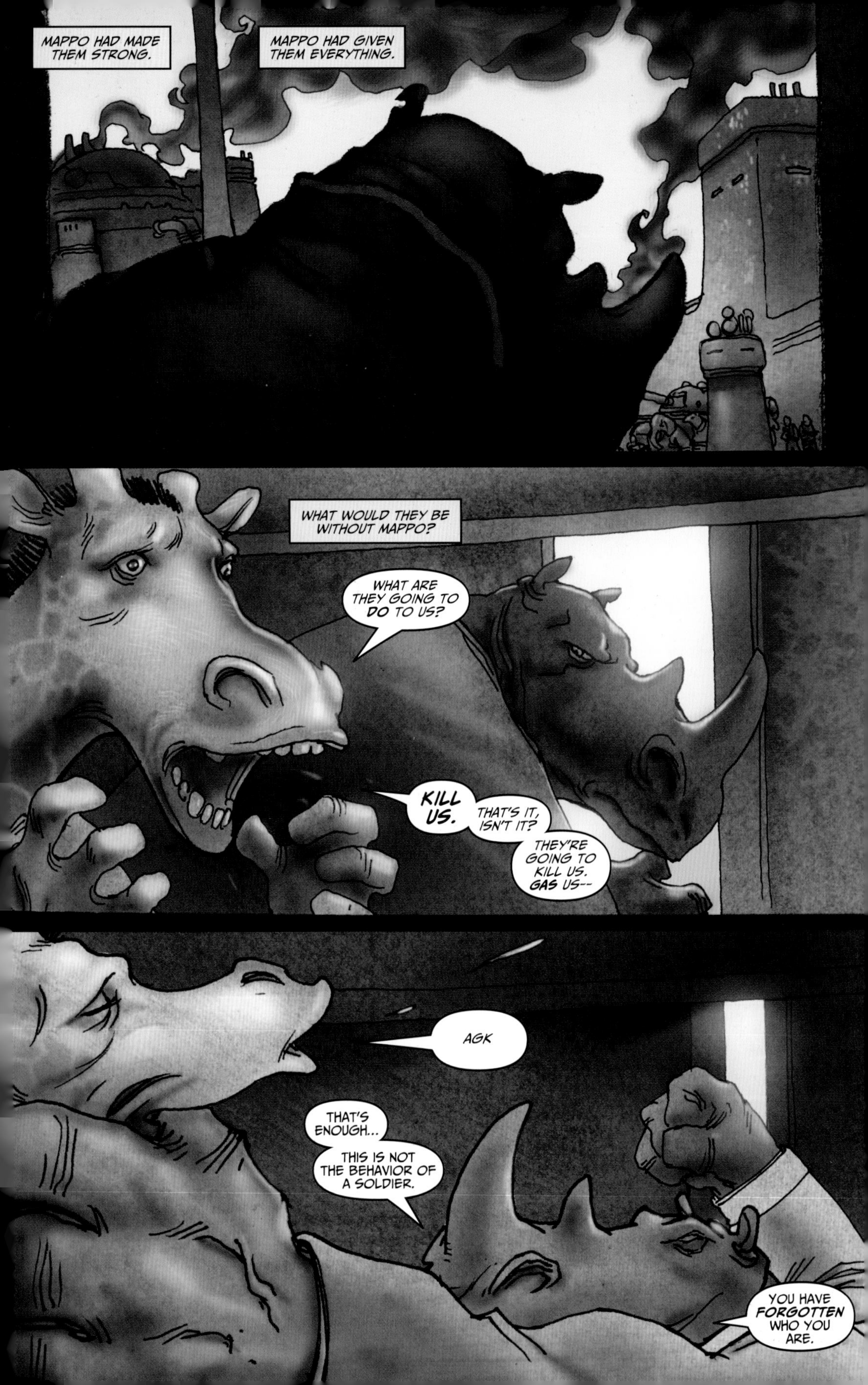
MAPPO HAD MADE THEM STRONG.
MAPPO HAD GIVEN THEM EVERYTHING.
WHAT WOULD THEY BE WITHOUT MAPPO?
WHAT ARE THEY GOING TO DO TO US?
KILL US.
THAT'S IT, ISN'T IT?
THEY'RE GOING TO KILL US. GAS US--
AGK
THAT'S ENOUGH...
THIS IS NOT THE BEHAVIOR OF A SOLDIER.
YOU HAVE FORGOTTEN WHO YOU ARE.

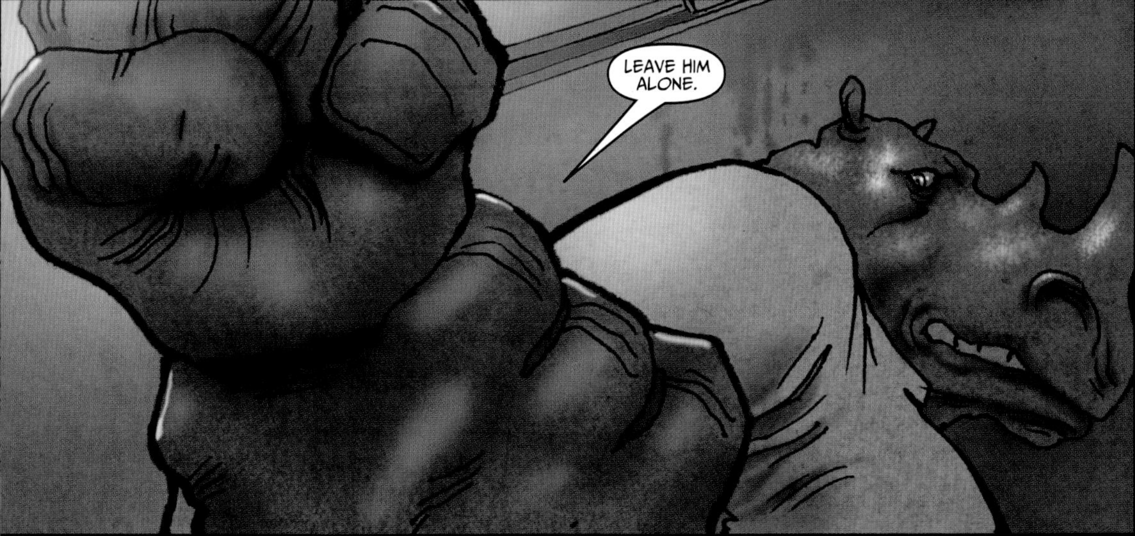
LEAVE HIM ALONE.

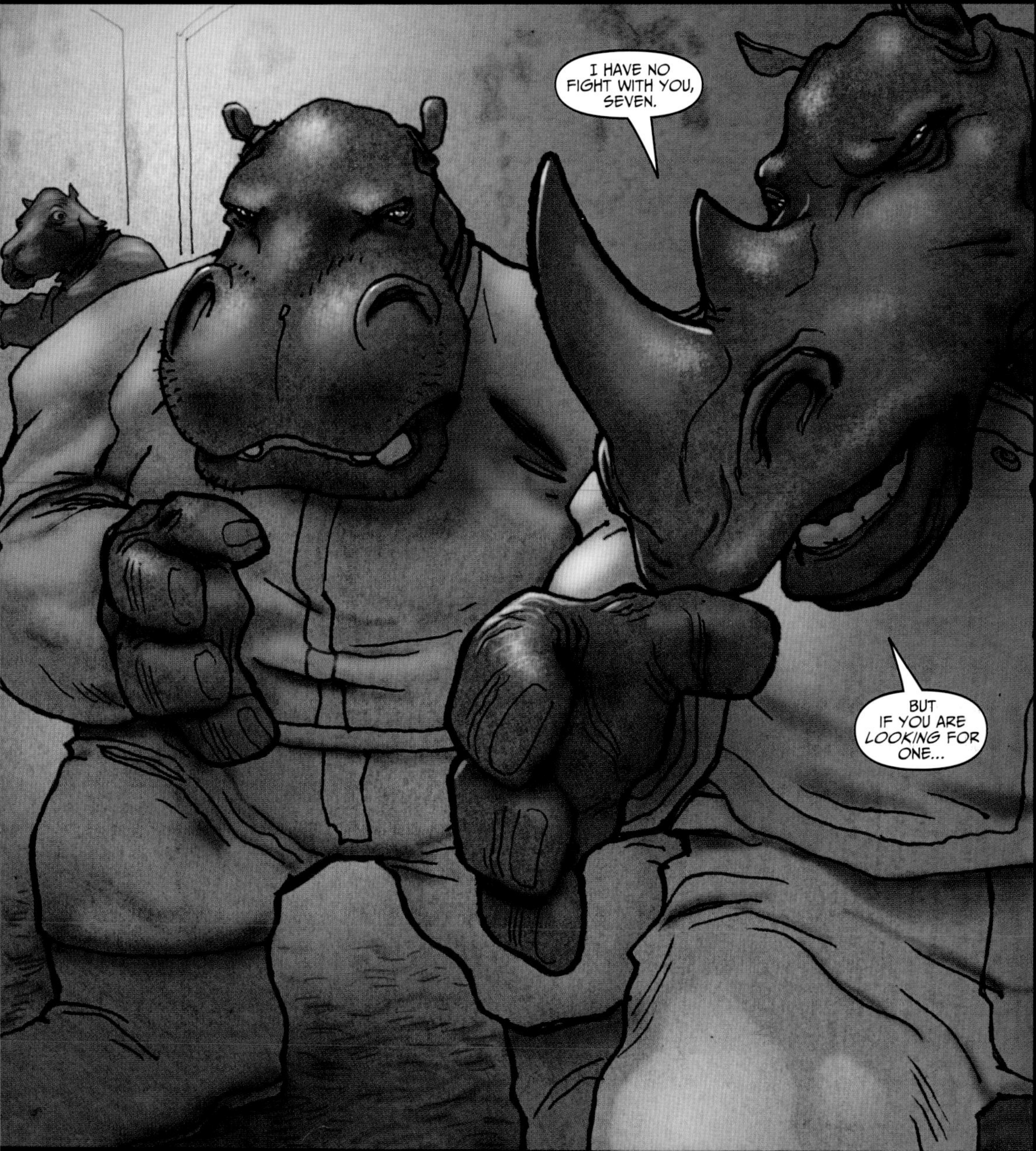
I HAVE NO FIGHT WITH YOU, SEVEN.
BUT IF YOU ARE *LOOKING* FOR ONE...

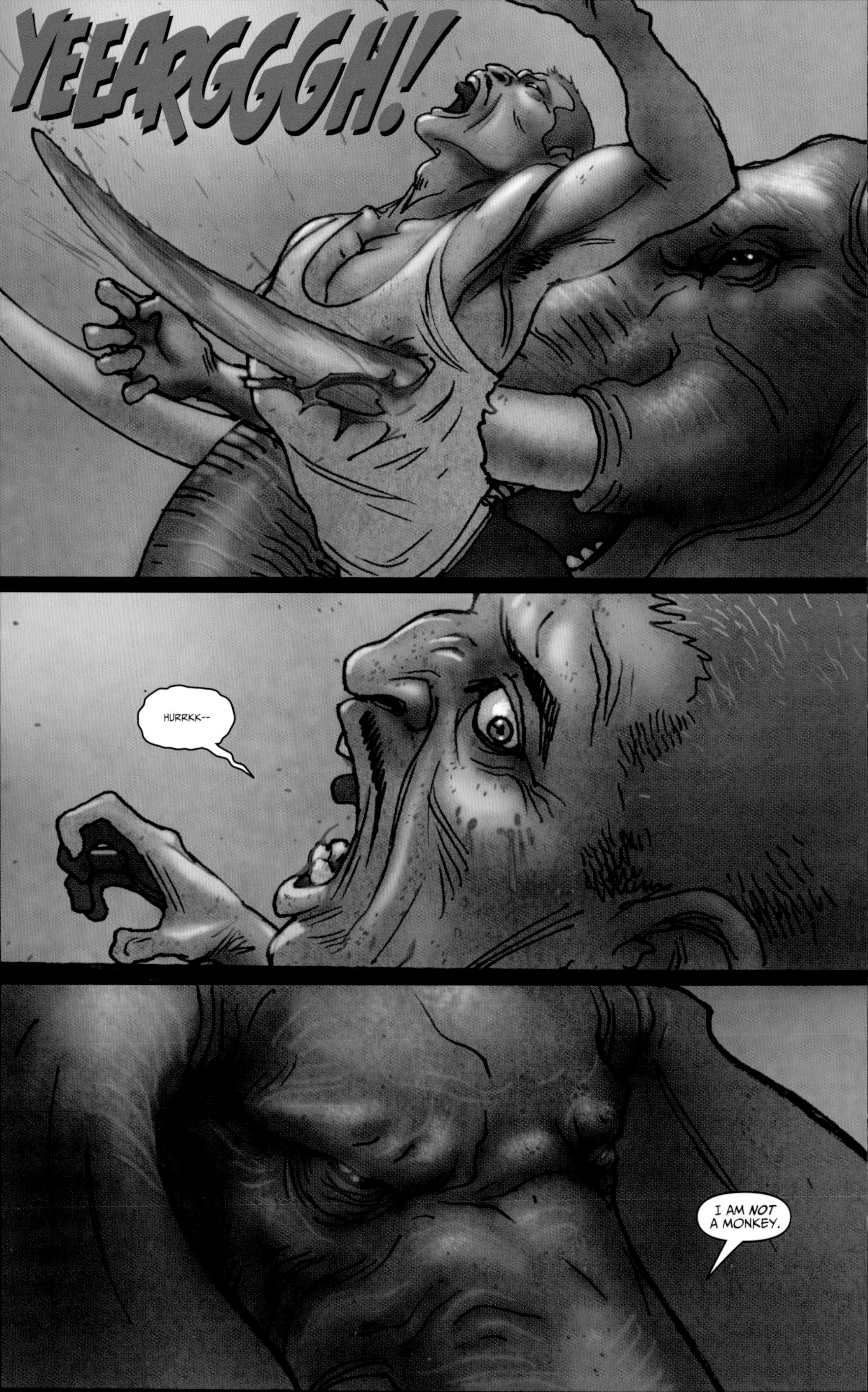
YEEARGGGH!
HURRKK--
I AM *NOT* A MONKEY.

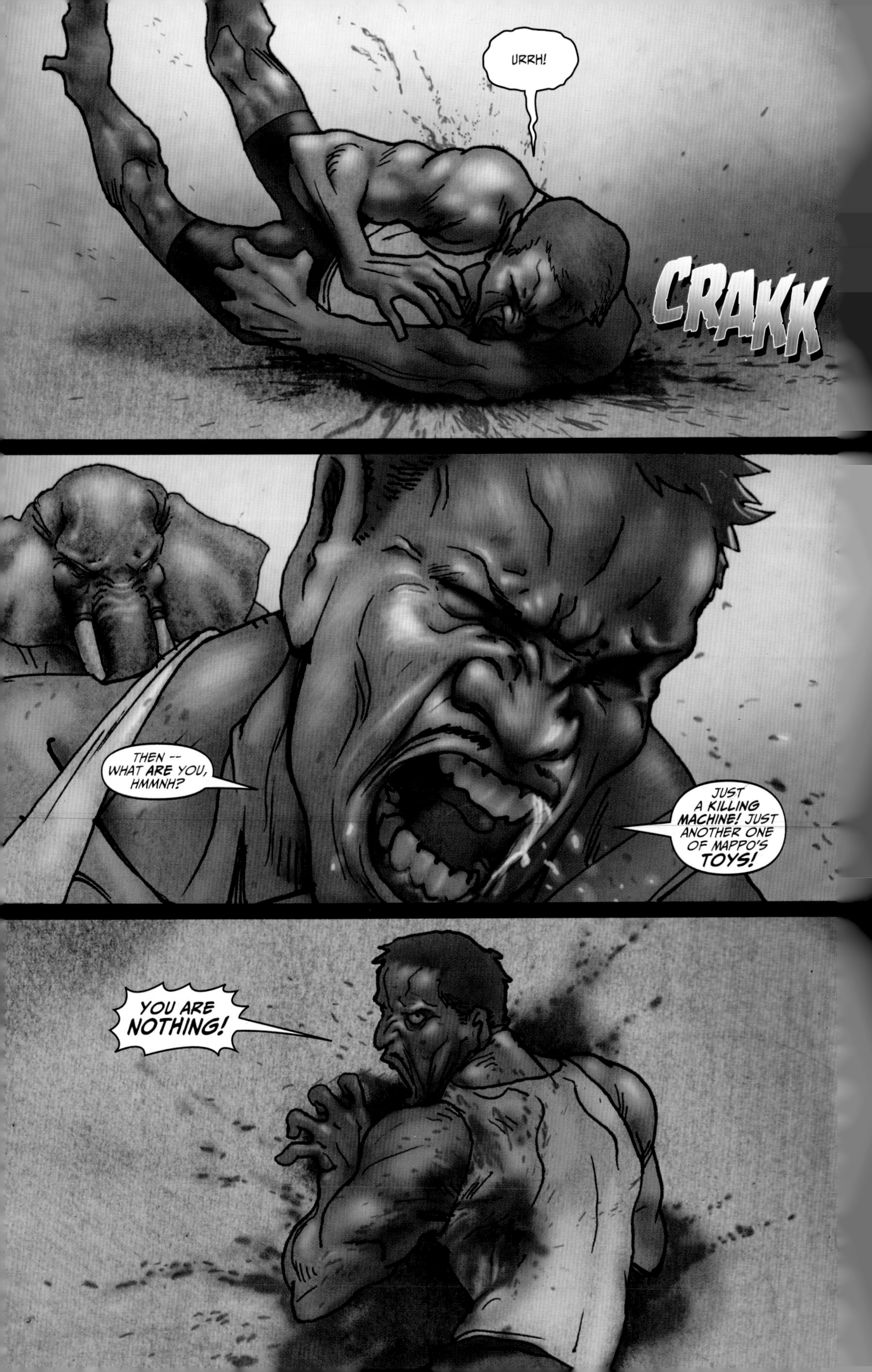
URRH!
CRAKK
THEN -- WHAT ARE YOU, HMMNH?
JUST A KILLING MACHINE! JUST ANOTHER ONE OF MAPPO'S TOYS!
YOU ARE NOTHING!

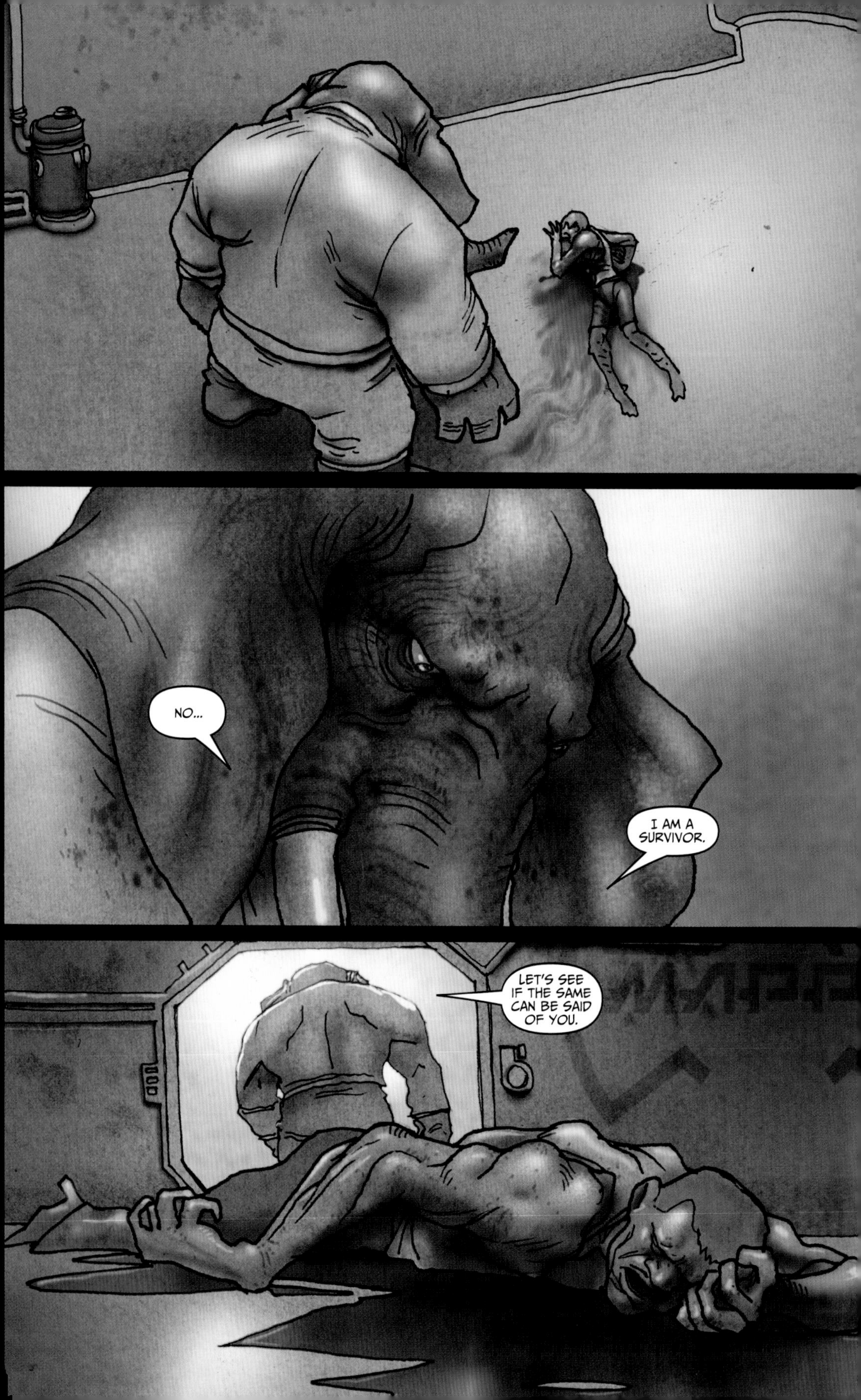
NO...
I AM A SURVIVOR.
LET'S SEE IF THE SAME CAN BE SAID OF YOU.

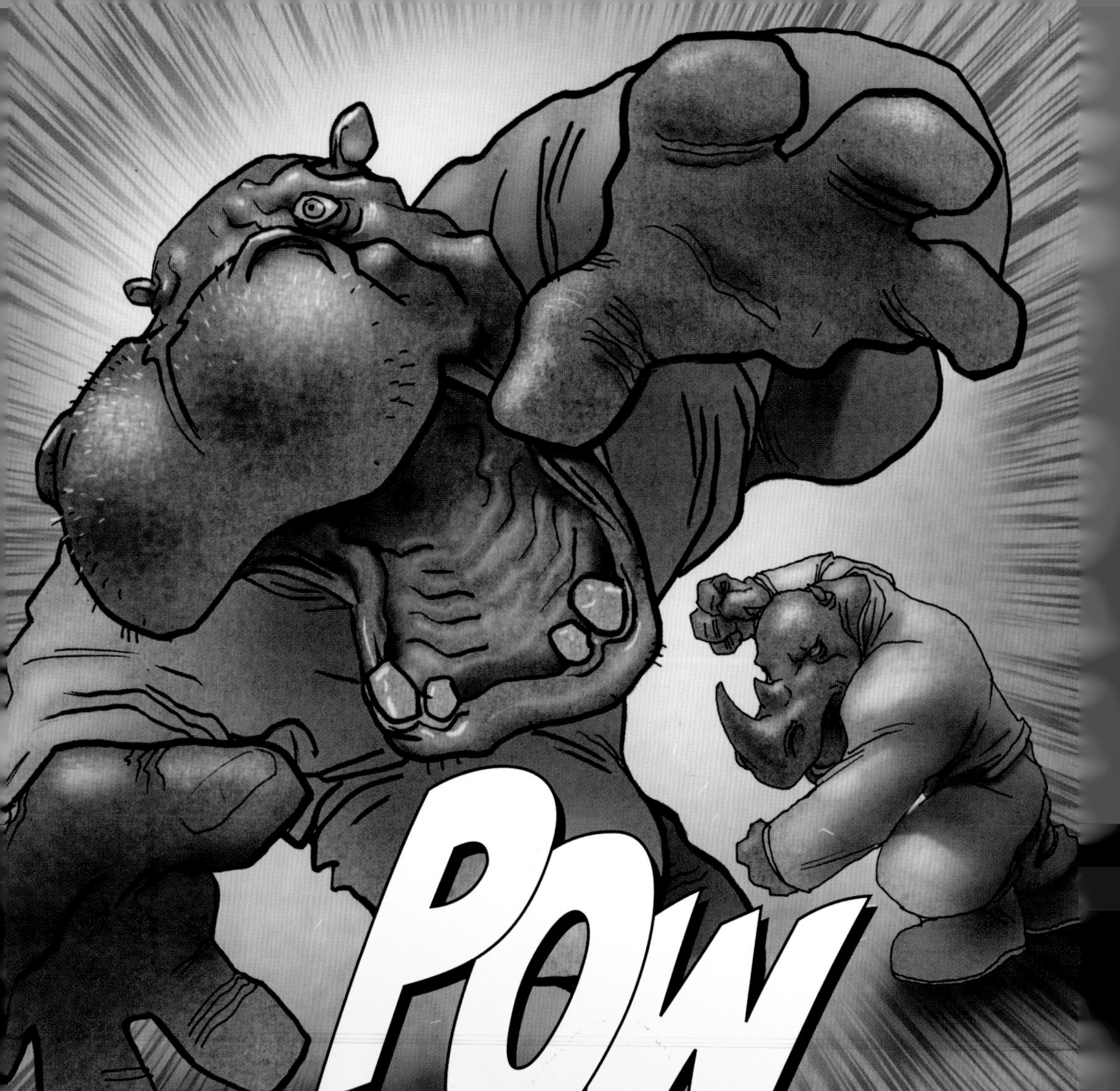
POW

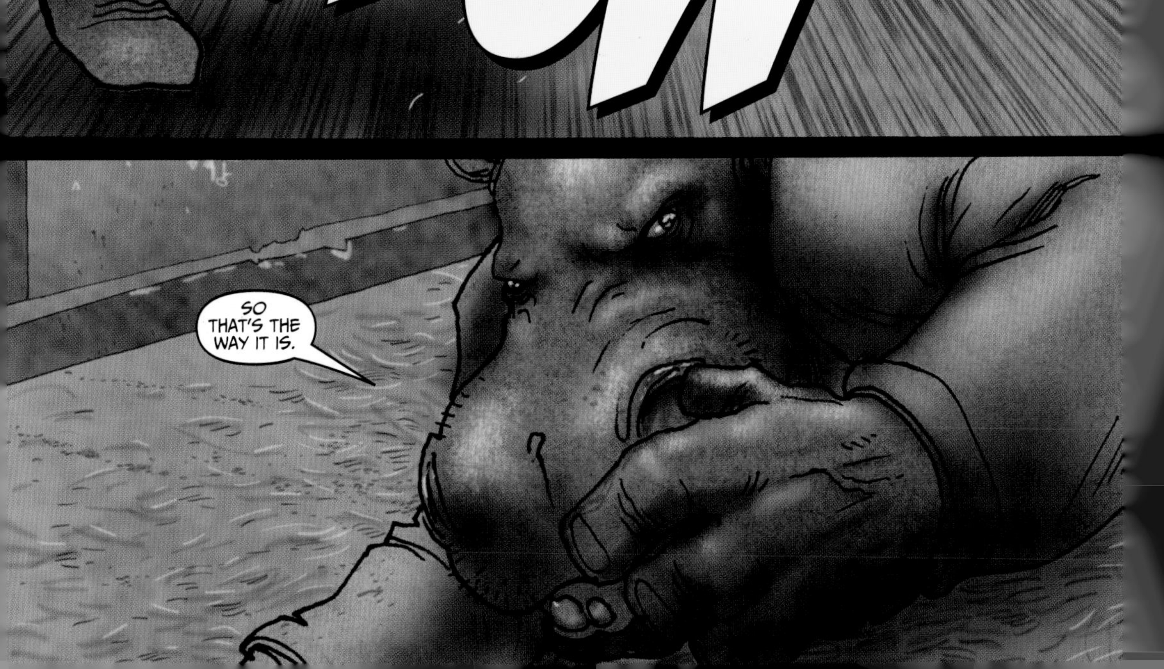
SO THAT'S THE WAY IT IS.

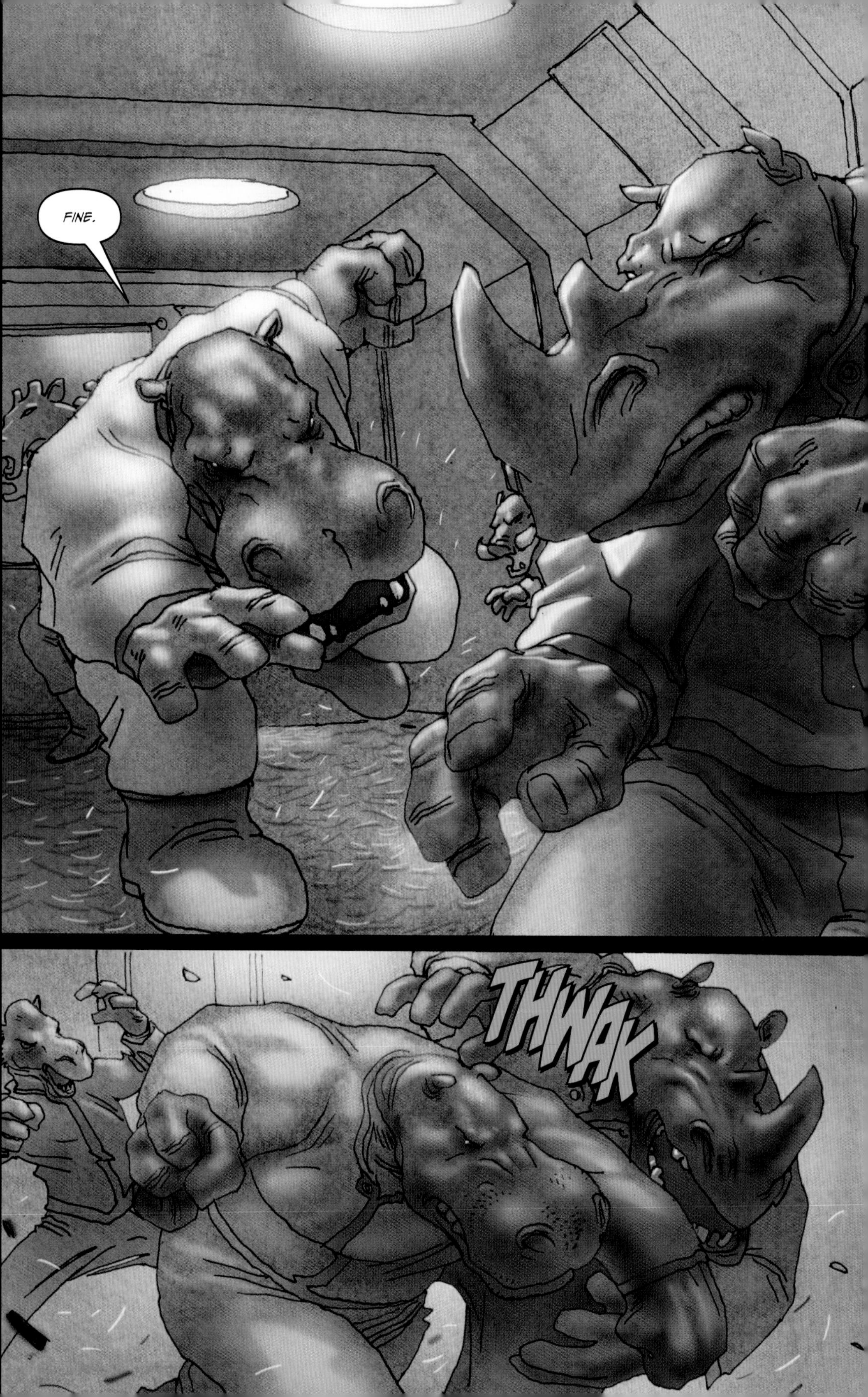
FINE.
THWAK

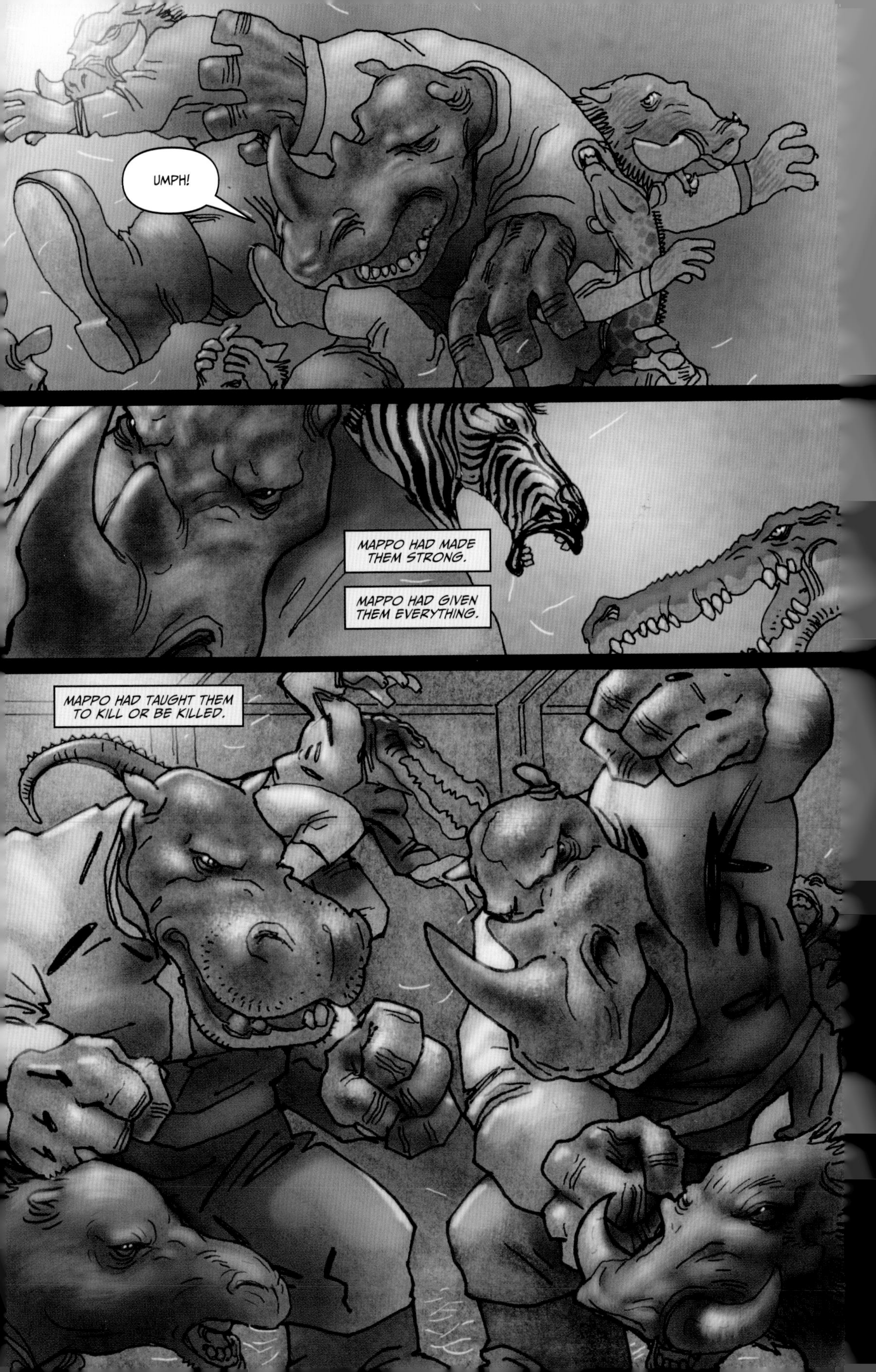
UMPH!
MAPPO HAD MADE THEM STRONG.
MAPPO HAD GIVEN THEM EVERYTHING.
MAPPO HAD TAUGHT THEM TO KILL OR BE KILLED.

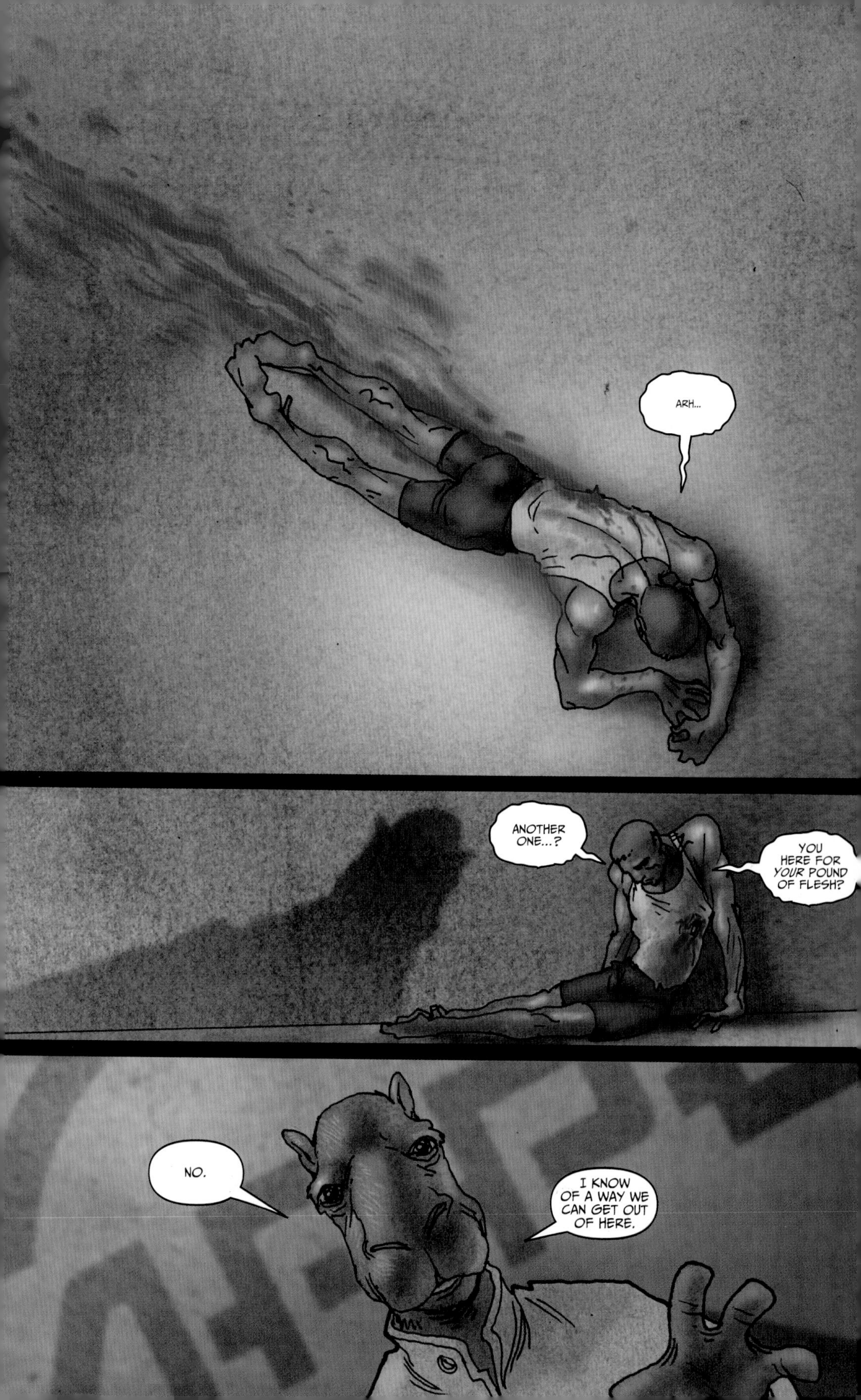
ARH...
ANOTHER ONE...?
YOU HERE FOR *YOUR* POUND OF FLESH?
NO.
I KNOW OF A WAY WE CAN GET OUT OF HERE.

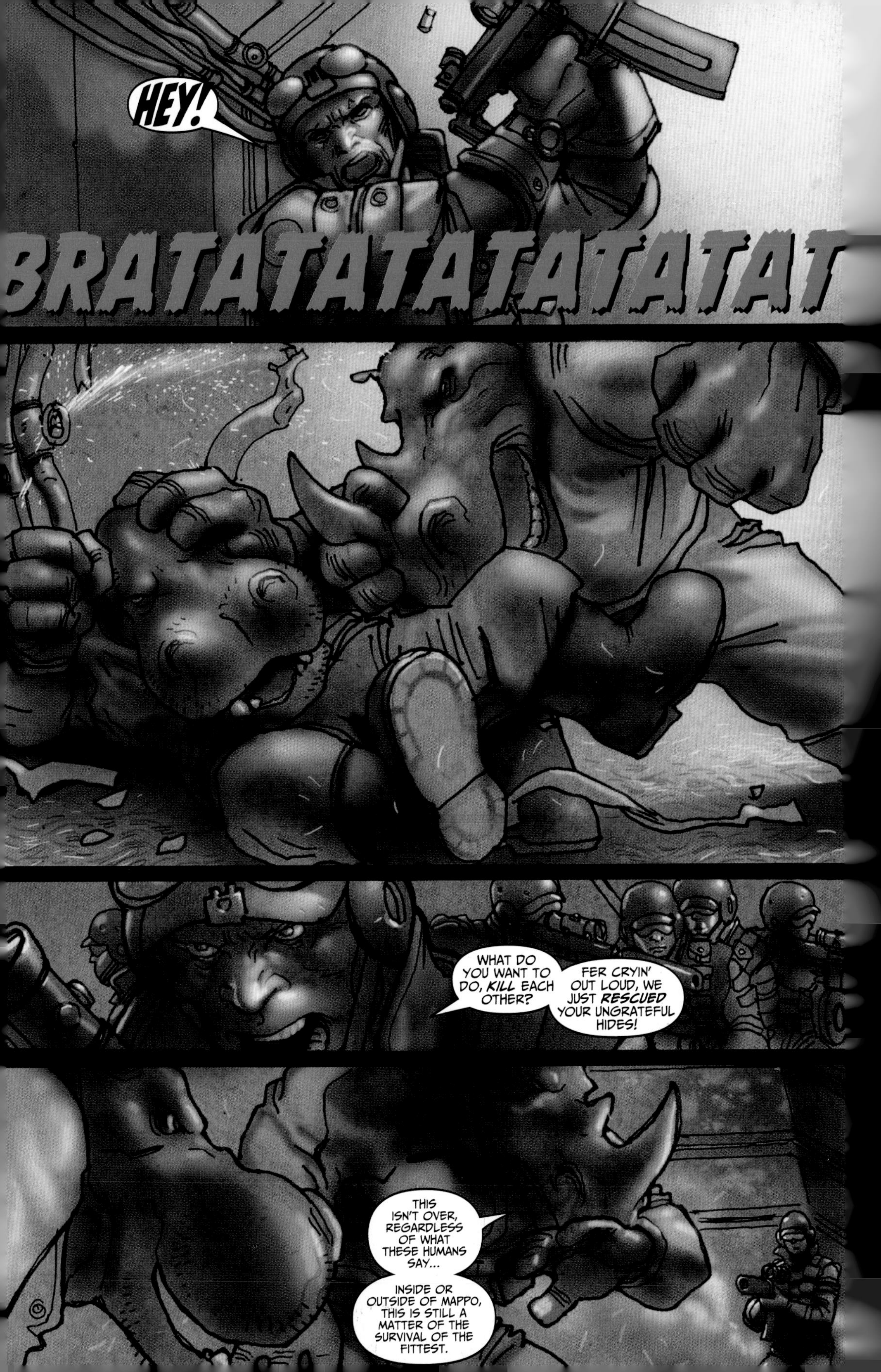
HEY!
BRATATATATATATAT
WHAT DO YOU WANT TO DO, KILL EACH OTHER?
FER CRYIN' OUT LOUD, WE JUST RESCUED YOUR UNGRATEFUL HIDES!
THIS ISN'T OVER, REGARDLESS OF WHAT THESE HUMANS SAY...
INSIDE OR OUTSIDE OF MAPPO, THIS IS STILL A MATTER OF THE SURVIVAL OF THE FITTEST.

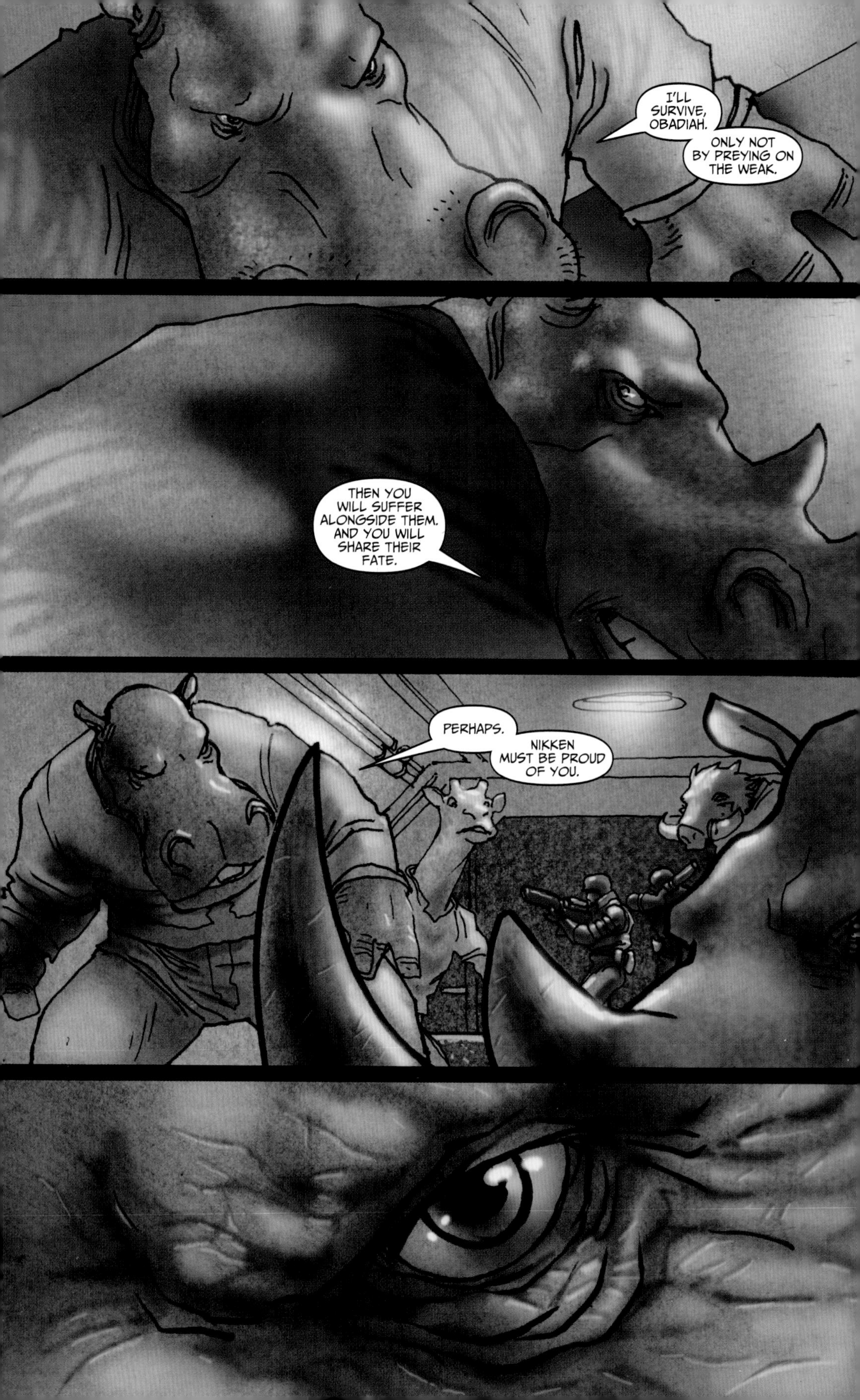
I'LL SURVIVE, OBADIAH.
ONLY NOT BY PREYING ON THE WEAK.
THEN YOU WILL SUFFER ALONGSIDE THEM. AND YOU WILL SHARE THEIR FATE.
PERHAPS.
NIKKEN MUST BE PROUD OF YOU.

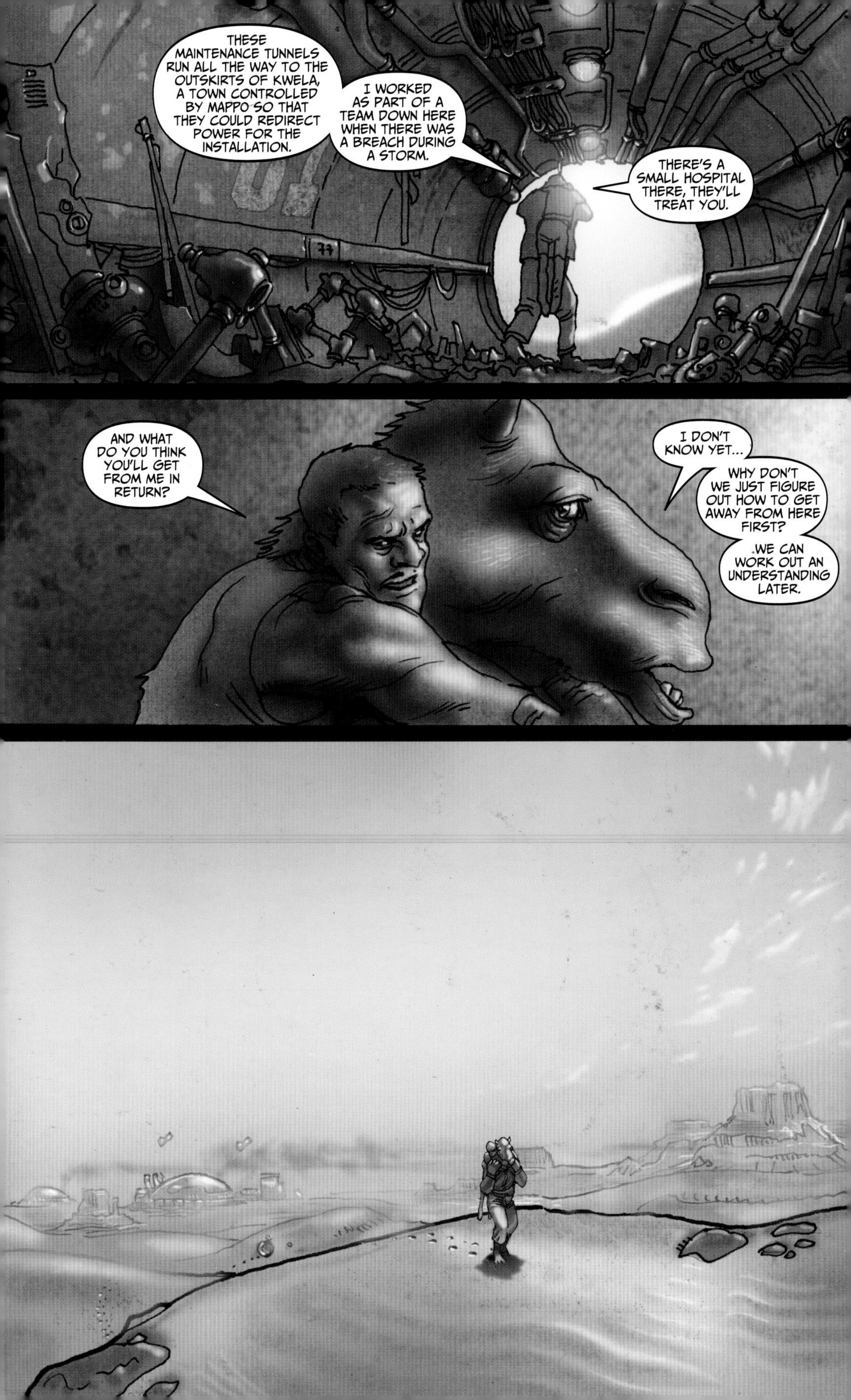
THESE MAINTENANCE TUNNELS RUN ALL THE WAY TO THE OUTSKIRTS OF KWELA, A TOWN CONTROLLED BY MAPPO SO THAT THEY COULD REDIRECT POWER FOR THE INSTALLATION.
I WORKED AS PART OF A TEAM DOWN HERE WHEN THERE WAS A BREACH DURING A STORM.
THERE'S A SMALL HOSPITAL THERE, THEY'LL TREAT YOU.
AND WHAT DO YOU THINK YOU'LL GET FROM ME IN RETURN?
I DON'T KNOW YET...
WHY DON'T WE JUST FIGURE OUT HOW TO GET AWAY FROM HERE FIRST?
WE CAN WORK OUT AN UNDERSTANDING LATER.

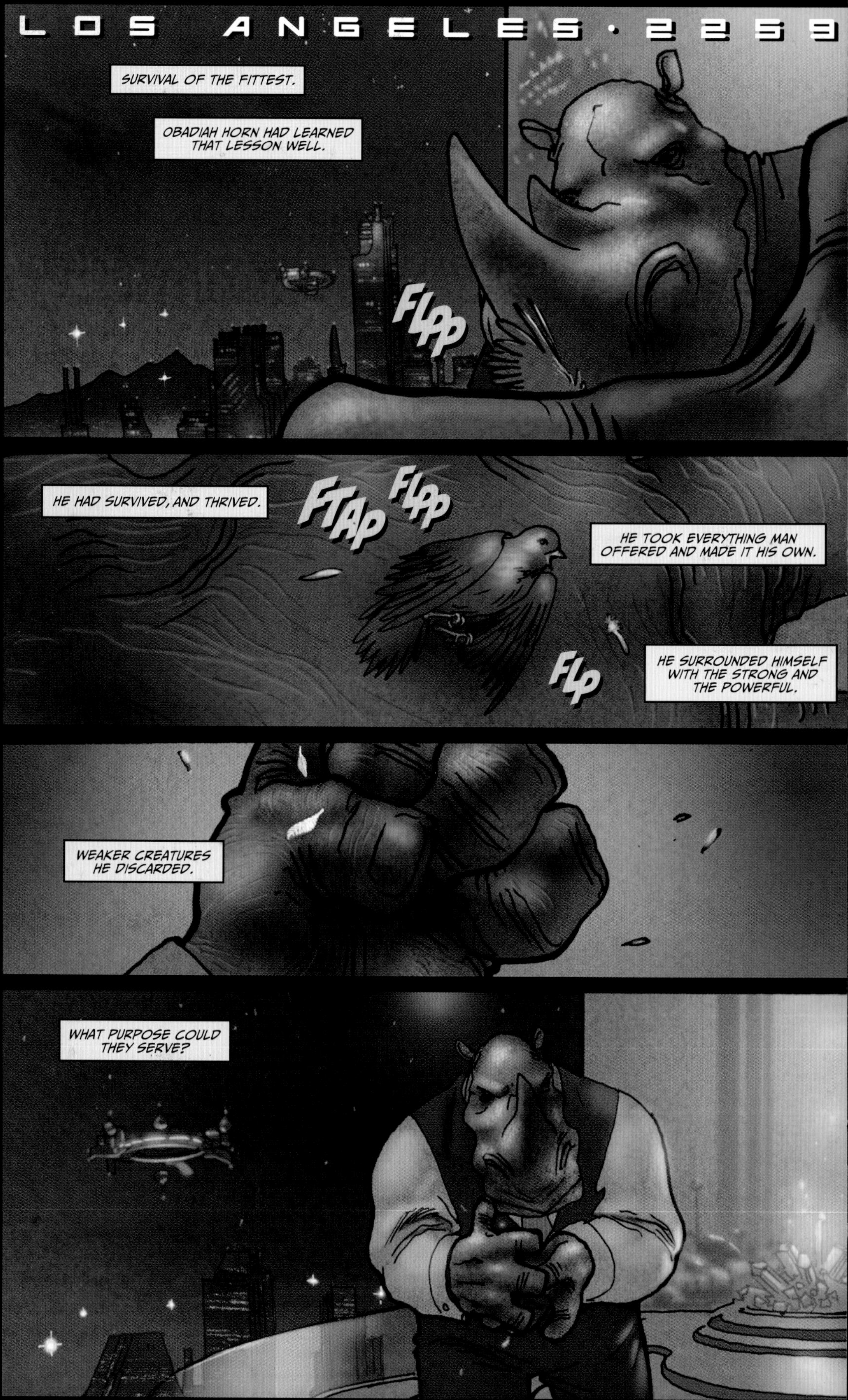
LOS ANGELES · 2259
SURVIVAL OF THE FITTEST.
OBADIAH HORN HAD LEARNED THAT LESSON WELL.
FLPP
HE HAD SURVIVED, AND THRIVED.
FTAP
FLPP
HE TOOK EVERYTHING MAN OFFERED AND MADE IT HIS OWN.
FLP
HE SURROUNDED HIMSELF WITH THE STRONG AND THE POWERFUL.
WEAKER CREATURES HE DISCARDED.
WHAT PURPOSE COULD THEY SERVE?

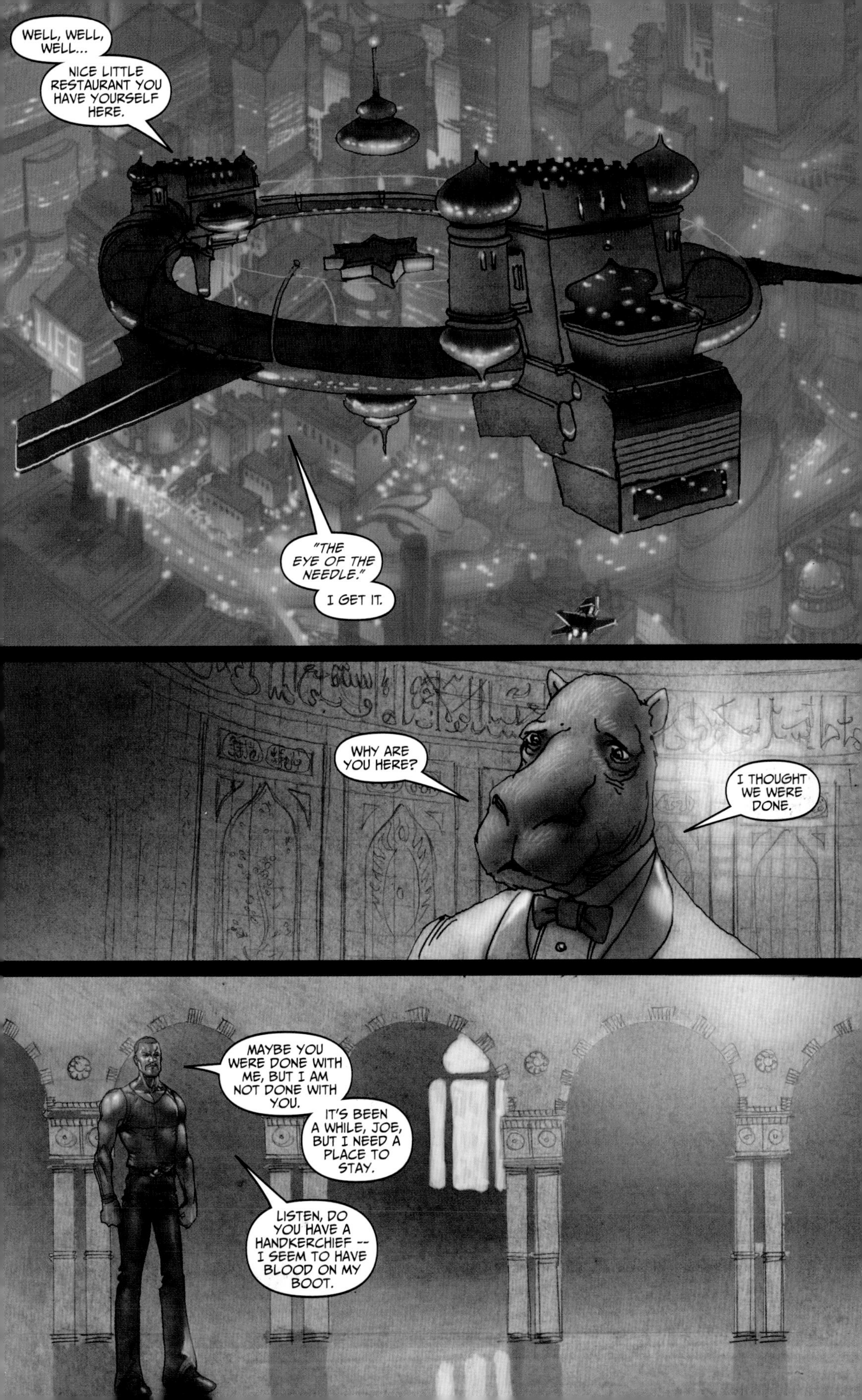
WELL, WELL, WELL...
NICE LITTLE RESTAURANT YOU HAVE YOURSELF HERE.
"THE EYE OF THE NEEDLE."
I GET IT.
WHY ARE YOU HERE?
I THOUGHT WE WERE DONE.
MAYBE YOU WERE DONE WITH ME, BUT I AM NOT DONE WITH YOU.
IT'S BEEN A WHILE, JOE, BUT I NEED A PLACE TO STAY.
LISTEN, DO YOU HAVE A HANDKERCHIEF -- I SEEM TO HAVE BLOOD ON MY BOOT.

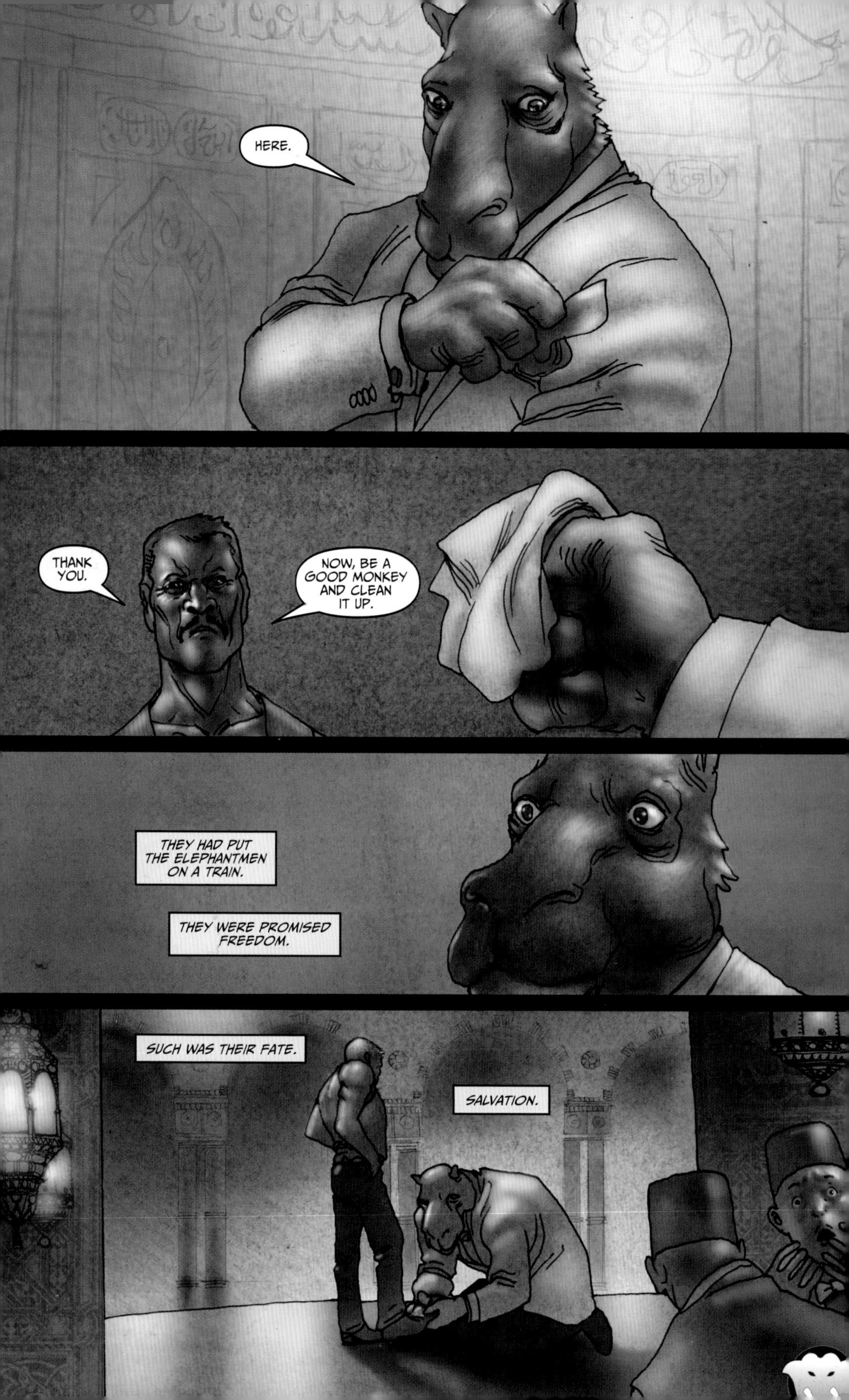
HERE.
THANK YOU.
NOW, BE A GOOD MONKEY AND CLEAN IT UP.
THEY HAD PUT THE ELEPHANTMEN ON A TRAIN.
THEY WERE PROMISED FREEDOM.
SUCH WAS THEIR FATE.
SALVATION.

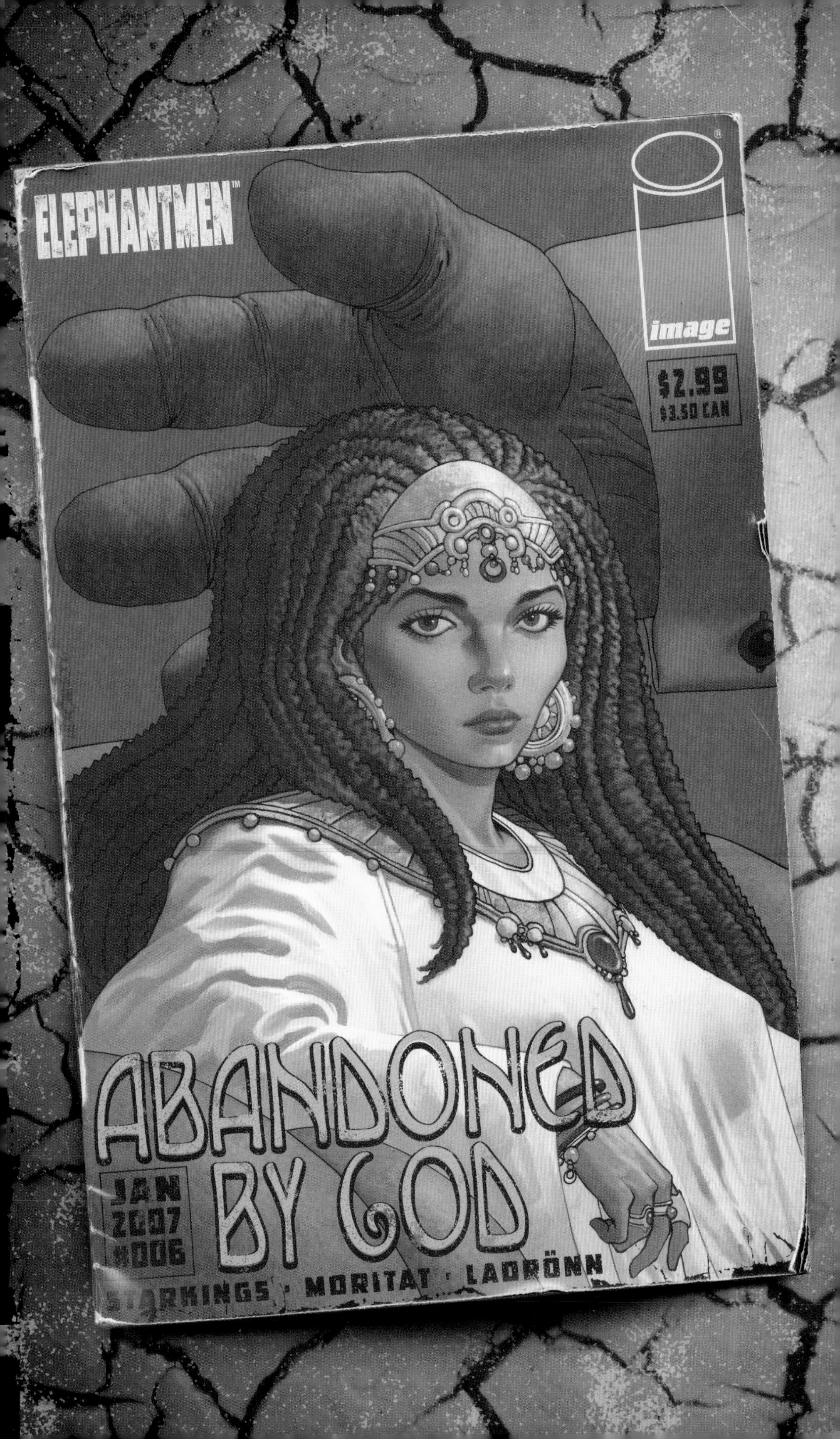
ELEPHANTMEN
image
$2.99
$3.50 CAN
ABANDONED BY GOD
JAN 2007 #006
STARKINGS · MORITAT · LADRÖNN

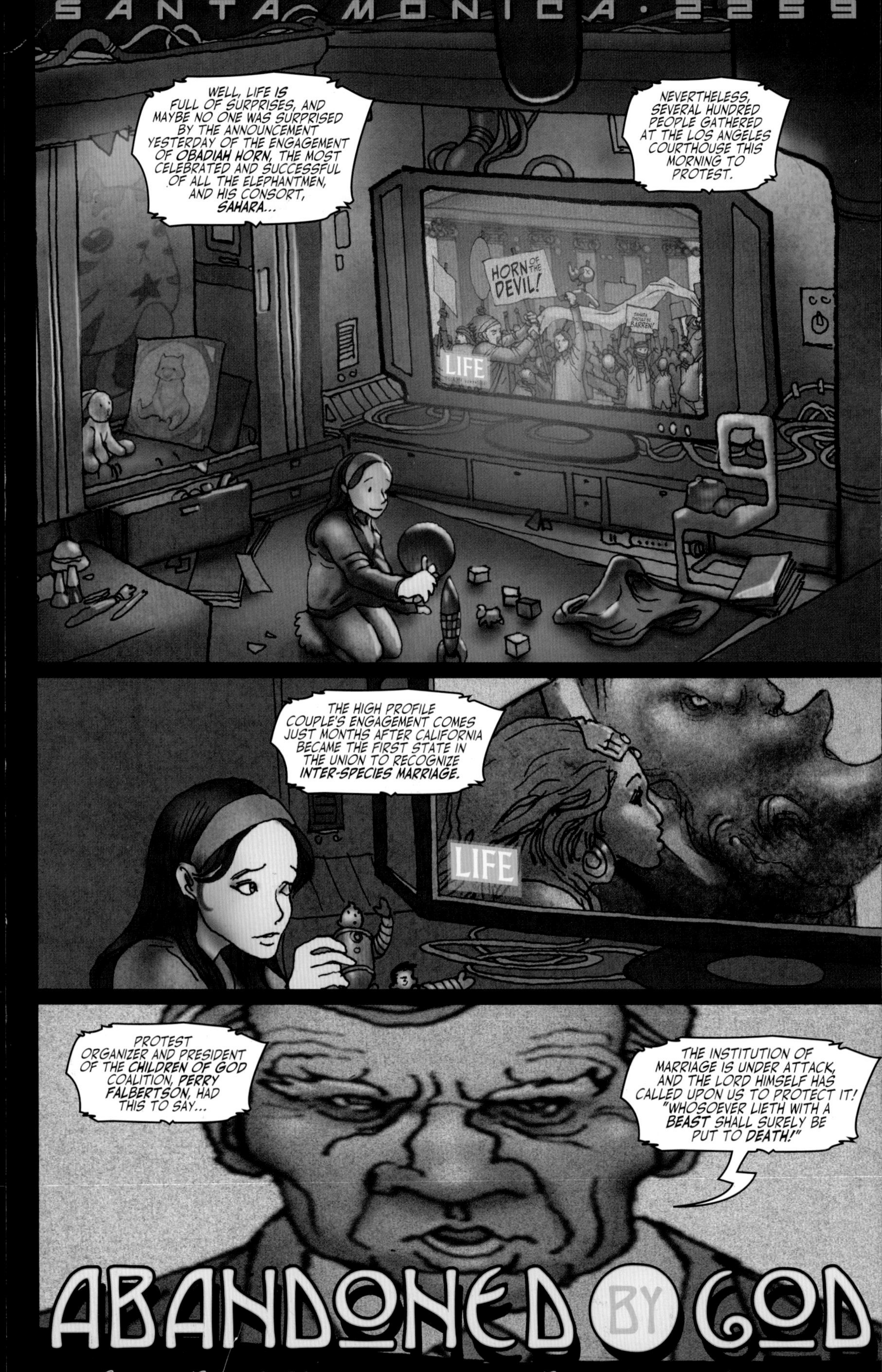
SANTA MONICA · 2259
WELL, LIFE IS FULL OF SURPRISES, AND MAYBE NO ONE WAS SURPRISED BY THE ANNOUNCEMENT YESTERDAY OF THE ENGAGEMENT OF OBADIAH HORN, THE MOST CELEBRATED AND SUCCESSFUL OF ALL THE ELEPHANTMEN, AND HIS CONSORT, SAHARA...
NEVERTHELESS, SEVERAL HUNDRED PEOPLE GATHERED AT THE LOS ANGELES COURTHOUSE THIS MORNING TO PROTEST.
HORN OF THE DEVIL!
SAHARA SHOULD BE BARREN!
LIFE
THE HIGH PROFILE COUPLE'S ENGAGEMENT COMES JUST MONTHS AFTER CALIFORNIA BECAME THE FIRST STATE IN THE UNION TO RECOGNIZE INTER-SPECIES MARRIAGE.
LIFE
PROTEST ORGANIZER AND PRESIDENT OF THE CHILDREN OF GOD COALITION, PERRY FALBERTSON, HAD THIS TO SAY...
THE INSTITUTION OF MARRIAGE IS UNDER ATTACK, AND THE LORD HIMSELF HAS CALLED UPON US TO PROTECT IT! "WHOSOEVER LIETH WITH A BEAST SHALL SURELY BE PUT TO DEATH!"
ABANDONED BY GOD

Another Great & Tall Tale from Mystery City by Starkings & Moritat

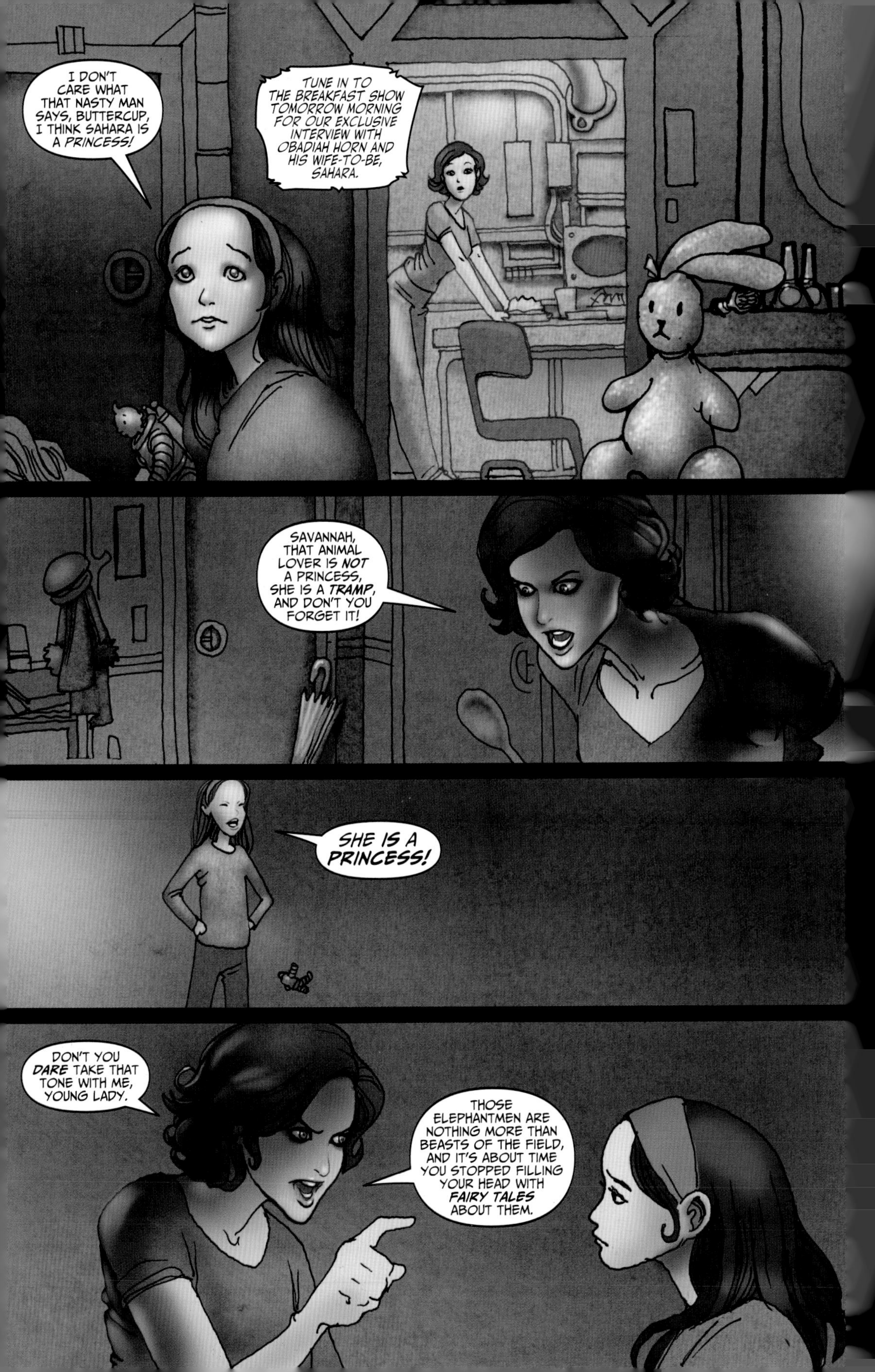
I DON'T CARE WHAT THAT NASTY MAN SAYS, BUTTERCUP, I THINK SAHARA IS A PRINCESS!
TUNE IN TO THE BREAKFAST SHOW TOMORROW MORNING FOR OUR EXCLUSIVE INTERVIEW WITH OBADIAH HORN AND HIS WIFE-TO-BE, SAHARA.
SAVANNAH, THAT ANIMAL LOVER IS NOT A PRINCESS, SHE IS A TRAMP, AND DON'T YOU FORGET IT!
SHE IS A PRINCESS!
DON'T YOU DARE TAKE THAT TONE WITH ME, YOUNG LADY.
THOSE ELEPHANTMEN ARE NOTHING MORE THAN BEASTS OF THE FIELD, AND IT'S ABOUT TIME YOU STOPPED FILLING YOUR HEAD WITH FAIRY TALES ABOUT THEM.

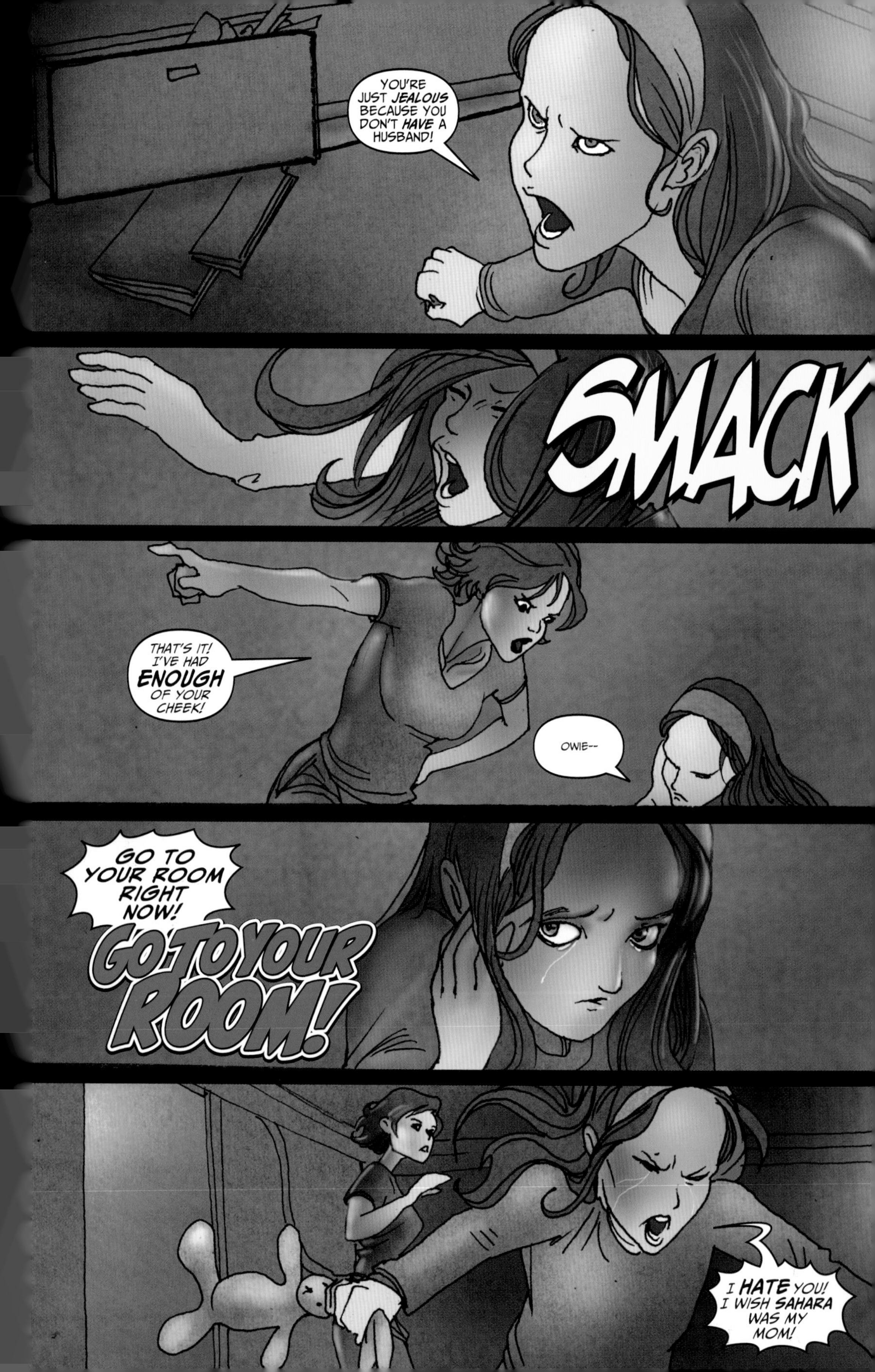
YOU'RE JUST JEALOUS BECAUSE YOU DON'T HAVE A HUSBAND!
SMACK
THAT'S IT! I'VE HAD ENOUGH OF YOUR CHEEK!
OWIE--
GO TO YOUR ROOM RIGHT NOW!
GO TO YOUR ROOM!
I HATE YOU! I WISH SAHARA WAS MY MOM!

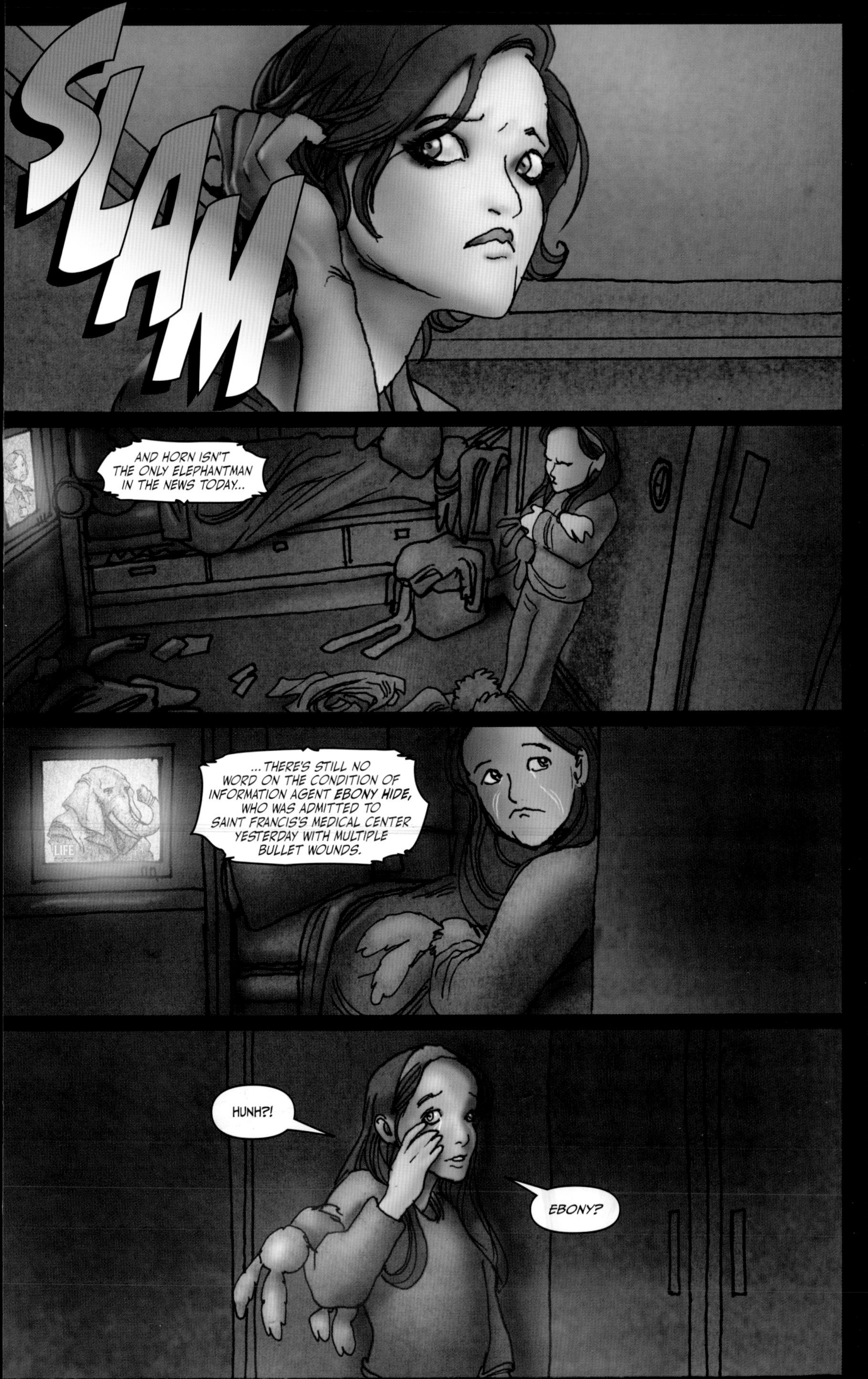
SLAM
AND HORN ISN'T THE ONLY ELEPHANTMAN IN THE NEWS TODAY...
...THERE'S STILL NO WORD ON THE CONDITION OF INFORMATION AGENT EBONY HIDE, WHO WAS ADMITTED TO SAINT FRANCIS'S MEDICAL CENTER YESTERDAY WITH MULTIPLE BULLET WOUNDS.
HUNH?!
EBONY?

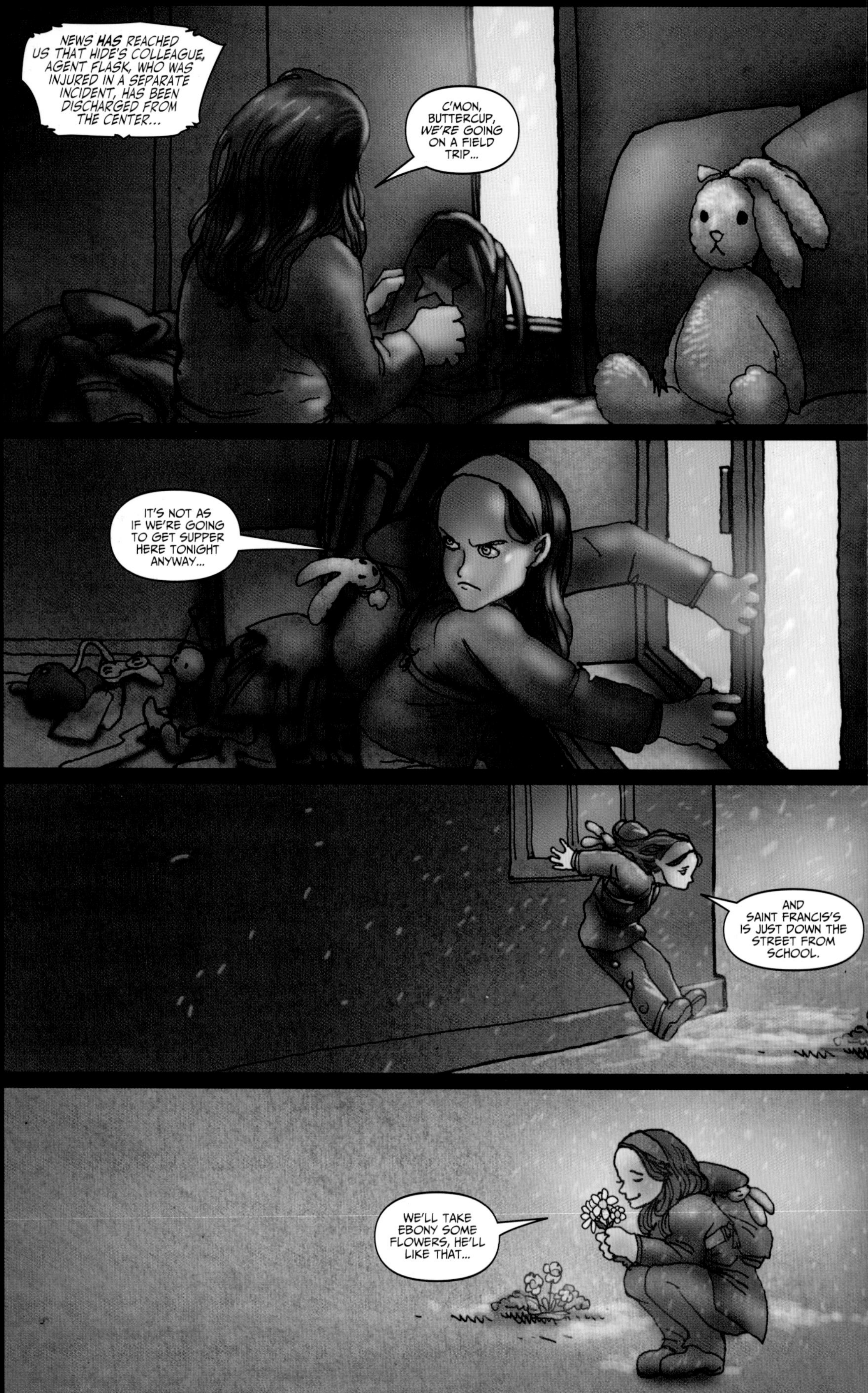
NEWS HAS REACHED US THAT HIDE'S COLLEAGUE, AGENT FLASK, WHO WAS INJURED IN A SEPARATE INCIDENT, HAS BEEN DISCHARGED FROM THE CENTER...
C'MON, BUTTERCUP, WE'RE GOING ON A FIELD TRIP...
IT'S NOT AS IF WE'RE GOING TO GET SUPPER HERE TONIGHT ANYWAY...
AND SAINT FRANCIS'S IS JUST DOWN THE STREET FROM SCHOOL.
WE'LL TAKE EBONY SOME FLOWERS, HE'LL LIKE THAT...

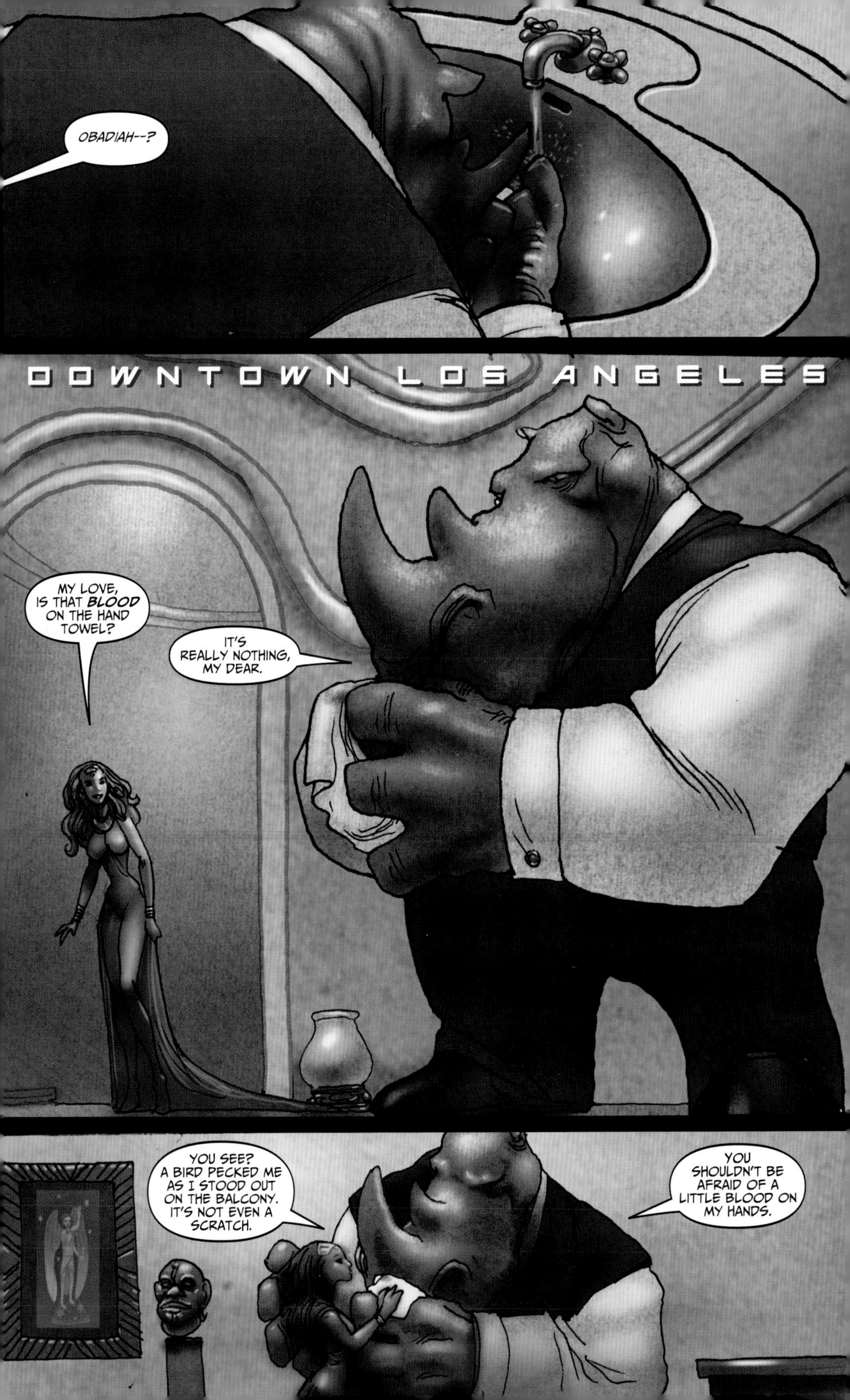
OBADIAH--?
DOWNTOWN LOS ANGELES
MY LOVE, IS THAT BLOOD ON THE HAND TOWEL?
IT'S REALLY NOTHING, MY DEAR.
YOU SEE? A BIRD PECKED ME AS I STOOD OUT ON THE BALCONY. IT'S NOT EVEN A SCRATCH.
YOU SHOULDN'T BE AFRAID OF A LITTLE BLOOD ON MY HANDS.

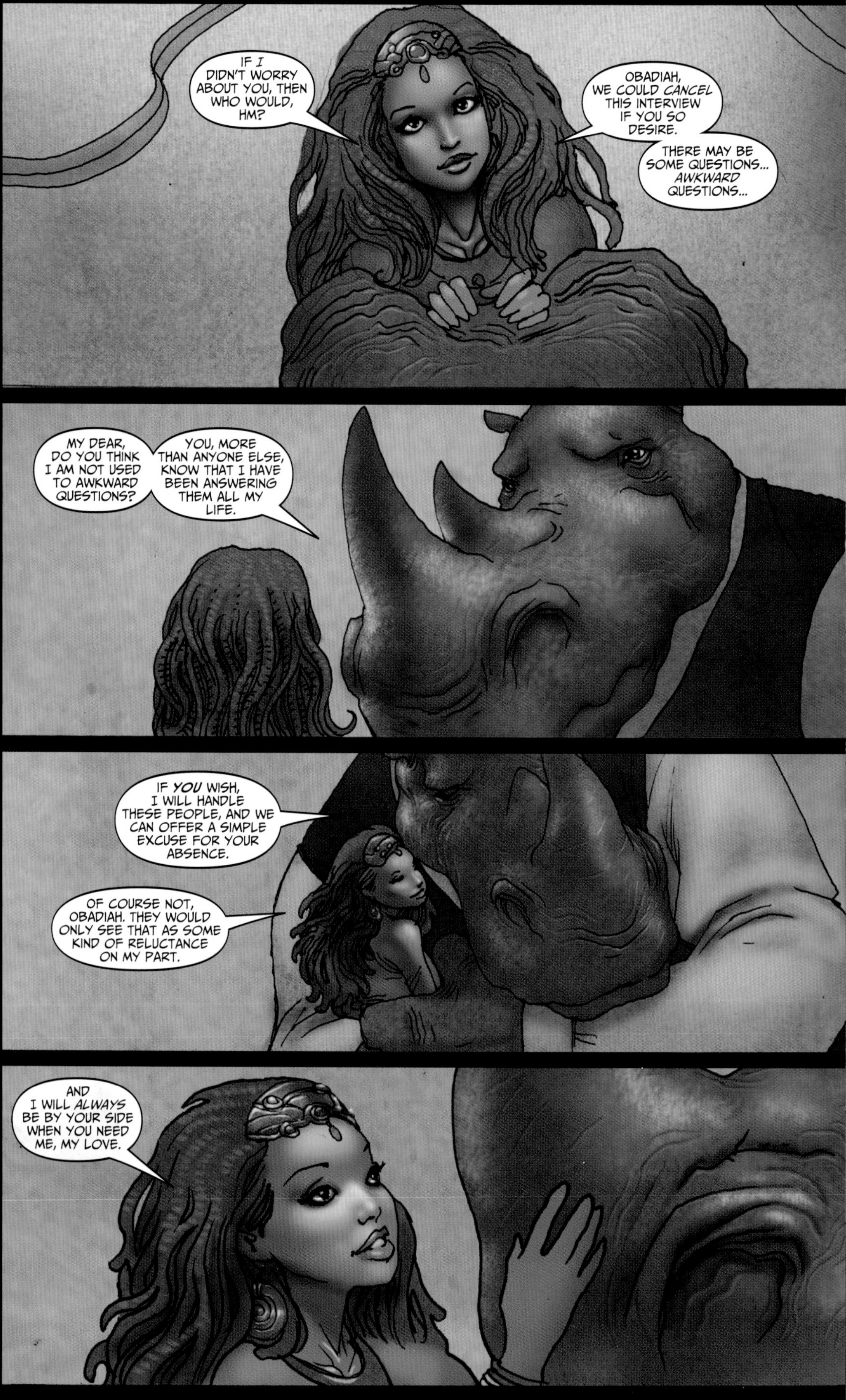
IF *I* DIDN'T WORRY ABOUT YOU, THEN WHO WOULD, HM?
OBADIAH, WE COULD *CANCEL* THIS INTERVIEW IF YOU SO DESIRE.
THERE MAY BE SOME QUESTIONS... *AWKWARD* QUESTIONS...
MY DEAR, DO YOU THINK I AM NOT USED TO AWKWARD QUESTIONS?
YOU, MORE THAN ANYONE ELSE, KNOW THAT I HAVE BEEN ANSWERING THEM ALL MY LIFE.
IF *YOU* WISH, I WILL HANDLE THESE PEOPLE, AND WE CAN OFFER A SIMPLE EXCUSE FOR YOUR ABSENCE.
OF COURSE NOT, OBADIAH. THEY WOULD ONLY SEE THAT AS SOME KIND OF RELUCTANCE ON MY PART.
AND I WILL *ALWAYS* BE BY YOUR SIDE WHEN YOU NEED ME, MY LOVE.

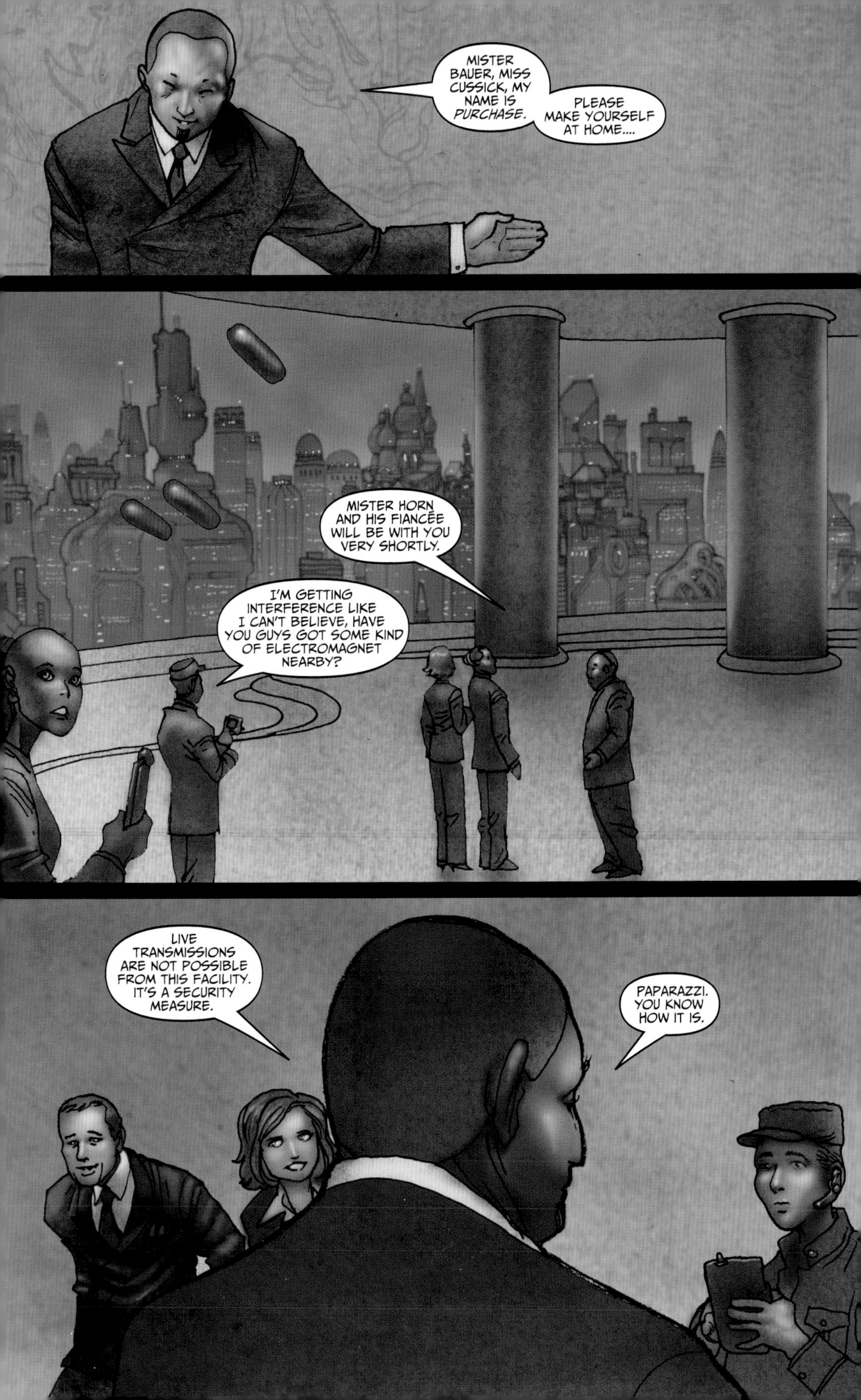

MISTER BAUER, MISS CUSSICK, MY NAME IS *PURCHASE.*
PLEASE MAKE YOURSELF AT HOME....
MISTER HORN AND HIS FIANCÉE WILL BE WITH YOU VERY SHORTLY.
I'M GETTING INTERFERENCE LIKE I CAN'T BELIEVE, HAVE YOU GUYS GOT SOME KIND OF ELECTROMAGNET NEARBY?
LIVE TRANSMISSIONS ARE NOT POSSIBLE FROM THIS FACILITY. IT'S A SECURITY MEASURE.
PAPARAZZI. YOU KNOW HOW IT IS.

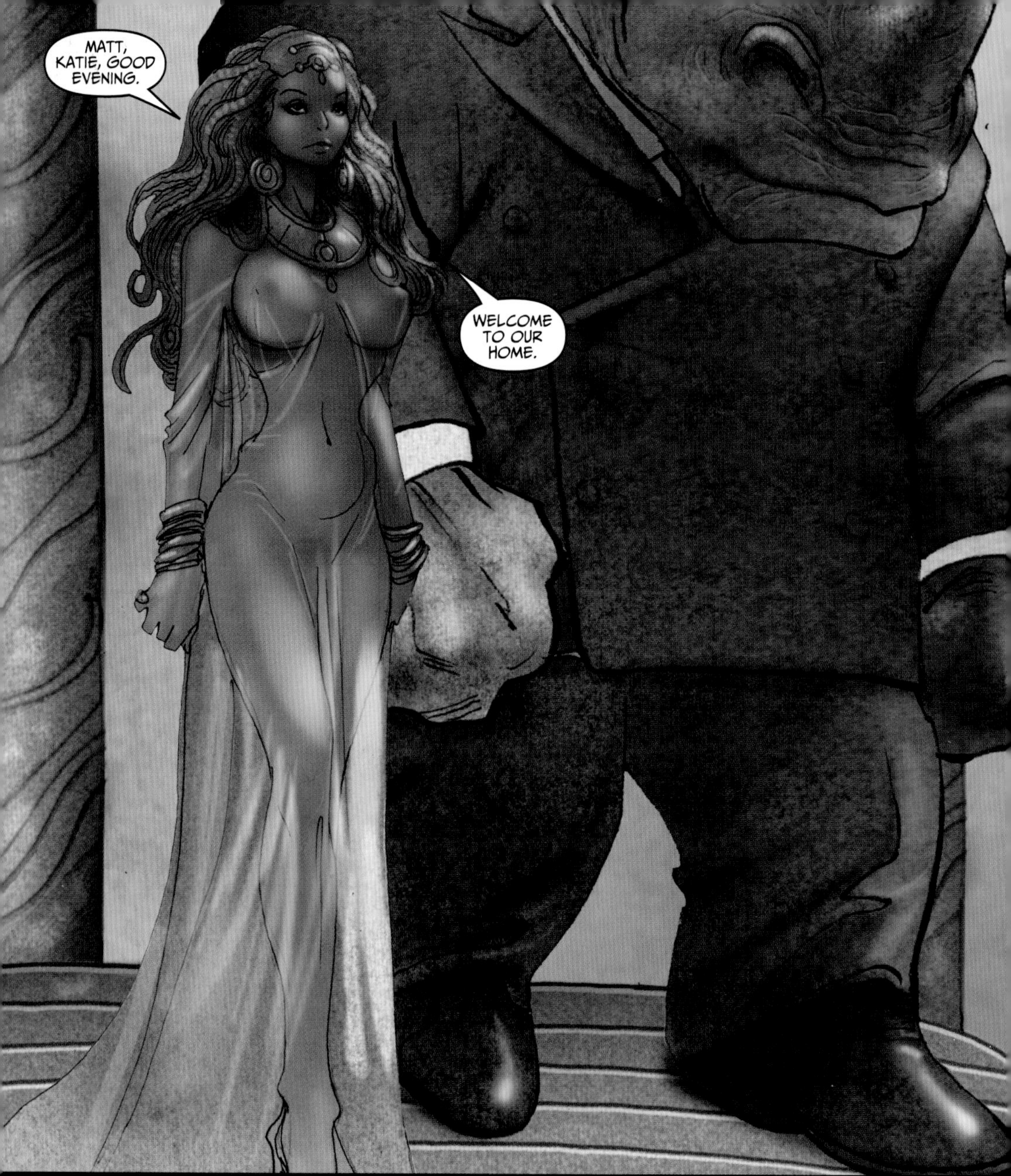
MATT, KATIE, GOOD EVENING.
WELCOME TO OUR HOME.
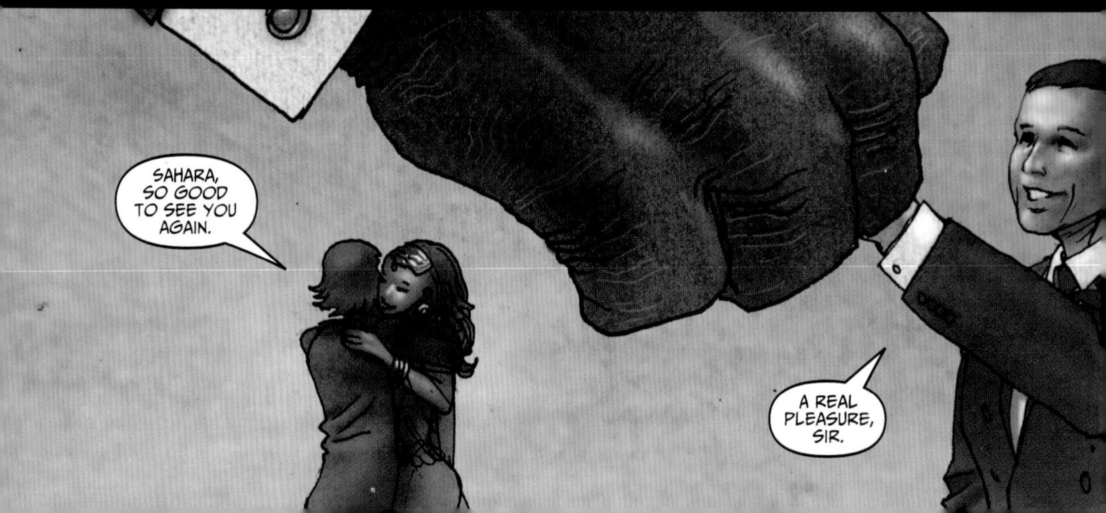
SAHARA, SO GOOD TO SEE YOU AGAIN.
A REAL PLEASURE, SIR.

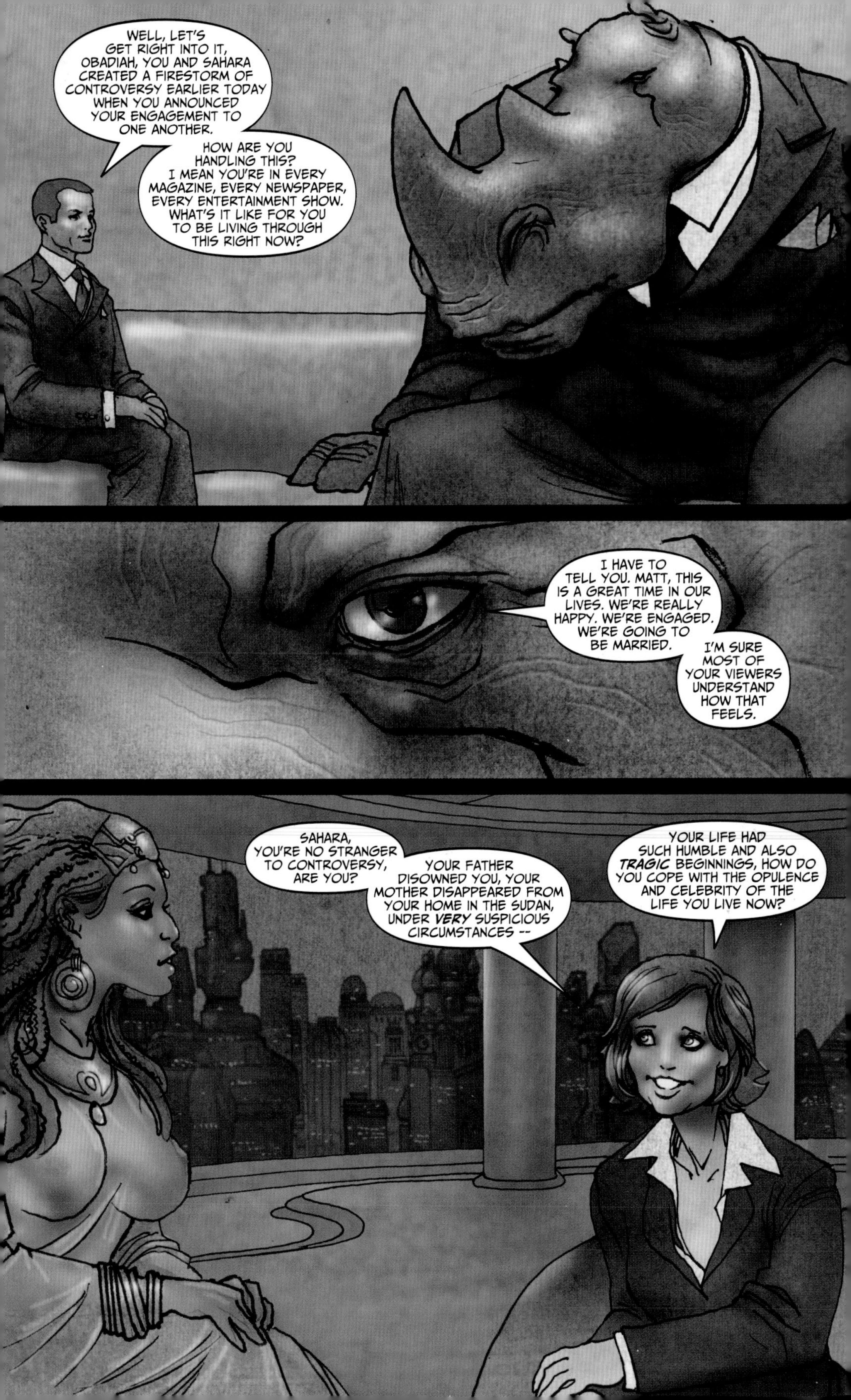
WELL, LET'S GET RIGHT INTO IT, OBADIAH, YOU AND SAHARA CREATED A FIRESTORM OF CONTROVERSY EARLIER TODAY WHEN YOU ANNOUNCED YOUR ENGAGEMENT TO ONE ANOTHER.
HOW ARE YOU HANDLING THIS? I MEAN YOU'RE IN EVERY MAGAZINE, EVERY NEWSPAPER, EVERY ENTERTAINMENT SHOW. WHAT'S IT LIKE FOR YOU TO BE LIVING THROUGH THIS RIGHT NOW?
I HAVE TO TELL YOU. MATT, THIS IS A GREAT TIME IN OUR LIVES. WE'RE REALLY HAPPY. WE'RE ENGAGED. WE'RE GOING TO BE MARRIED.
I'M SURE MOST OF YOUR VIEWERS UNDERSTAND HOW THAT FEELS.
SAHARA, YOU'RE NO STRANGER TO CONTROVERSY, ARE YOU?
YOUR FATHER DISOWNED YOU, YOUR MOTHER DISAPPEARED FROM YOUR HOME IN THE SUDAN, UNDER *VERY* SUSPICIOUS CIRCUMSTANCES --
YOUR LIFE HAD SUCH HUMBLE AND ALSO *TRAGIC* BEGINNINGS, HOW DO YOU COPE WITH THE OPULENCE AND CELEBRITY OF THE LIFE YOU LIVE NOW?

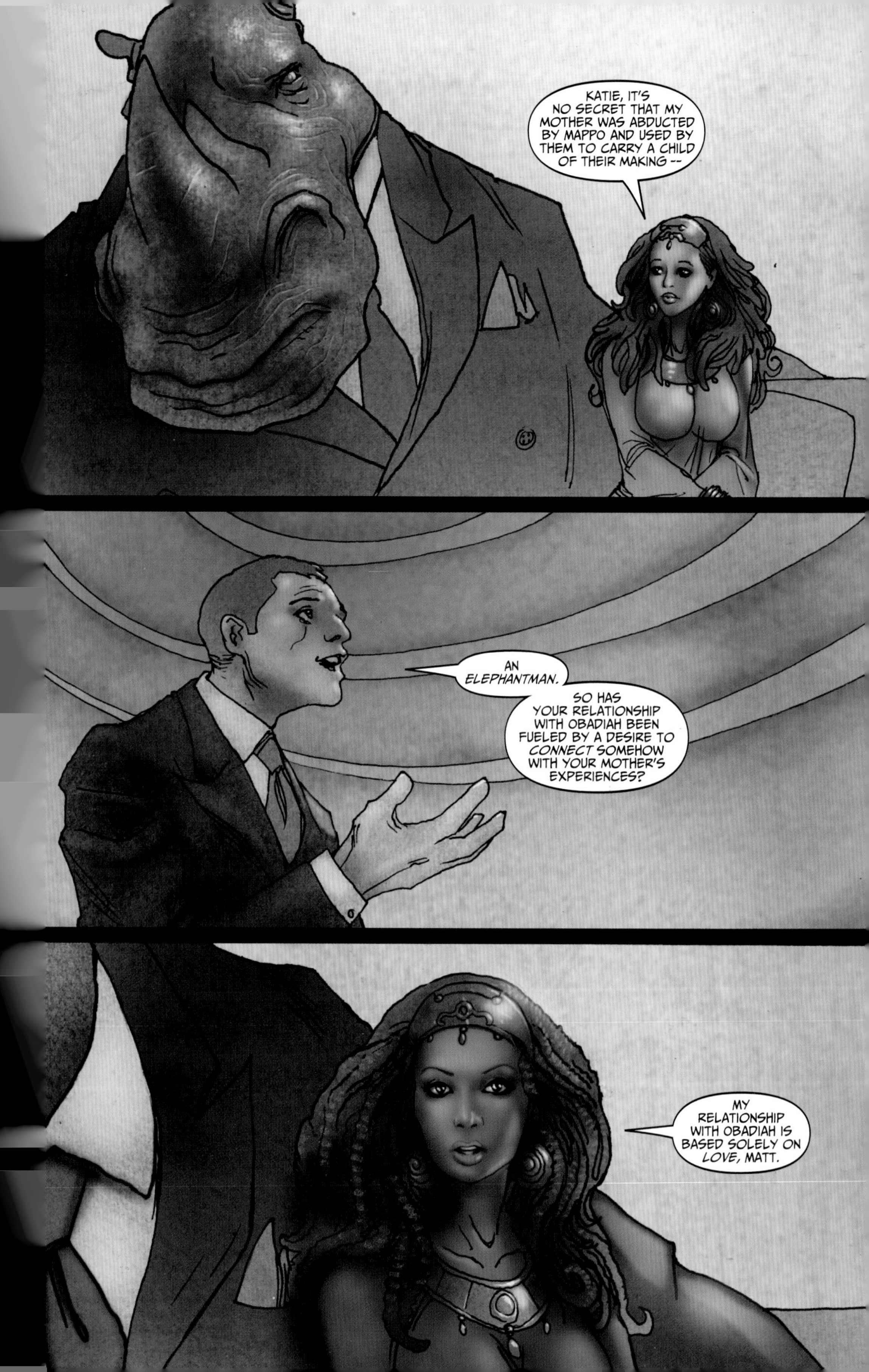
KATIE, IT'S NO SECRET THAT MY MOTHER WAS ABDUCTED BY MAPPO AND USED BY THEM TO CARRY A CHILD OF THEIR MAKING --
AN *ELEPHANTMAN.*
SO HAS YOUR RELATIONSHIP WITH OBADIAH BEEN FUELED BY A DESIRE TO *CONNECT* SOMEHOW WITH YOUR MOTHER'S EXPERIENCES?
MY RELATIONSHIP WITH OBADIAH IS BASED SOLELY ON *LOVE*, MATT.

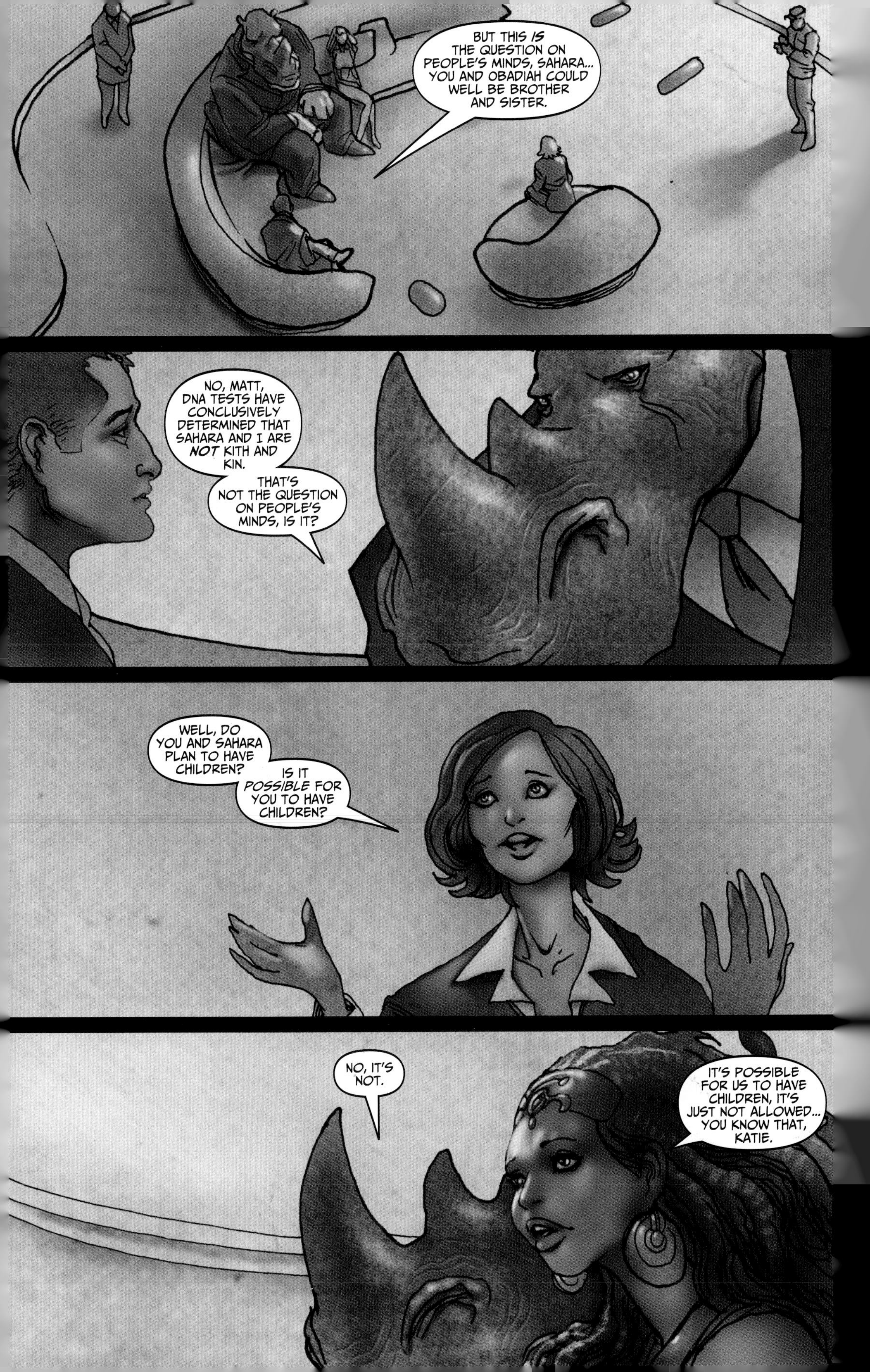
BUT THIS *IS* THE QUESTION ON PEOPLE'S MINDS, SAHARA... YOU AND OBADIAH COULD WELL BE BROTHER AND SISTER.
NO, MATT, DNA TESTS HAVE CONCLUSIVELY DETERMINED THAT SAHARA AND I ARE ***NOT*** KITH AND KIN.
THAT'S NOT THE QUESTION ON PEOPLE'S MINDS, IS IT?
WELL, DO YOU AND SAHARA PLAN TO HAVE CHILDREN?
IS IT *POSSIBLE* FOR YOU TO HAVE CHILDREN?
NO, IT'S NOT.
IT'S POSSIBLE FOR US TO HAVE CHILDREN, IT'S JUST NOT ALLOWED... YOU KNOW THAT, KATIE.

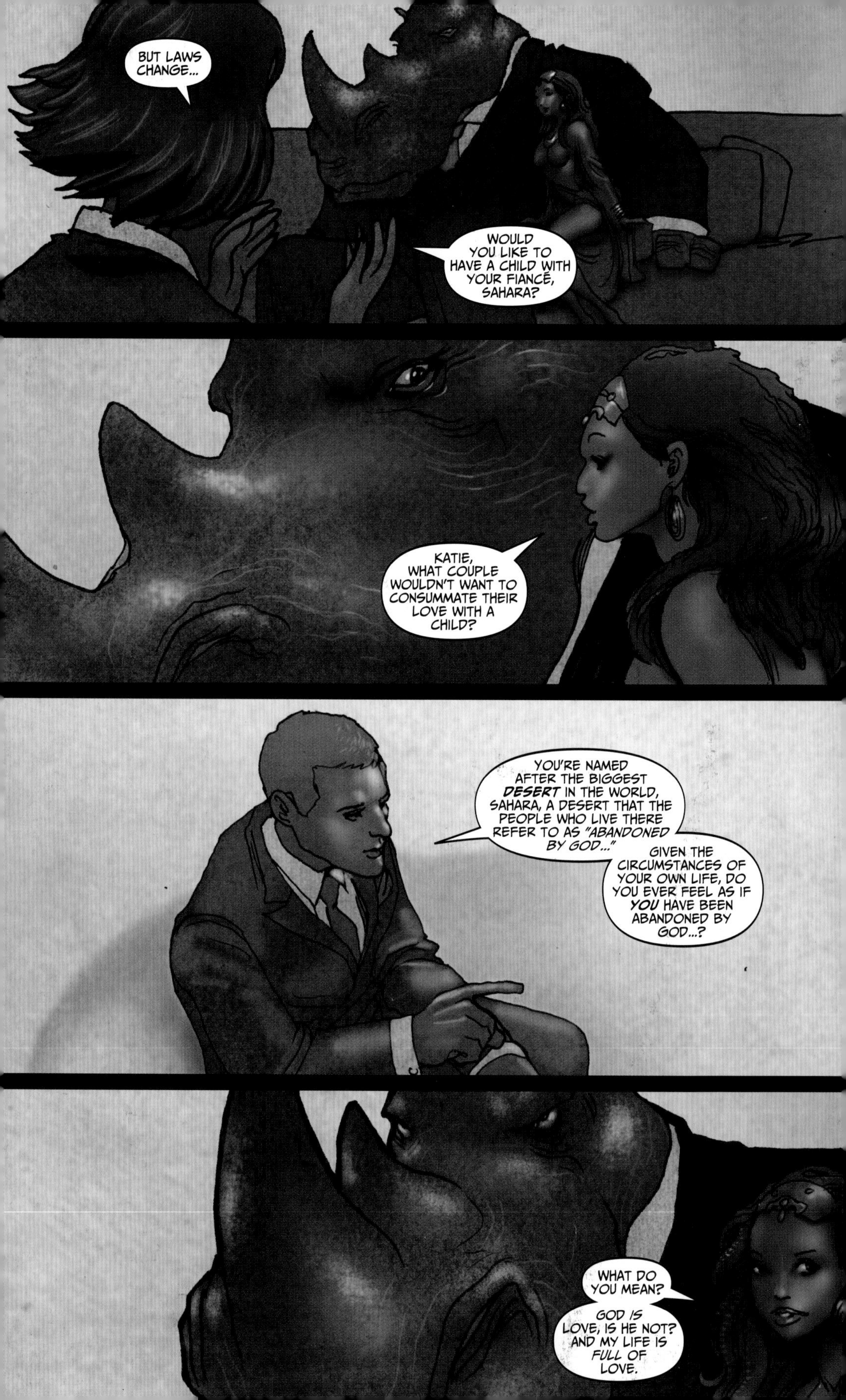
BUT LAWS CHANGE...
WOULD YOU LIKE TO HAVE A CHILD WITH YOUR FIANCÉ, SAHARA?
KATIE, WHAT COUPLE WOULDN'T WANT TO CONSUMMATE THEIR LOVE WITH A CHILD?
YOU'RE NAMED AFTER THE BIGGEST DESERT IN THE WORLD, SAHARA, A DESERT THAT THE PEOPLE WHO LIVE THERE REFER TO AS "ABANDONED BY GOD..."
GIVEN THE CIRCUMSTANCES OF YOUR OWN LIFE, DO YOU EVER FEEL AS IF YOU HAVE BEEN ABANDONED BY GOD...?
WHAT DO YOU MEAN?
GOD IS LOVE, IS HE NOT? AND MY LIFE IS FULL OF LOVE.

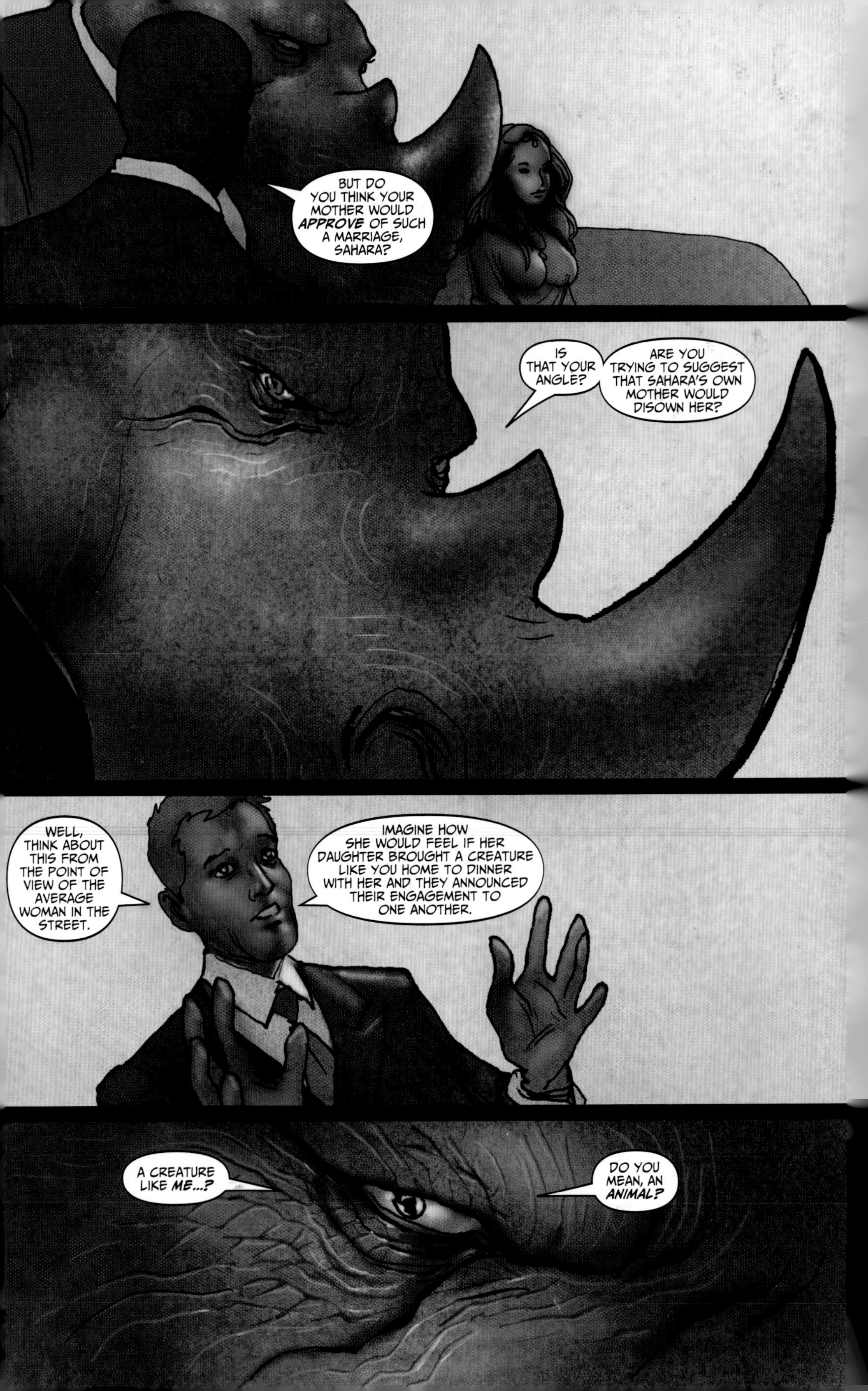
BUT DO YOU THINK YOUR MOTHER WOULD *APPROVE* OF SUCH A MARRIAGE, SAHARA?
IS THAT YOUR ANGLE?
ARE YOU TRYING TO SUGGEST THAT SAHARA'S OWN MOTHER WOULD DISOWN HER?
WELL, THINK ABOUT THIS FROM THE POINT OF VIEW OF THE AVERAGE WOMAN IN THE STREET.
IMAGINE HOW SHE WOULD FEEL IF HER DAUGHTER BROUGHT A CREATURE LIKE YOU HOME TO DINNER WITH HER AND THEY ANNOUNCED THEIR ENGAGEMENT TO ONE ANOTHER.
A CREATURE LIKE *ME...?*
DO YOU MEAN, AN *ANIMAL?*

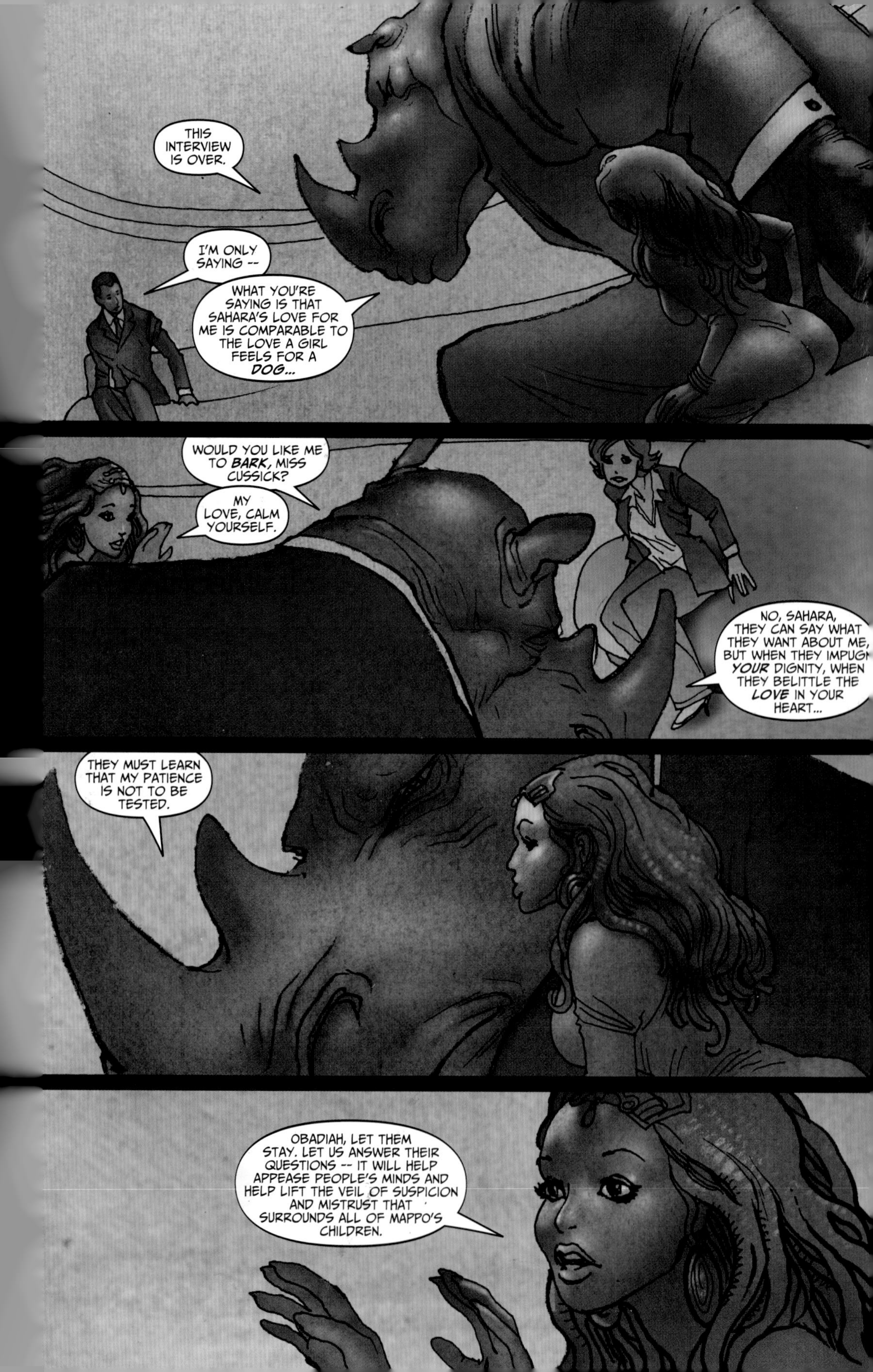
THIS INTERVIEW IS OVER.
I'M ONLY SAYING --
WHAT YOU'RE SAYING IS THAT SAHARA'S LOVE FOR ME IS COMPARABLE TO THE LOVE A GIRL FEELS FOR A DOG...
WOULD YOU LIKE ME TO BARK, MISS CUSSICK?
MY LOVE, CALM YOURSELF.
NO, SAHARA, THEY CAN SAY WHAT THEY WANT ABOUT ME, BUT WHEN THEY IMPUGN YOUR DIGNITY, WHEN THEY BELITTLE THE LOVE IN YOUR HEART...
THEY MUST LEARN THAT MY PATIENCE IS NOT TO BE TESTED.
OBADIAH, LET THEM STAY. LET US ANSWER THEIR QUESTIONS -- IT WILL HELP APPEASE PEOPLE'S MINDS AND HELP LIFT THE VEIL OF SUSPICION AND MISTRUST THAT SURROUNDS ALL OF MAPPO'S CHILDREN.

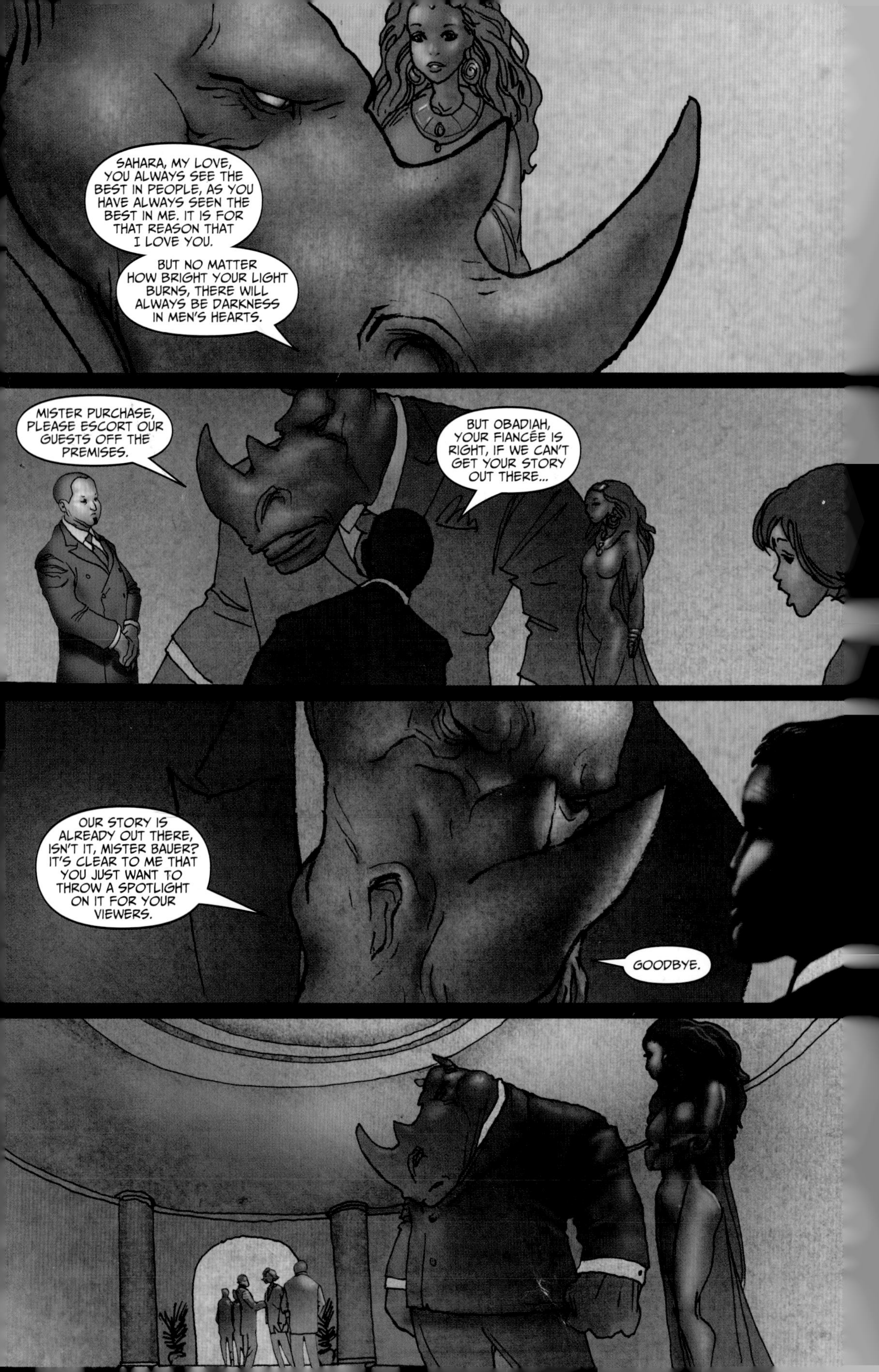
SAHARA, MY LOVE, YOU ALWAYS SEE THE BEST IN PEOPLE, AS YOU HAVE ALWAYS SEEN THE BEST IN ME. IT IS FOR THAT REASON THAT I LOVE YOU.
BUT NO MATTER HOW BRIGHT YOUR LIGHT BURNS, THERE WILL ALWAYS BE DARKNESS IN MEN'S HEARTS.
MISTER PURCHASE, PLEASE ESCORT OUR GUESTS OFF THE PREMISES.
BUT OBADIAH, YOUR FIANCÉE IS RIGHT, IF WE CAN'T GET YOUR STORY OUT THERE...
OUR STORY IS ALREADY OUT THERE, ISN'T IT, MISTER BAUER? IT'S CLEAR TO ME THAT YOU JUST WANT TO THROW A SPOTLIGHT ON IT FOR YOUR VIEWERS.
GOODBYE.

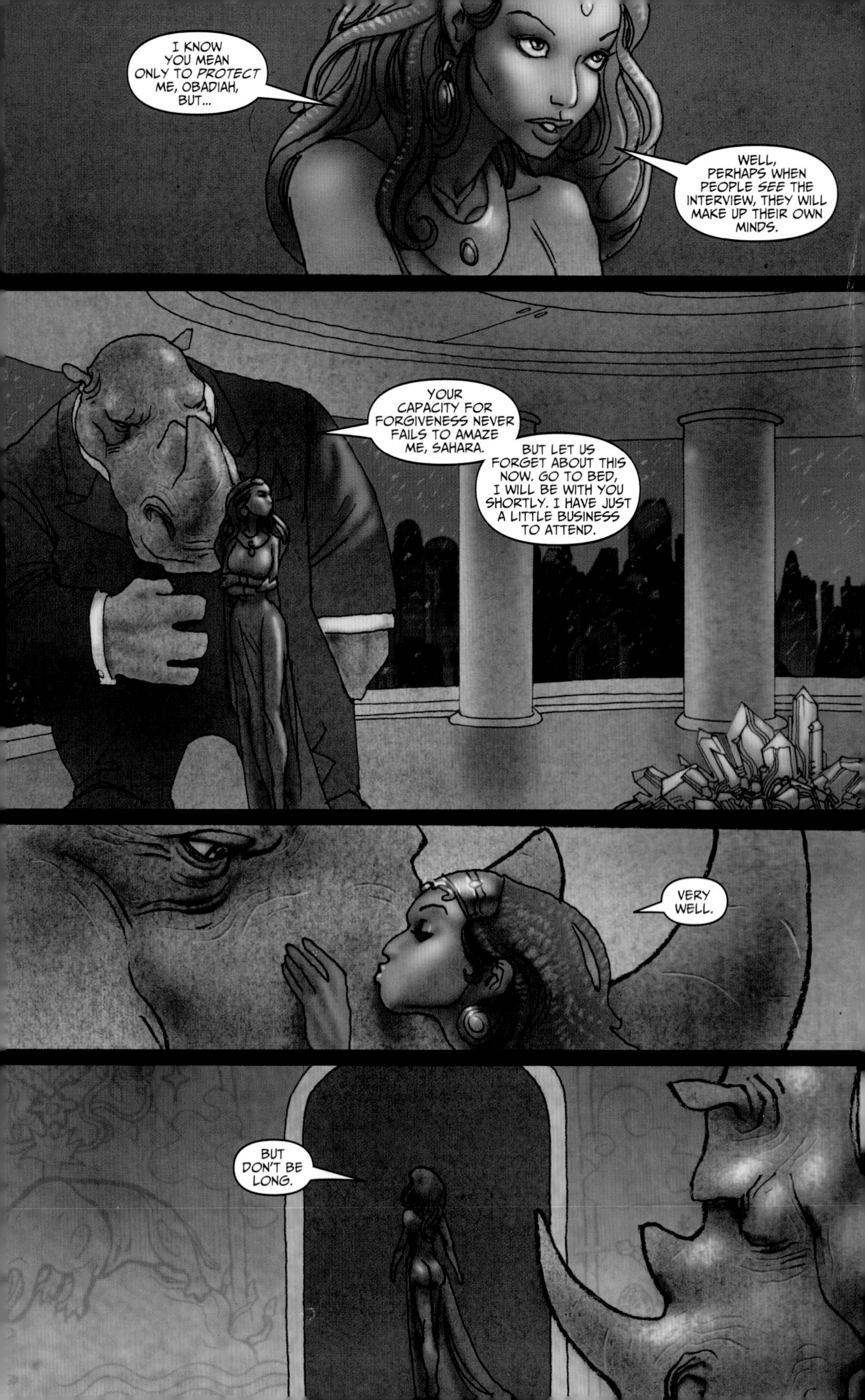
I KNOW YOU MEAN ONLY TO *PROTECT* ME, OBADIAH, BUT...
WELL, PERHAPS WHEN PEOPLE *SEE* THE INTERVIEW, THEY WILL MAKE UP THEIR OWN MINDS.
YOUR CAPACITY FOR FORGIVENESS NEVER FAILS TO AMAZE ME, SAHARA.
BUT LET US FORGET ABOUT THIS NOW. GO TO BED, I WILL BE WITH YOU SHORTLY. I HAVE JUST A LITTLE BUSINESS TO ATTEND.
VERY WELL.
BUT DON'T BE LONG.

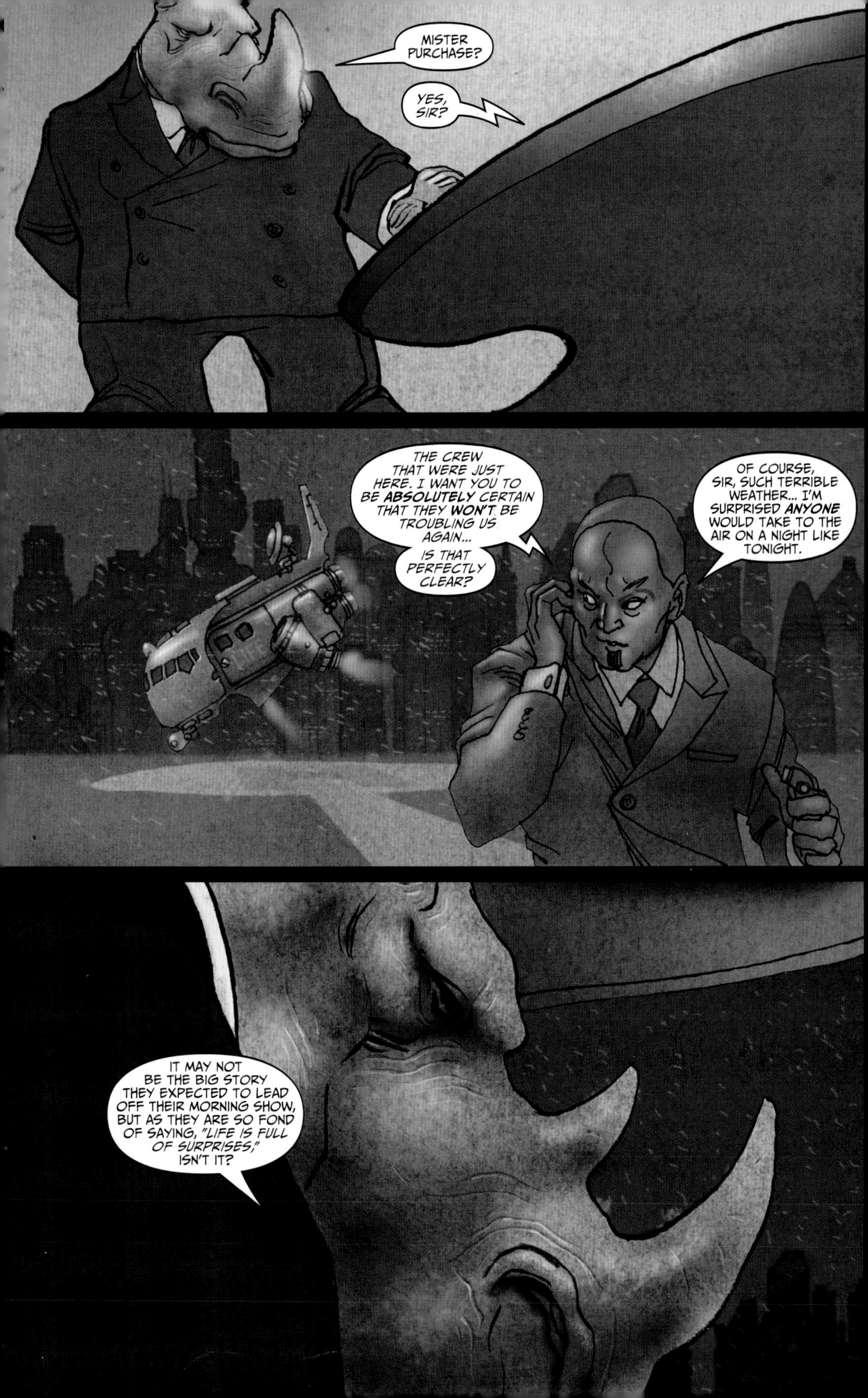
MISTER PURCHASE?
YES, SIR?
THE CREW THAT WERE JUST HERE. I WANT YOU TO BE ABSOLUTELY CERTAIN THAT THEY WON'T BE TROUBLING US AGAIN...
IS THAT PERFECTLY CLEAR?
OF COURSE, SIR, SUCH TERRIBLE WEATHER... I'M SURPRISED ANYONE WOULD TAKE TO THE AIR ON A NIGHT LIKE TONIGHT.
IT MAY NOT BE THE BIG STORY THEY EXPECTED TO LEAD OFF THEIR MORNING SHOW, BUT AS THEY ARE SO FOND OF SAYING, "LIFE IS FULL OF SURPRISES," ISN'T IT?

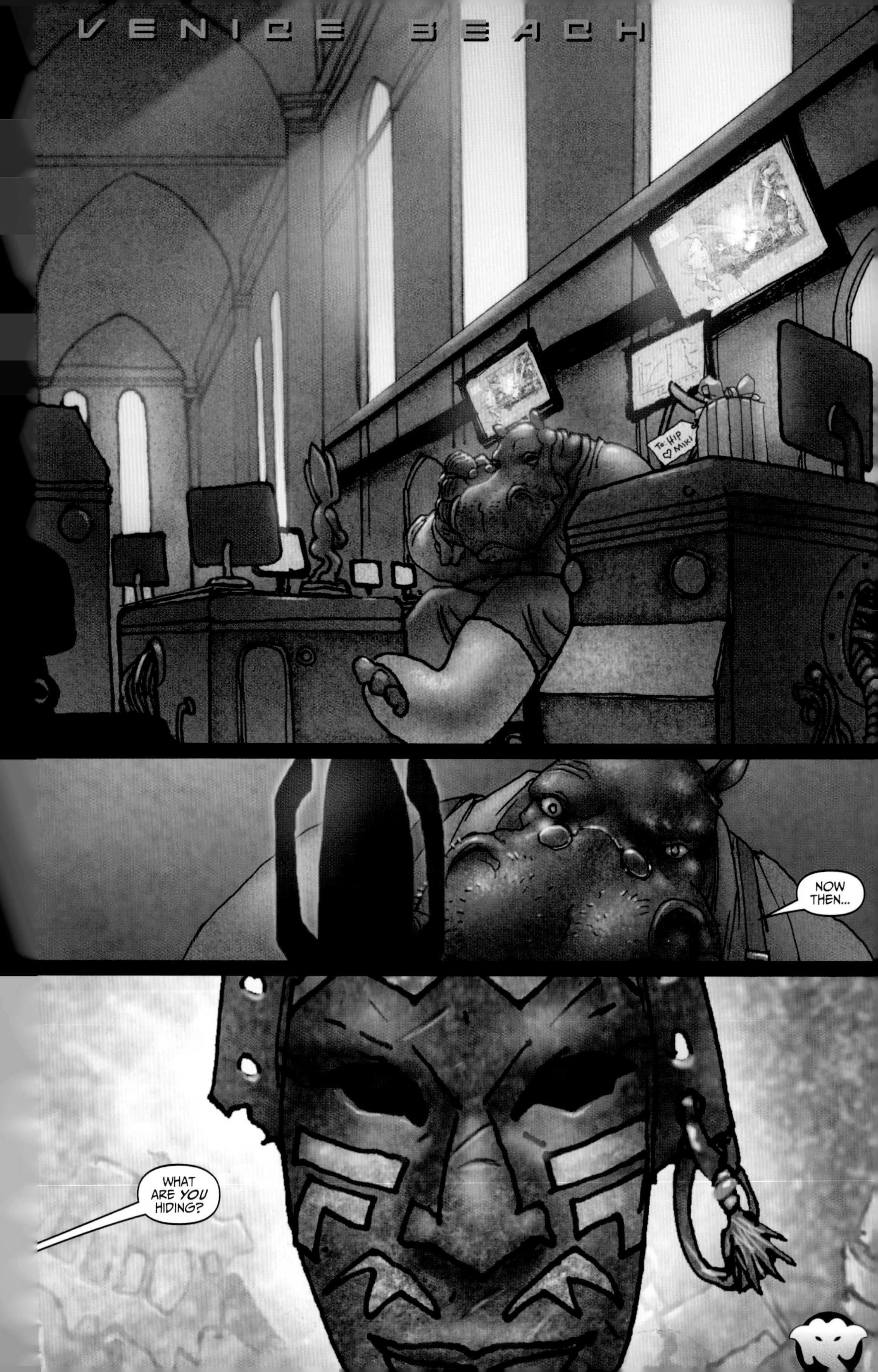
VENICE BEACH
To: HIP ♡ MIKI
NOW THEN...
WHAT ARE YOU HIDING?

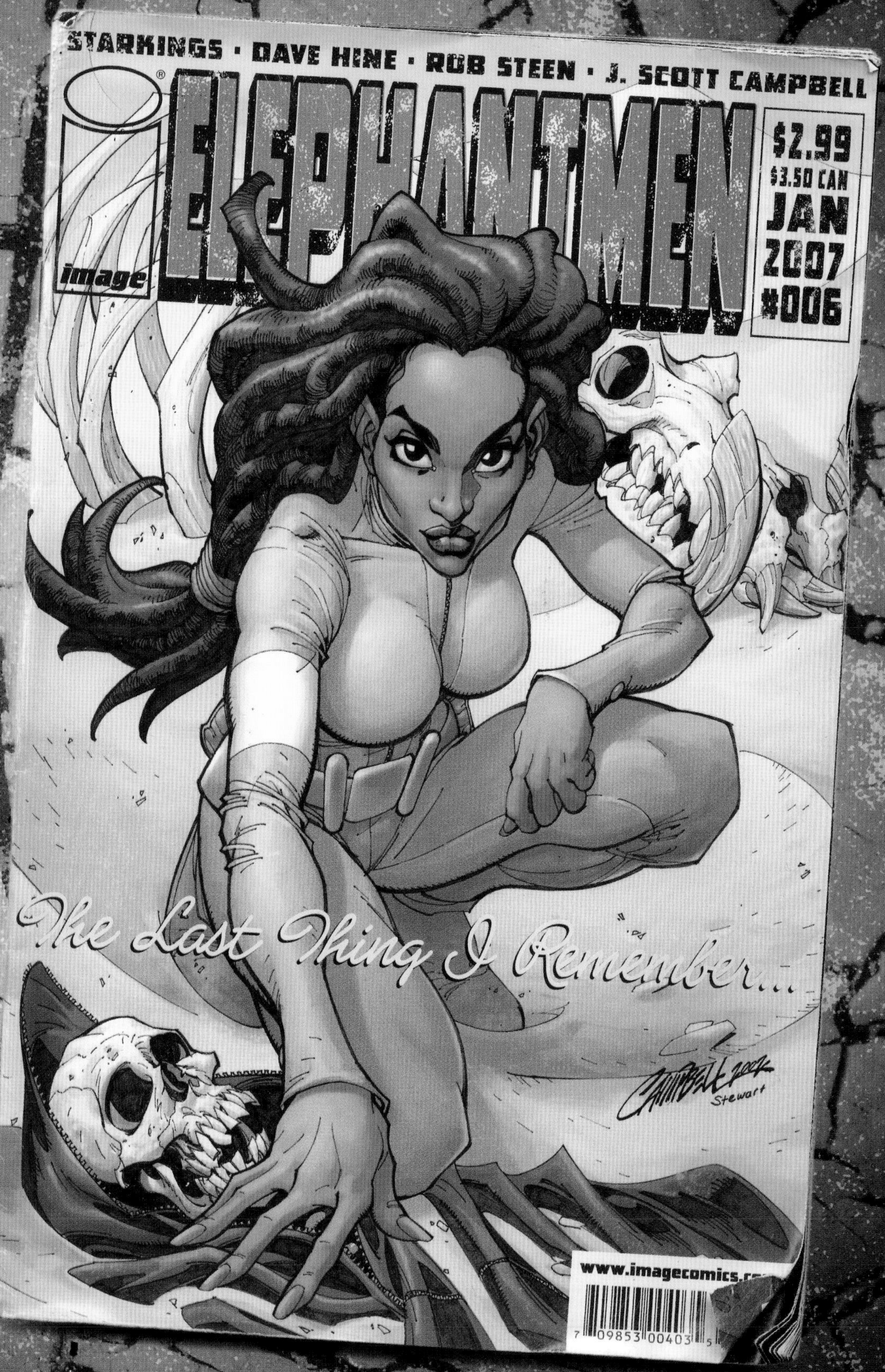

STARKINGS · DAVE HINE · ROB STEEN · J. SCOTT CAMPBELL
image
ELEPHANTMEN
$2.99
$3.50 CAN
JAN
2007
#006
The Last Thing I Remember...
Campbell 2006
Stewart
www.imagecomics.com

"AUSCHWITZ
BEGINS WHEREVER
SOMEONE LOOKS AT
A SLAUGHTERHOUSE
AND THINKS:
THEY'RE ONLY
ANIMALS."

THEODOR W. ADORNO

"THE MORE WE
DO TO YOU, THE
LESS YOU SEEM TO
BELIEVE WE ARE
DOING IT."

DOCTOR JOSEF MENGELE

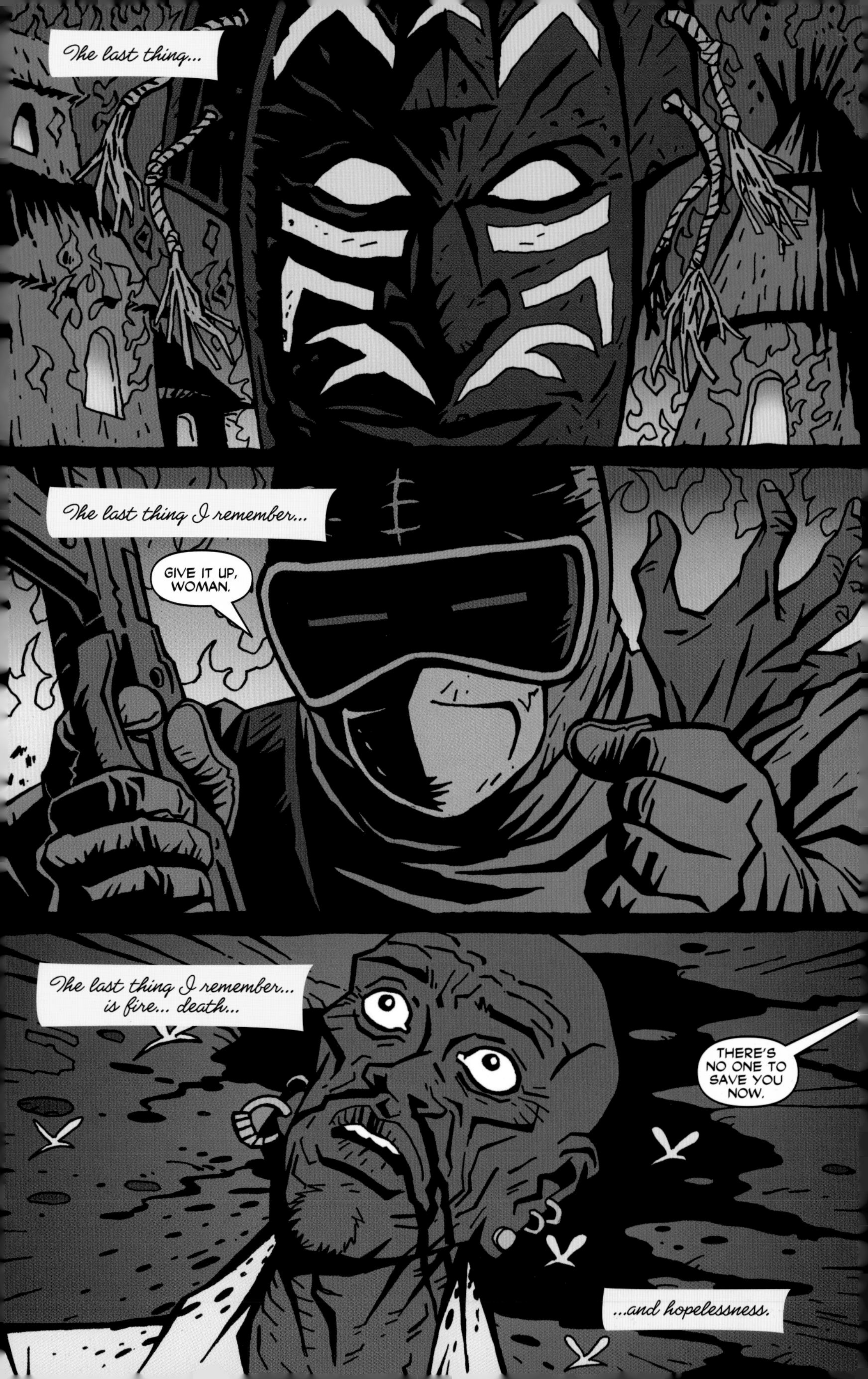
The last thing...
The last thing I remember...
GIVE IT UP, WOMAN.
The last thing I remember... is fire... death...
THERE'S NO ONE TO SAVE YOU NOW.
...and hopelessness.

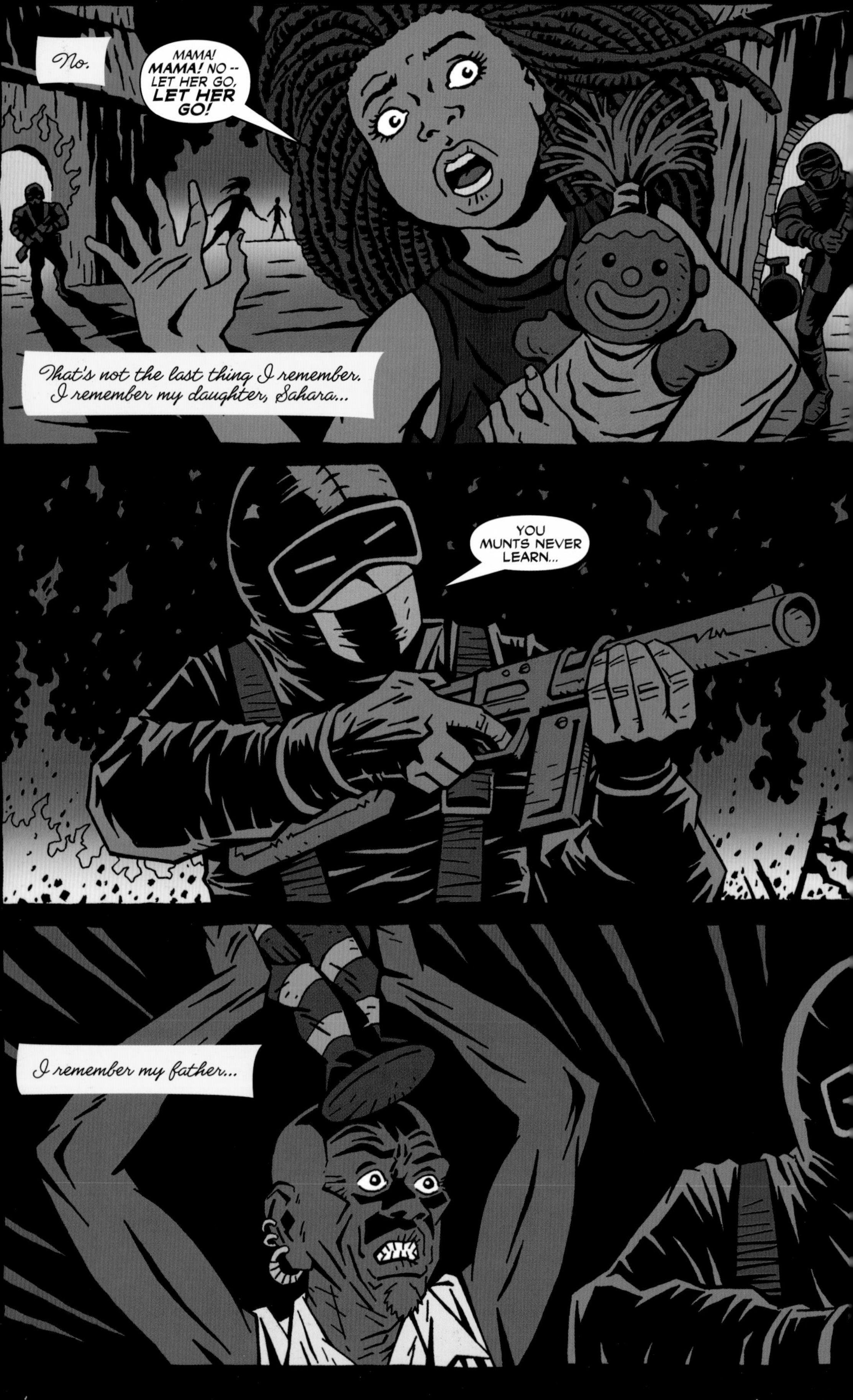
No.
MAMA! MAMA! NO -- LET HER GO, LET HER GO!
That's not the last thing I remember. I remember my daughter, Sahara...
YOU MUNTS NEVER LEARN...
I remember my father...

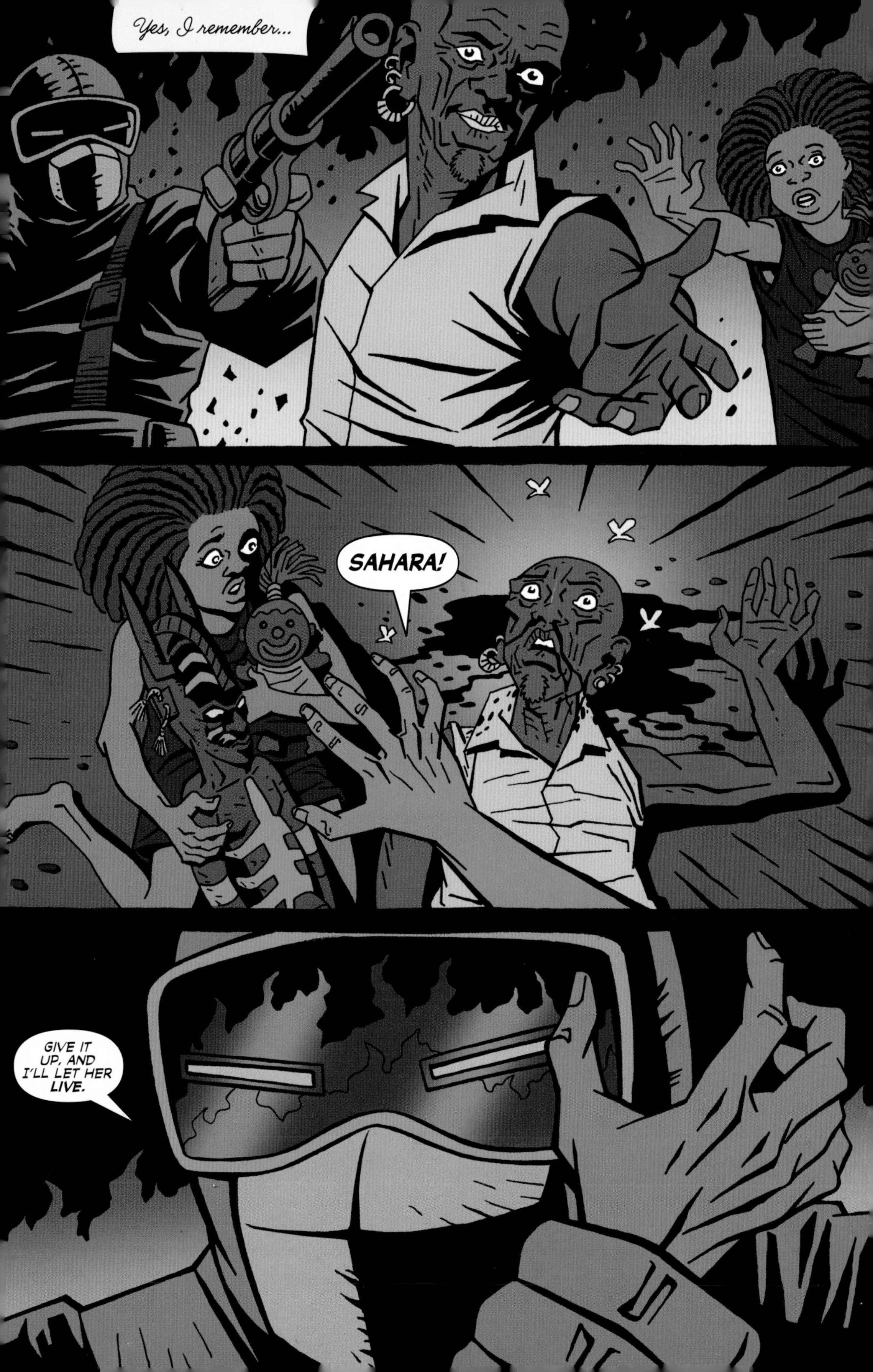
Yes, I remember...
SAHARA!
GIVE IT UP, AND I'LL LET HER LIVE.

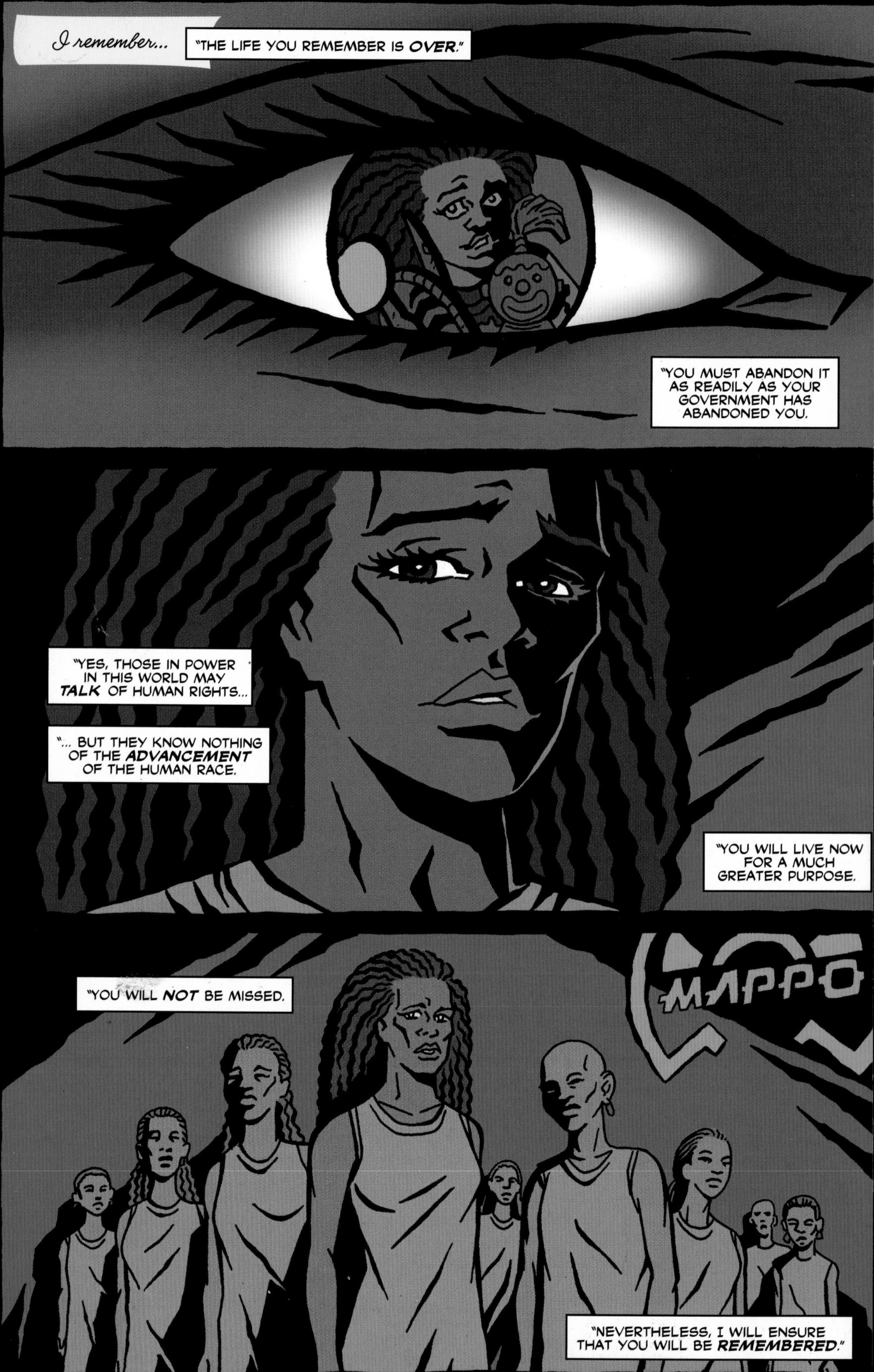
I remember...
"THE LIFE YOU REMEMBER IS *OVER*."
"YOU MUST ABANDON IT AS READILY AS YOUR GOVERNMENT HAS ABANDONED YOU.
"YES, THOSE IN POWER IN THIS WORLD MAY *TALK* OF HUMAN RIGHTS...
"... BUT THEY KNOW NOTHING OF THE *ADVANCEMENT* OF THE HUMAN RACE.
"YOU WILL LIVE NOW FOR A MUCH GREATER PURPOSE.
MAPPO
"YOU WILL *NOT* BE MISSED.
"NEVERTHELESS, I WILL ENSURE THAT YOU WILL BE *REMEMBERED*."

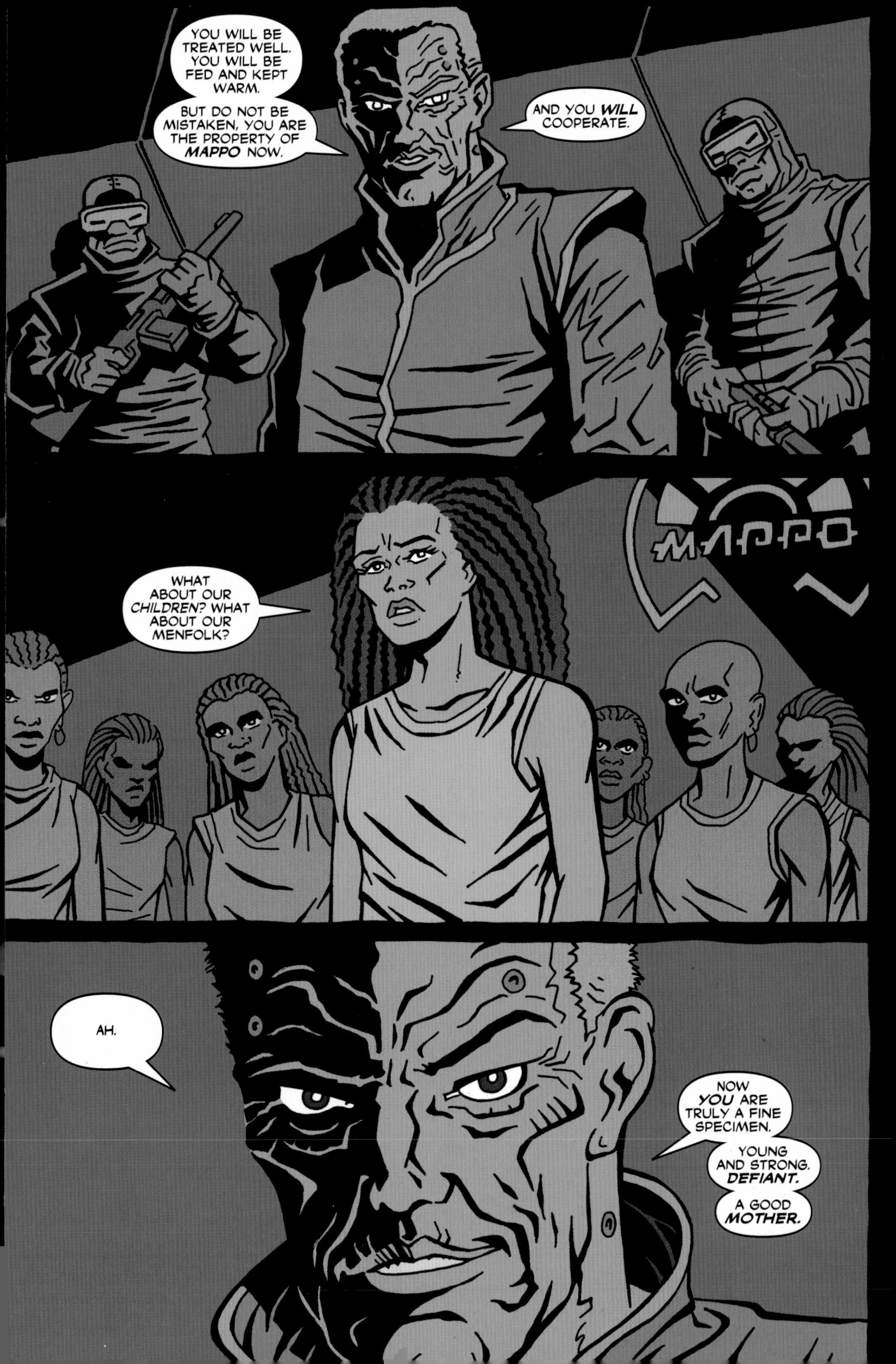
YOU WILL BE TREATED WELL. YOU WILL BE FED AND KEPT WARM.
BUT DO NOT BE MISTAKEN, YOU ARE THE PROPERTY OF MAPPO NOW.
AND YOU WILL COOPERATE.
MAPPO
WHAT ABOUT OUR CHILDREN? WHAT ABOUT OUR MENFOLK?
AH.
NOW YOU ARE TRULY A FINE SPECIMEN.
YOUNG AND STRONG. DEFIANT.
A GOOD MOTHER.

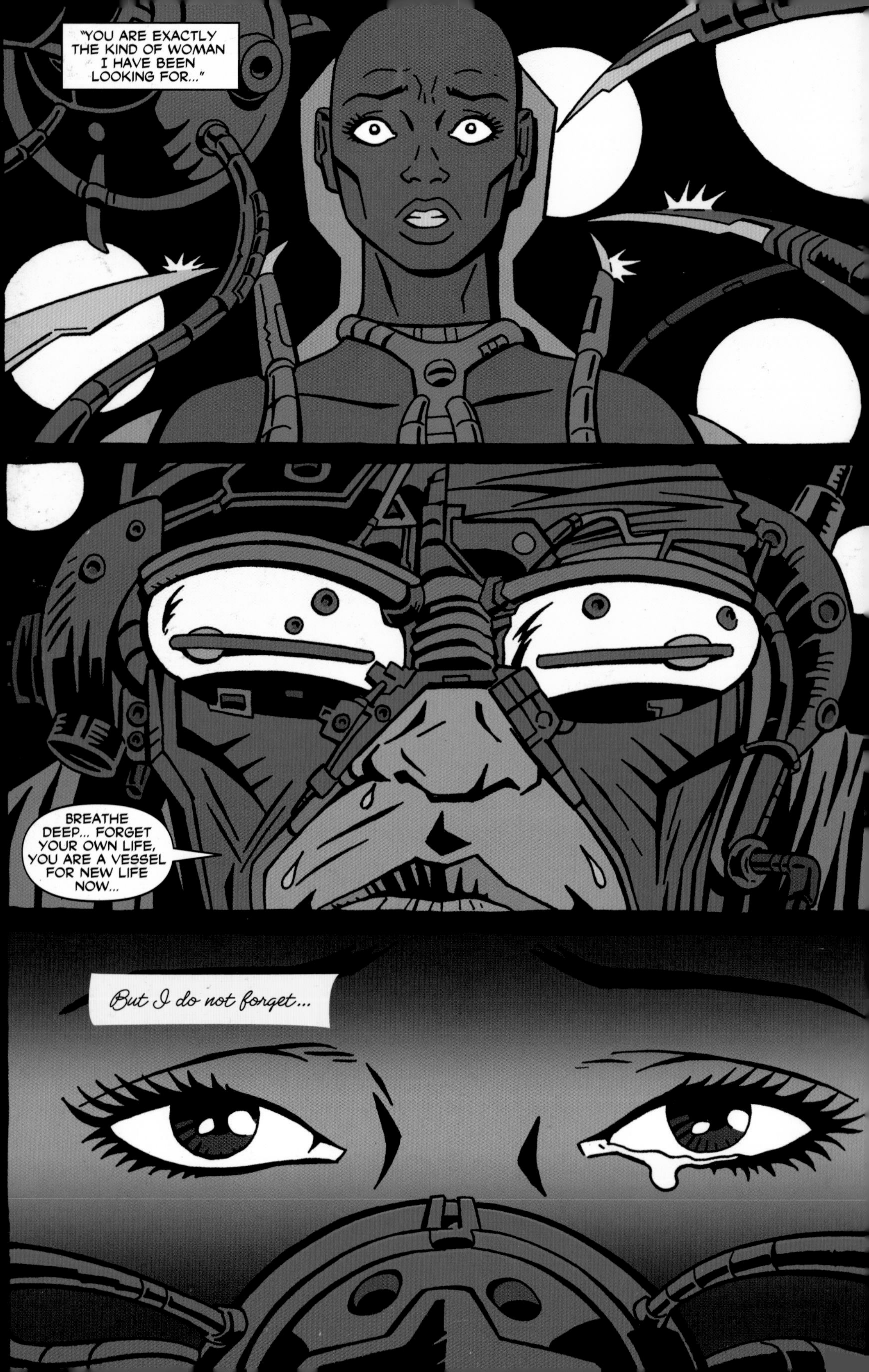
"YOU ARE EXACTLY THE KIND OF WOMAN I HAVE BEEN LOOKING FOR..."
BREATHE DEEP... FORGET YOUR OWN LIFE, YOU ARE A VESSEL FOR NEW LIFE NOW...
But I do not forget...

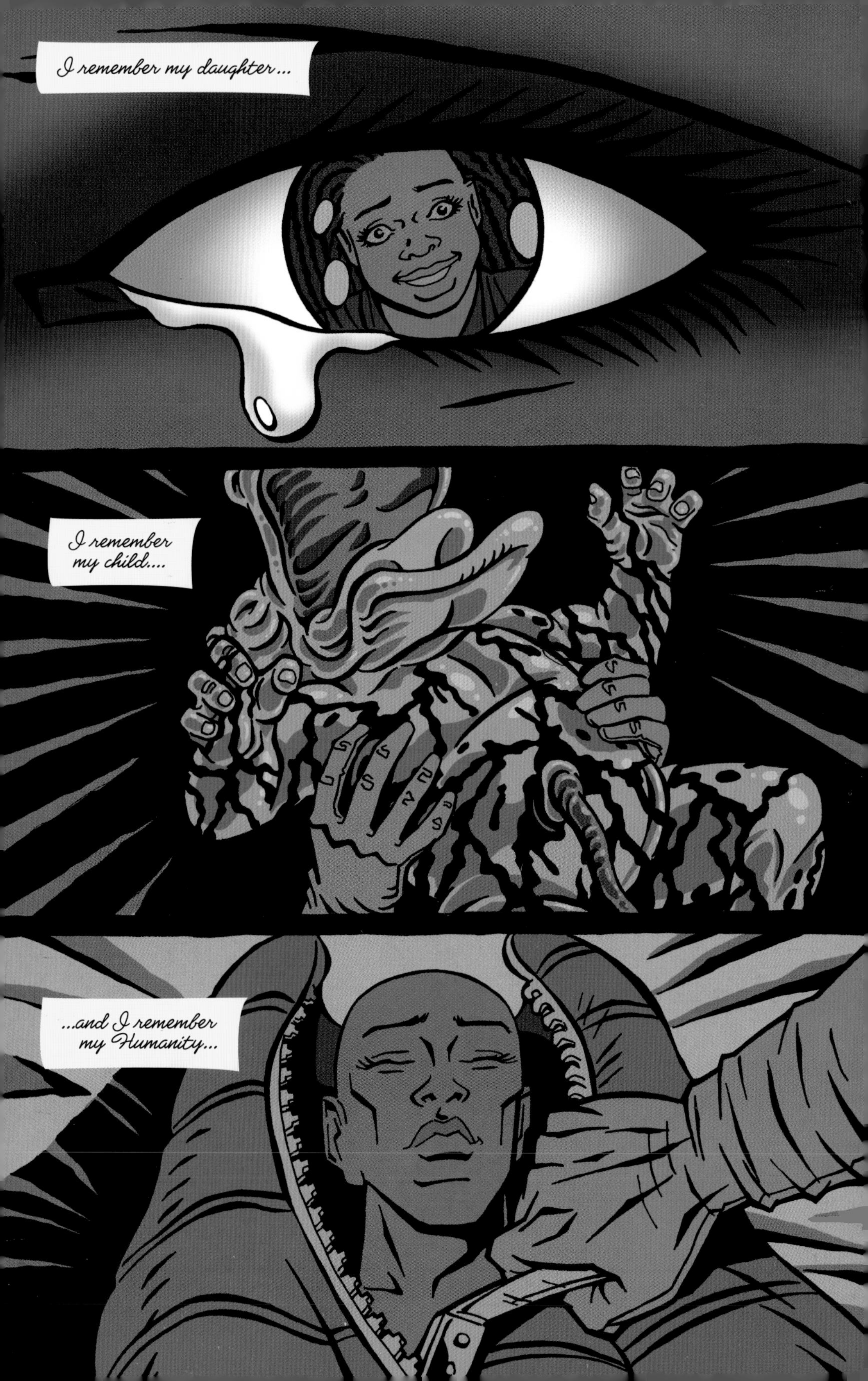
I remember my daughter...
I remember my child....
...and I remember my Humanity...

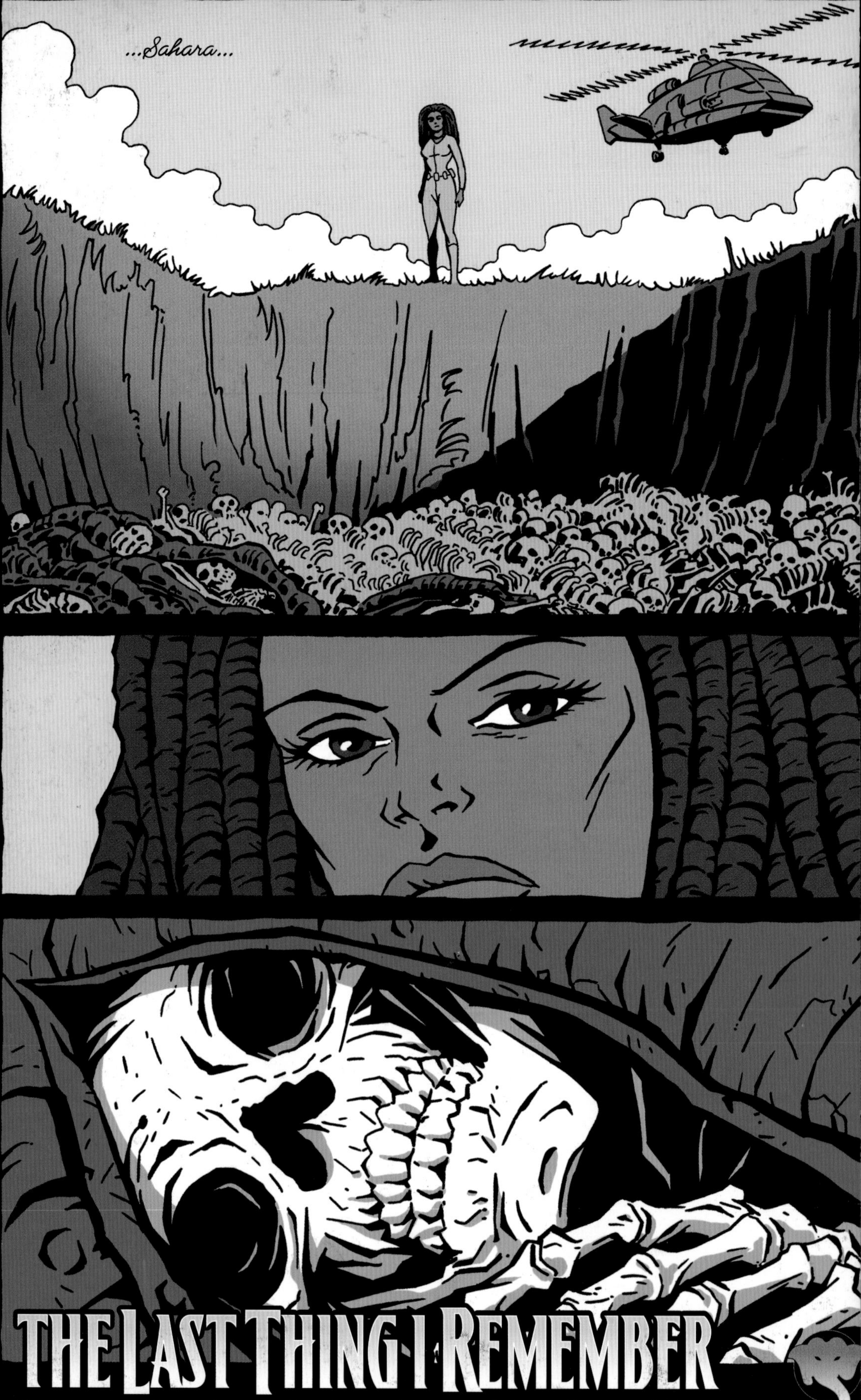
...Sahara...

THE LAST THING I REMEMBER

By Starkings, David Hine & Rob Steen • Cover by J. Scott Campbell & Dave Stewart

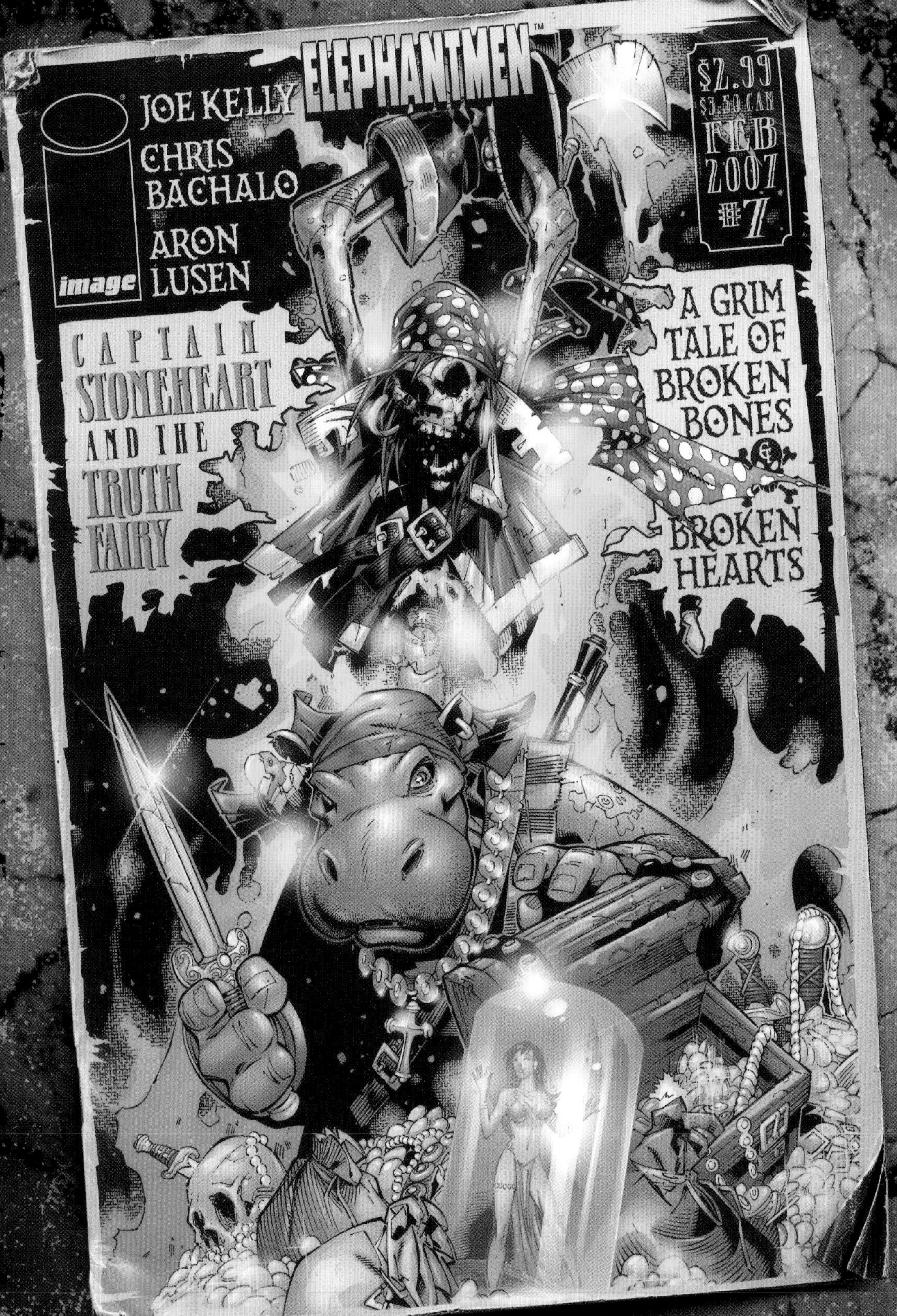

ELEPHANTMEN™
JOE KELLY
CHRIS BACHALO
ARON LUSEN
image
$2.99
$3.50 CAN
FEB 2007
#7
CAPTAIN STONEHEART AND THE TRUTH FAIRY
A GRIM TALE OF BROKEN BONES & BROKEN HEARTS

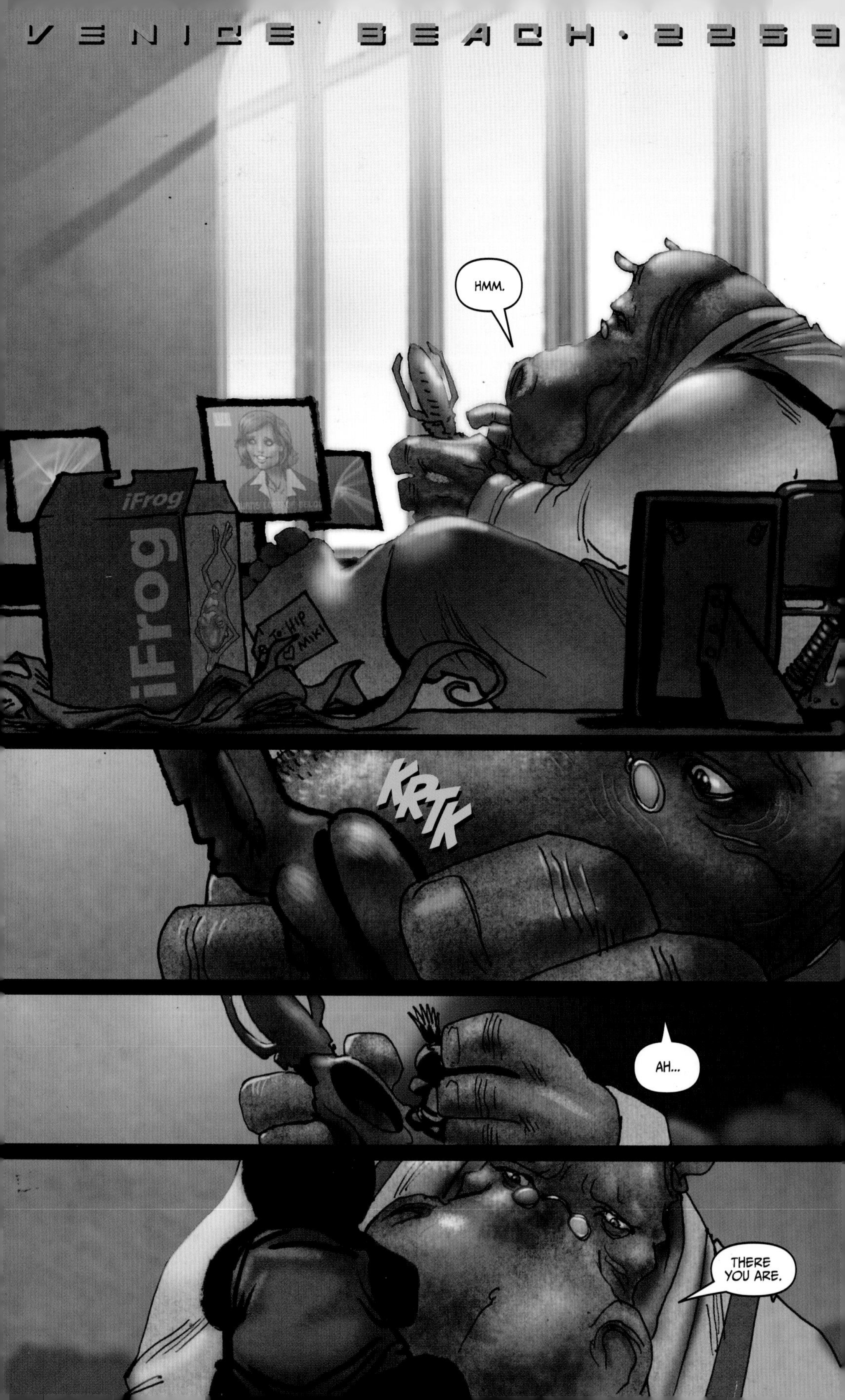
VENICE BEACH · 2259
HMM.
iFrog
iFrog
iFrog
To: HIP MIKI
KRTK
AH...
THERE YOU ARE.

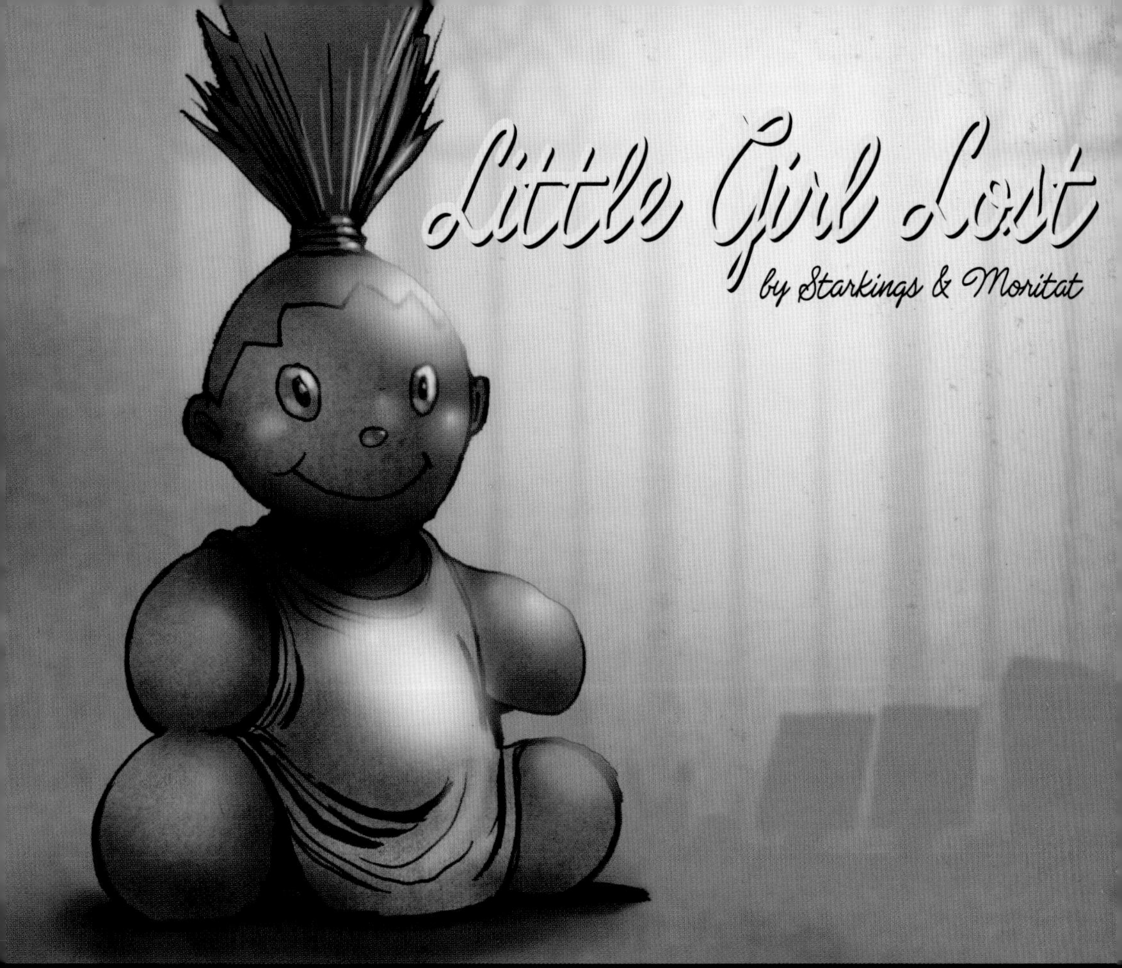
Little Girl Lost
by Starkings & Moritat

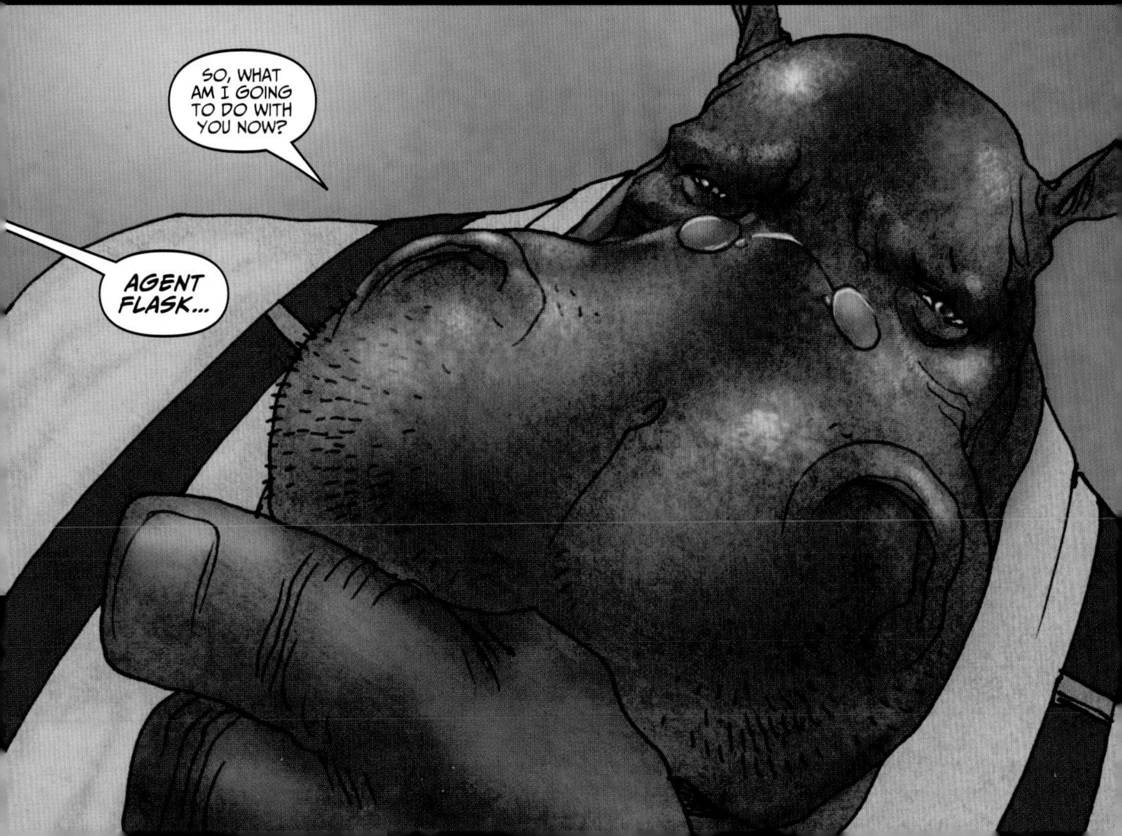
SO, WHAT AM I GOING TO DO WITH YOU NOW?
AGENT FLASK...

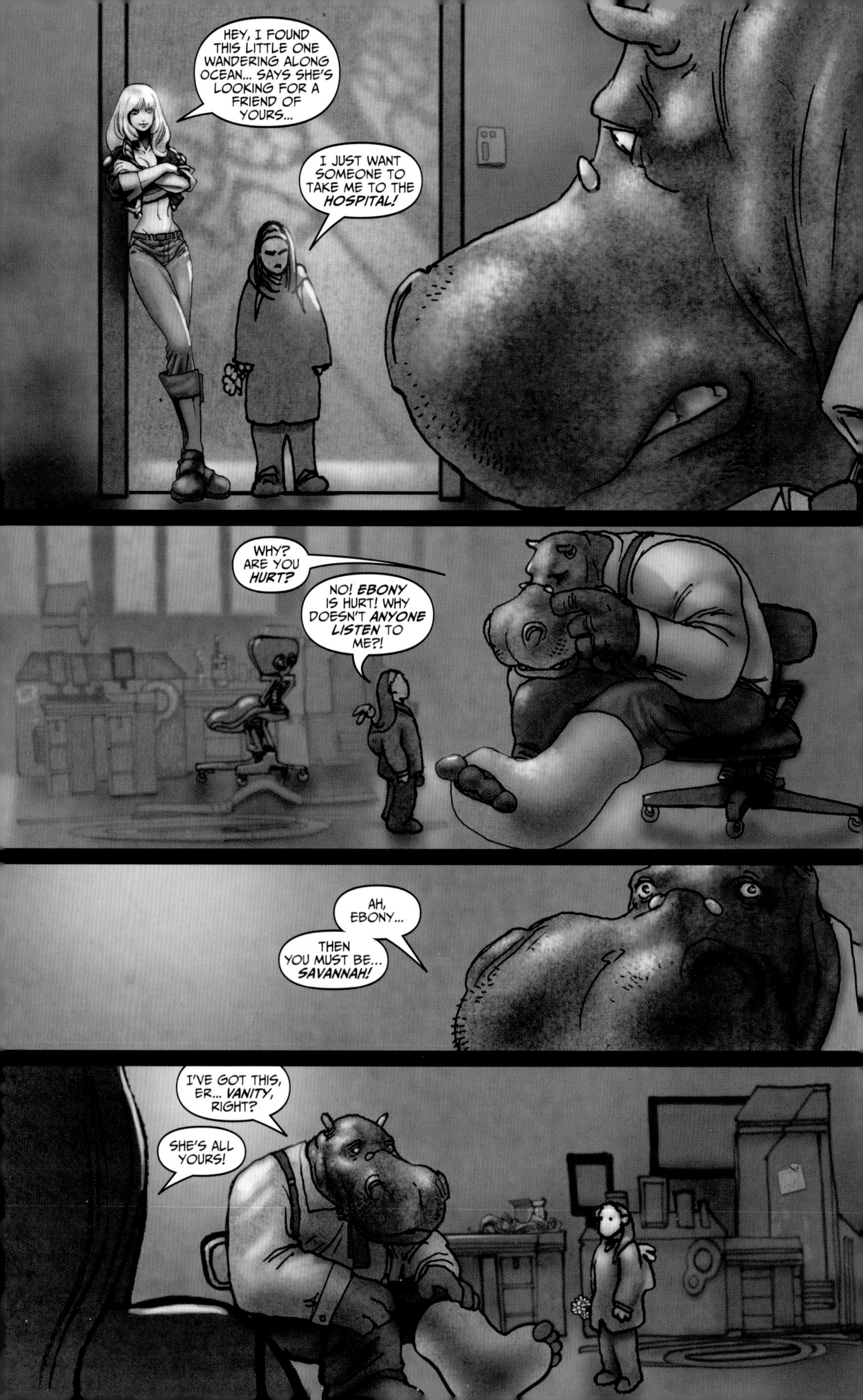
HEY, I FOUND THIS LITTLE ONE WANDERING ALONG OCEAN... SAYS SHE'S LOOKING FOR A FRIEND OF YOURS...
I JUST WANT SOMEONE TO TAKE ME TO THE HOSPITAL!
WHY? ARE YOU HURT?
NO! EBONY IS HURT! WHY DOESN'T ANYONE LISTEN TO ME?!
AH, EBONY...
THEN YOU MUST BE... SAVANNAH!
I'VE GOT THIS, ER... VANITY, RIGHT?
SHE'S ALL YOURS!

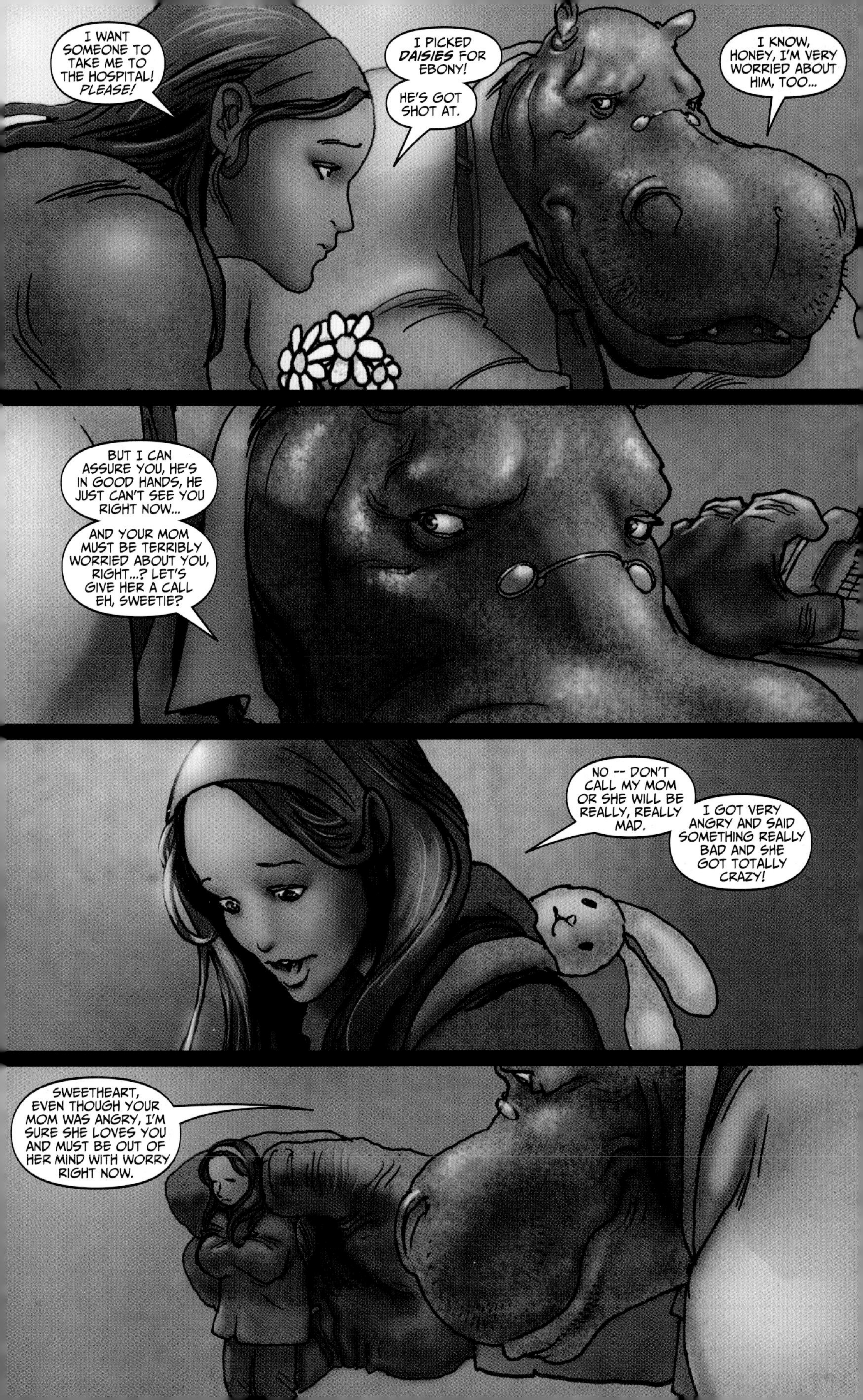
I WANT SOMEONE TO TAKE ME TO THE HOSPITAL! PLEASE!
I PICKED DAISIES FOR EBONY!
HE'S GOT SHOT AT.
I KNOW, HONEY, I'M VERY WORRIED ABOUT HIM, TOO...
BUT I CAN ASSURE YOU, HE'S IN GOOD HANDS, HE JUST CAN'T SEE YOU RIGHT NOW...
AND YOUR MOM MUST BE TERRIBLY WORRIED ABOUT YOU, RIGHT...? LET'S GIVE HER A CALL EH, SWEETIE?
NO -- DON'T CALL MY MOM OR SHE WILL BE REALLY, REALLY MAD.
I GOT VERY ANGRY AND SAID SOMETHING REALLY BAD AND SHE GOT TOTALLY CRAZY!
SWEETHEART, EVEN THOUGH YOUR MOM WAS ANGRY, I'M SURE SHE LOVES YOU AND MUST BE OUT OF HER MIND WITH WORRY RIGHT NOW.

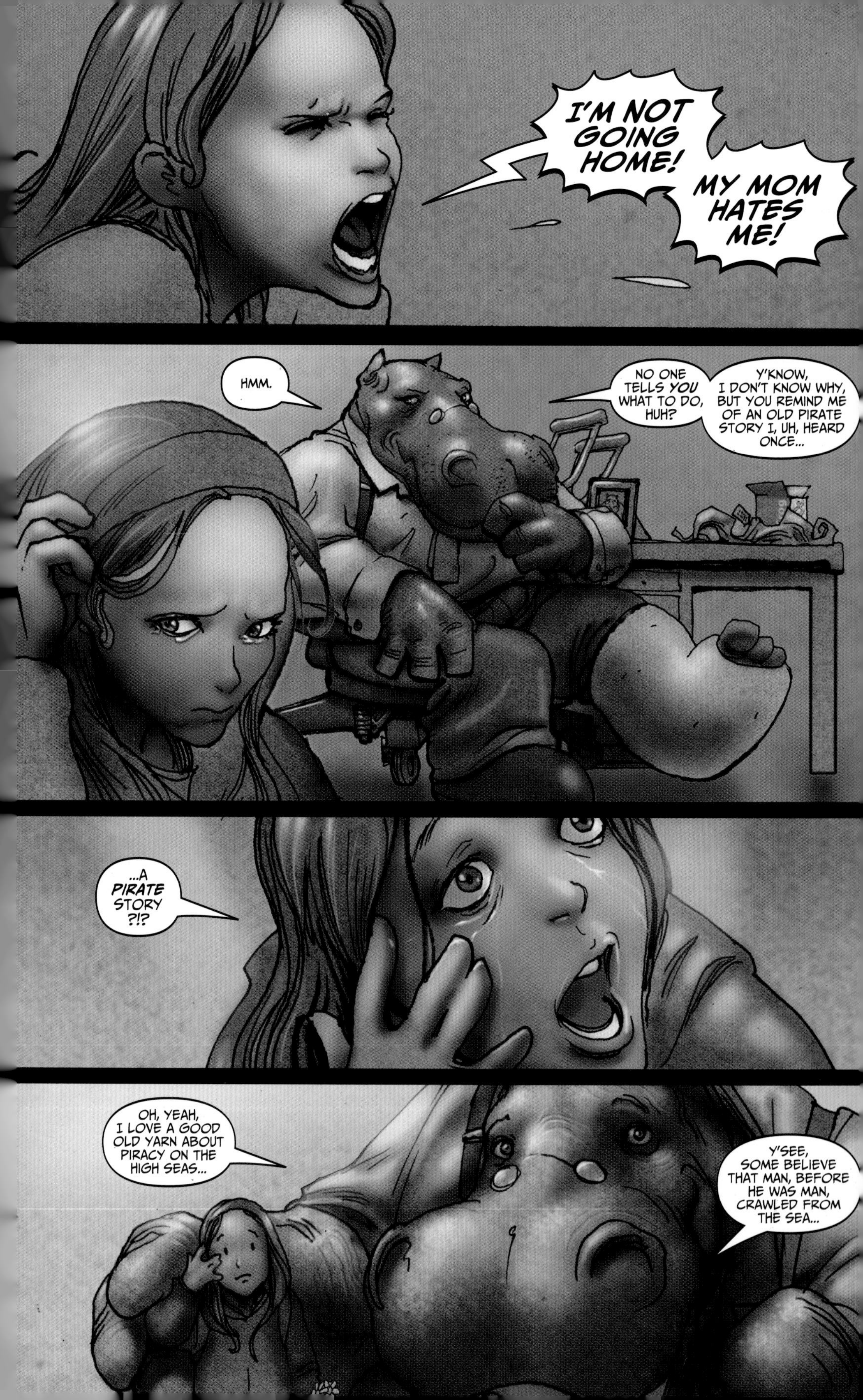
I'M NOT GOING HOME!
MY MOM HATES ME!
HMM.
NO ONE TELLS YOU WHAT TO DO, HUH?
Y'KNOW, I DON'T KNOW WHY, BUT YOU REMIND ME OF AN OLD PIRATE STORY I, UH, HEARD ONCE...
...A PIRATE STORY ?!?
OH, YEAH, I LOVE A GOOD OLD YARN ABOUT PIRACY ON THE HIGH SEAS...
Y'SEE, SOME BELIEVE THAT MAN, BEFORE HE WAS MAN, CRAWLED FROM THE SEA...

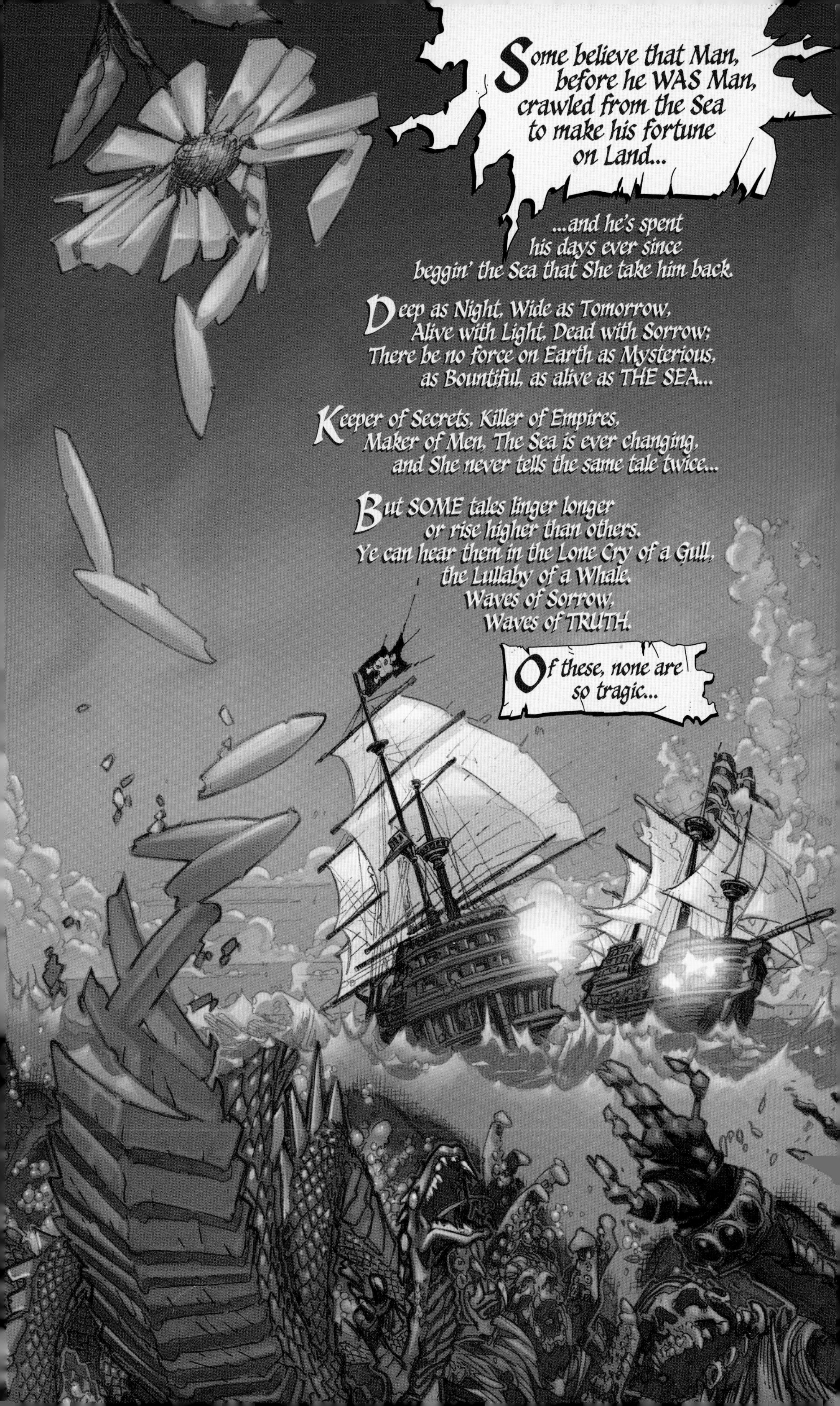

Some believe that Man, before he WAS Man, crawled from the Sea to make his fortune on Land...
...and he's spent his days ever since beggin' the Sea that She take him back.
Deep as Night, Wide as Tomorrow, Alive with Light, Dead with Sorrow; There be no force on Earth as Mysterious, as Bountiful, as alive as THE SEA...
Keeper of Secrets, Killer of Empires, Maker of Men, The Sea is ever changing, and She never tells the same tale twice...
But SOME tales linger longer or rise higher than others. Ye can hear them in the Lone Cry of a Gull, the Lullaby of a Whale. Waves of Sorrow, Waves of TRUTH.
Of these, none are so tragic...

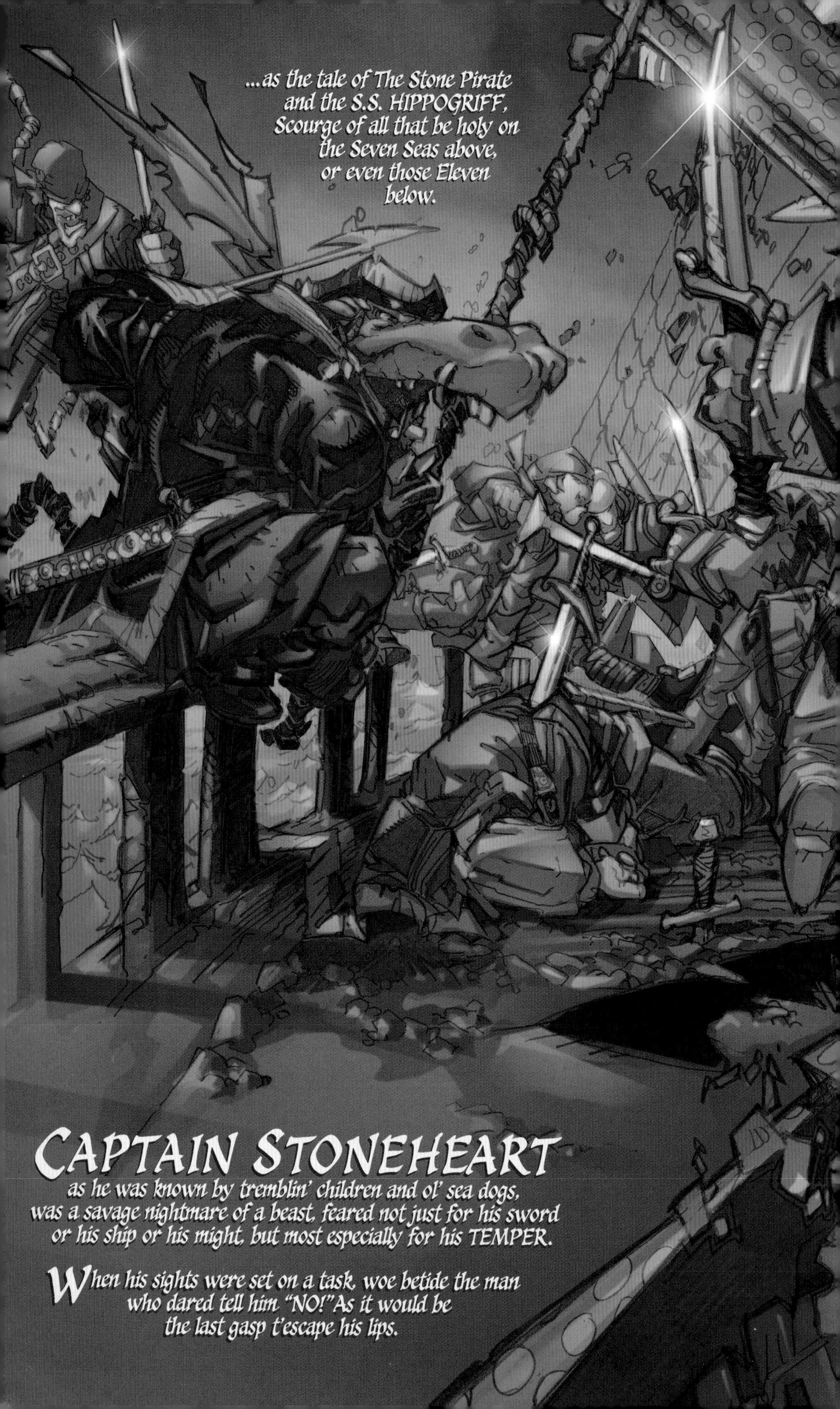
...as the tale of The Stone Pirate and the S.S. HIPPOGRIFF, Scourge of all that be holy on the Seven Seas above, or even those Eleven below.
CAPTAIN STONEHEART
as he was known by tremblin' children and ol' sea dogs, was a savage nightmare of a beast, feared not just for his sword or his ship or his might, but most especially for his TEMPER.
When his sights were set on a task, woe betide the man who dared tell him "NO!" As it would be the last gasp t'escape his lips.

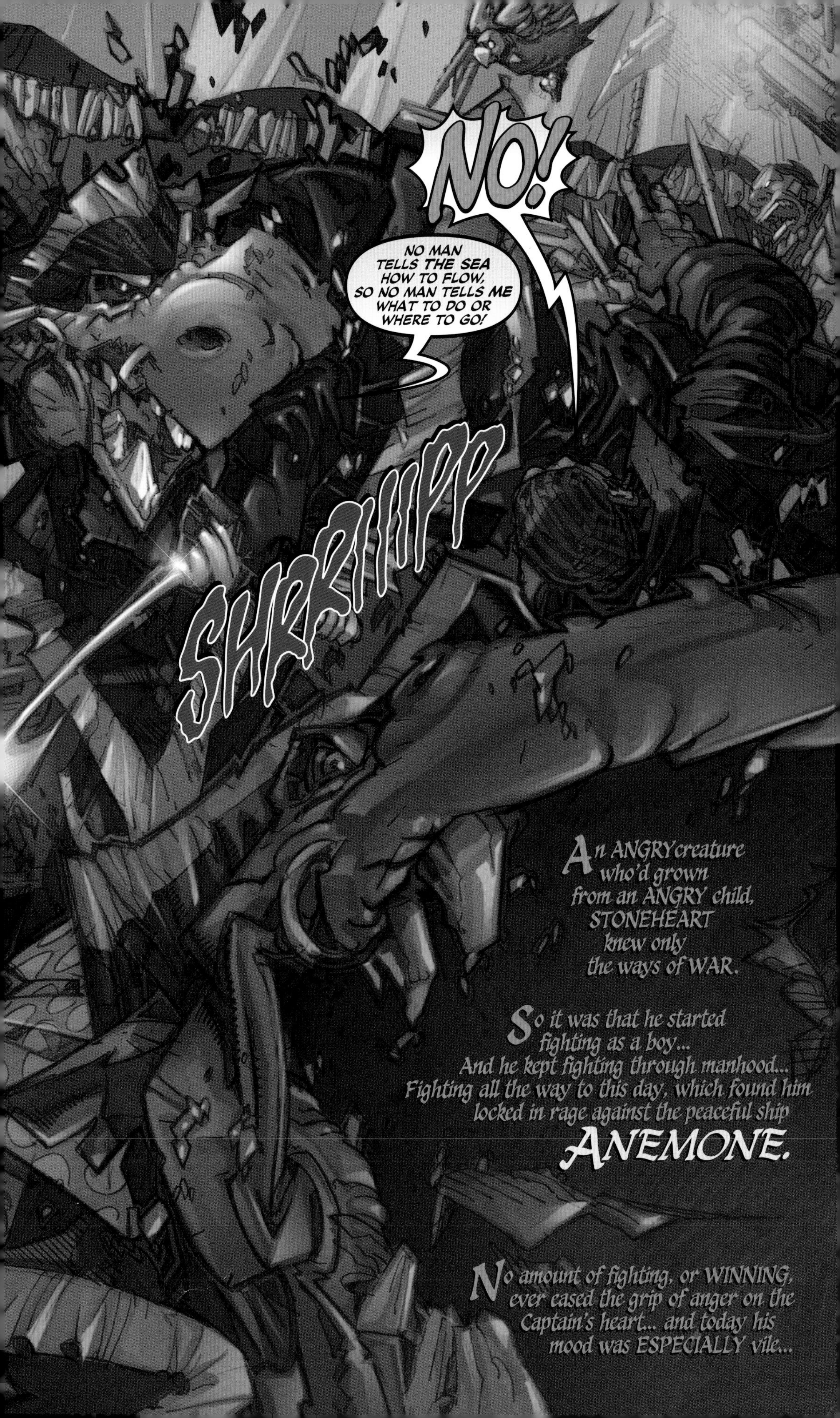
NO!
NO MAN TELLS THE SEA HOW TO FLOW, SO NO MAN TELLS ME WHAT TO DO OR WHERE TO GO!
SHRRIIIPP
An ANGRY creature who'd grown from an ANGRY child, STONEHEART knew only the ways of WAR.
So it was that he started fighting as a boy... And he kept fighting through manhood... Fighting all the way to this day, which found him locked in rage against the peaceful ship
ANEMONE.
No amount of fighting, or WINNING, ever eased the grip of anger on the Captain's heart... and today his mood was ESPECIALLY vile...

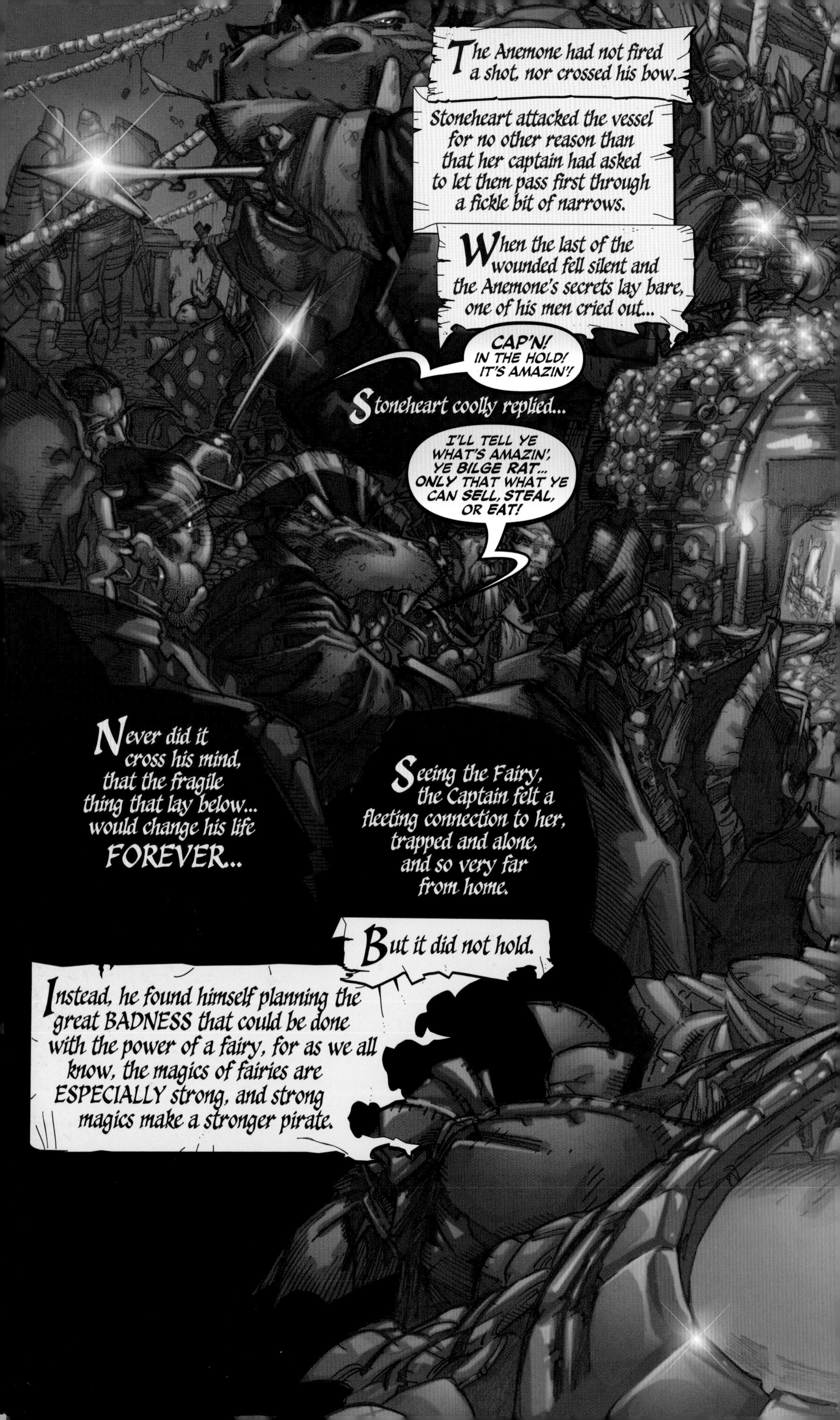
The Anemone had not fired a shot, nor crossed his bow.
Stoneheart attacked the vessel for no other reason than that her captain had asked to let them pass first through a fickle bit of narrows.
When the last of the wounded fell silent and the Anemone's secrets lay bare, one of his men cried out...
CAP'N! IN THE HOLD! IT'S AMAZIN'!
Stoneheart coolly replied...
I'LL TELL YE WHAT'S AMAZIN', YE BILGE RAT... ONLY THAT WHAT YE CAN SELL, STEAL, OR EAT!
Never did it cross his mind, that the fragile thing that lay below... would change his life FOREVER...
Seeing the Fairy, the Captain felt a fleeting connection to her, trapped and alone, and so very far from home.
But it did not hold.
Instead, he found himself planning the great BADNESS that could be done with the power of a fairy, for as we all know, the magics of fairies are ESPECIALLY strong, and strong magics make a stronger pirate.

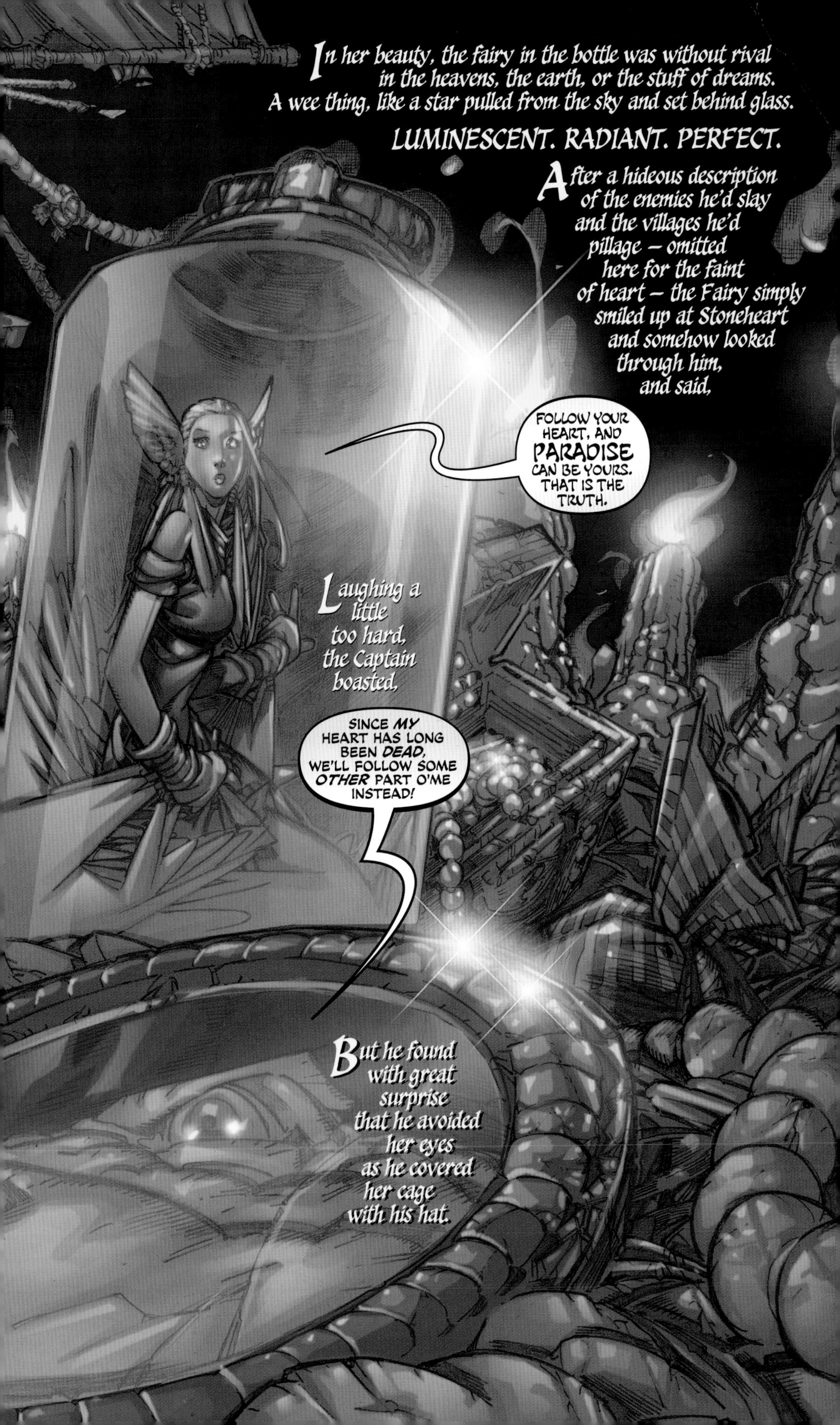
In her beauty, the fairy in the bottle was without rival in the heavens, the earth, or the stuff of dreams. A wee thing, like a star pulled from the sky and set behind glass.
LUMINESCENT. RADIANT. PERFECT.
After a hideous description of the enemies he'd slay and the villages he'd pillage – omitted here for the faint of heart – the Fairy simply smiled up at Stoneheart and somehow looked through him, and said,
FOLLOW YOUR HEART, AND PARADISE CAN BE YOURS. THAT IS THE TRUTH.
Laughing a little too hard, the Captain boasted,
SINCE MY HEART HAS LONG BEEN DEAD, WE'LL FOLLOW SOME OTHER PART O'ME INSTEAD!
But he found with great surprise that he avoided her eyes as he covered her cage with his hat.

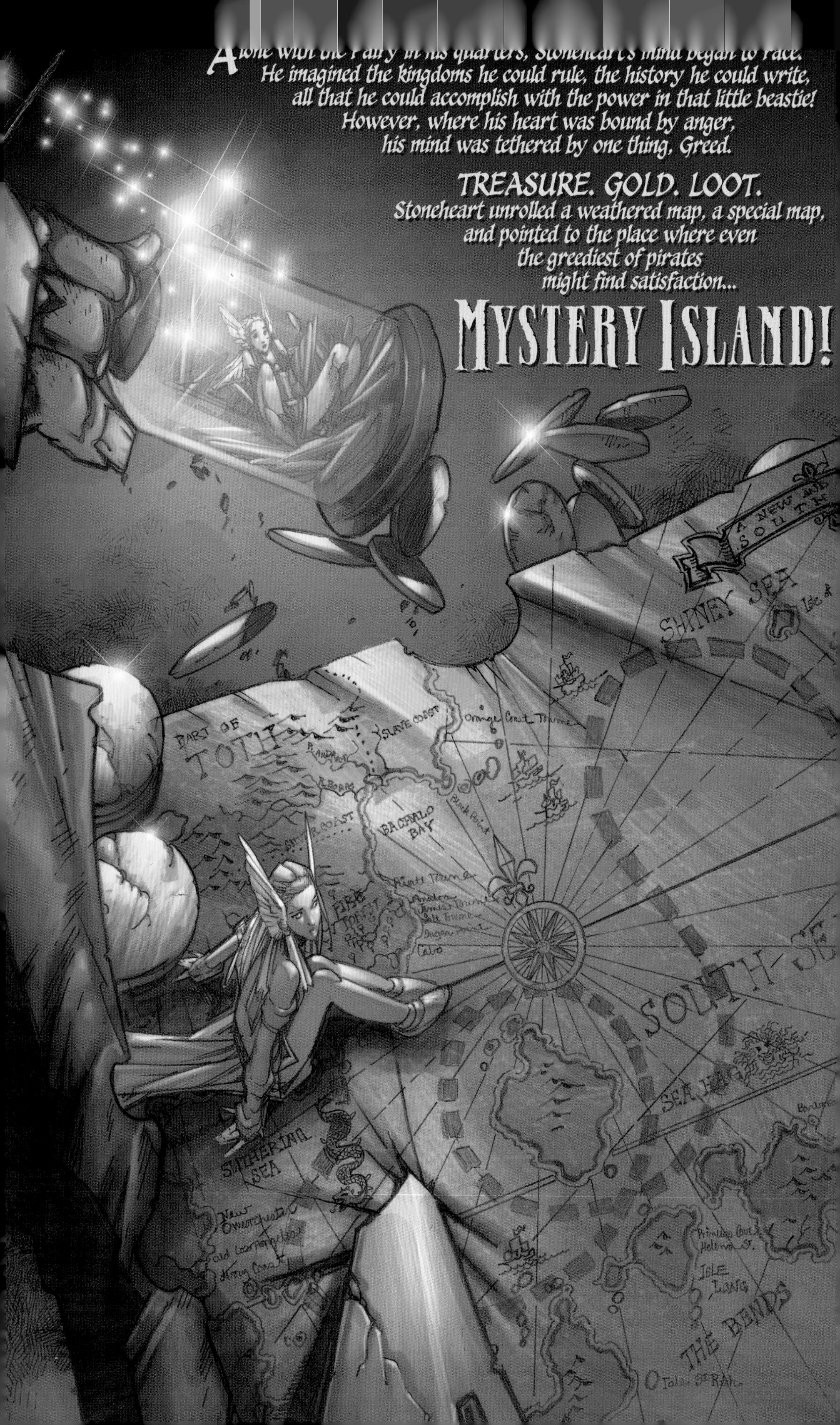
Alone with the Fairy in his quarters, Stoneheart's mind began to race.
He imagined the kingdoms he could rule, the history he could write,
all that he could accomplish with the power in that little beastie!
However, where his heart was bound by anger,
his mind was tethered by one thing, Greed.
TREASURE. GOLD. LOOT.
Stoneheart unrolled a weathered map, a special map,
and pointed to the place where even
the greediest of pirates
might find satisfaction...
MYSTERY ISLAND!
SHINEY SEA
PART OF TOTH
SLAVE COAST
BACHALO BAY
SEA HAG
SLITHERING SEA
ISLE LONG
THE BENDS

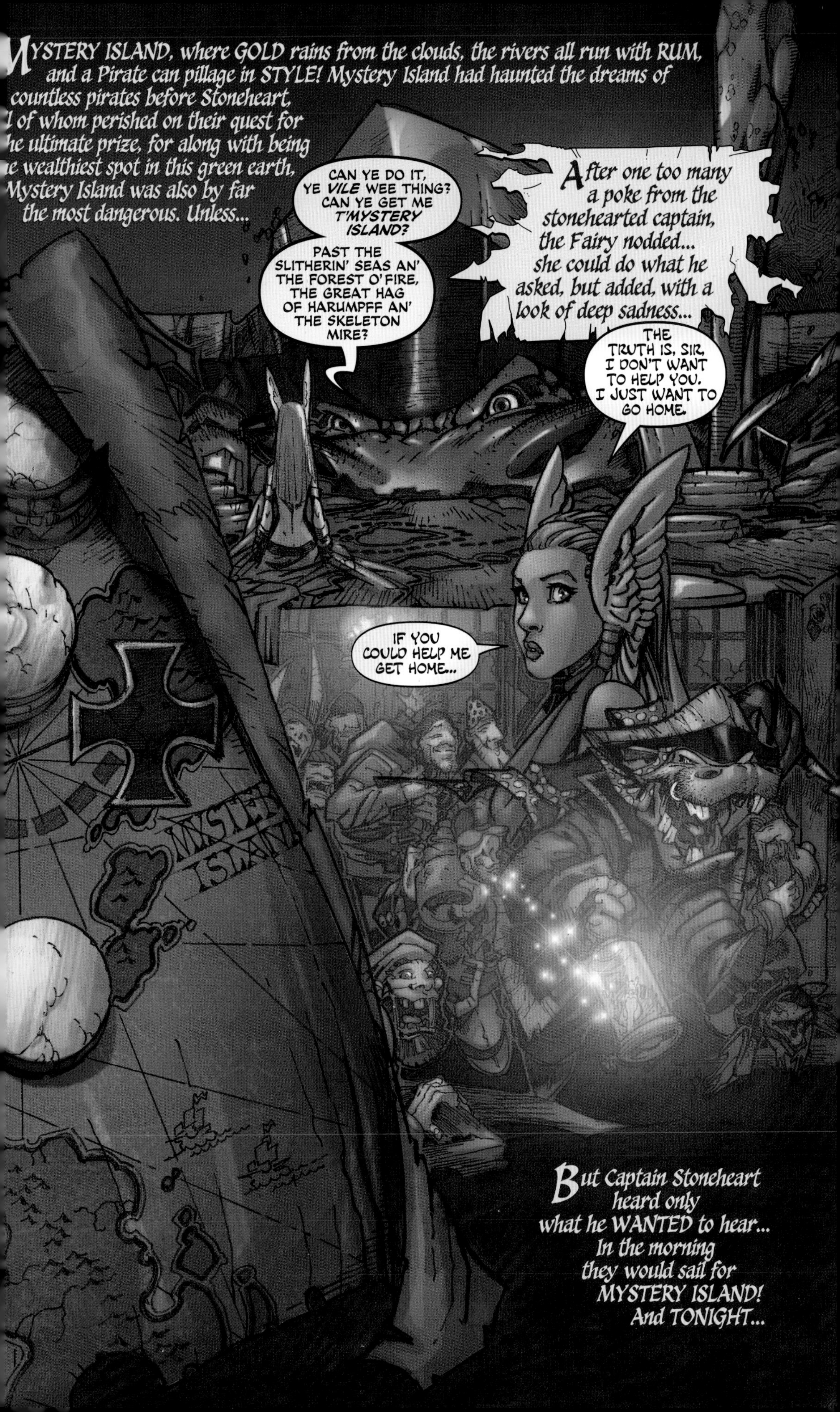
MYSTERY ISLAND, where GOLD rains from the clouds, the rivers all run with RUM, and a Pirate can pillage in STYLE! Mystery Island had haunted the dreams of countless pirates before Stoneheart, all of whom perished on their quest for the ultimate prize, for along with being the wealthiest spot in this green earth, Mystery Island was also by far the most dangerous. Unless...
CAN YE DO IT, YE VILE WEE THING? CAN YE GET ME T'MYSTERY ISLAND?
PAST THE SLITHERIN' SEAS AN' THE FOREST O'FIRE, THE GREAT HAG OF HARUMPFF AN' THE SKELETON MIRE?
After one too many a poke from the stonehearted captain, the Fairy nodded... she could do what he asked, but added, with a look of deep sadness...
THE TRUTH IS, SIR, I DON'T WANT TO HELP YOU. I JUST WANT TO GO HOME.
IF YOU COULD HELP ME GET HOME...
MYSTERY ISLAND
But Captain Stoneheart heard only what he WANTED to hear... In the morning they would sail for MYSTERY ISLAND! And TONIGHT...

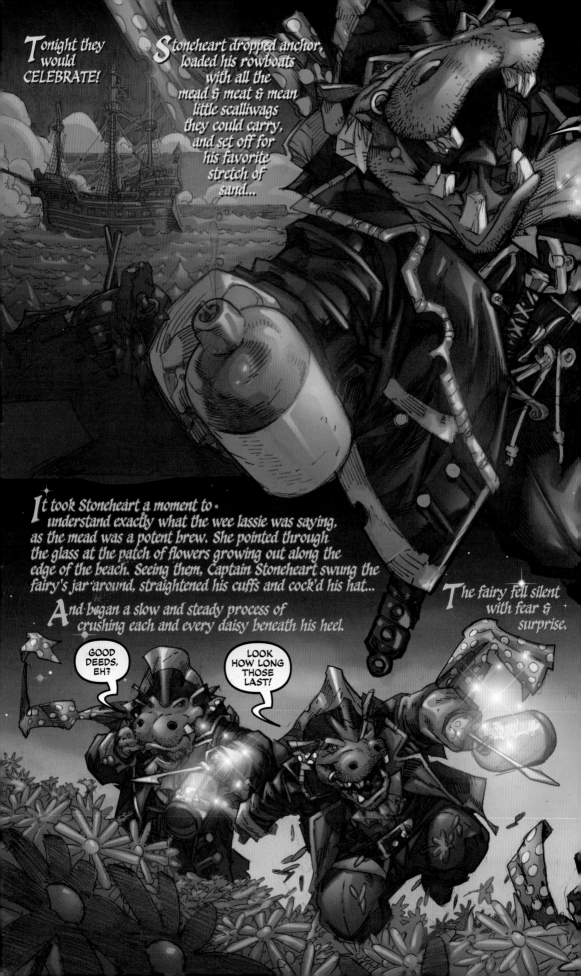

Tonight they would CELEBRATE!

Stoneheart dropped anchor, loaded his rowboats with all the mead & meat & mean little scalliwags they could carry, and set off for his favorite stretch of sand...

It took Stoneheart a moment to understand exactly what the wee lassie was saying, as the mead was a potent brew. She pointed through the glass at the patch of flowers growing out along the edge of the beach. Seeing them, Captain Stoneheart swung the fairy's jar around, straightened his cuffs and cock'd his hat...

And began a slow and steady process of crushing each and every daisy beneath his heel.

The fairy fell silent with fear & surprise.

GOOD DEEDS, EH?

LOOK HOW LONG THOSE LAST!

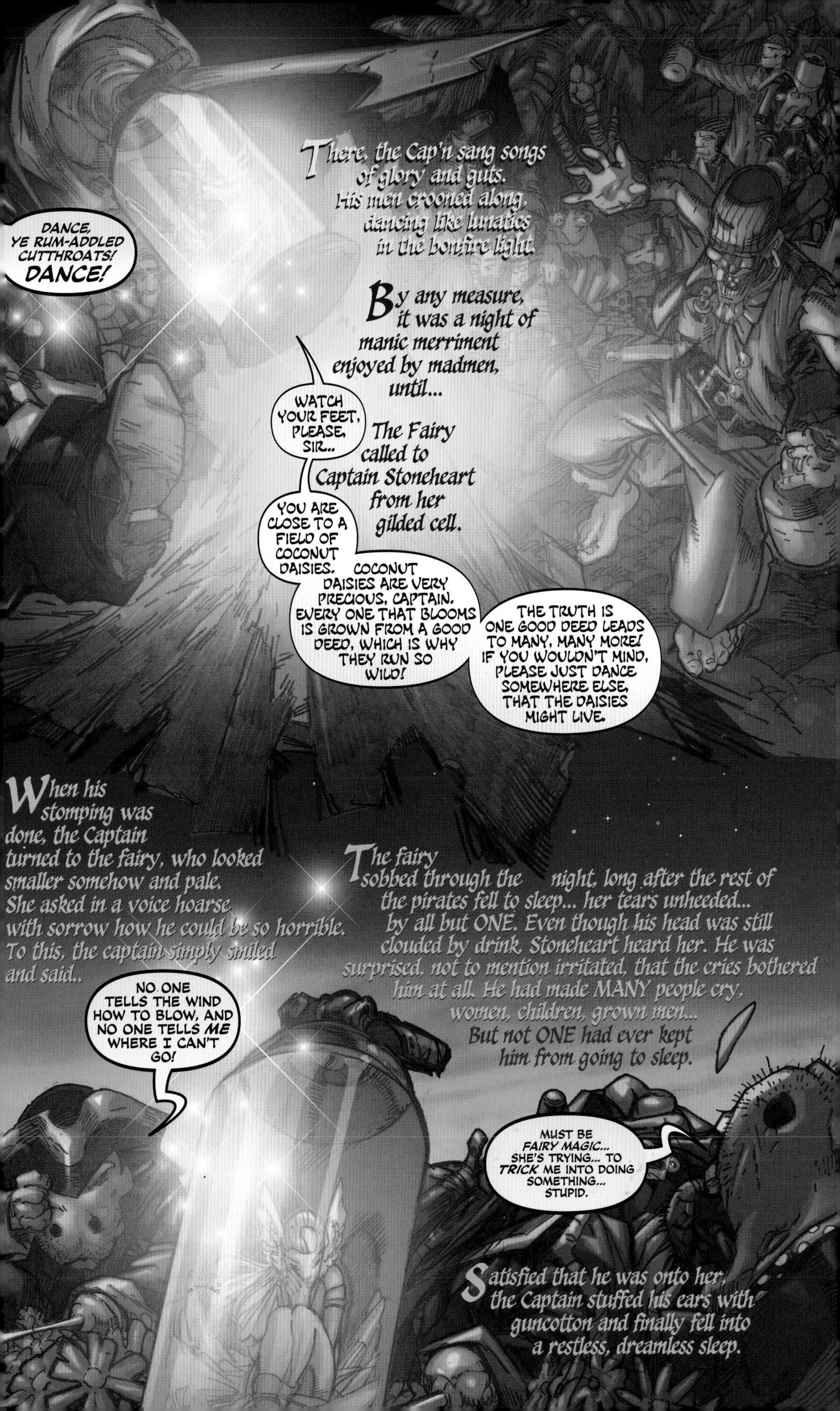
There, the Cap'n sang songs of glory and guts. His men crooned along, dancing like lunatics in the bonfire light.
DANCE, YE RUM-ADDLED CUTTHROATS! DANCE!
By any measure, it was a night of manic merriment enjoyed by madmen, until...
WATCH YOUR FEET, PLEASE, SIR...
The Fairy called to Captain Stoneheart from her gilded cell.
YOU ARE CLOSE TO A FIELD OF COCONUT DAISIES.
COCONUT DAISIES ARE VERY PRECIOUS, CAPTAIN. EVERY ONE THAT BLOOMS IS GROWN FROM A GOOD DEED, WHICH IS WHY THEY RUN SO WILD!
THE TRUTH IS ONE GOOD DEED LEADS TO MANY, MANY MORE! IF YOU WOULDN'T MIND, PLEASE JUST DANCE SOMEWHERE ELSE, THAT THE DAISIES MIGHT LIVE.
When his stomping was done, the Captain turned to the fairy, who looked smaller somehow and pale. She asked in a voice hoarse with sorrow how he could be so horrible. To this, the captain simply smiled and said..
NO ONE TELLS THE WIND HOW TO BLOW, AND NO ONE TELLS ME WHERE I CAN'T GO!
The fairy sobbed through the night, long after the rest of the pirates fell to sleep... her tears unheeded... by all but ONE. Even though his head was still clouded by drink, Stoneheart heard her. He was surprised, not to mention irritated, that the cries bothered him at all. He had made MANY people cry, women, children, grown men... But not ONE had ever kept him from going to sleep.
MUST BE FAIRY MAGIC... SHE'S TRYING... TO TRICK ME INTO DOING SOMETHING... STUPID.
Satisfied that he was onto her, the Captain stuffed his ears with guncotton and finally fell into a restless, dreamless sleep.

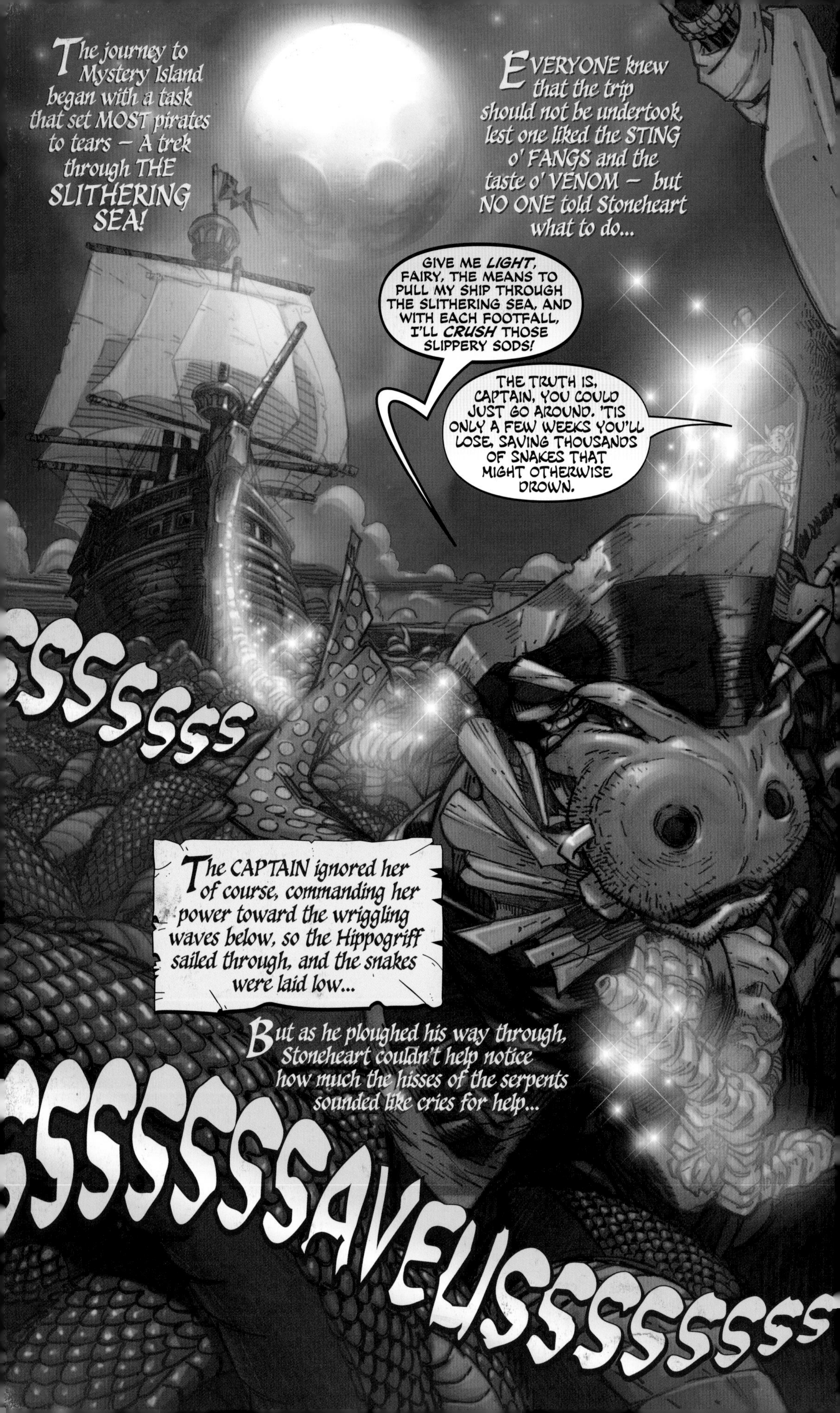
The journey to Mystery Island began with a task that set MOST pirates to tears — A trek through THE SLITHERING SEA!
EVERYONE knew that the trip should not be undertook, lest one liked the STING o' FANGS and the taste o' VENOM — but NO ONE told Stoneheart what to do...
GIVE ME LIGHT, FAIRY, THE MEANS TO PULL MY SHIP THROUGH THE SLITHERING SEA, AND WITH EACH FOOTFALL, I'LL CRUSH THOSE SLIPPERY SODS!
THE TRUTH IS, CAPTAIN, YOU COULD JUST GO AROUND. 'TIS ONLY A FEW WEEKS YOU'LL LOSE, SAVING THOUSANDS OF SNAKES THAT MIGHT OTHERWISE DROWN.
SSSSSSSS
The CAPTAIN ignored her of course, commanding her power toward the wriggling waves below, so the Hippogriff sailed through, and the snakes were laid low...
But as he ploughed his way through, Stoneheart couldn't help notice how much the hisses of the serpents sounded like cries for help...
SSSSSSSSAVEUSSSSSSSSS

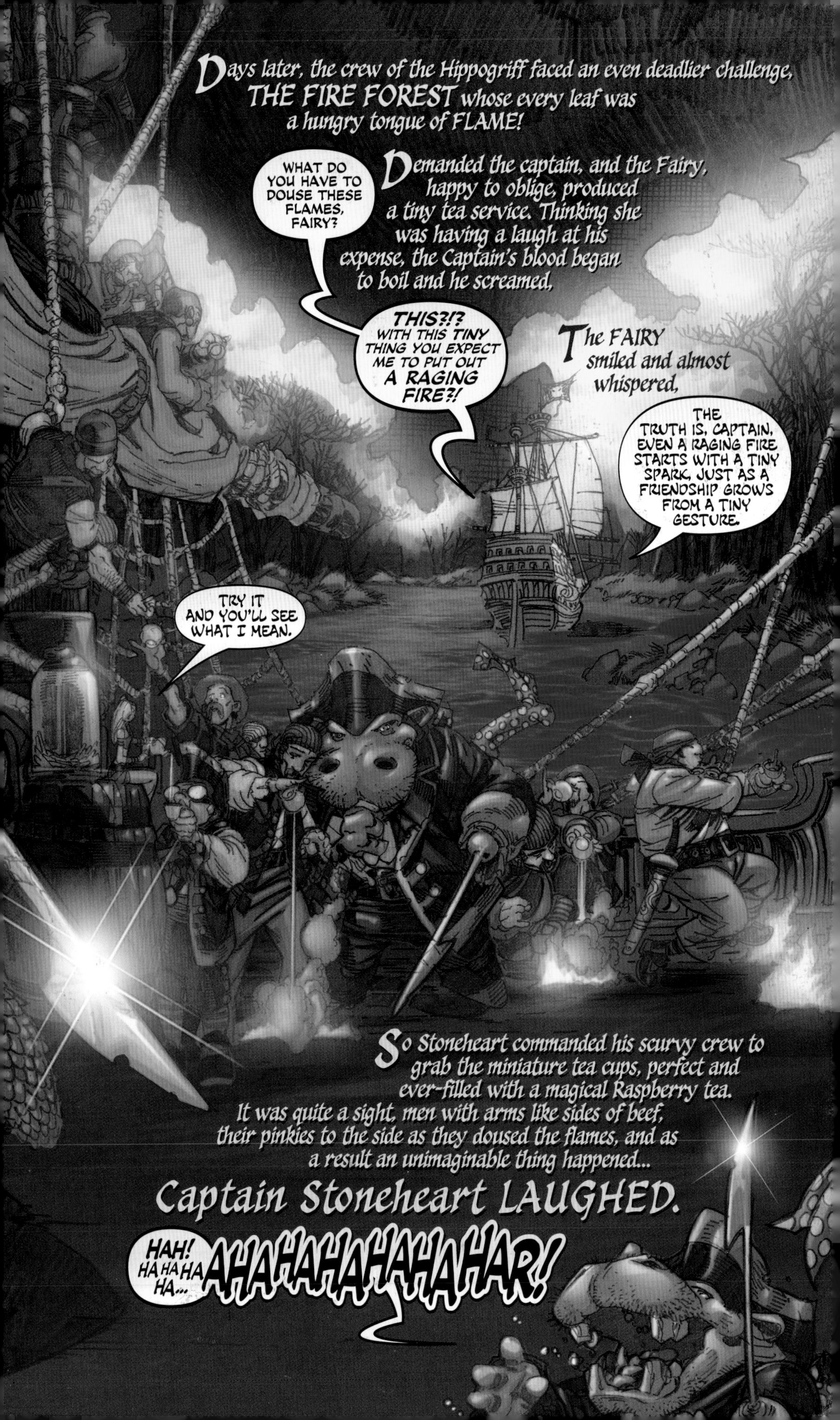

Days later, the crew of the Hippogriff faced an even deadlier challenge, THE FIRE FOREST whose every leaf was a hungry tongue of FLAME!
WHAT DO YOU HAVE TO DOUSE THESE FLAMES, FAIRY?
Demanded the captain, and the Fairy, happy to oblige, produced a tiny tea service. Thinking she was having a laugh at his expense, the Captain's blood began to boil and he screamed,
THIS?!? WITH THIS TINY THING YOU EXPECT ME TO PUT OUT A RAGING FIRE?!
The FAIRY smiled and almost whispered,
THE TRUTH IS, CAPTAIN, EVEN A RAGING FIRE STARTS WITH A TINY SPARK, JUST AS A FRIENDSHIP GROWS FROM A TINY GESTURE.
TRY IT AND YOU'LL SEE WHAT I MEAN.
So Stoneheart commanded his scurvy crew to grab the miniature tea cups, perfect and ever-filled with a magical Raspberry tea. It was quite a sight, men with arms like sides of beef, their pinkies to the side as they doused the flames, and as a result an unimaginable thing happened...
Captain Stoneheart LAUGHED.
HAH! HA HA HA HA...
AHAHAHAHAHAHAR!

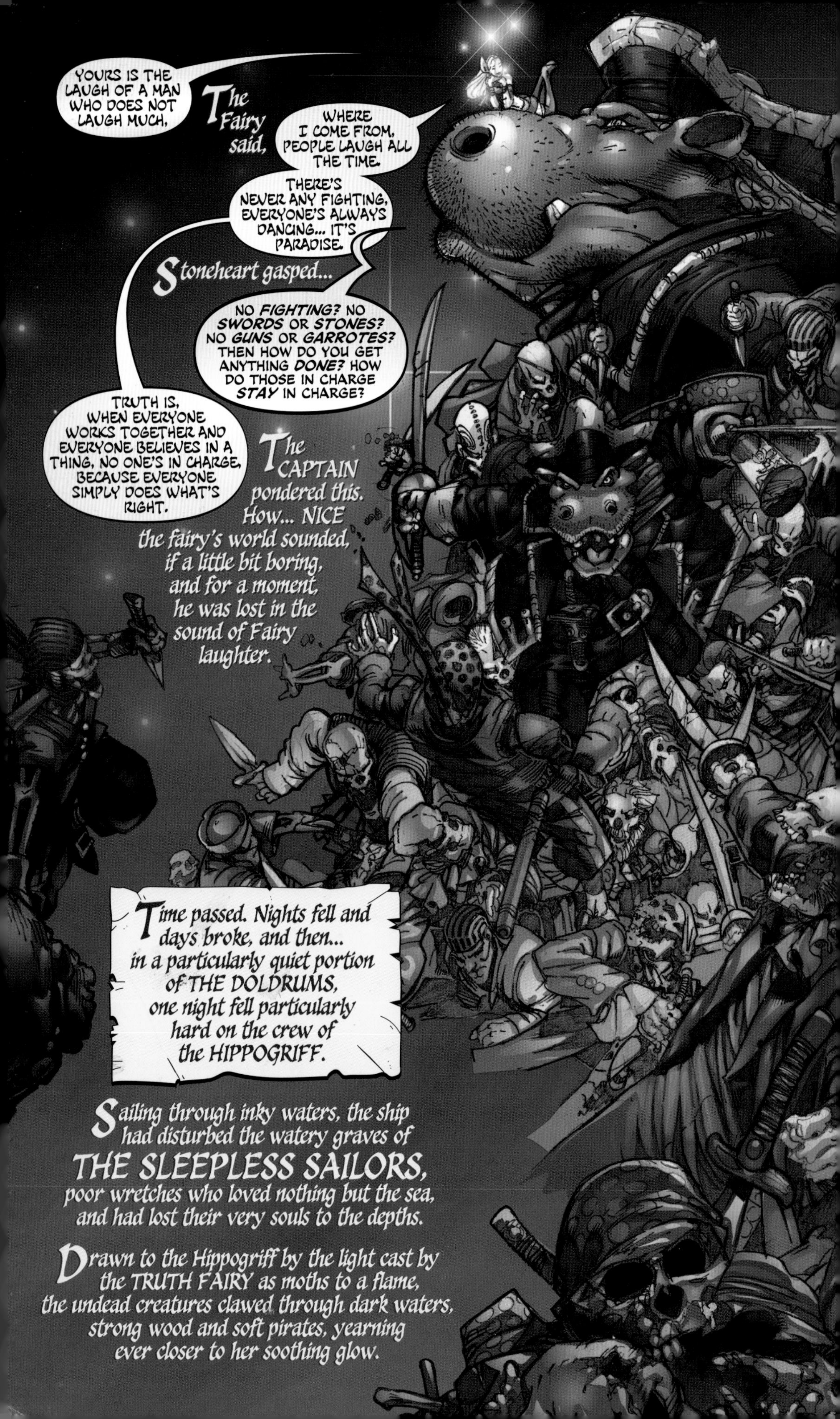
YOURS IS THE LAUGH OF A MAN WHO DOES NOT LAUGH MUCH,
The Fairy said,
WHERE I COME FROM, PEOPLE LAUGH ALL THE TIME.
THERE'S NEVER ANY FIGHTING, EVERYONE'S ALWAYS DANCING... IT'S PARADISE.
Stoneheart gasped...
NO *FIGHTING*? NO *SWORDS* OR *STONES*? NO *GUNS* OR *GARROTES*? THEN HOW DO YOU GET ANYTHING *DONE*? HOW DO THOSE IN CHARGE *STAY* IN CHARGE?
TRUTH IS, WHEN EVERYONE WORKS TOGETHER AND EVERYONE BELIEVES IN A THING, NO ONE'S IN CHARGE, BECAUSE EVERYONE SIMPLY DOES WHAT'S RIGHT.
The CAPTAIN pondered this. How... NICE the fairy's world sounded, if a little bit boring, and for a moment, he was lost in the sound of Fairy laughter.
Time passed. Nights fell and days broke, and then... in a particularly quiet portion of THE DOLDRUMS, one night fell particularly hard on the crew of the HIPPOGRIFF.
Sailing through inky waters, the ship had disturbed the watery graves of
THE SLEEPLESS SAILORS,
poor wretches who loved nothing but the sea, and had lost their very souls to the depths.
Drawn to the Hippogriff by the light cast by the TRUTH FAIRY as moths to a flame, the undead creatures clawed through dark waters, strong wood and soft pirates, yearning ever closer to her soothing glow.

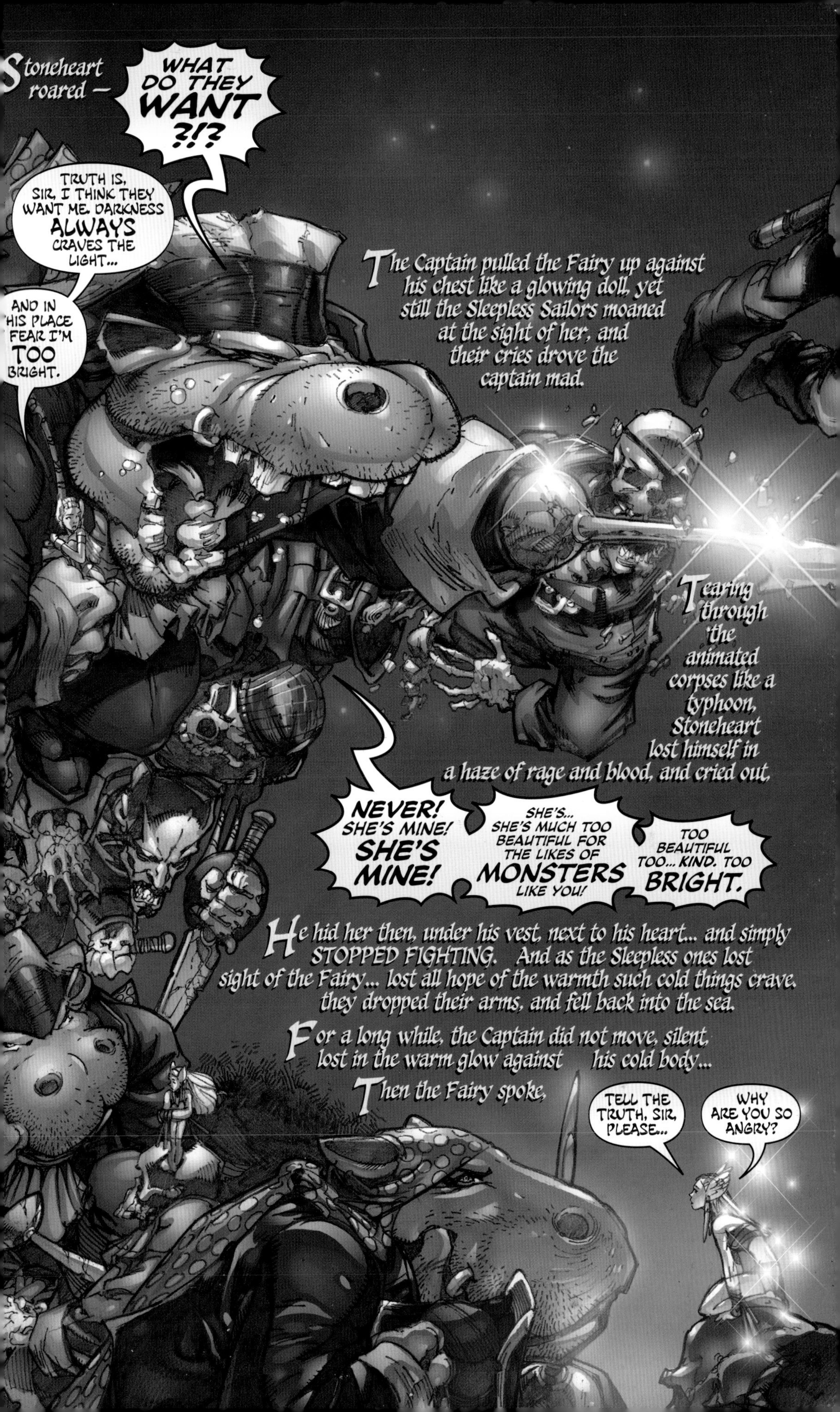
Stoneheart roared —
WHAT DO THEY WANT ?!?
TRUTH IS, SIR, I THINK THEY WANT ME. DARKNESS ALWAYS CRAVES THE LIGHT...
AND IN HIS PLACE FEAR I'M TOO BRIGHT.
The Captain pulled the Fairy up against his chest like a glowing doll, yet still the Sleepless Sailors moaned at the sight of her, and their cries drove the captain mad.
Tearing through 'the animated corpses like a typhoon, Stoneheart lost himself in a haze of rage and blood, and cried out,
NEVER! SHE'S MINE! SHE'S MINE!
SHE'S... SHE'S MUCH TOO BEAUTIFUL FOR THE LIKES OF MONSTERS LIKE YOU!
TOO BEAUTIFUL TOO... KIND. TOO BRIGHT.
He hid her then, under his vest, next to his heart... and simply STOPPED FIGHTING. And as the Sleepless ones lost sight of the Fairy... lost all hope of the warmth such cold things crave, they dropped their arms, and fell back into the sea.
For a long while, the Captain did not move, silent, lost in the warm glow against his cold body...
Then the Fairy spoke,
TELL THE TRUTH, SIR, PLEASE...
WHY ARE YOU SO ANGRY?

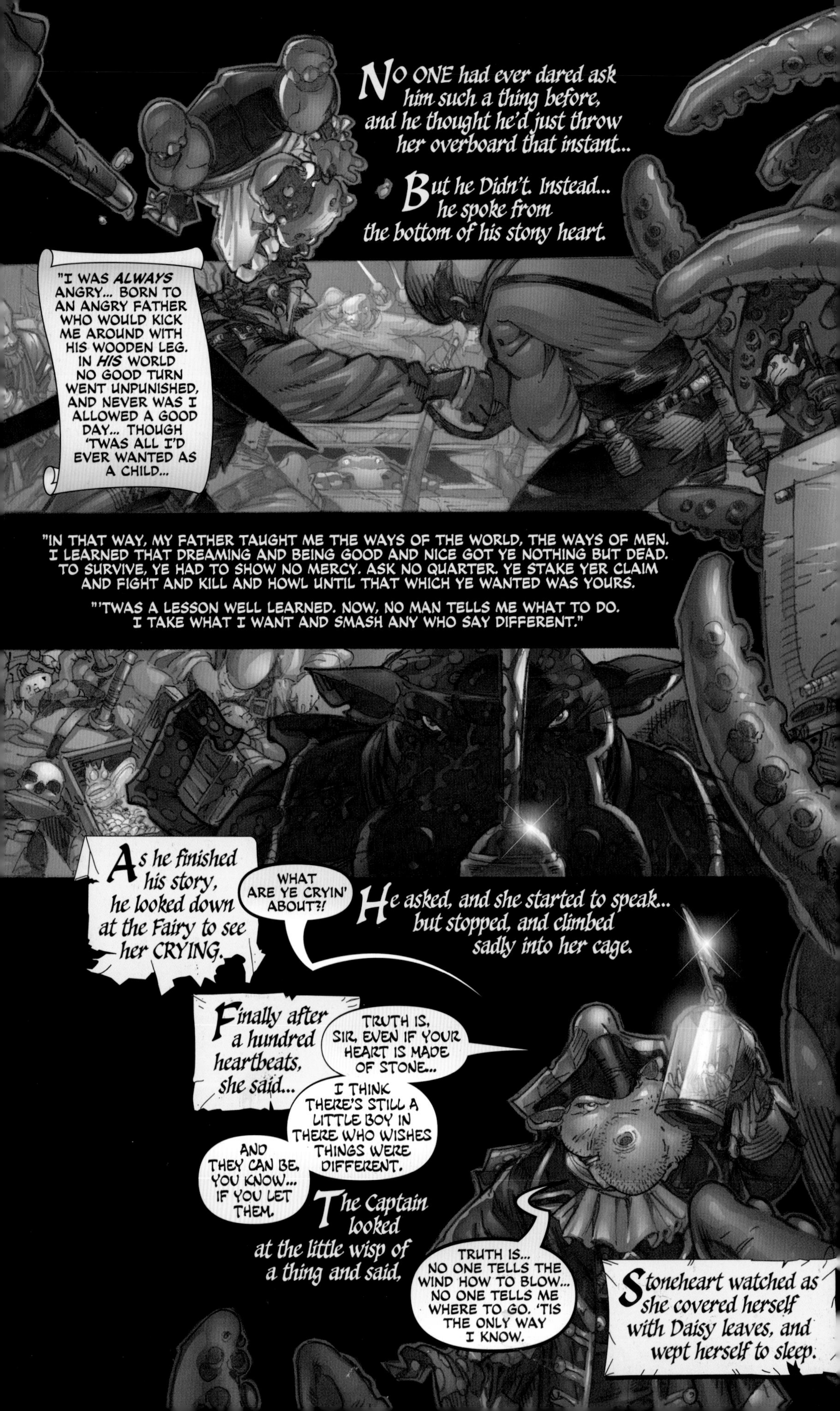
NO ONE had ever dared ask him such a thing before, and he thought he'd just throw her overboard that instant...
But he Didn't. Instead... he spoke from the bottom of his stony heart.
"I WAS ALWAYS ANGRY... BORN TO AN ANGRY FATHER WHO WOULD KICK ME AROUND WITH HIS WOODEN LEG. IN HIS WORLD NO GOOD TURN WENT UNPUNISHED, AND NEVER WAS I ALLOWED A GOOD DAY... THOUGH 'TWAS ALL I'D EVER WANTED AS A CHILD...
"IN THAT WAY, MY FATHER TAUGHT ME THE WAYS OF THE WORLD, THE WAYS OF MEN. I LEARNED THAT DREAMING AND BEING GOOD AND NICE GOT YE NOTHING BUT DEAD. TO SURVIVE, YE HAD TO SHOW NO MERCY. ASK NO QUARTER. YE STAKE YER CLAIM AND FIGHT AND KILL AND HOWL UNTIL THAT WHICH YE WANTED WAS YOURS.
"'TWAS A LESSON WELL LEARNED. NOW, NO MAN TELLS ME WHAT TO DO. I TAKE WHAT I WANT AND SMASH ANY WHO SAY DIFFERENT."
As he finished his story, he looked down at the Fairy to see her CRYING.
WHAT ARE YE CRYIN' ABOUT?!
He asked, and she started to speak... but stopped, and climbed sadly into her cage.
Finally after a hundred heartbeats, she said...
TRUTH IS, SIR, EVEN IF YOUR HEART IS MADE OF STONE...
I THINK THERE'S STILL A LITTLE BOY IN THERE WHO WISHES THINGS WERE DIFFERENT.
AND THEY CAN BE, YOU KNOW... IF YOU LET THEM.
The Captain looked at the little wisp of a thing and said,
TRUTH IS... NO ONE TELLS THE WIND HOW TO BLOW... NO ONE TELLS ME WHERE TO GO. 'TIS THE ONLY WAY I KNOW.
Stoneheart watched as she covered herself with Daisy leaves, and wept herself to sleep.

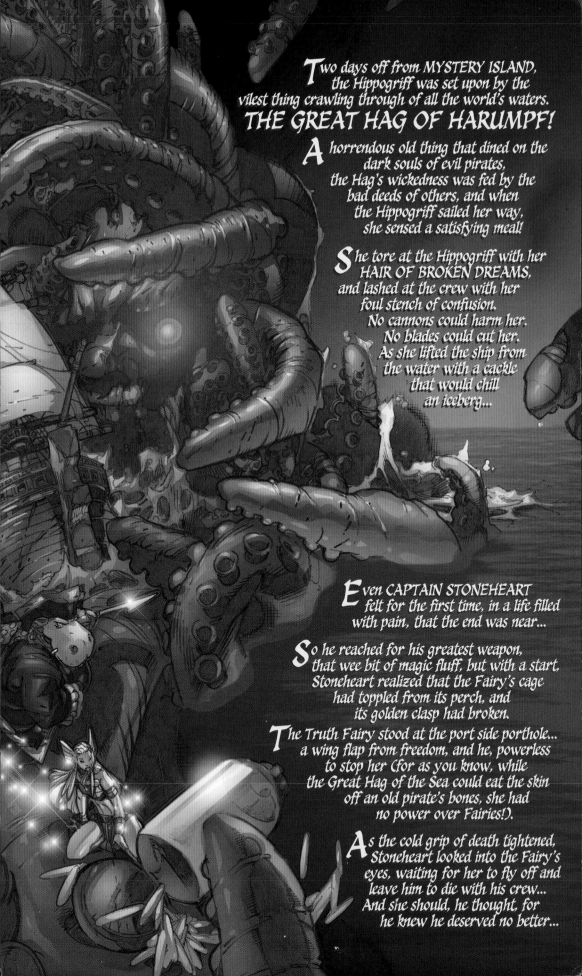

*T*wo days off from MYSTERY ISLAND,
the Hippogriff was set upon by the
vilest thing crawling through of all the world's waters.

THE GREAT HAG OF HARUMPF!

A horrendous old thing that dined on the
dark souls of evil pirates,
the Hag's wickedness was fed by the
bad deeds of others, and when
the Hippogriff sailed her way,
she sensed a satisfying meal!

*S*he tore at the Hippogriff with her
HAIR OF BROKEN DREAMS,
and lashed at the crew with her
foul stench of confusion.
No cannons could harm her.
No blades could cut her.
As she lifted the ship from
the water with a cackle
that would chill
an iceberg...

*E*ven CAPTAIN STONEHEART
felt for the first time, in a life filled
with pain, that the end was near...

*S*o he reached for his greatest weapon,
that wee bit of magic fluff, but with a start,
Stoneheart realized that the Fairy's cage
had toppled from its perch, and
its golden clasp had broken.

*T*he Truth Fairy stood at the port side porthole...
a wing flap from freedom, and he, powerless
to stop her (for as you know, while
the Great Hag of the Sea could eat the skin
off an old pirate's bones, she had
no power over Fairies!).

*A*s the cold grip of death tightened,
Stoneheart looked into the Fairy's
eyes, waiting for her to fly off and
leave him to die with his crew...
And she should, he thought, for
he knew he deserved no better...

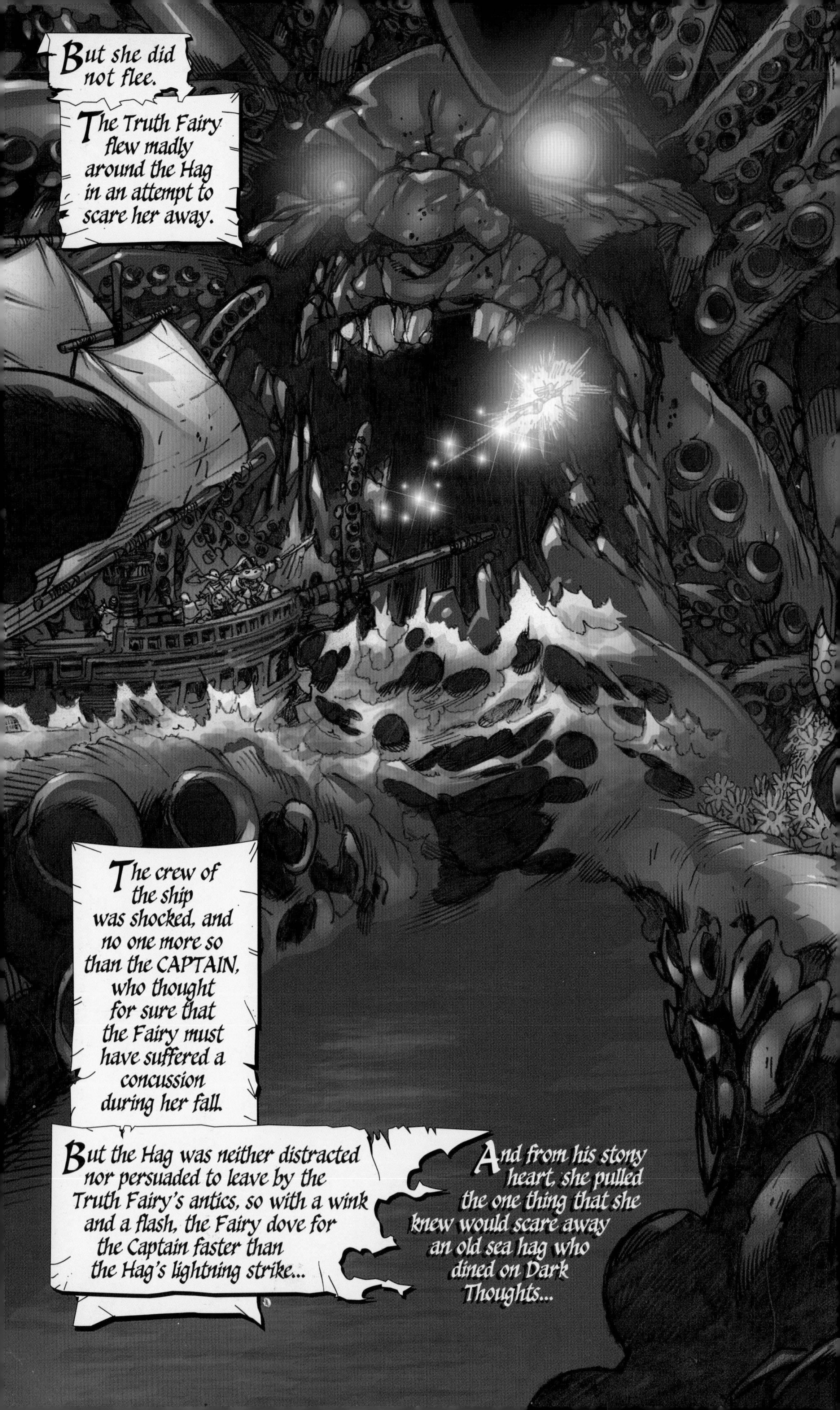
But she did not flee.
The Truth Fairy flew madly around the Hag in an attempt to scare her away.
The crew of the ship was shocked, and no one more so than the CAPTAIN, who thought for sure that the Fairy must have suffered a concussion during her fall.
But the Hag was neither distracted nor persuaded to leave by the Truth Fairy's antics, so with a wink and a flash, the Fairy dove for the Captain faster than the Hag's lightning strike...
And from his stony heart, she pulled the one thing that she knew would scare away an old sea hag who dined on Dark Thoughts...

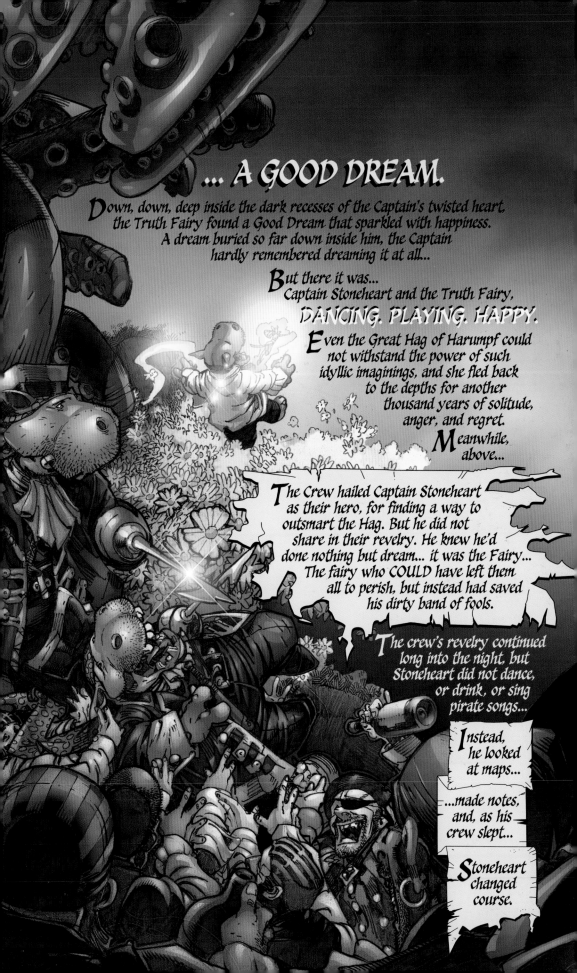

... A GOOD DREAM.

Down, down, deep inside the dark recesses of the Captain's twisted heart, the Truth Fairy found a Good Dream that sparkled with happiness. A dream buried so far down inside him, the Captain hardly remembered dreaming it at all...

But there it was... Captain Stoneheart and the Truth Fairy, DANCING. PLAYING. HAPPY.

Even the Great Hag of Harumpf could not withstand the power of such idyllic imaginings, and she fled back to the depths for another thousand years of solitude, anger, and regret. Meanwhile, above...

The Crew hailed Captain Stoneheart as their hero, for finding a way to outsmart the Hag. But he did not share in their revelry. He knew he'd done nothing but dream... it was the Fairy... The fairy who COULD have left them all to perish, but instead had saved his dirty band of fools.

The crew's revelry continued long into the night, but Stoneheart did not dance, or drink, or sing pirate songs...

Instead, he looked at maps...

...made notes, and, as his crew slept...

Stoneheart changed course.

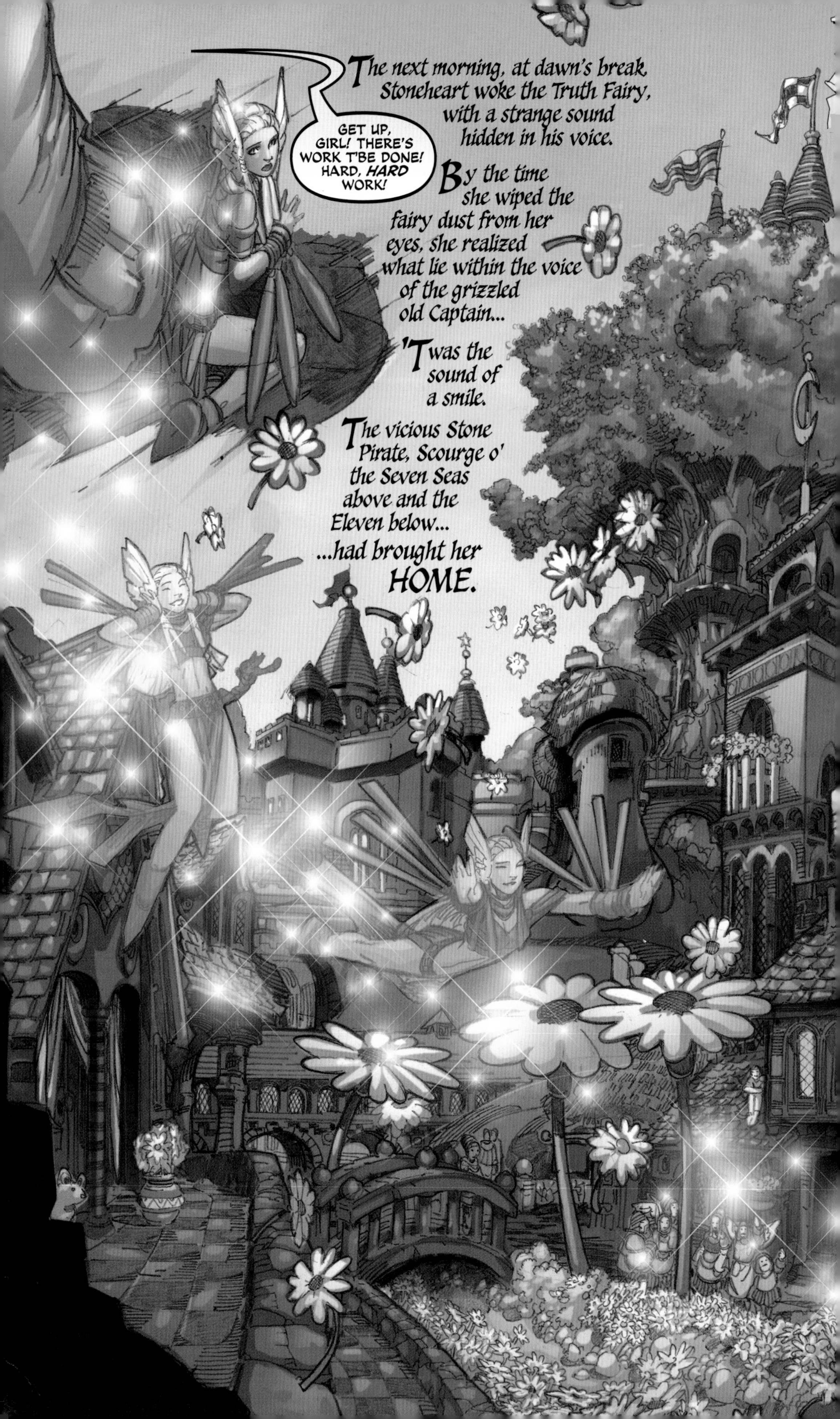
The next morning, at dawn's break Stoneheart woke the Truth Fairy, with a strange sound hidden in his voice.
GET UP, GIRL! THERE'S WORK T'BE DONE! HARD, HARD WORK!
By the time she wiped the fairy dust from her eyes, she realized what lie within the voice of the grizzled old Captain...
'Twas the sound of a smile.
The vicious Stone Pirate, Scourge o' the Seven Seas above and the Eleven below...
...had brought her HOME.

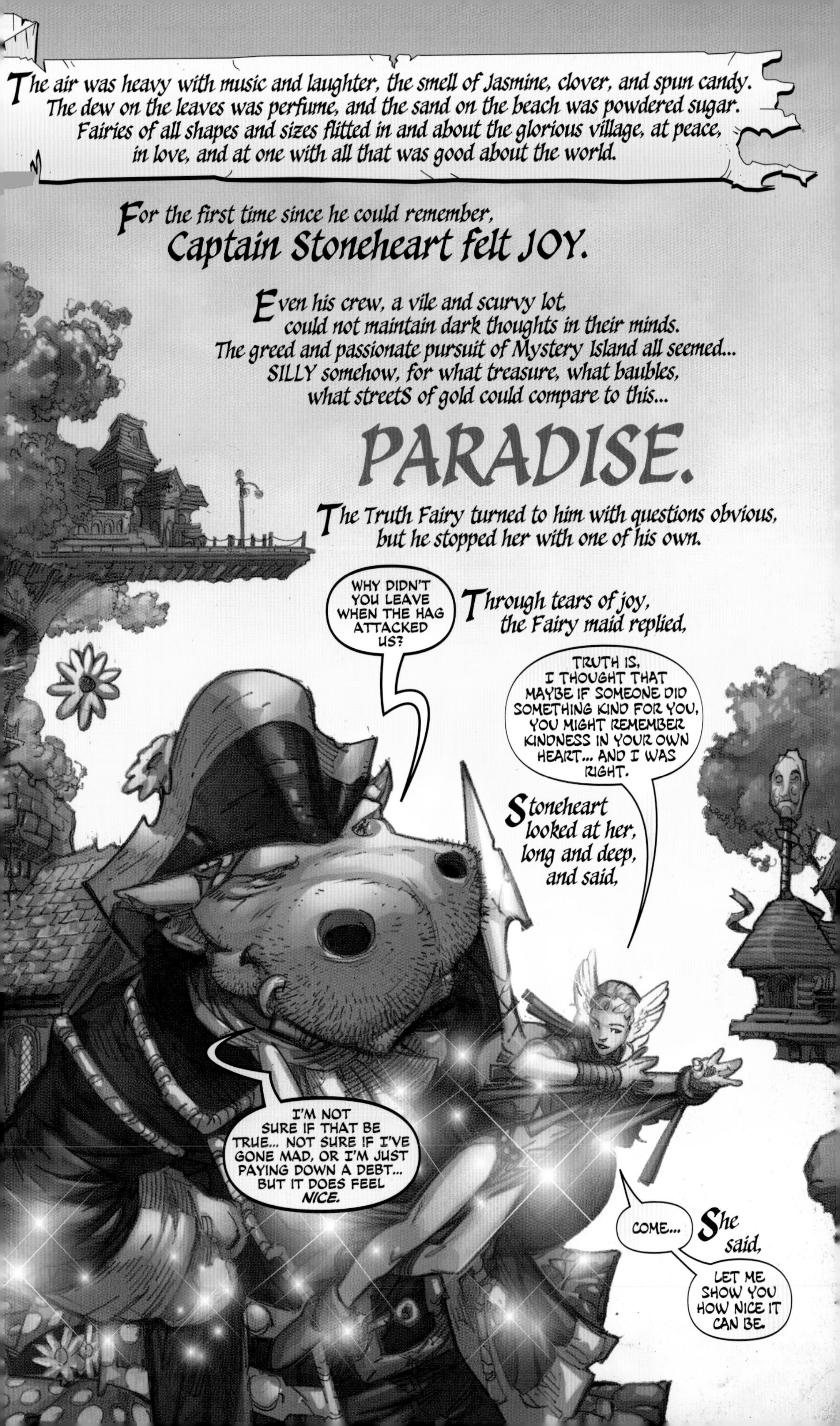
The air was heavy with music and laughter, the smell of Jasmine, clover, and spun candy. The dew on the leaves was perfume, and the sand on the beach was powdered sugar. Fairies of all shapes and sizes flitted in and about the glorious village, at peace, in love, and at one with all that was good about the world.
For the first time since he could remember, Captain Stoneheart felt JOY.
Even his crew, a vile and scurvy lot, could not maintain dark thoughts in their minds. The greed and passionate pursuit of Mystery Island all seemed... SILLY somehow, for what treasure, what baubles, what streets of gold could compare to this...
PARADISE.
The Truth Fairy turned to him with questions obvious, but he stopped her with one of his own.
WHY DIDN'T YOU LEAVE WHEN THE HAG ATTACKED US?
Through tears of joy, the Fairy maid replied,
TRUTH IS, I THOUGHT THAT MAYBE IF SOMEONE DID SOMETHING KIND FOR YOU, YOU MIGHT REMEMBER KINDNESS IN YOUR OWN HEART... AND I WAS RIGHT.
Stoneheart looked at her, long and deep, and said,
I'M NOT SURE IF THAT BE TRUE... NOT SURE IF I'VE GONE MAD, OR I'M JUST PAYING DOWN A DEBT... BUT IT DOES FEEL NICE.
COME...
She said,
LET ME SHOW YOU HOW NICE IT CAN BE.

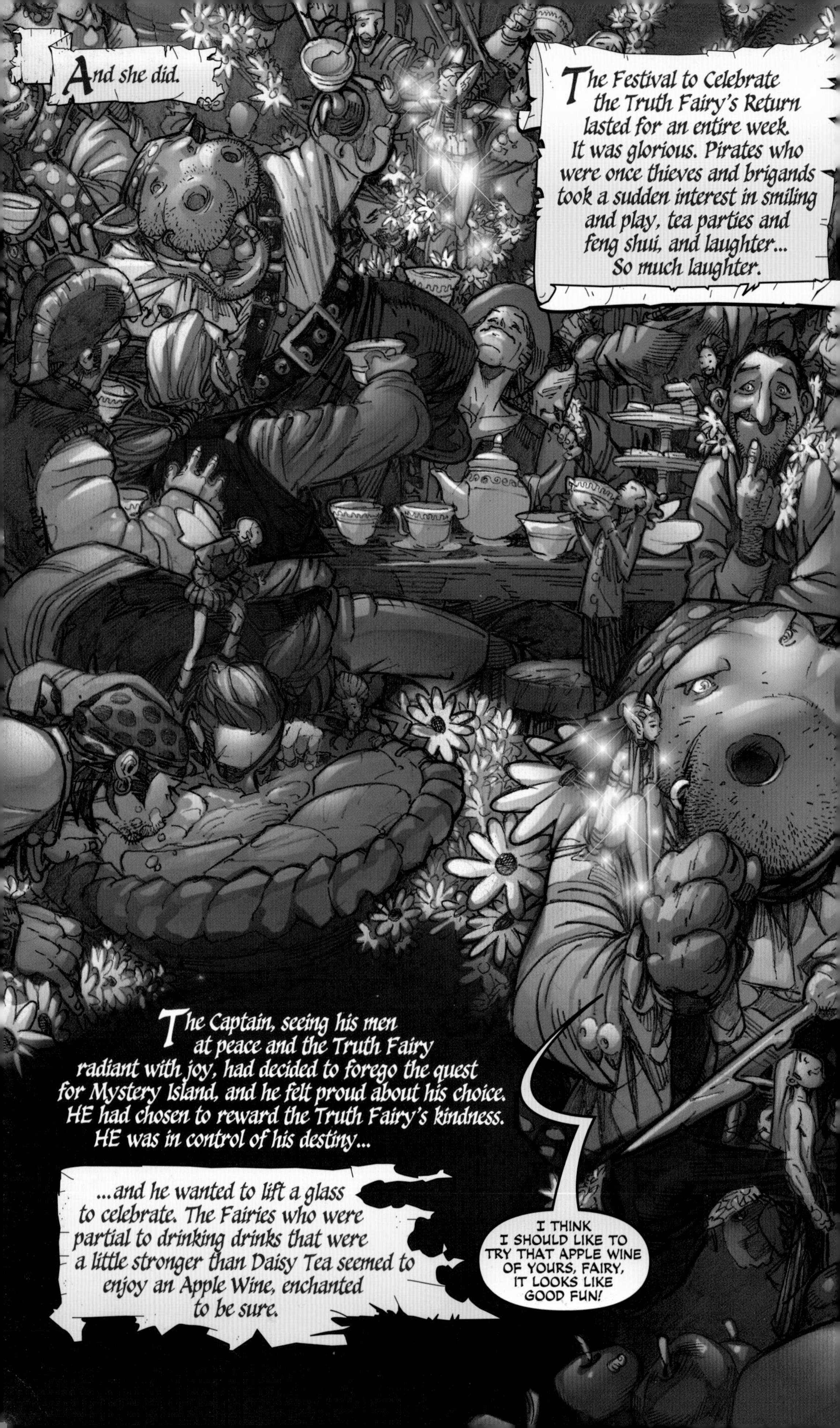
And she did.
The Festival to Celebrate the Truth Fairy's Return lasted for an entire week. It was glorious. Pirates who were once thieves and brigands took a sudden interest in smiling and play, tea parties and feng shui, and laughter... So much laughter.
The Captain, seeing his men at peace and the Truth Fairy radiant with joy, had decided to forego the quest for Mystery Island, and he felt proud about his choice. HE had chosen to reward the Truth Fairy's kindness. HE was in control of his destiny...
...and he wanted to lift a glass to celebrate. The Fairies who were partial to drinking drinks that were a little stronger than Daisy Tea seemed to enjoy an Apple Wine, enchanted to be sure.
I THINK I SHOULD LIKE TO TRY THAT APPLE WINE OF YOURS, FAIRY, IT LOOKS LIKE GOOD FUN!

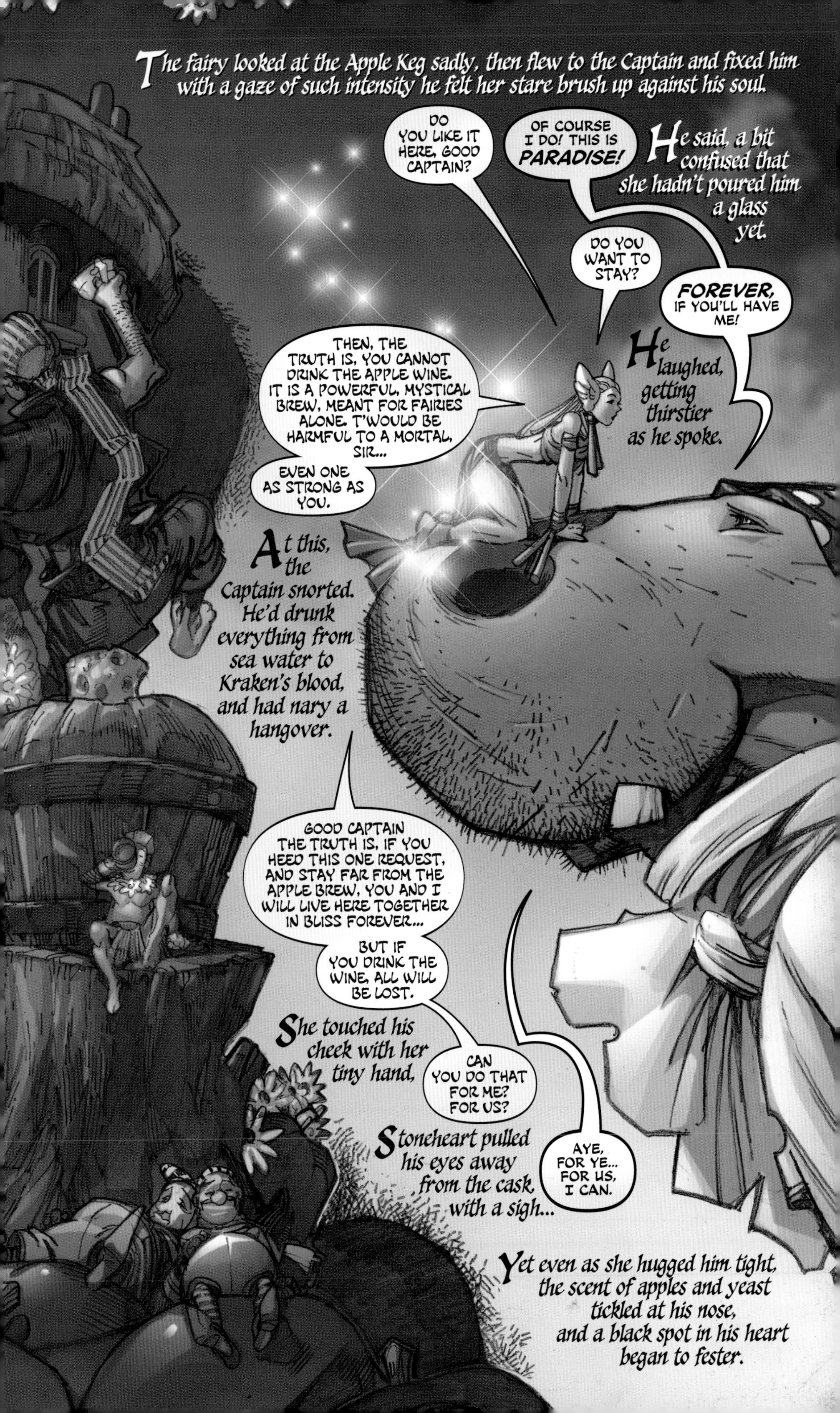
The fairy looked at the Apple Keg sadly, then flew to the Captain and fixed him with a gaze of such intensity he felt her stare brush up against his soul.
DO YOU LIKE IT HERE, GOOD CAPTAIN?
OF COURSE I DO! THIS IS PARADISE!
He said, a bit confused that she hadn't poured him a glass yet.
DO YOU WANT TO STAY?
FOREVER, IF YOU'LL HAVE ME!
He laughed, getting thirstier as he spoke.
THEN, THE TRUTH IS, YOU CANNOT DRINK THE APPLE WINE. IT IS A POWERFUL, MYSTICAL BREW, MEANT FOR FAIRIES ALONE. T'WOULD BE HARMFUL TO A MORTAL, SIR...
EVEN ONE AS STRONG AS YOU.
At this, the Captain snorted. He'd drunk everything from sea water to Kraken's blood, and had nary a hangover.
GOOD CAPTAIN THE TRUTH IS, IF YOU HEED THIS ONE REQUEST, AND STAY FAR FROM THE APPLE BREW, YOU AND I WILL LIVE HERE TOGETHER IN BLISS FOREVER...
BUT IF YOU DRINK THE WINE, ALL WILL BE LOST.
She touched his cheek with her tiny hand,
CAN YOU DO THAT FOR ME? FOR US?
Stoneheart pulled his eyes away from the cask with a sigh...
AYE, FOR YE... FOR US, I CAN.
Yet even as she hugged him tight, the scent of apples and yeast tickled at his nose, and a black spot in his heart began to fester.

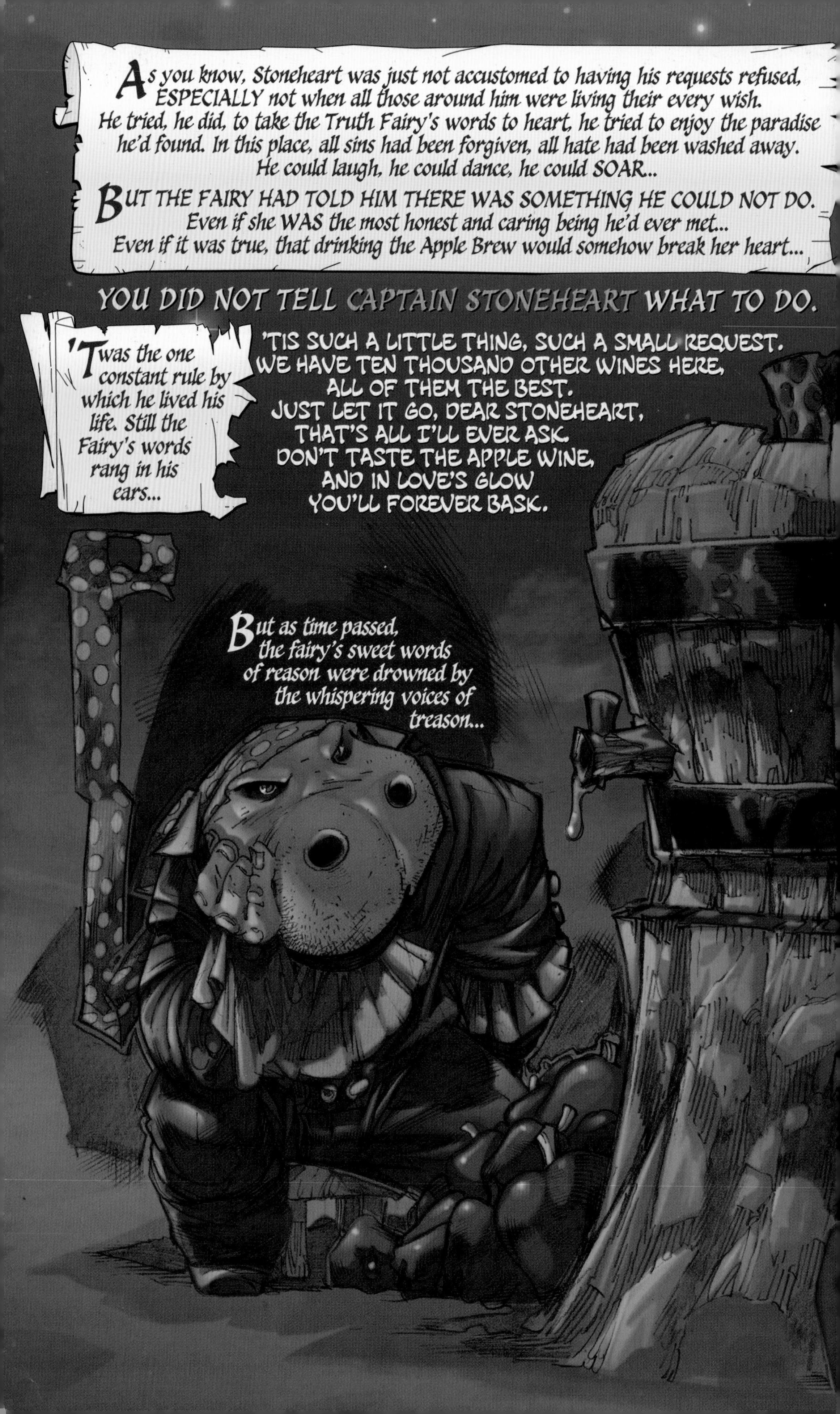
As you know, Stoneheart was just not accustomed to having his requests refused, ESPECIALLY not when all those around him were living their every wish. He tried, he did, to take the Truth Fairy's words to heart, he tried to enjoy the paradise he'd found. In this place, all sins had been forgiven, all hate had been washed away. He could laugh, he could dance, he could SOAR...
BUT THE FAIRY HAD TOLD HIM THERE WAS SOMETHING HE COULD NOT DO. Even if she WAS the most honest and caring being he'd ever met... Even if it was true, that drinking the Apple Brew would somehow break her heart...
YOU DID NOT TELL CAPTAIN STONEHEART WHAT TO DO.
'Twas the one constant rule by which he lived his life. Still the Fairy's words rang in his ears...
'TIS SUCH A LITTLE THING, SUCH A SMALL REQUEST. WE HAVE TEN THOUSAND OTHER WINES HERE, ALL OF THEM THE BEST. JUST LET IT GO, DEAR STONEHEART, THAT'S ALL I'LL EVER ASK. DON'T TASTE THE APPLE WINE, AND IN LOVE'S GLOW YOU'LL FOREVER BASK.
But as time passed, the fairy's sweet words of reason were drowned by the whispering voices of treason...

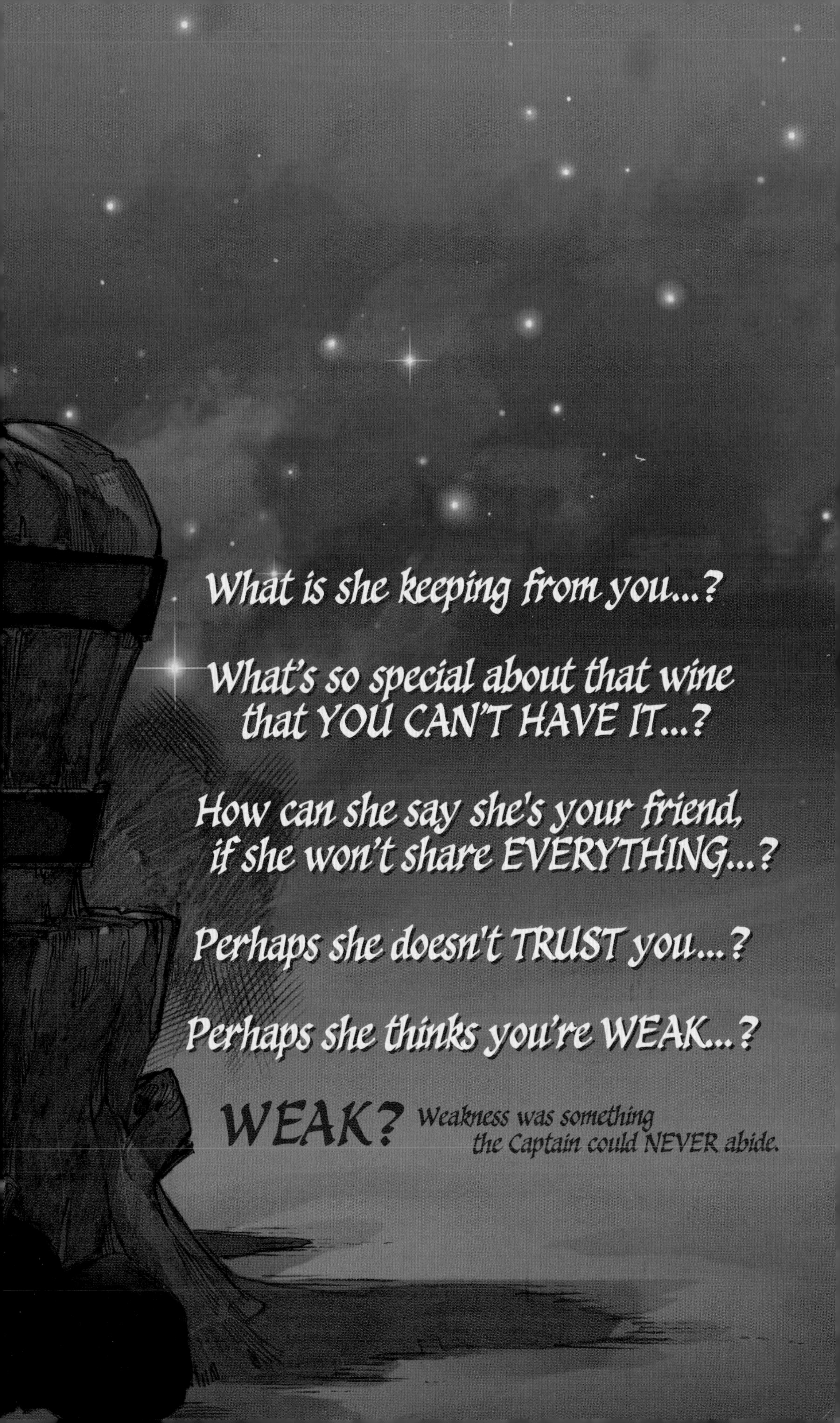
What is she keeping from you...?
What's so special about that wine that YOU CAN'T HAVE IT...?
How can she say she's your friend, if she won't share EVERYTHING...?
Perhaps she doesn't TRUST you...?
Perhaps she thinks you're WEAK...?
WEAK?
Weakness was something the Captain could NEVER abide.

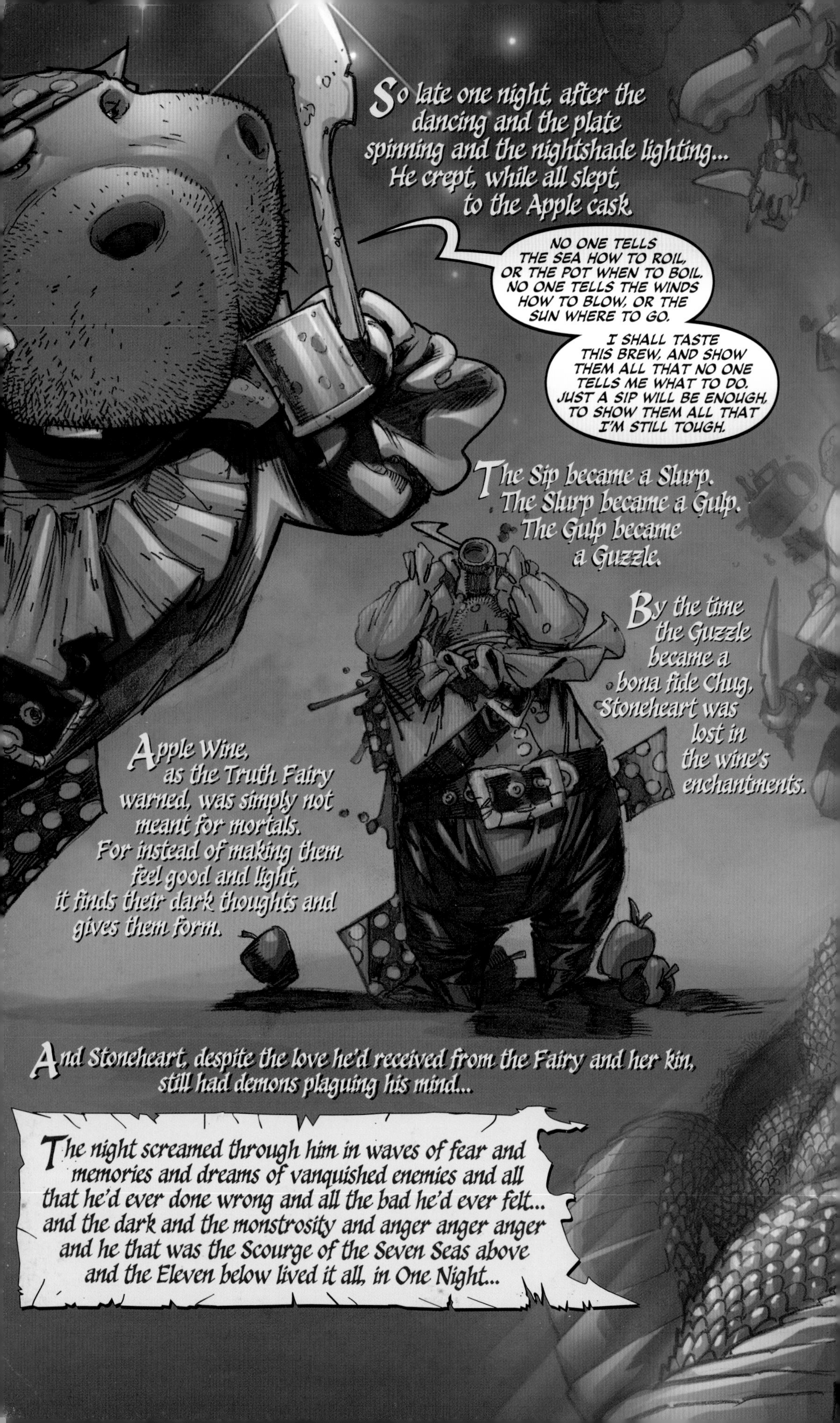

So late one night, after the dancing and the plate spinning and the nightshade lighting... He crept, while all slept, to the Apple cask.
NO ONE TELLS THE SEA HOW TO ROIL, OR THE POT WHEN TO BOIL. NO ONE TELLS THE WINDS HOW TO BLOW, OR THE SUN WHERE TO GO.
I SHALL TASTE THIS BREW, AND SHOW THEM ALL THAT NO ONE TELLS ME WHAT TO DO. JUST A SIP WILL BE ENOUGH, TO SHOW THEM ALL THAT I'M STILL TOUGH.
The Sip became a Slurp. The Slurp became a Gulp. The Gulp became a Guzzle.
By the time the Guzzle became a bona fide Chug, Stoneheart was lost in the wine's enchantments.
Apple Wine, as the Truth Fairy warned, was simply not meant for mortals. For instead of making them feel good and light, it finds their dark thoughts and gives them form.
And Stoneheart, despite the love he'd received from the Fairy and her kin, still had demons plaguing his mind...
The night screamed through him in waves of fear and memories and dreams of vanquished enemies and all that he'd ever done wrong and all the bad he'd ever felt... and the dark and the monstrosity and anger anger anger and he that was the Scourge of the Seven Seas above and the Eleven below lived it all, in One Night...

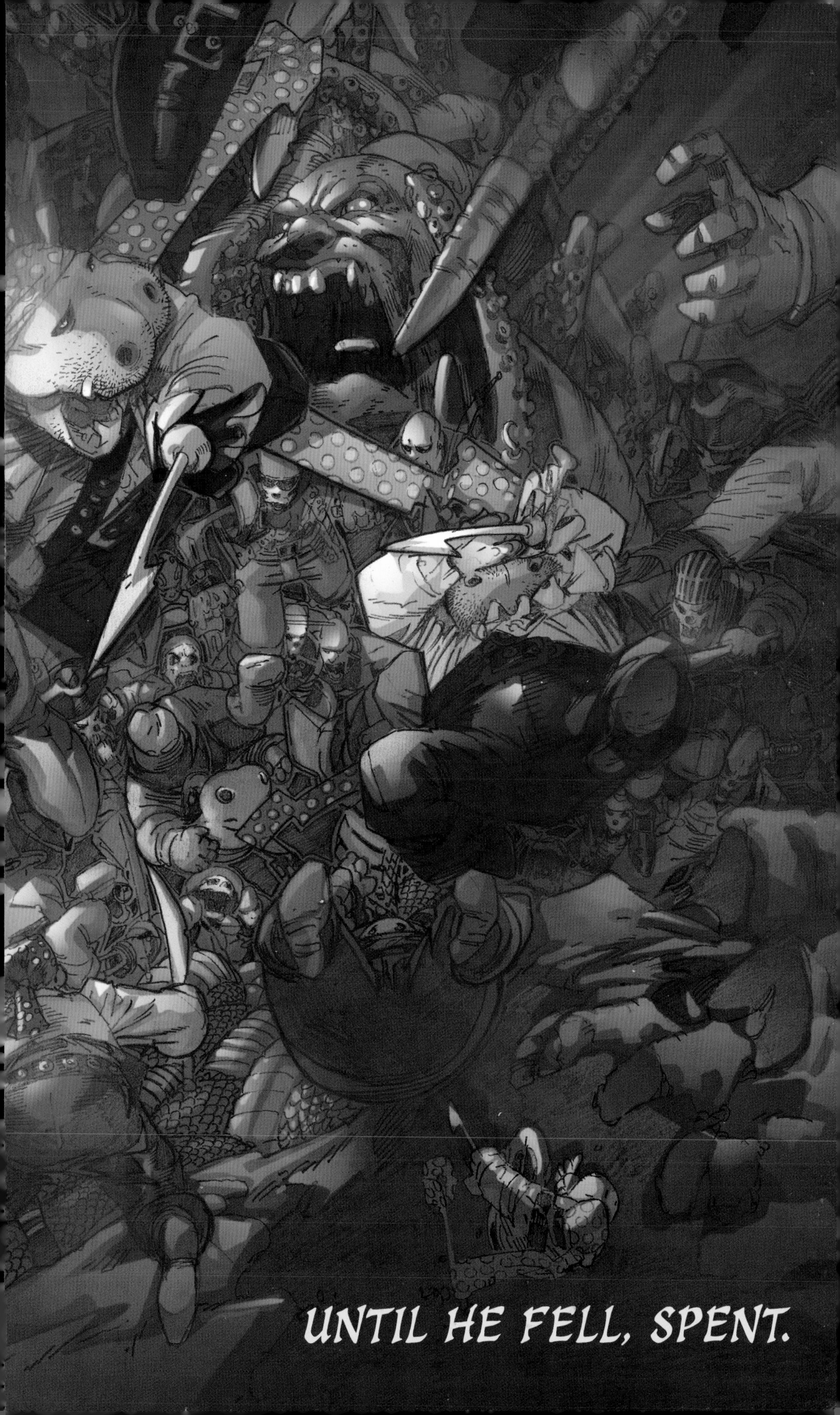
UNTIL HE FELL, SPENT.

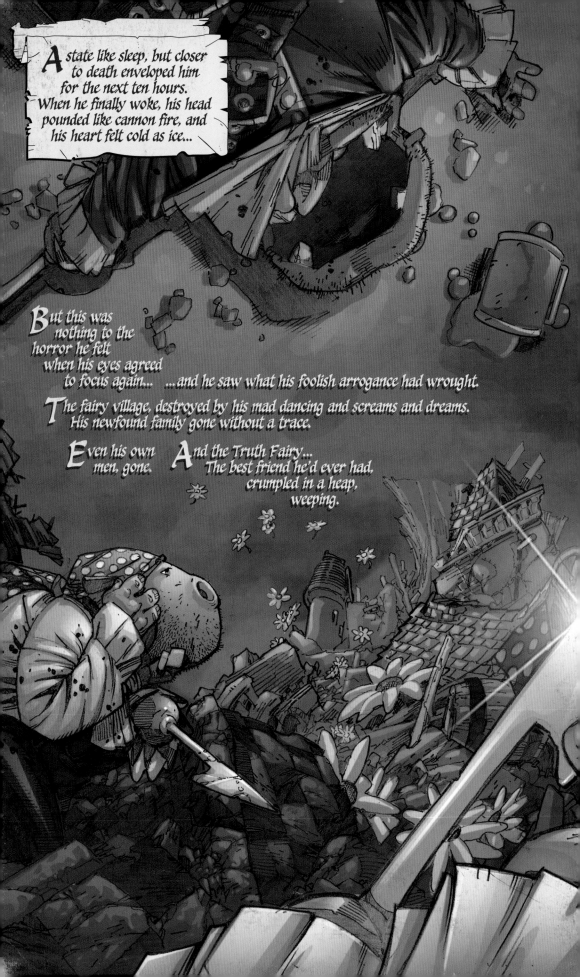

A state like sleep, but closer to death enveloped him for the next ten hours. When he finally woke, his head pounded like cannon fire, and his heart felt cold as ice...

But this was nothing to the horror he felt when his eyes agreed to focus again...   ...and he saw what his foolish arrogance had wrought.

The fairy village, destroyed by his mad dancing and screams and dreams. His newfound family gone without a trace.

Even his own men, gone.   And the Truth Fairy... The best friend he'd ever had, crumpled in a heap, weeping.

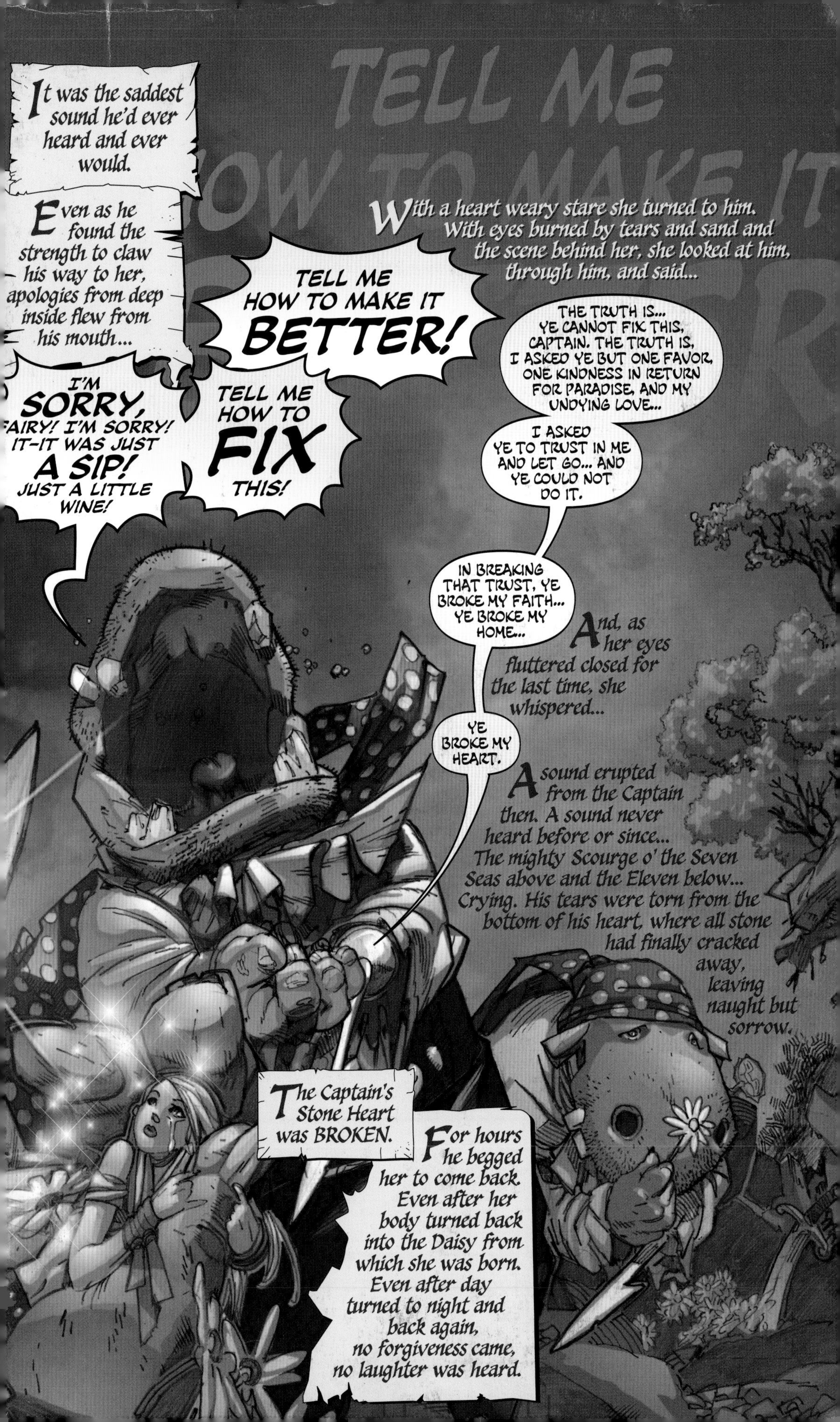
TELL ME HOW TO MAKE IT
It was the saddest sound he'd ever heard and ever would.
Even as he found the strength to claw his way to her, apologies from deep inside flew from his mouth...
I'M SORRY, FAIRY! I'M SORRY! IT-IT WAS JUST A SIP! JUST A LITTLE WINE!
TELL ME HOW TO FIX THIS!
TELL ME HOW TO MAKE IT BETTER!
With a heart weary stare she turned to him. With eyes burned by tears and sand and the scene behind her, she looked at him, through him, and said...
THE TRUTH IS... YE CANNOT FIX THIS, CAPTAIN. THE TRUTH IS, I ASKED YE BUT ONE FAVOR, ONE KINDNESS IN RETURN FOR PARADISE, AND MY UNDYING LOVE...
I ASKED YE TO TRUST IN ME AND LET GO... AND YE COULD NOT DO IT.
IN BREAKING THAT TRUST, YE BROKE MY FAITH... YE BROKE MY HOME...
And, as her eyes fluttered closed for the last time, she whispered...
YE BROKE MY HEART.
A sound erupted from the Captain then. A sound never heard before or since... The mighty Scourge o' the Seven Seas above and the Eleven below... Crying. His tears were torn from the bottom of his heart, where all stone had finally cracked away, leaving naught but sorrow.
The Captain's Stone Heart was BROKEN.
For hours he begged her to come back. Even after her body turned back into the Daisy from which she was born. Even after day turned to night and back again, no forgiveness came, no laughter was heard.

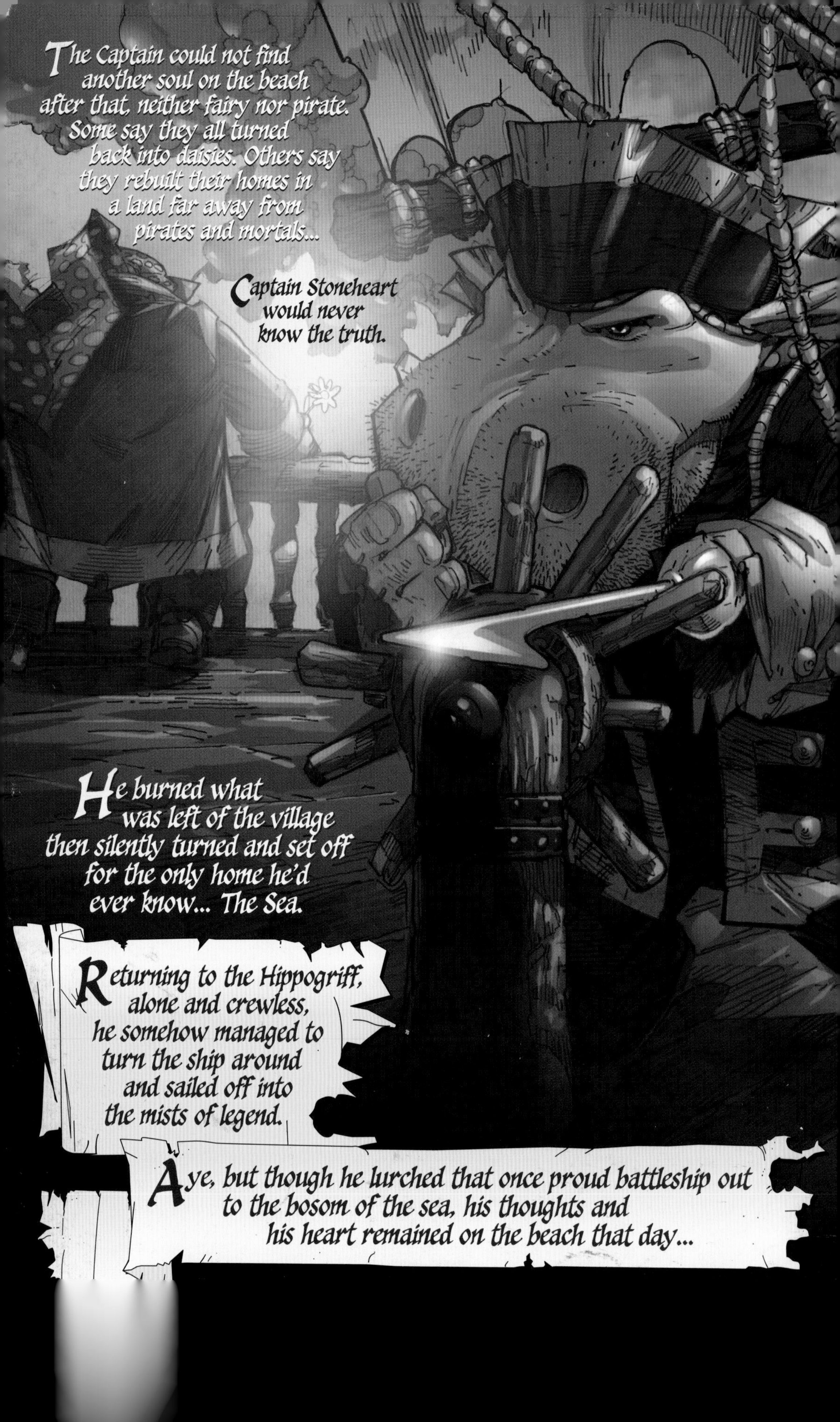
The Captain could not find another soul on the beach after that, neither fairy nor pirate. Some say they all turned back into daisies. Others say they rebuilt their homes in a land far away from pirates and mortals...
Captain Stoneheart would never know the truth.
He burned what was left of the village then silently turned and set off for the only home he'd ever know... The Sea.
Returning to the Hippogriff, alone and crewless, he somehow managed to turn the ship around and sailed off into the mists of legend.
Aye, but though he lurched that once proud battleship out to the bosom of the sea, his thoughts and his heart remained on the beach that day...

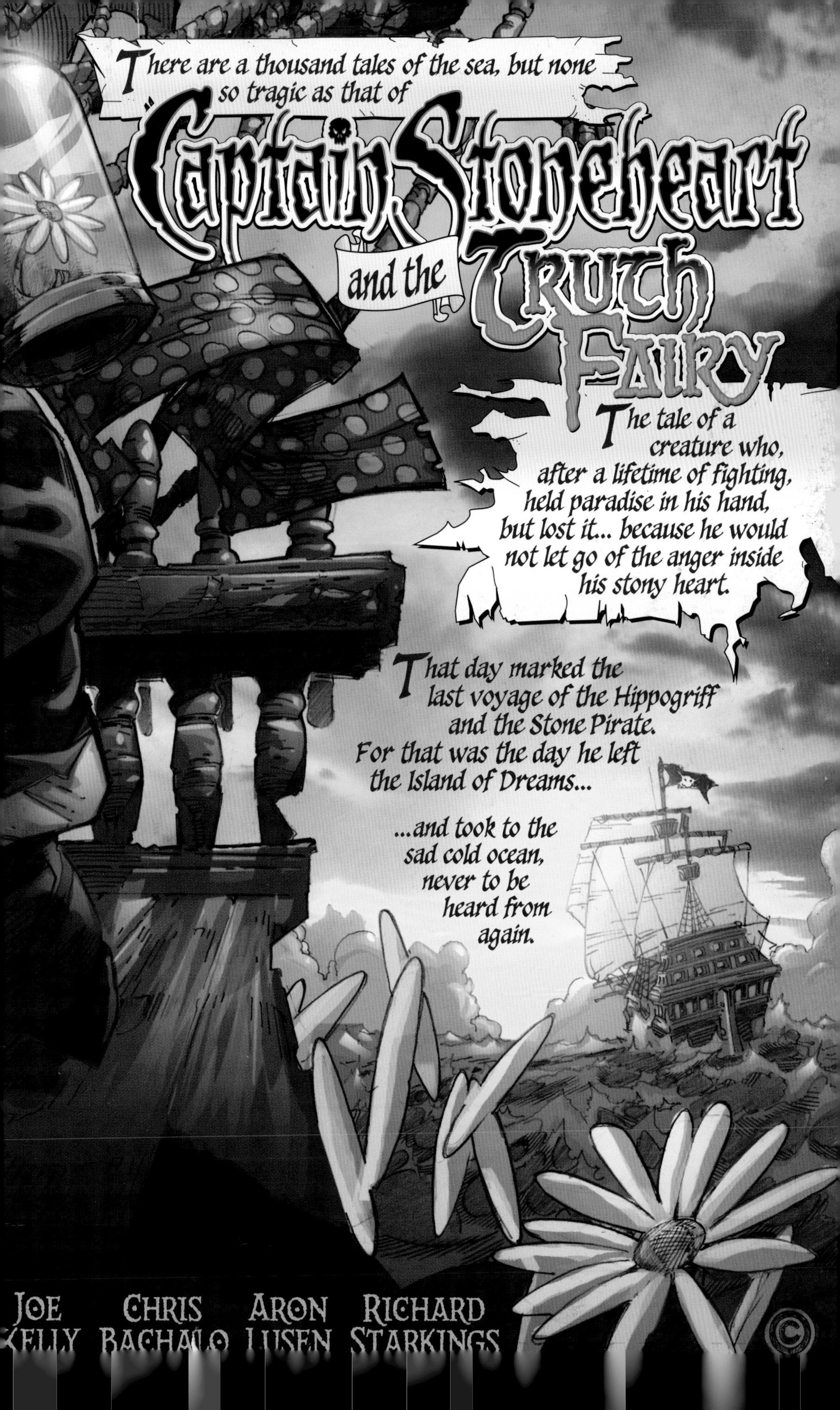

There are a thousand tales of the sea, but none so tragic as that of
Captain Stoneheart and the Truth Fairy
The tale of a creature who, after a lifetime of fighting, held paradise in his hand, but lost it... because he would not let go of the anger inside his stony heart.
That day marked the last voyage of the Hippogriff and the Stone Pirate. For that was the day he left the Island of Dreams...
...and took to the sad cold ocean, never to be heard from again.
Joe Kelly Chris Bachalo Aron Lusen Richard Starkings

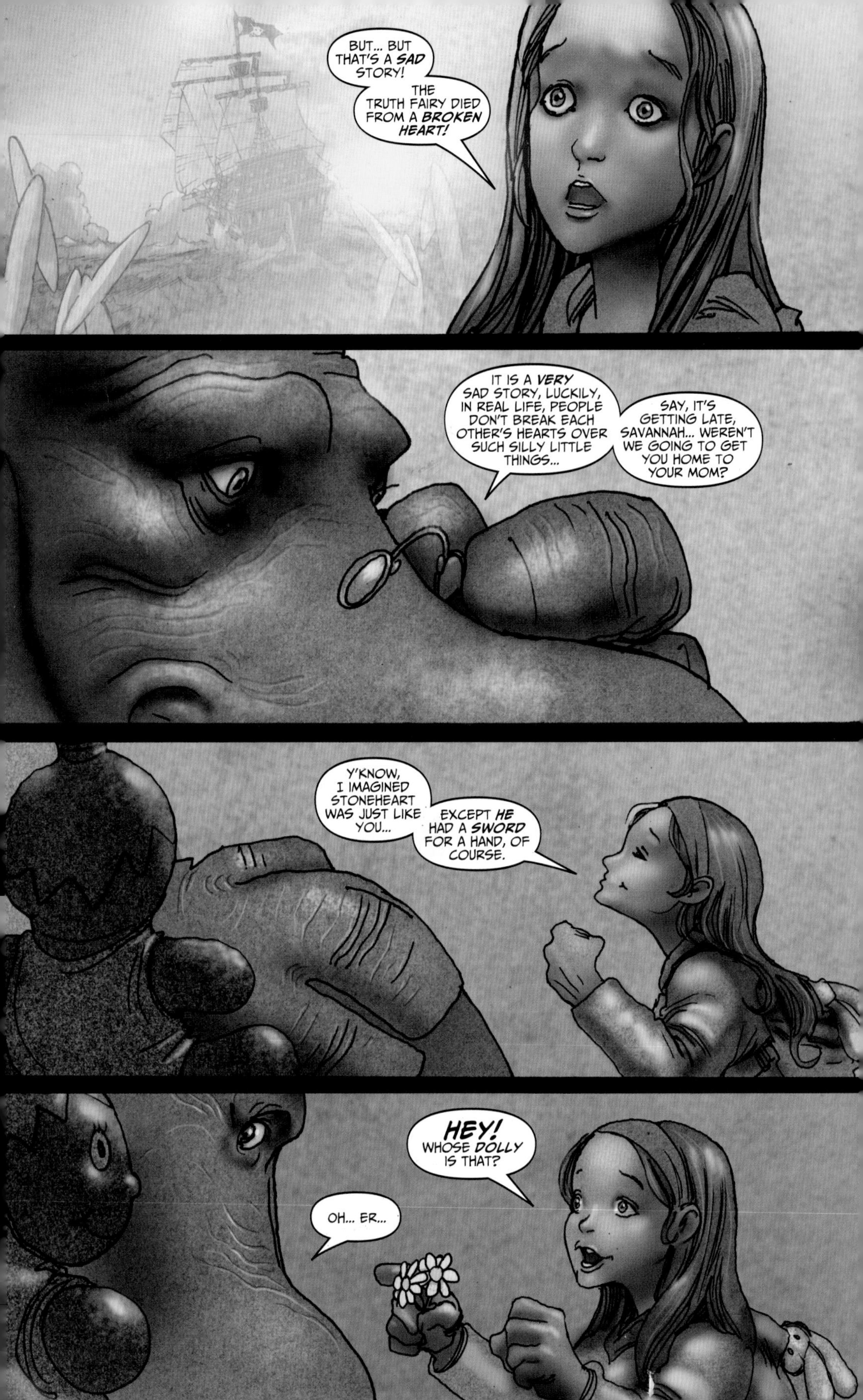
BUT... BUT THAT'S A SAD STORY!
THE TRUTH FAIRY DIED FROM A BROKEN HEART!
IT IS A VERY SAD STORY, LUCKILY, IN REAL LIFE, PEOPLE DON'T BREAK EACH OTHER'S HEARTS OVER SUCH SILLY LITTLE THINGS...
SAY, IT'S GETTING LATE, SAVANNAH... WEREN'T WE GOING TO GET YOU HOME TO YOUR MOM?
Y'KNOW, I IMAGINED STONEHEART WAS JUST LIKE YOU...
EXCEPT HE HAD A SWORD FOR A HAND, OF COURSE.
HEY! WHOSE DOLLY IS THAT?
OH... ER...

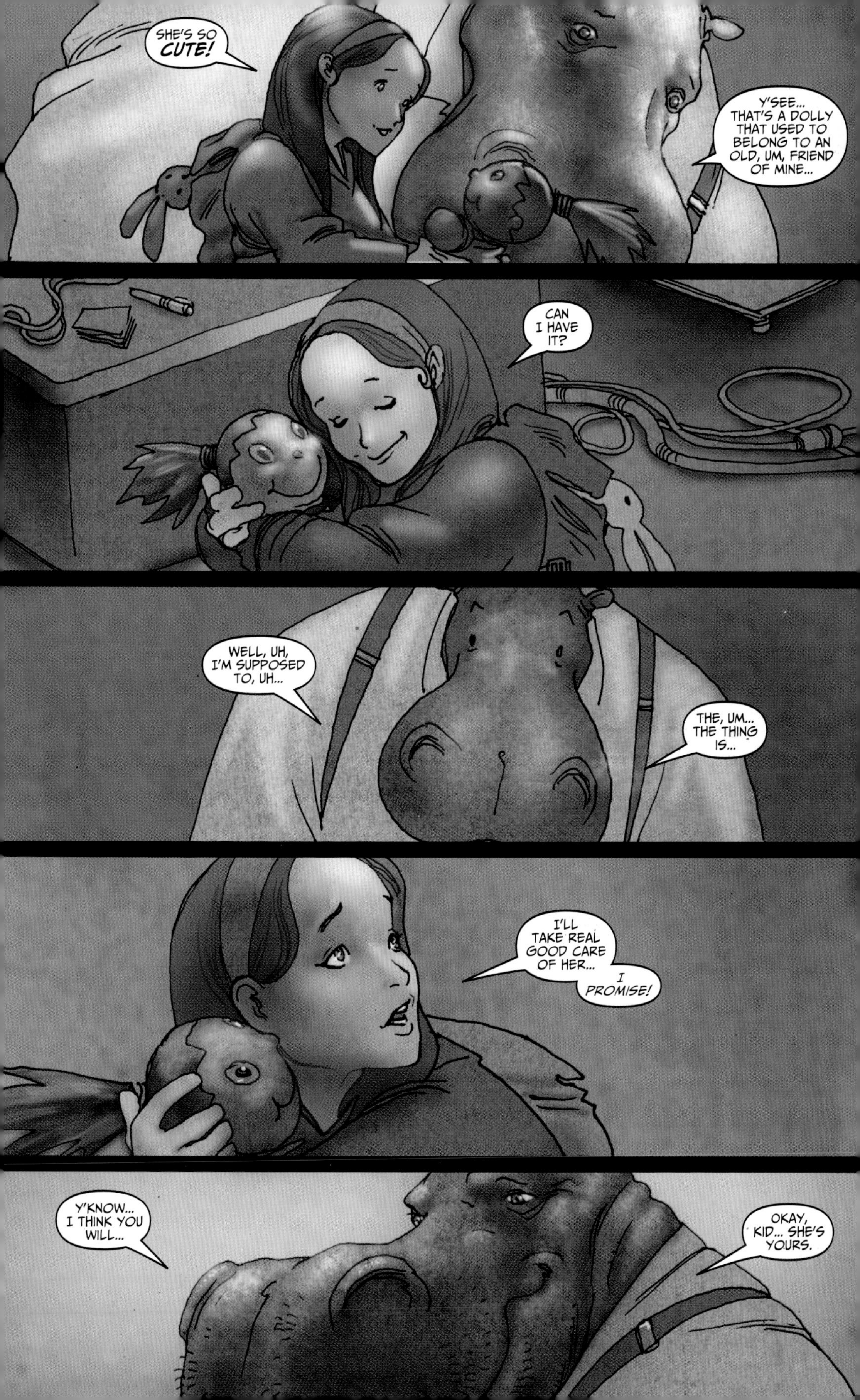
SHE'S SO CUTE!
Y'SEE... THAT'S A DOLLY THAT USED TO BELONG TO AN OLD, UM, FRIEND OF MINE...
CAN I HAVE IT?
WELL, UH, I'M SUPPOSED TO, UH...
THE, UM... THE THING IS...
I'LL TAKE REAL GOOD CARE OF HER...
I PROMISE!
Y'KNOW... I THINK YOU WILL...
OKAY, KID... SHE'S YOURS.

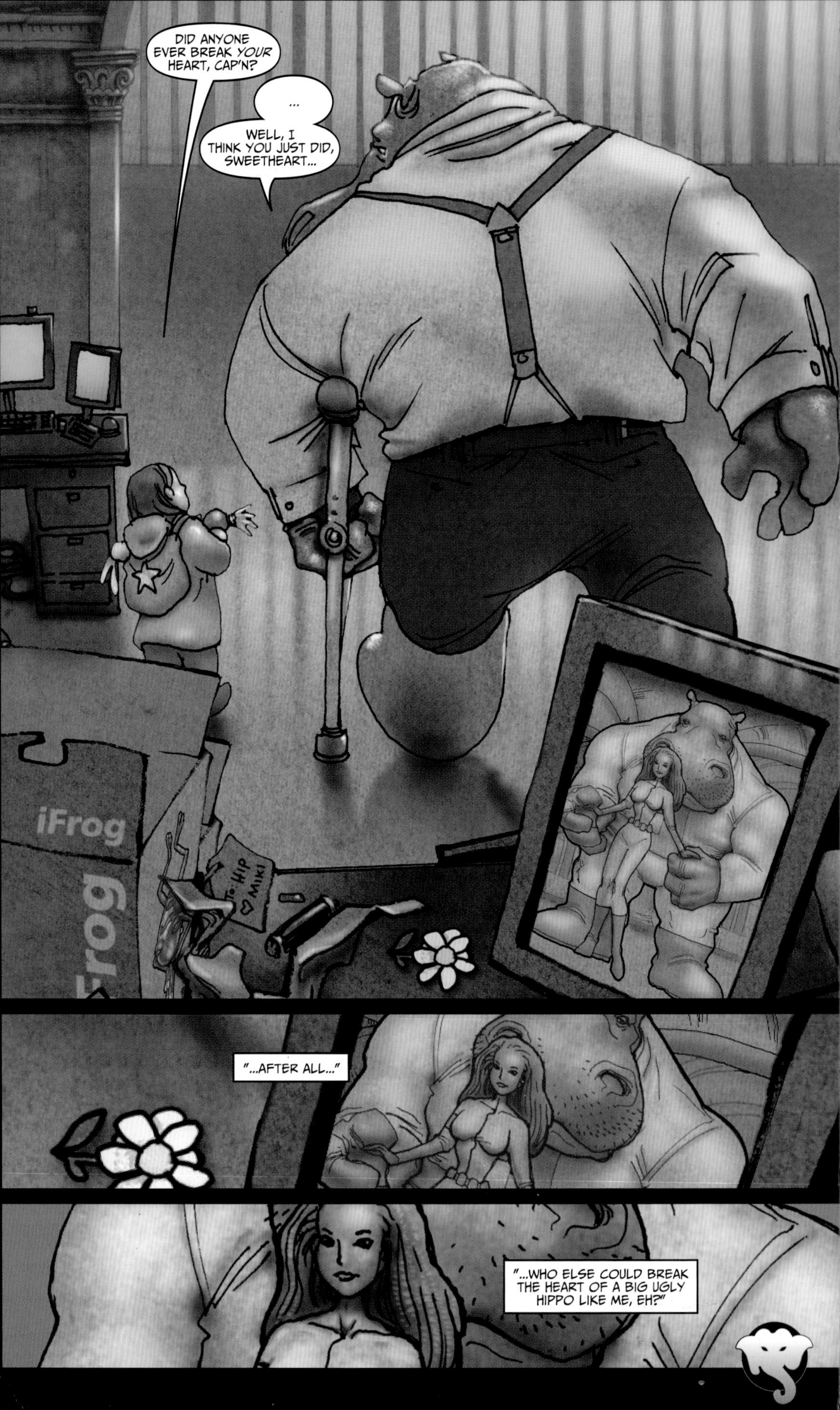
DID ANYONE EVER BREAK YOUR HEART, CAP'N?
...
WELL, I THINK YOU JUST DID, SWEETHEART...
iFrog
iFrog
To: HIP ♡ MIKI
"...AFTER ALL..."
"...WHO ELSE COULD BREAK THE HEART OF A BIG UGLY HIPPO LIKE ME, EH?"

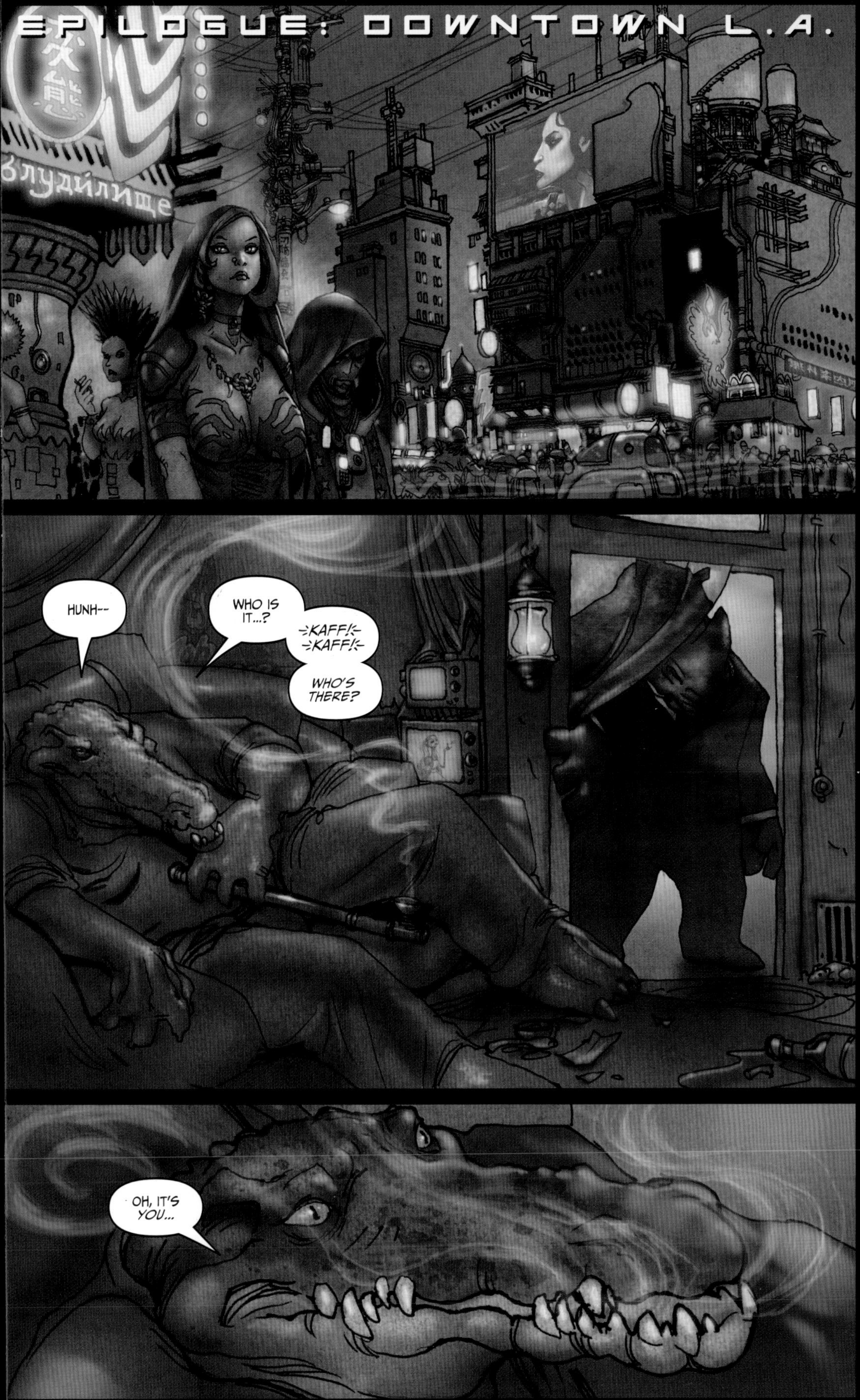
EPILOGUE: DOWNTOWN L.A.
HUNH--
WHO IS IT...?
-KAFF!- -KAFF!-
WHO'S THERE?
OH, IT'S YOU...

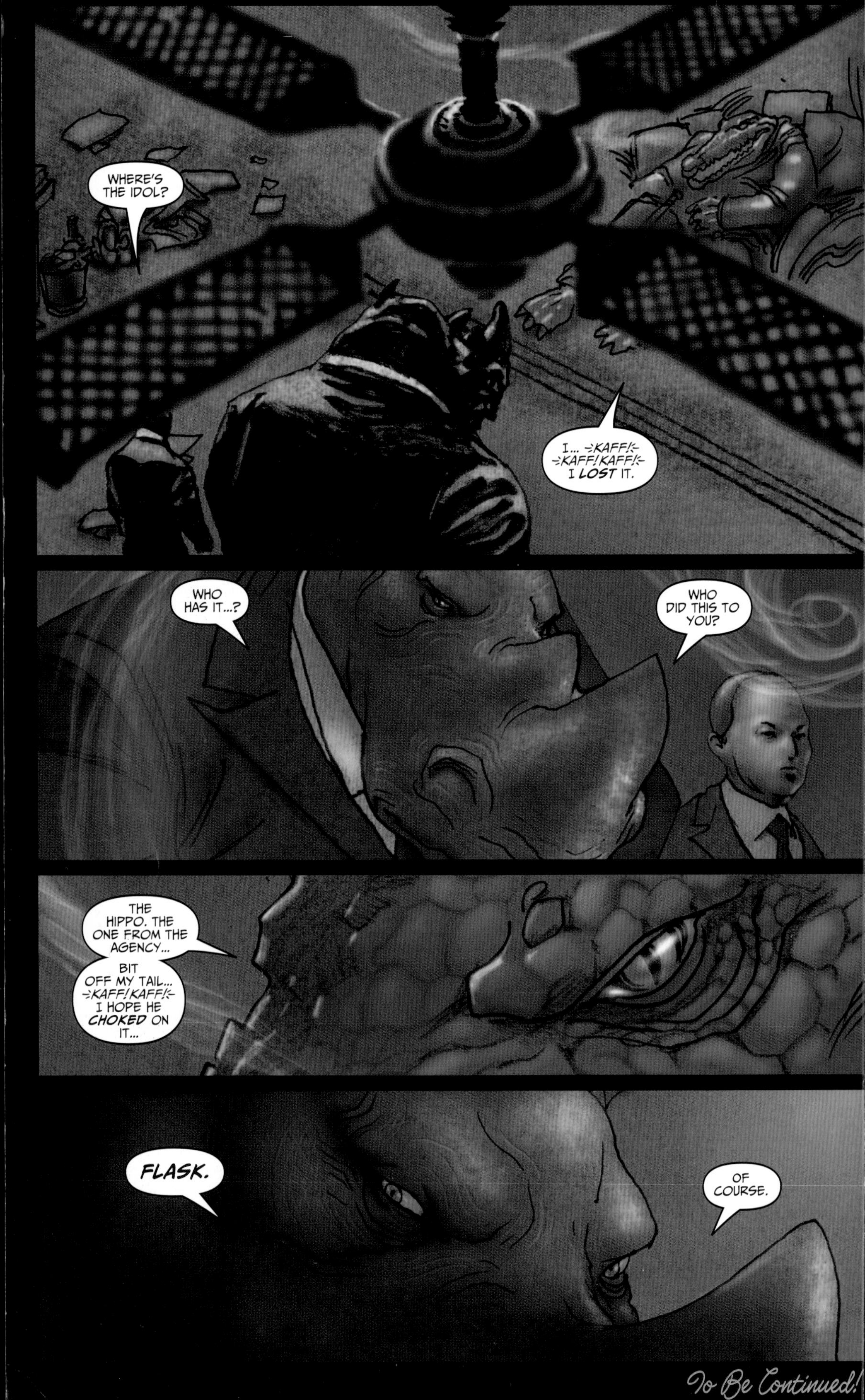
WHERE'S THE IDOL?
I... KAFF! KAFF! KAFF! I LOST IT.
WHO HAS IT...?
WHO DID THIS TO YOU?
THE HIPPO. THE ONE FROM THE AGENCY...
BIT OFF MY TAIL... KAFF! KAFF! I HOPE HE CHOKED ON IT...
FLASK.
OF COURSE.
To Be Continued!

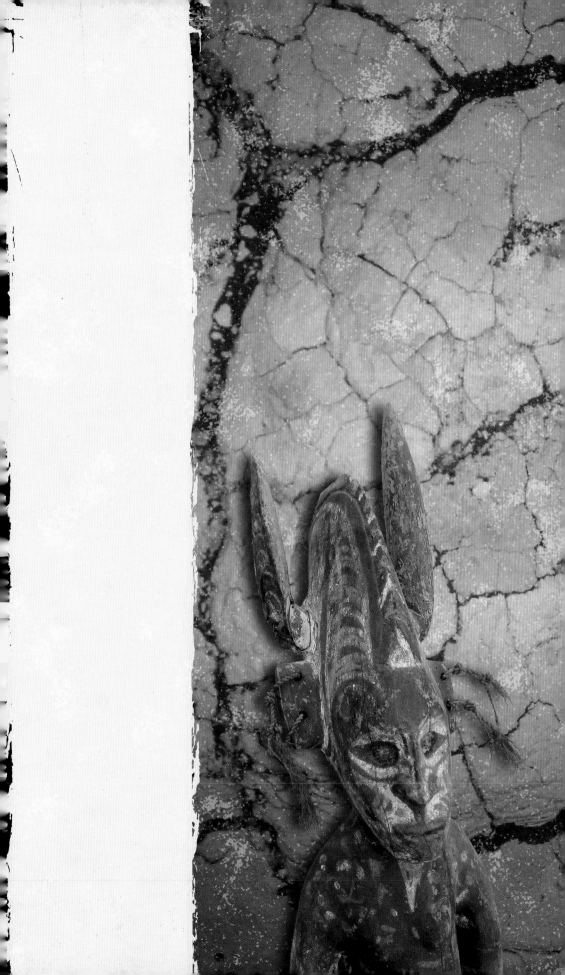

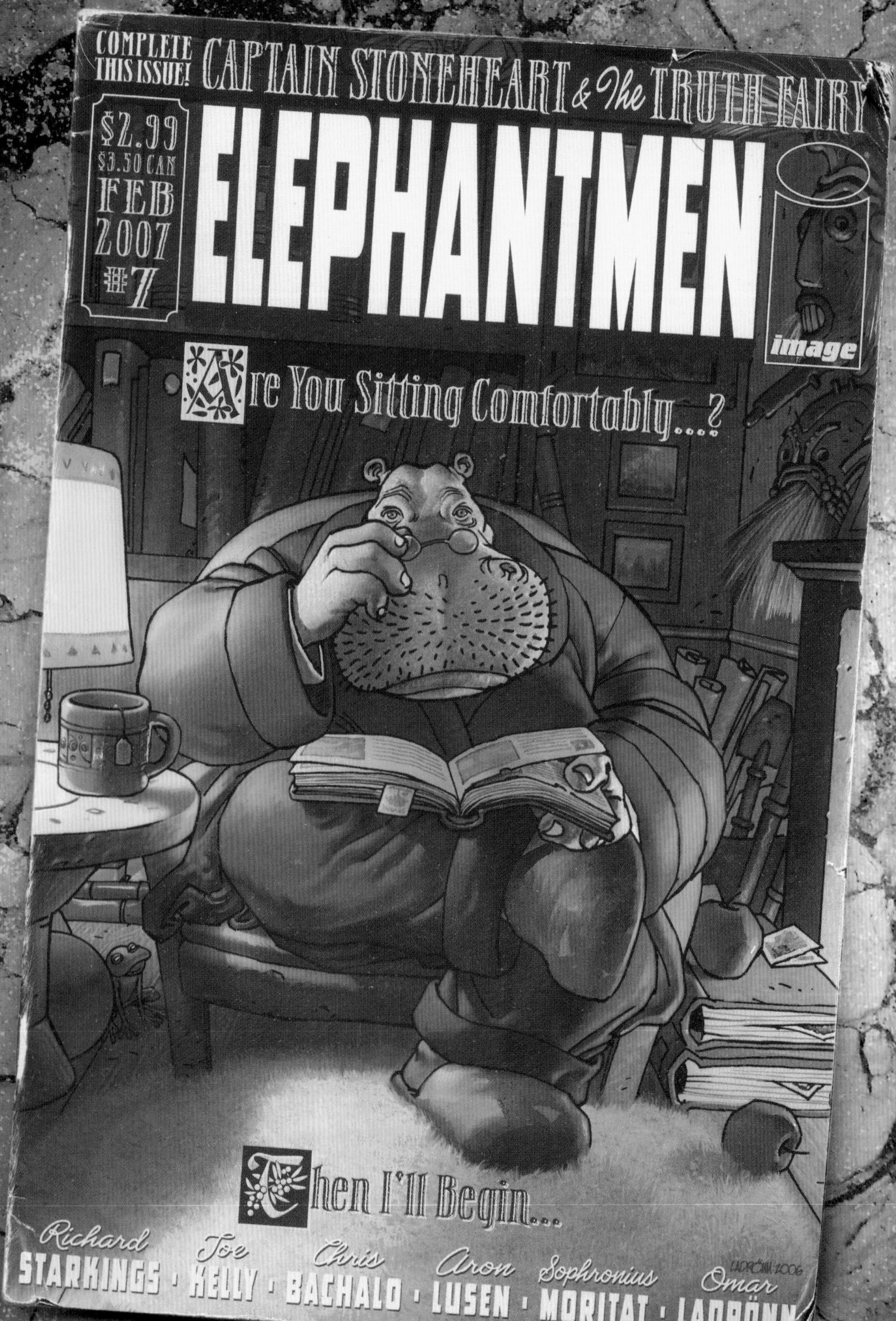
COMPLETE THIS ISSUE!
CAPTAIN STONEHEART & The TRUTH FAIRY
$2.99
$3.50 CAN
FEB
2007
#7
ELEPHANTMEN
image
Are You Sitting Comfortably....?
Then I'll Begin...
Richard STARKINGS · Joe KELLY · Chris BACHALO · Aron LUSEN · Sophronius MORITAT · Omar LADRÖNN
LADRÖNN 2006

ABOUT THE CREATORS

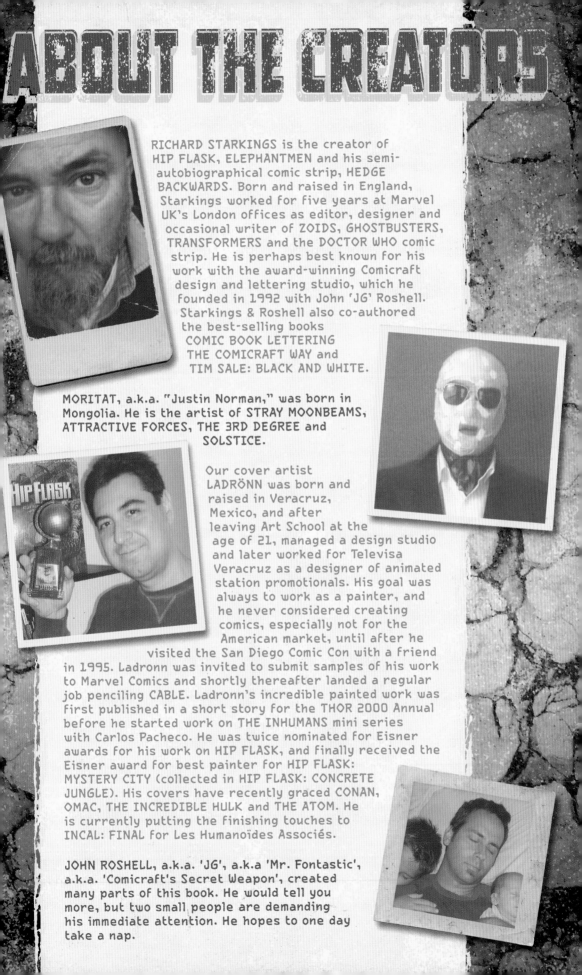

RICHARD STARKINGS is the creator of HIP FLASK, ELEPHANTMEN and his semi-autobiographical comic strip, HEDGE BACKWARDS. Born and raised in England, Starkings worked for five years at Marvel UK's London offices as editor, designer and occasional writer of ZOIDS, GHOSTBUSTERS, TRANSFORMERS and the DOCTOR WHO comic strip. He is perhaps best known for his work with the award-winning Comicraft design and lettering studio, which he founded in 1992 with John 'JG' Roshell. Starkings & Roshell also co-authored the best-selling books COMIC BOOK LETTERING THE COMICRAFT WAY and TIM SALE: BLACK AND WHITE.

MORITAT, a.k.a. "Justin Norman," was born in Mongolia. He is the artist of STRAY MOONBEAMS, ATTRACTIVE FORCES, THE 3RD DEGREE and SOLSTICE.

Our cover artist **LADRÖNN** was born and raised in Veracruz, Mexico, and after leaving Art School at the age of 21, managed a design studio and later worked for Televisa Veracruz as a designer of animated station promotionals. His goal was always to work as a painter, and he never considered creating comics, especially not for the American market, until after he visited the San Diego Comic Con with a friend in 1995. Ladronn was invited to submit samples of his work to Marvel Comics and shortly thereafter landed a regular job penciling CABLE. Ladronn's incredible painted work was first published in a short story for the THOR 2000 Annual before he started work on THE INHUMANS mini series with Carlos Pacheco. He was twice nominated for Eisner awards for his work on HIP FLASK, and finally received the Eisner award for best painter for HIP FLASK: MYSTERY CITY (collected in HIP FLASK: CONCRETE JUNGLE). His covers have recently graced CONAN, OMAC, THE INCREDIBLE HULK and THE ATOM. He is currently putting the finishing touches to INCAL: FINAL for Les Humanoïdes Associés.

JOHN ROSHELL, a.k.a. 'JG', a.k.a 'Mr. Fontastic', a.k.a. 'Comicraft's Secret Weapon', created many parts of this book. He would tell you more, but two small people are demanding his immediate attention. He hopes to one day take a nap.

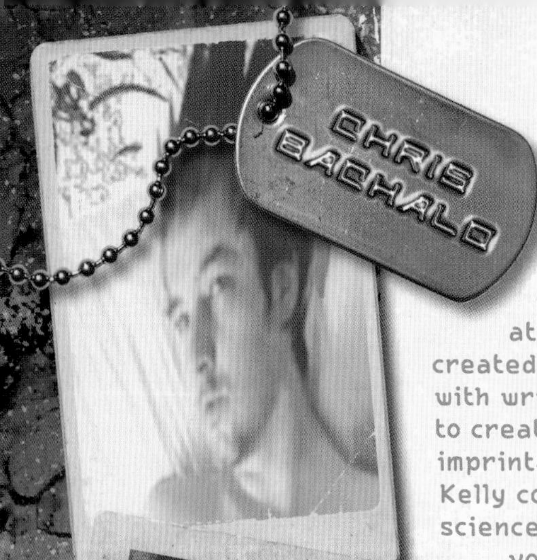
CHRIS
BACHALO

CHRIS BACHALO was born in Portage La Prairie, Canada, and is one of the most popular artists in the comic industry today. His work for DC's VERTIGO imprint on titles such as SHADE, SANDMAN and DEATH, THE HIGH COST OF LIVING, earned him acclaim and the attention of MARVEL COMICS where he co-created the quirky pop favorite GENERATION X with writer Scott Lobdell. Following an invitation to create a title for Wildstorm's CLIFFHANGER imprint, Bachalo and STONEHEART author Joe Kelly co-created STEAMPUNK, a retro-techno, science fiction fantasy epic -- the first two volumes are currently available from DC Comics; write to them and beg for more! Chris is currently the regular penciler on X-MEN, and resides in Southern California with his wife, Helen, son, Dylan and his Siamese fighting fish, Spike.

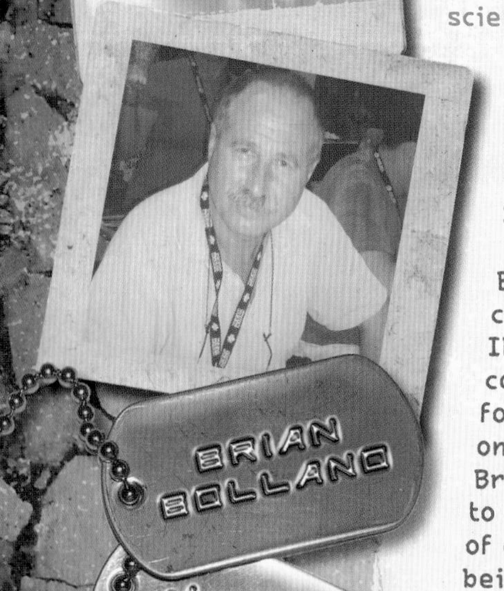
BRIAN
BOLLAND

BRIAN BOLLAND self published his first comics work, SUDDENLY AT TWO O'CLOCK IN THE MORNING shortly after he left art college in 1974. After acquiring an agent he found himself working alongside Dave Gibbons on POWERMAN for a comics company in Nigeria. Brian's association with Gibbons soon led him to 2000AD, for which he illustrated a string of covers and short stories before eventually being assigned to the strip with which he would become most closely associated, JUDGE DREDD. Bolland's work has also graced the pages of MYSTERY IN SPACE, CAMELOT 3000 and DETECTIVE COMICS, but he is best known for his collaboration, heh, with letterer -- and HIP FLASK creator -- Richard Starkings, on BATMAN: THE KILLING JOKE, written by some other British guy who probably wouldn't want to be named as the author of the work any moore, um, more. If you haven't already tracked down Brian's STRIPS or Image's huge THE ART OF BRIAN BOLLAND, do so immediately -- and don't forget to lick every page.

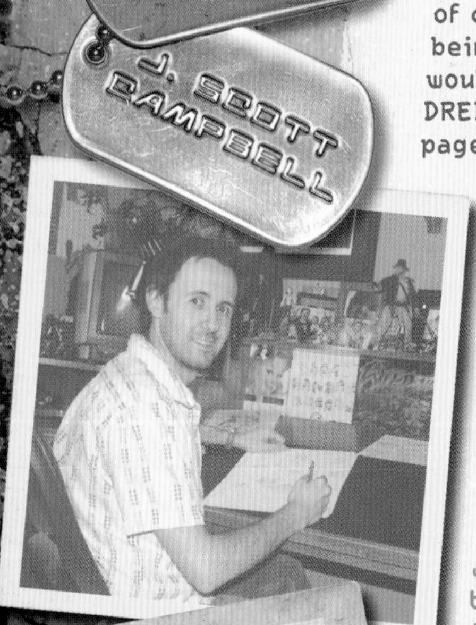
J. SCOTT
CAMPBELL

J. SCOTT CAMPBELL was initially discovered in the first Homage Studios talent search. His dynamic storytelling and animated style lent themselves perfectly to the smash-hit series GEN13 and his own DANGER GIRL. Campbell resides in Colorado where he currently draws WILDSIDERZ for DC comics and SPIDER-MAN for Marvel Comics.

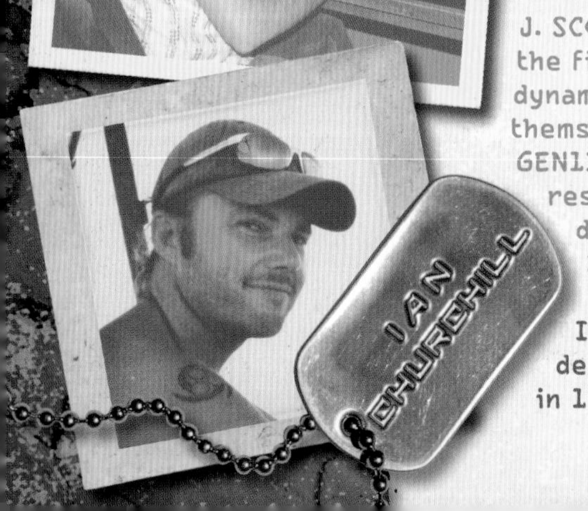
IAN
CHURCHILL

IAN CHURCHILL left a career in graphic design to work professionally in comics in 1994, when he was hired on the spot at a London comic convention by Marvel's editor-in-chief at the time, Bob Harras. Alongside Jeph Loeb, Churchill took Marvel's X-Men title, CABLE to new heights shortly before Joe Casey and Ladrönn created their memorable run on the book. Before landing his current assignment, DC's revamped SUPERGIRL, Churchill illustrated THE AVENGERS, UNCANNY X-MEN, SUPERMAN and a certain character by the name of HIP FLASK -- Huzzah!

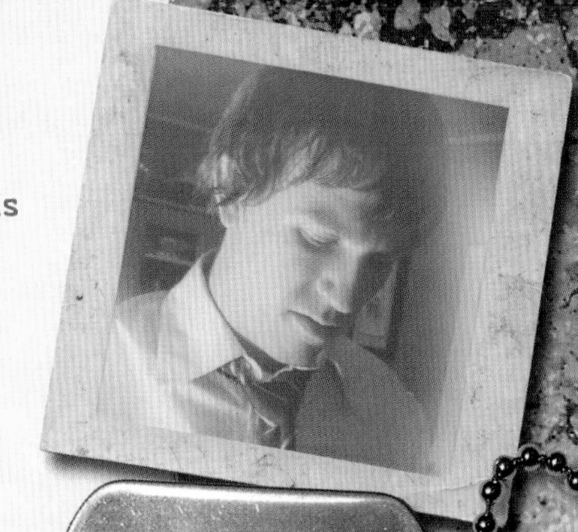

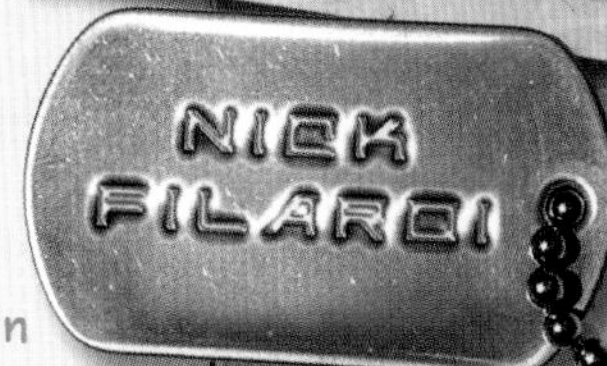
NICK
FILARDI

NICK FILARDI grew up in New London Connecticut watching BATMAN THE ANIMATED SERIES, reading SCUD: THE DISPOSABLE ASSASSIN, and hiding in the El 'n gee club listening to Small Town Hero. After graduating from Savannah College of Art and Design in 2004, he colored for Zylonol Studios under Lee Loughridge in Savannah, GA while maintaining the pretense of working an "office" job. Currently living in Philadelphia with his three-legged dog, Deniro, he also colors 24 SEVEN, GØDLAND, PIRATES OF CONEY ISLAND, and CROSS BRONX.

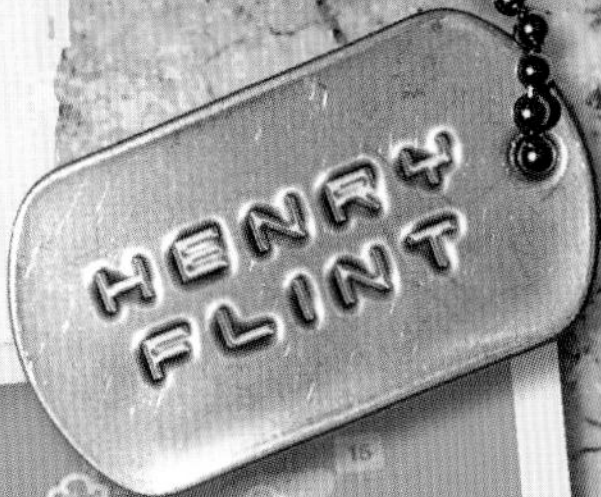
HENRY
FLINT

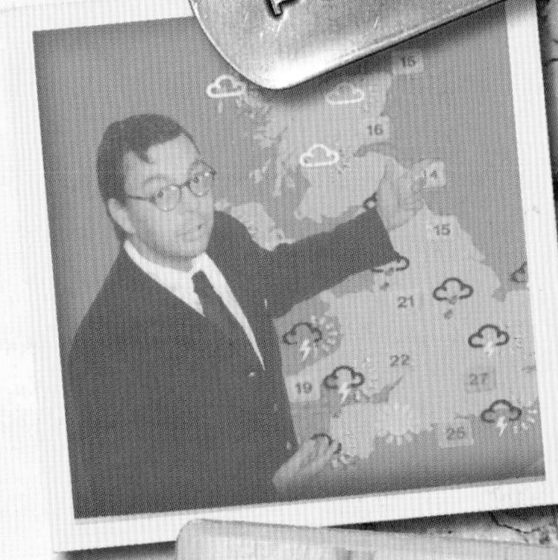

HENRY FLINT emerged from four years at Art College in Exeter and Falmouth, England to provide doses of Thrill Power for the ground-breaking British weekly 2000AD for 12 years. Under the watchful eye of Tharg, Flint worked on such characters as JUDGE DREDD, JUDGE DREDD vs ALIENS, NEMESIS THE WARLOCK, SHAKARA and ABC WARRIORS. Flint has also provided script and artwork on THARG'S ALIEN INVASIONS. Winner of Best Comic Artist in the 2004 UK National Comics Awards, Flint has recently finished an OMEGA MEN mini series for DC comics.

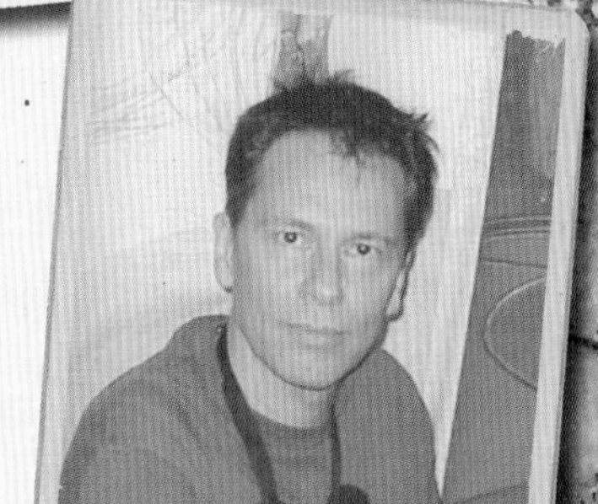

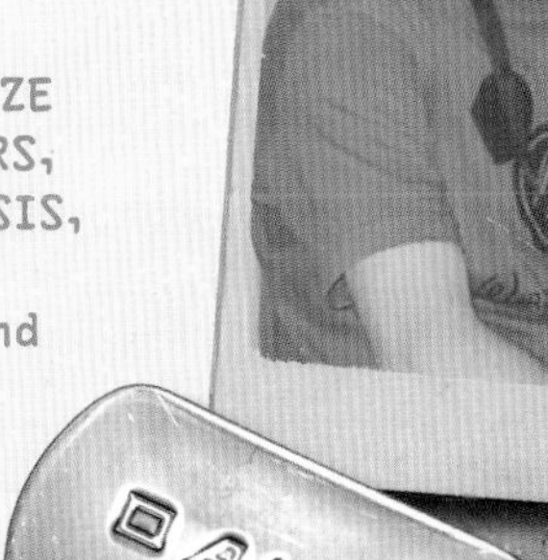
DAVID
HINE

DAVID HINE has been working in comics since the late 1980s. After creating a name for himself at Marvel UK as an inker on projects such as ZOIDS, SLEEZE BROTHERS and, sorry, Dave, CARE BEARS, he wisely fled licensed comics for CRISIS, for which he drew the series STICKY FINGERS (written by Myra Hancock), and a number of short pieces which he also wrote. For 2000 AD he drew TAO DE MOTO (again written by Hancock) and wrote and drew the futuristic police series MAMBO. STRANGE EMBRACE was originally published in black and white as a

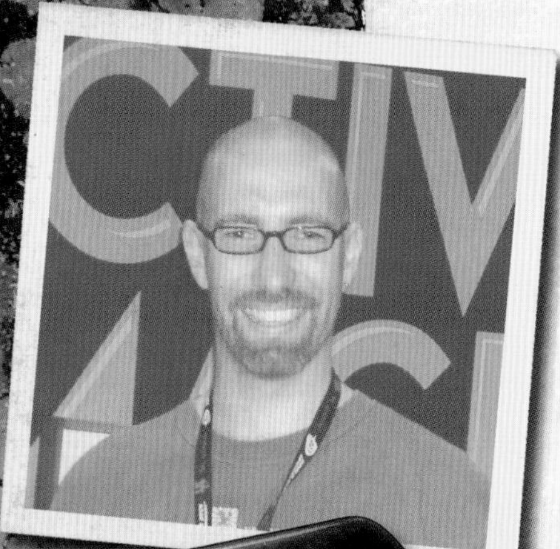

miniseries by Tundra, but it was the publication of the, now-hard-to-find, collected edition by Active Images which led to his current career as a writer at Marvel Comics on titles such as DISTRICT X/MUTOPIA X, DAREDEVIL: REDEMPTION, THE 198, SON OF M and CIVIL WAR: X-MEN. Dave's next project is SILENT WAR, a six-issue mini-series featuring THE INHUMANS with art by Frazer Irving. He is also the current writer of SPAWN for Image Comics.

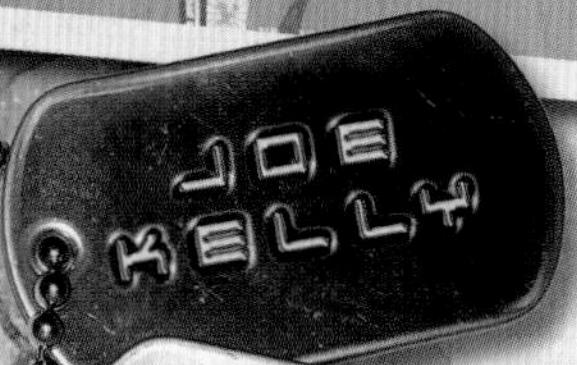
JOE
KELLY

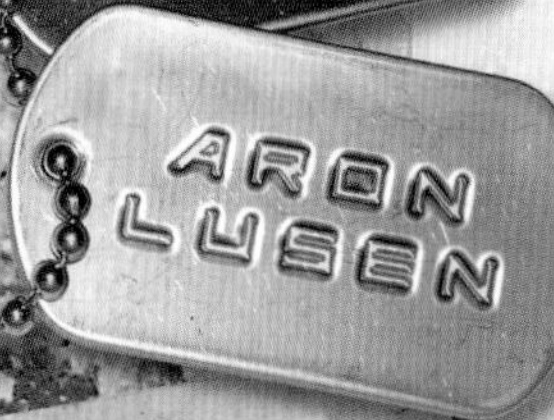
ARON
LUSEN

JOE KELLY is a New York based writer working in comic books and animation. His runs on X-MEN, ACTION COMICS, SUPERGIRL, JLA and SPACE GHOST stand as "exceptional works of genre-busting and emotional subterfuge," according to his elementary school aged children, and a hot dog vendor who bears a remarkable resemblance to Orson Welles. His writing for animation is pretty darn good too, and gets better all the time. Joe is 1/4 of MAN OF ACTION Studios (www.manofaction.tv), the creative juggernaut responsible for life-changing-mega-hit BEN 10 on CARTOON NETWORK. By most accounts his life is swell, bordering on rapturous.

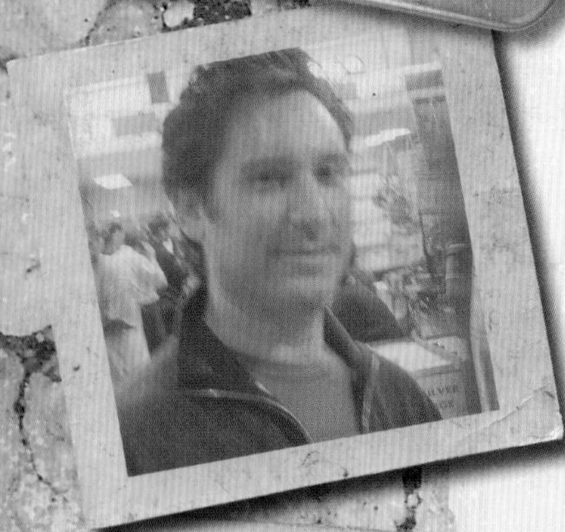

ARON LUSEN is not only the creator and writer of E.V.E. PROTOMECHA published by IMAGE COMICS in trade paperback in 1999 (and still available on Amazon.com), but also one of the founders of the award winning LIQUID! GRAPHICS studio, often described as the Industrial Light and Magic of comic book coloring. Alongside his LIQUID! co-founder, Chris Lichtner, Aron's work has graced the pages of UNCANNY X-MEN, THE FANTASTIC FOUR and Joe Madureira's BATTLE CHASERS. Aron's work over Salvador Larroca's pencils on XTREME X-MEN made him the perfect choice to color Chris Bachalo's pencils for CAPTAIN STONEHEART -- don't you just want to lick every page?! Look out for Aron's beautiful book DEAD SAMURAI, which he wrote and illustrated. If you see him in person, ask him when he's going to draw the next issue!

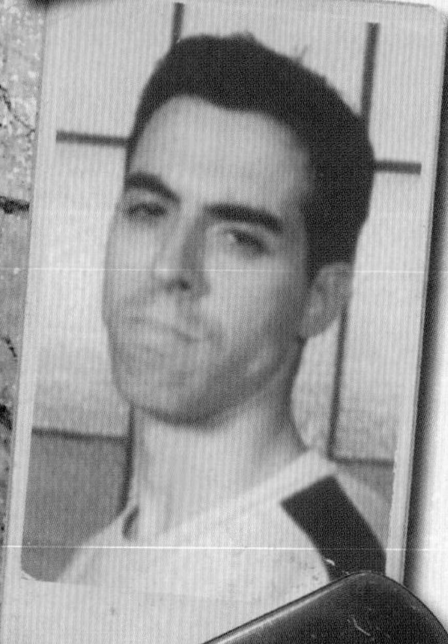

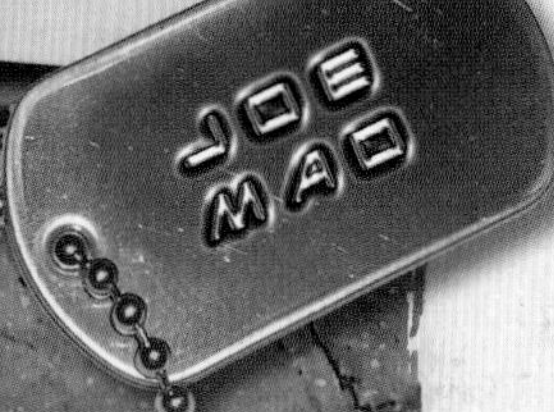
JOE
MAD

JOE MADUREIRA was hired by Marvel Comics as an intern at the tender age of 16. His first published comic strip work was an eight-page story for MARVEL COMICS PRESENTS but Joe's Marvel-meets-manga-via-Disney style propelled him onto THE UNCANNY X-MEN where he rapidly became one of the most popular artists in the industry.

Joe's creator-owned series BATTLE CHASERS helped launch Image Comics' CLIFFHANGER imprint before Joe left comics to design videogames. BOO! Nevertheless "Joe Mad" will be returning to comics next year for a brief stint on ULTIMATES by that Jeph Loeb guy.

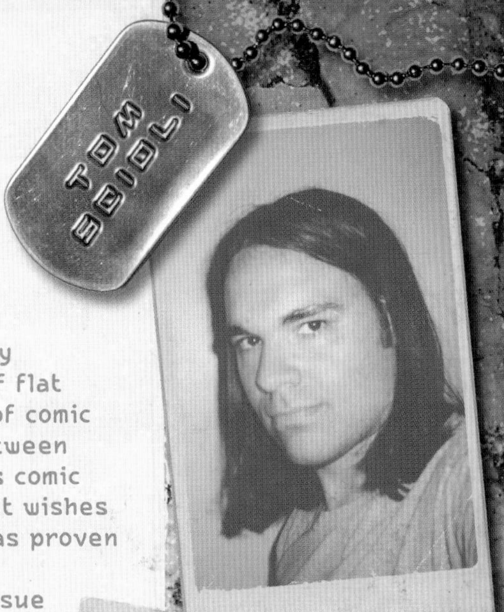
TOM
SCIOLI

TOM SCIOLI loves comic books, especially old ones. He likes the thin application of flat color on yellowed newsprint. The smell of comic books is really nice, too, somewhere between chocolate and lemon juice. He also makes comic books. He's very proud of his comics, but wishes they smelled like the old ones do. Tom has proven to be a veritable drawing machine and somehow manages to turn out a whole issue of GØDLAND every month while holding down a steady job as well.

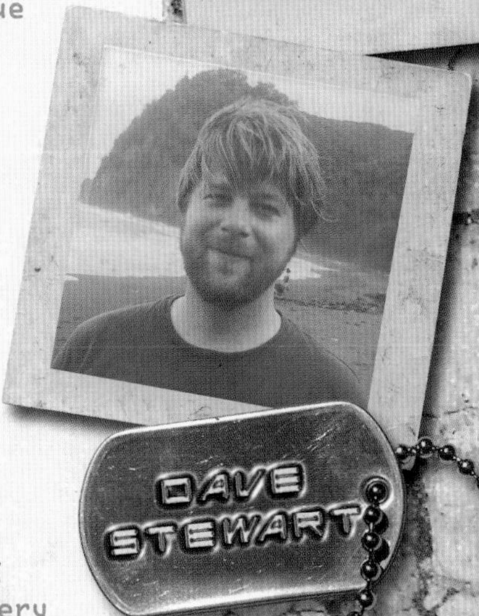
DAVE
STEWART

DAVE STEWART started out as a design intern at Dark Horse, and is now the award-winning colorist of HELLBOY, SUPERMAN, BATMAN and many, many other books. In addition to coloring some of the best artists in comics, he practices kung fu, speaks Cherokee, and raises Chihuahuas, which makes him a cross-cultural triple threat in his native state of Idaho.

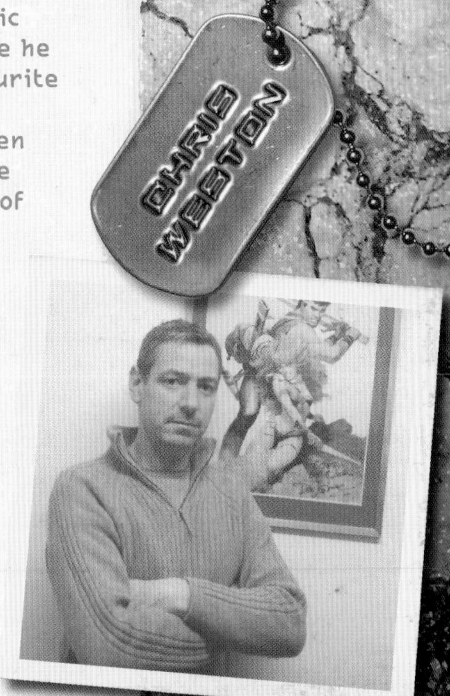
CHRIS
WESTON

CHRIS WESTON was raised on a diet of British adventure comics and the ASTERIX books of Goscinny and Uderzo . His discovery of the British weekly 2000AD cemented his desire to become a science fiction comic strip illustrator. In a bizarre twist of fate he discovered he lived near his all-time favourite artist, the late Don Lawrence, creator of STORM and THE TRIGAN EMPIRE. Weston then proceeded to stalk the poor fellow until he was offered an apprenticeship in the art of drawing comics. On completion of his year of tuition with Don, Chris had a portfolio good enough to get him his first job with 2000AD. For the next six years he worked on a vast array of stories, including JUDGE DREDD, NEMESIS, ROGUE TROOPER, NIKOLAI DANTE, INDIGO PRIME and CANON FODDER. Since then he has being plying his trade across the Atlantic, working on projects such as THE FILTH, BATMAN, LUCIFER and THE INVISIBLES. It remains his life-long ambition to draw the adventures of DAN DARE, PILOT OF THE FUTURE.

ALSO AVAILABLE

STARKINGS · CASEY · LADRONN
HIP FLASK
UNNATURAL SELECTION

ISBN #0-97405-670-7
PREVIEWS #STAR19898

STARKINGS · CASEY · LADRONN
HIP FLASK
CONCRETE JUNGLE

ISBN #1-58240-679-0
PREVIEWS #NOV061859

BY THE SAME CREATORS

COMIC BOOK
LETTERING
THE COMICRAFT WAY!

ISBN #0-97405-673-1
PREVIEWS #JAN031884

STEVEN T. SEAGLE
JUSTIN NORMAN
solstice
The shortest day of the year...
The longest day of their lives

ISBN #0-97667-611-7
PREVIEWS #APR052512

STEAMPUNK
MANIMATRON

ISBN #1-56389-762-8

GØDLAND
VOLUME ONE
"HELLO, COSMIC!"
JOE CASEY · TOM SCIOLI

ISBN #1-58240-581-6

MINISTRY OF SPACE
ELLIS · WESTON · MARTIN

ISBN #1-58240-423-3

THE ART OF BRIAN BOLLAND

ISBN #1-58240-603-0

24SEVEN, VOL. 1 TP
ISBN: 978-1-58240-636-7
$24.99

CASANOVA, VOL. 1:
LUXURIA HC
ISBN: 978-1-58240-698-5
$24.99

FELL, VOL. 1: FERAL CITY TP
ISBN: 978-1-58240-693-0
$14.99

THE FIVE FISTS OF SCIENCE GN
ISBN: 978-1-58240-605-3
$12.99

GIRLS
VOL. 1: CONCEPTION TP
ISBN: 978-1-58240-529-2
$14.99
VOL. 2: ERMERGENCE TP
ISBN: 978-1-58240-608-4
$14.99
VOL. 3: SURVIVAL TP
ISBN: 978-1-58240-703-6
$14.99
VOL. 4: EXTINCTION
ISBN: 978-1-58240-753-1
$14.99

JACK STAFF
VOL. 1: EVERYTHING USED
TO BE BLACK AND WHITE TP
ISBN: 987-7-58240-335-9
$19.95
VOL. 2: SOLDIERS TP
ISBN: 978-1-58240-392-2
$15.95
VOL. 3: ECHOES OF TOMORROW TP
ISBN: 978-1-58240-719-7
$16.99

LAZARUS CHURCHYARD:
THE FINAL CUT
ISBN: 1-58240-180-2
$14.95

PHONOGRAM, VOL. 1:
RUE BRITANNIA TP
ISBN: 978-1-58240-694-7
$14.99

ROCKETO: JOURNEY TO THE
HIDDEN SEA VOL 1
ISBN: 1-58240-585-9
$19.99

ROCKETO: JOURNEY TO
THE HIDDEN SEA VOL 2
ISBN : 978-1-58240-735-7
$19.99

WATERLOO SUNSET
ISBN: 978-158240-668-8
$17.99

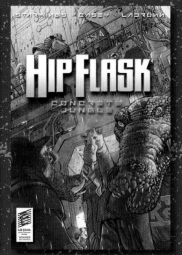